Praise for Robert Goddard:

KT-179-426

'He is a superb storyteller'
Sunday Independent

'Cliff-hanging entertainment'
Guardian

'Had me utterly spellbound . . . Cracking good entertainment'
Washington Post

'Takes the reader on a journey from which he knows he will not deviate until the final destination is reached'
Evening Standard

'Combines the steely edge of a thriller with the suspense of a whodunnit, all interlaced with subtle romantic overtones'
Time Out

'An atmosphere of taut menace . . . Suspense is heightened by shadows of betrayal and revenge'
Daily Telegraph

'A thriller in the classic storytelling sense . . . Hugely enjoyable'
The Times

'When it comes to duplicity and intrigue, Goddard is second to none. He is a master of manipulation . . . a hypnotic, unputdownable thriller'
Daily Mail

'Combines the expert suspense manipulation skills of a Daphne du Maurier romance with those of a John le Carré thriller'
New York Times

'A cracker, twisting, turning and exploding with real skill'
Daily Mirror

'His narrative power, strength of characterisation and superb plots, plus the ability to convey the atmosphere of the period quite brilliantly, make him compelling reading'

Books

www.booksattransworld.co.uk

Also by Robert Goddard

PAST CARING
IN PALE BATTALIONS
PAINTING THE DARKNESS
INTO THE BLUE
TAKE NO FAREWELL
HAND IN GLOVE
CLOSED CIRCLE
BORROWED TIME
OUT OF THE SUN
BEYOND RECALL
CAUGHT IN THE LIGHT
SET IN STONE

and published by Corgi Books

Also by Robert Goddard

DYING TO TELL

and published by Bantam Press

SEA CHANGE

Robert Goddard

CORGI BOOKS

SEA CHANGE
A CORGI BOOK : 0 552 14602 1

Originally published in Great Britain by Bantam Press,
a division of Transworld Publishers

PRINTING HISTORY
Bantam Press edition published 2000
Corgi edition published 2001

1 3 5 7 9 10 8 6 4 2

Copyright © Robert and Vaunda Goddard 2000

The right of Robert Goddard to be identified as the author of this
work has been asserted in accordance with sections 77 and 78
of the Copyright Designs and Patents Act 1988.

In this work of fiction, except in the case of historical fact, the characters, places and events are either the product of the author's
imagination or they are used entirely fictitiously.

Condition of Sale
This book is sold subject to the condition that it shall not,
by way of trade or otherwise, be lent, re-sold, hired out or
otherwise circulated in any form of binding or cover other than that
in which it is published and without a similar condition including this
condition being imposed on the subsequent purchaser.

Set in 10/12pt Plantin by
Phoenix Typesetting, Ilkley, West Yorkshire.

Corgi Books are published by Transworld Publishers,
61–63 Uxbridge Road, London W5 5SA,
a division of The Random House Group Ltd,
in Australia by Random House Australia (Pty) Ltd,
20 Alfred Street, Milsons Point, Sydney, NSW 2061, Australia,
in New Zealand by Random House New Zealand Ltd,
18 Poland Road, Glenfield, Auckland 10, New Zealand
and in South Africa by Random House (Pty) Ltd,
Endulini, 5a Jubilee Road, Parktown 2193, South Africa.

Printed and bound in Germany by
Elsnerdruck, Berlin.

It has been very judiciously observed that a commercial country has more to dread from the golden baits of avarice, the airy hopes of projectors and the wild enthusiastic dreams of speculators than from any external dangers.

John Millar, *An Authentic Account of the South Sea Scheme* (1845)

'I have made a profit of a thousand per cent – and I am satisfied.'

Robert Walpole (1720)

Contents

BOOK ONE

January–March 1721

CHAPTER ONE

Stags at Bay

It was dismal weather for a dismal time. The night was damp and clammy, clinging to London like a cold sweat. A fire burned in the grate, but Sir Theodore Janssen stood on the far side of the drawing-room from it, one arm propped on the sill of the open window, the other raised to his chest, his hand splayed across his brocaded waistcoat. He glanced out into Hanover Square and seemed to see in the drizzle-smeared gloom the deepening shadow of his future.

Until so very recently, he had been a man of high repute as well as substance. A baronet at the 'special request' of the Prince of Wales, a Member of Parliament, a director of the Bank of England, a landed gentleman, a financier of almost legendary acumen, he had been able to look forward to an old age of comfort and esteem. He had transformed himself from a friendless young Flemish émigré into a pioneer of a new era of commercial freedom. Yet now, here he stood, on the brink of ruin, a self-unmade man too close to the biblical term of life to delude himself with hopes of recouping what he was surely about to lose.

The South Sea Company was his mistake, of course, as it had been many men's. If he had resigned his directorship twelve months ago, or better still never accepted it in the first place, he would be free of this. Not of all

11

financial loss, naturally. No doubt he would have gambled on the stock continuing to rise, like everyone else. But he could have borne that. His wealth was such that he would scarcely have noticed. This was different, however. This was a shameful and unavoidable acknowledgement of his own greed and stupidity. And it would come with a price, one even he might be unable to pay.

To make matters bleaker still, on the other side of the room, warming himself before the well-stacked fire, stood the man who had lured him onto the board two years before: Robert Knight, chief cashier of the company, keeper of its accounts and guardian of its secrets. Knight too faced ruin, but did so with a blithe smile and an unfurrowed brow. He still looked ten years younger than he had any right to and retained a twinkle in his eye that owed nothing to the candlelight.

'Why are you here, Mr Knight?' Sir Theodore asked, turning from the window and coughing to clear the gruffness from his throat.

'Because I am to appear before the committee the day after tomorrow, Sir Theodore.' The committee to which Knight referred was the House of Commons Secret Committee of Inquiry into the South Sea scandal. It had been sitting like an army of occupation in South Sea House all week, interrogating whomever it pleased, appropriating whatever documents it deemed likely to lead it to the truth. But the truth was in essence already known. The South Sea scheme had always been an impossible dream, sustained only by a universal determination to believe in it. Now was the winter of cruel disillusionment, of frozen credit and frost-shattered fortunes. The search was on, not so much for truth as for culprits. Everyone was a victim. But not everyone could be a villain. 'I will be hard pressed, I think,' Knight continued. 'Do you not agree?'

'Very hard,' said Sir Theodore with a nod. 'I have no doubt of it.'

'What should I tell them?'

'You have come here for my advice?'

'Your advice – and your assistance.'

Sir Theodore frowned. 'Assistance with what?'

'The disposal – if I may so phrase it – of the contents of my valise.' Knight stooped to pick up the bag he had brought with him and advanced to a table halfway across the room. 'May I?'

With the faintest inclination of his head, Sir Theodore consented. Knight opened the valise and slid a thick leather-spined book out onto the table. The edges of its pages were marbled and well turned. Its cover was green.

'You look surprised, Sir Theodore.'

'I am.'

'You know what it is?'

'How should I?'

'How should you not? Unless—' Knight moved round the table and leaned back against it, trailing one hand behind him that came to rest on the cover of the book. 'Perhaps it is your intention to plead ignorance. And perhaps this is a rehearsal for such a plea. If so, let me spare you the effort. You know what this is. And I know that you know. You may fool others. I wish you luck in the endeavour. But you cannot fool me.'

'No.' Sir Theodore scowled. 'Of course not. It is quite the other way about, when all's said and done.'

'You were aware of the risks attendant upon our enterprise, Sir Theodore. Do not pretend otherwise.'

'Was I? I wonder now that I thought it could ever have succeeded.'

Sir Theodore was unlikely to be alone in that. All over England, the great and the good, the newly poor and the no longer rich, were asking the same question, if not of others then of themselves. How could they have supposed it would work? To snap one's fingers and convert thirty million pounds of the National Debt into the booming stock of a company whose hard commercial assets amounted to vastly less, but whose *potential* profits from the South Sea trade were surely limitless, had seemed magically appealing. And the smooth-tongued Mr Knight had swayed every doubter, if not with words then with . . . more tangible methods of persuasion. Now, however, the magician was exposed as a trickster. And those associated with him were left with the stark choice of proclaiming themselves either his dupes or his accomplices.

'I had hopes of more than my personal enrichment, Mr Knight,' Sir Theodore continued. 'I saw this as the beginning of a glorious new world for all. I believed we were engaged in the practice of philanthropy.'

'I should not recommend you to present that argument to the committee.'

'It is not an argument. It is the truth.'

'But will it keep you from prison? I think not.'

'Will anything?'

'Perhaps.' Knight's fingers drummed on the cover of the book. 'A harder kind of truth may save us.'

'*Us?*'

'You and me, Sir Theodore. You and me and your fellow directors and all their friends in high places. So many friends. So very high. Too high to be allowed to fall, I think. But the fear of falling will work wonders. And it is wonders we need.'

'I thought what you needed was assistance.'

'Precisely. A small thing to a great end.' His fingers stopped drumming. 'This book represents our salvation. But only so long as it remains safe, both from our friends, who would destroy it, and from our enemies,

14

who would shout its secrets from the rooftops.'

'Then I suggest you keep it safe, Mr Knight.'

'How can I? There is no safe place left at South Sea House. Mr Brodrick has sent his ferrets down every hole.' Thomas Brodrick was chairman of the Committee of Inquiry, a sworn opponent of the South Sea Company and all its works. Sir Theodore did not need to be told that he had set about his task with relish as well as dedication. It went without saying. 'If I stay, they will find it.'

'*If* you stay?'

'Or if I flee, like as not.'

'Do you propose to flee?'

'I did not say so.' Knight smiled. 'Now did I?'

Sir Theodore's eyes narrowed. He pulled the window shut behind him with sudden and excessive force. Then he said, as if tiring of their mutual prevarication, 'What do you want of me?'

'I want you to take charge of the book.'

'Why me?'

'Because you are the most eminent member of the board. Also the most reliable. And, I would judge, the least inclined to panic. Caswall and Master fell to blows in the street today outside South Sea House. It was not an edifying spectacle.'

'You flatter me, Mr Knight.'

'Not at all. I present you with the simple facts. You are the things I have said you are.'

'Supposing that to be so, why should my hands be safer than yours?'

'Because they are not the hands into which I might be expected to surrender such a document. And because you have acquaintances of long standing in your native land to whom it could be entrusted. In that event, I would not know where it was. The information could not be wrung out of me. And no-one would think to try to

15

wring it out of you. While the book remains abroad, so to speak, there would be limits to the action that could be taken against us. It would be an insurance policy for both of us. And for our colleagues.'

'You are thinking of them?'

'No.' Knight grinned. 'I mention them in case you are.'

'If it became known that you had handed it to me, it might be supposed that I was familiar with its contents.'

'Which you are not, of course.' Knight's grin broadened, then abruptly vanished. 'But it would not become known. Why should it? I have confidence in your choice both of recipient and of courier. I have confidence in you altogether.'

'I think you have as little of that in me as I have in you, Mr Knight.'

Knight looked genuinely hurt. 'How can you say so?'

'But confidence is no longer the issue, is it? If it were, we would all still be riding high.'

'What then is the issue?'

'Desperation.' Sir Theodore gave a heavy sigh and walked slowly to the table, where he halted and stared down at the green-covered book. 'Sheer desperation.'

'Perhaps so. I'll not argue the point. The question is a simple one. Will you do it?'

'I would be mad to.'

'And madder still not to. There is a great deal at stake. More than just our personal circumstances. Far more. But it so happens' – Knight's voice took on the syrupy tone he had used to persuade so many in days gone by that the South Sea project could not, would not, fail – 'that our interests and those of the nation coincide. Our salvation is the salvation of all.'

'How gratifying.'

'Will you do it?' Knight repeated.

Sir Theodore looked at him long and hard, then said, 'Let me not detain you, Mr Knight.'

'May I leave what I brought?'

'You brought nothing.' Sir Theodore cocked one eyebrow. 'I trust that is understood.'

Knight nodded. 'Very clearly.'

'Then there is no more to be said.' Sir Theodore picked up the book and carried it to a bureau in a corner of the room. He slid it into one of the drawers, turned a key in the lock and dropped the key into his waistcoat pocket. 'Is there?'

An hour later, with Knight long gone, Sir Theodore rose from his seat at the bureau in which the green-covered book was still locked. He drained his glass of port and looked down at the letter it had taken him the better part of that hour to write. Yes, on balance, it seemed to him, he had disclosed as much and as little as he needed to. And the precaution he had urged on his oldest and most trusted friend, though extreme, was undoubtedly necessary. He sealed the letter, crossed to the bell-pull and tugged at it.

A few minutes passed, during which Sir Theodore gazed into the dying fire. With the thumb and index finger of his right hand, he slowly revolved the gold and diamond ring that sat fatly on the little finger of his other hand. It had been a gift from the Prince of Wales, presented at the King's birthday party at St James's eight months before, when riches seemed to rain from the clear spring sky and no-one doubted, for no-one dared to, that a pound of South Sea stock would be worth ten tomorrow and a hundred the day after. His own holding must have amounted to a million then. A million pounds and a billion delusions. They were nothing now, nothing but ashes in his mouth.

There was a tap at the door. Nicodemus Jupe, Sir

17

Theodore's valet and loyal factotum, entered the room. A lean, grave-faced, hawk-nosed fellow of forty or so, Jupe had about him the air of one who never overestimated his importance in the world and yet never underestimated it either. He was humble without being obsequious, perceptive without being presumptuous. He had always been utterly reliable, yet the cold edge of efficiency in his soul that was the essence of his reliability was also the key to the understanding that subsisted between him and his master. He expected Sir Theodore to extricate himself from the difficulties that had overtaken them both. Indeed, he required it of him. And he himself would do anything he could to bring that about. That was the measure of his loyalty. It ran far. But it did not run to the ends of the Earth.

'There is a letter on the bureau,' said Sir Theodore. 'It must be on its way tonight.'

Jupe fetched it and glanced at the address. His face betrayed no reaction.

'I am sorry to ask you to turn out at such an hour. But it is a matter of the utmost urgency.'

'I understand, sir. I'll leave at once.'

'Before you do, there is one other thing.'

'Yes, sir?'

'The indigent mapmaker. Spandrel. We still have our eye on him?'

'Indeed, sir. I don't doubt he'll stray eventually. Then we'll have him. But for the present—'

'He adheres to the rules.'

'He does.'

'I wish to see him.'

Jupe's eyes widened faintly in surprise. 'And is that also . . . a matter of the utmost urgency?'

'It is, Jupe. Yes.'

CHAPTER TWO

The Idle Waywiser

Dawn came slowly and grudgingly to the ill-lit room William Spandrel shared with his mother beneath the eaves of a lodging-house in Cat and Dog Yard. Spandrel did not welcome its arrival. The grey, soot-filtered light only made the cracks in the plaster and the crumbling condition of the brickwork beneath more obvious. As he shaved himself with a blunt razor through a thumb's-smear worth of soap, he studied his fractured reflection in a shard of mirror, noting the ever hollower cheek-bones, the charcoal-shadowed eyes and the cringing look of defeat that tried to hide itself behind them. Who could welcome dawn when darkness was at least a kind of refuge?

He had nailed the mirror to the south-facing wall within the dormer-window, reckoning that would at least ensure enough light to cut his throat by, should he ever need to do so. It seemed likely enough that the need would one day arise, considering the intractability of his plight. If he glanced out of the window, he could see, looming beyond the sagging roof-tree of the Punch Bowl Tavern, the palisaded wall of the Fleet Prison, where he had been confined for ten purgatorial days last autumn, an unconsidered victim of the sudden tightening of credit following the bursting of the South Sea Bubble and several thousand fond dreams of wealth along with it. His own dream, strictly speaking, had not been among them, but commercial catastrophe on the scale of the South Sea runs deep and hard, afflicting even those who believe themselves immune from it.

His immunity, Spandrel now realized, had been imaginary, based as it was on the slender truth that he had not himself dabbled in South Sea stock. He had been far too busy assisting his father in the painstaking survey work for what was to have been their proudest achievement – An Exact and Definitive Map of the City and Environs of London in the Reign of His Britannic Majesty King George the First – to engage in stock market speculation, even supposing he had possessed any capital with which to speculate. But the world and his wife *had* speculated, at first successfully, at length disastrously. Those fine gentlemen who had assured William Spandrel senior that they would buy a copy of his map with which to adorn their soon-to-be-gold-leafed drawing-room walls had eagerly lent him the funds for his enterprise. But they had become equally eager to retrieve those funds when a financial chasm opened beneath their feet. The map was tantalizingly close to completion, but what use was that? Suddenly, there had been no customers, only creditors. William senior had fallen ill with the worry of it. William junior assumed responsibility for his debts to spare him a spell in prison he was not well enough to survive. And the bailiffs duly came for the younger man. But the older man had died anyway. Spandrel's sacrifice had been in vain.

So sombre had his situation then been that his mother was able to persuade her normally tight-fisted brother to donate the five guineas that bought him the freedom to live in lodgings within the rules of the Prison, but outside its walls. It was freedom of a limited kind. And it was certainly preferable to the horrors of the Fleet. But as those horrors faded slowly from his mind, so new ones took their place. Would he ever be truly free again? Was he to pass the prime of his life as a fly in a jar? Was there no way out?

On this dank January morning there certainly did not appear to be one. In the corner, half-hidden by the washing Mrs Spandrel had hung in front of the fireplace, stood one of the waywisers he and his father had pushed round the streets of London, calculating distances to an obsessive nicety. Now, its wheel was limned with rust. Everything was corroding, even hope. The sheets that made up as much of the map as they had drawn were with the engraver and seemed likely to remain there, since the fellow had not so far been paid for the work he had done. And while Spandrel stayed cooped up in Cat and Dog Yard, as the rules of the Fleet demanded, there would be no more sheets. That much was certain.

Surveying was all he knew. He had been his father's loyal apprentice. But no-one had need of a surveyor at such a time. And the only thing he could survey from this rotting garret was the wasteland of his future. To think of what he had lost was too much to bear. Last summer, he had entertained hopes of marriage, to the beautiful Maria Chesney. And the map had seemed like the best idea his father had ever had. Now, there was nothing. Maria was lost to him. His father was dead. His mother had become a washerwoman. And he had become a washerwoman's assistant.

At a sound from the door, he turned, expecting to see his mother, though surprised she should be back so soon. But, strangely, it was not his mother.

A thin man in dark clothes and a grey-black wig stood in the doorway, stooping slightly to clear the lintel. His eyes, deep-set and darting, combined with his sharp-boned nose, gave him the look of some strange bird of

21

prey, searching for carrion. And perhaps, it occurred to Spandrel, he thought he had found some.

'William Spandrel,' the man said. It was not a question. It had more the sound of an announcement intended to forestall any denial.

'Yes,' Spandrel cautiously admitted.

'My name is Jupe. I represent Sir Theodore Janssen.'

'You do? Well . . .' Spandrel put down the razor and wiped the remaining soap from his jaw. 'As you can see, there's nothing I can do for Sir Theodore.'

'You owe him a great deal of money.'

That much was undeniable. Sir Theodore was, in fact, his principal creditor by some way. Spandrel's father had surveyed an estate at Wimbledon Sir Theodore had bought a few years previously and had turned to him for backing when the idea for the map came to him. Sir Theodore, awash with cash at the time, had happily obliged. As a director of the South Sea Company, he was now likely to be a desperate man. Spandrel had gleaned that much from borrowed newspapers and overheard conversations in the yard. But he was surely not so desperate as to apply to the most hapless of his many debtors for help.

'Sir Theodore would like the debt settled,' said Jupe, advancing into the room and gazing round at the sparse and shabby furnishings.

'So would I. But I've better things to do than torment myself with thoughts of what I'd *like*.'

'So has Sir Theodore.'

'Then why are you here?'

'To present you with an opportunity to settle the debt – and your other debts along with it – by rendering Sir Theodore a small but significant service.'

'Is this some sort of joke?'

'Do I look like a man who makes jokes, Mr Spandrel?'

That he assuredly did not. 'What you should be considering is whether you can afford to ignore the chance I am offering of extricating yourself – and your mother – from the life you are leading here.' Jupe peered curiously at a sagging flap of plaster. 'If it can be called a life, that is.'

'Your pardon, sir.' Spandrel forced himself to smile. Perhaps, he told himself, Sir Theodore had decided to be generous to those his own malpractices had helped to bankrupt. Stranger things had been known, though he could not for the moment think of any. If it was true, maybe there really was a way out of his troubles. 'There's naturally no service I'd not be willing to render Sir Theodore in exchange for a remittal of the debt.'

'Naturally.' Jupe smiled back at him with thinly veiled superciliousness. 'As you say.'

'What would he require of me?'

'He will explain that to you himself, Mr Spandrel. When you meet.'

'He's coming here?'

'Certainly not.' Jupe beetled his brow to let Spandrel know how absurd the suggestion was. 'You are going to him.'

'But I can't.'

'You must.'

'Do you take me for a fool, Mr Jupe?' The outline of a crude but effective trap was forming in Spandrel's mind. 'If I set foot outside the rules, I'll be arrested.' And that, perhaps, was the sole object of the exercise.

'Not on Sunday.'

It was a valid point. No debtor could be arrested on the sabbath. It was Spandrel's weekly breath of liberty, when he walked the streets of London a free if penniless man. Occasionally, he would stray further, into the countryside, though never so far that he could not return

23

within the day. There was an invisible leash around his neck and always it tugged him back.

'Sir Theodore will see you then.'

'Very well.'

'Nine o'clock, Sunday morning. At his house in Hanover Square.'

'I'll be there.'

'Be sure you are, Mr Spandrel. And be on time. Sir Theodore values promptness.'

'Is there anything . . . I should bring with me?'

'Bring yourself. That is all Sir Theodore requires.'

'But . . . why? What can I—'

'No more questions.' Jupe's raised voice had suddenly filled the room. Now it dropped once more to its normal pitch. 'You will have your answers on Sunday. And I wish you well of them.'

Spandrel did not know whether to feel elated or perturbed by his summons to the presence of Sir Theodore Janssen. Just when he had least expected it, an escape route from all his difficulties had opened before him. But it might lead him into yet worse difficulties. There was the rub. The likes of Sir Theodore Janssen did not shower benefactions on the likes of him. It was not in the nature of things; not, at any rate, in the nature of merchant princes.

Folly and overconfidence had plunged Spandrel's father into debt. He had insisted on the most expensive equipment available for their project: brand-new theodolites, waywisers and measuring chains, of which none remained, the waywiser beside the fireplace being so old even the bailiffs had turned their noses up at it. He had lavished entertainment on potential customers, stinting them little in the way of food and drink while he explained the glory and precision of their map. He had thrown money around like a farmer sowing seed. But all he had reaped was broken promises and unpaid bills. And all Spandrel had inherited from him was a mapmaker's turn of mind and debts ratcheted up by interest to several hundred pounds.

Spandrel might as well have dreamed of flying through the window and mapping the city from the sky as of earning such a sum. Yet a way of earning it was what Sir Theodore had apparently decided to offer him. Why? And what did he have to do for it? What service could he render that was worth so much? It made no sense.

Yet he would go to Hanover Square on Sunday morning, of course. He would go and, like as not, he would agree to do whatever Sir Theodore asked of him. He had no choice. But that did not mean he had no doubt. Hope had been reborn. But doubt kept it company.

When Margaret Spandrel returned to Cat and Dog Yard later that morning, laden with dirty washing, she found her son staring out of the window of their room at a view so familiar to both of them that contemplation of it was surely futile. Already weary, she was at once irritated by his apparent listlessness.

'No tea brewed to welcome me back?' she snapped. 'Have you done nothing but sit there like a moon-calf while I've been gone?'

'I've been thinking,' William replied.

'Thinking?' Mrs Spandrel was a warm-hearted woman, who had married for love and been rewarded with five children, only one of whom had lived beyond the cradle, early widowhood and greater poverty than she had ever imagined descending into. Thinking was, on the whole, something she preferred not to do. 'I despair of you, boy, I really do.'

'No you don't, Ma.'

'I come close, believe me. Now, do let's have some tea before we set to scrubbing this load.' She dropped the vast bundle of washing on the floor and lowered herself into the fireside chair with a sigh. 'Then you can tell me who our mysterious visitor was.'

'We've had no visitor,' said William, as he threw some fragments of sea-coal onto the all but dead fire to warm the kettle by.

'I met Annie Welsh downstairs. She said a stranger called here earlier. Neat and clean-looking, she reckoned.'

'You know what a busybody that woman is.'

'But not often wrong.'

'Well, she is this time.'

'Are you saying she made it up?'

'No. He must have called on someone else, that's all.' William smiled at her, which was rare these days, and always cheered her. 'What would a neat and clean-looking stranger want with me?'

CHAPTER THREE

Knights Errant

It is doubtful if William Spandrel would have been able to guess the service Sir Theodore Janssen required of him, even had he been a fly on the wall of the board-room at South Sea House that Saturday, when, with candles lit against the gloom and rain drumming on the windows, the Secret Committee of Inquiry began its examination of Robert Knight. With his fluent tongue and agile mind, Knight was more than a match for his interrogators, but even he could be worn down eventually. That must have been Chairman Brodrick's calculation, at any rate. As the questions grew more specific and the answers more evasive, the crux of the scandal would inevitably emerge. Time was on the committee's side, after all. When they adjourned that evening, they had still not hacked a path through Knight's artfully cultivated thicket of obfuscations. But, on Monday, they surely would.

Sunday dawned grey and chill, the rain spent, the city silent. Spandrel had left his mother sleeping, but knew she would not worry when she woke to find him absent. His sabbath wanderings were familiar to her. But he was not wandering this sabbath morning. He had both a purpose and a destination. He strode along High Holborn with the vigour of a man refreshed by the knowledge that

27

he had business to attend to, even though he did not know what that business was.

The map he and his father had expended so much time and effort on might no longer be in his possession, but it was still in his mind, the great rats' maze of London printed indelibly on his memory. Few could know it as well as he did: the yards, the courts, the squares, the alleys. He could have chosen half a dozen circuitous routes to Hanover Square and negotiated them un-erringly. It was not caution but urgency that prompted him to press on along the most direct route, following the southward curve of Broad Street past St Giles. He literally could not afford to be late.

Soon, he was on the Tyburn Road, with elegant modern houses to his left and open fields, alternating with building sites, to his right. This was the very edge of the city, where new money had pushed out its tendrils into old land. But the South Sea disaster had cut those tendrils. Building had stopped. The half-built houses he saw to the north might never be finished now. His father had been assured by several potential customers that there would soon be a labyrinth of streets for them to map as far west as Hyde Park. But horses and cattle still grazed the pastures beyond Bond Street and surely would for many years yet.

Hanover Square was both the limit and the apogee of this abruptly halted surge of building. Here many of the favoured servants of the new monarchy had chosen to reside in Germanically ornate splendour, Sir Theodore Janssen among them. Whether the dukes and generals still wanted him as a neighbour was a moot point. The distinct possibility that he had become an embarrassment to them gave Spandrel some comfort as he approached the great man's door and rapped the knocker.

It was Jupe who answered, so swiftly that he must have

been waiting close at hand. He said nothing at first, merely looking Spandrel up and down as if wondering whether his clothes were the best he could find for a visit to such a distinguished person. (They were, in truth, the best he could find for a visit to anyone.) Then a clock began striking nine in the hall behind him and a flicker of something like surprised approval crossed Jupe's face.

He stood back, gesturing for Spandrel to enter, and closed the door behind him, then said simply, 'This way,' and led him along the hall and up the stairs. Spandrel's immediate impression was of great wealth, evident in gilded friezework and oil paintings as big as banqueting tables, weighed down by a pervading silence that magnified the striking of the clock into an ominous toll.

A door on the first floor opened and they were in a drawing-room, whose high windows looked out onto the square. There were paintings here too, along with busts and urns aplenty. A fire was burning, almost raging, it seemed to Spandrel, so unaccustomed was he to anything beyond the bare minimum of fuel. A man was standing in front of it, dressed in a purple shag gown and turban, sipping from a cup of chocolate. He was short and broad-shouldered, clearly old, but with none of the weakness of age. If he was desperate, he did not show it. Sir Theodore Janssen had not perfected a demeanour of calm authority for nothing.

'Mr Spandrel,' he said simply, handing his cup to Jupe, who left the room at once and without another word. 'I knew your father.'

'He spoke often of you, Sir Theodore.'

'Did he? As what, pray? A fine patron – or a merciless tormentor?'

'He did not enjoy being in debt.'

'No man does, Mr Spandrel. Yet you took on that state, to spare your father imprisonment.'

'There was nothing else I could do.'

'Some sons would not have taken that view of the matter.'

'Perhaps not.'

'Jupe tells me your present accommodation is . . . lacking in most comforts.'

'It's not Hanover Square.'

'No. Nor the Fleet Prison. There's that to console you.'

'So there is.'

'But I've not brought you here for consolation.'

'What have you brought me here for, Sir Theodore?'

'To business, yes? A sound principle. Well, our business is the money you owe me, Mr Spandrel.'

'I can't pay you.'

'Not in cash, no. Of course not. But in kind. Yes, yes. I rather think you *can* pay me in kind.'

'How?'

'By acting as my courier in a confidential transaction.'

'Your . . . *courier*?'

'I require an article to be delivered to a gentleman in Amsterdam who is known to me. And I require a trustworthy person to deliver it.'

'Me?'

'Exactly so.'

'But . . . why?' Spandrel could not have disguised his puzzlement even had he tried. The simplicity of what he was being asked to do was somehow more disturbing than had Sir Theodore wanted him to murder a business rival. 'Surely you have servants to run this kind of errand. Why not send Mr Jupe?'

'I have my reasons. And you have no need to know what they are. Indeed, the less you know the better. I will cancel your debt to me upon written confirmation that the article has been safely delivered. That is as much as you need to understand. Do you accept my terms?'

'Mr Jupe mentioned my debts to other parties than yourself.'

'There are no other parties. I have bought in all your debts. I am your sole creditor, Mr Spandrel. In passing, let me tell you that your debts came exceptionally cheap. No-one believes they will ever be paid. But no-one is likely to be as flexible as me in devising a means of payment.'

'And all I have to do to pay them off is to act as your postman?'

'Yes. That is all.'

'On this one occasion?'

'This occasion only.'

'That's very generous of you.' It was, indeed, suspiciously generous. How could Spandrel be sure further, more onerous, demands would not be made of him if he proved himself useful by accomplishing this straightforward task? The inescapable answer was that he could not.

'No doubt you are wondering what guaranty you would have that these terms would be honoured.' Sir Theodore seemed to find it easy to read Spandrel's thoughts. 'Well, you would have my word.'

'In my situation, Sir Theodore, would you find that . . . sufficient?'

'Your situation, Mr Spandrel, is that of someone who has nothing to lose and nothing to bargain with. In *your* situation, I would find any guaranty sufficient.' Sir Theodore raised his hand to forestall objections, though in plain truth Spandrel could conceive of none. 'I have to trust you with an article of some value and the money you will need to travel to Amsterdam. You have to trust me that your reward for undertaking the journey will be a release from indebtedness. You could abscond. But the consideration you showed your father suggests that you would not lightly abandon your mother. I could break my word to you. But to what purpose? I cannot profit from your imprisonment. I *may* profit from your feeling obliged to me. I still regard your father's map as a worthwhile commercial project. Only you can complete it. I have no wish to prevent you. Who knows but that if you do, we may not be in a position to contract more . . . orthodox business together.' Sir Theodore smiled. 'We all take a risk, Mr Spandrel, every day that we live. The one I am inviting you to take is not so very great, now is it?'

'I suppose not.'

'You agree, then?'

'Yes. I agree.' Spandrel refrained from adding that he really had no choice *but* to agree.

'Good.' Sir Theodore walked past him to a table in the centre of the room. Turning, Spandrel saw that an old leather satchel lay on the table. Sir Theodore pulled it upright and opened the flap. 'This is the article I require you to carry.'

Spandrel moved closer. Inside the satchel was a maroon leather despatch-box, with brass reinforcements, catches and lock.

'You are to deliver the box personally to Mijnheer Ysbrand de Vries at his home in Amsterdam. He lives on the Herengracht, near the centre of the city. You will have no difficulty finding the house. Mijnheer de Vries is well known. He will be expecting you. You will obtain a receipt and return here with it.'

'Is that all?'

'It is. The box is locked, Mr Spandrel, and I will retain the key. You understand?'

'Yes.'

'Mijnheer de Vries is a man of about my own age. We

32

are old friends. There must be no mistake as to the identity of the person to whom you deliver the box. You will say that you are instructed to ask him to recall to mind the third member of the party on the occasion when he and I first met. The person he will name is Jacob van Dillen. You have it?'

'Jacob van Dillen,' Spandrel repeated.

'Van Dillen is long dead. I should doubt if there is anyone now living who remembers him, other than Ysbrand de Vries and myself. And now you, of course.'

'I won't give him the box unless he can name van Dillen.'

'Good.'

'When do you want me to leave?'

'Immediately.'

'I must see my mother first.'

'There is no need for that. Write her a note. Say you will be away for a week or so, but do not say why. Jupe will deliver it to her and assure her that there is no need for her to worry.'

'Surely '

'That is how it will be, Mr Spandrel. Sit down and write the note. I have pen and paper to hand.'

Almost, it seemed to Spandrel, before he knew what he was doing, he was seated at the table, scrawling a few words that read as vaguely to him as he knew they would be baffling to his mother. Sir Theodore stood over him as he wrote, waiting for him to finish.

'Good enough.' Sir Theodore plucked the barely signed letter from Spandrel's fingers. 'You may leave that with me. Now, to your travel arrangements. You will be driven in my coach to Hungerford Stairs, where my skiff is waiting to take you to Deptford. The sloop *Vixen* is due to sail from Deptford for Helvoetsluys on the afternoon tide. Your passage is paid for. For your expenses beyond that . . .' Sir Theodore crossed to a bureau in a corner of the room and returned with a well-filled purse. 'This will be ample.'

'Thank you,' said Spandrel, pocketing the purse without examining the contents but judging by the weight of coin that it was, as Sir Theodore had said, ample. 'I'd, er, always understood the quickest passage to Holland was from Harwich.'

'I did not know you were an experienced traveller, Mr Spandrel.'

'I'm . . . not.'

'Have you ever been to Holland?'

'No.'

'Have you, in truth, ever left this country?'

'No.'

'Then accept the arrangements made for you by one who was born far from these shores. You will land at Helvoetsluys some time tomorrow. From there it should take you no more than two days to reach Amsterdam. Mijnheer de Vries will be expecting you on Wednesday. In the event of unforeseen difficulties, apply to my banker in the city – the firm of Pels. But do not do so unless absolutely necessary. It would be better for you, much better, to avoid all difficulties. And to return here for your reward.'

'That's what I intend to do, Sir Theodore.' Spandrel closed the flap of the satchel and laid his hand on it. 'You can rely on me.'

'Let us hope so,' said Sir Theodore unsmilingly.

Spandrel left Hanover Square in a daze. After months of hand-to-mouth misery at Cat and Dog Yard, he was suddenly riding through London in a well-sprung carriage, with money in his pocket and a liveried driver at the reins. He knew it was too good to be true. But he consoled himself that some things were good *and* true. Maybe this was one of them.

Maria Chesney was certainly another. His most recent encounter with the Chesneys' talkative footman, Sam Burrows, in Sam's favourite Sunday watering-hole, had yielded the information that Maria was still not engaged to be married. Spandrel had taken this to mean that her heart still belonged to him, which had only deepened his gloom at the time, since there was no way in the world that Maria's father would let her marry a debtor. But he might not be a debtor for much longer. Maybe, with Sir Theodore's grateful help, he could finish the map and make a commercial success of it. And maybe old Chesney could then be induced to approve of him as a son-in-law.

Unwise though he knew it to be, Spandrel let such thoughts fill his head. He had drunk his fill of despondency. For the moment, he could not resist the flavour of a sweeter brew.

Jupe delivered Spandrel's letter to his mother promptly, if peremptorily. Beyond assuring Mrs Spandrel that her son would be out of the Middlesex magistrates' jurisdiction throughout his absence and therefore not liable to arrest, he told her nothing and was gone almost before she had read the few lines William had written. They likewise told her nothing, other than not to worry, which naturally she did, especially when Annie Welsh expressed her certainty that Jupe was the man who had called there on Friday morning. William had been planning this since then at least, possibly longer. That much seemed clear. But nothing else was. And, until it became so, she would do little *but* worry. 'For that boy's sake,' she gamely informed Annie Welsh, 'I hope he's got a good excuse for leaving his old mother in the lurch.'

* * *

Whether his mother would regard his excuse as good or bad did not figure in Spandrel's thoughts as Sir Theodore's skiff nosed in to the dock at Deptford and drew alongside the *Vixen* beneath a gun-metal noonday sky. His confidence had already faded in the sobering face of a journey down the Thames during which the boatmen had said not a word to him, though they had exchanged many meaningful looks and mutters. He was cold and hungry and would soon be far from home. What was in the box? He did not know. He did not want to know. If all went well, he never would. And if all did not go well . . .

Why *had* Sir Theodore chosen him? And why had he not sent him by the Harwich route? There were questions, but no answers. Except one: he had to go through with it; he had no choice.

That would probably still have been Spandrel's conclusion had he been aware of the other sea crossing being made that day by a recent visitor to the house of Sir Theodore Janssen. Robert Knight was also on his way out of the country, boarding a private yacht at Dover by prior arrangement for the short voyage to Calais. When the Committee of Inquiry reconvened at South Sea House on Monday morning to continue his examination, it was going to find itself without an examinee.

CHAPTER FOUR

The Mapmaker's Journey

In other circumstances, Spandrel would probably have enjoyed his journey to Amsterdam, a choppy crossing on the *Vixen* proving, somewhat surprisingly, that he did not suffer from sea-sickness. Anxiety was a different matter, however. Once he had delivered the box to de Vries, he would be able to relish the sights and sensations of foreign travel. Until then, he could only wish the days and miles away.

He tried to keep himself to himself, but a loquacious tile merchant from Sussex called Maybrick wore down his defences in the passenger cabin of the *Vixen* and insisted on accompanying him from Helvoetsluys, where they landed on Monday afternoon, as far as Rotterdam. For Maybrick's benefit, Spandrel claimed to be what he would so like to have been: a mapmaker thinking of applying his talents to the cities of the United Provinces.

He could not complain too much about Maybrick, though, since the fellow took him to an inn in Rotterdam that was comfortable as well as cheap and told him how sensible he had been to avoid the Harwich run on account of the grasping ways of Essex innkeepers.

Spandrel was nevertheless relieved to continue on his own the following morning, by horse-drawn *trekschuit* along winding canals through flat, winter-stripped fields.

Rain of varying intensity, ranging from drizzle to down-pour, fell out of the vast grey dome of sky and the *trekschuit* kept up a slow if steady pace. It finally delivered its passengers to Haarlem nine hours later, in the chill of early evening, bone-weary and, in Spandrel's case, fuddled by spending all bar a few minutes of those nine hours inhaling other people's pipe smoke in the cramped cabin.

But Haarlem was only three hours from Amsterdam. Next morning, washed and refreshed, Spandrel felt his fragile confidence return. Before the day was out, he would have done what Sir Theodore had asked of him. Nothing was going to stop him. And nothing was going to go wrong.

The rain persisted. The Haarlem to Amsterdam *trekschuit* seemed draughtier and damper than the one Spandrel had travelled on the day before. Or perhaps it was simply that his tolerance was diminishing. The vast stretches of water between which the canal ran through a scrawny neck of land created the illusion that they were voyaging out to an island somewhere in the Zuyder Zee, well enough though he knew Amsterdam's location from his father's collection of maps.

At length they arrived, the canal running out into the moat that surrounded the city wall. Above them, on the wall, windmills sat like sentinels, their sails turning slowly in the dank breeze. It was early afternoon and Spandrel was eager to press on to his destination. Spending money with a liberality he reckoned he could easily accustom himself to, he hired a coach from the city gate to take him to the de Vries house. '*Ik heb haast*,' he told the driver, using a phrase he had picked up from merchant Maybrick. 'I'm in a hurry.' It was nothing less than the truth.

38

*   *   *

The houses of Herengracht were elegant and uniform, their high, narrow frontages lining the canal in a display of prosperity that convinced Spandrel he was entering the very heart of the city's mercantile community. The de Vries residence, which the coachman had seemed to know well, looked very much like its neighbours, a broad staircase leading up to a loftily architraved entrance at mezzanine level. Gazing up from the street, Spandrel noticed the hoist-beams jutting out above its topmost windows. Every house had such devices. His eye followed them round the curve of the canal. Suddenly, and unwelcomely, he thought how like a row of Smithfield meat-hooks they looked, waiting for a carcass. Then he thrust the thought aside and climbed the steps.

An elderly manservant answered the door. He had an unsmiling air of truculence about him, as if he sensed that Spandrel was not so important as to merit any show of respect. The fellow communicated by grimaces and hand signals, presumably because he spoke no English. He admitted Spandrel no farther than the marbled hall and left him to wait on a low chair literally overshadowed by a vast oriental urn on a plinth.

Five minutes passed, precisely timed for Spandrel by the long-case clock he was sitting opposite. Then a tall, dark-eyed man of about Spandrel's own age appeared. He had an intent, solicitous expression and was immaculately if plainly dressed. But there was also a languor about him, an impression of unstated superiority. And in those sea-cave eyes there was something else which disturbed Spandrel. He could not have said what it was. *That* was what disturbed him.

'Mr Spandrel,' the man said in perfectly enunciated

but accented English. 'My name is Zuyler. I am Mijnheer de Vries's secretary.'

'Is Mijnheer de Vries at home?'

'I regret not.'

'I must see him. It is a matter of some urgency.'

'So I understand.' Zuyler cast a fleeting glance at the satchel. 'You are expected. But the time of your arrival was unknown. And Mijnheer de Vries is a busy man.'

'I'm sure he is.'

'My instructions are to ask you to wait here while I fetch him. He is at the Oost Indisch Huys. It is not far. But I cannot say how . . . involved in business . . . I may find him. Nevertheless . . .'

'I'll wait.'

'Good. This way please.'

Zuyler led him towards the rear of the house and into what was clearly de Vries's library. Well-stocked book-cases lined the walls and the windows were shaded against the depredations of sunlight, an unnecessary precaution, it seemed to Spandrel, in view of the grey weather he had travelled through. Sure enough, more light was coming from the fire burning in the grate than from the world beyond the windows.

'I will return as soon as I can,' said Zuyler. And with that he was gone, slipping silently from the room with disconcerting suddenness.

Spandrel looked around him. Busts of assorted ancients were spaced along the tops of the bookcases. Lavishly framed oil paintings of less ancient subjects – Dutch burgher stock, for the most part – occupied the space between them and the stuccoed ceiling. Above the mirror over the fireplace was a painting of a different order, depicting a castle of some sort in a tropical setting, palm trees bending in an imagined breeze. An armchair and a sofa stood either side of the fireplace. There was a desk in front of one of the windows and a wide table adjacent to a section of bookcasing given over to map drawers. Spandrel was tempted to slide the drawers open and see what they contained, but he resisted. He did not want to complicate his presence in the house in any way. He wished, in fact, to know as little as possible about its owner; and that owner, in turn, to know as little as possible about him.

But that was easier thought than adhered to. There was a clock in this room too, ticking through the leaden minutes. Spandrel sat down in front of the fire, stood up and inspected the paintings, sat down again, stood up again. And all the while he kept the satchel in his hand.

Twenty minutes slowly elapsed. Spandrel had little hope that de Vries could be swiftly extricated from his place of business. He stood glumly in the centre of the room, examining his reflection in the mirror. It was a clearer and fuller version of himself than he had seen for many months and the hard times he had lived through during those months had left their mark – there was no denying it. He looked older than his years. He had acquired a faint sagging of the shoulders that would become a permanent stoop if he did not mend his posture, which he thereupon did, to encouraging effect. But it was only that: an effect. It could not last. As if admitting as much, he let his shoulders relax.

At which moment the door opened behind him and a dark-haired young woman in a blue dress entered the room. 'Excuse me,' she said, her accent sounding genuinely English. 'I did not realize . . .'

'Your pardon, madam.' Spandrel turned and mustered a bow. 'I was bidden to wait here for Mijnheer de Vries.'

'You may have a long wait, sir. My husband is at East

41

India House. I am not expecting him back before six o'clock.'

Spandrel registered the disconcerting fact that this woman was de Vries's wife. She could not be much above twenty-five, but Sir Theodore had described de Vries as a man of about his own age, so Mrs de Vries had to be more than thirty years his junior. To make matters worse, she was quite startlingly attractive. Not classically beautiful, it was true. Her nose was too long, her brow too broad, for that. But she had a poise and an openness of expression that overrode such considerations. Her blue dress set off her hair and eyes perfectly. There was a curl of some nascent smile playing about her lips. Her eyebrows were faintly arched. Around her neck she wore a single string of pearls, at her breast a white satin bow. Confined for so long to the female company of Cat and Dog Yard, Spandrel had forgotten how intoxicating close proximity to a well-dressed and finely bred woman could be. And even Maria Chesney had lacked something that Mrs de Vries quite obviously possessed: a confidence in her own womanhood that made her marriage to the crabbed old miser Spandrel had suddenly decided de Vries must be less a mockery . . . than a tragedy.

'Have you come far to see my husband, Mr . . .'

'Spandrel, madam. William Spandrel.'

'From England, perhaps?'

'Indeed.'

'It is always a pleasure to hear an English voice. You will have guessed, of course, that I am only Dutch by marriage. My husband speaks excellent English. So do most of the household. But . . .' She trailed into a thoughtful silence.

'I met Mr Zuyler.'

'Well, well, there you are. A fluent example, indeed. But fluency is not quite authenticity, is it?' She smiled.

42

'No,' Spandrel said hesitantly. 'I suppose not.'

'Where is Mr Zuyler now?'

'He has gone to fetch your husband.'

'To fetch him? With the expectation that he will wish to be fetched, I assume. You must be an important man, Mr Spandrel.'

'Hardly.'

'Has no-one offered you tea?'

'Er . . . no.'

'Then let me do so.' She moved past him to the bell-pull beside the fireplace and tugged at it. 'When did you arrive in Amsterdam?'

'This afternoon. By barge from Haarlem.'

'Then tea you will certainly need.'

'Thank you.' Spandrel smiled cautiously. 'It would be most welcome.'

'Please be seated.'

'Thank you.' Spandrel was aware of repeating himself. He sat down in the armchair and self-consciously lowered the satchel to the floor beside him.

Mrs de Vries sat on the sofa opposite him and seemed on the point of saying something when the door opened and a maid entered. There was a brief conversation in Dutch. The maid withdrew.

'How long,' Spandrel began, feeling the need to speak even though there was little he could safely say, 'have you lived in Amsterdam, Mrs de Vries?'

'Nearly three years, Mr Spandrel.'

'You speak the language . . . very well.'

'Not as well as I should. But Mr Zuyler has been as assiduous a tutor as his other duties will allow.'

'What part of England do you come from?'

'An obscure part. But your accent betrays you as a Londoner, I think.'

'You're correct.'

'How is the city these days?'

'The city is well. But the spirits of its citizens are generally low.'

'Because of the collapse in South Sea stock?'

'Indeed. I see you're well informed.'

'My husband is a man of business, Mr Spandrel. How should I not be? Besides, the South Sea Company has scarcely fewer victims here than in London. And those who have not thrown their money down that drain have consigned it to the pit of the Mississippi Company instead. Did London hold itself aloof from that?'

'I think not.' Spandrel had read various references to the Mississippi Company in the third- or fourth-hand newspapers that were his only informants on the world. It had been France's imitation of the South Sea scheme. Or was it the other way round? He could not rightly remember. 'But it seems . . . you know more about such matters than I do.'

'You would be unique among my husband's business associates if that were the case.'

'But I'm not his associate, madam. Merely the servant of one.'

'And would your master be Sir Theodore Janssen?'

Spandrel flinched with surprise. He had not expected to be seen through so easily.

'Forgive me, Mr Spandrel.' Mrs de Vries smiled at him reassuringly. 'The deduction required no great acuity on my part. Sir Theodore is my husband's oldest friend. My husband mentioned receiving a letter from him recently. Sir Theodore lives in London. You come from London. And Mr Zuyler hastens off to fetch Mr de Vries from the midst of his mercantile deliberations. You see? Simplicity itself.'

'Only when you explain it.'

'You flatter me.' Her smile broadened and Spandrel

44

realized that flattery had indeed been his intention. Then there came a stirring of the latch. 'Ah. Here's Geertruid with our tea.'

Geertruid it was, somewhat out of humour to judge by the sighs that accompanied her arrangement of the cups, plates, spoons and saucers. A rich-looking cake had arrived along with the tea and, as soon as Geertruid had left, Mrs de Vries cut him a large slice and watched approvingly as he tasted it.

'Travel makes a man hungry, does it not, Mr Spandrel?'

'It does, madam, I confess. And this is . . . excellent cake.'

'Good. You must eat your fill. There is no need for a man to go hungry in this house. My husband's prudence in matters of business has served us well of late.'

'I'm glad to hear it.'

'There is a saying in Dutch he often quotes. "*Des waereld's doen en doolen is maar een mallemoolen.*" "The ways of the world are but a fool's merry-go-round." But, if that is the case, I often think, it begs the question: are we all fools, then? For we must all live in the world.'

'I'm not sure there can be an answer to such a question.'

'Not one we would wish to hear, at any rate. Quite so. Let us try another, then. How long have you been in Sir Theodore's service, Mr Spandrel?'

'Not long at all.'

'And before?'

'I am a mapmaker by profession.'

'Indeed? I wonder you do not pursue your profession.'

'Times are hard. And in hard times people decide they can live without maps.'

'But without a map, there is always the danger of going astray.'

'As many do.'

'How did you take up your profession?'

'From my father.'

'An eminent mapmaker?'

'A prosperous one – for a while.'

'My husband has a Mercator Atlas. Is that the sort of mapmaking of which we speak?'

'Not exactly. I map . . . closer to home.'

'Ah. Then you may be interested in this.' Mrs de Vries rose and moved to the map drawers Spandrel had eyed earlier. She pulled one open, slid out a sheet and laid it on the table. 'A recent acquisition. Come and look at it.'

Spandrel set down his tea and joined her by the table. A map of London lay before him; one he well recognized as the work of a competitor.

'Is it good?' Mrs de Vries asked.

'It's . . . accurate. If a little . . . out of date.'

'Out of date?' Mrs de Vries laughed lightly. 'I shall look forward to teasing my husband with that remark.'

'All maps are out of date to some degree.'

'Then should we discard them, like an old newspaper?'

'They should be drawn so that you don't *want* to discard them.'

'Ah. Because of their beauty?'

'Yes.' He looked round at her to find that she was already looking at him. He was suddenly aware of her perfume enveloping him and of how close they were, the lace ruff at her elbow just touching his sleeve. 'Exactly.'

'So, your maps are works of art?'

'I only wish—'

The door opened abruptly, too abruptly for the arrival of a servant. And clearly the person who entered was nothing of the kind. He was a short, barrel-chested old man in russet greatcoat and black suit, the coat worn draped over his shoulders like a cape, the sleeves empty. His face was lined but mobile, broken veins reddening his sharp cheekbones beneath grey, wary eyes framed by a mane of his own snowy white hair. The absence of a wig and the way he had shrugged on the coat, presumably the more readily to shrug it off, conveyed at once a certain bluntness, if not brusqueness. Ysbrand de Vries, as Spandrel felt sure the newcomer was, lacked his old friend Sir Theodore Janssen's polish and perhaps also his subtlety. But he was the one of them who, according to his wife, had scorned the lure of South Sea and Mississippi alike. He, Spandrel reminded himself, was the better judge of the two.

'Mr Spandrel,' the man growled unsmilingly. 'I am de Vries.'

'Your servant, sir. I've come—'

'Enough of that.' He glanced at his wife. 'You may leave us, madam. *Ga weg.*' It sounded like what it undoubtedly was: a dismissal verging on the curt.

'Goodbye, Mr Spandrel,' said Estelle de Vries, so unembarrassed by her husband's manner that Spandrel could only suppose it was what she was well used to. 'I hope you enjoyed your tea.'

'I did. Thank you.' Already, as he spoke, she was on her way out of the room. As the door closed behind her, he looked at de Vries and summoned a respectful smile. 'Mijnheer—'

'Janssen sent you?'

'Sir Theodore Janssen, yes.'

'With an article for safe-keeping.'

'Yes. But . . .' Spandrel retreated to the armchair and retrieved the satchel. 'I must take precautions, mijnheer. You understand?'

'What precautions?'

'I'm instructed to ask you to name the third member

47

of the party on the occasion of your and Sir Theodore's first meeting.'

'Ha. *Spelletjes, spelletjes, spelletjes.* Janssen plays too much. You cannot always win.' De Vries pulled off his coat and tossed it over the back of the armchair. 'You liked the tea, Mr Spandrel? You enjoyed the . . . tart?'

'The cake was good.'

'The secret is in the spices.' De Vries scowled at him. 'No doubt.'

'Jacob van Dillen.'

'I beg your pardon?'

'The name you require . . . for Sir Theodore's game. Van Dillen.'

'Yes. Of course. I'm sorry.'

'So. The article. It is in the bag?'

'Yes.'

'Give it to me, then.'

Spandrel took the satchel to the table, laid it next to the map of London, opened the flap and slid out the despatch-box. De Vries's shadow fell across it as he did so, the old man's hand stretching out to brush the map aside.

'There were no . . . difficulties on your journey?'

'None, mijnheer.'

'That is good.' De Vries reached for the despatch-box and Spandrel noticed how swollen his knuckles were, how claw-like his fingers. He imagined them touching Estelle's soft, pale flesh and could not suppress a quiver of disgust at the thought. 'You are cold?'

'No. It's nothing.'

'Relief, perhaps.' De Vries slid the despatch-box towards himself. 'At a mission accomplished.'

'Perhaps.'

'You require a receipt?'

'Yes. Please. I do.'

De Vries smiled with half his mouth, then marched to the desk by the window and seized pen and paper. He did not sit down, but stooped to write, quickly, in a practised hand. Spandrel watched him, marvelling at how lightly his distorted fingers held the pen. Then he was done, and marching back to the table, holding out the receipt for Spandrel to take.

'Thank you, mijnheer.' Spandrel glanced down at the document and flushed at once with a sense of his own stupidity. 'But . . . it's in Dutch.'

'I *am* Dutch, Mr Spandrel.'

'I don't know what it says.'

'It is what you asked for. A receipt.' De Vries raised a wintry eyebrow. 'You doubt me?'

'I . . . must be sure.'

'Must you?'

'Yes. I think I must.'

'I think you must too.' De Vries gave another lopsided smile. 'I can also play games, you see? You write what you require.' He waved him towards the desk. 'I will sign it.'

Spandrel walked over to the desk, de Vries keeping pace behind him. He sat down, the old man looming at his shoulder, and wrote.

'Very good,' said de Vries when he had finished. 'But you have the date wrong. We are eleven days ahead of England here. And you are here, not there.' He took the pen, crossed out 25th January and wrote 5th February in its place. 'It is always better to be ahead than behind.' Then he added his signature. 'You are not an experienced traveller, I think.'

'No,' admitted Spandrel, shamed by his mistake.

'Dates can be confusing. It will still be January when you return to England. Those of us who make our profits and losses by the day' – he tapped his temple – 'keep such things in mind.'

'Yes. Of course.' Spandrel folded the receipt and slipped it into his pocket.

'Be sure not to lose that.'

'I will be.'

'When will you leave Amsterdam?'

'As soon as possible.'

'A pity, if this is your first visit. The city would repay a longer stay.'

'Sir Theodore will be anxious for confirmation of the box's safe delivery.' Spandrel stood up. 'I must go.'

'How will you travel?'

'The way I came. By barge.'

'You know the times?'

'I confess not.' Spandrel was once again brought up sharp by his own stupidity. He should have enquired about the return journey to Haarlem on arrival at the city gate. But, in his haste to reach de Vries's house, he had forgotten to do so. 'Do you, mijnheer, by any chance . . .'

'Keep them also in mind? No, I do not. But I employ someone who does.' De Vries strode to the door, opened it and bellowed into the hallway, 'Zuyler! *Hier! Onmiddellijk!*' Then, leaving the door open, he marched across to the table on which the despatch-box lay. But it was not the box he was looking at. 'Why did Estelle show you my map of London, Mr Spandrel?'

'She thought I would be interested.'

'Why?'

'Because I am a mapmaker by profession.'

'How did she know that?'

'I told her.'

'You tell too much.' De Vries turned and regarded him thoughtfully. 'It is a bad habit. You should—' He broke off at Zuyler's appearance in the doorway.

'Mijnheer?' There was a brief exchange in Dutch, then

Zuyler nodded and looked at Spandrel. 'You are bound for Helvoetsluys, Mr Spandrel?'

'I am.'

'Your quickest passage would be by the overnight *trekschuit* direct to Rotterdam. It leaves at eleven o'clock, from the Oudezijds Herenlogement on Grimburgwal.' De Vries intervened in Dutch at this and Zuyler smiled faintly before continuing. 'Mijnheer de Vries suggests I take you there. He doubts you will find the way. The Herenlogement is an inn. You may wish to take a meal before your journey.'

'Thank you. I'm sure I can find it myself.'

'It would be my pleasure to escort you, Mr Spandrel.'

'In that case . . .' Spandrel glanced from one to the other of them, 'I accept.'

'Goodbye then, Mr Spandrel,' said de Vries. 'Tell Sir Theodore . . .'

'Yes?'

'Nothing.' De Vries looked at him unsmilingly. 'That is always best.'

CHAPTER FIVE

Into the Darkness

It turned out to be but a short walk from the de Vries house to Grimburgwal. Spandrel was nonetheless grateful to have a guide. The network of canals and bridges and alleys that comprised Amsterdam seemed designed to confuse the stranger, so similar was one part of the whole to another. He jokingly asked Zuyler if this were deliberate, but the Dutchman responded with dry seriousness that he thought not and had himself found London equally bewildering without being driven to suspect a plot against foreigners.

Zuyler, of course, had only a swift return to his secretarial duties to look forward to, whereas Spandrel, his task accomplished, was already anticipating the transformation in his circumstances that awaited him in England. The disparity in their levels of humour did not really surprise Spandrel. Indeed, having met Ysbrand de Vries, he could not help feeling sorry for anyone who had to work for him. An attempt to put this into words, however, fell as flat as his joke.

'I imagine Mijnheer de Vries is a demanding employer.'

'That is the nature of employment,' Zuyler replied. 'It makes demands of one.'

'Indeed. But—'

'And it seldom rewards imagination.' Zuyler pulled up

and pointed to a handsomely pedimented building on the other side of the canal. 'That is the Oudezijds Herenlogement. The Rotterdam *trekschuit* will pick up from the landing-stage in front.'

'Well, thank you for showing me the way.'

'I hope you have a safe journey.'

'I'm sure I will.'

Zuyler gave him a faint little nod that hovered on the brink of becoming a bow but never did, then turned and walked away. Spandrel watched him for a few paces, then had to step beneath the awning over a hatter's shop while a coach drove by. It was mounted on sledge-runners, as if designed for harsher weather than the prevailing mild grey dismalness, but rattled across the cobbles briskly enough. When Spandrel looked in Zuyler's direction once more, he was nowhere to be seen.

The Oudezijds Herenlogement was as comfortable and congenial an inn as Spandrel could have wished for. The tap-room was full of smoke and warmth and chatter, even at this unpromising hour of the late afternoon. He ate a hearty stew, washed down with a mug of ale, and gleaned confirmation of the *trekschuit* departure time from the tapster. Then he smoked a pipe over a second mug of ale and considered how best to fill the evening he had at his disposal. Darkness had fallen over the city and he knew better than to stray far from the inn, for he would be certain to lose himself. This was not London. He carried no map, on paper or in his head. Much the safer course of action was to stay where he was.

But even the Oudezijds Herenlogement held its hazards. As more and more customers arrived, Spandrel was joined at his table by three drinkers of genial demeanour, one lean, animated and talkative, the other two paunchy, dough-faced and content to puff at their pipes and quaff from their mugs while their companion chattered on. The chatterer soon tried to involve Spandrel in the conversation and, upon realizing that an Englishman was among them, gleefully revealed his knowledge of the language.

Spandrel was half-drunk by then, nestled in a smoky swathe of self-satisfaction. Jan, the chatterer, evinced nothing but a grinning eagerness to hear his description of London life, while the puffing and quaffing pair – Henrik and Roelant – set a stiff pace of consumption which he felt obliged to match. A few desultory hands of cards were played, although Spandrel found it difficult to distinguish the clubs from the spades. Toasts were drunk to good health and fellowship. A venture to the jakes demonstrated to Spandrel that he was becoming unsteady on his feet, though he persuaded himself that a few lungfuls of night air aboard the *trekschuit* would cure the problem, ignoring the fact that the *trekschuit* was not due to leave for another few hours. Then he and Jan became embroiled in a comparison of Englishwomen and Dutchwomen that led to a fateful challenge. Jan knew a nearby *musico*, as he called it, where particularly delectable young women could be had at reasonable rates. Let Spandrel sample one and he would be bound to admit their superiority to anything London had to offer. Tea with Estelle de Vries had undeniably whetted Spandrel's sexual appetite, just as ale with Jan, Henrik and Roelant had fuddled his judgement. Assured by Jan that he would be back long before eleven o'clock, he accepted the challenge.

He knew it was a mistake as soon as he left the inn. Far from clearing his head, the night air administered a chill shock which set it reeling. That and the enveloping darkness disoriented him at once. Jan led the way, Spandrel several times needing Henrik's or Roelant's assistance to keep track of him through the cobbled gulfs of blackness between the few street-lamps, confusingly reflected as they were in the adjacent canal.

Then they left the canal behind, turning first right, then left, then right into a narrow alley lit only to the degree that it was less dark at its far end. Spandrel decided he had had enough. Lust had entirely deserted him. He hurried to catch Jan up, asking him to stop at the same time.

'I'm not sure about this, Jan. I don't feel—'

Suddenly, he tripped, on what he had no idea. He fell heavily to the ground and rolled into the central gutter, then struggled to his knees, looking around for assistance. But he did not receive assistance. Instead, he received a boot in the midriff that drove the breath from his body and was followed by a wave of nausea. A second boot added a sharp, disabling pain to the nausea. Then something blunt and heavy struck him round the side of the head. He fell helplessly into the gutter, his senses grasping little beyond fear and the impossibility of escape. He had been taken for a fool and he had acted like one. They were thieves and probably murderers too. He was done for.

He must have vomited at some point. He dimly saw a pale smear of it on one of their sleeves and heard the owner curse him. It was Henrik. Or Roelant. He could no longer tell. It earned him another cuff to the head and a deepening of the blear through which his brain struggled to understand what was happening. The ale he had drunk dulled his pain but sapped his ability to think or to act. He was dragged into a doorway and hauled into a sitting position. Then they began rifling through his pockets. One by one they were emptied, till finally his money-bag was pulled out, tearing off the button fastening the pocket it was in with such force that it bounced back onto his face from the wall next to him. '*Snel, snel,*' he heard Jan say. '*Het zand.*' Something else was being put in to replace the money-bag – something heavy and bulky. Whatever it was, the same was being thrust into his outer pockets. Then he was dragged upright and carried along the alley, held by his arms across Henrik's and Roelant's shoulders, his feet scuffing the cobbles.

He glimpsed lamplight to left and right and the vague outline of a bridge. They must be near a canal. That fact was as much as he had grasped before he was abruptly released and found himself falling. He managed to brace his arms in front of him to take the impact. But it was not the cobbles he hit.

The water was cold and darkly turbid, a soundless world that wrapped its muddy coils around him and held him fast. He could not swim, but even had he been able to he would probably have been helpless, so heavy did he feel, so resistant did the water seem. He recognized the end that he now confronted: a drowned drunkard, far from home. He struck out against it. He saw a shimmer of lamplight, refracted through the water. He was close to the surface, but not close enough. He sank back, abandoning the effort and with it himself to the oblivion that folded itself around him.

Then something caught at his shoulder and lifted him bodily through the water. He broke surface and gulped in the air, coughing convulsively. There were stone stairs at his back, leading down from the street into the canal. A boat-hook was being disentangled from his coat as he was dragged up the lower steps. Somebody was behind him, hands beneath his shoulders, knees braced at his side. 'Push yourself up,' said a voice he vaguely recognized. 'Push, damn your eyes.'

Spandrel did push, but it was the other man who did most of the work. When they were both clear of the water, he lay back, panting from the effort.

'We can't stay here.' Now Spandrel knew who he was. 'They may come back.'

'Zuyler? Is that . . . you?'

'Listen to what I'm saying,' Zuyler hissed. 'We have to go. Quickly.'

'I can't . . . move.'

'You'll have to.' Zuyler struggled to his feet, pulling Spandrel half-upright as he did so. 'Get up, man.'

'I can't, I tell you.' Spandrel gave way to a bout of coughing. His clothes were saturated, the stench of canal mud rising in a plume around him. 'I feel so weak.'

'This will help.' Zuyler bent over him, pulled something bulky from his right-hand coat pocket, then from his left, and tossed the objects into the canal. 'Sandbags,' he announced. 'To weigh down your corpse.'

'Oh God.'

'God will not help you, Spandrel. But I will. Now stand up.'

Afterwards the instinct for survival that lies dormant until it is most needed could alone satisfactorily explain to Spandrel how he was able to bludgeon his body into the action required of it that night. Quaking from the cold, and from the shock of what had happened, his clothes a chill, dripping weight around him, he somehow managed to follow Zuyler through a labyrinthine mile of alleys and canalsides to a chemist's shop, the meanly furnished basement of which constituted Zuyler's less than stylish residence.

Zuyler lit a fire for Spandrel to warm himself by, huddled in a blanket, his wet, mud-caked clothes discarded. A glass of schnapps and a bowl of soup slowly revived him, until he was able to offer the man who had saved his life some stumbling words of gratitude.

'You thank me,' Zuyler responded, puffing thought-fully at his pipe before adding, with a rueful smile, 'and I curse you.'

'What?'

'I curse you, Spandrel. For presenting me with such a choice.'

'I don't . . . understand.'

'What do you think happened to you tonight?'

'I . . . fell into bad company.'

'Indeed you did. But why?'

'Because I was . . .' He broke off to cough. The pain in his side every time he did so had convinced him that at least one of his ribs was broken. But the throbbing ache in his head had the meagre merit of distracting him from the injury. 'I was foolish.'

'And that is all?'

'What else?'

'What else is what brought me to your aid. Cornelis Hondslager is not a—'

'Who?'

'Hondslager. The thin one.'

'He said his name was Jan.'

'No doubt he did. Aliases are a natural condition of his occupation.'

'And what is his occupation?'

'He is an assassin, Spandrel. A hired killer.'

'Hired?'

'To kill you. The other two I don't know. His regular assistants, I think we can assume.'

'To kill me?' Spandrel was having difficulty keeping

58

pace with the implications of what Zuyler was saying.
'But that means . . .'

'It was arranged beforehand. Exactly.'

'How do you know?'

'I observed a meeting yesterday between de Vries and
Hondslager. It was the purest chance. The coffee-house
they chose for the purpose is not the kind of establishment where my employer is likely to be seen, in normal
circumstances. That is actually why I sometimes use it.
Well, clearly the circumstances were not normal.
Another customer had alerted me to Hondslager's occupation some time ago. I could have little doubt as to the
reason for their meeting and fell to asking myself who de
Vries wanted to have killed. Your arrival this afternoon
provided a possible answer. It could have been a coincidence, of course. De Vries has many enemies. He might
have felt obliged to eliminate one of them, though frankly
I doubted it. It is not the kind of sanction de Vries would
wish to invoke against a business rival, for fear another
rival might be inspired to use it against him. No, no.
A stranger to the city and its ways seemed much the
likelier target. Your arrival therefore seemed anything *but*
coincidental.'

'Why didn't you warn me?'

'Because you don't pay my wages, Spandrel. De Vries
does, albeit reluctantly. My interests are not served by
obstructing his affairs.'

'But you obstructed them this time.'

'Yes.' Zuyler took an irritated swig of schnapps. 'You
can thank my conscience for that.'

'I do. Believe me.'

'Which will profit me precisely nothing. But there it
is. What's done is done. After de Vries had finished with
me this evening, I decided to call at the Oudezijds
Herenlogement on my way home to see that you had

come to no harm. But you were already in Hondslager's
company, too drunk to notice me or indeed the trap that
was closing around you. Where did you think you were
going, by the way?'

'A *musico*.'

'Much as I thought. Well, you could say Hondslager's
done you a favour, Spandrel. At least you won't have a
dose of pox to remember Amsterdam by.'

'It's a great consolation.'

'There was nothing I could do while you were in their
hands. They'd have made short work of me. Fortunately
for you, however, they didn't linger after pushing you
into the canal. They must have thought the sand-bags
would keep you under. And they would have done if I
hadn't been standing by with the boat-hook. I'd guessed
what they were planning for you. Drowning's so much
easier to explain than a knifing, especially for a newcomer
to the city. *If* your body had ever been found, that is,
which I doubt. There must be more than a few murdered
men rotting in the mud at the bottom of our canals. So,
I borrowed the hook from a barge moored round the
corner and tried my hand at fishing you out.'

'You're a good fisherman, Zuyler. I'll say that.'

'Thank you. It's not often a mere secretary has the
chance to save someone's life.'

'If saving me's what you had in mind, I'm afraid your
work's not done yet.'

'How so?'

Spandrel sighed. His thoughts were ordered enough
now to reveal the bleakness of his plight. He was alive.
But, in many ways, he might just as well be dead. De
Vries could have had no reason to commission his
murder other than as a favour for a friend – his oldest
friend, Sir Theodore Janssen. Janssen had wanted
Spandrel to deliver the box to de Vries. But he had not

wanted him to return with proof that he had done so. That was clearly not part of his plan at all.

'Spandrel?'

'The letter Sir Theodore sent ahead of me to de Vries.' He looked sharply at Zuyler. 'Did you see it?'

'No.'

'So you don't know if, in that letter, Sir Theodore asked his good friend Ysbrand to ensure I didn't leave Amsterdam alive.'

'Do you think he did?'

'What else am I to think?'

'Why would he do that?'

'Because he required the services of a discreet and reliable courier.' Now Spandrel knew why he had been chosen for the mission, rather than Jupe or some other lackey. He was easily suborned and eminently expendable; he was the perfect combination. 'You understand, Zuyler? There's no more discreet kind of courier . . . than the dead kind.'

CHAPTER SIX

Plot and Counter-Plot

Spandrel slept little that night. He and Zuyler sat talking by the sputtering fire into the small hours, and even when Zuyler had retreated to his bed in the back room, leaving Spandrel to find what rest he could on the cot beside the chimney-breast, sleep proved elusive. His ribs pained him and there was no position he lay in that did not chafe a tender spot.

None of that would have kept him awake, however, so physically weary did he feel. It was the whirl of thoughts in his head that would give him no peace. It was the compulsive gaze of his mind's eye into the uncertainty of his future.

He was alive. De Vries, and hence soon Sir Theodore Janssen, must think him dead. But he was not. That represented his one advantage over them. Unhappily, it was outweighed by more profound disadvantages. He had delivered the despatch-box, but the receipt de Vries had signed for it had been stolen, along with all his money. He could not ask de Vries for a replacement without exposing himself to the danger of a second attempt on his life. But he could not return to England and demand Sir Theodore honour their bargain without such a replacement. Not that he supposed Sir Theodore *would* honour their bargain, under any circumstances.

His debts were not going to be cancelled. The map was not going to be finished.

What to do, then? He had no money with which to pay for safe passage out of the city. He scarcely even had clothes to his back, those in which he had been dragged from the canal being so badly soiled by mud and dirty water that it was doubtful he could wear them again, save in dire emergency. Zuyler had lent him a night-shirt, but he could hardly be expected to offer him the run of his wardrobe.

Zuyler had, in truth, already done enough. He had seemed, on first encounter, to be an arid, unbending sort of fellow. But his actions had spoken louder than his cautious words. The account he had given Spandrel of himself had revealed that they were alike in many ways. Educated above his station by a clever but impecunious father, Pieter Zuyler had learned English from the many English students attending the university in his home town of Leiden. He had befriended one of the more prosperous of them, who had offered him employment as a clerk in his father's shipping office in Liverpool. Zuyler had spent three years there before his talents had come to the notice of Ysbrand de Vries through a recommendation from the Dutch East India Company's Liverpool agent. The opportunity to return to the country of his birth had proved irresistible. But he had come to regret seizing that opportunity.

'De Vries is a hard man,' Zuyler had said, his tongue loosened by schnapps. 'Who expects anything else? Not me. But there's hard and hard. De Vries is granite, through and through. Also mean, vicious and cunning. As you've found out.'

'What manner of life does that mean Mrs de Vries leads?'

'I don't know. She never complains. Not to me, at any rate. She behaves as the model wife. And he parades her on his arm as a trophy, to make his rivals hate him the more. I comfort myself with the thought that he would not wish his trophy to be' – Zuyler had cast Spandrel a meaningful glance – 'damaged.'

'You think him capable of that?'

'I think him capable of anything.'

'A formidable enemy, then.'

'Extremely.'

'How can I hope to elude him?'

'By fleeing. And fleeing far. There is no other way.'

'I have to consider my mother.'

'It seems from what you tell me that you'll have to let her think you're dead. Janssen would be sure to hear of any communication between you.'

'Is that what you would do in my position?'

Zuyler had stared long and hard into the fire before replying. 'No. I confess not.'

'Then what *would* you do?'

'There comes a time, my friend, when a man must turn upon his enemy. I cannot say if that time has come for you. But, for me, in your shoes . . .'

'It would have done.'

'Yes.' Zuyler had nodded at him. 'I think so.'

And that was what Spandrel thought too as he lay on the cot and gazed sleeplessly into the darkness. If he fled, he fled from everything. There was nothing he could take with him, not even his past. And his future would be a blank sheet, a mapless void. This was his fate at the hands of powerful men. This was as much as he could hope for. Unless . . .

It was a drizzly dawn in Amsterdam. Spandrel saw the grey sheen of it on the pavement as he looked up through the basement window. He had found a twist of coffee and brewed it in a pot. The aroma woke Zuyler. They sat by the remains of the fire, drinking it, strangely shy of talk at first, perhaps because each of them was waiting for the other to mention the topic they had wrestled with so unavailingly a few hours before.

'I must be gone soon,' said Zuyler eventually, through a thin-lipped smile. 'De Vries does not appreciate lateness.'

'I should be gone soon myself.'

'Take any clothes that you need. Mine are all of a muchness. And all likely to be a little long in the arm and leg for you. I can't help that, I'm afraid. You could do worse than ask my landlord to bandage your ribs.' He nodded upwards. 'Barlaeus is a kindly sort. And a better doctor than many who call themselves doctors. I could spare you a guilder to see you on your way.'

'My way to where?'

'Far from Amsterdam is the only suggestion I can make.'

'You made a different suggestion last night.'

'It's true. I did. Have you decided to act upon it?'

'Yes.'

The two men looked at each other, coolly and soberly acknowledging the momentousness of Spandrel's answer.

'What should I do, Zuyler? How am I to strike back at him?'

'Are you sure you want me to tell you?'

'Oh yes. I'm sure.'

'Very well.' Zuyler leaned forward, an eagerness for intrigue lighting his features. 'Your only chance, as I see it, is to retrieve the box you delivered and find out what it contains. Then you will know why it was deemed necessary to have you killed. And with that knowledge

. . . you may be able to bring down your enemies.'

'De Vries *and* Janssen?'

'I think they stand or fall together in this.'

'But how am I to lay hands on the box now? De Vries will have it under lock and key.'

'Indeed he will.'

'Well, then?'

'It would be impossible, without the help of someone close to him.'

'Such as his secretary, you mean?'

'Exactly.' Zuyler grinned at him.

'You've risked enough for me already. I can't—'

'You misunderstand, Spandrel. The extreme measures taken against you convince me that the contents of that box can be used to break Mijnheer de Vries. To bring him down. To ruin him. Do you think, after all I have endured as his . . . creature . . . that I would baulk at a few small risks to bring about such a satisfying result?' Zuyler's grin broadened. 'Your salvation, my friend. And my pleasure. What say you to that combination?'

Spandrel said yes, of course, as he was bound to. And so Pieter Zuyler and he became co-conspirators. Zuyler had no doubt where the despatch-box was. De Vries kept all his most valuable – and secret – possessions in an iron chest in his study. The key to the chest never left his person, clipped as it was to his watch-chain. It would be necessary to break the chest open. But that was the beauty of Zuyler's plan.

'Tomorrow night,' he gleefully disclosed, 'Mijnheer and Mevrouw de Vries are attending a concert. De Vries wishes to be regarded as a music lover, even though the only music he really enjoys is the chink of coins in his purse. They will be gone from eight o'clock until midnight at least. They will probably go on to a supper party afterwards. De Vries likes me to stay at the house when he's not there. He doesn't think the servants are capable of dealing with any emergency that might arise. Though he's never spoken of it, I suspect burglary is what he truly fears. So, I'll oblige him . . . by supplying a burglar.'

'Me?'

'Exactly. You will enter at the rear. I can arrange for the gate next to the coach-house to be unlocked. I can also arrange for one of the library windows to be unfastened. There's a ladder in the shed next to the coach-house. You can use that to reach the window. The study is the room directly above the library. You'll have little to fear from the servants. They'll take the opportunity of de Vries's absence to huddle over the fire downstairs and complain about him. On this occasion, I think I'll join them. It would be as well for me to have witnesses to my whereabouts at the time of the burglary.'

'How strong is the chest?'

'I'm not sure.' Zuyler smiled. 'I've never tried to break it open. But by the look of the hasp . . .' He plucked the poker from the fireplace and weighed it in his hand. 'Not strong enough.'

To avoid evidence being turned up later of complicity between them, the two men agreed that they should part straight away. Zuyler lent Spandrel a suit of clothes, along with enough money to pay for overnight lodgings. He directed him to a discreetly located tavern, the Gouden Vis, where they would meet after the event to examine the contents of the despatch-box. They left separately, Spandrel first, with a farewell handshake to seal their agreement.

Spandrel walked slowly away from Barlaeus's shop that damp winter's morning, his ribs jarring at every step.

67

He would have to buy a bandage for them from some other chemist. But already the pain seemed less intense, dulled as it was by the contemplation of something he would never have expected to be able to inflict on the likes of Sir Theodore Janssen and his very good friend, Ysbrand de Vries: revenge.

Spandrel assumed – as why would he not? – that Sir Theodore was still comfortably installed at his house in Hanover Square, perhaps at that moment perusing his morning newspaper over a cup of chocolate, smug in his certainty that the courier he had chosen to carry the despatch-box and its so very important contents to Amsterdam was dead, his lips sealed for good and all.

Sir Theodore's situation was, in truth, rather different. Robert Knight's failure to appear before the Committee of Inquiry at South Sea House on Monday had led to a convulsion of righteous indignation in the House of Commons and the forced attendance there of those directors of the South Sea Company who were also Members of Parliament, followed shortly afterwards by their committal to the Tower pending further investigations by the committee, now vested with full executive powers. By the following day, the net had been widened to include all directors and officials of the company.

That morning, therefore, found Sir Theodore confined in an admittedly commodious but scarcely elegant chamber in the Tower of London. He had a view from his window of the traffic on the Thames and the wharves of Bermondsey, but the smell of the river at low tide was a heavy price to pay for such a prospect. The furnishings of the chamber might have been described as generous by someone not as accustomed as Sir Theodore was to the best. Happily, he had always possessed a pragmatical disposition and age had taught him patience if nothing else. Chocolate tasted the same wherever it was drunk, even if the Governor did exploit his monopoly on prisoners' supplies to charge scandalous amounts for portage. And though Brodrick and his fellow inquisitors might think they had him at their mercy, Sir Theodore was confident that they would eventually find it was quite the other way about.

There had been no objection to his valet waiting upon him in his altered place of residence and it was certainly a relief to Sir Theodore that he could begin each day with an expert shave. But Jupe's tonsorial talents, though considerable, were not those his employer valued most highly. Jupe's grasp of events was what Sir Theodore wished to call upon, every bit as much as his steady hand with a razor.

'Who is still at liberty, Jupe?' Sir Theodore accordingly enquired as his barber-cum-newsmonger slid the blade over the crown of his head. 'I'm told there are a dozen of us here.'

'That would be correct, sir. And more are sought. I believe there is not yet a warrant out for Deputy Governor Joye, however. The committee must expect to find him particularly helpful.'

'When does he go before them?'

'Today. Along with Sir John Blunt.'

'Blunt will tell them whatever he thinks will serve him best. And that, I suppose, will be nearly everything.'

'But not *quite* everything, sir?'

'They would need to speak to Knight for that.'

'As they would assuredly like to.'

'Do they know where he is?'

'Brussels has been mentioned.'

'An obvious choice. The Austrian authorities are unlikely to bestir themselves to do the committee's bidding.'

'But the King's bidding, sir?'

'A different matter – should it arise.'

'Rumour has it that the Duke of Wharton means to hire a hearse and drive it through the streets today in a mock funeral procession for the company.'

'The Duke of Wharton is a fool. He and his fellow Jacobites no doubt see this crisis as a gift from the gods. Well, well. Let them stage their funeral. Let them have their fun. What of the Government?'

'Lying low, I rather think, sir. Aislabie is said to be finished and Walpole to be certain of succeeding him as Chancellor.'

'Ah, Walpole. There *is* a man we must watch.'

'There is as yet' – Jupe cleared his throat – 'no word from Amsterdam, sir.'

'Too soon, Jupe.' Sir Theodore permitted himself a faint smile. 'Just a little too soon.'

CHAPTER SEVEN

Breaking and Entering

The Gouden Vis was a small, well-run, brightly painted tavern near the Montelbaanstoren, a disused harbourside watchtower to which a previous generation of Amsterdam's city fathers had added a clock, a decorative spire and a mermaid wind-vane. Spandrel had a good view of the tower from his room, as well as of the harbour, into which the Montelbaanswal canal ran past the front of the tavern. He watched the shipping plying back and forth, the comings and goings from the warehouses on the other side of the canal, the light silvering and fading over the city. He had little else to do for two whole days and a night, while he awaited his chance to turn the tables on Ysbrand de Vries and Sir Theodore Janssen. He could not wander the streets for fear of a chance encounter with the dreaded Hondslager or indeed with de Vries himself. Nor could he while away his time in the tap-room. He could not trust himself when in his cups. That was clear, painfully so, as his ribs and assorted other aches frequently reminded him. Not that he had the money with which to drink away the hours. The loan from Zuyler was strictly for necessary expenditure. And Spandrel's necessities – bed and board, a hammer and chisel to break open the chest in de Vries's study and a dark-lantern to find his way by – had consumed the greater part of it. There was nothing for it but to sit and wait.

Idleness, however, encouraged his mind to wander, even if his feet could not. What was in the despatch-box? What was the secret his death had been intended to conceal? De Vries and Janssen were old men as well as old friends. The answer might lie decades in the past. Or it might rest firmly in the present. Janssen's part in the South Sea disaster came irresistibly to mind. Did that have something to do with it? If so, Spandrel might be about to become involved in matters with which the likes of him should have no dealings.

But he was already involved. He had been from the moment he accepted Sir Theodore's offer. There was no way out – unless it was by plunging further in. His father would have told him to leave well alone. But then his father was partly responsible for the predicament in which he found himself. Dick Surtees, by contrast, would have urged him on. Spandrel had not thought of his harum-scarum schoolfellow in months, nor seen him in years; not since, in fact, Dick had thrown up the apprenticeship Spandrel had persuaded his father to offer him on the grounds that surveying was 'devilish tedious' and declared his intention of going abroad in search, he had told Spandrel, 'of adventures'. But Spandrel, he had added, should stay where he was. 'You're just not the adventuring kind, Billy. Take my word for it.'

Spandrel smiled at the memory. The joke was on Dick now. Adventures, it seemed, were not restricted to the adventuring kind. Anyone could have them. Even, perhaps especially, when they did not want to.

The weather changed during Friday afternoon, a stiffening breeze thinning and then clearing the cloud. The city changed with it, glowing in the sparkling light reflected from the harbour. When the sun set, it did so as a swollen scarlet ball, glaring at Spandrel across the

Amsterdam rooftops. He knew then that his waiting was nearly at an end.

When the clock on the Montelbaanstoren struck nine, he went down to the tap-room and drank two glasses of brandy. Dutch courage, they called it, and he had need of some. But two glasses were as much as he risked. Then he went back to his room to collect the hammer and chisel, concealed in a sack. He lit the lantern and set off.

The night was cold. The breeze of the afternoon had strengthened to a bone-chilling wind. There were few people on the streets and those who were did not dawdle. Nor did Spandrel. He followed the route Zuyler had said was the easiest, even if it was not the quickest, along the Montelbaanswal to the Amstel. He crossed the river by the first bridge to the west and traversed a deserted market-place. From the far corner of the market-place a narrow street led off between the rear walls of the houses on the Herengracht and the frontages of humbler dwellings. This, according to Zuyler, would take him to de Vries's coach-house entrance, which he would be able to recognize by the lamp-bracket on the coach-house door, worked as it was in the form of a monkey. The lamp would be lit, in readiness for the coach's return. If not lit, it could only mean that de Vries had not gone to the concert for some reason, in which case the attempt would have to be abandoned.

But it *was* lit. And there was the cast iron monkey beneath, grinning at him, it seemed, in the flickering glow of the lamp. Spandrel closed the shutter on his lantern, withdrew into the shadows and waited for the clock Zuyler had assured him was within earshot to strike ten, by which time Zuyler was confident the servants would all be in the basement, digesting their supper and regurgitating familiar complaints about their master.

It was a cold and nervous vigil that probably lasted

no more than ten minutes but felt to Spandrel like so many hours. He half-expected the coach to return, or Hondslager to leap at him out of the darkness. Less fancifully, he feared a passer-by would notice him and become suspicious. But there were no passers-by, save one savage-looking cat carrying a mouse in its jaws, who paid Spandrel no attention whatever. Only the stars watched him. Only the night listened. Eventually, the clock struck.

The narrow door in the wall beside the coach-house entrance opened with barely a creak. Spandrel stepped through into a short alley leading to the garden. It appeared as a gulf of blackness between him and the house, where lights shone dimly in the basement. Otherwise all was in darkness. He opened the shutter on his lantern and made his way along the coach-house wall until he reached the lean-to shed at its far end. He raised the latch and eased the door open. There was the ladder, just inside, standing among the hoes and rakes. He took the hammer and chisel out of the sack and wedged them in his pockets in order to free a hand for the ladder, then set off across the garden with his burden, holding the lantern at arm's length in front of him to light the path.

He was breathing heavily by the time he reached the terrace, sweating despite the cold. He glanced down into what looked like a pantry, into which light was spilling meagrely from a room beyond. Mercifully, there was no-one to be seen. Nor, when he paused to listen, could he hear any voices. The coast was clear.

Telling himself to go slowly and carefully, he propped the ladder against the sill beneath the farthest window of the library – the one Zuyler had said he would leave unfastened – and clambered up. There was a moment's resistance from the sash. Then, with a squeak, it gave. He pushed it halfway up, hung the lantern from one of the handles on the frame and scrambled in.

He was back in the room where Estelle de Vries had plied him with tea and Ysbrand de Vries had taken his contemptuous measure of him. He imagined them sitting next to each other at the concert, Estelle relishing the music while Ysbrand relished only the envy of other men that the sight of her would inspire. Spandrel wondered if she would be secretly pleased by what he was about to do. He could not help hoping she would. Maybe it would somehow set her free. If so—

Angry with himself for wasting time on such thoughts, he turned and pulled the ladder up after him. Leaving it in position would be to invite discovery. He laid it on the floor, then retrieved the lantern and closed the window. Silence closed about him as he did so, a silence broken only by the ticking of a clock. He looked round the room, at the bookcases and the paintings and the classical busts. They, like Estelle, were emblems of de Vries's wealth and power. He had no other use for them. They meant no more to him than did anything or anyone else.

Spandrel crossed the room, listened for a moment at the door, heard nothing, then turned the handle. The door opened onto the unlit hallway. The servants must have shut themselves in downstairs. Otherwise he would surely be able to see a glimmer of light in the stairwell. But there was none.

He closed the library door carefully behind him and stood still for a second, his senses straining. Clocks ticked. The wind mewed. He could detect nothing else – no sound, no movement. His luck, their luck, was holding. He moved to the stairs and started up them, avoiding the middle of the treads for fear of creaks.

The door to the study, located directly above the library, was to his left as he reached the top of the stairs.

Hurrying now in spite of himself, he strode across to it and opened it just far enough to slip inside. Then caution reasserted itself. He inched the door shut without letting go of the handle and slowly released it as the snib engaged. Then he turned and raised the lantern, his eyes casting about for the chest.

There it was, stowed against the far wall, between the fireplace and the window: a stout, brass-bound iron chest, fastened with a padlocked hasp. Spandrel walked over to it, ignoring the desk whose shadowy bulk he was aware of beneath the window to his right. He knelt down in front of the chest and tested the hasp with his hand. Zuyler was right, as he had been about everything else. It could be forced readily enough. There would be some noise made in the process. That was the biggest problem. But the servants were far from zealous. That was clear. Zuyler would no doubt be able to persuade them that any noise they did hear came from elsewhere. Spandrel set the lantern on the floor and took out the hammer and chisel.

As he did so, he noticed, out of the corner of his eye, some strange discrepancy in the shadow of the lantern. He turned and saw a dark, liquid patch on the floor-boards and on the rug laid in front of the desk. He picked up the lantern and raised it, directing the beam of light towards the patch.

It was blood, inky black in the lantern-light. And on the floor next to the desk lay a human figure. Spandrel caught his breath at the sight of Ysbrand de Vries's snowy white hair and at his own immediate certainty that the old man was dead. He had not gone to the concert after all. He had gone to meet his maker instead.

Spandrel stood slowly up and stepped towards the desk. He could see de Vries's face now, distorted by the agony of his death. There was blood on his chest and a thick pool of it beneath him where he lay. The toe of Spandrel's shoe touched something. Looking down, he saw a knife lying on the rug, its blade glistening. He looked back at de Vries, at the fixed grimace of his lips, at the staring blankness of his eyes. He tried to think what he should do, how he should react. It was the last thing he had expected, the very last. Whatever secrets the despatch-box contained, they could not hurt de Vries now.

Suddenly, the door was flung open. Light flooded into the room. Spandrel spun round to see the elderly manservant who had admitted him to the house on Wednesday standing in the doorway, holding a candle-lamp. The fellow's jaw dropped open as he took in the scene. Then Zuyler appeared at his elbow, holding a lamp in his left hand – and a pistol in his right. He moved towards Spandrel, his face expressionless, the weapon raised.

'You've killed him, Spandrel. You've murdered Mijnheer de Vries.'

'What? No. What are you—'

The truth silenced Spandrel in the instant that it burst upon his mind. The friendship unlooked-for; the ingenious plan; the unguarded house: they were all part of a plot in which he was a victim along with de Vries. He had been taken for a fool once again. And this time no-one was going to come to his rescue.

He made a lunge for the door, but it was too late. Even as he moved, Zuyler clapped the pistol to his head, halting him in mid-stride.

'Stay exactly where you are, Spandrel,' said Zuyler, cocking the firearm as he spoke.

'But for God's—'

'Shut your mouth.'

The muzzle of the pistol was boring into Spandrel's

temple, forcing him back against the edge of the desk. Zuyler's eyes were in shadow, but Spandrel could sense they too were boring into him.

Zuyler flung a volley of Dutch over his shoulder. The old fellow nodded and hurried away, his footsteps pattering down the stairs. 'I've sent him to alert the watchman,' Zuyler said, the tone of his voice altering now they were alone. 'They'll call out the Sheriff for this. The murder of an eminent citizen in his own home is a grievous thing. But it could be worse. At least the murderer didn't escape. Of course, he may still try. In which case, I'd have no choice . . . but to shoot him.'

'You're mad.'

'Far from it. I'm appalled and indignant at the slaughter of my cherished employer. Now, put the lantern on the desk.' Spandrel did so. 'Drop the hammer and chisel.' Again, he obeyed. They thumped down onto the rug. 'Walk over to the body.'

The pressure of the pistol relaxed just enough to let Spandrel move. He took three halting steps, shadowed by Zuyler, until they were both standing over de Vries.

'Kneel down.' Spandrel lowered himself to his knees. He felt the dampness of the blood seeping through his breeches. 'Lay your palms in the blood.' Spandrel hesitated for no more than a second, but it was enough to bring the pistol prodding at his temple. 'Do as I say.' The calmness in Zuyler's voice told Spandrel clearly that defiance was useless. With a shudder, he flattened his hands on the floor in front of him. 'Now, smear them across your chest.'

Spandrel did as he had been told, glancing up at Zuyler as he plastered the blood over his shirt and coat. 'Why did you kill him?' he asked, almost pleadingly.

'The question, Spandrel, is why *you* killed him. Stand up.'

78

'If you mean to shoot me, you may as well have done with it.'

'I'm not going to shoot you unless you force me to. I'd rather you were taken alive. Now, stand up.'

Spandrel began to rise, wondering if this was his best chance of springing at Zuyler. He had to do something before the Sheriff and his men arrived and convinced themselves of his guilt. He might be able to overpower Zuyler, perhaps even force the truth out of him. He braced himself on one knee, then lunged at Zuyler's midriff.

The pistol went off with a crack, deafeningly close to Spandrel's right ear. But the shot was wide. Spandrel's weight threw Zuyler off his feet. The two men fell together, the lamp rolling away and adding a tangle of shadows to their struggle. Zuyler had lost hold of the pistol as he struck the floor. Seeing it bounce clear, Spandrel made a grab for it, intending to use it as a club. But as he grasped the barrel and swung back towards Zuyler, he glimpsed too late the hammer in the Dutchman's hand, arcing up to meet him

CHAPTER EIGHT

The Arms of the Law

When Spandrel came to his senses, he thought for a moment that he was back in the Fleet Prison. All the ingredients were in place: the subfuscous light filtering down from a high, barred window; the coarse straw mattress he lay on; the coughs and oaths of his cellmates; the stale rankness of confined humanity. Then his mind began to piece together the truth of his situation, which was worse by far than it had been during his miserable days in the Fleet. He was not wherever he was because he could not pay his debts. He was there because he was suspected of murder. And not just any murder. Ysbrand de Vries was dead. Somebody would have to pay for that – with their life.

He sat up and was at once aware of a jolt of pain in his head so intense that he thought for a moment he had been struck with an axe. Then he remembered the hammer in Zuyler's hand, swinging towards him. He reached gingerly up and winced as his fingers touched the source of the pain. His hair was stiff with clotted blood. He did not know how bad the wound might be, but he was alive and capable of coherent thought. Looking around and catching the baleful eye of one of the other occupants of the cell, he reckoned that was the sum total of his blessings.

There was an exchange in Dutch between the man who had noticed Spandrel and another, gravelly voiced fellow in the shadows on the farther side of the cell who seemed to be called Dirk. Dirk then shuffled into clearer view, revealing himself as a gaunt scarecrow of a man, dressed in sewn-together rags that had surely never been clothes. There was a glint in his eye that made Spandrel think of a weasel peering from its hole.

'English, guard said. I speak bit.' He gave a toothless smile.

'I'm English, yes.'

'What you do, Englishman? What they have you for?'

'I did nothing. It's all a mistake.'

'Hah! Mistake. *Ja*. Right.' Dirk winked at him. 'All of us too.'

'I'm telling you the truth. I'm innocent.'

'*Ja, ja*. Who cares? You here. What *for*?'

'Murder,' Spandrel admitted bleakly.

'You kill?'

'So they say.'

'Who?'

'A merchant called de Vries.'

'De Vries? Ysbrand de Vries?'

'Yes. But—'

'De Vries dead?'

'Yes. He's dead.'

Dirk let out an eerie whoop of triumph and clapped his hands together. Most of the other half-dozen or so prisoners turned to look at him. 'You kill well, Englishman. De Vries a good man to kill. Very good.'

'I didn't do it.'

Dirk shrugged and grinned helplessly. 'Tell the executioner. Then you tell me what he says.' With that he sat down on the mattress at Spandrel's feet and winked again. 'You kill de Vries. Now . . .' Dirk mimed the looping of a noose around his neck and the jerking of a rope above his head. 'They kill you.'

Spandrel would have preferred to ignore Dirk, but no-one else spoke English and a few scraps of information were there to be gleaned amidst his alternately morbid and exultant ramblings. They were in a cell beneath Amsterdam's Stadhuis – the Town Hall. Spandrel had been brought in the previous night. The guards' reticence about his offence was now explained by the eminence of his alleged victim. They might expect a meal of stale bread and sour ale around noon. And Spandrel might expect to be questioned before the day was out. He was important, after all. At any rate, his crime was. Dirk was just a humble pickpocket, their cellmates little worse than vagrants. Some of them had been there for weeks, awaiting trial. When they had been tried – and found guilty, of course – a flogging or branding or both would follow. Spandrel would be dealt with in the same way, though perhaps more expeditiously; the authorities would not wish to be accused of dragging their feet in such a case. Only the end would be different. And, for Spandrel, it would be the end in every sense.

It was early evening when they came for him. Two guards marched him out of the cell and along a narrow passage lined on one side by the doors of neighbouring cells and on the other by a blank wall. They reached a large, high-ceilinged room, lit by candles at one end. In the shadowy reaches at the farther end, he thought he could make out the shape of a rack.

A long table stood beneath the chandelier in front of the empty grate. It was colder than in the cell, Spandrel's breath misting in the air. Three men sat at the table, one equipped with pen and paper. A fourth man stood by the shuttered window, smoking a pipe. He was older than the others and seemed to take no interest in Spandrel's arrival. The guards led Spandrel to a chair facing the table and gestured for him to sit. Then they shackled one of his legs to a large wooden block chained to the floor and left.

The two men at the table without pen and paper conversed briefly in Dutch, then one of them – a skinny, sallow-faced fellow with a squint that his narrow, bony nose seemed only to emphasize – said slowly in English, 'Your name is William Spandrel?'

'Yes.'

'This is your examination on the charge of the murder of Mijnheer Ysbrand de Vries. Do you admit the crime?'

'No.'

'You were caught in the act, Spandrel. You cannot deny it.'

'I can explain.'

'Do so.'

Spandrel had already decided that his only chance, and that a slim one, of escaping from the trap Zuyler had lured him into was to tell his inquisitors the truth – the whole truth – and to hope they could be persuaded to doubt Zuyler's version of events. He did not know precisely what that version of events was, of course, but he had little doubt that it painted him in the blackest of colours. He told his story from the beginning, therefore, and held nothing back. He could not judge how convincing it sounded. He was met only by the blankest of faces. When he had finished, there was a discussion in Dutch, then a brief silence, broken by a question he thought he had already answered.

'What did the despatch-box contain?'

'I told you. I don't know.'

'Where is it now?'

'I don't know. If it's not in the chest in Mijnheer de Vries's study, then Zuyler must have taken it.'

'Why would he do that?'

'*I don't know.*'

The man by the window barked a sudden intervention. The English-speaker reacted with no more than a rub of the brow, then said, 'You are an agent of the Marquis de Prié, Spandrel. This is known.'

'Who?'

'You told Mevrouw de Vries that you had come from London by way of Brussels. Why visit Brussels unless it was to attend on the Marquis for instructions?'

'I've . . . never been to Brussels in my life.' A sickening realization clogged Spandrel's thoughts. Estelle de Vries had lied. And that could only mean that she and Zuyler were in this together. 'You must believe me.'

'How can we? The Marquis's intelligence is faulty. Cornelis Hondslager was killed in a tavern brawl several weeks ago.'

'Zuyler must have lied to me about him too.'

'You are the liar, Spandrel. Admit it. Spare yourself a great deal of suffering.'

'I've told you the truth.'

'We will give you time to think. Then you will be re-examined.' The man rose, crossed to the doorway and shouted something in Dutch. One of the guards appeared and there was a murmured conversation.

'Zuyler killed him,' Spandrel shouted in desperation. 'Don't you understand?'

'We are moving you to a cell on your own,' came the unruffled reply. 'You may be able to think better there. For your sake, I hope you do.'

Solitary confinement made Spandrel yearn for the company of Dirk the garrulous pickpocket. A despair, blacker than the night beyond the small, barred window set high in the wall, closed around him. And daybreak did not dispel it. His head ached less and his ribs seemed to be healing well, but that only cleared his mind of a precious distraction from the bleakness of his plight. He had told the truth, but it had done him no good. Sooner or later, torture, or the threat of it, would force him to change his story. Then his guilt would seem to be confirmed and punishment would swiftly follow. Such was the cruel logic of the law in every land. He would admit he was the agent of a man he had never heard of. He would admit to a murder he had not committed. Then they would have done with him.

Why had Estelle de Vries lied? Only one answer made sense to Spandrel. She and Zuyler must be lovers. Now, she could inherit de Vries's wealth and marry the younger man. Yes, that had to be it. Spandrel was the unwitting means to their happy end.

And the three men who had tried to kill him? Were they really agents of de Vries? Or was all of that a piece of play-acting, commissioned by Zuyler? If so, Sir Theodore Janssen might have meant to honour their bargain after all. In that case, Spandrel need only have left Amsterdam when he had the chance and he could even now be contemplating a future free of debts and rich in opportunities.

Instead, he was contemplating four damp walls, a lousy palliasse and an early death. He had seen enough hangings at Tyburn to know how it would be. Whether men went bravely to the gallows, or quaking in terror, made no difference. Hanging was not beautiful. It was twitching limbs, loosened bowels, bulging eyes and frothing lips. It was a thing many were glad to watch, but none to experience, a just penalty for the guilty, occasionally visited upon the innocent.

*   *   *

Monday – morning or afternoon, he was not sure – brought a visitor. At first, Spandrel thought his examination was about to resume, but the guards made no attempt to remove him from the cell. Instead, they shackled him and chained him to a hook on the wall, then made way for his visitor.

He was a blond-wigged, dapper young man in a fawn-coloured coat, which he clutched close about himself, either because he was cold or because he was worried, not unreasonably, that the cloth might be soiled by brushing against something. A kerchief was bundled in his hand and he seemed to be restraining himself with some difficulty from holding it to his nose. There was an anxious frown on his face to complete the impression of someone who found himself where he had no wish to be with no intention of remaining one minute longer than he had to.

'You're Spandrel?' he said in a genuinely English voice.

'Yes.'

'Cloisterman. British vice-consul.'

'Have you come to help me?'

'The only help I can give you is to urge you to tell the Sheriff everything.'

'I have done that.'

'He seems to think otherwise. Why were you in Brussels, for instance?'

'I wasn't. Mrs de Vries is lying.'

'An unfortunate accusation to level at a grieving widow. She will be at her husband's funeral today. The Consul will also be there, seeking to make some manner of amends for the disgrace you have brought on the British community in Amsterdam.'

'De Vries was killed by his secretary, Mr Cloisterman:

86

Pieter Zuyler. Mrs de Vries knows that full well. She probably helped him.'

'Why should she have done that?'

'For the money she'll inherit, I suppose. The money they'll share.'

'But she won't inherit, Spandrel. Not much, at all events. De Vries had a son by an earlier marriage, now a V.O.C. officiary in Java.' By V.O.C. Cloisterman meant the Dutch East India Company – the Verenigde Oostindische Compagnie. Spandrel had learned that much from Zuyler. 'The younger de Vries, not the charming widow,' Cloisterman went on, 'is made rich by what you've done.'

'But I didn't do it. I didn't do anything. The Sheriff accused me of being in league with some marquess . . .'

'The Marquis de Prié.'

'Yes. But I've never heard the name before in my life, far less met him. Can you at least tell me . . . who he is?'

'You seriously claim not to know?'

'I tell you, sir, as God's my witness, I've no idea.'

'Well, well. This is a pretty turn-about, I must say.' Cloisterman seemed so struck by the notion that Spandrel might actually be innocent that he forgetfully released his coat and placed a thoughtful finger on his chin. 'The Marquis de Prié is Minister Plenipotentiary to the Governor-General of the Austrian Netherlands. He might have his reasons for wishing de Vries dead.'

'What reasons?'

'Who can say with certainty? I gather the Marquis favours the creation of a Flemish East India Company to rival the V.O.C., presumably to enrich the Flemish mercantile classes and so warm them to their masters in Vienna whom de Prié loyally serves. The V.O.C. has done all it can to prevent that happening. De Vries was a native of Flanders, with many friends in Antwerp and

Brussels. He may have wielded considerable influence to that end.'

'I know nothing about any of this. I never went to Brussels. I brought a package from London on behalf of Sir Theodore—'

'Janssen. Yes. Also of Flemish stock. Another wielder of influence. But Sir Theodore, as you must know, is a man in severely straitened circumstances. His present situation is indeed faintly comparable to your own.'

'How so?'

'When do you claim to have left London?' Cloisterman asked, ignoring Spandrel's question.

'A week ago . . .' Spandrel thought hard. 'A week ago yesterday.'

'Sunday the twenty-second of January, in the Old Style?'

'Yes. That's right. Sunday the twenty-second.'

'Would it surprise you to know that Sir Theodore was arrested by order of Parliament on Monday the twenty-third and consigned to the Tower?'

It did surprise Spandrel – very much. 'The Tower. Why?'

'Because the chief cashier of the South Sea Company, Mr Knight, fled the country the same day that you left: Sunday the twenty-second. It's all up with the South Sea. And with its directors. Mr Knight, incidentally, is reported to have fled . . . to Brussels.' Cloisterman gave a wan smile. 'These are deep waters, Spandrel. And the currents are treacherous. A man could easily drown in them.'

'I *am* drowning.' Spandrel reached out instinctively to clasp Cloisterman's sleeve, but Cloisterman stepped smartly back and the chain snapped taut. They looked at each other warily across three feet of fetid cell-space. 'Is there nothing you can do to help me, sir?'

'Very little.'

'But even a very little . . . might be enough.'

'I doubt it.' Cloisterman's expression softened marginally. 'Yet I will' – he gave a little nod that seemed intended to afford Spandrel some small comfort – 'see what I can do.'

With the proverbial celerity of bad news, word of his old friend's demise had already reached Sir Theodore Janssen. All the other reverses he had suffered in recent weeks had been anticipated and, in one way or another, allowed for. This, by contrast, was a blow he had not expected to receive. Death might call on men of his and de Vries's age at any time, of course. But murder, in the supposed safety of his own home? It could scarcely be credited. Yet it had happened. The report was not to be doubted. Ysbrand de Vries was dead. And amidst the sorrow Sir Theodore felt at the loss of the very last of his youthful contemporaries, he was gnawed also by an anxiety he dared not fully explain even to his loyal valet and prime informant, Nicodemus Jupe.

Today was the anniversary of the execution of King Charles I. As a mark of respect, Brodrick's Committee of Inquiry was not sitting. But tomorrow they would resume their work, fortified by whatever Blunt and Joye had told them. Sir Theodore's judgement was that by now they knew the worst. But knowledge was not proof. They might find that commodity rather more elusive. Nor were they alone in that. The news from Amsterdam had left the hunters and the hunted on dismayingly equal terms. And the news from Amsterdam was about to become more dismaying still.

'It's been confirmed, sir,' said Jupe. 'Mijnheer de Vries's killer was Spandrel.'

'It stretches credulity that the man should be capable of such a thing.'

'Yet it seems he was.'

'And this happened on Friday evening?'

'Yes, sir. At about ten o'clock. The weapon was a knife. Spandrel broke into the house and slew Mijnheer de Vries in his study.'

'I have lost a good friend, Jupe. I wish to know why.'

'Perhaps Spandrel isn't the fool he seemed to be.'

'But still a big enough fool to be caught in the act. There is something wrong here. Very wrong.'

'Do you wish me to make any specific inquiries . . . about the despatch-box?'

'No. That is . . .' Sir Theodore thought for a moment. 'How is the committee expected to proceed?'

'Rumour has it that Mr Brodrick will tomorrow set a date for them to report to the House of Commons. Within a fortnight, it's believed.'

'So soon?'

'A stiff wind's blowing, sir, no question.'

'Then we must take in sail. I want you to go to Amsterdam, Jupe. As soon as possible. Establish the facts – the *true* facts – of Ysbrand's death. And find the despatch-box. It must not fall into the wrong hands.'

'And whose are the right hands, sir?'

'Pels's Bank is a safe lodgement for the time being. But you understand, Jupe?' Uncharacteristically, Sir Theodore grasped his valet's wrist. 'It must be found.'

'Yes, sir.' Jupe's eyes met his master's. 'I understand.'

CHAPTER NINE

Meetings and Messages

Evelyn Dalrymple, chargé d'affaires at the British Embassy in The Hague, regarded the visitor to his office with measured caution. He had learned by occasionally bitter experience to hear out all those who claimed his attention on matters affecting the dignity of the Crown. Most were time-wasters, naturally. But the few who were not were unlikely to be correctly identified by his subordinates. Some, indeed, might be deliberately turned away in an attempt to embarrass him. In the Ambassador's absence on extended leave, Dalrymple had to be on his guard. The doubters and the enviers were ever alert for some slip on his part, however minor, that could be exploited to discredit him.

Kempis, the fellow sitting on the other side of his desk, was an especially difficult case to assess. He was a tall, dark-haired Dutchman in his middle to late twenties, smartly though soberly dressed, who spoke the perfect English of a well-educated man, but nonetheless had about him a suggestion of humble origins. What he did and where he came from were subjects he had declined to expand upon. In one sense, this had pleased Dalrymple, since it suggested they would come rapidly to the purpose of the visit. In another sense, however, it had worried him. The reticent, he had generally found, were more troublesome in the long run than the loquacious.

'What can I do for you, mijnheer?' Dalrymple ventured. 'An urgent matter, my secretary tells me, affecting' – he added a lilt of incredulity to his voice – 'the good name of the King.'

'King George is Governor of the South Sea Company, I believe,' Kempis said.

'Honorifically, yes.' Dalrymple's heart had sunk at the mention of the South Sea. He had lost enough money of his own on that foredoomed enterprise to need no reminding of it. So had many Dutchmen, who had insisted on dragging their consequent resentments to his door. If Kempis were another, this was likely to be a painful discussion, best cut short. 'But that is the full extent of His Majesty's involvement.'

'As far as you're aware.'

'You claim closer knowledge of the subject?'

'Some detailed information has come into my possession, certainly. Believe me when I say, Mr Dalrymple, that its wide dissemination would have consequences of the utmost gravity for your political – and your royal – masters in London.'

'I must take leave to doubt that, mijnheer.'

'Please do. I am not trying to convince you. I only want you to communicate my request to the appropriate person.'

'And what *is* your request?'

'In return for the surrender of the article I have come by, I require the payment of one hundred thousand pounds in high denomination Bank of England notes.'

Dalrymple could not suppress a flinch of astonishment. 'I beg your pardon?'

'One hundred thousand pounds, Mr Dalrymple. A round plum.'

'Very amusing.' Kempis's dark-eyed gaze did not encourage the notion that he was joking, but Dalrymple felt obliged to pretend that he thought he was. 'This is not the kind of request I can—'

'Tell them I have the Green Book.'

'What?'

'The green-covered ledger, lately in the keeping of the chief cashier of the South Sea Company. I have it.' Kempis leaned forward. 'And I know what it contains. I know everything.'

'There, mijnheer, you have the advantage of me.' Like a duck on the waters of the Hofvijver, which he could see if he turned and looked out of the window, Dalrymple was now engaged in strenuous efforts to remain afloat, efforts he could not allow to disturb the placid surface of his remarks. He knew that Robert Knight was presently in Brussels, taking his ease at the Hôtel de Flandre. He suspected that the Embassy there would already have applied for a warrant to arrest him. The Austrian authorities, however, could be expected to drag their feet about issuing one. They owed Britain no favours. Dalrymple knew nothing of green-covered ledgers, but he thought it safe to assume that Knight would have taken good care of his most sensitive documents. They were unlikely to be in the hands of an importunate young Dutchman. But he knew too little to be certain of that. The South Sea affair was riddled with many unlikelihoods, of which this would not be the most remarkable. Prevarication was therefore his only recourse. 'How, may I ask, did you arrive at your valuation of this information?'

'By asking myself what I would pay for its suppression were I the King's loyal minister.'

'I cannot imagine why you persist in mentioning His Majesty in this regard.'

'Then do not trouble to imagine. Simply convey my terms.'

'As they stand at present, mijnheer, I feel sure they would be dismissed out of hand.'

'That is because you do not know what the Green Book contains. But I do know. And so, of course, do those recorded in it. One could hardly forget such matters. I have some experience of book-keeping. The tale this book tells is clear and damning.'

'Perhaps you would care to show it to me.'

'Do you think me so foolish as to have brought it with me?'

'You are surely not implying that it would have been unsafe to do so, are you, mijnheer? This is the British Embassy, not a den of thieves.'

Kempis smiled, as if amused by the distinction. 'Mr Dalrymple,' he said steadily, 'will you present my request to your government?'

'Such as it is, I will.'

'That is all I ask. I will return here – shall we say one week from today? – for their answer. At that time I will specify how the exchange is to be made.'

'Exchange?'

'Of book for money. Time and place. Conditions. And so forth. It will have to be carefully managed.'

'If it is to be managed at all. I must say you seem remarkably confident of what answer you will receive.'

Kempis nodded in cool acknowledgement of the fact. 'Yes,' he said. 'I am.'

Somewhat against his better judgement, but adhering to the sound principle that it is wise to defer to other people's judgement in difficult cases, Dalrymple at once set about preparing a despatch for urgent transmission to the Secretary of State's office in Whitehall. It would take two days to arrive and another three or four days for a reply to reach him. A week should suffice for Kempis to have his answer. The nature of that answer would satisfy Dalrymple as to whether the man was an impertinent knave or an ingenious schemer. He could not for the moment decide which. And he would not have cared to bet on the outcome. He decided to take Kempis's advice and not trouble to imagine.

Imagination was one of the few indulgences left to William Spandrel, in his cell beneath the Stadhuis in Amsterdam. The days slipped slowly by, measured in the drift of light across the wall, in its strengthening and its weakening. Cloisterman did not return. Nor was Spandrel called for re-examination. It was as if he had been forgotten by all save the guards. His wounds healed, but the meagre diet of bread and ale sapped his strength. Only his thoughts roamed freely, back into his past and out across his uncharted future. Always they returned to the two questions he could not begin to answer. What was in the despatch-box? And why had de Vries been killed? Not for his money, it seemed. But there was a reason. There had to be. Spandrel's only hope of finding out what it was rested in other people. And that was hardly any hope at all.

Nicholas Cloisterman was perhaps the person upon whom Spandrel was relying the most. He had, after all, promised to see what he could do. Alas for Spandrel, he had decided in the days following his visit to the Stadhuis cells that what he *should* do, even if it was less than what he could do, was nothing. He was inclined to believe Spandrel's plea of innocence, but to involve himself in such a tangled affair unnecessarily would surely be folly. One did not thrive in the consular service by annoying the local authorities. If the Sheriff wished to persuade himself that Spandrel was an agent of the Marquis de

Prié, so be it. Spandrel was a person of no consequence. Nobody would care if he lived or died; nobody, at all events, who might ever call Cloisterman to account. Reluctantly, therefore, though not *very* reluctantly, he dismissed him from his thoughts.

Such a dismissal did not prove as simple a matter as he had supposed, however. Friday morning found him, as was his wont, lingering over a cup of chocolate and a quiet pipe in Hoppe's coffee-house at the western end of the Spui canal, perusing a fortnight-old copy of *Parker's London News*. He was several paragraphs into a chronicle of the latest outrages of highwaymen on Finchley Common when an ostentatious throat clearance drew his attention to a lean, lugubrious fellow who was standing by his table and looking at him critically down an eagle's beak of a nose.

'Can I help you?' Cloisterman snapped.

'I hope you may be able to, sir. My name is Jupe. I am in the service of Sir Theodore Janssen.'

'Janssen, you say?' Cloisterman closed his newspaper. 'That's odd.'

'Why, sir?'

'Never mind. What can I do for you?'

'I was told I might find you here. May I . . . join you?'

'Very well. But I . . .' He drew out his watch. 'I have very little time to spare.'

'Of course. We are all pressed.' Jupe sat down. 'You are Mr Cloisterman, the vice-consul?'

'Yes.'

'I wonder if you can help me. I am making inquiries on Sir Theodore's behalf, concerning . . .' Jupe lowered his voice. 'Mijnheer de Vries.'

'Mijnheer de Vries is dead.'

'Indeed, sir. Murdered, so I understand. By a fellow-countryman of ours. William Spandrel.'

'I know little of the matter, Mr . . .'

'Jupe, sir. Did I not say? Nicodemus Jupe.'

He had said. And Cloisterman had not forgotten. But he did not wish to imply that he was paying as much attention to this grave-faced emissary of the deep-dealing Sir Theodore Janssen as in truth he was. 'An Englishman called Spandrel is in custody, I believe.'

'I am told you have visited him in his place of confinement, sir.'

'You seem to have been told a good deal, Mr Jupe.'

'But not enough to satisfy Sir Theodore as to the circumstances of his old friend's death.'

'It is gratifying to know that Sir Theodore is able to spare a thought for a murdered friend in the midst of all his other . . . difficulties.'

'They were *very* old friends, sir.'

'And business partners of long standing, I'll warrant.'

'Since you mention business, sir, there's a matter on which I'd value your advice.'

'Oh yes?'

'Spandrel was engaged by Sir Theodore to deliver an article of some value to Mijnheer de Vries. Sir Theodore is naturally anxious to establish the whereabouts of that article.'

'Spandrel told me about the package. I wasn't sure whether to believe him.'

'You may believe him about that, sir. The question is: did he deliver it?'

'So he claims. If you're in doubt, ask de Vries's secretary – a fellow called Zuyler.'

'I would, sir, if I could. But Zuyler has left Amsterdam. As has the widow de Vries.'

'Really?' Cloisterman tried not to appear surprised. The fact remained, however, that he was. Spandrel had flung accusations of murder at Zuyler, mendacity at

97

Estelle de Vries and conspiracy at the pair of them. Cloisterman had been inclined to regard this as the desperate talk of a desperate man. Now, he was not so sure. 'How long have they been gone?'

'I don't know, sir. The staff at the house were not very forthcoming.'

'Did they go together?'

'There again . . .' Jupe shrugged. 'Their destination was likewise not disclosed to me.'

'Do you think they took the package with them?'

'It's possible, sir.'

'No doubt you feel unable to disclose to me its contents.'

'They have not been disclosed to *me*, sir.' Was Jupe lying? Cloisterman's instincts told him that, if not actually lying, he was at least dissembling. Whether he had been told or not, he knew what the package contained. 'Sir Theodore entrusted the package to Mijnheer de Vries. Mijnheer de Vries is dead. Sir Theodore therefore requires the return of the package. He is entitled to insist upon it.'

'Then let him come here and insist.'

'That is not presently possible.'

'Quite. Let us turn, then, to what is possible. Spandrel has told all who will listen that Zuyler murdered Mijnheer de Vries and conspired with de Vries's wife to incriminate him. The Sheriff prefers to believe that Spandrel murdered de Vries, acting on behalf of a hostile foreign power.'

'Spandrel is no assassin, sir.'

'He does not seem to have the makings of one, does he? And now the two people he accused have left Amsterdam, with, you believe, the package he delivered to de Vries.' Cloisterman paused, expecting Jupe to confirm this last point. When no confirmation came, he frowned at the other man and said, 'What is the package worth, Mr Jupe?'

'Worth, sir?'

'Yes. *What is it worth?*'

'I have no way of knowing, sir.'

Cloisterman gave an exasperated sigh. 'In that case, neither you nor I can say whether Spandrel's accusations are likely to have any substance.' He picked up his newspaper and reopened it with a flourish. 'And there would appear to be nothing more I can do for you.'

In London, that same Friday morning, Dalrymple's despatch reached the desk of James, Earl Stanhope, His Majesty's Secretary of State for the Northern Department. It did not find his noble lordship in a receptive mood. Recent weeks had been a trial for him. He had known little and understood less of the whole South Sea affair, preferring to leave financial matters to the management of his principal political ally and First Lord of the Treasury, the Earl of Sunderland, while he concentrated his endeavours on the creation of a new and stable order of relations between the European states. All his achievements in that regard were now imperilled, however, by the embarrassment, bordering on disgrace, that the failure of the South Sea scheme had brought to the Government.

Brodrick's committee, it was rumoured, had extracted evidence from Joye and Blunt of corruption extending to the most senior of ministers, including Aislabie, the Chancellor of the Exchequer, Craggs, the Postmaster-General, and Stanhope's own cousin, Charles, who as Secretary to the Treasury had personally conducted most of the negotiations leading to the South Sea Company's generous offer, as it had seemed at the time, to take over the lion's share of the National Debt. Some of the more alarmist rumour-mongers suggested that Sunderland himself was tainted. If so, the lease on power Stanhope had shared with Sunderland for the past four years might be about to expire. Sunderland could not be persuaded to tell him how great the danger was, but tomorrow, when the House of Lords was due to examine Blunt, it would surely become apparent.

These were nerve-testing times, therefore, for Lord Stanhope. As the responsible minister, he had instructed the Embassy in Brussels to secure Knight's arrest as soon as his whereabouts became known. Latest reports suggested that this was imminent. Stanhope was aware, however, that there was a constitutional objection in Brabant, within whose jurisdiction Knight had placed himself, to the extradition of criminal suspects, an objection the Austrian authorities could not readily override. He had pointed this out to Sunderland at their last meeting, only for Sunderland to reply enigmatically, 'That may be no cause to shed tears.'

What did the fellow mean by that? It was hard to resist the conclusion that Knight confined somewhere abroad, out of the committee's reach, was an outcome Sunderland distinctly approved of. But even if matters did resolve themselves in that way, it would not still the tongues of their accusers. And sooner or later those accusers would have to be answered. If ministers were forced to resign, especially if Sunderland was one of them, the King would be obliged to reconstruct the Government. Walpole was already talked of as Aislabie's successor at the Exchequer. The Treasury might soon be within his grasp. Then where would Stanhope's precious new continental polity be? Walpole was a narrow-minded Norfolk squire. He knew nothing of Europe. He would ruin everything Stanhope had worked so long and assiduously to bring about.

The threat of such ruin galled Stanhope the more because it had arisen from the greed and stupidity of other people. He was personally blameless. Yet it seemed he could not escape punishment. It was enough to drive a man mad. And it was certainly sufficient to fray his temper as he perused Dalrymple's urgent communication.

£100,000? For *what*? Dalrymple must be losing his reason. Perhaps it was time to send Cadogan back to The Hague if this was the measure of the man representing British interests in the United Provinces. It must surely be obvious, even to Dalrymple, that if the ledger spoken of by his mysterious Dutch visitor were truly a compendium of Knight's deepest secrets, it would not have left his side. Dalrymple seemed to suppose that the mere mention of what he semi-fabulously described, with breathless capitals, as 'The Green Book' would somehow justify his effrontery in passing on such a request. But Stanhope would show him his error. Kempis was clearly a mountebank. And mountebankery could only work its magic on fools. Stanhope had been visited by troubles enough on account of the foolishness of others. This was one instance where he could bear down hard upon it.

Stanhope seized his pen, dipped it in the ink-well, and began to write. Dalrymple would not have to wait long for his answer. He would have it short, but far from sweet.

Nicholas Cloisterman, meanwhile, was also composing a letter. His conversation with the odious Jupe had persuaded him that there were sinister ramifications to the murder of Ysbrand de Vries. The package Spandrel had delivered to de Vries on behalf of Sir Theodore Janssen contained something worth killing for, something connected with the fugitive Robert Knight and the failed South Sea Company. Cloisterman did not know what it was and in many ways was happy not to. But clearly he could no longer keep the little he did know to himself. Dalrymple, chargé d'affaires at the Embassy in The Hague, would have to be told. Let him make of it what he pleased. Cloisterman would have done his duty. At least, he would be seen to have done it. And that, he had tended to find, was more important in the long run.

CHAPTER TEN

Hell to Pay

Evelyn Dalrymple, chargé d'affaires at the British Embassy in The Hague, regarded the visitor to his office with suppressed apprehensiveness. Kempis had come for his answer. And Lord Stanhope had made it very clear what that answer should be. Indeed, he had made it very clear that Dalrymple should not have needed to be told how to respond to such a demand. But Stanhope had not met Kempis. Staring into the Dutchman's wine-dark eyes, Dalrymple detected no weakness, no lack of confidence in the terms he had set. He did not look like a man whom it was wise to dismiss out of hand.

Dalrymple was also troubled by various pieces of information that had lately come his way. From the Embassy in Brussels he had received notification that on Friday last, the day on which Stanhope had written to him, Robert Knight had been arrested while trying to leave Brabantine territory and removed to the citadel at Antwerp. No mention had been made of any papers found in Knight's possession. Dalrymple could only assume that any so found would by now be on their way to London and Stanhope's desk in Whitehall. Oddly, however, Cloisterman, the vice-consul in Amsterdam, seemed convinced that some vital South Sea document was now in the possession of the errant secretary and widow of a murdered V.O.C. merchant called de Vries.

He had written to Dalrymple, warning him to be on his guard, but failing, typically, to suggest what he should be on his guard against.

Matters were further complicated by a report that had reached him from London that very morning of the House of Lords debate of Saturday evening. Sir John Blunt, it seemed, had refused to tell their assembled lordships what he had confided to Brodrick's committee. Proceedings had been acrimonious and inconclusive. Lord Stanhope, it was stated, had been 'taken ill' in the midst of a furious exchange with the Duke of Wharton. His exact condition was not known.

Taken all in all, Dalrymple did not rightly see how he could be less comfortably placed. Knight's papers were in transit. Stanhope was ill. Cloisterman was on – or up – to something. And Kempis required an answer. Dalrymple tended, in these circumstances, as in so many others, to favour procrastination. But he doubted it would carry him through.

'If you insist upon an answer at this time, mijnheer—'

'I do.'

'I should not recommend you to, I really should not.'

'I will take my own advice, thank you, Mr Dalrymple.'

'As you please.'

'Are my terms accepted?'

'As I say, this really is not—'

'*Are they accepted?*'

Dalrymple took a long, calming breath. 'No, mijnheer. They are not.'

'Not?' Kempis cocked one eyebrow. He seemed not so much angry as incredulous. 'I cannot have heard you correctly.'

'His Majesty's Secretary of State for the Northern Department—'

'*Who?*'

'Lord Stanhope. The relevant minister.'

'Very well. What does he say?'

Dalrymple glanced down at Stanhope's letter and decided against direct quotation as likely only to prove inflammatory. 'He rejects your demands.'

'He does *what*?'

'He declines to entertain them, mijnheer. He is quite . . . unequivocal . . . on the point.'

'You did tell him what I told you . . . about the Green Book?'

'I did indeed.'

'Then he cannot say no to me.'

'But he has.'

'That is his last word on the matter?'

'I do not say that. The situation is somewhat volatile at present. Wait a while and it is poss—'

'*Wait?*' Now Kempis *was* angry. He jumped from his chair and glared across the desk at Dalrymple, his eyes flashing. 'You expect me to dally here while Lord Stanhope's agents come in search of me – and what I hold? You must think me mad, sir. Your masters have had time enough. If they won't pay me, someone else will.'

'Who might you have in mind, mijnheer?' Dalrymple asked, exerting himself to sound unflustered.

'Oh, I think I know where I will find a ready buyer, never fear. You may tell Lord Stanhope that the King will not thank him when he realizes who that buyer is. Or exactly what he has bought. Be it on his head. And on yours, Mr Dalrymple. Good day to you, sir.'

The discussion had gone as well, Dalrymple afterwards concluded, as it could have been expected to. Nobody would be able to reproach him. He had done what he had been bidden to do. And he had taken one significant precaution, instructing Harris, his secretary's clerk, to follow Kempis upon his departure from the Embassy. Harris was quick-witted and fleet-footed enough to trail Kempis to his lodgings. But he returned less than half an hour later with disappointing news.

'I think he must have been expecting something of the kind, sir. He walked to Prinsessegracht and I kept behind him, out of his line of sight, all the way. But a coach was waiting for him there. They took off at a tearing pace, I can tell you. I thought I glimpsed a woman in the coach. I couldn't get close enough to see any more. They crossed the canal at the next bridge and headed east.'

Kempis had eluded him. That too, Dalrymple felt, was to have been expected. All he could hope now was that he would hear no more from him – or even about him.

But Dalrymple's hopes were to be dashed that very evening. A reception at the Swedish Embassy promised only the blandest of entertainment, but an appearance by him, however brief, was inescapably called for. No sooner had he arrived, late and in unsociable humour, than other guests were sympathizing with him on a loss to his nation of which he was embarrassingly unaware. Lord Stanhope, it rapidly transpired, was dead.

Dalrymple's shock at the news seemed generally to be interpreted as grief for a fallen leader. In truth, grief had nothing to do with it. The excuse that he had only been following orders in turning Kempis away was an excellent one, so long as the giver of those orders remained alive. Now, the excuse would ring alarmingly hollow.

The Swedish Ambassador expressed his entire understanding of Dalrymple's need to leave early and the condolences of the gathering accompanied his departure. He hurried the short distance to the British Embassy, intending to roast any clerks still on the premises for not bringing the news to his door earlier in the evening. He found Harris in his outer office and was on the point of peppering him with abuse when he noticed a stranger warming himself by the fire.

He was a glower-faced ox of a man, with bulging eyes, a nose that would have done justice to a prize-fighter and a prominent scar on his forehead. His black hair, streaked with grey, was tied back in a pigtail. His clothes were old and dusty, but of good quality. Dalrymple had jack-a-dandyish tendencies and could tell fine cloth by its cut, even when it was frayed and travel-stained. He could also tell a fighting man by the hang of his sword. And this was a fighting man by temperament, even if he was perhaps too old to see much action.

'You're Dalrymple?' the fellow growled, with no pretence of civility. There was a Scots twang to his voice, which Dalrymple took as ample explanation of his abruptness.

'I am, sir. Who is this . . . gentleman, Harris?'

'McIlwraith,' the other said, before Harris could so much as open his mouth. 'Captain James McIlwraith.'

'And what can I do for you, Captain McIlwraith?'

'General Ross sent me.'

'Who?'

'General Charles Ross, M.P. A member of the House of Commons Committee of Inquiry into the failure of the South Sea Company. He's been deputed by the committee to secure the records of chief cashier Knight. I'm here on his behalf.' McIlwraith pulled a piece of paper from his pocket and held it out for Dalrymple to read. 'You're called upon to give me all necessary assistance.'

'Am I?' Dalrymple perused the document. It carried the House of Commons seal, Ross's signature and the counter-signature of Thomas Brodrick, chairman, as

Dalrymple well knew, of the committee in question. There appeared no reason to doubt its authenticity, other than McIlwraith's lowly rank and uncouth demeanour. 'Well, well. It would seem I am.'

'I'll thank you for a word in private.'

'Leave us, Harris.' Harris obeyed, with what looked like alacrity. Dalrymple moved to the desk and assumed what he judged to be a patrician pose beside it. 'You're personally acquainted with General Ross, Captain?'

'I served under him.'

'In the late war?'

'I had that honour.'

Dalrymple now had the measure of his man. Eight years had passed since the end of the War of the Spanish Succession, more like ten since any serious fighting. But still they were to be found in every tavern, these scarred, bemedalled survivors of shot and shell who dreamed of being under fire as others might dream of paradise. McIlwraith had no doubt struck terror into the enemy at Blenheim and Ramillies and Marlborough's various other blood-soaked victories. He could never have become an officer in peacetime and a mere captaincy suggested he had been a pretty truculent one in wartime. But General Ross trusted him, doubtless with good cause. He had his orders and would stick at nothing to carry them out.

'They have Knight locked up in the citadel at Antwerp,' said McIlwraith. 'I was there last night.'

'Should you not have remained there, Captain? If his . . . records . . . are what you—'

'Where's Kempis?'

'Who?' Dalrymple asked softly, trying hard to disguise his surprise.

'Kempis. The man you wrote to Lord Stanhope about.'

108

'My correspondence with the Secretary of State can be no business of a House of Commons committee.'

'Oh, but it can. When the subject of that correspondence is a green-covered ledger.'

'You seem to know a great deal, Captain.' (More, in truth, than was good for Dalrymple's peace of mind.) 'How did you come by such information, may I ask?'

'Never you mind. But Stanhope's dead. You know that, don't you?'

'Yes. I do. Sad tidings, indeed.'

'If you say so. Apoplexy, or something of the kind. Though whether brought on by the goadings of the Duke of Wharton in the House of Lords debate on Saturday or the prodigious quantity of Tokay he's said to have drunk at the Duke of Newcastle's the night before is uncertain.'

'He'll be greatly missed,' Dalrymple insisted stubbornly.

'By you, perhaps. Not by all.'

'By all men of feeling.'

'Feeling, is it? Why, I've a—' McIlwraith broke off and ran a hand over his chin and down his neck. Dalrymple heard with distaste the rasp of the stubble against his palm. 'I haven't the leisure to bandy words with you, Dalrymple. Where is Kempis?'

'I have no idea.'

'But you've seen him this very day, according to your clerk.'

'I'm really not at liberty to discuss my dealings with Mijnheer Kempis, or anyone else. I answer to His Majesty's ministers, not the House of Commons.'

'I wouldn't be too sure of that. Do you really want your name to go in the committee's report as a damned obstructive jack-in-office?' McIlwraith stepped closer. His voice dropped. 'I know what Kempis was trying to sell. And for how much. I also know what Lord Stanhope

109

instructed you to do: send Kempis away with a flea in his ear. Which I've no doubt you obediently did. It's a stroke of bad luck for you Stanhope's dead, meaning his instructions are so much waste paper you'd have done better to use as kindling for your fire. But there's good luck for you as well. Information will aid me more than your head on a platter. So, *where* is Kempis?'

'I don't know.'

'You surely can't mean you just let him walk away?'

How predictable it was that Harris had failed to mention his own part in the day's proceedings. 'He gave us the slip,' Dalrymple admitted through gritted teeth.

'I don't suppose he found that so very difficult.' McIlwraith stepped closer still, raking Dalrymple with a contemptuous glare. 'You must have something on him, man. For pity's sake.'

Dalrymple found himself wishing fervently that he did have something; anything, indeed, however insubstantial. And at that point his memory came to his rescue. 'I suspect his real name is Zuyler,' he said, enjoying the sight of contempt giving way to surprise on McIlwraith's face. And there was something else to relish in the moment. Cloisterman was going to regret that unhelpful memorandum. 'Perhaps our vice-consul in Amsterdam can assist your further inquiries.'

Spandrel knew nothing of such far-off events as the death of Lord Stanhope and the arrest of Robert Knight. His life had shrunk to the dingy confines of his cell and an occasional, much cherished walk in an enclosed courtyard. The guards did not know, or if they did would not reveal, why he had not been re-examined. The answer to this and all Spandrel's other questions being so consistently unhelpful, he stopped asking and lapsed into a strange, numb torpor in which his mind grew as empty as his days. He wondered if his mother would ever learn what had become of him, but no longer worried how anxious she might be. She and all the other people he knew were slowly becoming part of a dream he often had: a dream of maps and streets and clear, unwalled horizons. But waiting for him when he woke was the dim, dank reality of the cell. Through its high, barred window came snatches of sound from the city around him: hoofbeats, footsteps, the rumbling of cart-wheels, the shrieking of gulls. He listened to such sounds for hours at a stretch. He watched the movement of shadows on the wall and tried to guess what cast them. He held long, rambling conversations with his father in which he took both parts. Slowly, little by little, thoughts of the future left him. He asked nothing of the guards. Soon, he would ask nothing of himself. And then . . .

One winter's morning which Spandrel had no way, in his confinement, of distinguishing from any other, but which most inhabitants of Amsterdam knew to be Friday 21st February in the New Style, saw the customary tumult of commerce on the Dam, the square in front of the Stadhuis. Barges were loading and unloading at the wharfside. Merchants from the nearby Exchange were clustering round the Weigh-House. At the fish and vegetable markets, business was brisk.

Nobody was minded, therefore, to pay much attention to the man striding about impatiently at the foot of the steps that led up to the main entrance of the Stadhuis. And a fleeting glance at his face – scarred and balefully forbidding – was enough to discourage prolonged scrutiny. It was evident that whenever he paused to stare up at the columned and pedimented frontage of the Stadhuis, he was not doing so to admire the statues representative of Prudence, Justice and Peace, but to look at the clock on the dome above them.

111

The clock showed it to be eight minutes after ten when a figure rounded the north-eastern corner of the building and hurried to meet him. The newcomer was breathless and irritably flustered, softer-faced and sleeker than the first man. Neither of them looked pleased by their meeting. There was no handshake, far less a bow, but a curt nod on one part and a scowl of greeting on the other.

'Captain McIlwraith?'

'Aye. And you, I take it, are Cloisterman.'

'I am.'

'You're late.'

'I cannot order my affairs to suit your sole convenience. Had you arranged to call on me at my office, I dare say—'

'I've had enough of offices, man. There are no keyholes in the open air for clerks to listen at. The Amsterdammers seem to do their share of business here. It should be good enough for you.'

'Well, I'm here, am I not?'

'I was assured of your full assistance.'

'Then you'd best tell me what I can assist you with.'

'Spandrel. The fellow they have in there' – McIlwraith crooked a thumb towards the Stadhuis – 'for the murder of de Vries.'

'I'm aware of the case.'

'An assassin in the pay of the Austrians, do you think?'

'I do not.'

'A dupe, then? A pawn in a deeper game?'

'Perhaps.'

'If so, shouldn't you be doing something to help him?'

'It's a matter for the Sheriff.' Cloisterman shrugged. 'Spandrel's a person of no consequence.'

'But the reason he came here *is* of consequence. It's

crammed with consequences. And I'm here to unravel them.'

'I wish you luck.'

'I want more than your wishes, man. Zuyler stole the package Spandrel delivered to de Vries. He's been to The Hague trying to sell it to that booby who supposedly represents our nation's interests there.'

'You mean Mr Dalrymple?' Cloisterman looked unruffled by the disparaging reference to his superior.

'I mean the simpering clothes-horse who goes by that name, aye. He turned Zuyler away. But Zuyler's not returned here. Nor has the widow de Vries. They've gone in search of a buyer elsewhere. And some servant of Sir Theodore Janssen's called Jupe has gone after them.'

'Has he?'

'Oh, I think so. And I think I can guess where Zuyler and Mrs de Vries are heading just as readily as friend Jupe.'

'Where might that be?'

'Never mind. What concerns me is that I've never met Zuyler *or* Mrs de Vries. But Spandrel has.'

'Well, yes.'

'*And* he's had sight of the contents of the package he delivered to de Vries.'

'Presumably.'

'Why has the Sheriff not brought him before the magistrates for trial?'

'Who can say?' Cloisterman gave another shrug. 'The wheels of justice turn but slowly.'

'Not when a man of de Vries's standing in the community is murdered in cold blood by a foreigner.'

'Even so . . .'

'Why the delay, man? You must have some idea.'

'I could only guess.'

113

'Then do it.'

'Well, the sudden departure from the city of Zuyler and Mrs de Vries goes a little way towards supporting Spandrel's contention that they murdered de Vries. Only a very little way, it's true, but it may be sufficient to have persuaded the Sheriff that he should await their return before proceeding.'

'He'll have a long wait.'

'You think so?'

'And all the while poor wee Spandrel will moulder in gaol.'

'Inevitably.'

'Inevitably, is it? I don't think so.' McIlwraith clapped Cloisterman round the shoulder, sending him staggering to one side. 'Time you were bestirring yourself, Mr Vice-Consul, on behalf of a fellow-countryman in distress.' McIlwraith grinned crookedly. 'High time.'

CHAPTER ELEVEN

Dogs on the Scent

The Secretary of State is dead; long live the Secretary of State. That same Friday, dated eleven days earlier in England, was the first day in office of Lord Stanhope's successor as Secretary for the Northern Department. Charles, Viscount Townshend, had good reason to be pleased with himself as he sat behind Stanhope's desk in the Cockpit building off Whitehall. Four years previously, Stanhope and his great ally Sunderland had succeeded in ousting him from the very same post by playing on the suspicions of the King that he and the then First Lord of the Treasury, Robert Walpole, had deferred overmuch to the Prince of Wales during one of the King's sojourns in Hanover. Walpole, who happened to be Townshend's brother-in-law as well as his best and oldest friend, had resigned along with him. Now, thanks to the grievous inundations of the South Sea, they were back.

Walpole, it was true, had presently to be content with the post of Paymaster-General of the Forces. But he was certain to succeed Aislabie as Chancellor of the Exchequer in due course and, if the Brodrick Committee unearthed damning evidence against Sunderland, as it well might, he could soon be in sole dominion at the Treasury. Their partnership would then be fully restored. Yes, on the whole, Townshend had every reason to be delighted. An ill wind had blown much good to a deserving pair of plain-mannered Norfolkmen.

But much good was not all good. The Paymaster-General was, as it happened, presently slumped in the chair on the other side of the desk, chewing at an apple and scratching his stomach through the gap between two straining buttons of his waistcoat. The smile he often wore was absent. He had not even been cheered by the news Townshend had just conveyed to him that the Secretary for the Southern Department, James Craggs the younger, Stanhope's supposedly brilliant pupil, was mortally ill with the smallpox. Something was clearly amiss.

Townshend knew only too well what it was. The reason for the prevailing glumness was to be found amongst the papers scattered across the desk between them. Or rather, it was not to be found there. Its absence *was* the reason.

The slew of papers comprised Stanhope's most recent correspondence. Among the material that had arrived since his death was a bundle of documents sent post-haste from Brussels after their confiscation from Robert Knight following his arrest near the Brabantine border. They did not include a certain green-covered ledger by which so many set such very great store. And without that what they did include was of little significance. Bar one disturbing communication from chargé d'affaires Dalrymple at The Hague.

With a sudden oath, Walpole plucked what remained of the apple from his mouth and flung it into the fire, where it buried itself sizzlingly among the coals. 'Dalrymple should be grateful he's out of my reach,' he growled. 'Otherwise I'd be tempted to roast him on a spit for what he's done.'

'He was following orders, Robin,' Townshend ventured. 'As he wastes no time in pointing out. What can

116

Stanhope have been thinking of? To reject Kempis so . . . bluntly . . . was madness.'

'Stanhope took him for a rogue. It's understandable. We all assumed Knight would have the Green Book about him.'

'I assumed nothing. I hoped. That is all. Kempis should have been kept dangling till we knew for certain.'

'Stanhope seems to have been in no mood to temporize. Perhaps he was already unwell when he wrote to Dalrymple.'

'More likely Sunderland didn't trust him enough to explain how important the Green Book is.'

'I'm not sure I understand that myself.'

'None of us will, Charles.' Walpole paused to prise a fragment of apple skin from his teeth. 'Until we see for ourselves.'

'In that case, wasn't Stanhope right to rebel at the very notion of paying a hundred thousand pounds for it?'

'A hundred thousand may come to seem like a bargain.'

'Surely it could never be that. Unless—' Townshend broke off and eyed Walpole thoughtfully. 'Well, you always knew more of such matters than me, Robin.'

'The less you know the better.'

Walpole shaped a smile that failed to reassure his brother-in-law, but succeeded in deterring him from further enquiry. It occurred to Townshend that there was a distinct similarity between his own relative ignorance and that in which Sunderland had evidently kept Stanhope. The only difference was that Sunderland was a shifty and self-serving manoeuvrer, whereas Walpole, his boon companion and dear wife's loyal brother, would never betray him. Of that he felt certain.

'The question now,' said Walpole, slapping his thighs for emphasis, 'is what's to be done?'

*   *   *

Cloisterman had several reservations about the course of action he had embarked upon. The most serious of these was the impossibility of deciding what his masters in Whitehall, whoever they were following Stanhope's death, would later declare they had wanted him to do. Should he be helping McIlwraith, or obstructing him? Dalrymple had committed nothing to paper on the subject, presumably so that later he could either take credit for Cloisterman's actions or disown them, according to which way the wind blew. There was no way of extracting specific guidance from Dalrymple. Cloisterman knew better than to try. And the Consul had eagerly delegated full responsibility to him. 'I always leave dealings with the Sheriff to you, Nick. You have a sure hand in these matters.'

Cloisterman could only hope the Consul was right. A sure hand he certainly needed to play. Fortunately, Sheriff Lanckaert was a cautious and patriotic man, who could be expected to resist consular representations on behalf of the prisoner Spandrel. McIlwraith's suggestion, which Cloisterman had agreed to pass on, was that Spandrel should be given the chance, under close escort, to locate the chemist's shop beneath which, he claimed, Zuyler had lodgings, lodgings, indeed, where Spandrel said he had passed the night following the alleged attempt on his life. Zuyler had vanished before he could be questioned on the point, but de Vries's servants all said Zuyler lived in the house and had no outside lodgings. Nor was a chemist called Barlaeus known to anyone. But lies so easily nailed were scarcely worth the telling. It made no sense for Spandrel to make such things up. Perhaps, therefore, he had not made them up. Perhaps Zuyler had taken secret lodgings as part of the deception and given Spandrel a false name for his landlord just as he had for the hired assassin. If a chemist of some other name could be found who had recently let his basement to someone matching Zuyler's description, matters would be turned upon their head and Spandrel might be released – into McIlwraith's waiting arms.

But Cloisterman did not expect that to happen. He did not expect Lanckaert to agree to any part of the exercise. And if Lanckaert should confound his expectation, he did not foresee the result McIlwraith anticipated. Implicating Zuyler in de Vries's murder would not exonerate Spandrel. Spandrel might as easily have been his accomplice as his dupe, the lies he had told, if lies they were, merely desperate attempts to talk his way out of trouble.

From Cloisterman's point of view, Lanckaert's likely intransigence was a godsend. He would have assisted General Ross's representative as best he was able, without that assistance altering events in any way that could subsequently be laid at his door. McIlwraith would charge off in pursuit of Zuyler and Mrs de Vries, leaving Cloisterman in peace, with a ready answer to any criticism, readier still should that criticism emanate from the slippery Dalrymple.

It was thus with no apparent reluctance but very little enthusiasm that Cloisterman presented his request to Lanckaert's English-speaking deputy, Aertsen, in his cramped office beneath the eaves of the Stadhuis that Friday afternoon. Aertsen and he were occasional combatants in closely fought games of chess at Hoppe's coffee-house and pursued their official discussions in a similar vein, with every allowance for each other's tactical acumen. They had both questioned Spandrel and formed their views on the case. But their views were irrelevant and so they wasted no time on them. Lanckaert's judgement was all that mattered. And there Aertsen had a surprise for Cloisterman.

'An interesting proposition, Nicholas. I rather think it may commend itself to Mijnheer Lanckaert.'

'You do?'

'You look surprised.'

'I am. Are you sure?'

'I cannot be sure. But I am optimistic.'

'Why?'

'Because Mijnheer Lanckaert wishes to discover an Austrian conspiracy. Indeed, he *needs* to discover one. The V.O.C. expects it of him.'

'I'm asking for Spandrel to be given an opportunity to exonerate, not incriminate, himself.'

'You cannot have one without the other.'

Zuyler's flight had marked him down as Spandrel's co-conspirator, perhaps the arch-conspirator. That, Cloisterman clearly saw, was how it was. And now he had volunteered to help the authorities prove their point. Freedom would be dangled like a carrot in front of Spandrel, only to be snatched away once he had led them far enough in pursuit of it. It was the way of the world. It could not be helped. Certainly not by Cloisterman. He shrugged. 'So be it.'

'I will speak to Mijnheer Lanckaert as soon as possible.' Aertsen smiled, which had the disquieting effect of exaggerating his squint. 'And we shall see if I read him aright.'

But as to that there was no doubt. Aertsen was no more likely to advance an unfounded opinion than an un-defended pawn. Cloisterman already had his answer. And it was not the one he wanted.

When, the following afternoon, the guard he knew as Big Janus opened the door of his cell, the last thing Spandrel expected him to say – the last thing he would have dared to hope – was that he had a visitor. Big Janus seemed to sense this and went so far as to smile. 'Mijnheer Cloisterman,' he announced, as if genuinely pleased on Spandrel's account. He jangled the keys in his hand, then seemed to decide that manacling Spandrel was unnecessary. He stepped back, holding the door open for Cloisterman.

'Mr Cloisterman,' Spandrel said, struggling to control the surge of hope that had overcome him. 'Thank God.'

'Good afternoon.' Cloisterman's gaze revealed nothing. 'Are you being well treated?'

'Well treated?' Spandrel caught Big Janus's eye over Cloisterman's shoulder. 'I . . . have no complaints.'

'I'm glad to hear it.'

'I thought . . . I'd been . . .'

'Forgotten? Nothing of the kind, I assure you. I've been doing my very best for you.'

'Thank you.' Spandrel would have fallen at Cloisterman's feet had he thought the gesture likely to be appreciated. 'Thank you, sir.'

'And I have secured for you a significant concession.'

'Thank you. Thank you so much.'

'Do you think you could lead us to Zuyler's lodgings?'

'His . . . lodgings?'

'Yes. Where you went after he rescued you from the canal.'

'The canal.' Spandrel's mind grappled unfamiliarly with the process of connected thought. 'Of course. Zuyler's lodgings. Beneath the chemist's shop.'

'Exactly. Could you lead us there?'

'Yes. I . . . think so. I . . . I'm sure. I would know the way from . . . the tavern.' For the life of him, Spandrel could not remember the name of the tavern where he had spent the night before his ill-fated return to the house of Ysbrand de Vries. But he would eventually. It would all

121

come back to him in time. 'I could do it, Mr Cloisterman. I could.'

'I believe you. And you're to have the chance.'

'When?'

'Monday.'

'And when is . . .' Spandrel tried to calculate how many days had elapsed since he had last heard the church bells ringing for the sabbath. Was it five, or six? He shook his head helplessly.

'It's the day after tomorrow,' said Cloisterman, taking pity on him.

'Thank you. Of course it is. The day after tomorrow. And this . . . will help my case?'

'It may do.' Cloisterman hesitated, then said, 'We'll find out, won't we? On Monday.'

Although the Paymaster-Generalship of the Forces was a relatively lowly office, it enjoyed certain significant privileges. The most lucrative of these was custody of the Army pay-roll, which was handed over by the Treasury at the beginning of each year and gradually disbursed, the balance being invested by the Paymaster for his personal benefit until it was called upon. In time of war, when the Army was so much bigger, this practice could make a man fabulously wealthy. The Duke of Chandos, Paymaster-General during the War of the Spanish Succession, had been desperately trying to find ways of spending his money ever since and was rumoured to have lost £700,000 on South Sea stock without batting an eyelid. In time of peace, the riches that accrued to the fortunate incumbent did so at a slacker pace, but accrue they nonetheless did. This was Walpole's second spell in the post and he was now what careful husbandry of his Norfolk estate could never have made him: a man of considerable means.

He was also in occupation of the Paymaster's official residence, Orford House, attached to the Royal Hospital at Chelsea. It was a residence entirely suited to the dignity and pre-eminence he had resolved should be his and he had no intention of surrendering it when he assumed a more senior role in government. Indeed, as he took his Sunday morning ease there, strolling on the lawns that ran down to the Thames in sunshine warm enough for spring, he was already turning over in his mind ways of annexing more of the hospital's buildings and grounds for his private use. His wife had expressed a wish for an aviary and he himself thought a summer-house would look rather fine on the terrace where a few pensioners were currently taking the air. Yes, changes there would be, here and in Norfolk, when he came into his own.

His pleasing reverie was interrupted by the arrival of a visitor, someone he had been expecting and whom he needed to speak to. But it was nevertheless with a certain sinking of the heart that he watched the visitor approach across the lawn from the rear of the house. Colonel Augustus Wagemaker was not a man Walpole or anyone else looked forward to meeting.

He was a thick-set, bustling figure, with a head patently too large for his body, but a face that made this feature more menacing than ludicrous. There was something of the battering-ram in his jutting jaw and prow-like nose and something harsher still in his eyes: a dead, flat, shark's glare of hostility that even his deference to Walpole could not quite extinguish. He had been recommended for special services by Lord Cadogan after tirelessly hunting down remnants of the Earl of Mar's Jacobite army in the wake of the Fifteen and had shown himself to be reliable in all circumstances. He was also a man of notoriously few words and Walpole valued his reticence almost as much as his ruthlessness.

'Good morning, Colonel,' said Walpole. 'A fine day.'

'Lord Townshend has told me what you want of me, sir,' Wagemaker replied, the reference to the weather seeming to have passed him by. 'I'm anxious to be off.'

'Of course. And I'll not detain you long. But I wished to have a private word with you before you left. I trust Lord Townshend explained our difficulty.'

'He did, sir.'

'The item must be recovered. I cannot exaggerate the importance of your mission.'

'I understand, sir.'

'A great deal depends upon your success. A very great deal.'

'I don't intend to let you down, sir.'

'No. I'm sure you don't. And with that in mind . . .' Walpole placed an amiable hand on Wagemaker's shoulder. 'Bring this off for me, Colonel, and you'll be richly rewarded. I shall soon have many valuable offices at my disposal. To take but one example, I anticipate that the Rangership of Enfield Chase will shortly fall vacant. I could imagine you occupying that position with considerable distinction.'

Wagemaker nodded. 'So could I, sir. Since you mention it.'

'It is to me that you should deliver the item. Not Lord Townshend. You follow? To me personally.'

'I follow, sir.'

'And to me that you should then look for advancement.'

'Yes, sir.'

'Which you will not do in vain.'

'*If* I recover the item.'

'Exactly.'

'Would you really consider appointing a mere colonel to a rangership, sir?'

'Well . . .' Walpole smiled. 'Perhaps a general would be more appropriate.'

'Perhaps so, sir.' For a moment, Walpole thought Wagemaker might break into a smile himself. But there was only the faintest softening of his expression to indicate his eagerness for the prize that could be his. 'I'd best be on my way now, sir. I have work to do.'

CHAPTER TWELVE

Out of the Frying-Pan

Cloisterman had rarely felt less at his ease than during the journey he undertook on Monday morning. It led from the cells of the Stadhuis to the Goudene Vis tavern on Montelbaanswal and thence, by a circuit of initially wrong but eventually correct turnings, to the chemist's shop where Spandrel claimed to have been accommodated overnight in Zuyler's lodgings.

Cloisterman's unease was the result of a bad conscience. He had long believed his conscience to have been extinguished by the dulling effects of his vice-consular duties. To find that it could still be pricked and hence still existed was deeply disturbing and accounted in part for his distracted mood throughout the proceedings. The false nature of those proceedings was what troubled him. Spandrel believed that, if he could prove his claimed association with Zuyler, he would thereby prove his innocence. This belief could be seen shining in his pale and haggard face like a candle behind a mask. But he was wrong, as Cloisterman well knew. All he could achieve, if successful, was to prove his guilt in the eyes of the Sheriff.

They travelled in Aertsen's coach, Cloisterman and Aertsen sitting next to each other opposite Spandrel and his guard, the aptly nicknamed 'Big' Janus, to whom Spandrel was handcuffed. Spandrel's hands were also manacled together and Aertsen had supplied a constable to ride escort for them. A single glance at the prisoner suggested that these precautions were excessive, to say the least. Thin and weak from his confinement, Spandrel did not look capable even of trying to escape. Not that he was likely to, of course. He was in truth pitifully eager to do exactly what the Sheriff wanted him to do, though not, sadly, for the same reason. Cloisterman could hardly bear to look at him, knowing what he did. It was a rotten business and the sooner it was over the better.

The principal obstacle to its swift conclusion lay in Spandrel's uncertainty about the route he had followed from the chemist's shop to the Gouden Vis and the added complication of tracing it in reverse. Cloisterman wondered if there would ever be an end of trailing up one canal and down another, while Spandrel leaned out of the window of the coach, giving directions that then had to be translated by Aertsen for the benefit of the driver. Eventually, however, he saw true recognition dawn on Spandrel as they headed south along the Kloveniersburgwal. 'Stop, stop,' the poor deluded fellow shouted. 'This is it.'

They were indeed outside a chemist's shop, similar in appearance to dozens of others around the city, including the one where Cloisterman went for headache cures and condoms. The name of the proprietor was not displayed. A sign bearing the single word *Apotheek* hung above a grimy window filled with dusty jars. Steps led up to the shop doorway, while others led down to a shuttered basement. It would be in Spandrel's best interests, Cloisterman knew, for there to be nothing to connect Zuyler with these premises. He found himself hoping that such would be the case. But he was aware that Spandrel would do everything he could to substantiate his claim. And the sly half-smile on Aertsen's face

127

suggested he would offer him every encouragement to that end. 'I think,' Aertsen said, 'that we should go in, don't you, Nicholas?'

Cloisterman's consent was hardly needed and Aertsen did not wait for his answer. The party disembarked from the coach and entered the shop, Aertsen instructing the driver and escorting constable to remain where they were. 'This is Barlaeus's shop,' chirruped Spandrel as he and Big Janus made their entangled ascent of the steps like a pair of reluctant and ill-matched dancers. 'I'm certain of it.'

But Spandrel's certainty only took them so far. The proprietor, a thin, stooped fellow in a skull-cap, did not answer to the name of Barlaeus and displayed no flicker of familiarity with the name of Zuyler either. Aertsen insisted that he close the shop, then questioned him for some minutes, too quickly for Cloisterman's grasp of Dutch, before reporting what he had said. 'He is Balthasar Ugels. He has traded from these premises for nearly twenty years and says he has never had a lodger. He lives here with his wife and daughters. He says the rooms below are used for storage only. The family lives above. He says he is famous for his gout cure. Have you heard of the Ugels gout powder, Nicholas?'

'I do not happen to suffer from gout, Henrik,' Cloisterman replied with a measured sigh.

'Nor I. But it is perhaps—' Aertsen broke off at the appearance from the rear of the premises of a plump young woman with raven-black hair and eyes to match. 'One of the daughters, I presume.' Aertsen turned to Ugels and asked him in Dutch to confirm this, which the fellow did, adding something Cloisterman failed to catch. Whatever it was caused Aertsen to chuckle.

'Care to share the joke?'

'He says she knows nothing. But nothing about what? The denial betrays him, I think.'

'It does nothing of the kind.'

'Excuse me, sir,' put in Spandrel. 'Surely if—'

'Be silent, man,' snapped Cloisterman. 'Let me deal with this.'

'But—'

'*Silent, I said.*'

Everyone was struck dumb for a moment by the force of Cloisterman's words. Looks were exchanged. Ugels nervously licked his lips. The daughter began to tremble. Aertsen took a few slow steps towards her. 'Juffrouw Ugels?' he gently enquired. She nodded mutely in reply. He went on, asking her slowly and simply enough for Cloisterman to understand whether anyone had lodged in the house recently and whether the name Zuyler meant anything to her.

'*Nee,*' she said each time. '*Nee.*' But her face coloured as she spoke and she could not meet Aertsen's gaze. There was no doubt about it. She was lying. Cloisterman watched a tell-tale bead of sweat trickle down her father's brow.

'We will visit the store-rooms, I think,' said Aertsen. 'And see exactly what is being stored there.'

Ugels received this announcement with twitching anxiety and the implausible objection that he had mislaid the key. Aertsen let him babble on for a moment, then told him coldly and abruptly that he would be arrested and thrown into gaol if he did not do as he was told. With that, the key was found.

Ugels led the way to the front door and opened it. Cloisterman followed Aertsen out, expecting him to carry on down the steps. But he stopped dead on the landing at the top of them, so suddenly that Cloisterman collided with him. Before he could protest, however, he saw what had halted Aertsen in his tracks.

The coach was gone. So was the constable. They had been told to wait. It was unthinkable that they should have disobeyed. Yet gone they were. '*Wat betekent dit?*' said Aertsen irritably. 'What does this mean?' It was a good question.

Suddenly, it was answered. A figure burst out from beneath the steps and rushed up towards them. Cloisterman barely had time to recognize McIlwraith before he also realized that the Scotsman was carrying a double-barrelled pistol in each hand. 'Get back,' McIlwraith shouted, clapping one of the pistols to Aertsen's head and pointing the other at Cloisterman.

They stumbled back into the shop. Cloisterman heard the girl scream. Then McIlwraith kicked the door shut behind him. 'Tell her to be quiet,' he said in Dutch to Ugels, who whimpered some plea to his daughter that reduced her screams to sobs. 'That's better,' he declared in English. 'Now, I'm sorry to interrupt the pantomime, gentlemen, but I can wait upon the law no longer.'

'McIlwraith, are you mad?' asked Cloisterman disbelievingly.

'Far from it. Simply in a hurry. These pistols are primed and cocked. The longer we stand here debating my state of mind, the greater the danger I'll forget myself and blow Mijnheer Aertsen's head off. Is that understood?'

'It is understood,' said Aertsen in a wavering voice.

'I want Spandrel. Tell the big fellow to release him.'

Aertsen turned slowly round, the twin muzzles of the pistol pressing into his head as he did so. His face was fixed in a grimace of fear and there was a sheen of sweat on his upper lip. He murmured an instruction to Big Janus. The guard hesitated. He spoke again, more loudly. Now the guard responded and began sorting through the keys that hung at his waist.

'Be quick about it,' said McIlwraith. A glance over his shoulder through the window of the shop suggested he was more nervous than the steadiness of his tone implied. Perhaps he was worried that the constable might return. How he had got rid of him and the coachman in the first place Cloisterman could not imagine.

'What's happening, sir?' Spandrel whispered. 'I don't understand.'

'Just do as he says.'

There was a metallic clink as the handcuffs opened. 'The manacles too,' said McIlwraith. But Big Janus had anticipated that and was already working on them.

'I don't want to escape,' said Spandrel stubbornly. 'I'm not trying to.' But in the next moment the manacles were off him. Whether he desired it or not, liberty – of a sort – was his.

'Come over here, Spandrel,' McIlwraith ordered. 'Move, man.'

'I can't. I have to stay.'

'I'm offering you your only chance of freedom. I suggest you grab it with both hands.'

'No. I can prove my innocence. Here. Now.'

'You've gulled him good and proper, haven't you?' McIlwraith glared at Cloisterman. 'Well, it's time for a little enlightenment. Tell him the truth, Mr Vice-Consul.'

'The truth?' Incomprehension was written across Spandrel's face.

'You cannot prove your innocence, Spandrel,' said Cloisterman, perversely aware at some level far below his fear of what might be about to happen that he welcomed the course of action McIlwraith had forced upon him. 'If Zuyler can be shown to have lodged here, it will be taken

131

as proof that you and he conspired together to murder de Vries.'

'What?'

'Once that's been proved to the Sheriff's satisfaction, you'll be prevailed upon to admit it.'

'And by "prevailed upon" he doesn't mean by weight of reasoned argument,' said McIlwraith with a grim smile. 'Understand?'

Spandrel did understand. He looked at Cloisterman, who nodded towards the door in as open a gesture of approval as he dared risk. The girl was whimpering, but nobody else made a sound. Aertsen caught Cloisterman's eye and held his gaze for a moment. There was going to be some form of reckoning for this. And it was not going to be pleasant. But that lay in the future. In the present, Spandrel took several hesitant steps towards the door.

'*De sleutel*,' said McIlwraith to Ugels. '*Snel.*' The key to the door was proffered in a trembling hand. 'Take it from him, Spandrel.' Spandrel did so. 'We'll lock the door behind us, gentlemen. I advise you to be in no hurry about breaking it open. I'll not scruple to kill any man who follows us.'

'We will not follow,' said Aertsen. 'You have my word.'

'For what that's worth, mijnheer, I'm only a very little obliged. But thank you anyway. Open the door, Spandrel.' Spandrel obeyed. 'Your servant, gentlemen.' McIlwraith backed out onto the landing and nodded for Spandrel to follow. 'Close it, mijnheer. If you please.'

Aertsen stretched forward and pushed the door shut. McIlwraith and Spandrel were now visible only as blurred shadows through the frosted glass of the window. There was a click as the key turned in the lock. Then the shadows vanished.

No more than a second of silence and immobility followed. Then Aertsen rounded on Cloisterman, anger supplanting his fear. 'I hold you responsible for this.' He was ashamed. Cloisterman could see that. His parting assurance to McIlwraith – *'We will not follow'* – had been a craven and probably unnecessary surrender. 'You encouraged this . . . this madman.'

'Henrik—'

'And you'll answer for it, I assure you.'

Cloisterman summoned a smile. 'Do I have your word on that?'

Aertsen stepped closer. 'What does he intend to do?'

'At a guess, I'd say he intends to go after Zuyler and Mevrouw de Vries. He needs Spandrel to identify them and the article he delivered to de Vries, which McIlwraith believes them to be carrying.'

'"At a guess". That is all, is it? Just a guess.'

'What are you suggesting?'

'If I find any evidence that you knew what he was planning . . .'

'Shouldn't we be taking steps to catch them rather than arguing about who's to blame? There'll be a back door out of here, I've no doubt. Unless, of course . . .' Cloisterman looked Aertsen in the eye without flinching. Normally, he deferred to the judicial authorities in all matters. Now, however, the time had come to show a little defiance – a little, it occurred to him, of the spirit of McIlwraith. 'Unless you intend to honour your promise. And let them get clean away.'

CHAPTER THIRTEEN

Over the Water

'We'll be walking away from here as calmly as two professors on a promenade, Spandrel,' said McIlwraith, uncocking the pistols and slipping them into the pockets of his greatcoat. 'If you attempt to break away, however, I'll shoot you down without a moment's hesitation. Be in no doubt of that. I have need of you, but my need's not so pressing that I'll brook any resistance. And you're an escaped prisoner, remember. I'd probably be rewarded for my pains. We have a little way to go to a place of safety. Once there, I'll explain what I want from you. Until then, you'll keep your mouth shut and your ears open. Now, walk straight ahead.'

The simplicity of these instructions was strangely welcome to Spandrel. Who – or what – McIlwraith was he had no idea. But the fact remained that he was no longer in a cramped cell beneath the Stadhuis, nor were manacles chafing his wrists. He was free – up to a point. And, to judge by what Cloisterman had said, not a moment too soon. There was treachery everywhere. No-one could be trusted. But, for the present, he was walking the streets of Amsterdam and breathing the clear, sunlit air. It was enough. It was, in truth, all he had recently longed for.

The route they followed led through a busy market-place, then steadily north, by a series of alleys and canalside streets, to the harbour. As they reached the bustling waterfront, a view opened up between the rooftops to the east of the Montelbaanstoren. But they headed west, along the wharves and over the canal bridges. Slowly, Spandrel lost his sense of conspicuousness. Nobody knew who he was and nobody cared. By rights, he should have tried to flee the city. But out on the long straight roads through the flat fields of a country he did not know he really would be conspicuous. The city that had been his prison was also his only refuge.

At length, they entered a quieter district at the western end of the harbour. The warehouses here were mostly shuttered and unattended. A windmill loomed ahead atop a seaward bastion of the city wall. Some way short of it, McIlwraith directed Spandrel down an alley between a high wooden fence on one side and a row of warehouses on the other. Sawing and hammering could be heard from over the fence, but they had the alley to themselves. The far end was a wharf on some inlet of the harbour. A barge drifted by in the distance as they walked.

'This is far enough,' McIlwraith announced suddenly. They stopped by the doors of a warehouse that looked to Spandrel just like all the others to left and right. The number 52 and the word SPECERIJEN were stencilled over the lintel. McIlwraith took out a key and opened the wicket, then motioned for Spandrel to enter.

The interior was dark and cold as a tomb, but dry, the dust scented with sweetness. McIlwraith lit a lantern that hung from a beam, but its circle of light stretched no further than a nearby jumble of upturned boxes and a bench, on which stood a wicker hamper. Spandrel was left to imagine how far off the rear wall might be. There were patterings and scurryings from the darkness.

'We'll be here till nightfall,' said McIlwraith. 'There's

coal and a brazier somewhere, so we'll not freeze to death. And . . .' he crossed to the bench and unstrapped the hamper 'the rats haven't gnawed through this yet, so we'll not starve either.' He raised the lid. 'Bread. Cheese. Ham. A flagon of ale. And some tobacco. Plenty of everything. Just what you'll be needing after a couple of weeks on prison rations.'

'Why are you doing this?'

'Not because I'm sorry for you, Spandrel, if that's what you were hoping. My help comes with a price.'

'I have no money.'

'But you can pay me back, nonetheless.'

'How?'

'Eat something, man. You need to build your strength up.' McIlwraith kicked a box into position next to the bench and gestured for Spandrel to sit. He pulled a hunk of bread off a loaf and passed it to him with some thick slices of ham. Then he uncorked the flagon and stood it on the bench near Spandrel's elbow. 'Good?'

The bread was fresh and doughy, the ham lean and succulent. Their flavours surged through Spandrel. He coughed and took a gulp of the ale, then looked up at McIlwraith. 'Good,' he announced.

'Don't bolt it or you'll bring it up no sooner than you've got it down. There's plenty of time.' McIlwraith stowed his pistols away, then lit a pipe and sat up on the bench while Spandrel ate and drank more slowly. 'I'm Captain James McIlwraith. Acting on behalf of General Ross for the House of Commons Secret Committee of Inquiry into the South Sea Company. The Brodrick Committee, as it's known. Heard of it?'

'Yes. I think so. But what—'

'All in due course, Spandrel. Just listen, there's a good fellow. I have a House of Commons warrant authorizing me to do whatever's necessary to carry out the committee's wishes and requiring any British subject I encounter to assist me. Consider your assistance called upon. I've taken this warehouse on a short let. As far as the owner's agent is concerned, I need it to handle a consignment of cinnamon. But we're the consignment. You and me. And we're leaving rather than arriving. Aertsen will expect us to make for Rotterdam. His men will ride a stableful of horses into the ground chasing our shadows. They'd have overtaken us if we'd gone that way, no question. You'd have slowed me down too much to outrun them. As it is, we're leaving by ship. The *Havfrue* is a Danish vessel. It sails for Christiania tonight. We'll be on it. The master's agreed – for a generous consideration, naturally – to convey us to the eastern shore of the Zuider Zee. We'll be put off at Harderwijk. That's in the province of Gelderland. Be grateful for these Netherlanders' constitutional niceties, Spandrel. You can't be arrested outside Holland without all manner of swearing and affidaviting, for which there wouldn't be time even if Aertsen guessed our destination. And he's not likely to do that. We'll buy horses at Harderwijk and make for the border.'

'But why? Where are we going?'

'Lord save us, do you understand nothing, man? Isn't it obvious?'

'No. Not in the least.'

McIlwraith sighed. 'You delivered the Green Book to de Vries, didn't you?'

'I delivered something.'

'You must have seen what it was.'

'No. It was sealed in a despatch-box. I saw the box. Nothing more.'

At that McIlwraith loosed a guttural laugh that echoed in the rafters above them. 'I was hoping you'd know it by sight. That was one of my reasons for heezing you out of gaol. You *would* know Zuyler and the winsome widow by sight, wouldn't you?'

'Yes. Of course.'

'Then I'd best be grateful for small mercies. That pair have the Green Book, Spandrel. They tried to sell it to the Government – *our* Government – for a hundred thousand pounds.'

'*How much?*'

'A hundred thousand. And they'd likely have been paid it, but for numskullery in high places.'

'A hundred thousand . . . for a book?'

'Not just any book. The *Green* Book. The repository of the South Sea Company's darkest secrets. Who was bribed. When. How much. All the names. All the figures. Everything.'

'That's what I delivered?'

'It seems so. It wasn't with Knight when he was arrested. And Knight's known to have visited Janssen just before leaving England. It's what the committee's been looking for since it started work last month: the only true record of the company's dealings. The audited accounts were just a bundle of false figures and fictitious names. But even bribers need to keep tally. To root out the guilty men, high and low, the committee needs that book. And I mean to procure it for them.'

'How?'

'By catching up with Zuyler and his *amorosa*. It's clear they murdered de Vries and left you to take the blame. I'm not sure if Zuyler or de Vries was behind the attempt on your life – if that's what it was – and it doesn't much matter now anyway. According to Cloisterman, de Vries's money goes to his son. The widow doesn't even get her proverbial mite. Maybe the old man cut her out of his will for fear she might otherwise have a good reason to hasten his exit from this world. If so, he'd have made sure she knew that, which can't have filled her head with warm, wifely thoughts. Soon Zuyler was showing her what a younger man has to offer and they talked of running away together. But they needed money. And the Green Book offered them a way of getting more than they could ever hope to squeeze out of de Vries. They must have known it was on its way before you arrived. Between them, they must have weevilled into every one of de Vries's secrets. Oh, they've been clever. No question about it. But cleverness has a habit of foundering on simple bad luck. Our Embassy at The Hague's in the charge of a brainless popinjay. And the Secretary of State he answered to – the late, unlamented Lord Stanhope – had kept himself so calculatingly ignorant of the South Sea escapade that he didn't understand what Zuyler was offering for sale. So, the offer was rejected. How sad, how inconvenient, for our flitting pair of love-birds.' McIlwraith clapped his hands together. 'But how very fortunate for us.'

'Fortunate?'

'Aye, man. Fortunate for both of us. For me because, if the sale had been completed, the Government would have the Green Book. And we can safely assume too many ministers are named in it for them to allow it ever to see the light of day. Sunderland, for one. Why, if the committee could nail his dealings to the barn-door . . . Well, I still have a chance now of enabling them to do just that.'

'And me?'

'You? It's even better for you, Spandrel. You're out of gaol. And you'll stay out if you stick by me. The committee will be in your debt if we deliver them the Green Book. That means the Government will be in your debt, because it's certain we'll have a whole sparkling new set of ministers once the truth about the existing lot's known. No fear of being sent back here to face trial then. No need to hide from your creditors. The most eminent of them will likely be facing trial himself.' McIlwraith's tone turned suddenly sombre. 'That's if you help me, of course. Decide it's safer to run for it and you have my word you'll have to run for ever. I'll make sure you can't go home to England without being arrested and handed over to the Dutch authorities. You'll be back where you started – and where you'd have stayed but for me.' Then his tone softened again. 'But there's no question of that, is there? We're in this together.'

'All you want me to do is help you find Zuyler and Estelle de Vries?' It sounded simple, though Spandrel knew it was unlikely to be so. But what choice did he have? McIlwraith was right. They *were* in this together.

'That's all, my bonny fellow.'

'Then I'll do what I can. Though for the life of me I don't see *how* you hope to find them.'

'By putting myself in their shoes and using what God gave me to think with. Zuyler told Dalrymple – the popinjay at The Hague – that he knew where to find another buyer. And that the King wouldn't thank him and Stanhope when he learned who that buyer was. Those were his very words. Which he may come to regret uttering. Who would pay most dearly to disgrace His Majesty's Government in the eyes of his people? Who but one who would be King himself – who thinks he already is, by rights?'

'The Pretender.'

'You have it, Spandrel. They mean to try their luck with the Jacobites. They'd find a nest of them in Paris. But their dealings with Dalrymple and Stanhope will have left them wary of negotiating through intermediaries. I reckon they'll go to the court of James Edward Stuart himself.'

'In Rome?'

'Aye. But don't worry.' McIlwraith grinned. 'We'll catch up with them long before they set foot in the Eternal City. That's a promise.'

Spandrel still had no idea how McIlwraith meant to keep his promise when they boarded the boat sent for them by the master of the *Havfrue* at a nearby wharf early that evening and headed out across the moonlit harbour to where the ship was waiting for them at its anchorage beyond the boom. He was both more frightened and more excited by what had happened than he wanted McIlwraith to realize. His new-found companion might be his saviour – or a devil in disguise. There was no way to tell. Nor could Spandrel hazard the remotest guess at how, or where, or when, their journey would end. He had feared he might never leave Amsterdam and had hoped only for a safe return home. Now, instead, he had embarked on a voyage into the unknown. He was further from home than ever. And he could not turn back.

CHAPTER FOURTEEN

Cold Pursuit

The days following 'the abduction of the prisoner Spandrel', as the incident at Ugels's shop was drily described in Aertsen's formal report, were difficult ones for Cloisterman. He had to rebut any implication that he had connived with McIlwraith to spirit Spandrel away, but he could not do so as forcefully as he might wish in case Aertsen felt his own position was threatened. In that event, he would probably defend himself by persuading Sheriff Lanckaert to recommend that Cloisterman be declared *persona non grata* and sent back to England in disgrace. Cloisterman enjoyed life in Amsterdam and his courtship of the daughter of a wealthy tobacco merchant was at a promising stage. Banishment would spell disaster for all his plans and had to be fended off.

The only way he could see of doing this was to tread lightly where the issue of Spandrel's guilt or innocence was concerned. It was now obvious that Zuyler had murdered de Vries and manoeuvred Spandrel into taking the blame. To state that openly, however, would be to question the competence of the Sheriff and hence of his deputy. He refrained from raising the matter, therefore, and hoped that Aertsen would reciprocate his restraint.

In this regard, the authorities' failure to recapture Spandrel and to seize his abductor was actually quite satisfactory, since it meant that the issue need not be confronted. Spandrel's escape from custody was embarrassing, but not as embarrassing as an admission that the real guilty party had long since slipped through their fingers. It was also noticeable that Aertsen did not press the matter of McIlwraith's status as an agent of the Brodrick Committee. To do so might precipitate a formal complaint by the States of Holland to the House of Commons, with consequences too serious to contemplate for all concerned. Officially, therefore, McIlwraith was an anonymous confederate of Spandrel and, so long as he was not apprehended, that is what he would remain.

Cloisterman was obliged, of course, to report a reasonably accurate version of events to Dalrymple. He calculated, however, that Dalrymple, like Aertsen, would favour the line of least resistance. It had to be assumed that McIlwraith, with Spandrel as his willing or unwilling travelling companion, was no longer in the United Provinces. And it was unlikely that the pair would ever return. In that sense, they were no longer the concern of vice-consuls and chargés d'affaires. Let McIlwraith do his worst and leave others to worry about the consequences. Cloisterman's memorandum to Dalrymple on the subject bore the imprint of this agreeable urging between every reticent line.

It did not, though, yield the response Cloisterman expected, which was either silence or a testy but essentially approving little note. Instead, Cloisterman received by return of post a summons to The Hague. 'I should be obliged,' Dalrymple wrote in an abominable hand that suggested haste, perhaps even desperation, 'if you would wait upon me here at the very earliest juncture available transport will permit.' It did not augur well. In fact, it augured ill.

*　　　*　　　*

143

The urgency of the summons had the meagre advantage of justifying Cloisterman in the minor extravagance of travelling by coach rather than *trekschuit*. The journey nevertheless took the better part of a day and he was tempted to put off reporting to the Dalrymplian presence until the following morning, weary as he was and in need of supper and a bath. Reckoning, however, that he would find the chargé long since departed, he made his way to the Embassy and announced his arrival.

Dalrymple had indeed already gone home, but his secretary's clerk, Harris, was still there, instructed to remain, it transpired, with a late arrival by Cloisterman specifically in mind. 'Mr Dalrymple's anxious to see you, sir. Very anxious, I should say. I'm to escort you to his residence without delay.'

Dalrymple's residence was, in fact, only a short walk away. The simplest of instructions would have sufficed for Cloisterman to find it unescorted. Harris's company seemed intended, Cloisterman could not help but feel, to guard against his turning back rather than losing his way. The auguries were growing worse all the time.

A musical entertainment of some sort was under way when Cloisterman was admitted to the house. A snatch of jaggedly played Handel wafted out behind Dalrymple from the drawing-room. A disagreeable and faintly disturbing smile was hovering around the chargé's moist lips and Cloisterman hardly supposed it was because he was pleased to see him. Harris was told to wait in an antechamber, while they retired to the privacy of Dalrymple's study, where the smile rapidly faded.

'When did we last have the pleasure of seeing you here, Cloisterman?'

'The farewell reception for Lord Cadogan, as I recall.'

'As long ago as that?'

'It was, yes.'

'Well, well. Perhaps it's fortunate for you that it's me rather than his lordship you have to answer to. He was a hard taskmaster and wouldn't have been amused by your mishandling of recent events.'

'I afforded Captain McIlwraith every assistance,' said Cloisterman steadily. 'As you instructed me to.'

'My instructions did not include helping him to abduct a prisoner.'

'I didn't help him.'

'No? I'm not sure Sheriff Lanckaert would agree with you.'

'My report was detailed and accurate. If you've read it, you'll—'

'I've certainly read it. And a sorrier chronicle of mismanaged affairs I've seldom been obliged to peruse.'

'I'm sure I'd be diverted by your exegesis of what I should have done.'

'I haven't time to give lessons in adroitness, Cloisterman. It's lucky for you the Dutch don't seem disposed to make a fuss about it.'

'That's not entirely a question of luck.'

'Really?' Dalrymple eyed Cloisterman sceptically. 'How you've made your peace with the Amsterdam authorities I prefer not to know. I've not called you here for the purpose of recrimination. Circumstances do not afford me the leisure for such an exercise.' This, Dalrymple's expression implied, was something he regretted. 'Do you realize the degree of uncertainty that hovers over all our futures under the new Secretary of State?'

'Lord Townshend is clearly not the same man as Lord Stanhope.'

'He is not even his own man, Cloisterman. Walpole tells him what to think and do. And he will tell many more what to think and do before long. Brodrick's committee was due to report to the House of Commons today. Did you know that?'

'I confess not.'

'Their charges, whatever they are, will only strengthen Walpole's hand. It is his tune we must dance to now. You understand? We cannot allow him to doubt our loyalty.'

'I'm sure he will have no cause to.'

'In that case, you will be glad to learn that you have an opportunity to demonstrate your loyalty to the new order.'

'Oh yes?' Cloisterman did not feel glad. Quite the reverse. He felt an apprehensiveness amounting almost to dread. 'What manner of opportunity?'

'A special emissary of Lord Townshend – and hence Walpole – is waiting for you at the Goude Hooft. It's an inn not far from here. Harris will show you the way. The emissary's a military man. Colonel Augustus Wagemaker. A straighter sort than McIlwraith, but just as tough, I should say.'

'And he's waiting for *me*?'

'Yes. You know more about this whole damnable business than anyone else. You're the obvious choice.'

'For what?'

'Wagemaker will explain his requirements to you. You will do your best – your very best – to comply with them.'

'Can you give me no idea what they are?'

'Onerous, I shouldn't wonder. Though well within your compass. You're going on a journey, Cloisterman.' Dalrymple's smile had crept back out from its hiding place. 'And it could be a long one.'

The contents of the Brodrick Committee's report, at which Dalrymple could still only guess, were by now already known to the House of Commons in London. It had taken four hours for the document to be read, by

146

Brodrick until his voice gave out and then by the Clerk of the House. The complexities and obscurities of the tale it told were formidable but, so far as the Government was concerned, the charges were horribly simple. Bribes, in the form of free allocations of South Sea stock which could be sold later at a guaranteed profit, had been paid to certain ministers to ensure that they turned a blind eye to glaring irregularities in the National Debt conversion scheme, irregularities that had left the Company with liabilities for the year ahead of £14,500,000 to be set against income from the Exchequer of £2,000,000: insolvency, in other words, on a grand, not to say grotesque, scale. The ministers named as recipients of bribes were, as expected, Chancellor of the Exchequer John Aislabie, Postmaster-General James Craggs the elder, Secretary to the Treasury Charles Stanhope and, as less confidently anticipated . . . the First Lord of the Treasury and Groom of the Stole, Charles Spencer, third Earl of Sunderland.

How the House would proceed in the light of such a damning report was still unclear when it adjourned for the evening. Impeachment of the named ministers was the obvious course, but that would mean entrusting verdict and punishment to the Lords. Many favoured trying them, peers and all, along with the directors, in the Commons. The decision on that would have to wait for another day.

Some matters would not wait, however. The report had accused the Secretary of State for the Southern Department, James Craggs the younger, not of accepting a bribe himself but of negotiating bribes for the Duchess of Kendal and her so-called nieces. The Duchess, born Ehrengard Melusina von der Schulenburg, was none other than the King's openly acknowledged mistress. The King's wife had been confined in a German castle for the past twenty-seven years after being divorced on grounds of non-cohabitation following an affair with a Swedish count. The Duchess's 'nieces' were in reality her daughters by the King. Their corruption, if proved, would creep close to the person of the King himself. Craggs could not be interrogated on the point. Smallpox held him in its mortal grip. And his fellow Secretary of State, Viscount Townshend, had nothing to answer for. But one awkward duty did devolve upon him: that of explaining to his fretful monarch how the royal ladies' reputations were to be protected.

Thus it was that at an unheard-of hour for such summonses, Lord Townshend found himself being ushered into the royal closet at St James's Palace by the Turkish Groom of the Chamber, the notoriously inscrutable Mehemet. The scarcely less inscrutable Earl of Sunderland was already present. He had a narrow, skewed face that seemed forever suspended between a smile and a frown. His eyes were close-set and evasive. He greeted Townshend with his customary coolness, clearly unabashed by being accused in the Commons earlier that evening of accepting £50,000 worth of South Sea stock as virtual hush-money.

But if Sunderland was calm in the face of the storm, the King was not. He had always been a difficult man to read, what with his stilted English, his immobile features and his unsociable temperament, but it was apparent to Townshend that the committee's traduction of his beloved mistress had hit a tender spot. 'They had not the right to say these things,' he complained through gritted teeth. 'Mr Craggs was helping to the Duchess. What is wrong with that?'

'I'm sure Lord Townshend doesn't think there was anything wrong,' said Sunderland.

'Indeed not, Your Majesty,' Townshend swiftly

rejoined. 'And I'm confident the purchase of shares by the Duchess is not what will occupy the House in its consideration of the report.' (She had not purchased them, of course, but it was as well to subscribe to the fiction that she had.)

'The purchase of shares by *anyone*,' said the King with heavy emphasis, 'is out of their business.'

Townshend glanced at Sunderland. What – or rather whom – did the King mean by 'anyone'? It was a certain bet that his Groom of the Stole knew the answer. 'I fear, sir, that they will make it their business.'

'Perhaps your brother-in-law could dissuade them from doing so,' said Sunderland, with more of his smile than his frown.

'He did dissuade them from printing the report.'

'Printing?' The King's face was briefly lit by horror. 'We want no printing.'

'And there will be none, sir.'

'His Majesty is concerned about Mr Knight's . . . papers, Townshend. How is it that your department has failed to secure all of them?'

'Knight took steps to keep some of his more . . . sensitive . . . records from us. But we're on the track of them.'

'Track?' queried Sunderland. 'You speak literally?'

'Where is it?' the King put in, adding in an explanatory growl, '*Das Grüne Buch.*' He was apparently unable to bring himself to describe the article in English.

'We're doing everything we can to find it, sir.'

'We?' Sunderland's eyebrows twitched up.

'My department,' said Townshend levelly.

'Assisted and advised, no doubt, by your brother-in-law.'

'The Paymaster-General does what he can.'

'So he does. But you should beware. The robin is by nature a solitary bird.'

'In the present circumstances, Spencer, I should have thought you had more to beware of than me.'

'The report? It's nothing.' Sunderland flapped a dismissive hand. 'They can't touch me.'

'Without the Green Book, you mean?'

'I mean—' Sunderland broke off, apparently deciding that what he really meant was better not disclosed. 'They wouldn't have the nerve,' he eventually added. 'I made most of them. And I can break the rest.'

'Break them,' the King said suddenly, rousing himself from the reverie into which he had sunk while his two ministers bickered. '*Ja.* That is what you must do.'

'With the greatest respect, sir,' said Townshend, 'the Commons are not to be broken. But they may be controlled. With young Mr Craggs so ill and his father and Mr Aislabie accused of serious lapses, it is as well for us all that Mr Walpole is there to defend your Government. And that, I assure you, he is doing tirelessly.' Sunderland sniffed derisively but, holding the King's eye, Townshend went on. 'There is only so much that Lord Sunderland and I can accomplish in the Lords, sir. This will be settled by the Commons. Mr Walpole is trying his very best to hold them in check. If anyone can do it, he is the man.'

'Walpole,' said the King musingly. 'Can we trust him?'

'I trust him,' Townshend replied.

'And it seems,' Sunderland put in, 'that the rest of us will have to.'

Walpole was in truth a harder man to trust than Townshend cared to admit. He was so warm, so amiable, so vastly confiding. Townshend had been to Eton and Cambridge with him, had married his sister, had dined and hunted and argued and caroused with him down the years; yet still did not know, most of the time, what was in his mind. Beyond Walpole's many confidences, there were always other purposes he was set upon serving.

One such had taken him from the House of Commons that night to the Tower of London, a journey of which Townshend knew, and was to know, nothing. Walpole had been confined there once himself and wished for no reminder of that nadir of his political fortunes. But Sir Theodore Janssen could hardly be summoned to Westminster. And Sir Theodore he had to see.

'This is a surprise,' the elderly financier admitted when his visitor was shown in. 'And an honour, I suppose.'

'We must talk, Janssen,' Walpole said brusquely 'And we must do so to the point. If I want to thrust and parry, I shall hire a fencing master.'

'And what is the point, *Mr* Walpole?'

'You know Brodrick's committee reported to the Commons today?'

'Of course. A pretty scene, no doubt. And a distressing one, I should imagine, for several of your fellow ministers. The Governor will soon be running short of accommodation here.'

'I don't care about my fellow ministers, Janssen. I care about myself. I suppose *you* care about *yourself*.'

'Naturally.'

'This is no state for a gentleman of your age and distinction to find himself in.' Walpole glanced around the chamber. 'Now is it?'

'I'm forced to agree.'

'I want the Green Book.' Walpole smiled. 'And I have no time for shilly-shally.'

'So it would appear.'

'What do *you* want, Sir Theodore?'

'To live the years that remain to me in freedom and comfort.'

'Not likely, as things presently stand.'

'Alas no.'

'Where's your valet, by the by? I'm told he no longer visits. Who shaves you now I don't know, but, by the look of your chin, he's no barber.'

'The comings and goings of servants are surely beneath your concern.'

'Nothing is beneath my concern.' Walpole lowered his voice. 'Where is Jupe?'

'I wish I knew. As you're so kind to point out, I have need of him.'

'But I suspect he's serving those needs. Even if you don't know his whereabouts. I'll put it simply for you. Knight gave you the Green Book for safe-keeping. But you've lost it. And Jupe has gone in search of it.'

'That is the most—'

'Don't deny it. It would be a waste of your time as well as mine. Some weeks from now, the Commons will decide how to punish you for your part in this catastrophe. You'll need powerful friends then to escape imprisonment or penury or both. But you have none. They're all dead or fled or in the same boat as you. Your only hope is me. I can help you, Sir Theodore. And I will. If you help me.'

Several seconds of silence followed while the two men looked at each other. Then Sir Theodore said, 'What do you want?'

'I've told you. The Green Book.'

'I don't have it. Nor do I know where it is.'

'But that may change. If it should, I want to be the first to hear.'

'Very well. I agree.'

'You do?'

'What choice do I have?'

'You have the choice of thinking you may be able to deceive me. Knight gave you the book so that it could be

152

removed to a place of safety and used to bargain for clemency. There can have been no other reason. You may suppose that can still be done. But you would be in error. I cannot be forced to help you. I can only be persuaded.'

'Then I must try to persuade you.'

'So you must.'

'Persuasion is a two-edged sword, though. I have opened the book. I know what it contains.'

'I felt sure you did.'

'Do you?'

'How could I?'

'How indeed? But there's the strangest thing. I have the impression, you see – the very distinct impression – that you know exactly what the book contains. If so, you'll also know that prevailing on the House of Commons to treat me leniently would be a trifling price to pay for keeping those contents secret.'

'Trifling to me, perhaps.' Walpole winked. 'But everything to you.'

'Everything may be exactly what's at stake.' Sir Theodore rubbed his ill-shaven chin. 'If the book should fall into . . . the wrong hands.'

'It's certainly a pity you didn't take better care of it.'

'A pity, you say?' Sir Theodore summoned a defiant smile. 'As to that, Mr Walpole, it's a pity a great many people – a great many *grand* people – didn't take better care.'

As one conversation was ending at the Tower of London, so another, bearing on the same subject, was beginning at the Goude Hooft inn in The Hague. Cloisterman had found Colonel Wagemaker waiting for him in a balconied booth above the cavernous tap-room and had instantly formed a less favourable impression of Lord

Townshend's emissary than the one given him by Dalrymple: *'A straighter sort than McIlwraith, but just as tough.'* That was true as far as it went, but it did not capture the spine-shivering balefulness of the man. There was a flint-hard edge to him, but no spark of passion. Cloisterman was surprised to find himself thinking fondly of McIlwraith as he falteringly met Wagemaker's icy gaze.

'You travel light, Mr Cloisterman,' Wagemaker said. 'That's good.'

'As a matter of fact, Colonel, I don't travel light. An overnight journey from Amsterdam to The Hague is scarcely the Grand Tour.'

'Nor's the journey we'll be undertaking. But it may last as long.'

'Mr Dalrymple said something of the kind. I should appreciate—'

'You know what this is all about?'

'Knight's ledger. Yes, I know.'

'And you're skilled in the consular arts, I'm told.'

'I like to think so.'

'I can't afford to be held up. I'm a soldier, not a politician. But I may need to be a politician to win through. That's when you'll earn your keep.'

'I've no wish to "earn my keep", as you put it. I have duties in Amsterdam I'd be happy to return to.'

'You'll not see Amsterdam again in a hurry. We're heading south.'

'South?'

'That's where Zuyler and Mrs de Vries will have gone. I'm told you know Mrs de Vries by sight.'

'I've met her a few times in company with her late husb—'

'Good enough. You also know Spandrel.'

'Yes.'

'And Jupe.'

'Well, yes. Captain McIlwraith, too, if it comes to—'

'*I* know McIlwraith, Mr Cloisterman. Of old.' For the first time, there was a spark of some emotion in Wagemaker's eyes. And it was not friendship. 'You can leave him to me.'

'When you say south . . .'

'Zuyler and Mrs de Vries will try to sell the ledger to the Jacobites. It's obvious.'

'You mean they'll take it to the Pretender? In Rome?'

'They'll try. But we must overtake them before they reach their destination and retrieve the ledger. We must also overtake McIlwraith and Jupe. They're all ahead of us. But not so far ahead that they can't be caught. Any of them.'

'This sounds distinctly . . . perilous.'

'There'll be difficulties. There may be dangers. That's to be expected.'

'Not by me. I have no experience of such endeavours. I am *not* a soldier, Colonel.'

'You don't need to tell me that.' Wagemaker ran a withering eye over him. 'But it seems you're the best I'll get.'

Cloisterman did not sleep well that night. Wagemaker meant to leave at dawn and, reluctant though he was, Cloisterman would be leaving with him. He cursed Dalrymple for volunteering his services, suspecting as he did that they were a handy substitute for Dalrymple's own. He cursed his luck as well. Amsterdam had turned out to be the right place at the wrong time. Hard riding and harsh dealing lay ahead and he was not sure which he was worse equipped for. Yet there was no way out,

155

short of resigning his post and returning to England to face an uncertain and impecunious future. There was not much sign of a way *through* either. It was the very devil of a business. But it was the devil he was bound to serve.

CHAPTER FIFTEEN

The Road South

The pace McIlwraith set was predictably stiff. Spandrel, who had not ridden in over a year and had never done so regularly, was saddle-sore and weary before they left Dutch territory. He was sustained to that point by fear of recapture. Once they were on the winding high road of the Rhine Valley, however, he began to protest and plead for a day's rest. He was wasting his breath, of course. McIlwraith's hopes of overhauling Zuyler and Estelle de Vries rested on the likelihood that they were not naturally fast travellers and had no particular reason to fear pursuit. They were not fools, though. The Green Book was a slowly wasting asset and a dangerous article to possess. The sooner they reached Rome and sold it the better.

At the Graue Gans, Cologne's principal coaching inn, McIlwraith gleaned the first confirmation of their route. An English couple by the name of Kemp, the husband an excellent speaker of German, had stayed at the inn a week before. They had been travelling by chaise, but seemed embarked on a journey calling for a more robust vehicle. A wheelwright had been needed to replace some splintered spokes. And they had asked the landlord to recommend other inns on the road to Switzerland.

This discovery put McIlwraith in high good humour. He drank more, and talked more, in the tap-room that evening than he had at any time since leaving Amsterdam. Spandrel drank his fill as well and was soon too fuddled to follow what was being said. He retained a vague memory of McIlwraith reminiscing about the number of men he had killed in battle and an occasion on which, apparently, the Captain-General himself, the Duke of Marlborough, had sought his tactical advice. There was something too about secret missions behind enemy lines. But here Spandrel's memory grew vaguer still. As perhaps did McIlwraith's reminiscences.

The captain showed no ill effects of his over-indulgence next morning, rousing Spandrel before dawn and insisting on an early start. Spandrel, for his part, had a thick head that a few hours on horseback transformed into a ferociously aching one, the spot where Zuyler had hit him with the hammer throbbing to eye-watering effect. When he complained, McIlwraith suggested he should treat it as a useful reminder of the Dutchman's treachery, which he now had the chance to avenge.

But vengeance was far from Spandrel's thoughts. The simple joy of freedom had given place to a nagging fear that he was simply wading deeper and deeper into a morass. If his experiences since leaving London had taught him anything, it was that humble folk should never meddle – nor even allow themselves to become remotely involved – in the affairs of the great. Yet, here he was, straying still further into them. Green Books and Jacobites could easily be the death of him. If they were, he would have no-one to blame but himself. And no-one else would care anyway. But what was he to do? McIlwraith had him where he wanted him: by his side. And that was where he was bound to remain. Until . . .

When? That was the question. If the Kemps *were* Zuyler and Estelle de Vries, they were a week ahead of them. That could amount to three hundred miles.

Spandrel did not see how such a gap could be closed, however hard they rode. Much the likeliest outcome, it seemed to him, was that it would *not* be closed. They would reach Rome too late to prevent the sale of the book. In some ways, he hoped he was right. There would be nothing they could do, but he would have done what was required of him and might hope for some modest reward. In other ways, he knew that to be a fool's counsel. If they failed, there would be no reward for him, other than abandonment far from home.

It was better than imprisonment in Amsterdam, of course. Compared with what had seemed to lie in wait for him only a few days previously, this journey was a gift from the gods. It was just that with nothing but uncertainty waiting at the end of it and a cold head wind seeming to blow down the valley whenever a sleety drizzle did not descend from the mountains, a gift could soon feel like a curse.

'Don't look so long-faced, man,' McIlwraith upbraided him over supper that night, which they spent at an inn near Coblenz where the Kemps had not been heard of. 'I feed and horse you. I even think for you. Ah . . .' He pointed at Spandrel with his fork, on which half a gravy-smeared potato was impaled. 'That's it, isn't it? You've been thinking on your own account. You don't want to get into that habit. It's not a bit of good for you.'

Good for him or not, though, Spandrel continued to think – and to worry. About what would happen if and when they overtook their quarry. And about what would happen if they never did.

Spandrel might have been even more worried had he realized, as McIlwraith certainly did, that they were also being pursued. Their surreptitious exit from Dutch territory had necessitated an indirect and time-consuming route as far as Cologne. Their original lead had thus been pared down to barely a day. Wagemaker and Cloisterman spent that night at the Grau Gans, where they too heard about the English couple in the chaise – and about the pair of travellers who had expressed an interest in them the previous night.

It had been a physically exhausting and mentally wearing two days on the road for Cloisterman since their departure from The Hague. Wagemaker was a taciturn and unsympathetic travelling companion, who seemed to think Cloisterman's command of German and his ability to recognize several of the people they were looking for compensated for his poor horsemanship and lack of stamina – but only just. Cloisterman resented this, but had been poorly placed to do much about it. Revived and emboldened by the Grau Gans's food and wine, however, he decided to hit back in the only way he could, by questioning Wagemaker's tactics.

'We may be close to McIlwraith and Spandrel, Colonel, but we're all of us a long way behind the two people who actually have what we're trying to retrieve. I fail to understand how you hope to catch up with them.'

'I reckon we will.'

'And on what is your . . . reckoning . . . based?'

'It's based on the fact that when Zuyler and Mrs de Vries reach Switzerland, they'll have a hard choice to make. To cross the Alps? Or to take a boat down the Rhône to Marseilles, then look for a sea passage to Naples, say, and hope to travel up to Rome from there?'

'They can't go down the Rhône,' said Cloisterman, suddenly beginning to follow Wagemaker's reasoning.

'Why not?'

'Because of the outbreak of plague in Marseilles last summer. The port's still closed. There's no traffic on the Rhône. Most of Provence is reported to be in a state of chaos. Nobody in their right mind would try to go that way.'

'So I hear too. Which way will they go, then?'

'Over the Alps. They have to.'

'At this time of the year? I'd think twice about doing it alone. With a woman . . . it's asking for trouble.'

'What choice do they have?'

'They could wait for milder weather.'

'But that could mean waiting for a month or more.'

'So, they won't wait. But I don't think they're equal to it. I think they'll try the crossing and abandon the attempt when they realize how difficult and dangerous it is. And by then . . .' Wagemaker's right hand closed around an imaginary throat. 'They'll be within our reach.'

'And within McIlwraith's.'

'Yes. Jupe's as well. But if it had been easy . . .' Wagemaker unclenched his hand and stared at his palm. 'They wouldn't have sent me.'

The death from smallpox at the age of thirty-five of Secretary of State James Craggs the younger did not distract the House of Commons for many moments from its pursuit of the ministers named in the Brodrick Committee report. Walpole's recommendation of impeachment before the Lords was ignored, though whether this displeased him or not was hard to tell. Instead, the Commons voted to hear the cases themselves, which happened to mean that Walpole would be able to play a full part in the trials and influence their outcomes . . . one way or the other.

'The taking in, or holding of stock, by the South Sea Company for the benefit of any member of either House of Parliament or person concerned in the Administration (during the time that the Company's Proposals or the Bill relating thereto were depending in Parliament) without giving valuable consideration paid,' the House resolved after several days' debate, 'were corrupt, infamous and dangerous practices, highly reflecting on the Honour and Justice of Parliament and destructive of the Interest of His Majesty's Government.'

The charge was laid. Now, those accused would have to answer to it.

The trial of the first of those accused, Charles Stanhope, was still pending when McIlwraith and Spandrel crossed the Swiss border just outside Basle, one long and gruelling week after crossing the Dutch border nearly five hundred miles to the north. They had been detained at Heidelberg for the best part of a day by the need to obtain certificates of health from a hard-pressed doctor appointed by the local magistrate. Without them, Swiss customs officers were sure to turn them back on the grounds that they might be plague-carriers who had crept into the Palatinate from France. Another wrangle over certification had followed at Freiburg, where they had strayed into the Austrian enclave of Breisgau. McIlwraith had raged against these delays and pressed ever harder on the road to compensate for them. Spandrel's memory was of bone-weary rides in seemingly permanent twilight along frozen tracks through the snow-hushed fringes of endless forest. Travel, he had learned, was not the exhilarating experience he had dreamed it might be when gazing at his father's maps as a child.

Of Zuyler and Estelle de Vries there had been inter-mittent news suggesting that they were now only a few days ahead. Spandrel consoled himself with the thought that they were unlikely to be enjoying the journey any more than he was. Of Jupe, however, there was no trace, which had prompted Spandrel to suggest he might have given up. But McIlwraith had poured scorn on this idea. 'He's had the good sense to travel alone, man. That's all it is. I wish I'd followed his example, instead of hoppling myself with someone who rides like a nun on a donkey *and* never stops complaining.'

Despite the frequency of such insults, Spandrel had grown strangely fond of his companion. McIlwraith seemed to be just about the only person he had met since leaving England to have told him the truth, uncomfortable though it sometimes was. It was not so much that Spandrel trusted him, as that he felt safe with him. There was a reassuring solidity of body and purpose to the man. He had driven Spandrel hard, but nothing like as hard as he had driven himself.

In Switzerland, it seemed clear, their journey would reach its crisis. With the Rhône closed, the only route to Italy lay over the Alps. And in late winter, the only pass worth considering was the Simplon. McIlwraith expected the chase to end there. How it would end he did not say. Perhaps he did not know. Or perhaps, Spandrel reflected, he did not think it wise to disclose.

They left Basle early next morning and crossed the Jura ridge in fine, dry, cold weather. Spandrel had anticipated that the Alps would be craggier and perhaps snowier versions of the Black Forest peaks they had passed. When he first saw them massing on the horizon ahead, however, vast and white and forbidding, he realized just what kind of a barrier they represented and could hardly imagine that there was a way through them.

'They strike fear into your heart, don't they, Spandrel?' said McIlwraith. 'But remember. They'll do the same for our soft-bred Dutchman and his lady love. We have them now. Like rats in a trap.'

*   *   *

163

They descended from the ridge into the Aare valley and followed its winding course south as far as Berne. The city occupied a steep-banked lobe of land jutting out into a deep eastward loop of the river. They arrived at dusk, entering by one of the gates in the defensive wall on the western side. It was, for Spandrel, just one more in a succession of tired, travel-stained, twilit arrivals. Berne appeared no different from anywhere else they had been. The gateman recommended an inn: the Drei Tassen. They made their weary way to it along ill-lit, cobbled streets. They took a room, stabled the horses and went to the tap-room in search of food and drink. It was a routine they had followed in half a dozen other cities.

After the meal, McIlwraith lit his pipe and gazed broodily at the fire. This too was his custom. There had been no repetition of the drunken reminiscences he had permitted himself in Cologne. Spandrel was warm and replete now. Soon, he was having difficulty keeping his eyes open. He hauled his aching limbs out of the settle and announced he was off to bed. McIlwraith nodded a goodnight to him and stayed where he was. Spandrel knew it could easily be another couple of hours before the captain turned in. But he would still be up again before dawn. Sleep was not something he seemed to need much of.

Spandrel, on the other hand, needed every hour he could snatch. He paused in the passage leading to the stairs, then turned and headed for the yard at the rear of the inn. Cold as it was outdoors, a visit to the jakes before he crawled between the sheets could not be avoided.

A few minutes later, he was on his way back across the yard, hugging himself for warmth. As he neared the inn door, a figure stepped into his path from the darkness beyond the reach of the lantern that burned above the lintel.

'Spandrel.'

The voice came as no more than a whisper. Even so, Spandrel knew at once that he recognized it. He could not put a name to the voice, however. Stopping just before he collided with the man, he squinted at him through the shadows cast by the lantern.

'What are you doing here, Spandrel?'

'Who's there?'

'Don't you know me?'

'I . . . I'm not sure.'

The man stepped back, allowing the light from the lantern to fall across his face. Now Spandrel saw him plainly for who he was.

'You.'

'Yes.' The man nodded. 'Me.'

'What do you want?'

'An answer to my question. You're supposed to be in prison in Amsterdam, awaiting trial for murder. So, what are you . . . and your new-found friend . . . doing here – exactly?'

CHAPTER SIXTEEN

A Handful of Air

'I thought you were away to bed,' said McIlwraith, frowning up at Spandrel from his fireside chair. Then he looked across to the man who had accompanied Spandrel back into the tap-room. 'Who's this spindle-shanks?'

'I am Nicodemus Jupe, sir.'

'Sir, is it? I like the sound of you more than the look of you, Jupe, I'll say that. I suppose we were bound to tread on your coat-tails before long. But I didn't expect you to call on us to pay your respects. What do you want?'

'He thinks we should—'

'Let him speak for himself,' barked McIlwraith, cutting off Spandrel's explanation. 'Well?'

'Could we find somewhere a little more private?' Jupe glanced around. 'I'm sure you won't want our affairs widely known, sir.'

'*Our* affairs?' McIlwraith grunted. 'There's a reading-room of sorts on the other side of the passage. With no fire lit, we should have it to ourselves. The chill will keep you awake, Spandrel, even if Jupe's conversation fails to enthral. Lead the way.'

A few moments later, they were in the reading-room, with the door closed behind them. There were desks and chairs spaced around wood-panelled walls. A large bookcase held an assortment of atlases, almanacs and Bibles. A single copy of a Bernese newspaper lay on the table in the centre of the room, beneath a chandelier in which barely half the candles were lit. It was, as McIlwraith had predicted, breath-mistingly cold.

'Say your piece,' growled McIlwraith, propping himself against the table to listen. 'You can begin with how you knew we were here.'

'Apparently, the gatemen always recommend this inn, sir. No doubt the landlord makes it worth their while.'

'Are you staying here?'

'No, sir.'

'Then you were looking for us?'

'I knew someone would follow. It was inevitable. I've been . . . keeping my eye open.'

'But lodging elsewhere. Why's that?'

'I'll explain that in a moment, sir.'

'Stop calling me sir. You're not in my troop, thank God.'

'Very well . . . Captain.'

'How much has Spandrel told you?'

'Only that you're an agent for the Brodrick Committee. I was afraid you might represent the Government.'

'What do you care who I represent?'

'I care a good deal, Captain. We want the same thing. The Green Book.'

'Which your master did his best to put out of the committee's reach. The same thing? Aye. But not for the same reason.'

'Circumstances have changed. Our reasons now coincide.'

'How do you reckon that?'

'Sir Theodore's best hope of lenient treatment by the committee is to help them. By surrendering the Green

Book to them rather than the Government. He and Mr Knight originally planned to force the Government to protect them by threatening to publish the contents of the book. You see I tell you so quite openly. I'm concealing nothing.'

'And poor Spandrel here was to die to make sure that threat could be safely made.'

'It seems so. But that wasn't my fault. I only did what Sir Theodore told me to do.'

'And no doubt you're still doing his bidding.'

'Sir Theodore instructed me to retrieve the book and prevent it falling into the wrong hands. There'll be a Government agent not so very far behind you and I can't risk him succeeding where you or I might fail. My chances of securing the book alone are slim. I need your help.'

'But do we need yours, Jupe? That's the question.'

'You do. Because I know where the book is.'

'Oh, you do, do you?' McIlwraith pushed himself upright and took a step towards Jupe. 'Well, why don't you tell us?'

'May I see your House of Commons warrant first, Captain?' Jupe stood his ground unflinchingly. 'I need to be sure you're what Spandrel says you are.'

'Hah!' McIlwraith laughed, as if impressed by Jupe's steadiness of nerve. He plucked the warrant out from his pocket and handed it over. 'Satisfied?' he asked after a moment.

'Perfectly.' Jupe handed the warrant back. 'Your intention would be to deliver the book to General Ross in London?'

'Or Mr Brodrick. It makes no matter. But that *is* what I mean to do.'

'And you'd be willing to afford me safe passage back to London with you?'

'I could see my way to doing that, aye.'

'It's all I ask.'

'Consider it done. *If* you lead us to the book.'

'I can do that very easily.'

'How?'

'Zuyler and Mrs de Vries arrived here yesterday.'

'They're in Berne?'

'Yes. They've made no move to leave as yet. I've taken a room in the lodging-house they're staying in. They don't know me, of course. But I know them. Mr and Mrs Kemp, they call themselves. The Drei Tassen was obviously too popular for their liking. They preferred somewhere quieter. But not quiet enough. It didn't take me long to find where they're hiding. They've not been out much. When they do leave the house, they lock their door securely. But I expect they take the book with them wherever they go, so there'd be no point forcing an entrance when they're not there. And when they are there . . .' Jupe shrugged. 'Mijnheer de Vries's fate suggests Zuyler would be quite prepared to kill anyone trying to wrest the book from them.'

'Which is why you haven't tried to do so single-handed.'

'It is. I admit it.'

'Why haven't they headed on south?'

'Gathering their strength for the crossing of the Alps, perhaps. Making inquiries as to the best way to go about it. Who knows? You could ask them yourself, though. This very night.'

'So I could.' McIlwraith smiled. 'And so I believe I will.'

It was late now, but the taverns remained busy and a few hardy chestnut-mongers were still stooped over their braziers at the corners of the streets. They headed east along the main thoroughfare of the city, past a squat clock tower and on between tall, arcaded housefronts. A chill mist thickened as they neared the river, blurring the light from the lanterns that hung between the arches.

Whether McIlwraith had any doubts about the wisdom of what he seemed set upon doing Spandrel did not know. The captain was armed, of course, and had loaded his pistols before they set off. For his part, Spandrel felt torn between an eagerness to share in the humiliation of the two people who had happily let him take the blame for their crime and a suspicion that things could surely not fall out as simply as they promised to. Jupe had explained himself logically enough. And to take them unawares was the tactic most likely to succeed. Yet Spandrel could not rid himself of a nagging doubt. This silent march through empty streets reminded him of the night he had broken into the de Vries house in Amsterdam. His expectations had been confounded then. And, for all he knew, they might be again.

A slender church spire stretched up into the night sky behind them as they started to descend to the river, then was blotted out by the mist. Jupe led them down a narrow side-street and stopped at a door above which a lantern burned, illuminating the sign *Pension Siegwart* over the bell. He looked up at the windows on the upper floors, then pressed a cautionary finger to his lips.

'There's a light in their room,' he whispered.

'No matter,' McIlwraith replied, his own whisper sounding like a file scraping on rough wood. 'We'll take them as we find them.' He closed the shutter on the lantern he had been carrying and handed it to Spandrel. 'Open up, Jupe.'

Jupe slipped the pass-key from his pocket, unlocked the door and pushed it carefully open. There was a single lamp burning in the hall. More light – and a burble of voices – seeped up from the basement. They stepped inside and Jupe closed the door. 'Their room is the first floor front,' he said in an undertone. 'The best in the house.'

'Well, that'll save us a clamber up to the attics, won't it?' said McIlwraith. 'Lead on, man.'

Jupe set off up the stairs. McIlwraith signalled for Spandrel to follow and brought up the rear himself. There were a few creaks from the treads as they climbed, but Spandrel still caught the ominous click of a pistol being cocked behind him. He wanted to stop and ask McIlwraith if he was sure he was acting for the best. Above all, he wanted to slow the pace of events. But he knew it made no real sense to do so. McIlwraith was the hardened soldier and was well aware of the advantage of surprising the enemy. It was not an advantage he had any intention of letting slip.

But surprise comes in many guises. They reached the landing and doubled back to the door at the far end. A wavering line of light could be seen beneath it. And a moving shadow, as of someone pacing up and down between the lamp and the door. Then, as they drew closer, Spandrel caught the distinct sound of a sob. The voice, he felt sure, was female.

'A lovers' tiff, perhaps,' McIlwraith whispered in his ear. 'That could suit us well.' He moved past Spandrel to Jupe's shoulder. 'They lock the door when they go out, you said. What about when they're in?'

'I don't know.'

'Then try it, man.' McIlwraith stepped back and raised one of his pistols. 'Now.'

Jupe reached out, turned the handle and pushed.

The door opened and McIlwraith strode into the room. Over his shoulder, Spandrel saw Estelle de Vries turn and stare at him in astonishment. 'Cry out and it'll be the last sound you make, madam.' McIlwraith pointed the pistol at her and glanced around. 'Where's Zuyler?'

The best room in the house amounted to a sparsely furnished chamber boasting a four-poster bed that seemed to belong in more spacious surroundings, a single chair, a chest of drawers and a rickety dressing-table. There were no doors to other rooms and Zuyler was nowhere to be seen. Estelle de Vries was wearing a plain dress and shawl. Her hair was awry, one strand falling across her cheek. Her face was pale and drawn, her eyes red and swollen. As she pushed back the wayward strand of hair with a shaking hand, Spandrel saw that there was a bruise forming over the cheekbone. 'You,' she murmured, her shock turning to a frozen look of horror as their eyes met. 'Oh, dear God.'

'Where's Zuyler?' McIlwraith repeated.

'Not . . .' She shook her head. 'Not here.'

'Close the door, Jupe. Is the key in the lock?'

'Yes.'

'Turn it. We'll need warning of Zuyler's return.'

'Mr Spandrel,' said Mrs de Vries in a fluttering voice. 'How . . . did you . . .'

'Escape from the trap you set for me?' Spandrel hoped he sounded more bitter than he felt. She deserved every reproach he could fashion. Yet finding her as she was – distraught, deserted for all he knew – he could not help feeling a pang of sorrow for her. 'Why should you care?'

'It was thanks to me,' said McIlwraith, uncocking the pistol. 'Captain James McIlwraith, madam. Special representative of the House of Commons Secret Committee of Inquiry into the South Sea Company.'

'The . . . what?'

'This is Jupe,' he went on. 'Valet to Sir Theodore

Janssen. You may have seen him before. He's been following you. As have we.'

'I don't understand.'

'I think you do. We want the Green Book.'

'Book? What book?'

'Come, come, madam. You and your paramour tried to sell it to the British Government. And now you're on your way to Rome to hawk it round the Pretender's court. It's useless to pretend otherwise.'

'Useless?' She looked at McIlwraith, then at Spandrel, then back at McIlwraith.

'Utterly '

'And who did you say you represent?'

'The House of Commons Secret Committee of Inquiry into the South Sea Company.'

'You mean the Government?'

'No, madam. The House of Commons. You're English, for pity's sake. You must know the difference.'

'Of course. I . . . I thought . . .' She put her hand to her brow and squeezed her eyes briefly shut, then fingered away some tears from their edges. 'May I sit down?'

'By all means.' McIlwraith pulled the chair back for her with a flourish. She sank into it. 'Where is the Green Book?'

To Spandrel's amazement, she laughed, then took her handkerchief from her sleeve and dabbed at her eyes. 'Forgive me. It is . . . almost funny.'

'I pride myself on my sense of humour,' said McIlwraith, placing a heavy hand on the back of the chair. 'But I regret to say the joke has eluded me. Where's the book?'

'I don't have it.'

'Does Zuyler?'

'No.'

'Then what's become of it?'

'It's gone.'

173

'Gone where . . . exactly?'

'Into the river.'

'What?'

'I threw it into the river.'

'You destroyed it?' put in Jupe.

'Yes.' She nodded. 'I did.'

'We don't believe you,' said McIlwraith.

'I don't blame you. I hardly believe it myself. But it's true.'

'You threw it into the river?'

'Yes. I walked out onto the bridge down there' – she gestured towards the river – 'and tossed the book over the parapet. Then I watched it being borne away in the current. The river's in spate. It bobbed along like a piece of driftwood, until the water soaked into the pages and weighed it down. Then it sank. Or I lost sight of it in the turbulence. It makes no difference. Ink and paper don't fare well in water. There's a sodden lump of something on the riverbed a few miles downstream, I dare say. But for the only purposes you care about, it's gone.'

A brief silence fell. There had been such a ring of truth in what Estelle de Vries had said that the three men were momentarily struck dumb. Had she really done it? If so, only one question mattered. And it was McIlwraith who posed it. 'Why?'

'Because some things matter more than money. Such as love. Or the loss of it.' Her head fell. 'Pieter and I . . .'

'Fell out?'

'Everything I did was for him. For us. Our future.'

'Such as murdering your husband?'

'Have you ever been in love, Captain?'

'Aye. For my pains, I have.'

'But you're a man. You cannot love as a woman does. Not just with her heart. But with every fibre of her being. You do not understand.'

'Make me understand.'

'Very well. I adored Pieter. I worshipped him. I did whatever he said we had to do to escape . . .' She shuddered. 'From de Vries. Yes, I helped Pieter kill him. And I lied to blacken Mr Spandrel's name.' She turned and looked at Spandrel. 'For that I am truly sorry.'

'Not as sorry as I am,' said Spandrel, wondering if she grasped the doubleness of his meaning.

'All de Vries's money goes to his son,' she went on.

'We know,' said McIlwraith. 'But why should that worry someone who loves with every fibre of her being?'

'It didn't. But Pieter . . . said we had to have money if he was to keep me in the manner he wished to. He could not bear the thought of me living in poverty. And with the Green Book . . .'

'There was no need to see whether your love would thrive in adversity.'

'No. Exactly. We were greedy, of course. I don't deny it.'

'That's as well.'

'It wasn't all greed, though. Not for me.'

'But for Zuyler?'

'Perhaps.' She gave a crumpled little smile. 'When we arrived here yesterday, he told me that he would have to go on alone. That the Alpine crossing would be too much for me. I assured him it would not. But he insisted. He would leave me here, travel on to Rome alone and then return to fetch me when he had sold the book. But in his eyes I could see the truth. He wasn't coming back for me. It had all been for the money. And he didn't mean to share it. He didn't love me. He never had. I'd merely been the instrument of his enrichment. We argued. But he didn't change his mind. There was, of course, no possibility that he would. He had made it up a long time ago. He went out then. He had already arranged to sell the chaise, apparently, needing the proceeds to hire a guide for the crossing. While he was out, I took the book down to the bridge and threw it into the river. It was the last thing he had anticipated. Otherwise he would have taken it with him. He did not understand, you see, how deeply I loved him. And how little the money mattered once he was lost to me. But if I could not have him, he could not have his reward. It seemed very simple to me. And I was glad to do it, glad to hurt him as he had hurt me. When he returned, I told him at once what I had done.' She shook her head. 'He searched the room, you know. He didn't believe me. He thought I'd hidden it somewhere. When he realized the truth, he grew angry.' Her fingers moved to the bruise on her cheek. 'Very angry.'

'And then?'

'He left. I imagine he's in some tavern now, cursing my name and drowning his dreams of the wealth that won't now be his.'

'Nor yours.'

'Nor anyone's.' She looked from one to the other of them. 'Aren't you going to look for it? You surely won't take me at my word.'

McIlwraith sighed. 'No. I fear we can't do that.' He turned to Jupe and Spandrel. 'You both know what you're looking for. I suggest you set about it.'

'We're not going to find it,' said Spandrel. 'Are we?'

'Probably not. But look anyway.'

It did not take long. The chest of drawers contained only clothes and there were few places where such an object could be hidden. Jupe pulled a travelling bag from beneath the bed and opened it. Inside was the despatch-box. But it was empty, as Spandrel had known it would be. Then Jupe rolled aside the rug covering half the floor and crouched over the boards with the lantern, looking for some sign that one of them had been lifted. But there was none.

'Congratulations, madam,' said McIlwraith, when the search had come to its predictable conclusion. 'The Government will be grateful to you.'

'Why?'

'Because the Green Book's destruction serves them well. The guilty go free and—' He chopped the air with the edge of his hand. 'Love conquers all.'

'We should find Zuyler,' said Jupe grimly.

'Aye. So we should.'

'What will you do to him?' asked Estelle.

'I don't know.' McIlwraith looked at her. 'Whatever it is, I doubt it'll compare to what you've already done to him.'

'Tell him . . .'

'What?'

'That he's lost something more valuable than the Green Book.' She gazed into the guttering fire. 'And there will come a time when he regrets it.'

'Did you believe her, Spandrel?' McIlwraith asked as they walked away from the house a few minutes later.

'Yes.'

'Me too. Jupe?'

'She may be lying. She may be more cunning than you think.'

'You have no soul, man. "Heaven has no rage, like love to hatred turned, nor Hell a fury, like a woman scorned." Mr Congreve had it right, I reckon.'

'I'm a mere servant, Captain. What would I know of a playwright's moralizing?'

'Enough. If you wanted to. But to business. I doubt we'll have to look far for our despondent Dutchman.'

He was right. They found Zuyler in the third tavern they tried, a loud, smoke-filled establishment that was clearly as much a brothel as a drinking den. Zuyler seemed to have availed himself of both of the commodities on offer. He was leaning back in his chair at a corner table, with a girl on his knee and two bottles, one empty, one nearly so, in front of him. His left hand held a goblet, while his right was cradling one of the girl's ample breasts, barely concealed by her bodice.

'A charming scene, don't you think, gentlemen?' McIlwraith declared, dragging the girl to her feet and telling her to be on her way, which she promptly was. 'Mijnheer Zuyler!' Zuyler looked around in slack-jawed confusion, apparently uncertain where or why the girl had gone. 'Perhaps you prefer to be called Kempis. Or Kemp.'

'Who . . . are you?' Zuyler slurred.

'Surely you know Spandrel here.'

'Sp-Spandrel?' Zuyler gaped at him, his eyes visibly struggling to focus. 'That can't . . .' He tried to rise, then slumped back. 'No,' he said. 'You're not . . .'

'Oh but he is. Why don't you tell him what you think of him, Spandrel?'

'What would be the point?' Spandrel shook his head dismally.

'Maybe you're right,' said McIlwraith. 'An enemy in his cups is a contemptible thing. We have a message for you, Zuyler. From Estelle.'

'Estelle?' Zuyler spat. '*Die zalet-juffer.*'

Suddenly angry, Spandrel stepped forward and hauled Zuyler out of his chair. Then, staring into the eyes of the man who had all but condemned him to death, he realized how empty the prospect of revenge was. He pushed Zuyler away and watched him fall against the chair, then slide to the floor, toppling the table as he went.

'What did he call her?' asked McIlwraith, as the bottles rolled to rest at his feet.

'I don't know,' said Spandrel. 'And I don't care.'

'Is that so? For a moment, I thought you did. We'll forget the message, then, shall we?'

'He would.' Spandrel looked down at Zuyler where he lay, spilt wine dripping onto his face from the table. 'Even if we delivered it.'

They walked down to the river gate. McIlwraith tipped the gateman to let them through the wicket and they made their way to the middle of the bridge. The river was lost in mist and darkness, but they could see it spuming round the cutwater by the light of the gatehouse lanterns at either end and could hear the roar of it as it swept on round the bend to the north.

'This isn't how I'd expected the chase to end,' said McIlwraith. 'And it's far from what my superiors will want to hear. But hear it they must.'

'I'm still not convinced,' said Jupe. 'They may have lodged the book at a bank and be waiting for us to give up before retrieving it and carrying on to Rome.'

'You said yourself, man, that they've hardly set foot outside the house since arriving. So, they couldn't have known Spandrel and I were here. Are you suggesting they contrived all this just *in case* we came calling?'

'No,' Jupe admitted. 'I suppose not. But I shall keep my eye on them till their intentions are clear, nonetheless.'

'A wise precaution, no doubt.'

'I've been away from the house too long as it is.'

'Don't let us detain you.'

'I shan't. This is all very . . . unsatisfactory, you know.' There was a reproachful edge to Jupe's voice.

'Aye, aye. Life often is.'

'I'll bid you good night, then. You know where to find me.'

'And you us.'

McIlwraith and Spandrel watched Jupe walk away along the bridge until he had vanished into the shadow of the gatehouse arch. Several more moments passed with nothing said. The river rushed on below them. Then Spandrel asked plaintively, 'What are we to do now?'

'Now?' McIlwraith clapped him on the shoulder. 'Isn't it obvious?'

'No.'

'There's only one thing to do in a situation like this.'

'What's that?'

'We follow Zuyler's example. And get roaringly drunk.'

As McIlwraith and Spandrel walked up through the mist-filled streets of the city towards the Drei Tassen inn and the lure of its tap-room, Jupe was climbing the stairs of the Pension Siegwart. His room was on the third floor. But his climb ended at the first. There he paused, as if pondering some course of action, before heading along the landing to the door of the room taken by the couple known to the landlady as Mr and Mrs Kemp, where a light was still burning.

He knocked at the door with three soft taps. A moment later, it opened and Estelle de Vries looked out at him.

'Mr Jupe,' she said, with no inflexion of surprise. 'You're alone?'

'Yes, madam.'

'McIlwraith and Spandrel?'

'Have gone.'

'Do you think they were fooled?'

'Oh yes.' Jupe nodded. 'Completely.'

CHAPTER SEVENTEEN

Blood and Vanishment

The mist had all but gone by morning. The sun was up in an icy blue sky, glinting on the giant horseshoe of the Aare, within which were clustered the spires and turrets and jumbled rooftops of Berne. Spandrel looked down at the river from a high, buttressed terrace behind the cathedral. A line of broken water marked the course of a weir linking the southern bank to a landing-stage and dock away to his left. Smoke was rising from a mill adjoining the dock and the sound of sawing from a wood-yard carried up to him through the clarified air. A man with a fowling-piece under his arm was walking across a field on the opposite shore, a dog trotting beside him through the patches of snow. The world went on its way. And so did the people in it.

The thoughts filling Spandrel's head were not those he would have expected in the wake of his confrontation with the two people who had saddled him with the blame for a murder. Many times, languishing in his cell in Amsterdam, he had wondered what he would do if he ever set eyes – or laid hands – upon them. And never once had it occurred to him that he would simply walk away and leave them to their own devices. But what else could he do? They had worked his vengeance out for him. They had undone themselves. Estelle de Vries he now saw as beyond condemnation, Pieter Zuyler as beneath contempt. They hated each other more than he could contrive to hate either of them.

For Estelle he felt in truth no hatred whatever, rather a perverse kind of admiration. To risk all – and to lose all – in the name of love was somehow magnificent. Spandrel did not care that she had destroyed the Green Book. He faintly approved of the action. And he could not help worrying what its consequences would be for her. Zuyler's capacity for violence might yet cost her dear. She should leave Berne without delay. She should return to England and put behind her the follies and the evils Zuyler had tempted her into.

Whether she would he did not know. It had seemed to him, listening to her account of herself in that mean little room at the Pension Siegwart, that he could almost taste the blackness of her despair. She had abandoned her old life and now her new life had abandoned her. What would she do? 'She might drown herself,' McIlwraith had said at some late and drunken stage of the previous night, 'before Zuyler does it for her.' This suggestion, half-jest though it was, had lingered in Spandrel's mind, till he had convinced himself that something of the kind was horribly possible, that it might, indeed, have already happened.

It was to shake off the depression that this idea had plunged him into that he had left McIlwraith breakfasting morosely at the Drei Tassen and walked aimlessly about the streets of the city as it stretched and yawned and came to its Saturday morning self.

But he had not succeeded. The depression remained. And gazing down at the river, on which a barge had just now put out from the dock, he realized that there was only one way to be rid of it. He would have to return to the Pension Siegwart. And make some kind of peace with Estelle de Vries.

*   *   *

The door was answered by a twinkle-eyed butter-ball of a woman whom Spandrel took to be Frau Siegwart. Her command of English was evidently little greater than his of German and he did not help his cause by asking for Mevrouw de Vries. Once he had laughed that off and specified Mrs Kemp instead, there was a glimmer of understanding and he was invited to enter.

The stairs shook under Frau Siegwart as she led Spandrel up to the first floor and she was panting by the time they reached the door of the best room in the house. She knocked at it briskly, then more briskly still when there was no response. '*Ich verstehe nicht*,' she said with a frown. '*Wo sind sie?*' She listened, knocked again, then tried the handle.

The door was not locked. Frau Siegwart pushed it open and peered into the room. There was no-one there. Glancing in over her shoulder, Spandrel noticed at once what a sharp intake of the landlady's breath suggested she too had noticed. The drawers in the chest beneath the window were sagging open. And they were empty.

For a moment, while Frau Siegwart mumbled to herself and looked around, Spandrel struggled to understand what had happened. Where was she? Where were *they*? If Estelle had fled, as she well might have done, she would surely not have taken Zuyler's possessions with her. Unless, of course, they had fled *together*.

'Jupe,' he said aloud. 'Where's Jupe?'

'*Wie bitte?*'

'Jupe. He's staying here. *Mr Jupe.*'

'*Der Engländer?*'

'Yes. That's right. He's English too. Jupe.'

Grasping apparently that her other English guest might be able to shed light on the disappearance of Mr

183

and Mrs Kemp, Frau Siegwart clumped off towards the stairs. Spandrel followed.

Another two flights took them to a low-ceilinged landing at the top of the house. Frau Siegwart, breathing now like a bellows, rapped at one of the doors. There was no response. She tried again, with the same result. Then she grasped the handle and turned it.

Jupe's door was also unlocked, which somehow surprised Spandrel. But his surprise on that account was rapidly overborne by the shock of what he and Frau Siegwart found themselves looking at through the open doorway.

Jupe and Zuyler lay next to each other at the foot of the bed. There had been a struggle of some kind. The dressing-table had been overturned and the rug was bunched and ruckled beneath them. A pool of congealed blood extended across the rug and the floorboards around it. There was no movement, no sign of life. Both men, Spandrel realized at once, were dead.

'*Mein Gott*,' said Frau Siegwart, crossing herself as she spoke.

Spandrel stepped cautiously past her into the room and leaned forward, trying to see and understand what had happened. Zuyler was lying on his side, his face partly concealed by a fold of the rug. But enough of it was visible for there to be no doubt that he had died in agony. His eyes were bulging, his tongue protruding. There were splinters of wood scattered around him. One of his knees was sharply raised and the heel of his boot had gouged at the boards. He was wearing the greatcoat Spandrel had seen tossed over the back of the chair next to him in the tavern the night before. He did not seem to have been stabbed. There was blood beneath him, but no sign of a wound. The cause of his death looked to be the narrow leather strap wrapped around his neck. It was

184

loose now, but there was a deep red line beneath to show where it had been drawn tight.

The blood belonged to Jupe. He lay on his back, staring sightlessly up at the ceiling. A knife was buried to the hilt in his chest and his coat was sodden with blood. His left hand held the knotted loops of the strap, trailing in his stiffening fingers. It looked as if he had strangled Zuyler, who had managed to stab him with the knife as he did so. The wound had proved fatal, but not quickly enough to save Zuyler. Even as his life's blood had drained away, Jupe had finished what he had set out to do.

But why? What had they fought about? Spandrel's gaze moved to a knapsack lying open by the chest of drawers, with a bundle of clothes beside it. They were Jupe's, presumably. Had he been packing for a journey? If so, he would not have thrown his clothes on the floor. If he had stowed them in the knapsack, however, in readiness for his departure, and someone else had then pulled them out in search of something concealed beneath them—

'*Herr Jupe*,' Frau Siegwart wailed, suddenly realizing who the dead pair were. '*Und Herr Kemp.*' She clapped her hands to her cheeks. '*Fürchterlich.*'

'You should call for help,' said Spandrel.

But a different thought had struck Frau Siegwart. '*Wo ist Frau Kemp?*' Then she forced out the words in English. 'Where . . . Mrs Kemp?'

It was a good question. Indeed, it was a better question than Frau Siegwart could possibly know. Where was Estelle de Vries? And what did she have with her? Spandrel looked down at the two dead men. 'I don't know where she is,' he said, truthfully enough, though he could have hazarded a good guess at where she might be going. 'I don't know anything.'

*   *   *

185

'We've been a pair of fools, you and and I,' said McIlwraith an hour or so later, when Spandrel had finished describing to him the gruesome scene at the Pension Siegwart. 'You see what this means, don't you?'

'I think I do,' said Spandrel. 'Estelle de Vries didn't destroy the Green Book.'

'No more she did. But we'd have gone on believing her tearful little story save for something a sight more reliable than our judgement. Greed, Spandrel. That's what's undone them.'

'*Them?* Jupe was on their side, not ours?'

'You have it. He saw us arrive here, then went to Zuyler and his lady love and convinced them that, without his help, they'd not escape us. Remember her confusion about who I represented – the Government or the House of Commons? Jupe must have told them I was a Government agent. A natural enough assumption, in the circumstances.' McIlwraith pounded a fist into his palm. 'Jupe was the sceptical one, wasn't he? "I'm still not convinced." "I shall keep my eye on them." He over-played his hand and we still didn't see the cards up his sleeve.'

'He hid the book in his room?'

'Aye. Then they performed their touching masquerade in the hope that we'd give up and go away, leaving them to go on to Rome and sell the book, sharing the proceeds among the three of them.'

'What went wrong?'

'It sounds as if Zuyler caught Jupe in the act of decamping with the book. I don't suppose they trusted one another for an instant. It was an alliance of necessity. Realizing that there'd probably be a Government agent coming after them in due course as well must have cast its own shadow.'

'Will there be?'

186

'Aye, man, of course. You don't think we have the field to ourselves, do you?'

'You never told me that.'

'Did I not? Well, perhaps I didn't think you needed to worry your head over it. And no more you do.' But there, though he did not say so, Spandrel begged to differ. 'Nor about Zuyler and Jupe, now they've done for each other. There's only one person we need to consider.'

'Estelle de Vries.'

'The very same. She must have gone to Jupe's room when Zuyler didn't return and found them dead. Whether she shed a real tear for her lover to add to the false ones she sprinkled over us last night we'll never know. What we do know is that she took the book from Jupe's knapsack and—'

'We can't be sure she did.'

'You said you searched the room.'

'Yes. After the landlady rushed off to raise the alarm.'

'And the book wasn't there.'

'No. But—'

'For pity's sake, man. Why else would she leave without raising the alarm herself?'

'No reason, I suppose,' Spandrel reluctantly admitted. 'It must be as you say.' But it was such a cold-blooded thing to have done. Even now, he could hardly bring himself to believe it of her.

'She's gone and the book's gone with her,' said McIlwraith. 'The question is: where?'

It was not an easy question to answer. Even if she had lied to them about Zuyler selling the chaise, she could hardly have driven it away herself. She might have hired a driver, of course, but she would surely have realized it could not be long before they learned Jupe and Zuyler were dead and drew the correct conclusions. To attempt to outrun them on the road was futile. So, McIlwraith reasoned, she would prefer to travel by the first available public coach and set off for the Simplon Pass from wherever the coach took her.

The Drei Tassen happened to be the principal coaching inn of the city. Enquiries revealed that no services had left for any destination since the previous afternoon. At noon, however, the Basle and Interlaken coaches were both due to leave. She would hardly head back to Basle. Interlaken, lying forty miles to the south-east, was the obvious choice. Rather too obvious, however, for McIlwraith's liking.

And so it proved when they stood in the inn yard at noon and watched the coaches load and depart. There was no sign of Estelle de Vries. By then, word of the murders at the Pension Siegwart was abroad. The consensus of tap-room wisdom was that you could never tell with foreigners. It was at least a blessing that this pair had killed each other and left the locals un-molested. Old Frau Siegwart should choose her guests more carefully.

By dusk McIlwraith and Spandrel between them had visited just about every inn, stable and boarding-house in the city. No unaccompanied Englishwoman, or Dutchwoman come to that, was to be found. Nor was there any word of such a person hiring transport or even asking how it might be hired.

'Where can she be?' asked Spandrel, as they made their way back to the Drei Tassen through the darkening streets.

'She may be lying low,' said McIlwraith. 'Privacy can be bought, like most things.'

'Could she have persuaded some traveller to take her with him?'

'She could. There aren't many who'd refuse a woman like her . . . well, near enough whatever she wanted.'

'Then she could be anywhere.'

'Or on the road to it. Aye. But where do they say all roads lead? She won't give up now, Spandrel. Sooner or later, she'll turn south. It has to be the Simplon Pass. That's where we can be sure of catching her. She might be hiding here somewhere. But I'll waste no more time and boot leather looking. We'll leave in the morning.'

Nothing, Spandrel knew already, despite the brevity of their acquaintance, changed McIlwraith's mind once it was made up. He was a man of firm will and fixed decisions. But even firmness can be pushed aside by a greater force. There is no decision, however fixed, that cannot be out-decided.

As they walked along the passage towards their room at the Drei Tassen, a door ahead of them some way short of theirs slowly opened, the light from a lantern beyond the windows at the rear of the inn falling unevenly across a figure that stepped out into their path. McIlwraith pulled up at once and sucked in his breath. He knew who the man was. And Spandrel sensed that he did not like him.

'I saw you coming,' the man said. He was a squat, burly fellow, with a head too large for his body. His face was in shadow, but there was menace enough simply in his posture. Spandrel felt suddenly cold. 'You should be more careful.'

'Colonel Wagemaker,' said McIlwraith quietly. 'What brings you here?'

'The same wind that's blown you in.'

'Is that so?'

'I'm in the King's service, McIlwraith. I outrank you. In more ways than one.'

'I can only think of one, Colonel. And that wasn't always the case.'

'Where's the widow de Vries?'

'I don't rightly know.'

'Nor would you tell me if you did.'

'True enough.'

'But she does have the book, doesn't she?'

'Book?'

'Don't try to play blind-man's-buff with me, McIlwraith. Jupe and Zuyler are dead. But *she* slipped through your fumbling fingers, didn't she? Cloisterman's at the Town Hall now, trying to—'

'Cloisterman's with you?'

'He is. And that's Spandrel you have skulking beside *you*, isn't it? So, we have our seconds ready-made for us, don't we?'

'Seconds? You surely don't mean to—'

'Kill you? Most certainly. Unless you kill me. I told you that if we ever met again I'd finish it between us. Well . . .' Something in the tone of Wagemaker's voice revealed the smile that Spandrel could not see. 'We meet again.'

CHAPTER EIGHTEEN

Old Scores

'Quite a turn-up, eh, Spandrel?' said McIlwraith, as he sat by the window of their room at the Drei Tassen and gazed out at the blank Bernese night. By the flickering light of the single candle, Spandrel saw him raise his whisky flask to his lips and sip from it. 'Just what we didn't need. Just what *I* didn't want.'

'You're really going to fight him?'

'I have no choice. Despite appearances, I lay claim to be a gentleman. Colonel Wagemaker demands satisfaction. And I must give it him. Tomorrow, at dawn.'

'This is madness.'

'A form of it, certainly.'

'What's it about? Why does he hate you?'

'He blames me for his sister's death.'

'And are you to blame?'

'Aye. I am. But so is he. We share the blame. I believe that's what he can't stomach.'

'How did she die?'

'It's not a story I'm fond of telling. But since we need to consider the possibility that I may not be alive tomorrow to correct the cholerical colonel's version of events . . .' McIlwraith chuckled. 'As my second, you come close to being my confessor, Spandrel. You know that?'

'I haven't agreed to be your second.'

'You'll do it, though. I know you well enough by now. We may despise the forms of this world, but we observe them nonetheless. It'd be as cowardly for you to refuse to stand by me as for me to refuse to stand against him.'

'And, if so, I'm entitled to know why.'

'Aye. So you are.' McIlwraith took another sip of whisky. 'It goes back to the war. Like so much else in my misdirected life. Glorious days and grievous: they were the way of it. But we didn't mind. Not while Marlborough led us. A hard man. And a harder one still to read. But a leader, in his heart as well as his head. You'd have followed him into the fissures of Hell. Blenheim, Ramillies, Oudenarde, Malplaquet. I was at all of them. And proud to be. Then the politicians did him down, as good soldiers always are done down by backstairs intrigues and closet bargains. The Government changed its hue. The Captain-General was dismissed. Peace talks began. We surrendered in all but name. Most of the British troops went back to England, while the negotiations dragged on through the spring and summer of 1712. I was with Albemarle's Allied division during those months. Nobody knew what we were supposed to be about. Most of the officers were Dutch or German. There were precious few British left. And precious little spirit left either. The French seized their chance, crossed the Scheldt and attacked us at Denain. Seventeen battalions were lost. I was one of the many taken prisoner. We were sent to Valenciennes and confined there until a truce could be agreed. I fell in with an English officer from the garrison at Marchiennes, which the French had also captured. He was badly wounded and our captors made little effort to treat him. Before the truce was concluded, he was dead. His name was Hatton. Captain John Hatton. He was a good fellow. He made me promise to carry a letter he'd written to a young lady in England to whom he was engaged. His beloved Dorothea. You already know her surname.'

'Wagemaker.'

'The very same. The Wagemakers owned land in Berkshire. Still do, I dare say. When I was released and sent to rejoin what was left of my regiment, I was immediately discharged on half-pay. The country was done with us fighting men. Our time was over. I had no notion of what to do or where to go. I certainly had no wish to return to Scotland. I burned my boats there a long while ago. I had it in my mind to go back to what I knew best: fighting. There's always an army somewhere in the world that wants a recruit. But before I set to thinking about that, I had to deliver Hatton's letter to his betrothed. I wrote to her, warning her of my visit, then travelled to the Wagemakers' house, Bordon Grove, on the edge of Windsor Forest.'

'Was Colonel Wagemaker there?'

'He was. Though he was only a lieutenant then. Reduced to half-pay, like me, and cooling his heels at home. Our Augustus saw himself as head of the family, following his father's recent death, though his brother Tiberius had the running of the estate, such as it was. As for Dorothea, she was the pick of the bunch, as she'd have been of many another. Not merely beautiful, but sweet-natured and altogether lovely. A young woman of such breeding that you couldn't help wondering how she'd acquired so ill-bred a pair of brothers. A lamb to their wolves. She thanked me for my condolences and for bringing the letter. She urged me to stay awhile. And so I did. I stayed, indeed, too long. Brother Tiberius offered me the rent of a folly on the estate. Blind Man's Tower, it's called, on ironical account of the staircase to the top being on the outside of the building, open to the elements, with neither guard nor rail. But the ground floor's as cosy as a cottage. I took it just for the winter. By spring, I planned to be on my way.'

'And were you?'

'I was. But much had happened by then. What Wagemaker and I are to duel over was already done. I grew to know the family too well. That was my mistake. A soldier needs a billet. But he should never think he's found a home. The Wagemakers were pressed for money. Their father had been a poor manager of their interests and Tiberius wasn't the man to repair them. A loose-tongued aunt who lived with them and kept their invalid mother company muttered to me more than once about debts hanging round their necks. No doubt that explains why Tiberius was willing to rent me Blind Man's Tower. Any income was useful. And it also explains why he and Augustus weren't at all sorry that poor Hatton was dead. They never made any pretence that they were, speaking slightingly of him on several occasions, until they saw it tried my temper to do so and guarded what they said. They had a different, wealthier, husband in mind for Dorothea: Esmund Longrigg, owner of a neighbouring and better founded estate. Longrigg held the office of chief woodward or somesuch in the Forest hierarchy, which carried with it an enviable load of perquisites. He and Dorothea were put much together at balls and musical evenings that Christmas and Longrigg liked what he saw. But Dorothea didn't. I couldn't blame her for that. I didn't like the look of Longrigg myself. Tallow to her beeswax. But moneyed. To her brothers, that was all that mattered. They encouraged her to accept his proposal if, or, as they saw it, when it came. And come it did.' McIlwraith sighed and drank some more whisky. 'She asked for time to think. Then she turned to me for advice. She detested Longrigg. But she knew how important it was to the family's future that she marry him.

194

Yet still she detested him. Her life with him would be a misery. What was she to do?'

'What did you tell her?'

'To refuse him.' McIlwraith looked across at Spandrel, his face wreathed in shadow. 'If her brothers were so concerned about the family's future, by which they meant their own comfort, they should bestir themselves to secure it, rather than mortgage their sister's happiness.' He seemed to smile at the recollection of his words. 'Such was my advice.'

'Did she take it?'

'She refused him, right enough. Which displeased them mightily, as you can imagine. The more so because they knew she'd been to see me before giving Longrigg his answer and suspected I'd put her up to it. Nobly, she denied it. But when they accused me nonetheless, I chose not to deny it. I didn't care to be summoned to the house and cross-questioned like some tenant caught poaching. Longrigg was with them. The brothers seemed to think they had the right to tell me what to do simply because I was living on their property. Harsh things were said. Tempers were lost. Longrigg had the gall to suggest I was harbouring dishonourable intentions towards Dorothea. Then Augustus went further, implying they might not just be intentions. I demanded he withdraw the slur. He refused. So, I called him out. There was nothing else for it.'

'*You* challenged *him*?'

'Aye. But the duel was never fought. Dorothea was being held a virtual prisoner by then. I wasn't permitted to see her. But she knew what had happened. She smuggled a letter to me by her maid pleading with me not to fight her brother. She said she couldn't bear the thought of either of us dying on her account. I replied, saying it was a matter of honour and I had no choice but to fight, unless Augustus took back the remark, which I knew he wouldn't. Even then, he was too stubborn for that. And too brave. He'd deliberately provoked the challenge. He *wanted* to fight me. And I wanted to fight him, God forgive me. But we never did fight. Till now, anyway. A day and time were fixed for us to meet. The night before, Dorothea implored her brother to apologize to me. When he refused, she calmly said good night to him, walked up to the top floor of the house and threw herself over the balustrade into the stair-well.'

Spandrel caught his breath. 'She killed herself?'

McIlwraith nodded grimly. 'It was all of a sixty-foot drop to the stone-flagged hall. Certain death. And the only certain way she knew to prevent the duel. She had my letter, my pompous resort to honour as a justification for refusing to withdraw the challenge, concealed in the sleeve of her dress. Augustus found it, of course. He's a diligent searcher, if he's nothing else. And finding it somehow enabled him to forget his own responsibility for what she'd done. He laid it all at my door. The duel was called off, naturally, as a mark of respect, as Dorothea had known it would be. As far as Augustus was concerned, though, it was only a postponement, until after the funeral.'

'But not as far as you were concerned.'

'No. I couldn't go through with what Dorothea had laid down her life to avert. I withdrew the challenge.'

'What did Wagemaker do then?'

'He issued one of his own. Which I declined, on the tenuous grounds that a junior officer cannot challenge a senior. The actual grounds were rather different, of course. And seemingly beyond his comprehension. As it appears they still are. Now, however, he's no longer my junior. I cannot decline to meet him.'

196

'What will happen?'

'One of us will die. He hasn't waited eight years to content himself with a shot into the air. He's a man of his word. And he's given it.'

'But his sister's memory . . .'

'Is more likely to stay my hand than his.'

'But it won't, will it? You don't mean . . .'

'I don't know what I mean, Spandrel. It's late. And whisky inclines me to mawkishness. I'll tell you this for what it's worth, though. I lost no time in quitting Blind Man's Tower after the funeral and taking off on my travels. The Danish army found a use for me in its war against Sweden. That's how I came to learn enough of their language to be able to negotiate our passage aboard the *Havfrue*. I wasn't the Danes' only British mercenary, of course. There were a good many. And among them was one who'd met Lieutenant Augustus Wagemaker while serving in Ireland. He'd been a notorious duellist there, apparently. Quick to take offence. Determined to seek satisfaction for it. And never known to miss.' McIlwraith drained the whisky flask. 'I think Dorothea knew full well that it was far more likely to be me she was saving than her brother.' He sighed. 'There's a thought to ponder when we reach the standing-place tomorrow. If I'm right, Wagemaker knows it as well as I do. Perhaps she loved me a little. Perhaps more than a little. If so, that's really what he hates me for. And why he means to kill me.'

No candle burned in the room a few doors down the passage that Colonel Wagemaker was sharing with Nicholas Cloisterman. But only one of its occupants was still awake. Cloisterman lay on his bed, eyes wide open, staring anxiously into the darkness. From the other side of the room came the steady rise and fall of Wagemaker's slumbering breaths. How a man could sleep so soundly on the eve of a duel Cloisterman could not imagine. He had studiously avoided such affairs of honour himself, preferring any number of apologies and humiliations to the prospect of sudden, painful and, as he saw it, pointless death. He had never served as a second either and had no wish to do so now, but Wagemaker had insisted, deploying the ingenious argument that this was a heaven-sent opportunity to eliminate a dangerous rival in their pursuit of the Green Book and that Cloisterman was therefore obliged to assist him.

The possibility did not seem to have crossed Wagemaker's mind that he, rather than McIlwraith, might be eliminated by the morning's exchange of fire. He seemed, indeed, blithely confident of the outcome. 'McIlwraith's as good as dead,' had been his dismissive remark on the subject. As to the reason for the duel, which Cloisterman felt entitled to know if he was to stand as a second, about that too Wagemaker had been sparing with his words. 'He brought about my sister's death. Now he must pay for her life with his.'

If these two irascible old warriors were determined to take pot-shots at one another, that, so far as Cloisterman was concerned, they were welcome to do. He certainly could not prevent them. It was also undeniable that it would be easier to wrest the Green Book from Estelle de Vries, whom they would surely overtake before she reached the Simplon Pass, without McIlwraith trying to do the same. None of these considerations eased his mind, however. He did not like Wagemaker and he did not trust him. He did not subscribe to the colonel's notion that this would be a quick, clean kill, an old score settled and a present problem solved, free of consequences, devoid of penalty. In Cloisterman's experience, life was never that simple and nor was death.

A particularly disturbing thought was that he had no idea what the attitude of the Swiss was to duelling. For all he knew, it might be forbidden by some ancient cantonal law. If so, the seconds as much as the duellists would be in breach of it. During his visit to the Town Hall, he had represented himself to the Sheriff's officer with whom he had discussed the deaths of Zuyler and Jupe as a reputable and accredited agent of the British Government. How the Sheriff would react to such a personage involving himself in a duel he did not care to contemplate. But Wagemaker was Walpole's man. And Walpole seemed likely soon to be the arbiter of all their fates. Cloisterman had no choice but to do as he was bidden.

He did not have to like it, however. He especially resented his inability to think about anything else. There was surely much to ponder in the singular circumstances that had led to the fatal struggle at the Pension Siegwart. Zuyler and Jupe had killed each other and Estelle de Vries had fled with the Green Book. That seemed clear. But where had she fled to? The Simplon Pass was so obvious a destination that Cloisterman feared it might be too obvious. Mrs de Vries had shown herself to be a cool-nerved and resourceful woman. Just how resourceful he was not sure they yet knew. But he could not seem to concentrate on the clues to her intentions that he felt certain were scattered amidst the sparse facts of her behaviour to date. Instead, his mind was clogged with the brutal absurdities of a dawn duel between two men he scarcely knew over a long dead woman he had never known at all. It was a miserable scrape to find himself in. And somehow it seemed more miserable still because one of the duellists was sleeping like a baby in the same room where Cloisterman knew he was destined to toss and turn till the long night ended. Whereupon . . .

'Damn you, Dalrymple,' he muttered under his breath. 'I didn't deserve this.'

But deserving, as he was all too well aware, had absolutely nothing to do with it.

CHAPTER NINETEEN

The Wages of Honour

The roofs of Berne rose above them like those of some dream city, floating, girding mountains and all, on the mist that shrouded the river.

It was a still, chill, breathless dawn in the sloping, snow-spattered meadow where the four men assembled, between the mist-line and the Interlaken road. Few words were spoken at first and most of those were in the form of a stumbling effort by Cloisterman to call the duel off, to which Wagemaker responded with a grunted refusal and McIlwraith with a fatalistic shrug. Spandrel and Cloisterman were shivering and clearly ill at ease, whereas the two men who were about to hazard their lives were icily calm. They took off their greatcoats, then Wagemaker opened the pistol-case he had brought and offered McIlwraith his choice of the matched pair. They loaded the weapons themselves, apparently concluding, without the need of saying so, that their seconds were unequal to the task.

'We should toss a coin to see who has the right to fire first,' said Cloisterman, fishing one from his pocket. 'Unless . . .' But, with a shake of the head, he abandoned his last attempt at mediation.

'No need,' said Wagemaker, holding McIlwraith's gaze with his. 'Ten paces each, then turn and shoot. Agreed?'

'However you please,' said McIlwraith. 'Since you want this so badly, you may as well have the ordering of it.'

'Agreed, then. You can put your money away, Mr Cloisterman.'

'May I at least count the paces for you?' Cloisterman asked through pursed lips.

'You may,' said Wagemaker. 'Shall we get on?'

'One thing,' put in McIlwraith. 'Before we do.'

'Well?'

'Dorothea wouldn't have—'

'Don't mention my sister by name, sir. I don't choose to give you the right to.'

'What you *choose* to do is to defile her memory.'

'By God, you have a nerve. Now let's see how steady it is. Are you here to talk or to fight?'

'I'm here to give you satisfaction, Colonel. As I'm bound to. But we should be clear. Dorothea sacrificed her life to prevent us doing just this eight years ago.'

'Is that true?' asked Cloisterman.

'It's no business of yours whether it's true or not,' barked Wagemaker. 'Step back and let's be doing.'

'Very well.' Cloisterman retreated, signalling for Spandrel to follow.

When they were thirty yards or so away, Wagemaker cocked his pistol and McIlwraith cocked his. They nodded to one another, then took up position, back to back.

'Oh God,' groaned Cloisterman. 'This really is going to happen.'

'Did you think it mightn't?' asked Spandrel.

'I hoped.' He sighed, then shouted, 'Ready?'

'Ready,' came Wagemaker's reply.

'Ready,' McIlwraith confirmed.

'One,' Cloisterman called. And at that they started walking.

Duelling was no part of life in Spandrel's bracket of society. It was to him a strange and exotic indulgence of the upper classes, to which army officers, however humble their origins, also had habitual recourse. He had witnessed one once, thanks to Dick Surtees overhearing the arrangements being made in a coffee-house by the seconds and suggesting they go along and take a look at 'two pea-brained sparks using each other for target practice'. It had been a bloodless affray in Hyde Park, the 'pea-brained sparks' in question missing their targets by a country mile, looking heartily relieved to do so and departing arm in arm, like the best of friends. Spandrel found himself wishing there could be a similar outcome to the second duel he was ever about to witness. But he knew in his heart there could not be. Blood would be shed at the very least. A life – Wagemaker's or McIlwraith's – was likely to be lost in the exchange that now lay only a few seconds in the future. He fervently hoped it would not be McIlwraith's. But he greatly feared that it would. At the count of ten, he held his breath.

The two men were about twenty yards apart when they turned. Wagemaker spun on his heel, raised his arm and took aim a fraction of a second more swiftly – more naturally – than McIlwraith. The Scotsman's arm was still just short of the horizontal when Wagemaker fired. The loud crack of the pistol shot broke the silence that had followed Cloisterman's count of ten, only to be swallowed in a cawing rise of rooks from the mist-blurred trees further down the meadow. For a frozen instant, Spandrel did not know what had happened. There was no answering shot. The two men stood perfectly still, framing the city behind them, the cathedral tower seeming to mark, like a raised finger, the point from which they had measured their paces.

Then McIlwraith groaned and took one stumbling, sideways step. His arm dropped. His other hand moved to his chest. He seemed about to fall. Wagemaker slowly lowered his pistol. 'He's done for him,' said Cloisterman, stepping forward. 'As he swore he would.'

But McIlwraith did not fall. With a cry more like that of a beast than a man, he wrenched himself upright. Spandrel could see his chest heaving with the effort. He was hit, perhaps fatally, but something stronger than lead shot was holding him on his feet. He took one lurching step back to the position from which he had stumbled, his racing breath pluming into the air around him. Then he raised his pistol once more.

'He means to fire,' said Cloisterman, pulling up sharply.

'You're a dead man, Captain,' Wagemaker called to his opponent. 'You can't even stand straight, let alone shoot straight.' With that he threw his pistol to the ground. 'This is—'

There was a second pistol shot. Wagemaker's head jerked violently back as bone and blood burst out of it. He swayed for a moment, then fell backwards, hitting the frosted turf with a thud. There was no other movement. He lay where he fell, like a puppet whose strings have been cut, still and lifeless.

'Good God,' murmured Cloisterman. 'Good God Almighty.'

McIlwraith let his pistol fall to the ground. Then, slowly, as if stooping to pray, he slipped to his knees. Spandrel began running towards him. As he ran, he saw the captain topple over onto his side, his body convulsed by a series of spluttering coughs. Then he lay still.

'Captain?' Spandrel bent over him and touched his

elbow. There was blood on McIlwraith's waistcoat, oozing through the fingers of the hand he had clasped to the wound and darkening the frost-white grass beneath him. 'Can you hear me?'

'I can . . . hear you,' McIlwraith replied through clenched teeth. 'Wagemaker?'

Spandrel looked across at Cloisterman, who had hurried to where the colonel was lying and was stooping over him. Hearing the question, he looked over his shoulder and said, 'Quite dead, Captain, I assure you.'

'But he still has the . . . advantage of me.' McIlwraith seemed to be smiling. 'At least he died . . . cleanly.'

'You're not going to die,' said Spandrel.

'I wish you were right. But as usual . . . you're wide of the mark. Unlike . . . Wagemaker.'

'I'll fetch a doctor,' said Cloisterman. 'As fast as I can. Stay here, Spandrel. And go on talking to him. It may help.'

The two men exchanged nods, then Cloisterman took off across the field in a loping run, the tails of his coat flapping out behind him. He was heading towards the houses clustered around the bridge by which they had left the city, the bridge from which Estelle de Vries claimed to have thrown the Green Book into the river. Since she had uttered that claim, no more than thirty hours or so ago, Zuyler and Jupe and Wagemaker had all met their deaths, suddenly and violently, when they were least expecting to. And now McIlwraith seemed likely to join them.

'Has he gone?' McIlwraith's voice was hoarse and strained.

'Yes. Don't worry. He'll—'

'Stop jabbering and listen to me, Spandrel. I don't have long. I'm dying, man.'

'No. No, you're not.'

'Don't contradict me, damn you. I've seen enough death . . . in my time . . . to know what it's like. *Just listen to me.*'

'I'm listening, Captain.'

'Good. This is . . . important. You must leave here. Now.'

'I can't do that.'

'You must. Take my pouch. It's in my coat. There's money. Guineas. Louis d'or. And sequins. You'll need those for Rome.'

'Rome?'

'You have to go on . . . without me.'

'I can't leave you like this.'

'There's . . . no choice. I've been here before. Not to Berne. But to Switzerland. I know their ways. This is a Calvinist canton. They come down hard on . . . Catholic indulgences. That's what they see duelling as. You and Cloisterman will be arrested . . . as soon as the Sheriff hears what's happened. Do you want to go back . . . to prison? Maybe even a Dutch one? A warrant naming you as a suspected murderer . . . could find its way here from Amsterdam . . . while you're in custody. Do you . . . want that?'

'Of course not.'

'Then go. While you still can.'

'I won't leave you until the doctor's arrived.'

'There'll be nothing for him to do.' McIlwraith winced. 'An undertaker, now. He could be . . . useful.'

'Don't say that.'

'I'm only . . . facing facts, man. You should . . . do the same. You mustn't be here when Cloisterman returns. He's for the Government, remember, and . . . well capable of handing you over to the authorities . . . in exchange for his own freedom. I don't want him . . . spending the committee's money.'

'He wouldn't do that.'

206

'Wouldn't he? You're too trusting, Spandrel. That's your . . . big weakness. So, trust me . . . for once.'

'I do.'

'Good. In that case . . .' McIlwraith twisted round and clasped Spandrel's arm in a disconcertingly strong grip. 'For God's sake, go.'

Another half an hour had passed by the time Cloisterman returned to the meadow, accompanied by a doctor none too pleased to have been summoned from his breakfast-table and two of his manservants, equipped with blankets and a litter. McIlwraith was unconscious, though still breathing. But of Spandrel there was no sign. He had draped the captain's greatcoat over him and added Wagemaker's to keep him as warm as possible. And then . . .

'Where have you gone, Spandrel?' Cloisterman muttered, gazing suspiciously into the distance. 'What game are you playing?'

'This man is near death, mein Herr,' said the doctor, interrupting the drift of his thoughts. 'We must take him to my house.'

'Very well.'

'There has been . . . a duel?'

'Yes.'

'But it is Sunday. The sabbath. Have you no . . .' The doctor frowned at him. '*Verachtenswert.*'

'What?'

'We must go. We will not save him. But we must try.'

They loaded McIlwraith onto the litter, strapped him in and set off at a brisk pace across the meadow. Cloisterman made no move to follow.

'Come with us, mein Herr,' the doctor called back to him. 'There will be questions.'

'*Natürlich.*' Cloisterman made after them, quickly

enough at first to catch up, then more slowly. Questions. Yes. There would be. A great many questions. And not enough answers. He stopped and looked across at Wagemaker's body, the face white beneath the shattered brow, the clotted blood black against the frozen grass. He remembered the colonel's steady, sleeping breaths of the night before. So much certainty, so much strength, undone in an instant.

'Mein Herr!' The doctor's voice carried back to him through the cold, clearing air. 'We will send someone for the other. *Einen Leichenbestatter. Kommen Sie!*'

'I'll follow. In a moment.'

What should he do? Spandrel had fled. That was obvious. And who could blame him? Not Cloisterman. He was inclined to do the same himself. He had been told to assist Wagemaker. But Wagemaker was dead. Dalrymple had said nothing about trying to complete Wagemaker's mission in the event of the colonel's demise. Strictly speaking, Cloisterman's duties were at an end. He could not be blamed for returning to The Hague and reporting the dismal facts as they stood. He *would* be blamed, of course. But he could bear that a good deal better than having to answer to the Bernese authorities for the havoc he might be accused of wreaking in their peaceful city – on the sabbath, as the doctor had pointed out. The doctor, however, did not know his name and was presently preoccupied with McIlwraith. There was an opportunity for Cloisterman to slip away. But it would not last long. If he did not take it, he might come to regret it. And, so far, he had come to regret just about everything that had happened since his departure from Amsterdam. It was time to think of himself.

'Excuse me, Colonel,' he said under his breath as he turned towards the road. 'I really must be going.'

CHAPTER TWENTY

Chances and Choices

The trial before the House of Commons of Charles Stanhope, Secretary to the Treasury, was closely argued and narrowly decided. The evidence presented seemed damning, but Walpole spoke vigorously for the defence and rumours abounded that the King had pleaded with certain Members to abstain. Abstentions, indeed, were what ultimately saved Stanhope. Three members of Brodrick's own committee left the House before the vote was taken, the aptly named Sloper among them. Stanhope was eventually acquitted by 180 votes to 177.

The public reaction to thus being cheated of a prime victim was predictably querulous. A mood of simmering riot prevailed for some days afterwards. Once more, it was widely and plausibly asserted, the politicians had spat in the eye of Justice.

To avoid inflaming the situation still further, it was decided that the funeral of James Craggs the younger, lately deceased Southern Secretary, should be held at night. Under the cover of darkness, therefore, late in the evening of the day following Stanhope's acquittal, many of the great and the good of Augustan England – or the greedy and the grasping, according to taste – filed into Westminster Abbey to pay their obsequial respects to one for whom death had forestalled many reproaches.

Near the front of the sombrely clad gathering,

Viscount Townshend found himself awkwardly seated between Walpole and the Earl of Sunderland, between the coming man in the political firmament and its fading force.

For one whose power was draining away almost by the hour, however, Sunderland contrived to seem remarkably unconcerned by the difficulties that confronted him. 'Carteret will be confirmed as Craggs' successor within days, I believe,' he casually ventured. 'You think you will find him pliable, Townshend?'

'He has not been recommended for his pliability, Spencer.'

'Has he not? For his ability, then? Ability can be a dangerous thing.'

'Except in oneself,' Walpole muttered.

'Oh, quite, quite,' said Sunderland. 'And securing Stanhope's acquittal undoubtedly suggests ability of a high order . . . in someone.'

'It certainly augurs well for those yet to answer to the case,' said Walpole with a sidelong smile.

'His Majesty would be pleased if all his traduced ministers could be acquitted,' said Sunderland. 'Preferably by handsomer majorities.'

'That may be asking for too much.'

'The prerogative of kings, Walpole. If you don't understand that . . .' Sunderland shrugged and flipped open his prayer-book, then closed it again and tapped the cover. 'What of the other matter so much on His Majesty's mind?' He smiled. '*Das Grüne Buch*, as he coyly refers to it.'

'In hand.'

'But not *in our hands*.'

'Not yet.'

'Soon?'

Walpole curled his lip. 'I trust so.'

'You sent Wagemaker, didn't you?' Townshend did his best not to look surprised by this disquieting evidence that Sunderland's information network was functioning as efficiently as ever. 'What if he should fail – or fall by the wayside?'

'Don't worry, Spencer,' Walpole replied. 'Whatever happens, we shan't ask you for advice.'

'No? Well, here's some anyway. You should—'

Before Sunderland could let fall his pearl of statesmanly wisdom, the funeral drum sounded and a noise from behind them of shuffling feet and clearing throats signalled the arrival of the coffin. The three men rose, along with those to right and left of them. There was a second drum-beat. Then, in the instant before the dirgeful music began in earnest, Sunderland leaned towards Townshend and finished what he had been saying, though in too hushed a tone for Townshend to think that Walpole would be able to catch the words.

'Always assume the worst.'

Assuming the worst had become second nature to Nicholas Cloisterman since his departure from The Hague in the company of the late Colonel Wagemaker. Nothing had gone right and almost everything had gone wrong. Wagemaker was dead, the Green Book was probably already on the other side of the Alps and Cloisterman's own recent conduct, he could not but admit to himself, bore no close inspection. He had fled Berne with a singular lack of vice-consular dignity and no clear plan other than to return to Amsterdam and face down any criticism that Dalrymple threw at him.

The lapse of days had made that plan seem less and less prudent, however. At Burgdorf he had sold his horse, being no natural horseman, in favour of travelling by *post-wagen*, a slow but reliable mode of transport that had taken him first to Lucerne, then Zürich, then the spa town of Baden, where he had thought to sample the waters in the hope that they might have some tonic effect on him, before heading north to the Rhine and seeking a passage downstream. It was at Baden, on the evening of Craggs' funeral in London, the waters as yet unsampled, that he finally realized it would not do; it simply would not do.

He reviewed matters over a mournful pipe as he paced the chill and empty promenade by the banks of the Limmat. Turn it over how he might, his situation was even less appetizing than the meal he had just consumed at the Rapperswil inn. But sometimes it was as necessary to confront uncomfortable truths as it was to swallow unpalatable food. He would be expected to have done more than he had. Ultimately, he served the same master as Wagemaker. And that master would be satisfied by nothing less than retrieval of the Green Book. Failure would only be excused if it could be shown that no effort had been spared in the attempt. Thus far, Cloisterman's efforts did not look unstinting so much as grudging, if not minimal. He was going to have to do better.

He stopped and gazed soulfully down into the river. This sort of business did not suit him. It really did not. Yet it was business he would have to attend to. As from tomorrow. He sighed, turned up his greatcoat collar and started back towards the inn. There was an early call to be arranged.

An early call did not figure in William Spandrel's intentions for the following day. His flight from Berne had been far from the aimless retreat Cloisterman had contrived to make, but had yielded strangely similar results. Feeling unable to risk returning to the Drei Tassen for his horse, he had walked south along the

212

Interlaken road to the first post-house, where he had used some of McIlwraith's money to have himself driven on to Thun. There he had stayed overnight, heavy-hearted and lonely, before boarding a southbound coach early the following morning. Many jolting hours later, he had discovered that what the Thun innkeeper meant by south was not the Simplon Pass but Lake Geneva. He had finished his second day on the road at Vevey, as far from his destination as he had begun his first.

Naturally, he had intended his stay at Vevey's Auberge du Lac to be brief, but he had been woken in the night by the onset of a violent ague that kept him abed for the next two days, too ill even to think of leaving his room, let alone the inn. It was, according to the not unsympathetic landlady, Madame Jacquinot, '*La grippe; c'est partout.*' There was nothing to be done but to sweat it out. The evening of Craggs' funeral in London and of Cloisterman's about-turn in Baden found Spandrel decisively out of action.

Some semblance of normal health began to return to him the following day. By the afternoon he felt well enough to sit by the window of his room and watch the comings and goings of ferries and barges from the quay below the inn. The sun sparkled on the lake and warmed him through the glass. There was a springlike bloom to the weather. But for anxiety born of the knowledge that he had accomplished precisely nothing towards fulfilling his promise to McIlwraith to hunt down Estelle de Vries, he might have been able to summon a degree of content-ment as he surveyed the scene.

He thought of McIlwraith more wistfully then than at any time since leaving him to die in that snow-patched meadow outside Berne. It was not only that he missed him more acutely than he would ever have expected. It was also that it had been so easy to let him decide what to do and when to do it. Now, Spandrel had to think and act for himself. Tomorrow, he would set off for the Simplon Pass. If Estelle had gone that way, she was almost certainly beyond the Alps by now, perhaps even beyond Milan, although his grasp of Italian geography was far too insecure to guess where she might be, or how long it might take her to reach Rome. He should have paid more attention to McIlwraith's references to the journey that lay ahead while he had the chance. As it was, he would have to rely on whatever information he could glean along the way.

Luck would be bound to play its part, of course. So far, he did not seem to have enjoyed his share of it. But luck, he reflected as he watched an elegant pink-sailed yacht nose in towards the quay, always turned in the end, one way or the other.

And there below him, as the yacht tied up and the passengers disembarked, it did so, in that instant, just for him.

There were three passengers: two men and a woman. The men were both wearing plush hats, beribboned wigs and extravagantly swag-cut greatcoats, flapping open to reveal frilled stocks and brocaded waistcoats. They were of about the same age – mid to late twenties – and clearly neither lacked for funds, at any rate to lavish on expensive tailors. Physically, they could hardly have been more different, however. One was tall and cadaverously thin, with a narrow, pale, bony face to which his fruitily feminine lips seemed scarcely to belong. He struck a pose with every step, flourishing a cane as counterpoint to his daintily flexed ankles. The other was short and fleshy, poised between youthful plumpness and middle-aged corpulence, with puddingy features set in a smirking

214

face, the high colour of which suggested a toping disposition. He clumped along the quay in what was
presumably intended to be a confident swagger.

They were both English. Spandrel could hear their
braying tones from where he sat, though he could not
make out more than the odd word. Their female
companion was also English. This he knew, even though
she was saying nothing as far as he could tell. Nor was it
her taste in clothes that gave her away. The sky-blue
dress visible beneath the mushroom-grey travelling coat
was undeniably fetching, but also curiously anonymous.
What settled the issue beyond doubt was that he recognized her very well. She was Estelle de Vries.

Spandrel put on his boots and coat so quickly that the
exertion induced a coughing fit, from which he had
barely recovered when he left his room and hurried
downstairs. Estelle and her new-found friends had been
ambling along the quay when last glimpsed, admiring the
view of the lake and the snow-capped mountains beyond.
But Spandrel was convinced he would find them
nowhere in sight or already going back aboard the yacht.
The chance that fate had handed him was a fleeting one.
He had to seize it, though how to do so was still unclear
to him as he reached the hall and turned towards the
front door.

But he need not have hurried. There they were, in
front of him, being ushered into the dining-room by
Madame Jacquinot, no doubt attracted, as he had been,
by the Auberge du Lac's freshly painted air of welcome.
Estelle glanced along the hall at him as they went. He saw
her catch her breath and look quickly away. Then she
stopped and said something to Madame Jacquinot.
It seemed to be a request of some kind. The two men
moved ahead into the dining-room. But Madame

Jacquinot led Estelle further down the hall. Spandrel moved back up the stairs out of sight. A door opened below him. He glimpsed a wash-stand and mirror in the closet it led to. '*Merci, madame,*' said Estelle. She stepped inside and closed the door. Then Madame Jacquinot bustled off to attend to the men, whose laughter could be heard echoing in the low-ceilinged dining-room.

Spandrel moved cautiously to the closet door. It opened as he approached and Estelle stepped out to meet him. 'Mr Spandrel,' she said. 'This is . . . a surprise.' And not, her expression suggested, a pleasant one.

'There's a small garden.' Spandrel nodded towards the rear quarters of the building. 'We can talk there.'

'I can't be gone long.'

'I don't know who those two preening ninnies are, Mrs de Vries, but I'd wager they know nothing of the murdered husband you left in Amsterdam, not to mention the dead lover in Berne. In the circumstances, I think you can be gone as long as you need to be. Shall we?'

'You don't look well,' she said, as they reached the daylight and turned to face each other.

'You, on the other hand, look uncommonly well.' It was true. Perhaps it was the lake air, or the thrill of the chase, that had given a heightened colour to her cheeks. She did not seem at all frightened. She seemed, indeed, utterly calm, inconvenienced by this turn of events, but undismayed.

'Where is Captain McIlwraith?'

'Dead.'

She frowned. 'That I am sorry to hear.'

'A Government agent caught up with us. There was a duel.'

'And the agent?'

216

'Also dead.'

'So much death. I am sorry, Mr Spandrel. Though I don't suppose you believe me.'

'Why should I? You lied *about* me in Amsterdam. You lied *to* me in Berne.'

'Those lies seemed . . . necessary.'

'You still have the Green Book?'

'It's in a safe place.'

'Where?'

'A bank. In Geneva.'

'Why didn't you make for the Simplon Pass when you left Berne?'

'I'm not sure. I was confused. Pieter's death was so violent, so . . . stupid. I could scarcely think for the shock of what had happened. They killed each other, he and Jupe. You know that?'

'I saw their bodies. Left by you for someone else to discover.'

'I couldn't remain. You must understand how it was.'

'Oh, I do.'

'You think me very callous, don't you?'

Spandrel nodded. 'Yes.'

'I suppose I must seem so. But it isn't—' She glanced back towards the door by which they had left the building. 'I shall be missed soon.'

'Who are they?'

'Mr Buckthorn and Mr Silverwood are two young English gentlemen sent abroad by their fathers to improve their minds. I met them in Geneva and persuaded them to add me to their party. We are due to set off for Turin in just a few days. I gather the Mont Cenis Pass is scarcely more formidable than the Simplon.'

'Why did you go to Geneva?'

'Because I could not hope to complete my journey

217

unaided and alone. Geneva was the closest city where I was likely to find the sort of help I needed.'

'And you weren't disappointed.'

'What brought you to Vevey?'

'Chance. *Mis*chance, so far as you're concerned.'

'I would deny anything you told them.'

'Would your denials suffice?'

'Perhaps. Perhaps not. I would prefer . . .' She looked at him with a faint, self-mocking smile. 'Not to find out.'

'You don't have to.'

'Are you proposing a partnership, Mr Spandrel?'

'Either I go with you. Or you don't go at all.'

'The Green Book?'

'We share the proceeds of the sale.'

'What of Mr Buckthorn and Mr Silverwood?'

'Tell them I'm your cousin. Tell them whatever you think they're likeliest to believe. But persuade them to let me join the party. Do you think you can do that?'

'Probably.'

'And will you?'

'It seems I must.' She arched her eyebrows at him. 'Does it not?'

CHAPTER TWENTY-ONE

Between the Covers

Estelle Plenderleath, only daughter of Josiah Plenderleath, led a comfortable if not cosseted childhood amidst the rural quietude of Shropshire, untroubled – because no-one could bear to tell her – that the family estate was entailed and would pass to a male cousin when her father died. This the hale and affectionate Squire Plenderleath did not seem likely to do for many years. But a riding accident plucked him inconsiderately away, obliging his widow to explain the sombre consequences to Estelle and the pair of them to take refuge with relatives in London, while the cousin took prompt and unceremonious possession. The Spandrels were as welcoming as the constraints of space and money would permit, but those constraints were far from negligible and Estelle's mother encouraged her to seek a moneyed husband who could rescue both of them from their sadly reduced circumstances. A Dutch merchant called de Vries, whose dealings with Mr Spandrel in connection with his mapmaking business led to an encounter with Estelle, became instantly and fortuitously enraptured. There was a significant difference in age, it was true, but de Vries showed himself to be a good man and Estelle could scarcely allow her heart to rule her head. They were married and, for several years thereafter, Estelle lived quietly and dutifully with her husband in

Amsterdam, while her mother, supported by an allowance from de Vries, retired to Lyme Regis. Then, quite suddenly, de Vries died. Estelle, now a wealthy widow, decided that the time had at last come to enjoy herself. De Vries had often promised to show her the wonders of Rome, but had always been too busy to take her. Now, she would take herself. When news of her departure reached her mother, the old lady was thrown into a state of high anxiety by the thought of a vulnerable young woman undertaking such an arduous and hazardous journey on her own. The Spandrels were persuaded to send their son William after her to afford such protection and assistance as he could. William was not to know, of course, that when he found Estelle he would not find her alone, but enjoying the solicitous attentions of two excellent young gentlemen whose path had crossed hers in Geneva: Giles Buckthorn and Naseby Silverwood.

Spandrel was given no cause to doubt, during the days following his addition to the travelling party, that Buckthorn and Silverwood believed this version of events. (It was not a question of Buckthorn *or* Silverwood; the two men were as similar in their opinions and modes of expression as they were *dis*similar in appearance.) Why should they not believe it? The account of themselves to which Estelle and Spandrel had agreed to subscribe at the conclusion of their hasty negotiations in Vevey contained enough of the truth to disguise that which was not true. The exact proportion was unknown to Spandrel. Had Estelle ever been Miss Plenderleath, the demure Salopian lass? He was inclined to think not. But since, as Estelle at one point remarked, the secret of successful lying was to invent as little as possible, perhaps she really had been.

What was undeniable was the dexterity with which she accommodated Spandrel in the tale she had already told Buckthorn and Silverwood, a tale that grew around him in the telling and wove their separate pasts into an interdependent present. There were times, posing as Estelle's cousin, when he actually believed that was what he was. Certainly, he could not afford to do other than consistently pretend he was. The fiction, once agreed upon, had to be maintained – for both their sakes.

Fortunately, Buckthorn and Silverwood were an incurious pair, at least so far as Spandrel was concerned. They were not interested in him at all. They affected, indeed, to ignore him. Their attentions were devoted to Estelle and not, even then, to the circumstances that had thrown her into their company, but to the alluring possibilities that arose as a result. Amidst all their exaggerated courtesies and languid drolleries, it was obvious that they were as besotted with Estelle as she had intended them to be. They were just down from Oxford, bored, idle, vain and arrogant, acquainted, if they were to be believed, with a legion of great men and beautiful women. But they had never met anyone like Estelle de Vries. Of that Spandrel felt certain.

Spandrel, for his part, was obliged to simulate a degree of cousinly familiarity with Estelle, as she was with him. This sharing of secrets was undeniably exciting. It was all too easy to dream of a future more delectable than any he had previously envisioned. But tempting prospects, he well knew, made bad guides. Their partnership was not likely to be an enduring one. He reminded himself of his intention to wrest the Green Book from her at the first possible opportunity and deliver it to the Brodrick Committee in accordance with McIlwraith's dying wish.

But no such opportunity presented itself during the three days the party spent in Geneva. Estelle argued, not unreasonably, that the book was best left where it was – in a safe at Turrettini's Bank – until their departure. Buckthorn and Silverwood believed it was a jewel-box she had deposited there. And why would they not, since that was what she had told them? As to the Alpine crossing, they favoured a delay until after Easter, but Estelle was keen to proceed at once, purportedly on account of her thirst for a sight of those Roman antiquities her late husband had evocatively described to her. Spandrel was rather pleased with himself for settling the issue by suggesting that Buckthorn and Silverwood had been taken in by blood-curdling travellers' tales of ravening wolves in the mountain passes at this time of the year. Their fear of personal discomfort, let alone danger, was only surpassed by their fear of losing face before Estelle. A departure upon the morrow was instantly agreed.

That afternoon, Estelle asked them to escort her to the bank so that she might collect her jewel-box. They were clearly delighted that this honour was conferred upon them rather than Spandrel. And Spandrel had no choice but to give every appearance of feeling slighted by being passed over for such a duty. What he actually felt was a growing suspicion that opportunities of laying his hands upon the Green Book during the journey to Rome were going to be few and far between. Estelle, indeed, had probably already resolved that he would have none. But, as to that, she might yet be surprised.

If Spandrel believed himself capable of surprising such a woman as Estelle de Vries, he failed to allow for the probability that she would spring a greater surprise on him. That evening, when the ill-matched party of four met for supper at the Clé Argenté, the comfortable inn near the cathedral where they had been lodging, Buckthorn and

Silverwood proposed an evening of cards and music at the house of the tirelessly hospitable Monsieur Bouvin, whose acquaintance they had recently made. Estelle excused herself on grounds of a headache and retired to her room. Spandrel claimed to have a letter to write. After some grumbling about the unsociability of their companions, Buckthorn and Silverwood headed out into the night.

Spandrel had no letter to write, of course. He left the inn a short time afterwards and sought out a humble tavern where he could drink and smoke at his ease and not mind his manners and turns of phrase, as he felt obliged to do while playing the part of Estelle's cousin. An hour or so later, feeling less fretful and altogether more himself, he made his way back to the Clé Argenté.

As he entered his room, he noticed something pale lying on the dark boards at his feet. It was a note, apparently slipped under the door in his absence. He held it up to read by the light of the lamp he was carrying.

I must see you tonight. Come to my room. E.

She was waiting for him, seated by a well-stacked fire, wearing some kind of loosely belted dressing-gown in which threads of gold glimmered in the firelight. A bottle of brandy and two glasses stood on a small table beside her chair.

'What can I do for you . . . cousin?' Spandrel began.

'Sit down. Join me in a glass.'

Spandrel fetched the upright chair from its place by the dressing-table and set it down on the other side of the hearth from her, then poured them both some brandy. He felt wholly unsurprised by her masculine taste in liquor.

'Where have you been? Not to Monsieur Bouvin's, I assume.'

'No.' Spandrel seated himself and sipped some brandy. 'Not to Monsieur Bouvin's.'

'We should trust each other, William,' she said. 'Really we should.'

The only response Spandrel could summon was a rueful smile.

'I'm perfectly serious.'

'I'm sure you are.'

'We have a long journey ahead of us. Too long, I think, to be spent in watching each other for signs of impending treachery.'

'How's that to be avoided?'

'By putting what unites us before what divides us.'

'The Green Book unites us. And the money it's worth. Nothing else.'

'Nothing? Come, William. Why do you think we've been able to convince Mr Buckthorn and Mr Silverwood that we are cousins?'

'Because they're easily convinced . . . by you.'

'And by you. We seem like cousins. There's a similarity, a . . . kinship. Fate has handed us this chance to transform our lives. We must take the chance. Together.'

'Is that what you told Zuyler?'

'Pieter was greedy. But you are not. You are in truth rarer than you look. You are a good man.'

'And an easily flattered one, you seem to think.'

'Not at all. Do you think me beautiful?'

He looked at her in silence for a moment, then said, 'Yes. I do.'

'Is that flattery?'

'It's the truth.'

'Exactly. The truth. The book is in a case in the dressing-table drawer, William. Would you like to see it? I think you should.'

He frowned at her in puzzlement, then rose and

carried the lamp he had brought from his room across to the dressing-table. He stood it on the table and slid open the drawer. A red, padded-leather jewel-box lay within. This he lifted out and set down by the lamp.

'It's not locked,' said Estelle from behind him. 'In ordinary circumstances, it would be, of course. But these are not ordinary circumstances.'

Spandrel released the catches and raised the lid. There was the book: a plain, green-covered ledger, with leather spine and marbled page edges. For this, and what it contained, men had died. He had nearly been one of them. Yet now, here it was, in his grasp. He hooked a finger under the cover and opened it.

The pages were ruled in columns. In the middle were listed names, on the left and right amounts at dated intervals, paid in and paid out. But for most of the names nothing had been paid in, only out. And the sums involved were massive: £10,000 here, £20,000 there. The transactions on the page he was looking at dated from about a year before. Each was recorded in the same hand, the initials of the writer, R.K., added in minute script above each entry. Spandrel turned to the next page, then the next. Thousands more, in a forest of zeros, met his gaze. He turned back to the beginning and ran his eye down the names. Then he caught his breath.

'Are you surprised?' Estelle's voice was scarcely more than a whisper. She was standing beside him now, her shadow, cast by the fire, flickering across the page. 'So many of them. The proud and the mighty. All that they took, down to the last farthing.'

'But . . . I never thought . . .'

'That there would be so many? Or that they would have taken so much? Some paid for less than they received. Others paid nothing at all. Every one of them was, and is, a bought man. And what men they are.

Dukes, marquesses, earls, Members of Parliament, courtiers, ministers, persons of distinction. Abundant largesse, showered on the great and the wealthy, while the seaside widows and the humble shopkeepers scraped together their pennies to buy stock these people were made a gift of. Do you wonder that Pieter asked a hundred thousand pounds for this book?'

'No. I don't.'

'The book you carried from London to Amsterdam . . . for how much?'

'The promise of hardly anything, compared with . . .' He nodded glumly at the ranks of figures.

'Where we're going . . . we might reasonably ask for more than a hundred thousand.'

'Might we?'

'I think so. See . . .' She turned the page and pointed to an entry. 'Here.'

Spandrel stooped for a clearer view. On the line where Estelle's finger rested was written, *Rt. Hon. J. Aislabie, on behalf of H.M.*

'The Chancellor of the Exchequer,' said Estelle. 'On behalf of His Majesty. The King.' Her finger moved to the right. 'One hundred thousand pounds' worth of shares. That is why Pieter fixed on the figure. And how much paid for them?' Her finger moved to the left. 'Twenty thousand pounds. Just twenty. Then the whole allocation was sold back to the company, when the price was near its zenith, at a colossal profit. What do you think the London mob would do if they knew?'

'I think they might do almost anything.'

'Exactly. Which means the Pretender will pay handsomely for possession of this book – our book.'

'Why didn't the King pay handsomely, when he had the chance?'

'The message must have gone astray. Pieter dealt

through intermediaries. We won't make that mistake.'

'Won't we?'

'We won't make any mistakes. Trust me.'

'That word again. *Trust.*'

'It comes in many guises. And pledges come in different forms. Not just words, William.'

'What else?'

'Can you not guess?'

Spandrel felt a slither of something soft and silken across his hand. He turned towards Estelle and saw that she had released the belt of her gown. It hung open. Beneath, she wore only the thinnest of shifts. His mouth was dry, his mind aswarm with competing instincts. A good man? There she was surely mistaken. He wanted her, even more than he wanted the money. But it seemed he could have both. They were his for the asking.

Estelle slipped off the gown. It fell about her feet. The firelight behind her revealed the outline of her body through the shift. Desire engulfed Spandrel. He had to have her. What he would not even have dreamt to be possible when they had met in the library at her husband's house in Amsterdam was suddenly and deliriously about to happen. He reached out. She grasped his hand and slowly led it to her breast, full and soft beneath the shift. The warmth of her thrilled through him.

'Estelle—'

'Don't say anything.' She drew him closer. 'Whatever pleasure I can give . . . is yours to take.'

CHAPTER TWENTY-TWO

Over the Mountains

There were times – most of them when he was swaying
in a strange kind of litter on the shoulders of four mountain porters with nothing but their sureness of hand
between him and a sheer drop into a chasm of pure white
snow and stark black rock – when Nicholas Cloisterman
came seriously to doubt that he would survive the Alpine
crossing. He remembered his Classics master at King's,
Canterbury, pondering the puzzle of which route
Hannibal had taken, elephants and all, back in 218 B.C.
and was now quite certain on one point: it could not have
been the Simplon Pass.

Arriving at Brig after a three-day journey from Baden,
Cloisterman had joined a small party of travellers bound
for Milan, happy as they were to accept his share of the
cost of hiring guides and porters. The journey that
followed was occasionally awe-inspiring, so vast and
majestic were the Alps in their late winter grimness. But
it was more often bone-numbingly cold and hair-
raisingly hazardous. For Cloisterman the relief that he
felt as they descended to Lake Maggiore was tempered
only by the awareness that he would have to come back
this way, though not, it was true, in late winter.

As to what season it would be, spring or summer, he
had no way to tell. There had been no word at Brig of a
lone female traveller. His enquiry on the subject had

yielded nothing beyond the suggestion that, at this time of the year, he had to be joking. Nor did the British Consul at Milan, an amiable sinecurist called Phelps, prove any more helpful. Of Estelle de Vries there was no trace. Where she was remained a mystery. But where she was going was certain. And Cloisterman would have to follow.

'Business in Rome, is it?' remarked Phelps. 'I don't envy you, I must say. Concerns the Pretender, does it?'

'What makes you think so?' Cloisterman responded warily.

'Nothing else seems to take Government men that way. You know the wretched fellow has a son and heir now?'

'Of course.' News of the birth of a male to the Stuart line a couple of months previously had travelled fast.

'Horribly healthy, I gather.'

'How pleasing for his parents.'

'But not our employers, eh? Well, I wish you luck, whatever your business.' Phelps grinned. 'I expect you'll need it.'

A man in still greater need of luck than Cloisterman was Chancellor of the Exchequer John Aislabie, whose trial commenced at the House of Commons in London on the very afternoon of Cloisterman's unilluminating conversation with Consul Phelps in Milan.

Alas for Aislabie, luck did not come his way. The consequences of another acquittal following Charles Stanhope's evasion of justice were too serious to be contemplated. Walpole said nothing in defence of Aislabie, whose explanation that he had burnt all records of his dealings in South Sea stock because they were of no importance once settled was not well received. Small wonder, since those dealings had netted him a profit of £35,000. He was convicted, expelled from the House and consigned to the Tower, there to languish until occasion could be found to anatomize his estate and decide how much of it, if not all, should be forfeit.

Celebratory bonfires were lit across London as the news spread. Public anger was appeased. 'Sometimes,' remarked Walpole, watching the flames light the night sky from Viscount Townshend's Cockpit office, 'a sacrifice there has to be.'

'Will Aislabie be enough for them?' asked Townshend.

'I'd happily give them Sunderland as well. But the King's uncommonly fond of the fellow. And the King expects me to persuade the House to spare him.'

'Will you be able to?'

'I think so. Just so long as no new evidence turns up.'

'Such as the Green Book? I worry about it, Robin, I really do.'

'So you should. If it fell into the wrong hands . . .' Walpole cast his brother-in-law a meaningful look. 'They might be lighting bonfires for us as well.'

The four English travellers who arrived in Turin the day after Aislabie's conviction in London had a no less arduous Alpine crossing than Cloisterman to look back on. The vertiginous scramblings of their porters over the wind-scoured Mont Cenis Pass had caused Estelle de Vries no apparent alarm, however. It had therefore been necessary for her male companions to affect a similar unconcern, their true feelings concealed behind devil-may-care quips and high fur collars.

The performance of Buckthorn and Silverwood in this regard had scarcely wavered, although Buckthorn had mentioned wolves often enough to suggest a preoccupation with the subject and Silverwood had manifestly not been amused by the porters' discontented mutterings about his weight.

Spandrel for his part had found it easy to assume an uncharacteristic jauntiness of manner. The frozen beauty of the Alps was something he had never expected to experience. Nor, for that matter, was the sexual favour of such a woman as Estelle de Vries. He had entered a new world in more ways than one and his elation left little space for fear, nor indeed for the thought that Estelle did not and could not love him. She had used the act of love to bind him to her and she had succeeded. The memory of their night together in Geneva was sometimes clearer to Spandrel than the events taking place around him. Like a white flame of refined pleasure, it burned within him. He was hers, completely. And she was his, reservedly. He was aware of the disparity, what it meant and why it existed. He knew the promises he was breaking and the dangers he was ignoring. But he also knew that what she had given him he could not resist.

The cramped accommodation available to Alpine travellers had prevented any immediate repetition of their night of passion. Buckthorn and Silverwood could be given no hint of how matters stood between them. It was one more secret for them to share – the darkest and most delicious of all. At a spacious inn of the sort the Savoyard capital might be expected to boast, however, that secret might both be kept and enjoyed.

But Estelle did not agree. 'We must be careful,' she counselled during a few snatched moments of privacy. 'If Mr Buckthorn and Mr Silverwood should learn that we are lovers, they would be consumed by jealousy. They might also come to doubt that we have given them a true account of ourselves. They are not above spying at corners and listening at keyholes. We must give them nothing to spy upon.'

'We don't need them any more,' Spandrel protested. 'Let's go on alone.'

'It was agreed that they would accompany me to Florence. I cannot spurn them now. To Florence we must go – together.'

'And after Florence?'

'You'll have me all to yourself.'

It was a promise and a lure. Florence was the better part of a week away. Until then . . .

'Don't spoil what we have, William. There's so much more to come. Very soon.' She kissed him. 'Trust me.'

He did not trust her, of course. He could never do that. But he did adore her. And he was not sure that he would ever do otherwise.

'Mr Walpole,' the Earl of Sunderland announced in a tone of mock geniality as he stepped into the Paymaster-General's office at the Cockpit the following morning. 'I'm a little surprised to find you here, I must say.'

'No more than I'm surprised to see you here,' growled Walpole.

'I only meant that so many posts are said to be within your grasp – more I sometimes think than are not – that it's a touch disconcerting to realize that in truth you're still only' – Sunderland looked about him and smiled – 'the Army's wages clerk.'

'What can I do for you, Spencer?'

'It's what *I* can do for *you* that brings me here, my dear fellow.'

'Good of you to think of me when you've so much else on your mind.'

'The trial, you mean? Next week's . . . grand entertainment.'

'*Your* trial.'

'We all have trials. Some bear them better than others.'

'Some have more to bear.'

'Indeed.' Sunderland plucked his snuff-box from his

coat pocket and took a pinch, as if needing to clear his nose of some unpleasant smell. 'I have . . . disappointing news for you. I'm sure you'll . . . bear it well.'

'What news?'

'A Secret Service report, the contents of which I thought it kinder to convey to you personally than . . . through the normal channels.'

Soon, very soon, Walpole consoled himself, the Secret Service would be reporting to him, not Sunderland. Then he would be the one doling out their nuggets of intelligence to those he judged fit to hear them. Then *he* would be master. But for the moment, Sunderland still stood above him, albeit on a crumbling pedestal. 'Kind of you, I'm sure.'

'As to kindness, you might not think it so when you hear what I have to tell you.'

Walpole leaned back in his chair and scratched his stomach. 'Well?'

'Colonel Wagemaker. Your . . . agent.'

'Is that what you think he is?'

'It's what I think he *was*. Until he was killed in a duel at Berne on the twenty-sixth of last month.'

Walpole summoned a grin to cover his discomposure. 'Wagemaker? Dead?'

'As the mission you sent him on.'

'How's this . . . said to have happened?'

'A duel of some sort. Details are sparse. But dead he undoubtedly is. It seems you did not choose wisely. As for Townshend's assurances to the King that you and he would soon have the Green Book under lock and key . . .' Sunderland cocked his head and treated Walpole to a look of distilled condescension. 'What are they worth now?'

'I never put all my eggs in one basket, Spencer. Any more than you do.'

233

'A hard policy to follow, when the basket is so distant.'

Walpole shrugged. 'Hard, but prudent.'

'Prudent, but unlikely.' Sunderland propped himself on the corner of the desk and held Walpole's gaze. 'Your eggs are smashed, Mr Paymaster. Every last one.'

'I doubt it.'

'Of course you do. Doubt's your stock-in-trade. I'll send you a copy of the report. That should still a few of those doubts.'

'I'm obliged.'

'Obliged to me. Yes. I'm glad you understand that.' Sunderland stood up. 'And I'd be gladder still if you remembered it.' He moved towards the door, then stopped and looked back. 'The King accepts that Aislabie had to go. But he wishes it to end there. He wants no more ministers led away to the Tower.'

'No more than you do, I'm sure.'

'If you aim to win his favour, you'd do well not to disappoint him.'

'I'll see what I can do.'

'If you'll take my advice . . .' Sunderland's gaze narrowed. 'You'll make sure you do enough.'

The gloom of a London winter seemed far away amidst the balmy pleasantries of a Tuscan spring. Relaxing in the walled garden of the British Consul's Florentine palazzo beneath a sapphire sky, warmed by good food, fine wine and mellow sunshine, Nicholas Cloisterman felt that his journey from Amsterdam was at long last beginning to yield some rewards. His host, Percy Blain, was an intelligent cynic after Cloisterman's own heart and his hostess, Mrs Blain, was proof that cynicism might be a sure guide to many things but not to womankind. After but two nights beneath their roof, he felt that he was among friends.

Nor was friendship the only gift the Blains had bestowed upon him. Blain, in whom he had confided all but the exact nature of the book he was so earnestly seeking on the British Government's behalf, had suggested a precaution they might take, there in Florence, to reduce the likelihood of that book's arrival in Rome.

The precaution depended on the co-operation of the Tuscan authorities and it was the securing of that co-operation which Cloisterman and Blain were now toasting over a glass of excellent local wine beside a plashing fountain and a table still bearing the remnants of a splendid repast.

'How were you able to bring it off?' Cloisterman asked, still unclear on the point. 'The Dutch authorities would have sent me away with a flea in my ear if I'd ever put such a request to them.'

'But the Dutch are a powerful and independent people,' replied Blain. 'What is the Grand Duchy of Tuscany but a pawn on the great powers' chessboard? The Grand Duke is an old man, his son and heir a childless degenerate. The treaty with Spain our late Lord Stanhope spent so much time and effort negotiating cedes Tuscany to the Spaniards when the Medici line fails, which it surely soon will. But Stanhope is dead. New ministers mean new policies. Treaties can be re-negotiated. That is the Grand Duke's hope. And that is why *his* ministers are so keen to oblige us.'

'Every customs post will be on the look-out for Mrs de Vries?'

'Any Englishwoman *or* Dutchwoman, travelling alone *or* in company, whatever name she gives, will be stopped and searched. Believe me, the customs men need no encouragement to perform such a task with the utmost diligence.'

'She might not pass through Tuscany.'

'It is a considerable diversion to go round. And from her point of view surely an unnecessary one.'

'True,' Cloisterman conceded. Estelle de Vries would head for Rome by the most direct route. That was certain. And that was indeed the one problem Blain could not solve for him. 'But by the same token . . .'

'She may already have passed through.'

'Yes. She may.'

'My enquiries suggest not. But it's possible, of course. I can't deny it.'

'I shall have to press on, then.'

'A pity. Lizzie and I have enjoyed your visit.'

'So have I.'

'As for what awaits you in Rome . . .' Blain smiled. 'The Pretender's so-called court is a warren of squabbling Scots. We have one of them in our pay, of course. More than one, I dare say. Our masters in Whitehall don't trust me with all their secrets. Colonel Lachlan Drummond is a name I *can* give you, though. I shouldn't rely on him overmuch. But he's there to be used. As for—' Blain broke off at the sight of his wife hurrying out to them from the deep shade beneath the loggia at the rear of the palazzo. 'What is it, my dear?'

'A message from Chancellor Lorenzini.' She handed him a note and smiled across at Cloisterman. 'I thought you'd wish to see it at once, in case it had some bearing on your discussions.'

'Let's hope he hasn't had second thoughts about granting your request,' said Cloisterman.

'Surely not.' Blain tore the note open and looked at it, then frowned. 'Well, I say . . .'

'What is it?'

'The Pope is dead.' He passed the note to Cloisterman for him to read. 'It seems you'll find Rome in the fickle grasp of an interregnum. I was just about to tell you that His Holiness keeps the Pretender on a tight rein. But now, it seems . . .' Blain shrugged. 'The reins are off.'

If Cloisterman had known that Estelle de Vries was at that moment not in Rome, more than a hundred miles to the south, but in Genoa, more than a hundred miles to the north, he would no doubt have remained in Florence, contentedly waiting for the Tuscan authorities to seize his prey for him. But he did not know. And ignorance can sometimes be a useful ally.

The journey from Turin to Genoa along mud-clogged roads had been neither fast nor agreeable. Along the way, an idea had formed in Spandrel's mind, an idea that had taken him down to Genoa's bustling harbour on the very afternoon of the party's arrival in the city. There he had chanced upon the British merchantman *Wyvern*, bound for Palermo by way of Orbitello and Naples. It was a two-day voyage to Orbitello, the master's mate told him, and a day by coach from there to Rome, a much quicker route to his destination than overland all the way; and paying passengers could be readily accommodated. A deal was thereupon struck.

It was a more fortuitous deal than Spandrel knew, for Orbitello lay in the tiny Austrian enclave of the Presidio, sandwiched between Tuscany and the Papal States. By this route, he and Estelle would never set foot on Tuscan territory; Cloisterman's trap would never be sprung.

Spandrel would no doubt have rubbed his hands in satisfaction had he been aware of this happy consequence of his negotiation of a swift coastal passage south. But he was not aware. And yet rub them he nonetheless did, as he left the *Wyvern* and hurried back towards the *albergo* where he and his companions had taken lodgings. Silverwood had complained of sea-sickness on the placid waters of Lake Geneva. The Mediterranean would surely be too much for him to contemplate. Besides, Orbitello was closer to Rome than Florence. And it was Florence that Silverwood and Buckthorn had proclaimed as their destination from the start. No, no. Only two passengers would be leaving aboard the *Wyvern* in the morning. Estelle had promised him he would soon have her all to himself. And now he would – even sooner than she had expected.

But Spandrel's reckoning was awry. Giles Buckthorn had no intention of allowing his friend's sea-sickness to separate them from Estelle.

'The arrangement is an excellent one, Mr Spandrel. So excellent that we will come with you. I'm sure the *Wyvern* can accommodate two more passengers.'

'Oh, I don't—'

'Leave it to me. I'll cut down there now and hire a berth for us.'

'But Mr Silverwood's clearly no sailor.'

'Nonsense. It was because Lake Geneva was a millpond that he felt it. The ocean wave is just what he needs.'

'And this will keep you from Florence.'

'No matter. We will simply turn our itinerary about and take Florence after Rome. Ah, *la città eterna*. With a veritable Venus for company. What could be better?' Buckthorn struck a classical pose, arm outstretched, and gave Spandrel a fruity-lipped grin. 'Nothing, I rather think.'

CHAPTER TWENTY-THREE

Whither all Roads Lead

The trial by the House of Commons of the First Lord of the Treasury, Charles Spencer, third Earl of Sunderland, was fixed, by fateful chance, for the Ides of March. Legally, the event was without precedent, a peer of the realm being traditionally answerable only to the House of Lords. The fact that the trial was to be held in the absence of the accused, Sunderland not even deigning to watch from the gallery, added piquancy to the uniqueness of the occasion, while rumours that Walpole had been making free with bribes to save his old enemy's neck rumbled darkly in the background.

The debate, when it came, was fast and furious. The accusation that Sunderland had received £50,000 worth of South Sea stock without paying a penny for it was stark, but by no means simple, with neither chief cashier Knight nor his infamous account book on hand to settle the issue. That rested instead on votes, some freely given, some expensively bought. In the end, as many had predicted, Sunderland was acquitted.

The public were outraged, but unsurprised. And, as the dust settled, the delicacy of Walpole's judgement became apparent. Sunderland had survived, but the margin of votes by which he had done so – 233 to 172 – was too narrow for him to claim exoneration. He had escaped the Tower. But he could not remain at the

Treasury. His days were numbered. His era was over. While that of Walpole was about to begin.

Unless, of course, there was something even Walpole had failed to foresee.

The following morning saw a solitary and travel-weary Englishman present himself at the Porta del Popolo, northernmost of the gates set in the ancient wall surrounding Rome. It was a hot, glaringly bright spring day that would have been considered a fine adornment to high summer in Amsterdam, let alone London. Harassed by the customs officer into administering a bribe, Nicholas Cloisterman was at length allowed to pass through into the piazza on the other side, where he paused to admire, despite his fatigue, the Egyptian obelisk standing at its centre. Beyond this haughty finger of Imperial plunder from times long gone by, three streets led off into the city like the prongs of a trident. Cloisterman was bound for the right-hand prong, the Via di Ripetta, and, some way along it, the Casa Rossa, an *albergo* recommended to him by Percy Blain. Anglo-Papal relations being as cool as they were, the British Government had no consular representation in the city. Cloisterman was on his own. But he did not expect that to prove a problem. Early communication with the Government's spy at the Pretender's court, Colonel Drummond, would establish whether or not Estelle de Vries had already reached Rome. If not, Cloisterman could safely return to Florence and let Blain and the Tuscan authorities do what needed to be done. If she had, on the other hand . . . But Cloisterman was too tired to confront that issue unless and until he needed to. Succumbing to the importunate blandishments of one of the many *servitori di piazza*, he engaged a fly and bade the driver take him directly to the Casa Rossa.

*   *   *

If Cloisterman had lingered in the Piazza del Popolo until late afternoon, he would have been taken aback to witness the arrival in Rome not just of Estelle de Vries, but also of William Spandrel, in the company of two Englishmen, one shaped like a bean-pole, the other like a water-butt – Giles Buckthorn and Naseby Silverwood. The latter pair administered as many loud complaints as lavish bribes before progressing beyond the customs-house, while Mrs de Vries and her supposed cousin attracted little attention. Buckthorn and Silverwood had it on good authority, so they declared, that the best accommodation was to be found in or near the Piazza di Spagna. By strange chance it was the very same fox-faced *servitor* who had earlier obliged Cloisterman who now earned another fee by leaping aboard their carriage and directing its driver to their destination.

The light was fading fast as they drove along the Via del Babuino, the sky turning a gilded pink. Spandrel saw the alternately grand and dilapidated buildings to either side as purple-grey monuments to a world he had never expected to experience – ancient, exotic and mysterious. He should have felt exhilarated. Instead, the bile of regret and resentment lapped at his thoughts – regret for the promise he had given McIlwraith and was now busily breaking; resentment of Buckthorn and Silverwood for forcing Estelle to maintain a seemly distance from him. His only consolation was that they had finally arrived where their bold project of enrichment could be enacted. Once the book presently nestling in Estelle's travelling-case was sold, Buckthorn and Silverwood could be forgotten, along with everything else comprising their past. Only the future would matter then. And it was the future that seemed to glitter in Estelle's eyes as she glanced across at him. Nothing would be denied him then.

The Palazzo Muti, Roman residence of the self-styled King James III of England and VIII of Scotland, was a handsomely columned and pedimented gold-stuccoed building at the northern end of the Piazza dei Santi Apostoli, close to the heart of the old city. The Pretender had spent all but the first six months of his life exiled from the country he claimed the right to rule. The failure of the Fifteen had led to a still more humiliating exile from France and the past four years had found him sheltering in Rome, further than ever, both metaphorically and geographically, from where he wanted to be. Yet those four years had also seen his marriage, to the beautiful Polish princess, Clementina Sobieski, and her obliging production of a bonny baby boy. With the British Government mired in unpopularity, half its ministers on trial and the other half scrabbling for position, the Pretender's prospects did not currently seem as negligible as they often had.

Surveying the Palazzo Muti from the *trottoir* on the other side of the piazza, the lanterns flanking its entrance newly lit against the encroaching dusk, Cloisterman reflected that, grand though it was, it was far from grand enough for a king. Nor were its surroundings – narrow, rubbish-strewn streets rank with mud and *merda* – in any way flattering to James Edward Stuart's dignified view of himself. All in all, the Pretender's home-from-home looked what it was: a tribute to his past failures. But they would not matter if he could achieve one crowning success. And for that, Cloisterman suspected, the Green Book might be enough.

He moved away then, walking smartly towards the other end of the piazza. Before reaching it, he turned right, back towards the Corso, middle and longest of the three streets leading south from the Piazza del Popolo. He crossed the Corso, headed up it a little way, then turned off along a narrow street consumed by the shadows of unlit buildings, before stepping through a low arch into a dank courtyard, where he felt his way to a doorway and rang three times at the bell.

A minute or so passed, then the sound of shuffling feet and the glimmer of a candle seeped around the door. It creaked open and a small old woman with no more flesh on her than a sparrow squinted out at him. '*Si?*'

'For Colonel Drummond,' said Cloisterman, thrusting a letter into her ice-cold hand. 'You understand?'

'Colonel Drummond,' she repeated, comprehendingly enough. '*Si, si.*'

'It's important.' He raised his voice. '*Importante.*'

The candlelight made a shadowy chasm of her toothless grin. There was the rattle of something that might have been a laugh. '*Si, si. Sempre importante.*' Then she closed the door in his face.

Circumstances had meanwhile conspired to smile on the wishes and desires of William Spandrel. The Piazza di Spagna was a broad concourse, centred on a fountain fashioned in the likeness of a leaking boat, separating the Spanish Embassy from a muddy, cart-tracked slope, at the top of which stood the twin bell towers of the church of Trinità dei Monti. The *servitor* who had accompanied them from Piazza del Popolo persuaded Buckthorn and Silverwood that the most charming lodgings in the area were to be found in the Palazzetto Raguzzi, at the northern end of the piazza. Buckthorn and Silverwood were indeed charmed by the two first-floor rooms that were available, though chagrined to discover that the whole party could not be accommodated under the same roof. After much courteous proposing and chivalrous disposing, it was agreed that Estelle had to be given the benefit of one of the rooms and Spandrel that of the other, while Buckthorn and Silverwood contented themselves with rooms at the Albergo Luna in Via Condotti, just off the piazza.

The Palazzetto Raguzzi was well named so far as Spandrel was concerned. His room, like Estelle's, was palatially proportioned, with high windows overlooking the piazza, and was richly furnished. Such odd stains and frays as there were did not prevent it being just about the grandest lodgings he had ever secured. But grandeur was something he was already looking forward to becoming accustomed to. And meanwhile there was a priceless pleasure to be enjoyed.

After dinner with Buckthorn and Silverwood at the Albergo Luna, they retired early to the Palazzetto on grounds of fatigue following the long day's journey. Fatigued they certainly were. But for Spandrel that counted for nothing compared with his four days' worth of pent-up longing for Estelle. She seemed as delighted as he was to end their self-denial. An evening of irksome attendance on Buckthorn and Silverwood's by now all too familiar vapidities gave way to a night of physical release in which the joy Spandrel had felt in Geneva bloomed anew. It was a joy he knew at the back of his mind he should not make the mistake of supposing that Estelle shared. But by morning, suppose it he nonetheless did.

By morning also their thoughts had turned to the purpose for which they had come to Rome. 'We must deposit the book at a bank this morning,' said Estelle, as

244

they lay in bed together at dawn. 'Mr Buckthorn and Mr Silverwood will be eager to show me some of the antiquities I have assured them I am equally eager to see. I propose you complain of some minor illness and absent yourself. They will not question your absence.'

'I reckon not.'

'In fact,' said Estelle with a smile, 'they will be rather pleased by it.'

'And won't hide their pleasure well.'

'Exactly. At all events, while I am yawning my way round some ruin or other, you will go to the Palazzo Muti and seek an audience with the Pretender's secretary.'

'What if he won't see me?'

'If you are persistent, he will. It may take a little while. We must be patient. When you tell him what we have to sell, he will understand its significance. And he will pay what we ask to gain possession of the book. For the Pretender, it will promise an end to exile.'

'Is that truly what the Green Book means, Estelle? Revolution in our homeland? A Stuart king back on the throne?'

'Who knows? And who cares?' Estelle inclined her head to look at Spandrel. Her eyes were deeper shadows amidst the shadows of the room. The scent of her flesh was all about him, the cunning and the daring of their scheme wreathing itself around his intoxicating memories of the night before. 'This is for us, William. Us and no-one else.'

'I wish you could come with me.'

'So do I. But such negotiations are best conducted by a man. It is the way of the world.'

'Who'd have conducted them for you if we hadn't met in Vevey? Buckthorn? Or Silverwood?'

'Neither.'

'But you just said—'

'Enough.' She silenced him with a kiss. 'We met. We made our pact.' She stretched out her hand to touch him beneath the sheets. 'Now we look forward. Not back. Ever again.'

CHAPTER TWENTY-FOUR

Skinning the Bear

'Mr Spandrel, is it?' said James Edgar, as he looked up from his desk.

It was the late afternoon of the following day. The glaring Roman light of noon had faded to a purpling pink in the sky and to a blackening grey in the office of the private secretary to King James VIII and III, as Mr Edgar would undoubtedly have described himself. He was a spare, round-shouldered, bespectacled man who looked, though he probably was not, much older than the thirty-two-year-old king-in-exile whom he served. Mr Edgar was the dry-as-dust inky-fingered quintessence of a Scottish solicitor, transplanted with no apparent change of habit to the land of dead Caesars and dissolute cardinals.

Spandrel had waited many hours to see Mr Edgar. He had been left to cramp his haunches during those hours on a narrow chair in a draughty passage near the main stairway of the Palazzo Muti, while a contrasting assortment of whispering clerics, grumbling Scots and pinch-mouthed servants passed him heedlessly by. He had waited as patiently as he could, bearing Estelle's prediction of delay in mind. The Green Book was now safely lodged at the Banco Calderini, while Estelle was being shown the wonders of the Pantheon and the Campidoglio by the ever attentive Buckthorn and Silverwood. It was Spandrel's demanding lot to await his

247

opportunity of a conversation with the dour Mr Edgar and to ensure that the opportunity, when it came, was not wasted.

'My name is Spandrel, yes. May I come straight to the purpose of my visit?'

'I'd be grateful if you did. I'm a busy man, Mr Spandrel. And we have more than our fair share here of uninvited visitors. I can't afford to waste my time hearing all their stories.'

'I'm obliged to you for seeing me, then.'

'I was told you gave no sign of meaning to leave.'

'I've come too far to do that without explaining myself . . . to someone close to . . .'

'The King?'

Spandrel shrugged. 'Yes. The King.'

Edgar smiled thinly. 'You don't sound like a true believer, Mr Spandrel.'

'My beliefs don't matter.'

'Do they not? How far *have* you come, by the by?'

'That doesn't matter either. It's what I've come *with* that's important.'

'And what is that?'

'The secret account book of the chief cashier of the South Sea Company.'

Edgar raised one sceptical eyebrow, but seemed otherwise unmoved. 'The Green Book?'

'You've heard of it?'

'I've *heard* of many things. The King's loyal friends in England make sure I do. The South Sea disaster is a judgement on those who let in a German prince and his greedy minions to rule the Stuart domain. I'm aware of all the highways and byways of the affair. But I'm not aware of a single reason why I should suppose that a . . . man like you . . . might have charge of the errant Mr Knight's sin-black secrets.'

'It's a long story. Chance and treachery are about the sum of it.'

'As of many a story.'

'I have the book, Mr Edgar. Believe me.'

'Why should I?'

'Because you can't afford not to. It represents a heaven-sent opportunity for you.'

'You don't look like a heavenly messenger to me.'

'The Green Book lists all the bribes paid to secure passage of the South Sea Bill last year. Exactly how much. And exactly who to.'

'Tell me, then. *Exactly* how much was it?'

'I'm no accountant. It would certainly take one to tease out the pounds, shillings and pence. Many hundreds of thousands of pounds is as close as I can get. More than a million, I'd guess.'

'Would you, though?' Edgar's gaze was calm but penetrating. He looked neither disbelieving nor convinced. 'And *exactly* who received this money?'

'I can give you some names.'

'Do.'

'Roberts; Rolt; Tufnell; Burridge; Scott; Chetwynd; Bampfield; Bland; Sebright; Drax.'

'Members of Parliament to a man.'

'You'd know them better than me, Mr Edgar. They're all listed.'

'Who else?'

'Carew; Bankes; Forrester; Montgomerie; Blundell; Lawson; Gordon—'

'Sir William Gordon? The Commissioner of Army Accounts?'

'Sir William Gordon, yes.' Estelle had insisted he memorize some of the names and now he realized how right she had been to. Edgar's expression was softening. His doubts were receding. 'And various peers.'

249

'Which ones?'

'Lord Gower; Lord Lansdowne; the Earl of Essex; the Marquess of Winchester; and the Earl of Sunderland.'

'Sunderland?'

'Yes.' Spandrel looked at Edgar with the confidence of knowing that what he said was absolutely true. 'The First Lord of the Treasury's isn't the most eminent name in the book.'

'No?'

'Far from it.'

'Whose is, then?'

'His master's.' Spandrel paused for effect. He was beginning to enjoy himself. 'The King.'

'The King?' Edgar smiled. 'I take it you are referring to the Elector of Hanover.'

'I beg your pardon.' Spandrel felt himself blushing at his mistake. In the looking-glass world of the Palazzo Muti, it was important to remember who was notionally a king and who was not. 'I do mean the Elector of Hanover. Of course. But whatever we call him . . .'

'He is listed.'

'Yes.'

'To the tune of what?'

'An allocation of one hundred thousand pounds in stock for a payment of only twenty.'

'When was the allocation made?'

'The fourteenth of April.'

'Then it signifies nothing. That was when the First Money Subscription opened. Twenty per cent would have been a normal first instalment.' Edgar shook his head. 'Dear me, Mr Spandrel. You seem to be just another bearskin jobber, of the kind the Stock Exchange always has in plentiful supply.' Seeing Spandrel's uncomprehending look, he added, 'You are trying to sell me the bear's skin before you have killed the bear.'

'No, no. You must let me finish. The K—' Spandrel gulped back the word. 'The Elector of Hanover,' he continued slowly, 'sold the stock back to the company on the thirteenth of June at a profit of sixty-eight thousand pounds. He never paid any more instalments.'

'No more instalments?' Edgar queried softly.

'None.'

'Sold back . . . and treated as fully paid?'

'Yes.'

Edgar pursed his lips. 'Were any other members of the Elector's family similarly treated?'

'Yes. The Prince of Wales. That is, I mean—'

'Let it pass. I know who you mean.'

'Also the Princess.'

'Aha.'

'As well as the Duchess of Kendal and her nieces.'

'As one would expect.'

'And the Countess von Platen.'

'Both mistresses. What a considerate lover the Elector is.'

'I should also mention . . .' Spandrel hesitated. He knew from what McIlwraith had told him of the political situation at Westminster that the name he was about to let fall was in many ways the most significant of all. 'Walpole.'

'*Robert* Walpole?'

'Yes.'

Edgar looked straight at him. 'You're sure of that?'

'I'm sure.'

'How much?'

'I can't say.'

'Why not?'

'Because . . .' Spandrel had employed Estelle's tactics faithfully and was not about to stop. He had told Edgar

251

enough. Now it was time to name their price. 'We need to agree terms, Mr Edgar.'

'Terms?'

'For your purchase of the book.'

'You are not making a gift of it to the cause, then?'

'No.'

'You are merely a thief, seeking to sell what he has stolen.'

'Do you want to buy it . . . or not?'

'How much did Walpole receive?'

'How much are you willing to pay to find out?'

'*How much*, Mr Spandrel' – Edgar let out a long, slow breath – 'are you demanding?'

'One hundred thousand pounds.'

'Absurd.'

'I don't think so.'

'The King hasn't the resources to pay such money.'

'It's not so very much . . . for a kingdom.'

'For a kingdom?' Edgar leaned back in his chair and rested his hand thoughtfully on the papers strewing his desk. A moment of silence passed. Then he looked up sharply. 'Why are you offering this to us instead of to the Elector? He'd pay handsomely to retrieve the evidence of his own corruption.'

'I lost all the money I spent on South Sea stock. Every penny. I was cheated. I want the people who cheated me to suffer for what they did.'

'Revenge, is it?'

'Partly.'

'But mostly greed.'

'Call it what you will. The price is a fair one.'

'The price is extortionate. But . . .' Edgar drummed his fingers. 'I will apprise the King of your proposition.'

'When can I have an answer?'

'Return here at noon tomorrow. By then, I should have something for you, be it an answer or no.'

'The Green Book blasts the reputation of every man in it, Mr Edgar. It can topple a throne. You'll never have—'

'I know what it can do. *If* what you say is true.'

'It's true.'

'Then be patient, Mr Spandrel.' Edgar nodded towards the door. 'Until noon tomorrow.'

Colonel Lachlan Drummond must once have cut an imposing figure. He was broad-shouldered and square-jawed enough to have led many a man into battle and many a woman into bed in his time. But that time was gone. Exiled in Rome with his make-believe king, he had sought consolations where he could find them. Now, bloated and bedraggled, his mind fuddled and his words slurred by drink, he slumped at a table in a private booth at the rear of L'Egiziano, a coffee-house just off the Corso, gazing blearily across at Nicholas Cloisterman, while a smile hovered complacently on his lips.

'The King's been entertaining no Dutch widows, my friend. You can be sure of that. The Queen would scratch out the eyes of any woman who—'

'You seem deliberately to misunderstand, Colonel. Mrs de Vries is no courtesan.'

'Whatever she is or isn't, she hasn't shown her face at the Palazzo Muti.'

'Is there anything to suggest that valuable information might have reached your master? Talk of another rising, perhaps?'

'There's always talk.'

'A recent change of mood. Anything.'

'We've been drinking Prince Charlie's health for the past three months. The birth of a son and heir has put

253

everyone in good spirits. I don't know about anything else. There's some . . . nervousness . . . now the Pope's up and died. But that's to be expected.'

'What I'm referring to would be known only to a few.'

'Aye. But I'm one of the few, d'you see?' Drummond tapped his nose. 'There's not a whisper in a corridor I don't get to hear in due course. Your Mrs de Vries is a bird that hasn't flown into our parish.'

'I wish I could be sure of that.'

'You can. She's not been here, my friend. She's not been near.' Drummond leaned forward, the brandy on his breath wafting over Cloisterman. 'Do you mean to wait in case there's sign of her?'

'I haven't decided.'

'Either way, vigilance doesn't come cheap.'

'You don't, Colonel, certainly.' Cloisterman lifted a purse from his pocket and slid it across the table. 'I'll bid you good afternoon,' he added, rising to his feet.

'Good afternoon to you, my friend.'

Leaving Drummond to count his money, Cloisterman hurried from the booth and threaded his way between the settles and tables in the main room of the coffee-house. Blain had assured him of Drummond's reliability as an informant, though whether Blain had ever met the fellow Cloisterman did not know. It was difficult to place much confidence in the good colonel's self-proclaimed vigilance. The only reassurance Cloisterman had obtained for his money was that the Green Book – and the havoc it might wreak – was not the talk of the Palazzo Muti.

The likelihood, Cloisterman consoled himself, was that Estelle de Vries had not yet reached Rome. It was therefore also likely, given the precautions Blain had taken for him in Florence, that she never would. Telling himself to feel more satisfied with his afternoon's work than he did, he stepped from L'Egiziano into the chill onset of a Roman night and strode down the street to its junction with the Corso, intending to cross the thorough-fare and make for his lodgings at the Casa Rossa.

A lantern illuminating a sign on a tobacconist's shop at the corner was all that saved him from a collision with a man hurrying along the Corso. As Cloisterman pulled sharply up, the man headed on across the side-street, apparently unaware of what had happened.

Cloisterman, for his part, stepped back to the wall of the shop and leaned against it for support, his heart racing. He had caught a clear sight of the man's face in the light of the lantern and had recognized him immedi-ately. He could still do so, in fact, by the set of his shoulders as he pressed on into the shadows.

'Spandrel,' Cloisterman whispered incredulously to himself. 'What are you doing here?' Instinctively, he started after him.

As he did so, another man brushed past him, heading in the same direction as Spandrel. He was short, thin as a whippet and almost as fleet-footed. Something in the angle of his head and the intent, forward tilt of his body told Cloisterman at once what he was about. He was following Spandrel too. There were others, it seemed, who wanted to know what the bankrupt English mapmaker was doing in Rome.

James Edward Stuart, Pretender to the thrones of Scotland and England, was nothing if not assiduous in his pretensions. He addressed himself seriously to every stray chance and frail hope of the restoration of his dynasty. In his dedication to the cause, however, stood revealed his weakness. He was a king by birth and upbringing, who clung to the title because it was the only thing he knew. Long-faced and lugubrious, he was

255

no-one's vision of the ideal monarch. As to whether he had the heart of a king, or his newly born son had for that matter, only time would tell.

But time was suddenly of the essence, as James Edgar's unaccustomed urgency of manner made clear. It was early evening at the Palazzo Muti and the king whose kingdom its walls comprised had intended to visit the nursery before dinner to dandle his celebrated infant. Instead, he found himself closeted with his secretary in earnest discussion of a potentially earth-shaking development.

'How important might this book be to us, Mr Edgar?'

'It proves the Elector of Hanover, his son, his daughter-in-law, his mistresses and most of his ministers, past and present, to be self-serving scoundrels.'

'Surely we knew that already.'

'But this *proves* it, sir. The nation is on its knees, brought low by the South Sea fraud. If your subjects understood how the prince who rules them had profited from their ruin, I believe they would rise against him and demand the return of their true king. I believe, in simple fact, that this book represents a surer prospect of success than any you or your father before you have ever enjoyed.'

'Then we must have it.'

'Indeed, sir. So we must.'

'How is it to be obtained?'

'This fellow Spandrel demands a sum of one hundred thousand pounds for its surrender.'

'So much?'

'I will persuade him to accept a lower figure. I have had him followed, naturally, but I feel sure he will not have the book about him. Some payment will probably be necessary. But if I may speak freely, sir . . .'

'Please do.'

'Our friends say London is in a ferment. Stanhope's acquittal has outraged the populace. Sunderland will doubtless have been acquitted by now as well, with Walpole's connivance. They are all in it together. And the Green Book will damn every one of them. Whatever we have to pay for it . . . will be a bargain.'

While in Rome the Pretender and his secretary contemplated the sudden opening of a host of attractive vistas, in London the Postmaster-General, James Craggs the elder, foresaw only ruin on the eve of his trial before the House of Commons. Beset by grief for his son and a keen knowledge of the truth of the charges laid against him, he resolved the matter by taking a fatal dose of laudanum. The last of the trials of senior ministers implicated in the South Sea scandal was thus over before it had begun. While in Rome other forms of trial were just about to begin.

CHAPTER TWENTY-FIVE

Bend or Break

Where was Estelle? It was nearly ten o'clock, yet still she had not returned to the Palazzetto Raguzzi. Spandrel was growing anxious. He had called at the Albergo Luna earlier on his way back from the Palazzo Muti, intending to claim a partial recovery from the illness that had supposedly prevented him accompanying Estelle on her afternoon tour with Buckthorn and Silverwood, but neither they nor she had been there. Perhaps they had decided to dine before returning to their lodgings. Perhaps Rome by night had proved as diverting as Rome by day.

This Spandrel doubted. Estelle would be as eager to hear how he had fared at the Pretender's court as he was to tell her. She would have found some way to prevail upon Buckthorn and Silverwood to that end. But clearly something had prevented her. What could it possibly be?

He had waited long enough. Another visit to the Albergo Luna would relieve his anxiety to some degree. For all he knew, Buckthorn and Silverwood might by now have arrived there with Estelle. He flung on his coat, extinguished the lamp and made for the door.

Cloisterman had spent several chill hours lurking in the shadows of the Piazza di Spagna, waiting for Spandrel to emerge from the Palazzetto or for Estelle de Vries to

258

enter. So far, neither had. The whippety fellow likewise dogging Spandrel's trail had vanished. The night had deepened. Cloisterman had grown cold and bored and less and less certain of what he should do.

Now, as ten o'clock struck in the tower of Trinità dei Monti, palely lit by the moon on the hill above the piazza, he decided to try his luck at the Albergo Luna, where Spandrel had called briefly on his way along the Via Condotti. Perhaps that was where Estelle was hiding. Certainly he did not doubt that she was somewhere close at hand.

Pulling his hat down over his eyes and his greatcoat collar up to meet it, he turned and hurried away across the piazza.

A few minutes later, Spandrel emerged from the Palazzetto Raguzzi and set off across the piazza, following unwittingly in Cloisterman's footsteps.

As he turned into the Via Condotti, he was surprised to see that a small crowd had gathered outside the Albergo Luna, which lay a hundred yards or so ahead. A coach had pulled up in front of the inn and there were shouts and whistles from the crowd. As Spandrel drew nearer, he saw that the coach was not one of the low-slung gilded conveyances he had already become accustomed to seeing on the streets, but was darkly painted and soberly styled, with shutters at the windows.

Then he stopped dead in his tracks. From the inn emerged two tall, black-greatcoated figures, holding between them a shorter, slighter man, whose hat toppled from his head as he was marched out and loaded into the coach to reveal a blond wig and a pale, disbelieving face. It was the face of Nicholas Cloisterman.

'The Romans do so savour every little drama of life, don't they?' The voice came from behind Spandrel as the coach door slammed and Cloisterman was driven away. Spandrel turned to find Buckthorn standing virtually at his shoulder, smiling blandly. 'Do you happen to know the poor fellow they've arrested?'

'Arrested?'

'Looks like it to me.' Buckthorn's gaze drifted towards the departing coach, then moved back to Spandrel. 'So, do you know him?'

'Of course not.'

'Really? That's odd. He's been keeping watch on the Palazzetto Raguzzi for the past few hours. Now he strolls down to the Luna and gets himself dragged off to the clink. *Deuced* odd, I'd say.'

'I know nothing about him. Where's Estelle?'

'With Naseby.'

'And where is he?'

'Not at the Luna. And just as well, it seems.'

'What do you mean, Buckthorn?'

'Don't be testy, old man. I'll be happy to explain.'

'Why not just tell me where they are?'

'Because it's not as simple as that. Let's go back to the Raguzzi. We can talk there.'

'We can talk here.'

'And be overheard? I'd really rather not take the risk. You'll agree a few precautions are in order when you hear what I have to say. And if the lovely Estelle's welfare is at the forefront of your concern – which as an ever-attentive cousin I'm sure it is – you'll indulge me on the point.' Buckthorn's smile broadened. 'Come along, do.'

It took them no more than five minutes to reach Spandrel's room at the Palazzetto Raguzzi. Nothing was said on the way, but in the silence Spandrel could read more than was good for his peace of mind. Buckthorn had changed from the rich, dunderheaded young wastrel he had seemed to be. He was somehow older, subtler, worldly-wiser. Or perhaps that was what he had been all along. Perhaps Giles Buckthorn, the spoilt and shallow Grand Tourist, was nothing but an artful impersonation. If so, Naseby Silverwood, his similarly minded friend, probably was as well. In which case . . .

'How are the beds here?' Buckthorn enquired, as Spandrel lit the lamps. 'Soft enough?'

'The accommodation's very comfortable.'

'I'm sure it is.'

'Do you mind telling me where—'

'Your cousin is? Haven't the vaguest, old man.'

'But you just said Estelle—'

'Estelle? Oh, is that who you mean? Sorry. I thought we'd dropped that pretence. Let's be honest. She's no more your cousin' – he smiled – 'than Naseby and I are chums from Oxford.'

'Where is she?'

'Somewhere safe and secure.'

'What do you mean by that?'

'I mean she's our prisoner. And she'll remain so until our business is concluded.'

'Your . . . *prisoner*?'

'Quite so. And in case you doubt me, here's something to convince you we're keeping a very close eye on her.' Buckthorn took something from his pocket and tossed it across to Spandrel.

Spandrel caught it in his right hand and gazed down in astonishment at what he saw nestling in his palm: a blue silk garter, of the kind, if it was not the very same, that he knew Estelle wore; that he knew oh so well.

Rage flooded into him. He made to lunge at Buckthorn, but the other man was too quick for him. A punch to the pit of the stomach doubled him up, then Buckthorn was behind him, pulling him half-upright. He

261

saw the blade of a knife flash in the lamplight. Then it was at his throat. He felt the edge of it pressing against his skin.

'We'll kill her if we have to, Spandrel,' Buckthorn rasped in his ear. 'You too.'

'What do you want?'

'Those jewels of hers she's so prudently lodged at a bank in every town we've stopped in. Not that we think they are jewels, of course. But treasure. Yes. Treasure they certainly are, of some kind, at any rate, which your anxiety to reach Rome suggests is worth more here than anywhere else. That's why we let you get this far.'

'I don't know what you're talking about.'

'But you do. You must do. You see, you're named on the Calderini receipt along with Estelle.' So he was. Estelle had insisted on a joint receipt. She was to keep it in case he ran into trouble at the Palazzo Muti. But both their signatures were required to reclaim what the receipt described as a *scatola di gioielli rossa*: a red jewel-box, containing a green book; *the* Green Book. 'Tell me one more lie, Spandrel, and I'll slit your throat.' Buckthorn's voice was as hard and sharp as the knife in his hand. 'Do you understand?'

'Yes.'

'Good. Now, what's in the box?'

'A book.'

'What kind of book?'

'An account book. It belongs to the chief cashier of the South Sea Company. It records all the bribes the company paid last year to get their bill through Parliament.'

'Does it, indeed? Whom did they bribe?'

'Members of Parliament. Government ministers. The royal family.'

'Hence Rome. You're trying to sell it to the Pretender, aren't you?'

'Yes.'

'What's your asking price?'

'One hundred thousand pounds.'

'Estelle does fly high, doesn't she? Well, I doubt you'd ever have got that much. But never mind. Who's the fellow we saw being marched out of the Albergo Luna?'

'Cloisterman. British vice-consul in Amsterdam.'

'Whence he followed you and Estelle, presumably. Who was de Vries?'

'A merchant there, entrusted with the book by one of the directors of the company.'

'I take it de Vries didn't meet with a natural death.'

'No.'

'So, you're murderers as well as thieves. Well, I'm sorry to have to disappoint you, I really am. Your efforts were all in vain. What are your arrangements with the Pretender?'

'I'm to meet his secretary, Mr Edgar, at noon tomorrow.'

'The arrangements have changed. I'll be going in your place. At eleven o'clock tomorrow morning, you'll meet me at the Banco Calderini, where you'll withdraw the box and surrender the contents to me. We'll already have persuaded Estelle to countersign the receipt and to give us the key to the box, so there'll be no difficulty. In exchange, I'll tell you where you can find her, alive and relatively unharmed. At that point, our business will be concluded. Should we meet again thereafter, it'll be the worse for you. For both of you. You follow?'

'I follow.'

'And you agree?'

'Yes.'

'I thought you would. Strictly between you and me, I'm not sure Estelle would, if your positions were reversed. But that's women for you, isn't it?' Suddenly, the knife was whipped away from Spandrel's throat. Buckthorn was in front of him now, backing towards the door, the knife held defensively before him. 'A piece of parting advice, Spandrel. *Always* look a gift-horse in the mouth. Oh, and don't try to follow me. You're simply not up to it.' He opened the door behind him. 'Good night,' he added. Then he stepped out into the passage and closed the door.

Spandrel raised a hand to his throat. He stared at the smear of blood on his fingers, then moved unsteadily across to the bed and sat down. He heard his breathing as if it were that of someone else, slowly returning to normal. His thoughts did so at the same pace, settling bleakly on the certainty that Buckthorn was right. He was no match for them. This was the end of his fond dream of wealth. As for Estelle, all he could do now was whatever it took to save her life. And then . . . But no. He could not look so far ahead. He could not bear to.

Cloisterman's ride in the shuttered black coach was a short one, so short that he was still struggling to understand what had happened when a change in the note of the horses' hoofbeats told him they were passing beneath a covered gateway into a courtyard of some kind. There he was bundled out and up some steps into a large, lamplit building. His guards marched him along an echoing, high-ceilinged corridor, then up a winding, stone-flagged staircase, finally delivering him to a first-floor room of some magnificence, decorated with frescoes, tapestries and a pair of opulent chandeliers in which every candle was burning.

In the centre of the room, behind a desk as large as

many a banqueting-table, sat a corpulent, heavy-lidded, goatee-bearded man of advanced age, dressed in the red robes and cap of a cardinal. He cast Cloisterman a darting, reptilian glance, but said nothing. Then Cloisterman looked towards the only other occupant of the room: a brawny, bright-eyed priest with cropped black hair and a cherubic flush to his cheeks, who was standing at one end of the table. He fixed Cloisterman with a twinkling gaze and said, in Irish-accented English, 'Good evening, Mr Cloisterman. Welcome to the Quirinal Palace. I am Father Monteith. This is His Excellency the Pro-Governor of the City of Rome, Cardinal Bortolazzi. He speaks no English, so you'll pardon me if I . . . articulate his thoughts.'

'What the devil is going on here, sir?' demanded Cloisterman, summoning as much outraged dignity as he could. 'Why was I dragged from the Albergo Luna like some . . . common criminal?'

'Because you were enquiring after a Mrs de Vries and had already displayed an interest in her travelling companion, Mr Spandrel.'

'What's that to you?'

'The Pro-Governor is responsible for the maintenance of peace and order in the city.'

'I'm threatening neither.'

'What are you here for?'

'To see the antiquities.'

'Come, come. That won't do. You've not been near the Colosseum, have you? But you have been near the Palazzo Muti. You've conferred with a notorious spy at King James's court. And Mr Spandrel has been in discussion with the King's private secretary.'

'I know nothing about any spy. Or what Spandrel may or may not have been doing.'

Monteith sighed. 'These denials are futile, Mr

Cloisterman. If the Pro-Governor is so minded, you can be consigned to a dungeon at the Castel Sant'Angelo for the rest of your life, with neither charge nor trial. You are not in the United Provinces now.'

'How did—' Cloisterman broke off, instantly regretting the admission.

'A guess, based on the Dutch ring to Mrs de Vries's name. But it's unimportant. Where you've come *from* does not concern us. Why you've come *here* does.'

'I'm the British vice-consul in Amsterdam.' The mention of dungeons had settled the issue in Cloisterman's mind. He could not continue trying to brazen his way out of whatever he was in. 'My Government—'

'Is no friend of His Holiness the Pope.' Monteith rounded the table and moved closer. 'As I'm sure you're aware, however, there is no pope at present. His Holiness Clement the Eleventh was gathered unto the Lord last week. Several more weeks are likely to elapse before his successor is elected by the College of Cardinals. When he is, he will no doubt wish to be assured that he finds his temporal realm in good order. The Pro-Governor is determined to ensure that he does.'

'So,' Cloisterman ventured, believing he had at last caught the priest's drift, 'the Pro-Governor's prime concern is to maintain the affairs of state . . . *in statu quo nunc.*'

'Indeed it is.' Monteith's head bobbed like that of a bird pecking at seed. '*Exactly* as they are now.'

'A sudden enhancement of the prospects of a restoration of the Stuart line to the British throne would not therefore be—'

'Any more compatible with that policy than their sudden extinction.'

'I see.'

'I'm glad you do. Now, the Pro-Governor does not wish to know what Mr Spandrel has been hawking around the Palazzo Muti. But he does wish to know whether your presence in Rome indicates that the consequences for your Government of His Majesty King James's acquisition of . . . whatever the article is . . . would be – how shall I put it? – disastrous.'

'That would be to put it lightly.'

'Would it, now?'

'I'm afraid so.'

'Well, well.' Monteith frowned. 'As bad as that.' Then his expression brightened. 'We shall just have to see what we can do.' He beamed at Cloisterman. 'Shan't we?'

Spandrel was still lying on his bed at the Palazzetto Raguzzi an hour later, staring sleeplessly into the darkness above his head, when he heard a noise at one of the windows. He sat up. The noise returned. It was surely that of a pebble striking the glass. He rose from the bed and crossed to the window. He had not bothered to close the shutters earlier and now had a clear view down into the moonlit piazza. A man was standing below him, preparing to throw another pebble. As he raised his head to aim, Spandrel recognized him. And froze in astonishment.

CHAPTER TWENTY-SIX

Lie Ledger

The Banco Calderini occupied the ground floor of a middling-sized palazzo near the Ponte Sant'Angelo. From the pavement in front of the bank, there was a clear view across the bridge of the Castel Sant'Angelo, the papal fortress that loomed above the Tiber. But Spandrel did not so much as glance towards it. In a deep shadow cast by the razor-sharp Roman sun, he waited, head bowed, as eleven o'clock struck on unseen church towers all around him.

Before the clocks had finished striking, his waiting ended. Buckthorn, dressed to the nines as usual, sauntered round the corner of the building and bade him an icy-smiled good morning. Spandrel said nothing, for nothing needed to be said. He led the way into the bank.

The marble-floored, high-ceilinged interior was cool and echoing, murmured consultations and shufflings of paper joining above them like the rustling of bats' wings. As they moved towards the counter, Buckthorn took something from his pocket and passed it to Spandrel. 'Duly countersigned,' he said softly. It was the receipt. 'And lo, what do we have here?' He jiggled the key to the jewel-box in his gloved palm.

The first clerk they approached spoke no English. There was a delay while a bilingual clerk was found. Then a further delay while he descended to the vault to fetch the jewel-box. Spandrel fell to studying Estelle's two signatures on the receipt. There was no discernible difference between them, no sign of suffering at the hands of her captors.

'She is well enough,' said Buckthorn, as if reading his thoughts. 'We have treated her better than she treated her husband.'

'Where is she?'

'All in good time. The book first.'

The clerk returned, carrying the scarlet jewel-box. He placed it on the counter and invited Spandrel to confirm that it had not been tampered with.

'Let's open it and see,' said Buckthorn. He unlocked the box and raised the lid. A green-covered book lay within. 'Is this a ledger which I see before me?' He chuckled, then closed the box. 'Sign for it, Spandrel.'

The clerk, who had displayed no reaction whatever on seeing what the jewel-box contained, offered Spandrel a pen. Spandrel countersigned the receipt and passed it to the clerk, along with two sequin coins: the agreed storage fee. '*Grazie, signore*,' said the clerk. The transaction was at an end.

Buckthorn gathered up the box and started towards the door. Spandrel took several hurried steps to catch up with him. He wanted to ask once more where Estelle was, but something held him back.

He was still hesitating when they reached the street. There Buckthorn stopped and turned to him with a smile. 'Your meek compliance is much appreciated, Spandrel. If I were you, I'd try some other kind of work. You're not equal to this kind. Nor, to speak candidly, are you equal to Estelle. But you'll be wanting to know where she is, nonetheless. And you'll be needing this.' He handed him a key – larger and heavier than the one that had opened the jewel-box. 'Go to the Theatre of

Marcellus. Look for a door with the letter E on it: E for Estelle. This is the key to the door. She'll be waiting for you inside.'

'But where is . . . the Theatre of Marcellus?'

'You'll find it, I'm sure. And now I really must be going. Naseby will be growing anxious, which isn't good for him. And we have an appointment at noon we really can't afford to miss.' He patted the jewel-box. 'Goodbye, Spandrel. It's been a pleasure.'

No sooner was Buckthorn out of sight than Spandrel hastened towards the Ponte Sant'Angelo. At the side of the road adjoining the bridge stood a calash, its driver seated and holding the reins, as if expecting a passenger. Spandrel climbed smartly aboard.

'*Dove?*' queried the driver.

'The Theatre of Marcellus,' Spandrel replied.

'*Si. Il Teatro di Marcello. Andiamo.*' The driver geed up the horses and they started away.

The Theatre of Marcellus stood close to the Tiber a mile or so to the south, where the river divided round the Isola Tiberina. It was an ancient Roman amphitheatre, atop which some later generation had added two storeys of their own to form a strange, hybrid palazzo. This too was now in decay, at a faster rate, it seemed, than the ruin it had squatted on. The lower arches of the amphitheatre had also been filled in, to form workshops and store-rooms. Business was being conducted in some, but most were closed, their heavy wooden doors firmly shut on whatever lay within.

Telling the driver to wait, Spandrel jumped down from the calash and began running round the curve of the building, shading his eyes as he trained them on the doors. Then he saw what he was looking for: a large E, crudely daubed in yellow paint.

He turned the key in the lock and pulled the door open. Sunlight flooded into a narrow, windowless chamber in which dust swirled, but nothing else moved. There was a table to one side, with a lamp standing on it. Otherwise the room was empty. Then, as his eyes adjusted to the gloom that lay beyond the sun's reach, he saw another door, in the middle of the rear wall. There was a barred vent above it, and through the vent came a voice from the space beyond. 'Is someone there?' It was Estelle. 'Help me. Please.'

'It's me,' Spandrel called. 'William.' Then he strode to the door, pulled back the bolts and flung it open.

She was crouched on a mattress that was actually too big for the floor it lay on and curled up against the wall at either end. The air was damp and fetid. Her face was smudged with dirt, her hair streaked with dust, her once-lovely pink moiré dress creased and stained. 'Thank God you found me,' she said, rising unsteadily to her feet. 'What has—' She swayed slightly and Spandrel stepped forward to support her.

'You're safe now. My God, Estelle, I thought they might have killed you.' He tried to put his arm round her, but she pushed him away.

'I'm sorry,' she said, squinting into the sunlight behind him. 'I can't bear to be touched while I'm so filthy.'

'That doesn't matter. At least you're alive.'

She stumbled past him into the outer room. 'Where are Buckthorn and Silverwood? Where are they, William?'

'I don't know. Possibly at the Palazzo Muti.'

'You didn't—' She looked round at him sharply. 'You didn't give them the book?'

271

'Not exactly.'

'Then where is it?'

'I'll explain later. We must get away from here.' He gathered up her cape, which lay crumpled on the mattress, and tried to put it round her, but she shook it off.

'Explain now.'

'It'll be better if—'

'*Now.*'

'Estelle—'

'Tell me, William.' Her gaze was stern, her ordeal forgotten, it seemed, in the face of what she deemed far more important. 'Where is the Green Book?'

'Gone.'

'Gone where?'

'Back to England. With Cloisterman.'

'What?' She stared at him disbelievingly.

'Buckthorn and Silverwood have a green-covered ledger filled with gibberish. Whether they realize that before, during or after their meeting with the Pretender's secretary at noon is in the lap of the gods. Whenever it is, though, they'll come looking for us, quite possibly with a pack of angry Highlanders at their backs. That's why we have to leave here. Now.'

'I'm going nowhere until you explain what's happened.' Estelle's voice was as cold and implacable as her face. Already, moments after being rescued, she was thinking more about what she had lost than about what she might have gained.

'Buckthorn and Silverwood must have told you what they meant to do.'

'Of course they told me. I was trusting you to find some way to outwit them.'

'How could I? They had your countersignature on the receipt.'

'I had to sign. They held a pistol to my head.'

'I feared for your life, Estelle. Buckthorn gave me . . . proof that they were holding you captive.'

'The garter. Is that it? Were you afraid they might rape me?'

'Yes.' Why the answer sounded foolish Spandrel could not tell. Yet, strangely, it did. 'Of course I was.'

'As they meant you to be. Poor credulous William. You agreed to their demands?'

'Yes. And I'd have given them what they wanted. But Cloisterman changed my mind.'

'How?'

'He came to me late last night and told me how matters stood. Apparently, the authorities know everything that happens at the Palazzo Muti. They weren't willing to let the sale of the book proceed in case the new pope didn't approve of the consequences. So, we had to be stopped. But without the Pretender realizing who'd stopped us. Cloisterman was to take the book back to the British Government. If we refused to let him and tried to sell it, we'd be arrested. When I told him about Buckthorn and Silverwood, he suggested giving them a fake ledger. The authorities instructed the bank to open the jewel-box with one of their skeleton keys. The real ledger was then impounded and handed over to Cloisterman. He's been given safe-conduct to the Tuscan border.'

'That book would have made us rich.'

'Not here, Estelle. Not in Rome. It wasn't destined to be.'

'And what is destined to be?'

'I've agreed we'll go south. To Naples. There's a trader sailing from the river-port at two o'clock. It's expecting to take on two passengers. I've packed our belongings. They're on the calash.'

'And what will we do in Naples?'

273

'I don't know.'

'No.' She looked at him sadly, almost pityingly. 'Exactly.'

Nothing was said as the calash bore them across the bridge onto the Isola Tiberina, then over the next bridge to the west bank of the Tiber and down to the vast riverside hospital of San Michele, beyond which lay their destination: the Porto di Ripa Grande, principal riverport of the city.

They found the trading ketch *Gabbiano* tied up and loading at the embankment steps. All they had to do was go aboard. But when their driver made to take their bags off the calash, Estelle told him to leave them where they were. The fellow looked helplessly at Spandrel, clearly unsure whose orders he should obey.

'We can't stay, Estelle,' reasoned Spandrel. 'You must understand that.'

For answer she merely sighed and began slowly pacing to and fro along the embankment, staring up into the blue vault of the sky and smoothing her hair as she walked. Tangled though it still was, it shimmered in the sunlight. A memory of running his fingers through those dark tresses came to Spandrel with a jag of pain, as of something precious that he had already lost.

'It's nearly one o'clock. They'll be looking for us by now. They're bound to be. We should be below decks – out of sight.'

'Hiding?' She stopped and tossed the word back at him.

'Yes.'

'And fleeing?'

'We have no choice.'

'*I* have a choice.'

She had never looked more beautiful than in that

moment, standing on the embankment above the jumble of boats and masts and furled sails, her hair awry, her dress stained, her eyes wide and accusing. It was futile. There was nothing she could do to retrieve the book. And yet it was magnificent. There was nothing she could *not* do. 'We have to go,' said Spandrel. 'I gave my word.'

'Your word. Not mine.'

'For God's sake, Estelle. Please.'

She looked at him long and coolly, then said, 'No. I will not go. Not this way.'

'Then how?'

'I'm going north.'

'You can't mean . . .'

'I'm not giving it up. I'm not letting *Mr* Cloisterman steal my future from under my nose.' She began walking towards the calash. 'You go to Naples, William. You keep your word. But don't ask me to go with you. I intend to be on the next coach north. Cloisterman can't be at the border yet. And even if he is—' She reached the calash, grabbed Spandrel's bag and heaved it to the ground, stumbling with the effort. Then she turned to the driver. '*Piazza del Popolo. Subito. Rapidamente.*'

CHAPTER TWENTY-SEVEN

Every Man's Hand

Spandrel stared down at the busy scene of loading and making ready aboard the *Gabbiano*. Half an hour had passed since Estelle's departure, but still he had not moved from the embankment. He had never felt less certain about anything in his life. To go with Estelle in pursuit of Cloisterman was folly, to remain in Rome madness. Yet, as Estelle had said, what was there for them to do in Naples? What was there for *him* to do? McIlwraith's money would soon run out. With the Green Book gone, only destitution awaited him, in an unknown city far from home – destitution and despair.

He had done his best. He had played the cards fate had dealt him as adroitly as he could contrive. But there had always been those cleverer and more ruthless than him to steal the hand. It would have been Buckthorn and Silverwood but for Cloisterman's intervention. 'You've thrown in your lot with a murderess,' Cloisterman had said to him the night before. 'You should be grateful to be let off so lightly.'

Grateful? No. He was not that. But lonely and home-sick, riddled with guilt and self-pity, he most certainly was. He knew why he had thrown in his lot with a murderess, if that was what Estelle really was. Money was not the half of it. For as long as he had been her secret lover and co-conspirator, life had been a revel of dreams and sensations he had never expected to experience. It had been . . . glorious. And now the glory was done. He had been given much and promised more. But all he was left with was the little his existence had previously amounted to.

Then he understood at last. He had to follow her. What they would achieve by going after Cloisterman he did not know. But at least they would achieve it – or fail to – together.

He hired a fly that had just delivered a passenger to the hospital. The most direct route to the Piazza del Popolo lay back the way they had come, crossing the Tiber uncomfortably close to the Theatre of Marcellus. Loth to take such a risk, Spandrel told the driver to cross by the next bridge up.

No sooner had they set off than a curricle, hard-driven by the look of the dust-cloud it was raising, bore down on them from the direction of the city. Spandrel's driver had to pull in to avoid a collision. As the curricle swept past, Spandrel realized that Buckthorn and Silverwood were aboard. They were heading for the river-port. How had they known where to look for him? Had someone overheard him talking to the calash-driver at the Theatre of Marcellus?

It hardly mattered now. Looking over his shoulder, Spandrel saw to his horror that they were reining in. They had seen him. And they would outrun the fly. There was no doubt of it. Even if they did not, what could he achieve by pressing on? He would simply endanger Estelle if he led them to the Piazza del Popolo.

The neighbourhood to his left was a warren of alleys and courtyards, where a man could travel faster on foot than by any carriage. His decision was made in the instant the thought came to him. He leaped from the fly, abandoning his bag, and began to run.

'Spandrel!' He heard Silverwood's piping voice from behind him. 'We want a word with you.'

He did not stop.

Spandrel was soon safe, at any rate from Buckthorn and Silverwood. Trastevere was an unfathomable maze of jumbled dwellings, where the poorest inhabitants of Rome lived in a seething squalor that made Cat and Dog Yard look almost desirable. The dull-eyed children and blank-faced women watched Spandrel plunge past them with indifference, but his peacock-clad pursuers would find themselves – not to mention their gold pocket-watches and silver snuff-boxes – the objects of considerable attention, once they had given up the curricle, as the narrow going would force them to.

Just as Spandrel could not be tracked through Trastevere, however, so he could not keep track of where he was. Whichever turn he took seemed only to lead uphill, away from the river and further from his destination. He could not turn back for fear of blundering into Buckthorn and Silverwood, so on he went, by crumbling steps and winding paths, till he suddenly emerged onto a wide road flanked by high-walled gardens. He was on the Janiculum Hill, commanding a view so extensive that he thought he could make out the twin domes of the churches that stood where the Corso reached the Piazza del Popolo. But what use was that – other than to tell him just how far he was from where he wanted to be?

There was nothing for it but to follow the line of the city wall round to the Vatican and hope to pick up a fly there. The afternoon was already well advanced. Every hour he lingered in Rome added to his peril. But the

Gabbiano would have sailed by now. He had thrown away one chance and not yet grasped another.

His pace quickened.

Spandrel entered the Piazza di San Pietro as an ant might stray onto a beach: as one tiny, insignificant speck in a vast landscape. The colonnades seemed to circumscribe a space too huge for him to comprehend. The sunlight sparkled in the fountains and cast a stretched and mina-tory shadow of the central obelisk to meet him, while the pillars and dome of St Peter's itself soared shimmeringly above the steps on the farther side of the piazza. It struck him for a moment that he had never seen anything made by man more beautiful than this.

But he could spare no time to relish even unparalleled beauty. He headed towards the steps leading up to St Peter's, at the foot of which were gathered several carriages, some of which might well be for hire.

He was about halfway between the obelisk and the steps when he realized someone was keeping pace with him away to the right. Glancing towards him, he saw that it was Silverwood. He stopped. So did Silverwood. Then a twitch of the fellow's head told him where Buckthorn was: no more than twenty yards to Spandrel's rear, osten-tatiously flicking back his coat to reveal the handle of the sword he was wearing.

Spandrel was outflanked and outmanoeuvred, his retreat cut off. They had either guessed where he would go in search of transport or had simply struck lucky; it hardly mattered which. His only hope now was the safety of holy ground. He ran to the steps and started up them. Silverwood rushed to intercept, but his rush was another man's dawdle. Buckthorn posed the greater threat and Spandrel could not afford to look back to see how close he was.

He reached the top of the steps and headed for the nearest door into the basilica. There were footsteps behind him now, pounding on the flagstones. Then a hand closed around his shoulder. 'Hold hard,' shouted Buckthorn, wrenching Spandrel round to face him. 'You'll answer to us before you do any praying.'

There was a knife in Buckthorn's hand. Spandrel had seen it before and knew how adept the fellow was with it. He moved instinctively away, but suddenly Silverwood was behind him, panting and swearing and pinning his arms at his back.

'Where's the Green Book, Spandrel?' Buckthorn feinted a lunge with the knife. 'Where is it, damn you?'

'I . . . don't have it.'

'Estelle must have, then. Where is she?'

'Out of your reach.'

'If that's true, I'll—'

Buckthorn never finished the sentence. Suddenly, the blunt end of a halberd struck his wrist and the knife clattered to the ground. Buckthorn cried out in pain. Then he and Silverwood were seized by tall, broadly built men in helmets and brightly striped uniforms. They were men of the Pope's Swiss Guard and Spandrel did not think he had ever been so pleased to see a soldier in his life.

'Take your hands off us,' bleated Silverwood. 'You can't treat English gentlemen like this.'

Clearly, however, the Swiss Guards believed they could. More probably, they neither spoke nor understood English and did not think people brandishing knives at the very door of St Peter's were at all likely to be gentlemen. They dragged the pair unceremoniously away.

'We'll come after you, Spandrel,' shouted Buckthorn. 'Don't think you've seen the last of us.'

A friar standing close by shook his head disapprovingly. '*Un coltello, qui*,' he said, to no-one in particular. '*Un sacrilegio.*' Sacrilege? Yes. Spandrel supposed what they had done could well count as that. And he also supposed sacrilege was something the papal authorities bore down on very hard indeed. On the whole, he reckoned he probably *had* seen the last of them.

He turned away and hurried back down the steps.

The Piazza del Popolo was empty. Not of people, of course. There was the normal assortment of *servitori*, tradesmen, travellers and idlers, the customary comings and goings through the gate. But of Estelle there was no sign. And to Spandrel, casting about him as he circled the piazza, it seemed that all he saw was emptiness.

More in hope than expectation, he approached a group of men sitting on the plinth at the foot of the obelisk. They were smoking and enjoying the afternoon sunshine. They looked as if they had been there some time. '*Parla inglese, signori?*' he ventured. But the only answer he received was a deal of squinting and shrugging. 'Has a coach left here for Florence? *Una carrozza? Per Firenze?*'

One of the men, the shortest and slightest built, stood up then and moved to Spandrel's elbow. 'Why should you want to know?' he asked, in a heather-soft Scottish accent.

Suddenly, the other men were on their feet as well, clustering round Spandrel. His arms were seized and held. 'Let go of me,' he protested. 'Who are you?' But he knew who they were. And he knew they were not going to let him go. There were no Swiss Guards to come to his aid here.

'There's a coach leaving this minute, Mr Spandrel. It's not going to Florence, I'm afraid. It's going to the Palazzo Muti. And you'll be riding in it.'

281

* * *

'A change of plan, Mr Spandrel?' said James Edgar, surveying him across his desk at the Palazzo Muti half an hour later. 'Where is the Green Book, pray?'

'I don't have it.'

'Did you ever?'

'Oh yes.'

'How did you come to lose it?'

'It's difficult to explain.'

'Really? I suggest you find a way to do so. And I suggest you adhere strictly to the truth while you're about it. Otherwise the Tiber will have another nameless corpse floating down it tonight.' Edgar frowned. 'You understand?'

Spandrel nodded. He understood. All too well.

The light was failing by the time Spandrel finished. It was the same chill point of late afternoon as when he had previously sat in Edgar's office, just twenty-four hours before. But everything had changed since then. He had nothing to sell and nothing to dream of. He did not even have any lies left to tell. And for that at least he was strangely grateful.

'Confession to a priest is seen in the true faith as a means of absolution, Mr Spandrel,' said Edgar, after a lengthy silence. 'A pity for you I'm not a priest.'

'I've given you what you asked for: the truth.'

'I believe you have. But it's not the truth I wanted to hear. Nor yet to carry to the King. The Green Book on its way to Tuscany with an escort of Swiss Guards. And treachery even in the Quirinal Palace. Cardinal Bortolazzi is a great friend of the Bishop of Osimo, who many believe will be the next pope. If the King cannot trust such people . . .' Edgar sighed. 'Some truths are better for kings not to know.'

'I'm sorry.'

'What use to me is your sorrow?'

'None, I suppose.'

'I'm glad you understand that.'

'But . . .'

'What's to become of you? Is that the question teetering on your lips?'

'Yes.'

'What's to become of any of us?' Edgar took an irritable swipe at the papers on his desk, then rose and strode to the window. He gazed out thoughtfully at the gathering dusk for several long moments, before turning round to face Spandrel once more. 'You are a lucky man, Mr Spandrel.'

'I am?'

'I have a proposition for you.'

'What is it?'

'Go before the King and tell him you never had the Green Book. Tell him you are an errant clerk of the South Sea Company, seeking to profit from the scraps of information you accumulated in the course of your work. Tell him that, as far as you know, the Green Book was seized from Mr Knight when he was arrested in Brabant and has been in the keeping of the Elector's ministers ever since.'

'But . . . that's not . . .'

'The truth? No. Exactly. It is a version of events that will make me look a fool and you a still more contemptible rogue than you actually are. But it will merely disappoint the King, not destroy him. And that is the most I can hope to gain from this sorry affair. For you, there is a reward.' Edgar smiled grimly. 'Survival.'

'You'll . . . let me go?'

'Not quite. I will persuade the King to spare you. And then I will send you away. There is a ship sailing from

Cività Vecchia on Wednesday. The master is a friend of ours. A true friend. You will be aboard. The ship is bound for Brest. And there you will be delivered. What you do then – so long as you never return to Rome – is none of my concern.'

'If I refuse . . . to tell this tale?'

Edgar shrugged. 'The Tiber awaits.'

'I had hoped . . . to go to Tuscany.'

'Fashion a different hope.'

'Can I not—'

'No.' Edgar looked straight at him. 'You cannot.'

'I have no choice but to accept?'

'No sane choice, certainly.'

'Then . . .'

'You accept?'

Brest, or Naples. What difference did it make? What had he achieved by going after Estelle other than to lose her over again? Even the truth was forfeit now. He had no choice. Perhaps he had never had one. He had no hope. But he did have life.

'Mr Spandrel?'

'Yes.' He nodded. 'I accept.'

INTERLUDE

April 1721–March 1722

CHAPTER TWENTY-EIGHT

Ways and Means

At the beginning of April, 1721, the Earl of Sunderland bowed to the seemingly inevitable and resigned as First Lord of the Treasury. Robert Walpole succeeded him with immediate effect, combining the office with that of Chancellor of the Exchequer. The nation's finances were thus squarely under Walpole's control. So indeed was the nation's mail, since he at once appointed his brother Galfridus Postmaster-General, or Interceptor-General, as some suspicious letter-writers dubbed him.

Sunderland was not quite a spent force, however. He remained Groom of the Stole and the King's principal confidant, with control of the Secret Service. He was willing to lie low for a while, but not to accept defeat. There were Members, actual and prospective, to be bribed and blackmailed before the general election due to be held the following March. If more of Sunderland's bought men than Walpole's found a seat in the new Parliament, their fortunes might yet be reversed.

The South Sea Sufferers Bill had meanwhile to make its way through the old Parliament. It was intended to be the last word on the notorious Bubble, recovering as much as possible from the estates of the directors and other convicted parties to defray the company's losses. But the last word was a long time being uttered. Each director was allowed to offset certain inescapable liabilities against his declared assets, necessitating lengthy argument at every stage. Deals were done, bargains struck, favours rewarded. Aislabie, the disgraced former Chancellor, escaped with the bulk of his fortune intact. The heiresses of the deceased Postmaster Craggs were leniently treated. And Sir Theodore Janssen, when his turn came, was mysteriously allowed to keep more than any other director.

The public knew what all this amounted to, of course: corruption in its normal nesting-ground – high places. But what was to be done? Robert Knight remained locked up and incommunicado in the Citadel at Antwerp. (Though not if persistent rumours of his secret removal elsewhere were to be believed.) Of his most sensitive records there was no apparent trace. Walpole waited until most Members had slipped away to their country seats before bringing the matter to the vote early in August. Despite the audible protests of aggrieved creditors outside the House, the Bill was passed. Legally, the South Sea affair was closed.

In Rome, the Pretender continued to believe that discontent over the issue would lead to his restoration. As a plot-hatchery, the Palazzo Muti remained busy. But plots and risings, especially the successful kind, were not quite the same thing. The newly elected Pope Innocent XIII – the former Bishop of Osimo – assured James Edward of his full support, before giving a very good impression of forgetting about him altogether.

At the end of September came news of Knight's escape from the supposedly escape-proof Antwerp Citadel and his abscondence across the border into France. The Brodrick Committee's oft-repeated demands for his extradition had finally been answered, though scarcely in the fashion its members had hoped. Another deal had clearly been done. Before the year was out, Knight had established himself in Paris as a financial consultant. As the former chief cashier of a bankrupt company with debts of £14,500,000, his credentials for such a role were manifestly impeccable.

That portion of the British public still hoarding South Sea shares certificates and notes of credit bore such events in a mood of half-stifled fury. Out of pocket and humour alike, they came to hate Walpole even more than the delinquent directors who had bilked them. 'The Screenmaster-General', as they called him, had screened his enemies as well as his friends, leaving the poor and the innocent to pay the price.

They can hardly have been surprised when it became known that the presses used for printing the Brodrick Committee's reports had been smashed on the orders of Viscount Townshend. There were to be no second editions. Not that those reports contained more than a fraction of the truth, of course. Only a certain green-covered ledger could tell the whole story. And nobody seemed to know where that might be found, or indeed whether it still existed.

With a collective sigh of relief on the part of those who had lost less by it than they had gained, the sorry saga of the South Sea was consigned, if not to history, then at least to history's waiting-room, whence it was likely to be retrieved only in the most extraordinary circumstances. The political world's attention shifted back to more familiar ground: a struggle for power between two able and ambitious men, to be decided by that orgy of auctioned loyalty known as a general election.

BOOK TWO

April–June 1722

CHAPTER TWENTY-NINE

Death of a Statesman

Viscount Townshend hurried across St James's Square through a breezy spring morning. His destination was the London residence of the Earl of Sunderland and the circumstances were sufficiently extraordinary for him to feel disconcertingly torn between elation and apprehension. The election results were still arriving, in their customary dribs and drabs, and those so far received had left the issue between Sunderland and Walpole tantalizingly undecided. But those results had suddenly become irrelevant. The issue *was* decided. Sunderland was dead.

News had reached Townshend the previous evening of Sunderland's sudden and as yet unexplained demise. It had been conveyed to him by the Lord Privy Seal, the Duke of Kingston, considerably put out at being instructed by Walpole to secure all the dead Earl's papers at once, even if it meant breaking into his study to do so. Kingston had not cared much for the propriety of this move and nor had Townshend. But he had nevertheless told Kingston to proceed. His brother-in-law's instincts, though sometimes brutal, were always to be trusted.

It was undeniable that the long struggle with Sunderland had taught Walpole some unedifying lessons. He had become more secretive, more devious, more downright egotistical. He hid the traits well, beneath bonhomie and bluster, but they were there for those who knew him best to detect. This latest turn of events was an example. With Sunderland scarcely cold in his death-bed, let alone his grave, Walpole was laying claim to documents that were technically the property of his family, trampling on the feelings of his pregnant widow and blithely incurring the wrath of his mother-in-law, the formidable Duchess of Marlborough. All this, moreover, he had embarked upon without troubling to consult Townshend.

A consultation of sorts was presumably what awaited Townshend at Spencer House. But it would be of the kind he was growing all too used to: one held after the event. Perhaps he should protest. 'Remember, my dear,' his darling Dolly had said to him more than once, 'Robin owes such a lot to you.' Townshend certainly remembered. But he was no longer sure his brother-in-law did.

Spencer House should have been a place of hushed mourning. Instead, it was a tumult of scurrying servants and bustling Treasury clerks. Several of the latter were loading tea-chests crammed with papers into a closed cart under the sheepish supervision of the Duke of Kingston, who cast Townshend a doleful look and shrugged his massive shoulders.

'He's been busy in Sunderland's study since dawn,' Kingston said, neither troubling nor needing to specify whom he meant. 'I found it locked, you know. I had to force the door open. Every drawer as well.' It was unlikely that Kingston had personally forced anything, but his point was made. 'Damned unseemly, I call it.'

'But necessary, no doubt,' said Townshend.

'Who's to say? All this' – he gestured at the tea-chests – 'is bound for Chelsea.' Walpole's London residence, then, not the Treasury. It was an eloquent distinction.

'How's the Countess?'

'In a torrent of tears, as you'd expect. And horror-struck to find a pack of inky-fingered clerks clumping about her home, as you'd also expect. She may have miscarried by now, for all I know.'

'Where's the, er . . .'

'Corpse? Taken away, thank God.' Kingston lowered his voice. 'They're talking of a post mortem.'

'Why?'

'Why do you think? The fellow was in rude good health when I last saw him.'

'You're surely not suggesting—'

'I'm suggesting nothing. But others won't be so circumspect, will they?'

'I dare say not.'

'Well, don't let me keep you. He's in no mood to greet late arrivals.'

'I'm not late.'

'No?' Kingston's voice sank to a whisper. 'If you ask me, we're all late when it comes to keeping up with him.'

There was unquestionably an air of pre-emptive industry in Sunderland's plundered study. Walpole sat at his dead foe's desk, a late breakfast mug of cider at his elbow and a drift of papers before him, his face flushed and beaming, like that of a farmer in their native Norfolk at the conclusion of a tiring but ample harvest.

'Ah, there you are, Charles. Welcome, welcome. How's the day?'

'Well enough,' Townshend conceded, though in truth he had only the faintest awareness of the weather.

'Better than well, I reckon. This is a day I didn't think we'd see.'

'What have Sunderland's papers revealed?'

'Much. You might almost say all. But—' He broke off and glared across at a pair of clerks filling boxes on the other side of the room. 'You two! Get out!'

'Yes, sir,' they chorused. 'At once, sir.' And out they got.

'Close the door behind you!' It clicked respectfully shut. 'I've had them under my feet all morning, damn their eyes.'

'It looks as if you've needed them.'

'For porterage, yes. It's about all they're good for. But sit down, Charles. Make yourself comfortable. You may as well.'

'Comfortable? In a dead man's study? I don't know about that.' Nevertheless, Townshend drew up a chair. As he did so, his eye was taken by a portrait above the fireplace of a good-looking young man in military costume of the Civil War era. 'An ancestor?'

'The first Earl. Killed at the battle of Newbury, a few months after he was given the title.'

'Sunderland's grandfather?'

'Yes. Note that. The grandfather, not the father. The second Earl was the same brand of scheming trimmer as his son. Maybe Sunderland wanted someone more inspiring to look at over his mantelpiece.'

'Have you found anything inspiring to look at?' Townshend nodded at the slew of papers on the desk.

'You could say so. Sunderland seems to have been mighty selective about passing on what the Secret Service brought him.'

'Has he held back anything important?'

'It's only the important stuff he *has* held back. You and Carteret can pick out the bones when it's all been collated. Carteret tells me, by the way, that he may have found someone who can give us more reliable information on the doings of the Pretender than the kilted drunkards we normally employ.'

'Baron von Stosch.'

'That's his name. The genuine article, you reckon?'

'About as genuine as a diamond necklace on a Haymarket whore. But he could be useful.'

'He'll need to be if I read these runes aright.'

'What is it, Robin?' Townshend sat forward, his curiosity aroused. 'Jacobite rumblings?'

'There are always rumblings. This is something more. What do you make of these?' Walpole plucked a batch of papers from the pile before him and tossed it across the desk.

It was a list of names, running to several pages, arranged under county headings. The names were familiar to Townshend. Many of them were known Jacobites. Many more were not. 'These surely don't all belong in the same basket,' he said. 'You're not suggesting . . .'

'Look at Norfolk.'

Townshend leafed forward to their own county and read the names, with rising incredulity. 'Bacon, l'Estrange, Heron, North, Wodehouse.' He stopped. 'Some of these are our bought men.'

'But some men sell themselves twice over. Ever hear of a lawyer called Christopher Layer?'

'I don't think so. Hold on, though. Not Layer of Aylsham?'

'You have him. Not a credit to his profession, as you know. That list seems to be his handiwork. And Secret Service reports say Layer visited Rome last summer.'

'He's gone over to the Pretender?'

'To the extent of boasting he'll be Lord Chancellor under King James, apparently.'

'Then . . . how did Sunderland . . . come by his list?'

'There's the question, Charles. How indeed? Perhaps he was simply sent it. Perhaps he asked for it to be drawn up. Sudden death leaves no time for the disposal of incriminating documents. That's the best of it. On the one hand the Secret Service is busy telling Sunderland that Layer's an active Jacobite plotter known to be in regular communication with one James Johnson, an alias, they believe, of none other than George Kelly.'

'Secretary to the Bishop of Rochester.'

'Exactly. Our least loyal prelate. That, as I say, is on the one hand. On the other, Sunderland has Layer's list in his possession, bearing every appearance of a muster-roll of traitors and their camp-followers, including twenty-three peers and eighty-three Members of Parliament.' Walpole grinned. 'I counted.'

'How long has he had the list?'

'Who knows? Long enough to alert the King's ministers to its contents, I'd have thought. But he didn't, did he? And this may be the reason.' Walpole slid a single sheet of paper across the desk to join the pages of Layer's list.

Townshend picked up the sheet of paper. It was a letter, addressed to Sunderland. As he read it, his mouth fell open in surprise. Then he read it again, this time aloud. '"I am greatly obliged to your lordship for the service you have rendered my cause and wish to assure your lordship that such service will be well rewarded. Your privileged foreknowledge of the Electoral itinerary will be our sure and certain guide in determining when it would be most propitious to set our enterprise afoot. It will be an enterprise of honour and of right and to find that you have as keen a sense as did your grandfather of where honour and right abide is to me a distinct and pronounced pleasure."'

'You didn't know the Pretender had such a florid style of expression, did you, Charles?'

'"Jacobus Rex."' Townshend read the signature in no more than a murmur. Then he looked at the date. 'This was written less than a month ago.'

'So it appears. In perfect confidence, so it also appears. But I could hardly ask Galfridus to rifle through Sunderland's post-bag, could I? There are limits.' Walpole sighed. 'This is what comes of abiding by them.'

'I can hardly believe it, Robin. Sunderland . . . and the Pretender.'

'He'd have thrown in his lot with the Devil himself to get the better of me.'

The use of the singular pronoun registered somewhere in Townshend's confused thoughts. *Me*, not *us*. It was telling, in its way. But not as telling as the letter in his hand. 'What's meant by the . . . "Electoral itinerary", do you suppose?'

'The date of the King's departure for Hanover, I'd surmise. He's set on going this year. As to precisely when, who'd know sooner than his Groom of the Stole?'

'They plan to strike when the King's out of the country?'

'Or worse – to assassinate him on the road to Hanover.'

'Surely Sunderland wouldn't have put his name to that.'

'He put his name to something. Of course, if he'd succeeded in packing the House with his creatures and ousting us from office, he could have exposed the plot and claimed the credit for saving the kingdom. No doubt he only meant to go through with it if the elections went against him. As our managers seem to reckon they generally have. A desperate man, our Sunderland. And now a dead one.'

'What are we to do?'

'Nothing, for the moment. I want the ringleaders, Charles. And I mean to have them.' Walpole sat back in his chair. 'So, let them think they're safe for a little longer yet. Let them plot away their days while we gather the evidence to damn them.'

'Where's such evidence to be found? This letter condemns Sunderland, not his co-conspirators.'

'We must draw them out.' Walpole smiled. 'And I think I may have found a way to do just that. Sir Theodore Janssen came to see me a few days ago.'

'Is he still complaining about his treatment?'

'With decreasing energy. No, no. He came to see me because of an undertaking I secured from him while he was in the Tower – an undertaking to keep me advised of any developments in the matter of the Green Book.'

'How can there be any developments now?'

'I expected none, certainly. But what Janssen said gives me—' There was a sudden commotion outside. Kingston's voice could be heard above that of another man. 'Ah! That'll be Lord Godolphin.'

'Godolphin? What will he say when he finds us taking our ease in his brother-in-law's study?'

'Very little, when we show him that letter. I suggested he call, as a matter of fact.'

'Why?'

'So that one of Sunderland's relatives could witness our destruction of the letter.'

'You mean to destroy it?'

'Certainly. As an act of compassion, to spare the noble Earl's reputation and his family's feelings. That should take the wind out of Madam Marlborough's sails, don't you reckon?' Walpole winked. 'It's not the dead we need to snare, Charles. It's the living.'

CHAPTER THIRTY

The Wanderer Returns

'Hello, Ma.'

Spandrel's greeting was hardly equal to the momentousness of the occasion. His mother gaped at him in astonishment for fully half a minute, seemingly – and understandably – unable to believe that he was standing before her, alive and well, alive and *uncommonly* well, to judge by his healthy complexion and newish clothes. Fifteen months of unexplained absence, during which she had often been reduced to believing him dead, had ended on an April morning of fitful sunshine, with her opening the door in answer to a strangely familiar knock and finding her son standing before her, smiling a smile she knew so well.

'Aren't you going to give me a kiss?'

She did kiss him, of course, and hugged him too. Tears started to her eyes. She hugged him again, then stood back and frowned at him. 'I thought you were dead, boy. You know that?'

'Not dead, Ma. As you can see.'

'Come inside and close the door before we have half the neighbourhood goggling at you.'

'I bumped into Annie Welsh in the yard.'

'What did she say to you?'

'Something about a bad penny.'

'She probably remembers what I said to her when you first went missing.'

'What was that?'

'That I hoped for your sake you had a good excuse for leaving me in the lurch.'

'I don't know about in the lurch.' Spandrel looked around the room. The piles of washing and the rack-load drying before the fire indicated that his mother was still plying her trade as a washerwoman. 'You probably found living was cheaper without me.'

'Cheaper, maybe. But not easier.' She grabbed his left ear lobe, as she often had when he misbehaved as a child. 'What have you been up to?'

'Ow!' Spandrel's exaggerated cry persuaded her to let him go. 'Some breakfast would be nice.'

'I'm surprised you don't expect a fatted calf.'

'Have a heart, Ma.'

'Lucky for you I've a bigger heart than's good for me. I'll make breakfast. While *you* explain yourself.'

Explaining himself was something Spandrel had already given much thought to. The Green Book – and the secrets it contained – was a subject he had no intention of broaching to his mother. He doubted she would be able to comprehend what he himself now found difficult to believe. The year that had passed since his departure from Rome had cast the events that had led him there in the first place into a semi-fabulous compartment of his memory. And he was content for them to remain there. Accordingly, while admitting that Sir Theodore Janssen had sent him on a secret errand to Amsterdam, he claimed that he had no idea what the package he had been charged to carry might have contained. He had been robbed of it in a tavern in Amsterdam, so he related, and, ashamed of such foolishness, had remained abroad rather than return home empty-handed to face Sir Theodore's wrath.

His account grafted itself at this point onto the truth. For the past year, he had worked as a surveyor's assistant in the French city of Rennes. He had met the surveyor, a kindly but ailing fellow much in need of assistance, by the name of Jean-Luc Taillard, during a coach journey (from Brest, a detail he omitted). Taillard, having no family of his own, had appointed Spandrel his heir. And Taillard's recent death had left Spandrel in possession of his life savings, amounting to 15,000 livres – about £1,000. This was a fraction of what Spandrel had dreamt the Green Book might bring him. But it was also far more than he had ever had to his name. And it meant he could return to England without fear of being imprisoned for debt.

'All the debts are paid, Ma,' he said, as he finished his breakfast. 'And there's plenty left over.'

'To spend on what, may I ask?'

'Somewhere better for you to live, to start with. You'll be sending washing out, not taking it in. And I'll be finishing the map.'

'That old dream of your father's?'

'This is one dream that's going to come true.'

'You mean that?'

'I certainly do.'

'All our troubles are over?'

'Yes. Thanks to Monsieur Taillard.' He plucked a flagon of gin from his bag and pulled out the cork. 'Let's drink to happier times.'

'You'll be the ruin of me, boy,' said his mother, unable to stifle a grin.

Viscount Townshend hurried into the Treasury that morning with an altogether lighter tread than he had felt capable of when entering Spencer House the previous day. This time, he had news for Walpole, not the other way about, and it was a rare enough experience for him to relish.

Walpole was standing by the window of his office, munching an apple and gazing out at a leash of deer in St James's Park. He looked exactly what Townshend knew him not to be – a man without a care in the world. But Townshend also knew that the cares of state were what lent him such a genial aspect. They were what made him happy.

'What do you have for me, Charles? Something, I'll be bound. I've seen that twinkle in your eye too often to be wrong.'

'A despatch from Sir Luke Schaub.' (Schaub was the British Ambassador in Paris, second only to Rome as a centre of Jacobite plotting.) 'Sent two days ago.' (Sent, then, on the day of Sunderland's death.)

'What does Sir Luke have to say?'

'Cardinal Dubois has alerted him to a request from the Pretender for the use of three thousand French troops.'

'When?'

'Within weeks.'

'How fortunate we are that the French Foreign Minister is such a devious man.' Walpole raised the window and tossed his half-eaten apple out through the gap, then turned to Townshend with a broad smile. 'It seems we'd have known something was afoot even without the run of Sunderland's study. But no doubt Sunderland would have persuaded the King there was nothing to worry about.'

'We should inform His Majesty.'

'I agree. We'll see him this afternoon. You'd better bring Carteret with you. It'll give the impression we're all of one mind.' Walpole chuckled. 'But then we are, of course.'

Shopping for anything but the barest necessities was for Margaret Spandrel a half-forgotten indulgence. Shopping for a new home was something she had not expected to do this side of Heaven. But that afternoon, equipped with a copy of the *London Journal* and the addresses of several reputable house agents, she accompanied her son on a tour of properties which were considerably larger and more elegant than many of those where she had latterly called to collect washing and which – miracle of miracles – William assured her they could afford.

Yet she was not to be lured into extravagance. Such money as they had should be used wisely. There were only two of them. They deserved no more than they needed: a modest level of comfort. This they found to her satisfaction – though not entirely to William's – on the second floor of a house on the southern side of Leicester Fields.

'Four rooms and a palace in view whenever you look out of the window for fourteen shillings a week,' observed the agent. 'You'll not do better.'

The palace in question was actually Leicester House, whither the Prince of Wales had fled after falling out with his father a few years previously and being expelled from St James's. It was not a palace and it did not look like one. But the square was quiet and its residents respectable. It would do. It would do very well indeed. They took the lease.

In the King's closet at St James's, which really was a palace even though some had been rude enough to suggest that it looked no more like one than Leicester House, what would do and what would not do were also matters of moment.

The King was not in one of his more pliable moods. Sunderland's death had shocked him to whatever lay at the core of his Germanic being and his reaction veered between the lachrymose and the suspicious. The triumvirate of ministers facing him – First Lord of the Treasury Walpole and Secretaries of State Townshend and Carteret – wished, it seemed, to vex him with problems beyond his fathoming while failing to answer the questions that most troubled him.

'What made Lord Sunderland to die?' he demanded, not for the first time that afternoon.

'Pleurisy,' said Walpole. 'According to the doctors.'

'Pleurisy? So sudden?'

'It is a puzzle,' remarked Lord Carteret, despite a sharp look from Walpole. The youngest and best bred of the three, Carteret impressed the King by his fine manners and independence of mind. Would that he could have more such courtiers about him, instead of coarse-tongued, beetle-browed Norfolkmen. 'But of puzzles we have no lack.'

'Nor of plots, Your Majesty,' said Townshend. 'There seems no doubt that the Pretender is set upon another attempt.'

'They tell us his son may die also.'

The ministers needed to exchange several glances before realizing that the King was referring not to the Pretender's son but to the Honourable William Spencer, youngest son of the late Earl of Sunderland. 'The boy has smallpox, sir,' said Walpole. 'It's not connected with—'

'Where is the Duke of Newcastle?' barked the King. 'We are needful.'

'I'm sure the Lord Chamberlain will wait upon you

306

directly, sir,' said Townshend. 'He has as yet, however, no knowledge of the threat to your person.'

'Person? Threat?'

'We fear it does amount to that,' said Carteret.

'Who? When? How?'

'The Jacobites,' said Walpole darkly. 'When you travel to Hanover. An assassin on the road. Simultaneous with—' He broke off, then began again, expressing himself more simply. 'At the same time as a rising here in London.'

'In the circumstances . . .' Townshend began.

'It would be best to postpone your visit to Hanover,' Walpole continued. 'We must have regard for Your Majesty's safety.'

'I will go to Hanover.'

'Perhaps not this year.'

'*I will go.*'

'There is still much resentment among your subjects on account of the *Angelegenheit South Sea*,' said Carteret, smiling faintly at his own Germanism. 'That is what the Jacobites hope to exploit. We should give them no opportunity.'

'It is easy enough to frustrate their plans now we know of them,' said Townshend. 'We can station troops in Hyde Park and expel all papists and non-jurors from the city. That, together with Cardinal Dubois' refusal of assistance for the Pretender and his withdrawal of Irish regiments from the Channel ports—'

'And the postponement of your visit to Hanover,' put in Walpole.

'Should render us safe,' Townshend concluded.

'*Ja, ja.*' The King chewed at his knuckles. 'I stay here,' he conceded glumly.

'But for the moment,' said Walpole, 'we should do nothing.'

'Nothing?' The King glared at him. '*Nichts?*'

'Nothing to alert them to our knowledge of their plans. Once they know the game is up, they will go to ground. We will not catch them then.'

'So how will we – how will *you*, Mr Walpole – catch them?'

'By luring them into betraying themselves.'

'We believe the Bishop of Rochester to be at the bottom of it,' put in Townshend.

'No doubt he dreams of becoming Archbishop of Canterbury,' Carteret remarked.

'*Verräter*,' growled the King. 'Why do we let Atterbury to give sermons in Westminster Abbey when he plots behind us?' Francis Atterbury was Dean of Westminster Abbey as well as Bishop of Rochester. His sermons in the former capacity, uttered a mere stone's throw from the Palace, had often been thinly veiled dalliances with treason. Small wonder that the King did not understand why he had to tolerate him. But there *were* reasons. And they were good ones.

'He is undeniably popular,' said Townshend.

'A veritable darling of the mob,' said Carteret, smiling weakly. 'Against whom there is a singular lack of evidence.'

'Evidence that would secure his conviction in court, that is,' added Townshend.

'But give me a few weeks,' said Walpole, 'and I think I can gather such evidence.'

The King frowned at him. 'How?'

'You'll remember, sir, the . . . Green Book?'

'*Das Grüne Buch?*' The inflexion of horror in the King's voice suggested he was hardly likely to have forgotten it.

'Indeed, sir.' Walpole smiled at him reassuringly. 'I believe we can use it to bait a trap . . . that will snap shut round Bishop Atterbury's overweening neck.'

Margaret Spandrel returned to Cat and Dog Yard that afternoon to commence the less than daunting task of packing her belongings in readiness for the move to Leicester Fields. William did not accompany her. On the pretext of visiting the engraver who was holding the completed sheets of the map (and who he would later say had not been at home), he left her to make her way back there alone. He headed north to Bloomsbury, an area of the city favoured by those who had sufficient money to buy themselves a charming view of the meadow-patched hills of Hampstead and Highgate. George Chesney, a director of the New River Company, which piped Hertfordshire spring water to a goodly portion of Londoners from its reservoir at Islington, was one such person. His home in Great Ormond Street backed onto this vista of rural meadowland, while presenting an imposing Palladian face to the city.

The Chesney residence was not Spandrel's destination, much as he would have liked it to be. The year he had spent working for Monsieur Taillard had rid him of many delusions, most notably the idea that anything could be had for nothing, be it beauty *or* wealth. Life could only be bettered by honest endeavour. He was financially independent because of such endeavour, whereas fortune-hunting across half of Europe had yielded only fear and a fugitive's despair. All that was behind him. He missed old Taillard, he really did. He wished the poor fellow could have lived longer. But his death had handed Spandrel an opportunity to improve his station in society. For that he needed a wife, not a dangerously alluring dream-lover. And as a wife Maria Chesney would be ideal. But was she still available? He could hardly knock on her father's door and ask. He could, however, enquire of the Chesneys' loquacious footman, Sam Burrows, who was unlikely to let a Saturday afternoon pass into evening without calling at his favourite local tavern, the Goat.

'Mr Spandrel, as I live and breathe.' Sam was already pink-gilled and grinning when Spandrel found him. He had enjoyed a profitable afternoon at the cock-fights, so he explained, and was celebrating. But an excess of ale did not quite swamp his surprise. 'I had you down as dead – or in the clink.'

'You were nearly right on both counts.'

'Instead of which, here you are, looking the real gent.'

'That's because I am one.'

'If you say so, Mr Spandrel.'

'I do.'

'What brings you out this way?'

'Can't you guess?'

'Oh, that's it, is it?' Sam put down his mug and wiped his mouth. 'You're still set on Miss Maria.'

'I might be.'

'I'm sorry, Mr Spandrel.' To his credit, Sam actually looked as if he was. 'You're too late.'

'She's married?'

'All but. She'll be Mrs Surtees come July.'

Spandrel sighed. 'I suppose I should have—' Then he stopped and looked at Sam intently. 'Did you say Surtees?'

'I did.'

'Not . . . Dick Surtees?'

'Well, he calls himself Richard, but . . .' Sam frowned. 'Do you know him, then?'

310

CHAPTER THIRTY-ONE

A Friend in Need

As apprentices, William Spandrel and his then very good friend Dick Surtees had often marked the close of the working day by adjourning to the Hood Inn near Smithfield. Spandrel had nominated it as a rendezvous in the note he had persuaded Sam to deliver for the highly practical reasons that he could be sure it would be open on a Sunday and that Dick knew where it was. Waiting there the following afternoon, however, the choice of venue began to prey on his mind, weighed down as it was by memories of the things he had lost in the years since they had been regular customers there, Dick's friendship not least among the losses.

Spandrel had been prepared to hear that Maria was married, or engaged to be so. He had almost expected it. But that her betrothed should be none other than Dick Surtees, failed mapmaker and aspiring man of the world, was a shock he had still not recovered from. He could have no fundamental complaint. Dick owed him nothing. Except an explanation. Yes, on that point Spandrel was clear. He *was* owed an explanation.

It seemed that Surtees agreed with him, for it was only a few minutes past the time Spandrel had specified in the note when a familiar figure threaded through the smoke-wreathed ruck to join him. The slim, slope-shouldered physique was the same, as were the dark, evasive eyes.

311

But Surtees' appearance had nonetheless been transformed. There were braided buttonholes and deep, embroidered cuffs on his coat, and the cream cravat and grey-black wig beneath the fancily brimmed hat singled him out not just as a gentleman but as a well-heeled student of fashion.

'Billy, I can't tell you how good it is to see you,' he said, clapping Spandrel on the shoulder and sitting down beside him. 'How long has it been?'

'Seven years.'

'Seven years that have treated you well, by the look of you. New suit?'

'Not as new as yours.'

'This?' Surtees flexed his cuffs. 'Well, you have to put on a show, don't you?'

'Not for old friends.'

'No. I suppose not.' For a moment, Surtees looked almost sheepish. 'I had your note.'

'I was surprised when Sam told me of your engagement.'

'Ah, that. Yes. Well, you would be.'

'How did it happen?'

'I sometimes wonder myself.' Surtees grabbed the sleeve of a waiter as he wandered by and ordered some brandy. 'Yes, I sometimes do.'

'My father died.'

'I know. I was sorry to hear of it.'

'How *did* you hear of it?'

'When I came back to London last autumn, I thought I'd look you up. For old times' sake. Reports had it your father had got into debt and then into the Fleet Prison and then . . .' Surtees shrugged. 'Sorry.'

'Did these . . . reports . . . mention me?'

'Oh yes. They said you'd fled abroad.'

'I didn't flee.'

'You don't have to explain yourself to me, Billy.'

'I'd be happy to. If you explained *yourself* to *me*.'

'Me? I made good. Simple as that.'

'Abroad?'

'Yes. Paris. You've heard of the, er . . .' Surtees lowered his voice. 'Mississippi Company?'

'I thought it crashed, like the South Sea.'

'Oh, it did. But I sold just at the right time. *Acheter la fumée; vendre la fumée.* It's a game. You have to know the rules.'

'A game of buying and selling smoke.'

'You, er, *parlez le français*, Billy?' Surtees looked quite taken aback.

'I spent some time there myself.'

'In Paris?'

'No. Rennes. Where I made good as well, out of something more substantial than smoke. And I came home, hoping I might still be able to . . .'

'Capture Maria's heart.'

'Yes, Dick. Exactly.'

Surtees' brandy arrived. He poured them a glass each. 'Sorry,' he said, by way of apologetic toast.

'But I find *you've* captured her heart.'

'Yes. Well, she's a lovely girl. You know that.'

'Yes. I do.'

'I'll, er, make her happy. You have my word.'

'How did you meet her?'

'That was . . . thanks to you, actually.'

'*Me?*'

'I remembered you'd said what a treasure she was. Even when she was no more than fifteen. So, when I heard you'd left London, I, er, decided to try my luck.'

'You seem to have had a lot of that – luck.'

'More than my fair share, probably. The father *and* the daughter have taken to me.'

'The mother too, I expect.'

'Since you mention it . . .' Surtees grinned nervously. 'Yes.'

'And you're to be married in the summer.'

'The thirtieth of June.'

'Perhaps I should congratulate you.'

'No need to be sarcastical. It couldn't be helped.'

'Couldn't it?'

'No-one had seen hide or hair of you in months and no-one expected to. I thought you'd forgotten all about her. So did she.'

'Encouraged by you, no doubt.'

'Be reasonable, Billy. How was I to know you'd turn up like this?'

Spandrel looked at his former friend long and hard before admitting, 'You weren't, I suppose.'

'It's damned unfortunate, but . . .' Surtees grimaced. 'There it is.'

'Be sure you *do* make her happy.'

'I will. You can rely on it. You could even, er, help me to.'

'What's that supposed to mean?'

'You've left her life, Billy. No sense trying to come back into it.'

'Are you warning me off?'

'Good God, of course I'm not. I'm just . . .'

'Asking me to give you a clear run.'

'Well, I, er, wouldn't put it quite like that, but . . .' Surtees shaped a smile that somehow suggested he was both grateful for not having to express the sentiment himself and a little ashamed of letting Spandrel do it for him. 'Yes. That's what I'm asking you to do. Leave well alone. For Maria's sake.'

*   *   *

Spandrel made his way back to Cat and Dog Yard as the sunny afternoon gave way to a pigeon-grey evening. Dick Surtees was right, of course. Spandrel would achieve nothing by trying to come between Maria and her intended, unless it was to make a fool of himself. He had had his chance and it had slipped through his fingers. Now, the only sensible course was to seize the other chances that had come his way. As Maria had forgotten him, so he would have to forget her.

'William Spandrel?'

The voice echoed like a muffled bell in the cramped passage as Spandrel entered from the yard. A tall, broadly built man in dark clothes loomed in front of him and the shadow of another man fell across him from behind. He was suddenly surrounded.

'William Spandrel?' came the question once more.

'Yes. I . . .'

'Come with us, please.'

Powerful hands closed around Spandrel's elbows and shoulders. He was marched back out into the yard almost without being aware of it. 'What . . . Who are you?' An absurd thought came into his mind. 'I've paid my debts.' Then he remembered: it was Sunday. 'You can't be bailiffs.'

'We don't collect debts, Spandrel. We collect people.'

'What?'

'You're wanted.'

'Who by?'

'You'll find out soon enough. There's a carriage waiting. Do you want to go quietly?' The cold head of a cudgel pressed against Spandrel's cheekbone. 'Or very quietly?'

*   *   *

315

The carriage was shuttered and Spandrel was held fast by his captors, who remained as reticent as they were threatening. He could see no more than twilit shards of street corners through the gap between the shutters. But he had not mapped every alley and highway of London for nothing. He tracked their route in his mind, judging every turn and every sound. Fleet Street and the Strand to Charing Cross; down Whitehall to Westminster Abbey, where the bells were summoning the faithful to evensong; round the southern side of St James's Park to Buckingham House, then out along the King's Road, through the darkening fields to Chelsea.

Why Chelsea? He could think of only one reason. And he did not want to believe it. But when they reached the Royal Hospital and drew to a halt in a courtyard to the rear of Orford House, residence, as all Londoners knew, of Robert Walpole, First Lord of the Treasury and Chancellor of the Exchequer . . . he had to believe it.

CHAPTER THIRTY-TWO

Reopening the Book

The room was high-ceilinged and ill-lit, the windows overlooking some inner courtyard engulfed in shadow. Shadow, indeed, seemed to fill the room, despite, or perhaps because of, a roaring fire, whose flames cast flickering ghosts of themselves across the walls and the gold-worked tapestries that covered them.

For a moment, Spandrel thought he was alone. Then he saw a figure stir on the vast day-bed that covered half the length of the far wall – a big, swag-bellied, red-faced man of middle years, in plain waistcoat and breeches, scratching under his wig as he hauled himself upright. He hawked thickly as he crossed the room, spat into the fire, then turned to face Spandrel, who had, with as much reluctance as incredulity, come by now to realize that this was the master of Orford House – Robert Walpole.

'Colic does not put me or any man in the best of tempers,' Walpole said in a gravelly voice. 'Try me, sir, and you'll regret it.'

'I have no wish to try anyone, sir,' said Spandrel.

'Nor to be tried, I dare say.' Walpole moved closer. 'Though the Dutch authorities would like to try you, I'm told, for the murder last year of one of their more eminent citizens.'

'I didn't—'

'Save your denials for your Maker, sir. I'll not hear them. You are William Spandrel?'

'Yes, sir.'

'The same William Spandrel who escaped from custody in Amsterdam in February of last year and still stands accused in that city of murder?'

'Well, I . . .' Something in Walpole's gaze told him prevarication was worse than futile. 'Yes, sir.'

'The United Provinces are a friendly nation. Surrendering a fugitive to them would be a common courtesy.'

'I am innocent, sir.'

'That's for them to say. However—' Walpole flapped his hand. 'I didn't have you brought here for the pleasure, if it would be one, of loading you aboard a ship bound for Amsterdam.'

'No, sir?'

'But I want you to understand that it can be done. It *will* be done.' Walpole snapped his fingers so sharply and suddenly that Spandrel jumped. 'Unless . . .'

The pause grew into a silence that Spandrel felt obliged to break. 'Is there something . . . I can do for you, sir?'

'There is.' Walpole moved to a circular table in the middle of the room and lit the lamp that stood on it. Then he unlocked one of the shallow drawers beneath the table, opened it and pulled out a book, which he let fall with a crash next to the lamp.

Spandrel flinched at his first sight of the book. It was a plain, green-covered ledger, with leather spine and marbled page edges.

'I see you recognize it.'

'I'm not sure. I—'

'I know everything, Spandrel. The whole squalid tale

of scheming and double-dealing. Including your part in it. You do recognize this book, don't you?'

'Yes, sir.'

'And you're familiar with the contents?'

'I . . .' Spandrel strained to decide what it was best to say. Walpole's own name was to be found listed within those green covers. If Spandrel admitted he knew how big a bribe Walpole had taken, he was surely a dead man. But if Walpole already knew he knew . . . 'The contents made no sense to me, sir. I have no head for figures.'

'No head for figures? A bold try, sir. Yes, I compliment you on that. What about Dutch widows? Do you have a head for their figures?'

'I . . . don't understand, sir.'

'When I said I knew everything, that is exactly what I meant. *Everything*.'

Spandrel gulped. 'I . . .'

'Do you still not understand?'

'I do understand, sir. Yes.'

'Good. The book was delivered to me a year ago by an acquaintance of yours, Mr Cloisterman, of whose safe return from Rome you'll doubtless be glad to learn. Mr Cloisterman, incidentally, is now His Majesty's Ambassador to the Sublime Porte.' Catching Spandrel's blank look, he smiled and added, 'The Ottoman Empire.'

'Mr Cloisterman's an ambassador?'

'Thus is assiduous service rewarded. Yes indeed. Cloisterman is sampling the pleasures of Constantinople, which are many and varied, so I'm told. I've never been abroad myself. You know that? You, sir, are a better travelled man than me. But *not* a better informed one. Before he left, Cloisterman made known to me every detail of the Green Book's journey from

London to Rome and back again. So, whatever lies you are tempted to tell, save your breath. I don't care how you managed your own exit from Rome. It matters not to me. Here you are, though, home again. Like the Green Book.' Walpole patted its cover, almost affectionately. 'And ready to do my bidding, I rather think.'

'How did you know . . . I'd come home?'

'Sir Theodore Janssen alerted me to the repayment of your debt to him, which could only mean you planned to return, wrongly supposing you were no longer of interest to the likes of me.'

'I did suppose that, sir, yes.'

'An expensive mistake, as it turns out. You passed Westminster Abbey on your way here?'

'I . . . think so, sir, yes.'

'*You think so.* You know so. Don't play the fool with me.'

'We did pass the Abbey, sir. Yes.'

'Are you acquainted with the Dean of Westminster?'

'No, sir.'

'The Right Reverend Francis Atterbury, Bishop of Rochester.'

'I, er . . . have heard of him.'

'As what?'

'As, er . . .'

'As a stiff-necked, silver-tongued Tory who was all for proclaiming the Pretender King when Queen Anne died. The Right Reverend Atterbury is a right renegade Jacobite.'

'Yes, sir.'

'And a plotting one to boot.'

'I know nothing of such things.'

'High time you learned, then. Certain papers have come into my possession following the recent death of the Earl of Sunderland. You knew his lordship had

320

breathed his last? It's been the talk of the town, doubt-less even your neck of it.'

The copy of the *London Journal* Spandrel had bought the previous day had been much given over to Sunderland's sudden death. Spandrel had not bothered to read the reports, wrongly supposing that the deaths along with the doings of such men were none of his concern. 'I heard, sir, yes.'

'Those papers leave no room for doubting Lord Sunderland's complicity in Atterbury's plotting.'

'Lord Sunderland?'

'Yes. *Lord Sunderland.* Don't look so surprised, man. Your perusal of the Green Book can hardly have left you with a glowing impression of your political masters' capacity for loyalty.'

'You're very frank, sir.' Walpole was being, in truth, disturbingly frank. Spandrel had felt safer being hectored than confided in.

'I'm frank when I need to be. Your value to me lies in your attested knowledge of the Green Book. Tomorrow is St George's Day. We can rely on Dean Atterbury presiding at evensong in the Abbey in order to lavish some patriotic prayers on the congregation. That'll be his brand of patriotism, of course, not mine. You will attend the service and afterwards bring yourself to the Bishop's attention. How you manage that is up to you, but manage it you must. Tell him you have something of inestimable value to the cause which you wish to discuss with him, something entrusted to you by the Earl of Sunderland.'

'But—'

'But nothing. He will rise to the bait. Sunderland's death has him all a-quiver, fearful about what it means and what it portends. He will agree to see you in private. You will ensure he does. At that meeting, you will tell him about the Green Book.'

'But—'

'Save your buts for a hogshead of ale!' roared Walpole, suddenly reddening. 'What do you mean by them, sir?'

'It's just that . . .'

'*What?*'

'If the Bishop is in secret communication with the Pretender . . .'

'As he is.'

'Then he'll know of my attempt to sell the book in Rome – and how it ended.'

'So?'

'I, er, got myself off the hook by telling the Pretender I'd made up the story. I said the Green Book was seized and sent to London when Mr Knight was arrested. I said I was a South Sea Company clerk trying to swindle him.'

'He believed you?'

'He seemed to.'

'Well, it's reassuring to know he's as big a fool as we'd always hoped. I suggest you make Atterbury believe that you were lying. Not difficult, since you were. Say Cloisterman made off with the book, leaving you to talk your way out of it as best you could. When you returned to London this spring, you were picked up by the Secret Service and taken before Sunderland. Sunderland had charge of the Secret Service, damn his memory, until the day he died, so that'll seem likely enough. Here's the wrinkle. Cloisterman was acting for Sunderland, not me. It was to Sunderland that he delivered the book and through Sunderland's influence, not mine, that he secured the Turkish posting. Well, Atterbury can hardly write to Cloisterman and ask him, can he? He'll swallow it. You'll say Sunderland seemed nervous, frightened almost, and threatened to have you sent to Amsterdam in irons unless you agreed to deliver the Green Book into Atterbury's hands. The nervous-

322

ness is a nice touch. It'll play on the crazy suspicion that seems to have got about that I had Sunderland poisoned. His little son died last night, which only seems to have added to the rumours. You'll explain that you weren't supposed to reveal the source of the book, but, now Sutherland's dead, there seems little point in keeping his name out of it. You'll also explain that, now he *is* dead, you're free to impose your own terms. How much did you ask the Pretender for? A hundred thousand, wasn't it?'

'How did—' Spandrel bit his lip. 'Yes. It was.'

'You've learned from your mistake. Your price now is twenty thousand.'

'You want me to . . . try to sell it?'

'I want you to persuade Atterbury that it can be bought. The price is neither here nor there. I want him to believe this . . . bookful of gunpowder . . . is within his grasp. Then . . .' Walpole smiled. 'A letter to Rome, asking for instructions, or boasting of what the book will do for the Pretender's standing here – its publication as a prelude to a rising. It doesn't matter. But something, anything, to incriminate him. That's what I want. And that's what I mean to have.'

'I . . .' Spandrel's heart sank. There was no way out. He would have to do this. And that was not all. He was a pawn. And pawns tended to be sacrificed in quest of a bishop, especially pawns who knew too much. Perhaps Atterbury's involvement in his murder was just the kind of incrimination Walpole had in mind. 'I'm not sure I . . .'

'Do you want to be hanged as a murderer?'

'No, sir. Of course not.'

'Well then?'

'I, er . . .' Spandrel tried to look as if he meant what he was about to say. 'I'll do my best.'

'So you will.' Walpole slipped the Green Book back

323

into the drawer, locked it and dropped the key into his waistcoat pocket. 'And you'd better pray your best is good enough.'

'Yes, sir.'

'No-one else knows where the book really is, of course, apart from Cloisterman, far away in Constantinople. No-one but you and me. We make a strange pair to share such a secret, don't we? Of course . . .' He fixed Spandrel with his gaze. 'Should anyone else find out, I'll know who must have told them, won't I? That's the beauty of it.'

'I won't tell a soul, sir.'

'Be sure you don't.'

'And, er, when I've, er . . . accomplished the task?'

'How can you be sure I won't hand you over to the Dutch authorities anyway? Is that what's worrying you?'

'Well, no. I mean, not exactly.'

'I rather think it is. And, if it isn't, it should be. But the answer's very simple. You have my word. As a gentleman and a statesman.' Walpole treated Spandrel to a broad but fleeting grin. 'I can't say handsomer than that, now can I?'

Spandrel was left to make his own way back to London. Night had fallen and, as the lights of the Royal Hospital fell away behind him, darkness closed in on every side. Only his own footfalls and the mournful hoots of an owl somewhere to the north kept him company. He could not recall feeling so miserably desperate since his escape from Amsterdam. He should have left his debts unpaid and his mother unaware that he was still alive. Perhaps that was still the answer: to flee while he had the chance. But he could not abandon his mother so soon after re-entering her life and promising to transform it. There had to be another way out of this. There had to be. For if not . . .

He pulled up his collar against the deepening chill of the night and pressed on towards the city; and towards the task that awaited him there.

CHAPTER THIRTY-THREE

A Worm on the Line

The move from Cat and Dog Yard to Leicester Fields was accomplished with fewer difficulties than Spandrel's mother seemed to have anticipated. Her meticulous oversight of the removal man's work suggested that she half-expected some disaster to intervene before she could lay claim to being mistress of a respectable household at a reputable address. But, as the removal man muttered at one point, 'Nobody's going to make off with any of this,' nodding towards a cartload of their possessions. 'I've seen better stuff dumped in the Fleet Ditch.'

If Mrs Spandrel had overheard such insolence, she might have boxed the fellow's ears. Spandrel, for his part, would probably have told him to button his lip, had he been less preoccupied with a disaster whose proportions threatened to eclipse his mother's worst fears. 'Don't look so miserable,' she rebuked him as they stood together in their new and sparsely furnished drawing-room. 'I'll soon have this fit for the Princess of Wales to take tea in.'

'I'm sure you will, Ma,' Spandrel managed to say. And sure he was. But that did not make him any less miserable. 'Happy St George's Day.'

'Well, it's a happier one than I thought I'd ever see again, I'll say that.'

'Me too.'

'Then put a smile on your face, boy. And help me unpack.'

'I can't. I have to go out.'

'I might have known. Why?'

'Let's just say . . .' He put together some kind of a smile. 'I have to see a man about a dragon.'

Whether the congregation for evensong at Westminster Abbey that afternoon was larger because it was St George's Day Spandrel had no way to tell, since he had only ever been a reluctant churchgoer at best and then only on Sunday mornings. Evensong, especially in the august surroundings of Westminster Abbey, was for him a strange experience. His atheistical tendencies would not have made it an agreeable one in any circumstances. The circumstances that had led to his attendance, however, were such as to override religious scruples. What would have been merely disagreeable became instead an ordeal.

The nave was well filled with worshippers and Dean Atterbury made his entrance only after the choir had filed in. Spandrel caught a glimpse of an erect, sombre-faced figure in flowing robes soon lost to him behind a pillar. Even a glimpse was subsequently denied him by the Dean's position in the choir-stalls in relation to Spandrel's own beyond the screen.

But the Dean's voice was denied no-one. It tolled sonorously, like a bell, echoing in the vaulted roof. 'When the wicked man turneth away from his wickedness that he hath committed, and doeth that which is lawful and right, he shall save his soul alive.' What did Atterbury consider lawful and right? Spandrel wondered. Who *was* the wicked man? 'Dearly beloved brethren, the Scripture moveth us in sundry places to acknowledge and confess our manifold sins and weaknesses.' Sins and weaknesses.

Yes. They were what had brought Spandrel to this pass. And very possibly the Dean too. 'Almighty God, the Father of our Lord Jesus Christ, who desireth not the death of a sinner, but rather that he may turn from his wickedness, and live; and hath given power and commandment to his Ministers, to declare and pronounce to his people, being penitent, the absolution and remission of their sins . . .'

'The grace of our Lord Jesus Christ, and the love of God, and the fellowship of the Holy Ghost, be with us all evermore. Amen.'

'Amen.' Evensong was at an end, after nearly an hour of psalms and lessons and prayers. Most of the congregation was still kneeling, but the Dean was already leading the choir out. Spandrel's long-awaited chance had come, a chance he had no choice but to take. He had deliberately sat at the end of a pew and now rose and walked rapidly and unnoticed across the south aisle to the door that led out into the cloister next to the Deanery.

There was a pearly early evening light in the close. The choir was progressing round the cloisters towards the school. But the Dean, attended by a flock of chaplains, was bearing down on Spandrel, or rather on the side-entrance to the Deanery, next to which Spandrel had emerged from the Abbey.

'My lord,' he said, standing his ground. 'I must speak to you.'

Atterbury stopped so abruptly that several of the chaplains carried on past him, only to have to scuttle back when they realized what had happened. One of them advanced menacingly on Spandrel, as if intending to remove him from the Dean's path. But Atterbury held up a restraining hand. 'One moment, Kelly.' He examined Spandrel through cool blue eyes. 'Well?'

'It is a matter of the utmost importance, my lord. Affecting . . . a subject close to your heart.'

'What subject?'

'I cannot . . . speak of it openly.'

'Can you not?' Atterbury thought for a moment, then said, 'Deal with this, Kelly,' before sweeping past Spandrel and into the Deanery.

'But my—'

Kelly's broad black-robed back was suddenly between Spandrel and his quarry. The Deanery door slammed shut. The Dean and his retinue were gone. Save only Kelly, who slowly turned and gazed down at Spandrel from a considerable height, before cocking one bushy eyebrow and baring a fine set of teeth in what might as easily have been a snarl as a smile. 'Your name?'

'William Spandrel.'

'Your business with the Dean?'

'Is, begging your pardon, sir, with the Dean alone.'

'I'm the Dean's ears and eyes.'

'Even so.'

'I'll not bandy words with you, sir.' Spandrel was suddenly seized by the collar and hauled onto tiptoe in an unclerically muscular grasp. 'I am the Reverend George Kelly, confidential secretary to my lord the Dean and Bishop. What you tell me you tell him. And tell me you will.'

'Very well. I . . .' Slowly, Spandrel was lowered back to the ground. His collar was released. 'I'm sorry. I . . . didn't . . .'

'Out with it.'

'It concerns . . .' Spandrel took a deep breath. He was about to plunge into waters of unknown depth. 'The cause.'

'What cause might that be?'

'There is surely only one.'

'Hah! And so there is.' Kelly gave Spandrel a cuff to the shoulder that nearly felled him. 'Well, we have the cloister to ourselves. I'll allow you one circuit to tell your tale. One only, mind. I have no time to waste.'

'Nor have I, sir.' They started walking. And Spandrel started talking. But his thoughts travelled faster than his words. Walpole had told him to speak to Atterbury. Intermediaries, however confidential, however trusted, would not suffice. Yet Kelly would know half a story for the fraction it was. He would not be fobbed off, nor easily taken in. He had to be given enough – but not too much. 'I'm placed in a difficult position. I'm instructed to deliver an article to the Dean in person.'

'Instructed by whom?'

'The late Earl of Sunderland.'

'And what were you to the Earl?'

'Nothing. I . . . came to his attention.'

'By reason of the article you're charged to deliver?'

'You could say so, yes.'

'What is the article?'

'Something that will make the people of this country cry out for the restoration of King James.'

'And what is that?'

'The secret account-book of the chief cashier of the South Sea Company.'

'Hah!' Kelly pulled up and pushed Spandrel back against a pillar. 'You expect me to believe that?'

'It's true. I can give the Dean the Green Book.'

'And what will that avail him?'

'It lists all the people the company bribed. Up to and including . . . the Elector of Hanover.'

'"The Elector of Hanover." You choose your words like a man picking lice, Spandrel. What's the meaning of them?'

'The meaning's clear.' Spandrel looked Kelly in the eye. 'I have the Green Book. And with Sunderland dead, no-one knows I have it. Except you.'

'Why should Sunderland have entrusted such a thing to you?'

'Of all people, you mean?'

'Yes. *Of all people.*'

'I'll explain that to the Dean. I can answer all his questions. And I can give him what the King needs more than any number of loyal priests.'

'What does he need?'

'Ammunition. To fire a cannonade that will blast the Elector back to Hanover, where he belongs, and clear the way' – Spandrel nodded towards the Abbey – 'for a coronation.'

Kelly stared at Spandrel long and hard. Then a priest appeared in the far corner of the cloister and moved along the walk parallel to the one they were standing in. Kelly followed him with his eyes. A door opened and closed. He was gone.

'I must see the Dean.'

'But must the Dean see you? It's for him to say.'

'And for you to advise.'

'As I will.' Kelly nodded thoughtfully. 'Be at the Spread Eagle in Tothill Street this time tomorrow. I'll bring you your answer there.'

'But—'

'Be there.' Kelly stabbed Spandrel in the chest with a powerful thrust of his forefinger. 'That's all I have to say.'

Spandrel returned to Leicester Fields that evening by way of several inns other than the Spread Eagle. He fell to wishing that the matter could have been settled, one way or the other, rather than deferred for another twenty-four hours. Even then, there was no saying that his meeting with Atterbury, if he was granted one, would not be on yet a subsequent occasion. He did not seriously doubt that such a meeting would take place eventually. The lure was too strong for a true Jacobite to resist. But when would it be? And what would it yield? The uncertainty gnawed at him like hunger. And, as with hunger, time only made it gnaw the worse.

He was almost grateful to be able to spend most of the next day arguing with Crabbe, the engraver, over how much interest should be added to the long outstanding payment due for the completed sheets of the map. Crabbe drove a hard bargain, but had taken good care of the sheets and wished Spandrel well, though with a typically gloomy qualification. 'This is no time to be venturing into the market, young man. You'll get no subscribers till things look up. And it'd be best to wait until they do.' He was probably right. But Spandrel could not presently see more than a matter of days into the future. And he did not care for what those days promised to contain. He thanked Crabbe for the advice and went on his way.

Spandrel's mother was busy interviewing candidates for the post of maid-of-all-work in her new household when Spandrel arrived home. He took the sheets into his room and sat with them in the thinning late afternoon light, casting his eye over the intricately drawn and precisely scaled patterns of parks and streets and squares and alleys – and his memory across the weeks and months of labour needed to produce them. A map, his father had once said, is a picture of a city without its inhabitants. And how beautiful it looked without them, how clean and elegant. The people who had made the city were also those who had marred it. And even a mapmaker had to live among them. He could not walk the empty ways he had drawn. No-one could.

The Spread Eagle was one of several coaching inns serving the route from Westminster west out of the city. Its proximity to the Abbey made it a logical enough choice, even though Spandrel was surprised that a priest should nominate an inn as a rendezvous. But the Reverend Kelly was about as unpriestly as could be imagined, so the surprise was muted. Waiting in the tap-room that evening, Spandrel found himself wondering whether Atterbury employed Kelly more for the power of his arm than the depth of his piety. Perhaps, if he really was as busy a plotter as he was a preacher, he had need of such men about him.

Sure enough, when Kelly ambled in, he looked more like a half-pay army officer than a bishop's secretary. There was nothing remotely clerical in his dress and the set of his powerful shoulders, taken together with his swaggering gait, confirmed that humility was not a prominent feature of his character. He ignored Spandrel at first, preferring to buy a drink and exchange several guffawing words with the tapster before moving to speak to some lounging fellow in a corner. Then both men walked across to Spandrel's table.

'Good evening, Spandrel,' said Kelly, in a genial growl. 'This is a friend of mine, Mr Layton.'

Mr Layton was a smaller, less imposing figure than Kelly, with quick, darting eyes and a louche smile. He had been flirting with the pot-girl earlier. Spandrel had paid him no heed. But clearly Layton had paid him considerable heed.

'Mr Layton tells me you came alone and at the agreed time,' Kelly continued. 'That's reassuring.'

'No-one else is involved in this,' said Spandrel. 'I told you that.'

'Indeed you did. You also told me you had an article to deliver to my employer.'

'Yet you came empty-handed,' said Layton, with a feral twitch to his smile.

'You came without your employer.'

'You'd hardly expect a bishop to set foot in a tap-room,' countered Kelly.

'Is he willing to see me?'

'He wants to see what you have for him, certainly.'

'So he can, when we've agreed terms.'

'Terms, is it?' Layton snorted. 'I warned you, George. The fellow's out for what he can get.'

'Sunderland's dead.' Spandrel smiled gamely. 'I'm no longer bound by his instructions.'

'How much do you want?' asked Kelly, mildly enough, as if merely curious.

'I'll name my price, when I meet your paymaster.'

Kelly chuckled. 'You're the cool one and no mistake.'

'Perhaps we should warm him up a touch,' said Layton. 'See if he punches as well as he pleads.'

'No, no,' said Kelly. 'Let it go.'

'If you're sure.' Layton looked positively disappointed at being overruled on the point. 'Shall we send him up?'

'Yes,' Kelly replied. 'It's time.'

'Time for what?' asked Spandrel.

'Climb the steps to the galleried room across the yard,' said Kelly. 'Third door you come to. He's waiting for you.'

'The Dean?'

'*He's waiting.*'

Spandrel could see an ostler busying himself in the stable at the rear of the yard, but there was no-one else about. It was cool and quiet, away from the bustle of the tap-room. He glanced up at the windows of the galleried

334

rooms above him, but there was no sign of movement.

He took the steps two at a time and marched smartly along to the third door. Through the window, he could see a fire burning, but the chair beside it was empty. He knocked at the door.

There was no answer. He knocked again. Still there was nothing. He turned the handle and pushed at the door. It yielded.

As he entered, a figure moved in the corner of the room, detaching itself from the shadow of the chimney-breast.

'So there you are, Spandrel.' The voice was not Atterbury's. Nor was the bearing. Nor yet the face. 'About time.'

Spandrel could neither move nor speak. He stared at the figure advancing upon him in a paralysis of disbelief.

'What's wrong with you, man?' said McIlwraith. 'You look as if you've seen a ghost.'

CHAPTER THIRTY-FOUR

Back From the Dead

'Why don't you sit down, Spandrel?' said McIlwraith, gesturing to one of the two chairs flanking the fireplace. 'Before you fall down.'

'Captain . . .' Spandrel sat unsteadily down and gaped at the gaunt but otherwise unaltered figure of James McIlwraith. 'You're not dead?'

'Not unless you are too and Lucifer's decided to entertain himself by making us think we're alive.'

'I don't understand. Cloisterman said he left you for dead.'

'Left for dead and being dead aren't quite the same thing.'

'But you said . . . yourself . . . that you were dying.'

'I thought I was.'

'I wouldn't have left you if . . .' Spandrel shrugged helplessly. 'If I'd thought you'd live.'

'I'll do you the honour of believing that.' McIlwraith smiled. 'Have some brandy.' He poured a glass from the bottle standing on the mantelpiece and handed it to Spandrel, who gulped some gratefully down. 'Let me tell you it tastes even better when you've thought you might never taste it again.'

'How did you survive?'

'I don't know. I just did. It surprised that Bernese doctor even more than me. Must be the pure Swiss air.

Or my long years of clean living. It was touch and go. Very nearly go. In the end, though, I came back. Maybe my immortal soul didn't care to leave so much business unfinished. That ball Wagemaker put in me hasn't gone, by the by.' He slapped the left side of his chest and winced. 'Still in there somewhere, they tell me. And still capable of killing me, if it lodges in something vital. So, if I drop dead in mid-sentence, you'll know the cause. But if I were you . . .' He moved to the back of Spandrel's chair and closed a crushing grip on his shoulder. 'I wouldn't count on it.'

'Count on it?' Spandrel looked up into McIlwraith's hooded eyes. 'I can't tell you how glad I am to see you alive, Captain. You surely don't think . . .'

'That you'd rather I'd stayed dead?' McIlwraith chuckled. 'Well, if you don't now, you soon will.'

'What do you mean?'

McIlwraith walked slowly across to the other chair and sat down. 'I've thrown in my lot with the Jacobites, Spandrel. With Atterbury and those two fellows downstairs: Kelly and Layer.'

'Layer? Kelly introduced him as Layton.'

'A clumsy alias. His name's Christopher Layer. He's a lawyer. And a plotter. Not that there's a lot of difference.'

'But the Jacobites? You? Why?'

'Ah well, that's the question, isn't it? You see, it took me months to recover. By the time I was fit to leave Berne, there was no point going on to Rome. I knew the chase had ended long ago by then, one way or the other. So, I started back for England, by slow boat down the Rhine. I wasn't up to riding. And I was in no hurry. If I had been, I might have reached Cologne sooner. Which would have been a pity, because then I'd have missed Cloisterman.'

'You met Cloisterman?'

'I did. He was on his way south.'

'To Constantinople?'

'Aye. Constantinople. An embassy, no less. His reward . . . for services rendered.'

'What did he tell you?'

'Everything, Spandrel. Everything you and he did in Rome.'

'I see.'

'Do you now?'

'I can repay . . . the money you gave me.'

'It wasn't my money. It was the committee's. And they've disbanded. So, don't worry your head about the money. We'll let that pass. Breach of faith, now. That's a different matter.'

'I . . .'

'Why don't you tell me you never meant to sell the book? Why don't you say Buckthorn and Silverwood intervened just before you were planning to spring some sort of a trap on Mrs de Vries?'

'Because . . .' It had been bad enough to break his word to a dead man. Spandrel had often consoled himself with the thought that he would never have to account to McIlwraith for what he had done at Estelle's bidding. She had been worth it, after all. But she was lost to him now. And he *did* have to account to McIlwraith. 'Because it wouldn't be true.'

'No. It wouldn't be true. Nor would whatever you were intending to say to Atterbury, would it? Cloisterman delivered the book to Walpole, not Sunderland. He told me so. He was pleased to tell me. And he wasn't lying, was he?'

'No. Walpole has the Green Book.'

'And he has you, in his pocket.'

'Yes.'

'He set you on Atterbury.'

'Yes.'

'In the hope that the Green Book could be used to tempt the Bishop into betraying himself.'

'Yes.'

'And you had little choice but to do his bidding because otherwise he'd have handed you over to the Dutch authorities.'

'Yes.'

'Who don't know that de Vries was murdered not by you but by his secretary, with the connivance of his wife.'

Spandrel sighed. 'I should never have come back to England.'

'No more you should.' Then McIlwraith also sighed. 'And neither should I. They'd all given up by then, you see. Brodrick, Ross and the other members of the committee. They'd thrown in their cards. They'd abandoned the struggle. Walpole was cock of the dunghill. The Green Book was a dead letter. As for me, well, General Ross made it obvious I was an embarrassment to them now the game was up. They had to look to the future and make . . . accommodations . . . with their new master. I was politely encouraged to vanish. And so I did. As far as they were concerned. But when you've come as close to death as I have, when the Grim Reaper's brushed the hem of his cloak across your face and you can still catch the cold, grave-damp smell of it in your nostrils, you don't see things as other men do. You're not interested in accommodations. You can't be sent away. You won't be stopped.'

'Jacobitism is treason, Captain.'

'High treason, Spandrel. As high as Tyburn gallows.'

'You're really one of them?'

'Sworn and enlisted.'

'But why? You're no Jacobite. You were trying to stop the Green Book reaching Rome.'

'The case is altered. I won't let them win.'

'Won't let who win?'

'Walpole and his cronies. I'll have them yet.' There was a look in McIlwraith's eyes Spandrel had never seen before. His brush with death truly had altered him. Determination had become obsession. 'By hook or by crook, I'll have them.'

'It'll mean blood in the streets.'

'Then let it flow. I swore to make the truth known. No matter that those I swore to have sheathed their swords and slunk away. I still mean to make it known.'

'You won't succeed. Walpole knows everything. He has Sunderland's papers.'

'But he's biding his time. Because he thinks he has plenty of it. He doesn't know about me. If he did, he'd never have sent you to Atterbury. That's his mistake. And he'll pay for it, I promise you.'

'You can't win.'

'Oh, but I can. Not by listening to fools like Layer or waiting for instructions from Rome. They have some crazy plan to assassinate the King – the Elector, as they call him – on his way to Hanover. And they still mean to go through with it, despite Sunderland's death. But there's no need. There's another way to snare our fat Norfolk Robin. A surer way, by far. The Green Book, Spandrel. You saw it?'

'Yes.'

'My fellow plotters have persuaded themselves that Walpole destroyed it. But I never fell for that notion. He didn't get where he is by destroying the secrets that come his way.'

'You're not thinking of . . .'

'Stealing it back from him?' McIlwraith caught Spandrel's eye. 'No. It's a tempting thought, but a fatal one. Orford House is well guarded. And where would

340

we look? He's not likely to keep it wherever you saw it. He'd like us to try, no doubt. A few of us shot down as common housebreakers would suit his purpose very well. It'd look bad for you, of course. Who but you could have told us he had it there? So, you'll be glad to know I have no intention of blundering into that trap.'

'What do you mean to do?'

'Nothing that you need worry your head about.' McIlwraith rose from his chair with more of an effort than he would once have needed to exert and leaned against the mantelpiece. 'You have more than enough to think about already. Such as what you're going to report to Walpole.'

'What can I report? I've failed.'

'No need to tell him that. *I* won't tell. Say Atterbury's agreed to meet you, down in Bromley, at his palace, next week.'

'Why next week?'

'Because by then Walpole will have more important things to worry about. I'll see to that.' McIlwraith grinned. 'I'm doing you a favour, Spandrel, though God knows why I should. I'm letting you off the hook.'

Off the hook? Spandrel did not feel as if he was. Quite the reverse. If he lied to Walpole and Walpole found out, he was finished. But if he told him the truth . . . he was also finished.

'Aren't I more trustworthy than Walpole, man? Aren't I just about the only one you *can* trust in all this?'

'It's hopeless, Captain. Don't you understand? He's too powerful. You can't defeat him.'

'Wait and see.' McIlwraith's smile grew wistful. 'Every man has his breaking point.'

'Not Walpole.'

'Oh, he has his weaknesses, never doubt it. One of

341

them's the same as yours, as a matter of fact. *Exactly* the same as yours.'

'What do you mean?'

'Estelle de Vries.' McIlwraith refilled Spandrel's brandy glass. 'He keeps her as a mistress.'

'That's not true. It—' Spandrel stopped and stared into the fire. Estelle, with Walpole? It was not possible. It was not to be believed. 'It can't be.'

'But it can. It is. How is not for me to say. What did you think she meant to do when you left Rome?'

'We left . . . separately.'

'She had no more use for you once the Green Book was gone, then. Well, you can't have been surprised.'

'She went after Cloisterman.'

'Ever the huntress. You can't fault her for spirit. But Cloisterman went by sea from Leghorn. That put him out of her reach. And the Green Book likewise. Perhaps this . . . connection . . . with Walpole is her way of profiting from it nonetheless.'

'I don't believe it.'

'As you please. I hardly did myself. But I've seen her with my own eyes, man, riding with him in a coach. It's common knowledge. Walpole doesn't hide his vices any more than his virtues. He's installed her in a house in Jermyn Street. Phoenix House, near the corner of Duke Street, should you wish to see for yourself. An easy toddle from the house he keeps in Arlington Street. A wife in Chelsea and a mistress in St James's. That no doubt appeals to his sense of . . . husbandry. Oh, she calls herself Davenant now, by the by. *Mrs* Davenant, of course. I haven't told my . . . accomplices . . . who she really is.'

'I still don't believe it.'

'Yes you do. You just don't want to. Walpole didn't

342

mention it to you, of course. He was hardly likely to. He needs your compliance, not your envy.'

'God rot him.' Surprised by his own vehemence, Spandrel pressed a fist to his forehead and closed his eyes. If only he could truly have said that it made no sense. But it did. It was, in some perverse way, just what he might have expected. He had thought he had succeeded, not in forgetting Estelle – for how could he forget such a woman? – but in setting aside his attraction to her. The months in Rennes, the women he had had there, the level-headed aspiration to Maria Chesney's hand . . . amounted to scarcely anything compared with the meagre portion of his life he had spent with her. And scarcely anything was virtually nothing.

'Do you hate him now, Spandrel?' McIlwraith's voice came as a whisper, close to his ear. 'Because, if you do, I have good tidings for you.'

Spandrel opened his eyes and looked up at McIlwraith. What was the captain planning? What could he do against someone like Walpole? What could he really do?

'I have the breaking of him.' McIlwraith's smile was broad and contented. He looked like a man at peace with himself – and at war with another. 'It's him or me.'

CHAPTER THIRTY-FIVE

The Devil and the Deep Blue Sea

St James's was better lit than most parts of London, but there were still plenty of shadows large and deep enough to shroud Spandrel from view. He stood in the entrance to a service alley on the northern side of Jermyn Street, watching for signs of life at Phoenix House, handsome residence of one Mrs Davenant, a little way down the opposite side of the street. So far, there had been none.

Spandrel had several times asked himself what he was expecting to see at this hour of the evening. Estelle, if she truly did live there, was not likely to show herself to suit his convenience. The afternoon was a better time by far to watch for her. But he could not risk loitering in the area in daylight, any more than he could knock at the door and demand to see Mrs Davenant.

It made little sense, in all honesty, for him to be there at all. But the alternatives were hardly better. He could go home and listen to his mother describing the girls who might – or indeed the girl who had – become the maid their new station in life enabled them to employ. Or he could slink into a tavern and drink as much as he needed – which would be a lot – to forget the dilemma that McIlwraith had placed him in.

Should he tell Walpole that McIlwraith was alive and well and intent on meting out his own brand of justice? If he did, he would have to admit in the process that his attempt to gull Atterbury had failed miserably. Nor did he know what he would be warning Walpole against. It would certainly be easier to tell him the lie McIlwraith had suggested. But Walpole was a dangerous man to lie to. Only if McIlwraith really could destroy him, as he had pledged to, was such a risk worth taking.

Tomorrow, though, he would have to decide. Walpole required a report by then on what progress he had made, to be submitted by hand to the Postmaster-General – none other than Walpole's brother. Spandrel had to say something. And whatever he chose to say might easily rebound on him.

The need to see Estelle and to assure himself that what McIlwraith had told him about her was true was thus a distraction, in some ways, from a problem he had no hope of solving. More and more, he felt like a man trapped in a quagmire, whose every attempt at extrication only sucked him in deeper. Even his pleasure at McIlwraith's return from the dead was soured by the knowledge of the peril it exposed him to. And now—

There was a movement at one of the illuminated upper windows of Phoenix House. Spandrel caught his breath as a curtain was twitched back. A figure, outlined against the glow of a lamp, glanced down into the street. From where he stood, Spandrel could see that it was a woman. Her long dark hair flowed over bare shoulders above a low-cut gown. He could not make out a single detail of her face. And yet he knew, by the way she stood, head thrown back slightly, arm raised, that it was Estelle. He stared up at her, knowing full well that she could not see him, yet half-hoping, half-fearing, that she would somehow sense his presence. Then she released the curtain. Her shadow dwindled away behind it. She was gone.

Spandrel stood there for several more minutes, wondering what he had gained from this paltry glimpse.

McIlwraith had told him she lived there and he had not seriously doubted it. Yet he had felt driven to see her for himself. And now he had. It told him little. It proved nothing. Strictly speaking, he could not even be sure it was her he had seen. But it was enough.

With sudden decisiveness, Spandrel emerged from the alley-mouth and started walking east along Jermyn Street, head bowed, moving fast. He regretted now that he had ever allowed himself to be drawn to the area. Estelle rediscovered as Walpole's mistress was Estelle lost to him more conclusively than if she had been removed to the other side of the world.

He paid the few passers-by little attention as he pressed on. Seeing a man come round the corner of Eagle Street ahead of him, he did no more than move slightly to the left to accommodate him. But the man moved into his path, as if deliberately. He was a big, bulky fellow in a broad-collared greatcoat, full-bottomed wig and low-brimmed hat, flourishing a stick. And, far too late to avoid the encounter, Spandrel recognized him.

'Mr Walpole,' he said nervously, coming to a halt.

'*Mr* Spandrel.' Walpole prodded him in the chest with the point of his stick. 'What are you doing here?'

'I—' Spandrel broke off, but only momentarily. One of the few advantages conferred on him by his mis-adventures of the year before was speed of thought. Walpole was going to pay a late call on his mistress. He was not likely to believe that coincidence had led Spandrel to the very street where she lived. And Spandrel could not allow him to catch him out in a lie. But there were lies . . . and then there were lies. 'I saw . . . Estelle de Vries . . . in Pall Mall and followed her here . . . to Phoenix House.'

'Estelle de Vries? Here?'

'It seems so, sir.'

'You're sure?'

'I saw her with my own eyes.'

'Well, well.' Walpole lowered the stick and stepped towards the area railings of the house beside them, lowering his voice as he did so and beckoning Spandrel closer. 'Phoenix House, you say?'

'Yes, sir. Near the corner of Duke Street.'

'Very well. You may leave me to have this matter looked into. You'll do nothing about it. You'll make no attempt to approach her. You'll give her no means of knowing that you've returned to London. Is that understood?'

'Yes, sir.'

'Good. Now, then.' The stick tapped at Spandrel's shoulder. 'What of other matters? Since we have this chance of a private word, you needn't trouble to call at the G.P.O. tomorrow.'

Such relief as Spandrel felt at outwitting Walpole over Estelle was instantly banished by the realization that he could equivocate no longer about what he should report concerning Atterbury and McIlwraith. He paused only long enough to draw a deep breath, then chose his course. 'I have . . . secured an appointment . . . to call at the Bishop's Palace.'

'When?'

'A week today.'

'A week? Why so long?'

'He's a busy man, sir.'

'But busy with what? That's what we want to know.'

'It was the best I could do, sir.'

'Who gave you this appointment?'

'His secretary, sir. The Reverend Kelly.'

'See Kelly again. Tell him you can't – won't – wait so long.'

'But—'

'See him again.' The stick moved to Spandrel's chin and pushed it up, forcing his head back. 'Report to my brother the day after tomorrow. I want prompter progress. You understand?'

'Very clearly, sir,' Spandrel said, as distinctly as the extension of his neck would allow.

'So I should hope.' Walpole whipped the stick away. 'Now, be off, damn you.' And with that the First Lord of the Treasury and Chancellor of the Exchequer strode past Spandrel and on along the street.

Even Robert Walpole could not always have what he wanted. Spandrel's problem was how to fend off the evil hour when he would have to explain that to him, hoping McIlwraith would spare him the necessity. It condemned him to an agony of uncertainty throughout the next day, during which his mother believed him to be scouring London for mapmaking equipment, while he was in truth wandering its streets in a state of aimless anxiety.

Thursday found him no better placed. Quite the contrary, since before it was out he would have to submit his report to Walpole's brother. He composed this work of fiction in a Covent Garden coffee-house, after searching the newspapers for some portent of McIlwraith's intentions – and finding none. *I have been unable to secure an earlier appointment,* he wrote. *I would have done my cause more harm than good had I persisted in the plea.* A nice touch that, he thought. *I am confident, however, of achieving much of what you require of me when I visit Bromley next week.* He was, of course, confident of absolutely nothing, except that he would not be going to Bromley next week.

He left delivery of the report as late in the afternoon as he dared, trudging out along the Strand and Fleet Street, then up Ludgate Hill to St Paul's and round by narrow ways he still remembered from his waywising days to the General Post Office on Lombard Street.

He was expected. The doorman directed him up to see the Postmaster-General's secretary, a taciturn fellow who conveyed all he needed to by way of acknowledgement in one lingering look and a dismissive nod. The report was received.

Spandrel's apprehensiveness amounted now to a fluttering of the heart and a tremor of the limbs. He walked round to Threadneedle Street and looked into the courtyard of South Sea House, where only an air of neglect about the stuccoing and paintwork revealed the savage decline of its fortunes. He had never set foot across its threshold, yet, thanks to the Green Book, he knew the darkest secrets of its bankrupt workings – and wished to God he did not.

From South Sea House he wandered along Lothbury towards the cluster of inns between Lad Lane and Love Lane, eager to drown his identity as well as his sorrows in one of their cavernous tap-rooms. The route took him within sight of Guild Hall. A glance in its direction was enough to remind him of a visit with his father to one of the regular prize draws held there when the War of the Spanish Succession was still on and the Government took to organizing lotteries to raise money for Marlborough's army.

Two giant drums had been set up in the banqueting hall, one containing numbered tickets, the other tickets representing either blanks or prizes. Tickets drawn from the first drum won whatever was drawn next from the second drum. 'Look at these men's faces, William,' his father – an avowed non-gambler – had said. 'Can you tell which of them will be lucky?'

'No, Pa,' William had replied.

'No more you can, son. And no more you'll ever be

349

able to. Just remember: the more desperately you need to win, the more certain it is that you won't.'

Good advice, then and now. Good advice, but bleak counsel. Spandrel's need of a prize to match his ticket was so acute that desperation was hardly the word for it. And the draw could not much longer be delayed.

Spandrel arrived home late enough to find his mother already abed, for which he was grateful, having no wish for her to see how drunk he was and hardly feeling equal to the task of pretending for her benefit that all was well. He took to his own bed at once and plunged instantly into a dark well of slumber.

From which he was roused by a commotion of raised voices and pounding feet in what the light seeping through the window suggested was early morning. He heard his mother protesting at something, with alarm bubbling in her throat. Then the door of his room burst open and several large, burly men, one holding a lantern, strode in.

'Take him,' came a shout.

'Who are you?' Spandrel wailed, as he was hauled from the bed. 'What do you want?'

'We want you, Spandrel. Put some clothes on. Mr Walpole won't want to see you in your nightshirt.'

'Mr Walpole?' The name hit Spandrel like a bucketful of cold water. Suddenly, he knew. It had happened. Whatever McIlwraith had planned to do . . . he had done.

CHAPTER THIRTY-SIX

The Biter Bit

Whitewash and a drizzle of sunlight through one of the barred windows set high in the wall did little to brighten the cellar of the Cockpit building in Whitehall to which Spandrel had been delivered. It was cold and damp, moisture clinging to the iron rings fitted to the floor, the vapour of his breath dissipating but slowly in the stale, frozen air.

The only other occupant of the room strode back and forth between the far wall and a trestle-table separating him from Spandrel. Robert Walpole was flushed about the face despite the prevailing chill and breathing heavily, his jaw working rhythmically, as if chewing on some irreducible lump of gristle. An intimidating presence at the best of times, he seemed now, in his evident anger, purely frightening, like a bull pawing the ground and choosing its moment to charge.

'You live with your mother, I'm told,' he growled, the remark striking Spandrel as just about the last thing he might have expected Walpole to say.

'Yes, sir.'

'She loves you?'

'Yes, sir.'

'Even if nobody else does. Because she *is* your mother.'

'Er . . . yes, sir.'

'And your father loved you too?'

'He . . . did, sir, yes. But I—'

'I have three sons and two daughters, Spandrel. My eldest daughter, Kate, is racked with illness. The doctors can do nothing for her. Such fits and fevers and purges as would grieve even you to see. She's not yet nineteen, but there's no hope for her. Not a one.'

'I am . . . sorry to hear it, sir.'

'You're sorry? Do you think that lightens my heart?'

'Well . . .'

'*No, sir.*' Walpole slammed his fist down on the table. 'It does not. She's dying slowly, at Bath, in an agony of mind and body. And I can't ease her suffering. Only my other children console me for that. Robert, Mary, Edward and little Horace. They're all well, thank God.'

'I'm glad to—'

'Or so I thought they all were. Until last night. When the news came from Eton.'

'What news, sir?'

'You don't know, of course. You don't know a damned thing about it.' Walpole rounded the table and clapped his hand to Spandrel's throat. His hand was large, his grip vicelike. 'Isn't that so?'

Spandrel tried to speak, but only a hoarse splutter emerged. He looked into Walpole's glaring eyes and could not tell whether the man meant to strangle him or not. He was about to try to push him away, indeed, when Walpole released him and stepped back.

'Yesterday afternoon, my son Edward was set upon by two masked men while returning to Eton College from some sport by the river. The boys who were with him say he was forced into a carriage at the point of a sword and driven away in the direction of Datchet. Those boys were given a letter and told to deliver it to the Provost, Dr Bland, a friend of mine from my own days at Eton.'

352

Walpole whipped a folded sheet of paper from his pocket and handed it to Spandrel. 'Read it.'

Spandrel looked down at the letter. It was short, jaggedly scribed if elegantly worded, unsigned and very much to the point.

26th April 1722
Sir,
Be so good as to inform your friend, Mr Walpole, that his son will be released unharmed provided only that the full contents of the Green Book are published in the May Day edition of the *London Gazette*. Failure so to publish will result in his son's execution. Be warned. We are in earnest.

Walpole plucked the letter from Spandrel's trembling fingers and replaced it in his pocket. 'In earnest,' he said. 'Yes, I rather think they are.'

'I don't . . .' Spandrel's words dribbled out with his thoughts. 'I can't . . .'

'Account for it?'

'No, sir. I can't.'

'It's no more than a coincidence that this should happen so shortly after your approach to Atterbury?'

'What else . . . can it be?'

'It can be cause and effect, Spandrel. Damnable cause and bloody effect. Poke your stick into a beehive and you can expect to be stung. Prod a bishop and . . . what?'

'I'm sure there's no connection, sir.'

'Well, I'm not. Why else should Atterbury delay seeing you until next Tuesday?'

'You mean . . .' Spandrel uttered a silent prayer of thanks to whatever deity had decreed this one true coincidence. 'Because by then he believes he won't have to buy what I'm offering to sell him.'

'So it would seem.'

'I never had any inkling of such a response on his part, sir. As God is my witness.' This much was true. What Spandrel did not add, of course, was that he also had not the slightest suspicion that Atterbury was responsible for the abduction of Walpole's son. McIlwraith had taken him. McIlwraith might even have written the letter. But McIlwraith was supposed to be dead. 'This is . . . dreadful.'

'Did you recognize the writing?'

'No, sir.'

'The boys say one of the men spoke with a Scotch accent. Kelly's Irish. They could have mistaken that for Scotch. Or it could be some bloodthirsty Highlander Kelly's recruited. Either way, Jacobites have done this. Oh yes. There's no doubt of that. Who else would stoop to punishing the child for their hatred of the father?'

'They say . . . he'll come to no harm, sir, if . . .'

'If I gazette the Green Book. Do you think I'm likely to do that, Spandrel?'

'I . . . don't know, sir.'

'You know what it contains. There's your answer.'

'But—'

'Which poses another question. How do the kidnappers know I *can* publish it?'

'I don't understand, sir.'

'You were to tell Atterbury that the book came from Sunderland, not me. Why then are the people he obviously put up to this so sure that I have it?'

'I didn't tell them, sir.' But he had told them. He had told McIlwraith, as McIlwraith had obliged him to, little thinking that the admission would rebound on him in such a fashion as this. 'I swear I didn't tell them.'

'Who did, then?'

Spandrel swallowed hard. 'There is . . . Mr Cloisterman.'

'So there is.' Walpole stepped closer. 'But Cloisterman is far away and greatly beholden to me. What would you say if I told you I was certain it wasn't Cloisterman?'

'What could I say, sir? It wasn't me. That's all I know.'

'And you truly have no idea who it might have been?'

'I truly have none, sir. None at all.'

'It really is a coincidence?'

'It must be.'

'Indeed.' Walpole took a slow walk to the wall beneath the windows and gazed up at the rectangles of milky sunlight that revealed the brickwork beneath the white-wash like the ribs beneath a starving man's skin. Then he turned. 'It's just a pity for you I don't believe in coincidences. Anyone who lays a hand on my son – or any child of mine – strikes at me as if he were thrusting a sword into my heart. And I strike back, as best I can. It may be that they saw through your offer of the Green Book. Or it may be that you know more than you're telling. I can't be sure which. And I haven't the time to spend deliberating on the point. I'll save my son if I can. What's certain is that I'll have the men who are holding him and I'll see them hanged, drawn and quartered for what they've already done, let alone what they've threatened to do. If I find that you bear so much as a shred of responsibility for their actions, I'll have you sent to Amsterdam to be hanged as a murderer . . . and I'll have your mother hanged as a thief.'

'My mother?'

'An honest woman, I'm sure. But no-one will believe that with her son swinging from a Dutch gallows and one of my wife's necklaces found about her person.'

'You wouldn't . . .'

'I would. And I will.' Walpole moved back to where

Spandrel was standing and looked him in the eye. 'Is there nothing you want to tell me?'

There was much. But to confess the truth now was to confess to not having warned Walpole that McIlwraith was moving against him. 'There's nothing I *can* tell you, sir.'

'Then get out. And be sure you can be found when I want you. If you run, it's your mother who'll answer for it.'

'Should I still go to Bromley . . . on Tuesday?'

'Of course not. Do you think any of that will matter a damn by—' Walpole stopped and took a deep, soulful breath. Fear simmered beneath his fury: a fear of what would happen to his son. But it would not deflect him. It would not defeat him. 'Just get out of my sight, Spandrel. Now.'

CHAPTER THIRTY-SEVEN

Allies in Adversity

'It was nothing, Ma. A misunderstanding. They were bailiffs who didn't know I'd settled my debts. And they were full of apologies once they realized their records were out of date.'

'Bailiffs?' Margaret Spandrel eyed her son doubtfully. 'They seemed more like, well, like Revenue men to me. And they didn't breathe a word about debts.'

'A hasty crew and no mistake. But that's all it was. A mistake.'

'We can't have this sort of thing going on now we've moved to a respectable neighbourhood, William. I have Jane starting on Monday.' Jane? Spandrel was momentarily at a loss. Then he remembered. The maid. Of course. 'How am I to keep staff if we have such carry-ons as this?'

'We won't, Ma. I promise. I've put a stop to it.'

'I surely hope you have, boy. Now, when are you going to get down to some work? Maps don't draw themselves.'

'This very minute. I have to see Marabout.'

'Marabout? Your father could never abide the man. What do you want with him?'

'A matter of business, Ma. He has something I need. Whether I can abide him or not, I still have to see him.'

Gideon Marabout kept a shop in Portsmouth Street, near Lincoln's Inn Fields, where he peddled more or less

357

anything that came his way, from broken-down automata to wobbly clerks' stools . . . and 'maps for the discerning traveller', as he usually put it.

'Cheaper than hiring a guide and safer than leaving it to chance,' was another phrase of Marabout's that had lodged in Spandrel's mind as he hurried along Long Acre. If anyone could supply him with a more or less reliable map of any area he cared to name, it was Marabout. And this was more than a matter of business. It was a matter of life and death. So to Marabout he was bound to turn.

A few extra layers of dust on the stuffed bear still standing just inside the door were about the only changes Spandrel noticed as he entered the dilapidated premises. Marabout himself, a stooped and shuffling figure with strange flecked blue eyes the colour of lapis lazuli, abandoned sifting through a jumble of bent and chipped spectacles, gave Spandrel a coal-toothed grin and welcomed him as if he had been in only last week, rather than some time in the previous decade.

'Still not finished that map of your father's, then? You'll have to start all over again if you leave it much longer. Things do change that fast.'

'But not you, Mr Marabout.'

'No indeed. There has to be a still point to every spinning top.'

'It's maps I've come about.'

'Oh yes? Going a-travelling?'

'You could say so. How are you for Windsor Forest?'

'Well supplied. Not the call there was in the old Queen's days, see. This German King we have is no hunting man. Nor are you, though. It'll not be stag you're after.'

'I have business that way.'

'Then be on your guard. They say Maidenhead Thicket's thicker with highwaymen than trees.'

358

'What do you have, Mr Marabout?'

'Come through and see.'

Marabout twitched aside a curtain that looked more like a plague victim's winding-sheet and led Spandrel into a windowless, low-ceilinged back room, where a broad, shallow-drawered cabinet housed his collection of maps. They came in all sorts and sizes, ranging from fanciful impressions of the Americas to allegedly accurate street-plans of provincial towns. The light was too dim for Spandrel to tell one from another, but Marabout's eyesight was evidently equal to the task. He sifted through a well-filled drawer, then plucked out a large canvas-backed sheet and carried it out into the shop, where he laid it on the counter and weighed down the corners with four scratched and dented pocket-watches that came magically to hand.

'There you are. Reading to Egham one way, Cookham to Sandhurst the other. Every road and lane and most of the houses besides. Less than twenty years old, what's more, which is as good as yesterday in those parts.'

'I see no date.'

'No need. Datchet Bridge, look.' Marabout pointed to a span across the Thames east of Windsor. 'The old Queen had that built, in the year nought-six.'

Datchet Bridge. Spandrel's eye lingered on it. That was the direction Edward Walpole's kidnappers had taken. And there was the reason. They could not cross the Thames at Windsor for fear of being delayed by the toll long enough to be overtaken by any pursuit there might be. The Datchet route was obviously a safer way back into the Forest, whose bosky expanse the mapmaker had represented with dozens upon dozens of tiny tree-symbols. And the Forest was a place where they could hold the boy, safely out of sight, for the few days needed to force his father's hand – if forced it could be.

'What do you think?' asked Marabout.

'Not bad. Not bad at all.'

'To you, a guinea.'

'A guinea? That's steep.'

'You'd charge more if you'd drawn it yourself.'

'*Every* house, did you say?'

'I did not. But every house that matters, that's for sure. See for yourself.'

'You see more keenly than me, Mr Marabout. Can you find Bordon Grove?'

'Whereabout would it be?'

'Near the edge of the Forest.'

'Which edge?'

'I don't know.'

Marabout grunted and shook his head, but rose to the challenge nonetheless, as Spandrel had known he would. He traced a wavering circle round the ragged perimeter of the Forest with his forefinger, muttering, 'Bordon Grove,' repeatedly under his breath as he went. He was about three quarters of the way round when he stopped and tapped at the place. 'There it is.'

And there it was. Bordon Grove, family home of the Wagemakers. It lay about halfway between Bagshot and Bracknell, in the south-east quadrant of the Forest, no more than ten miles from Eton College. The boundary of its parkland was clearly shown and, within the boundary, additional to the inked square of the house itself, a smaller, narrower mark that could only be Blind Man's Tower.

'Do you want to buy the map – or commit it to memory?' Marabout was losing patience. 'I can go to nineteen and six.'

'Then you've gone far enough.'

'So I should think. It's tantamount to—'

The jingle of the door-bell caused Marabout to break

off. Another customer had entered the shop, one more elegantly attired than most of his patrons: a woman, wearing an embroidered burgundy dress beneath a masculine-style jacket and fitted waistcoat. Her dark hair fell in ringlets to her shoulders. There was a white silk cravat, held by a brooch, at her throat. In her gloved hands she carried a feather-trimmed tricorn hat. She looked at Spandrel quite expressionlessly as she moved towards them, slowly removing the glove from her right hand.

'What can I do for you, madam?'

She made no immediate reply to Marabout's question, but gazed down at the map laid out on the counter. Then she said, more as a statement than an answer, 'A map of Windsor Forest.'

'This one's sold.'

'It will do.'

'But, as I say, it's sold.'

'No matter.' She smiled sweetly enough to charm even Marabout. 'I'm sure William can tell me what's to be found on it.'

Marabout looked round incredulously at Spandrel. 'You know this lady?'

'Oh yes.' Spandrel nodded. 'I know her.'

'This is appalling,' said Townshend, pacing to and fro across his office at the Cockpit. 'Kidnapped?'

'There's no doubt of it,' said Walpole, who might have seemed to an observer – had there been one – less distressed on his son's behalf than the boy's uncle-in-law. 'Nor any of their terms for his release.'

'How has Catherine taken it?' Townshend had little regard for Walpole's wife, but this calamity compelled him to spare her a thought.

'She hasn't.'

'What?'

'She doesn't know, Charles. And I don't want you to tell Dolly either.'

'His mother? His aunt? They aren't to know?'

'They'll be upset. Distraught in all likelihood. I can't have their feminine weaknesses brought to bear on the matter. I have to set aside my feelings – and theirs. I have to forget that he's my son.'

'But how can you?'

'I don't know. But I must. There can be no question of yielding to their demands. Can you imagine the consequences of publication? I can. Revolution, Charles. It would come to that, never doubt it. Blood and butchery. The city aflame. The King deposed. And you and I? The Tower, if the mob didn't get to us first. What would Edward's life be worth then? Not a groat. Even supposing his kidnappers released him, which I doubt.'

'What are we to do, then?'

'Find him. And rescue him. Before Tuesday.'

'But how?'

'I'm sending Horace to Windsor to organize a search. You and he and Galfridus are the only ones outside Eton College who know.' Walpole's two brothers, then, and his brother-in-law: so was the trusted circle defined. 'And I want it to go no further.'

'The King?'

'Must not be told.'

'He won't be best pleased when he finds out.'

'With luck, he won't find out at all. With luck, we'll have Edward free and safe by Sunday and those blackguards—' Walpole closed a fist on his invisible prey.

'He may be far from Windsor by now.'

'Yes. He may. Which is why I want you to conduct operations here in London. I want all the Jacobite bolting-holes and hiding-places watched. Discreetly,

362

Charles. Very discreetly. If there's any suspicion that you've found where he's being held, I'm to be told before anything's done.'

'I'll see to it at once.' Townshend made to leave, then turned back and squeezed Walpole's slumped shoulder. 'He's a brave and resolute boy, Robin. He'll probably escape without any help from us.'

'A nice thought, Charles.' Walpole looked up into his old friend's face. 'But I can't afford to count on it.'

'I never thought we'd meet again,' said Estelle, as she and Spandrel walked slowly along one of the gravelled paths that quartered the rectangle of rank greenery known as Lincoln's Inn Fields. A group of ragamuffin boys were playing chuck-farthing ahead of them. Behind lay the narrow mouth of Portsmouth Street, from which they had recently emerged. Under his arm, Spandrel was carrying a canvas-backed roll, tied with string. 'Did you?'

'No,' Spandrel bleakly replied.

'You think very badly of me, don't you?'

'I think nothing.'

'Your mother told me where you were. *I* told *her* that we were acquaintances from your days in Rennes.'

'And who told you about my days in Rennes?'

'I think you know. My benefactor. The lessee of Phoenix House.'

'Walpole.'

'He's not the monster you think.'

'He threatened to have my mother hanged as a thief this morning. I'd call that monstrous. Wouldn't you?'

'He fears for his son's life. And he'll do anything to save him. Except what the kidnappers demand.'

'Then it's hopeless.'

'I don't think so. You have an idea, don't you? You

363

think you know where the boy's being held – and who by.'

'Do I?'

'Yes. You do. I can read you as well as you can read that map.'

'Maps? They're my province, Estelle. You're right there.' He looked at her. 'But the human heart? I don't know my way around that.'

'A rebuke, William? Because I settled for the best I could hope for when I realized the Green Book was out of my reach? Well, rebuke me, then. I have nothing to apologize for.'

'How did you bring yourself to his attention?'

'I was taken in for questioning when Cloisterman reported my presence in London. I'd hoped he might not have surrendered the Green Book by then, that he and I could . . .' She sighed. 'I was too late, of course. He was on the point of setting off for Constantinople and keen to oblige his master in every way that he could. As for the master, he was curious about me. Cloisterman's reports had . . . whetted his appetite.'

'An appetite you were happy to satisfy.'

'I don't deny it. Why should I? A house in Jermyn Street. Liveried servants. My own carriage. Fine clothes. Expensive jewellery. What I give in return is little enough.'

'An ideal arrangement, then.'

'An acceptable one, certainly. But now endangered.'

'By what?'

'The Green Book. He's sure one of us has betrayed him. Possibly both, thanks to your encounter with him not far from my door. I deny it, of course. So do you. We may both be telling the truth. But that won't help us. Not if Edward Walpole dies. Then his father will seek vengeance. And he'll wreak it upon us. Even upon your mother. The boy's not yet sixteen. And Robin has such high hopes for him.'

'Robin?'

'He won't give in to the kidnappers, William. He'd rather let his son be killed than do that. And if he is killed . . . we're as good as dead.'

'There's nothing I can do.'

'You're going to Windsor Forest, aren't you?'

'Am I?'

'I'm coming with you.'

'No.'

'We'll make better time together in my chaise than you will alone on a hired nag.'

'You're not coming with me.'

'I'll go anyway and be waiting for you when you arrive. Why waste time when we have so little of it? We can be in Windsor by nightfall. It's my neck as well as yours. You can't refuse me.' She stopped and looked at him. 'Can you?'

CHAPTER THIRTY-EIGHT

The Sylvan Chase

Acting against his better judgement was scarcely a novel experience for Spandrel. Nor had it always been a disastrous one. There was the rub. Estelle's arguments for combining their efforts were sound enough. About one thing he was sure she did not deceive him. Walpole would destroy both of them if his son did not escape alive. And he would almost certainly carry out his threat to destroy Spandrel's mother. With time pressing and their interests aligned, it made good sense for them to act in concert.

But past treacheries and present doubts travelled with them in Mrs Davenant's fine black and yellow chaise out along the Exeter road that afternoon, through the villages strung along the route, dappled and dozing in the warm spring sunshine. Spandrel still remembered Estelle as she had been at the river-port in Rome, proud and stubborn and untameable. That was her true nature and it would never change. Strangely, though, she was relying on him now, confident that he could yet avert the catastrophe that threatened to overtake them. He had refused to say precisely where they were going or why, but even this had failed to discourage her.

They knew each other too well, in their strengths and their weaknesses. That was the problem. There was too much understanding – too much bitter experience – for any form of trust. They were together because they needed to be. And in the silence that Spandrel strove to maintain lay his best hope of remembering that there could be no other reason. But silence held no appeal for Estelle.

'You keep to the Exeter road, I see,' she said as they failed to fork right beyond Hounslow. 'So, we aren't going to Windsor. Our destination must lie somewhere in the southern reaches of the Forest.'

'We'll put up at Staines tonight.'

'And in the morning?'

'We'll see whether this is a fool's errand or not.'

'You're not a fool, William.' (Of that Spandrel was presently far from sure.) 'You may have been once. But no longer.'

'Wrap your cloak about you.'

'I'm not cold.'

'It's not your comfort I'm concerned about. Hounslow Heath has more than its share of footpads. I don't want your fine clothes attracting unwelcome attention.'

'Then drive the horse faster. We can leave any footpad choking in our dust.'

'We'll need him fresh for tomorrow.'

'Why? Are we going much further?'

Spandrel smiled grimly. 'Do you never give up?'

'Why don't you just tell me where we're going?'

'I'll tell you tomorrow.'

'Why not tell me now?'

Why not, indeed? Because, as Spandrel could hardly admit, he feared that, if he did, he might wake in the morning to find her and the chaise gone. And this time he had no intention of being left behind.

Tired though he was, Spandrel did not sleep well at the inn in Staines. The landlord had a single room only for

Estelle, condemning Spandrel to share a bed with a drugget merchant from Devizes who snored like a walrus and rolled much like one as well. Not that Spandrel could have hoped for carefree slumber in any circumstances. It was hardly more than a guess that McIlwraith was holding Edward Walpole in the vicinity of Bordon Grove, even if the guess had come to Spandrel with an eerie weight of conviction. If he *was* right, they still had to find the place and persuade McIlwraith to release the boy, an outcome which did not seem remotely likely, however Spandrel argued it out in his head. All he knew for certain was that he had to try. And then, of course, there was Estelle . . .

'Wagemaker?' The surprise in Estelle's voice was matched by the frown of disbelief on her face. It was the following morning, they were ready to start . . . and the time had come to reveal their destination. 'Surely that was the name of the Government agent who died in the duel with Captain McIlwraith.'

'Yes. It's his brother's house we're looking for. Bordon Grove. A few miles into the Forest, beyond Egham.'

'But why? What does Wagemaker's brother have to do with this?'

'I'll tell you when we find it.'

'How do you know where he lives?'

'I'll tell you that as well.'

Spandrel had never related McIlwraith's story of his feud with the Wagemakers to Estelle. Keeping it to himself had been his small act of homage to McIlwraith's memory. But McIlwraith was not dead. And soon, very soon, Estelle would have to find that out.

The horse began to show signs of lameness as soon as they set off. They were obliged to turn back and spend the better part of an hour waiting on a blacksmith to have him re-shod. It was late morning when they reached Egham and well gone noon by the time they came within sight of Bagshot. The weather was clear and fine, a gentle breeze coursing like a murmur through the deep stands of the Forest that flanked their route. Spandrel should have felt fortunate to be riding in a handsome carriage with a beautiful woman on a perfect spring day. But what he actually felt was a growing sense of dread.

They stopped at the Roebuck Inn in Bagshot to water the horse. Spandrel suggested they take a meal there and overrode Estelle's objection that this was a waste of valuable time by pointing out that he wanted to ply the tap-room gossips for information concerning the master of Bordon Grove.

'What information do you need?'

'Any I can obtain.'

'To what end?'

It was the same, insistent question in disguise. Why had they come here? The answer was close now, whether Spandrel supplied it or not. He could delay the moment of revelation only a very little longer.

The wiseacres of the tap-room exchanged knowing looks when Spandrel mentioned the Wagemakers. A fresh flagon of ale between them sufficed to loosen their tongues. Bordon Grove had been a well-run and prosperous estate in the days of old Henry Wagemaker. But misfortune and mismanagement had been its undoing. The sudden death of young Dorothea Wagemaker (whether by accident or suicide opinion differed) so soon after her father's demise had sucked the vitals from the family and Tiberius, her brother, had subsequently proved himself to be the sottish wastrel all present had predicted from early in his feckless existence.

Another brother, Augustus, had enjoyed a successful military career and his remittances were presumed till lately to have sustained Tiberius, their invalid mother and a soft-headed aunt who, together with no more than a couple of servants, comprised the household. Certain it was that the estate yielded nothing but thistles and vermin, being utterly neglected and overgrown. Augustus was reported to have been killed in a duel, somewhere abroad, a year or so before, so the family's fortunes could now be assumed to have reached their nadir. This doubtless explained why Tiberius had taken to filling his larder with royal game, earning himself a heavy and quite probably unpaid fine from the Swanimote Court at the rumoured bidding of chief woodward Longrigg, whose long ago courtship of Dorothea was sure to have a bearing on the case.

The name McIlwraith, dropped by Spandrel into the murky waters of so much rumour and reportage, sank at first without a ripple. Then, slowly, certain memories were dredged to the surface. McIlwraith. Yes, he was the last tenant of Blind Man's Tower, a folly on the estate, before it was abandoned, its windows bricked up, its outer staircase left to crumble. It had been used for a while as a store-house for coppicing gear, but coppicing was but a distant memory at Bordon Grove. You could hardly see the tower now above the straggling trees. Owls had long been its only residents. As for McIlwraith, he had vanished shortly after Dorothea Wagemaker's death. And that, the stranger could rest assured, was no coincidence.

When Spandrel returned to the dining-room, he found, as he might have foreseen, that Estelle had already gleaned much of the same information from the land-lady. Estelle had had no reason to mention McIlwraith, of course, so Spandrel could at least be sure that that element of the story was still unknown to her. It was, as it happened, the vital element. Blind Man's Tower was an overgrown ruin. No-one lived there any more; no-one went there. But might not its very abandonment make it ideal for McIlwraith's purpose? Where better to hold a prisoner in secret for a few days? Where else, conveniently close to Eton College, could he be held?

Marabout's map showed a lane leading through the Forest to Bracknell, passing Bordon Grove about halfway along its winding route. They made slow going in the chaise through the many puddles and deep wheel ruts. The boundary pale of Bagshot Park – residence, according to Spandrel's tap-room informants, of the Earl of Arran – curved slowly away from them into the Forest. After that, only dense, unfenced woodland met their gaze to either side. They glimpsed a group of barkers working in a small clearing at one point. Otherwise, the Forest was an empty domain of greenery and birdsong and filtered sunlight.

A low stone wall, moss-covered, fern-shrouded and much broken down, became visible away to their right. Spandrel stopped to study the map before confirming that they were now at the edge of the Bordon Grove estate, if estate it could any longer be called, rather than an indistinguishable part of the surrounding forest. 'The entrance should be about a quarter of a mile ahead.'

'And what do you propose to do when we reach it?' asked Estelle sharply. 'Drive up to the house and politely ask Mr Wagemaker to release Master Edward Walpole?'

'No.' Spandrel sighed. The time had come. 'It isn't Wagemaker we're looking for.'

'Who, then?'

'Captain McIlwraith.'

Estelle should have been dumbstruck by such an

apparently perverse answer. Instead, she looked calmly at Spandrel and said, 'He didn't die in Berne, did he?'

'No.'

'I began to suspect something of the kind when you first mentioned the Wagemakers. I'm not sure why.'

'He's determined to see the contents of the Green Book made public.'

'Does he know what the contents are?'

'Oh yes. I told him.'

'Poor foolish William. You told him?'

'Yes. Strange, isn't it? Yesterday you said with such confidence that I wasn't a fool.'

'You aren't. You don't have to be one in order to do foolish things.'

'Good. Because I'm about to do another.'

'Which is?'

'I think I know where he's hiding the boy. And I think I can persuade him to let him go.'

'How?'

'By convincing him that Walpole won't yield to his demands under any circumstances. The captain isn't a cruel man. He won't want to harm the boy. If we can persuade him—'

'We?'

'He knows what you are to Walpole. He'll believe you understand him better than I do.'

'I'm not sure he'll believe a word I say.'

'He must.'

'Yes. If all's to end well.'

'It still can.'

'Perhaps. Perhaps not. You seem to have forgotten that young Edward was seized by two men. Captain McIlwraith has at least one accomplice, who won't necessarily share this kindly nature you credit him with.'

'Convince Captain McIlwraith and we convince

however many others there are. He'll carry them with him.'

'You're sure of that, are you?'

'I'm sure of nothing.'

'Except that walking unarmed into a nest of kidnappers is a risk worth taking?'

'You don't have to come with me.'

'If I don't, you're even less likely to succeed than if I do.'

'But the choice is yours.'

'Yes.' Estelle looked away into the world of green shadows beyond the tumbled wall. 'And I made it when we left London.'

The entrance to Bordon Grove comprised two lichen-patched stone pillars between which gates no longer hung. The drive they stood guard over was a mud-clogged track, thick with weeds, but still passable. The house itself was nowhere to be seen through the tangle of trees. Not that the house was their destination. The map marked the tower away to the north-west of it, on rising ground. And Spandrel proposed to make straight for it.

They left the chaise in a glade a little way into the forest on the other side of the lane, the horse tethered and grazing. Such pathways as presented themselves in the woodland of Bordon Grove were no better than badger-runs. Estelle's dress soon became soiled with mud and frayed by thorns. But she made no complaint and kept pace with Spandrel as he steered a course by map and compass up the heavily wooded slope. She, indeed, was first to sight the tower ahead of them.

It looked like the turret of some strange castle that had otherwise vanished into the surrounding trees: a squat, three-storey-high structure of stone and flint, with arrow-loops for windows on the upper floors and a battlemented parapet round the roof. That these were mere architectural conceits was confirmed by the open, external staircase that zigzagged up one face of the building, serving doors on each level, not to mention the large, domestic windows on the ground floor. These had been bricked up, however, leaving the tower blind in fact as well as name.

'There doesn't seem to be any sign of life,' whispered Estelle, as they surveyed it from the shelter of the trees.

'They won't want to attract any attention.'

'Then how do you think they'll react to receiving some?'

'I'll approach slowly, but openly. Let anyone who's there see that I mean no harm. Wait here.'

He set off, breathing fast but walking as slowly as he had said he would. The undergrowth thinned as he reached a track leading to the tower entrance – a broad, stout-hinged door at the foot of the staircase. Looking back along the track, which soon curved out of sight, Spandrel guessed that it led to the house. Glancing down, he saw recent boot-prints in the mud, proving that Blind Man's Tower was not as neglected as some supposed. He turned and started towards the entrance. Still nothing stirred. A woodpecker began to hammer at a trunk somewhere close by. A rook flapped lazily from one tree to another above him, cawing as it went.

He reached the door. There was no knocker and rapping at it with his knuckles made little impression through the thick panels. He pounded at it with his fist and raised a muffled echo within, but no kind of answer. Then he tried the handle. The door was locked, as he had assumed it would be. He stepped away and stared up at the arrow-loops above him – then stumbled back in astonishment at the sight of a face staring down at him from the roof.

374

'Who the blazes are you, sir?' came the imperious demand.

'I—'

'Stand where you are. I'm coming down.'

He was a thick-set, red-faced fellow in a threadbare coat and stained waistcoat, a narrow-brimmed hat worn low and crookedly on his wigless head. He was carrying a fowling-piece under one arm that threatened to trip him at every stage of his unsteady descent. If not actually drunk, he was clearly far from sober. Spandrel had never met him before, but there was something familiar about him. And very soon the reason for that familiarity was revealed.

'I own this tower. And the land around it. You're trespassing, sir, and you'll explain yourself, if you please.'

'You're Mr Tiberius Wagemaker?'

'I am.'

'My name's Spandrel. William Spandrel.'

'Never heard of you. You don't look like a Forester to me.'

'I'm from London.'

'Then you can take yourself off back there.'

'I've come a—'

'Mr Wagemaker?' Estelle's voice carried up to them from the trees. Spandrel turned and saw her walking purposefully towards them. When he turned back, Wagemaker was smiling.

'Is this lady with you, Spandrel?'

'Yes, sir.'

'Then perhaps I should go to London more often. Your servant, ma'am.' Wagemaker plucked off his hat and essayed a stiff-backed bow, presenting a patchily shaved head for their inspection. 'You have the advantage of me.'

'I am Mrs Davenant, Mr Wagemaker. Mr Spandrel and I are here on a mission of mercy.'

'Mercy, you say?' Wagemaker creaked upright and replaced his hat. 'I shouldn't have thought you'd have any difficulty extracting that from the hardest of hearts, madam. And mine must rank as one of the softest for many a mile. How can I help you?'

'Mr Spandrel is my brother. I am a widow, as is my sister, who has a son at Eton.'

'A credit to the family, I'm sure.'

'He's been—' Estelle turned aside, apparently needing to compose herself. 'He's been kidnapped.'

'Kidnapped? Good God.'

'We think he's being held somewhere in the Forest,' said Spandrel.

'Have you informed Colonel Negus?'

'We're not acquainted with the gentleman, sir.'

'Deputy Lieutenant of Windsor Castle. If the Forest's to be searched—'

'The kidnappers have sworn to kill the boy if we approach the authorities,' said Estelle. 'We've had to let the college believe he's simply run away. Whereas, in truth . . .' She paused to take the calming breath that she so evidently seemed to need. 'The ransom is beyond our family's means, Mr Wagemaker. Our sister is beside herself. She fears she will never see her son again. Nor will she, unless we can find the place where they've confined him before the ransom falls due.'

'When does—'

'May Day,' put in Spandrel.

'And today is the twenty-eighth,' said Estelle dolefully.

'We're doing our best in the short time available to us,' Spandrel continued. 'Searching every disused or out-of-the-way building in the hope of finding him. Blind Man's

376

Tower was mentioned to us at the Roebuck in Bagshot as meeting both of those requirements.'

'So it does,' said Wagemaker. 'Built by my grandfather, to celebrate the Restoration. I've, er, had no use for it in recent years. The strange thing is, though . . .'

'Yes, sir?' Spandrel prompted.

'Well, my housekeeper – an idle baggage, it's true, but sharp-eyed when she wants to be – reckons she's seen strange men in these woods over the past couple of days. I came up here this afternoon to take a look. No sign of anyone. Until you turned up.'

'There are fresh boot-prints yonder,' said Spandrel, pointing down the track.

'Probably mine.'

'I'd say they were the prints of more than one pair of boots.'

'Even so, you can see for yourselves the tower's empty. I keep it locked. And I'd swear no-one's so much as tried to force the door.'

'Do you have the key about you, Mr Wagemaker?' asked Estelle.

'Yes, but—'

'I'd esteem it a great favour if you'd let us look inside.'

'You would? Well, in that case . . .' Wagemaker fumbled in his waistcoat and produced the key – large, old and rusty. 'Anything to oblige a lady.' He propped his fowling-piece against the staircase, stepped past Spandrel to the door and slid the key into the lock. At first it would not turn, but after pulling the door tight against the frame – and deepening the colour of his face alarmingly in the process – Wagemaker succeeded. He turned the handle and pushed the door open. 'I'm sorry to say the only living creatures you're likely to find in here are mice and spiders, but you're welcome to see for yourselves.'

The door gave directly onto a dusty, cobwebbed chamber as wide and about half as deep as the tower itself. The floorboards were bare and large, jagged gaps in the plaster on the walls revealing the brickwork beneath. There were doors in each corner of the room, standing open to smaller rooms at the rear. The fireplace was a bare hole from which a fallen bird's-nest and other debris had spilt across the floor.

Spandrel stepped inside, disappointment already leaching away his hopes. Then he heard it: a scuffling, shuffling noise, followed by something midway between a moan and a whimper. 'Is there someone here?' he called. And for answer a figure half-fell, half-rolled into view in the doorway of the back room to his left: a youthful figure in plain shirt and breeches, his hands and feet tied, his mouth gagged.

'God's blood,' said Wagemaker. 'It's the boy.'

And so it surely was, though not the boy Estelle had said they were looking for. Spandrel hurried towards him, aware of Estelle's footfalls on the boards behind him.

'Have they harmed him?' she said breathlessly.

'I don't think so.' Spandrel stooped over the boy, resisting the urge to recoil from the stench of urine. 'Never fear, young sir. We're here to help.' He prised at the knot securing the gag as the youth's wide, frightened eyes stared up at him from beneath a fringe of sweat-streaked hair. After a moment, Spandrel gave up trying to untie the knot, took out his pocket-knife and cut through the cloth. 'You are Edward Walpole?' he asked, pulling away the gag.

'You didn't say your sister had married a Walpole,' called Wagemaker from the front door. 'And it's strange you don't seem to recognize your own nephew.'

'We can explain, Mr Wagemaker,' said Estelle, turning back towards him.

'No need, madam.' Wagemaker smiled. 'I already know.' Then he pulled the door shut with an echoing crash. And darkness engulfed them even before they heard the key turn in the lock.

CHAPTER THIRTY-NINE

Blind Treachery

The only light on the ground floor of Blind Man's Tower was a glimmer between the front door and its frame and a still fainter glimmer down the chimney. Spandrel moved across the room to the door and put his eye to the keyhole, but Wagemaker had made sure the escutcheon was back in place. There was nothing to be seen. And seemingly nothing to be done. Their attempt to rescue Edward Walpole had ended in them joining him in his imprisonment.

'Didn't you know that fellow was one of them?' snapped the boy, some of his father's arrogance revealing itself despite the dire straits he was in. 'There's a Scotchman in it too. And some other slinking rascal.'

'We did not know,' said Estelle softly.

'Did my father send you?'

'No.'

'I thought not. He'll have chosen people who know what they're about.'

'Perhaps,' said Spandrel. 'But we found you. And I doubt anyone else can.'

'What help are you to me?'

'Not much. Nor to ourselves, it seems.'

'Mr Wagemaker plays his part very convincingly,' said Estelle.

'Why have they done this to me?' There was a petulant note to young Walpole's voice that Spandrel sensed he would soon find irksome, understandable though it was.

'They're trying to force your father to do something he's determined not to do,' said Estelle.

'Papa can't be forced.'

'They think otherwise.'

'What have they said they'll do to me?'

'They've said they'll kill you,' put in Spandrel.

Silence fell, long and heavy. Spandrel made his tentative way back across the room and began trying to untie the knotted ropes at the boy's wrists and ankles. But the knots were tight and in the darkness he could make little of them.

'You have a knife.' Edward Walpole had not been cowed for long. 'Cut them.'

'I was about to.' Spandrel took out his knife and went to work. 'But I'll have to be careful I don't cut through you as well as the ropes.'

'Hurry up, can't you?'

'You'll gain nothing by railing at us,' said Estelle.

'Will I not?' There was a thud as the boy kicked the wall with his pinioned feet, followed by a rustle of falling plaster. 'My father is the King's first minister. I can't be treated like this.'

'Perhaps you should have explained that to your kidnappers,' said Spandrel, sure though he was that young Walpole had done so just as often as he had been given the chance. 'Now, hold still.' Reluctantly, the boy did hold still. 'There. You're free.' Spandrel pulled the ropes away.

'Free of these ropes, but not this prison. What's to be done, damn it?'

'How often do they visit you?' asked Spandrel levelly.

'That fellow – Wagemaker – brings me bread and

water. I can't tell at what intervals. I can't tell anything' – the boy's voice cracked – 'in this confounded darkness.'

'Calm yourself, Edward,' said Estelle gently.

'I'm Master Walpole to you, madam.'

'As you please.' There was an icy edge to Estelle's voice as she continued. 'Well then, *Master Walpole*, be so good as to keep to yourself any further reproaches of us that may come to your mind. We will all have to wait as patiently and as calmly as we can.'

Silence fell once more. But Spandrel reckoned it would not last for long. 'There might be something worth trying,' he said, rising to his feet and feeling his way round the wall to one of the bricked-up windows. There he stopped, took out his pocket-knife and gouged at the mortar between two of the bricks with the point of the blade.

'What are you doing?' called Estelle.

'Trying to scrape out enough mortar to dislodge a brick.'

'Do you think you can?'

'Eventually.' Mortar began to patter at Spandrel's feet. 'I doubt Wagemaker employed master craftsmen when he had this place sealed.'

'How long will it take?'

'I don't know.' Spandrel looked over his shoulder, sensing Estelle's presence close behind him, but seeing nothing. 'I may as well find out, though. Unless you have any better ideas.'

'I don't have any better ideas.' There was a touch of her hand at his elbow. 'But I'm sure there's a way out of everything – if you look hard enough.'

'One day there won't be. You know that, don't you?'

'One day. But not this day.'

'If you think you can do it, why don't you get on with it?' came a familiar whine from behind them.

'Out of the very mouth of babes and sucklings,' murmured Estelle.

'And spoilt brats,' added Spandrel, turning back to the wall.

Spandrel had loosened one brick, but was still a long way from dislodging it, an uncountable portion of time later, when Estelle called from the front door for him to stop.

'I think I can hear someone outside,' she explained. 'Footsteps. Voices. I'm not sure.'

But by the time Spandrel had joined her at the door, she *was* sure. And so was he. There was a burble of conversation. Who was speaking or what they were saying was not distinguishable. Then a boot scraped against the doorstep and the key was thrust into the keyhole. They moved back as the door opened.

The flood of daylight was at first dazzling. A figure loomed in the doorway, haloed by the glare. 'I'd bid you good afternoon,' came the voice of Captain James McIlwraith. 'But I fear it's not likely to be good for any of us.' He was holding a pistol in his right hand, which he proceeded to cock and point, not at Spandrel, but at Estelle. 'Particularly you, madam.'

'What became of your gallantry, Captain?' said Estelle, smiling defiantly at him. 'Imprisoning boys and threatening women is sorry work indeed.'

'As you say. Sorry work. But in a glad cause.'

'You'll pay for this,' said young Walpole, who for all his defiance hung back in the doorway of the rear room. 'You whoreson villain.'

'Another word from you, sir,' said McIlwraith, 'and I'll have my friend here tie and gag you again.' Tiberius Wagemaker loomed at his shoulder. 'Just one word, mind, is all the provocation I need.'

Edward Walpole stared dumbly at his captors,

tempted to answer back, it was clear – but knowing better than to do so.

'What are we to do with you two, then?' McIlwraith pondered the point. 'The rat and the vixen we find in our trap. Have you succumbed to her charms again, Spandrel?'

'We have to talk to you, Captain,' said Spandrel. 'That's why we're here.'

'You *are* talking to me.'

'Alone.'

'Oh, alone, is it? So that Mrs de Vries can pour another sweet lie into my gullible old ear? I don't think so.'

'We risked our lives by coming here.'

'So you did.'

'Won't you grant us one small favour in return?' Spandrel looked McIlwraith in the eye. 'A private word, Captain. It's not much to ask.'

'Don't trust them,' said Wagemaker.

'I don't trust *you*.' McIlwraith sounded more than slightly testy. His strange alliance with an old enemy had clearly not been ordained in Heaven. 'But still I speak to you. Very well, Spandrel. You and Mrs de Vries go up to the roof. I'll join you there for your "private word". Lock the door behind them, Wagemaker. And stand by. Plunket!' A lean, narrow-faced fellow dressed like a scarecrow and closely matching young Walpole's description of a 'slinking rascal' appeared from round the corner of the building as Spandrel and Estelle stepped outside. 'Get back to the road and keep watch. And make it a keener watch than you managed earlier.'

'Yes, sir.' Plunket took off at a lope along the track.

'After you, madam.' McIlwraith uncocked the pistol and waved Estelle towards the stairs. 'And watch your step. Wagemaker is behindhand with his repairs.'

Spandrel followed Estelle up the stairs. There was a

384

muttered exchange between McIlwraith and Wagemaker that he could not catch. Then the captain started after them.

The roof was a shallow pyramid of lead, centred on the chimney, with a walkway round all four sides behind the castellated parapet. Windsor Forest defined the horizon in every direction, green and deep and hazy in the mellowing sunlight. The sun was drifting through a cloud-rack away to the west and from its position Spandrel judged that the afternoon was turning towards evening. There was a chill to the air, though whether enough to account for the shiver he saw run through Estelle he rather doubted.

'Cold, madam?' McIlwraith, standing at the top of the stairs, had evidently seen the same thing. 'Or nervous?'

'Neither, Captain. A touch of vertigo, I rather think. I'm prone to it.'

'Then you shouldn't climb so high, should you?'

'I like to conquer my weaknesses, not be governed by them.'

'So I've seen. Now, this private word of yours, Spandrel. We'll make it quick, if you please. Mrs de Vries may not be nervous, but I have the impression Wagemaker is.'

'Does he know you killed his brother?' asked Spandrel.

'Oh yes. I told him myself. Little love lost there of late, apparently. The brothers had fallen out. Over this, as a matter of fact. The Forest. Walpole's been installing his favourites here just as he's been installing his whores in St James's. And those favourites have ridden roughshod over local rights and traditions. Tiberius blames the likes of Lord Cadogan, who's building a palace to rival Blenheim over at Caversham, for all his misfortunes. And the Jacobites have enabled him to dignify his resentment

385

as a noble cause. There's no shortage of Jacobites around here, thanks to old King William's periodic expulsions of Catholics from London. The Earl of Arran lives nearby. And Lord Arran, as I'm sure Walpole knows from his perusal of Sunderland's papers, is thick with the Pretender.'

'This rising they plan cannot possibly succeed,' said Estelle.

'Not as things stand. But after Tuesday's edition of the *London Gazette* reaches the coffee-houses and taverns of England, it may not be so certain.'

'He won't do it, Captain,' said Spandrel. 'That's what we're here to tell you. Walpole won't give in. Tuesday's *Gazette* will make no mention of the Green Book.'

'We'll see as to that.'

'All you'll see,' said Estelle, 'is his son's blood on your hands.'

'I've no wish to harm the boy, in need of a thrashing though he clearly is.'

'What you wish is beside the point. What will you *do*, when Walpole defies you?'

'He won't.'

'He will. Trust me, Captain. I know him. As you so charmingly put it, I am his whore. His nature is clearer to me than it can ever be to you. He is immovable. He loves Edward. But he loves power more. And he will not give it up.'

'Then he'll have to—'

'You see?' Estelle stared intently at McIlwraith. 'You'll kill the boy, won't you? Or Wagemaker will. Or Plunket. Or the Earl of Arran's gamekeeper. It doesn't matter who. Someone will do it, rather than admit defeat and let him go free.'

'I cannot foretell the future.'

'We can. Tell him about your mother, William.'

386

'He says he'll have her hanged as a thief, Captain,' said Spandrel. 'After I've been hanged as a murderer.'

'And he means it,' said Estelle. 'He's only stayed his hand for fear of forcing yours.'

'And what does he say he'll do to you, madam?'

'He does not say. But he knows one of us must have told you what the Green Book contains.'

'How big a bribe he was paid, you mean? How much room he had to make in his pocket? I wouldn't worry your beautiful head too much about answering for that. If it comes to the point, I'm sure Spandrel here will manfully bear the responsibility, being the noble fool that he is.'

'It *is* my responsibility,' said Spandrel bleakly.

'There you are. It's back to the bedroom in safety for you, madam. Back where you belong.'

'Walpole takes nothing on trust,' said Estelle. 'He won't give me the benefit of the doubt.'

'You'll pardon me if I lose no sleep over that.'

'I hardly think you'll have much sleep to lose, with the forces Walpole can command on your trail. But that's beside the point. I'm not asking for your pity.'

'That's as well, since you'll get none from me.'

'I only want you to understand that we're here on our account, not Walpole's. We're here to save his son – and to save ourselves.'

'And you too, Captain,' said Spandrel. 'He doesn't know of your involvement. And he needn't. If it ends here.'

'In meek surrender? Is that your proposal?'

'You don't want murder on your conscience. That's what it'll be. Plain murder. And of a boy. An innocent boy, what's more, however guilty his father may be.'

'I told you, Spandrel. It's him or me.'

'Then it's him. I don't believe you're ruthless enough

to go through with this. But he is. *I* told *you*. You can't win.'

'Only choose the manner of my defeat? That's no course for a soldier.'

'Release the boy,' said Estelle. 'We'll say we don't know who you are or where you've gone. I promise.'

'I know how reliable your promises are, madam.'

'You can rely on this one.'

'I think not. The brat knows too much already for you to protect my anonymity. Besides, what could have brought you here – other than that story of lost love I told Spandrel in Berne?'

'You could be out of the country long before anything was sworn against you.'

'Exile and hiding. What riches you do promise me.'

'Not riches, perhaps. But the best we can contrive.'

'And your reward? A long lease on Phoenix House, perhaps.'

'Perhaps.'

'But Spandrel's mother allowed to live out her days in peace. And Spandrel spared a miscarriage of Dutch justice. That's the sum of it, is it?'

'Yes.'

'The sum of all things.' McIlwraith sighed and looked past them across the rolling canopy of the Forest. 'Walpole's a keen huntsman, so they tell me. And it seems he no more wants for foxes than for hounds. He breeds the one as he breeds the other. What a grasp of economy the man does have. You're right, of course, Spandrel. My quarrel's with the father, not the son.'

'You'll let the boy go?' asked Spandrel, hope blooming suddenly within him.

'It seems it's either that or kill him. And I'd sooner hang for murdering the First Lord of the Treasury than his son. You may take it I—'

'McIlwraith!' It was Wagemaker's voice, raised in a shout of alarm. 'We're discovered.'

McIlwraith swung round even as did Spandrel and Estelle. There, below them, hurrying up the track, came a troop of infantry, their musket barrels glinting in the sun. Discovered they had clearly been. Or betrayed.

'Well, well,' said McIlwraith. 'It seems my mind's been made up for me.'

CHAPTER FORTY

Under Siege

'Stand where you are!' came a shout.

For a second, Spandrel thought the order was directed at all of them. Then he realized that Tiberius Wagemaker was the real target. He had started up the stairs, a pistol clutched in his right hand, glaring upwards as he climbed. 'They've done for us, McIlwraith,' he bellowed. 'Spandrel and that she-devil.'

'*Halt or we fire!*'

But Wagemaker did not halt. It seemed to Spandrel that he did not even hear. Nor did he see, as they could from the roof, the musketeers taking aim below him.

'*Halt, I say!*'

Wagemaker raised his pistol, cocking it as he did so, and pointed it at Spandrel. In the same instant, there was a barked order and an explosion of musket shots.

Several of the shots took Wagemaker in the back. He arched backwards and fired into the air, the roar of the shot swallowing a last, grimacing cry. Then he fell, striking his head against the stairs behind him before plunging to the ground with a heavy thud like that of a laden sack being tossed from a barn-loft.

'Don't move,' said McIlwraith quietly, lowering his pistol out of sight behind the parapet. 'And say nothing unless I tell you to. I reckon Wagemaker's shown us what's likely to come of acting hastily.'

'You three on the roof!' The musket-smoke cleared to reveal the stout figure of a heavily braided senior officer. 'I'm Colonel Negus, Deputy Lieutenant of Windsor Castle. I have reason to believe an oppidan of Eton College, Master Edward Walpole, is being held here against his will. I require and demand his immediate release.'

'You'll find the boy in the room below,' McIlwraith shouted back. 'And you'll find the key to the door in the pocket of the fellow your men have just shot.'

'What's the boy's condition?'

'He's alive and well enough, though none too happy.'

'It'll be your neck if he's come to any harm.'

'I dare say it'll be my neck either way, Colonel.'

To this Negus did not respond. He sent two men scurrying over to Wagemaker's body. As they began searching his pockets, McIlwraith said to Estelle in an undertone, without turning to look at her, 'Have we you to thank for this, Mrs de Vries?'

'Yes,' she softly replied. 'The landlady of the Roebuck named you as the last person to live here and a rumoured lover of Dorothea Wagemaker. I'd already guessed you were still alive and that's when I realized William suspected you were holding the boy here. William was in the tap-room at the time, unaware of what I was doing. I paid the stable-boy to ride to Windsor Castle with a message for Walpole's brother, Horatio, whom he sent there yesterday to organize a search.' She paused, then added, 'I'd thought they might arrive sooner.'

'All this . . . negotiating . . . was just a delaying tactic, then?'

'Partly. But I bear you no ill will, Captain. I'd have been happy to—'

A sudden commotion below marked the discovery of the key. Negus sent his adjutant forward to open the door. He disappeared from their view, but they could hear the rattle of the key in the lock, followed by a creak of the door on its hinges.

'We were supposed to be in this together,' said Spandrel, slowly recognizing the deception to which Estelle was calmly admitting. 'We were supposed to trust one another.'

'But you didn't trust me, did you? If you'd told me where we were going and why, it mightn't have come to this.'

'That won't do,' objected McIlwraith. 'How did you know Walpole had despatched his brother to Windsor? He told you, didn't he? And he also told you to send a message to him there if and when you succeeded in gleaning the boy's whereabouts from Spandrel. So, if Spandrel had told you from the outset what was in his mind, you'd only have betrayed him the sooner.'

'What a hard woman you think me, Captain.'

'What a hard woman you are.'

'We could have ended this as I'd hoped,' said Spandrel, seeming to see in his mind a dream slipping away from him. 'We could all have escaped, with no harm done. There was no need for . . .'

'A military resolution,' said McIlwraith. 'Need or not, though, that's what we're to have. And in short order, I imagine, now they have the brat.'

At that moment, Edward Walpole appeared below, limping slightly as he walked towards the soldiers, supported by the adjutant. He cast a glance across at Wagemaker's body, then up at them on the roof, as he went. It was not a glance in which either mercy or gratitude was to be readily detected.

Colonel Negus led the boy away, patting his shoulder as he talked to him. Their discussion lasted several minutes, during which not a word was spoken on the roof. Spandrel stared at Estelle, daring her to look him in the eye. But she trained her gaze firmly on the scene below. Then Negus strode back to his position, leaving young Walpole in the care of someone who looked to be a doctor.

'Captain McIlwraith!' Negus called.

'Aye, Colonel?'

'Where's your other accomplice?'

'Taken to his heels, I assume.'

'Your companions there are Mrs Davenant and Mr Spandrel?'

'So they are.'

'Send them down. Mrs Davenant first.'

'As you please.' McIlwraith moved clear of the head of the stairs, waving Estelle forward.

The walkway was so narrow that she could not avoid brushing against Spandrel as she passed him. But still she kept her gaze averted. He watched her walk slowly to the gap in the parapet and turn to start her descent.

At that moment, McIlwraith moved smartly forward, raised the pistol and clapped it to her temple. 'That's quite far enough, madam,' he said, cocking the trigger. 'You surely don't suppose I'm going to let you go.'

'Don't do it, Captain,' Spandrel cried. 'She's not worth it.'

'There I must disagree, Spandrel. It seems to me she's eminently worth it, especially considering that killing her's unlikely to increase the severity of my punishment.'

'Lower the pistol,' shouted Negus. 'At once.'

'I can't oblige you there, Colonel,' McIlwraith replied. 'And if your men open fire, I should say they're as likely to blow Mrs Davenant's head off as mine. I advise you to stay your hand.'

'Let me go, Captain,' said Estelle, too calmly to sound as if she was pleading.

'Why should I?'

'Because, if you let me live, I can save William from the gallows. Kill me and you condemn him to hang alongside you.'

'And will you save him?'

'If you give me the chance to, yes.'

'No doubt I can have your word on that.'

'Would my word mean anything to you?'

'Not even if this tower was built of bibles.'

'I swear it, even so.'

'You're right anyway, damn it, whether you swear or no. A ball through your head is a noose round Spandrel's neck. And I'm as sure as you probably are that Negus will have been instructed to take me at any cost – even your life.' McIlwraith lowered the pistol. 'Go down and join your friends, madam. And remember your promise.'

'I shall.'

Spandrel watched her as she slowly descended the stairs, disdaining to put a hand to the wall to steady herself, an eddying breeze stirring her hair beneath the hat and tugging at her dress. As she reached the first landing and turned, she glanced up at him, but her eyes were in shadow and what her gaze might have conveyed he could not tell. Then she went on down, without a second upward glance.

'Spandrel may follow,' called Negus.

'Do as the man says,' said McIlwraith. 'You're better off down there than up here.'

'Will you surrender, Captain?' Spandrel asked as he moved to the head of the stairs.

'Do you think I should?'

'Walpole told me he'd have his son's kidnappers hanged, drawn and quartered.'

'Aye. And their heads left to rot on spikes at Temple Bar, no doubt. If that should happen to me, Spandrel, will you climb up there one dark night, take mine down and give it a decent burial, for the sake of the miles we rode together?'

'Yes, Captain. I will.'

McIlwraith smiled. 'Good man. I'll do my best to spare you the need. Now, look lively on the stairs. We don't want Colonel Negus to suspect you of collusion with the enemy.'

Spandrel started down. He looked up twice during his descent, but McIlwraith was not watching him. He seemed to be scanning the horizon, his eyes narrowed against the sun.

It was no more than thirty yards from the foot of the stairs to where Colonel Negus was standing. In the few moments it took Spandrel to cover the distance, he became aware of a difference in the manner of his reception compared with that of Estelle. She was some way off down the track, with young Walpole, the doctor and a junior officer. Around the group they made hovered an atmosphere of solicitude and deference. But for Spandrel there was only Negus's stern gaze and gravelly voice.

'Place this man under arrest, Captain Rogers,' he said to his adjutant. 'We're unsure as to his allegiance.'

A pair of burly soldiers seized Spandrel by the arms and led him aside. He did not resist. He did not even protest. It was only what he had half-expected. As to what it portended, he could not find the energy to imagine.

'Captain McIlwraith!' he heard Negus call. 'Discharge your pistol into the air, lay down your sword and descend the stairs with your arms held aloft.'

'I'm a soldier like yourself, Colonel. I don't surrender lightly.'

'Your position is hopeless.'

'Aye. So it is. Whether I surrender or no.'

'Give it up, man. You've not harmed the boy. That'll count in your favour.'

'With God, perhaps. But not with Walpole. I advise you to withdraw your men.'

'Surrender, Captain, or prepare to be stormed.'

'You'll never take me, Colonel. And you'll lose most of your men in the attempt.'

'I'll bandy words with you no longer.' Negus turned to his adjutant. 'Captain Rogers—'

'Wait, sir,' said Rogers. 'What's he doing?'

The two soldiers holding Spandrel looked round at this, enabling Spandrel to do the same. He did so in time to see McIlwraith scrambling up the roof to the chimney and round to the far side of the stack.

'The man's mad,' declared Negus, his patience exhausted. 'Deploy your best marksmen and end this, Rogers.'

'I'll decree the ending of this, not you, Colonel,' shouted McIlwraith. He threw his gun down the roof to the walkway, then pulled something from inside the chimney-pot and fumbled in his pocket.

'Finish the man, Rogers. Now!'

'Yes, sir. But—'

There was a flash of some kind from where McIlwraith was standing, then a duller, trailing flame.

'He's lit a fuse, sir. Do you think—'

'My God, he must have mined the chimney. Fall the men back. Quickly!'

The realization of what McIlwraith was about communicated itself to the troops before Rogers could even issue an order. Once he did, they began a withdrawal down the track that soon became a pell-mell retreat. Spandrel's guards, intent upon saving themselves, left him where he was, staring up at the gaunt figure on the roof.

McIlwraith's coat flapped behind him in the breeze, his bare, grey-maned head lit by the sun. Though he could not be certain amidst the confused shouts and pounding footfalls, it seemed to Spandrel that McIlwraith was laughing with genuine amusement at the scene below him. Then he stopped laughing. And slowly, with seeming relish, drew his sword. The sunlight glinted on the blade. McIlwraith held it out before him, as if to meet the charge of some other, invisible swordsman.

Then, with a flash and a roar, the mine exploded. The whole upper half of the tower vanished in a gout of flame and smoke and flying stone. And Spandrel's last thought, before something struck him near his right ear and darkness swallowed him, was that McIlwraith could not be hanged, drawn and quartered now. Nor would his head need rescuing from Temple Bar. He was out of Walpole's reach. For good and all.

CHAPTER FORTY-ONE

Full Circle

Spandrel had a dim awareness of a wound above his ear being washed and dressed and of a bandage being wrapped round his head, but it was some unmeasurable time after that when he regained consciousness to find himself lying in bed in a bare, twilit chamber. The granular light from the window suggested either dusk or dawn, but he had no clear idea which and felt a strange lack of curiosity on the point. He fell asleep.

When he woke, the light was stronger and his mind once more in command of logical thought. The bed was soft and generously blanketed and there were no bars at the window, but nevertheless there was something cell-like about the chamber. He rose, slowed by a dull, pounding headache, and fingered the bandage round his head, faintly surprised to discover that he still had a head to be bandaged. Then he walked unsteadily to the window and looked out.

A high wall and a steep escarpment below it combined into a sheer and vertiginous drop beyond the mullioned panes. The river at the foot of the escarpment was surely the Thames and the town huddled on the other side Eton, to judge by the ecclesiastical building seeming to float above it that could only be the college chapel. He was in Windsor Castle. And not, the bareness of the room suggested, as an honoured guest. He crossed to the door and tried the latch. But the door was locked, as he had expected. So, he was a prisoner, as he had also expected.

He banged on the door loudly and for long enough to rouse any guard who might be near. But there was no response. Perhaps they had not supposed he would wake so soon. He went back to the window and pushed it open.

Church bells were ringing. It was Sunday morning. The events of the day before lay in the past. But they were fresh in his memory. In his mind's eye, clearer by far than the vista below of river and field and chapel, Spandrel saw McIlwraith standing on Blind Man's Tower, sword in hand, the instant before he and it were blasted into oblivion. 'You'll never take me,' he had said. And he had been as good as his word.

He was gone now, that strange, curmudgeonly warrior. He had used up the last of his lives. Spandrel wandered back to the bed and lay down, tears stinging his eyes as a grief he had never thought he would feel swept over him. It was a grief, he realized, sharpened by fear. McIlwraith had rescued him once before, when no one else could. What would happen to him now? Who – if anyone – would rescue him this time?

The church bells had fallen silent, and the angle of the sun across the rooftops of Eton had altered with the advance of the day, when the door of Spandrel's room was at last opened, to an overture of jangling keys. A grim-faced guard, built like a bear but clearly not given to dancing, looked in at Spandrel, then made way for a kitchen-boy, who brought in a meal that smelt surprisingly good, deposited it at Spandrel's feet and scuttled out.

'What am I—' But Spandrel's admittedly tardy question was cut off by the slamming of the door. And a further jangling of keys.

Half an hour later, the door opened once more. Expecting the kitchen-boy, Spandrel picked up the licked-clean plate and held it out for collection. Only to find himself confronted by the corpulent, scowling, Sunday-suited figure of Robert Walpole.

'Put the plate down, sir. Do you take me for a turn-spit?' Walpole looked round at the guard. 'Close the door behind you. And stay within call.'

'Yes, sir.' The door closed.

'Well now, Spandrel, how do I find you? Barely scratched, according to the doctor.' Walpole ambled across to the window and gazed out. 'And handsomely accommodated, I see.'

'Am I a prisoner, Mr Walpole?'

'Certainly you are, sir. But a well fed and softly bedded one, thanks to Mrs Davenant. She assures me you did your best to rescue my son. And he *was* rescued. But since you bear a large measure of responsibility for the peril he was placed in—'

'I had nothing to do with it.'

'*Don't interrupt me.*' Walpole turned and glared at him. 'You knew McIlwraith was still alive, yet you said nothing. I suspect you also knew what he intended to do, but still you said nothing, calculating that his plan, if it succeeded, would bring me down. Only when you realized that I would not yield to his demands and that you would therefore be complicit in my son's murder did you attempt to retrieve the situation. In which attempt you were only partially successful.'

'Your son *is* alive.'

'Indeed he is. But Colonel Negus's adjutant and two other members of his detachment of troops are not, having been killed by flying lumps of stone of the kind that merely grazed you. Nor are my son's kidnappers available for questioning. Two are dead and one is in hiding. How am I to prove Atterbury's involvement in this plot without the evidence only they could have supplied?'

'But your son is alive,' Spandrel hopelessly repeated.

'Yes. And if I believed you'd tried to save him out of Christian charity rather than a concern for your own skin, I'd thank you fulsomely enough. But I don't believe it. And I doubt you have the gall to try to persuade me otherwise.'

'I did my best, sir.'

'To serve two masters and outwit each of them in turn. That's what you did your best to accomplish, Spandrel, and you failed, as you were bound to. Well, there's a price for failure. And you'll have to pay it. Mrs Davenant tells me she gave McIlwraith some sort of undertaking to save your neck, but I have to tell you she was in no position to give such an undertaking. Your neck is at my disposal, not hers. And her whims are not my will. That is something both of you need to understand. She seems to think I should set you free. But then Kelly would squeeze the truth out of you and Atterbury would know better than to carry on with his treasonable designs. As it is, he still doesn't know the extent to which I've seen through them and I mean to keep him in ignorance as long as possible. I also mean to teach you – and Mrs Davenant – that disobeying me is a grievous offence.'

'What are you going to do with me?'

'Send you to Amsterdam.'

'To hang?'

'That'll be a matter for the Dutch court to decide.'

'But you know what they'll decide.'

'Not at all.' For a moment, Walpole seemed about to smile. Then his face hardened. 'You must address yourself to your own salvation, Spandrel. I'm done with you.

401

Tomorrow, you'll be moved to the Tower of London and held there while a message is sent to the Sheriff of Amsterdam and a reply awaited. You'll be allowed no visitors, I'm afraid. I can't have your situation becoming the talk of the city. As for letters, you may send one to your mother if you wish. I'll read it before it's delivered, of course, courtesy of the Postmaster-General, so you'll need to watch what you say in it. A flight to foreign parts might be a merciful lie to tell in the circumstances. Your mother needn't know anything of events in Amsterdam. I shan't inflict them upon her. Nor, if you conduct yourself with suitable reticence at your trial, will my wife's jewellery ever be found about her. You have my word on that.'

'Your word . . . as a statesman?'

'That blow clearly hasn't addled your memory. Yes. My word as a statesman.' Walpole walked slowly across the room towards the door, then stopped and looked round at Spandrel. 'We shan't meet again. Nor will you and . . . Mrs Davenant. If you have a message for her . . .'

'There's no message.'

'Good.' Walpole permitted himself a grin. 'I wouldn't have passed it on if there had been.'

Spandrel was surprised by the mildness of his own reaction. This was, after all, the plight he had been struggling to evade, one way or another, for more than a year. Perhaps that was the reason for the fatalistic lethargy that held him in its grasp. He could do nothing. There was no escape. He was done for. Days would pass, journeys be undertaken, procedures followed. But the end was fixed and known. In that certainty lay a strange kind of comfort. He did not have to think any more. He did not need to struggle. Everything would be done for him. Except dying, of course. He would have to do that for himself.

Looking through the window, he thought how easy it would be to scramble out onto the chamfered sill and decree his own end, falling through the Windsor air to the ground far below. It would spare him a deal of suffering later. But he had not the courage for that. And his store of hope, he realized, was not quite exhausted, though why not he failed to understand. 'While there's life,' his father had often said, 'there's hardship.' And so it seemed there was.

Spandrel pulled his bed across to the window and sat by it to write the one letter Walpole had said he could write and for which a single sheet of paper had been provided. He would tell the lie Walpole had suggested. He would let his mother go on believing that she might yet see him again. At least she did not have to do so as a washerwoman living within the rules of the Fleet Prison. As a well set up widow, she might find a new husband and forget her wayward son. She might, indeed, be better off without him. She could hardly be worse off.

The letter written, he lay down on the bed and stared out at the sky, watching the afternoon wear towards evening. How odd it was, he thought, that a man who has never done anything wrong, nor borne anyone the least ill will, should nevertheless be required to pay with his life for the crimes and conspiracies of others. It was not fair. It was not right. But it was how the world turned. From light to dark. And back again. For some.

Robert Walpole's arrival that evening at the Townshends' London residence was a surprise, though a pleasant one, for the Viscountess. The Viscount pretended for his wife's benefit that he shared her surprise. The truth was, however, that Walpole had said he would call upon his return from Windsor, to speak of matters which his sister knew nothing about.

After an exchange of family gossip which the Viscountess found disappointingly short and shallow, Walpole and his brother-in-law retired to the Viscount's study, where, behind closed doors, fortified by port and tobacco, they turned at once to urgent debate.

'Edward is well?' Townshend asked, knowing already that his nephew-in-law was safe, but not yet certain that safe also meant sound.

'Oh yes,' said Walpole, smiling the broad smile of a relieved parent. 'He doesn't seem to have had to endure anything worse than I was put through at Eton in the normal course of a typical day. You oppidans never knew the brutalities we collegers were subjected to.'

'I did, Robin. You complained to me of them in unfailing detail at the time and have often reminded me since.'

'Lest you forget.' Walpole laughed. 'Edward will be able to entertain you with tales of his incarceration when you see him in the summer. He's likely to mention a dark-haired lady who'll sound confoundedly like Mrs Davenant.' He held up a hand. 'I know you've always wanted to know nothing about my mistresses, Charles. I blame your prudery on a happy marriage. And I thank God for it as well, of course. You and Dolly are luckier than you know. It was because of your . . . sensibilities . . . that I failed to tell you of the lady's involvement in this matter.'

'Say no more.' Townshend gave his brother-in-law a knowing look. 'I gather there was . . . some kind of explosion.'

'The tower where Edward was held turns out to have been mined. It was blown to blazes.' Walpole chuckled.

'My son seems to have enjoyed the fireworks.'

'Were many killed?'

'Negus's adjutant and two soldiers. Along with two of the kidnappers. A third made off. I needn't tell you I'd like to have had at least one of them to squeeze for evidence. As it is, we're back where we started so far as Atterbury's concerned. The fugitive's called Plunket. He's known to the Secret Service as a Jacobite hanger-on. The smallest of fry, but worth landing if we can catch bigger fish in the same net.'

'This dishes your efforts to tempt Atterbury with the Green Book, I assume.'

'I fear it does, Charles. That, as you might say, is now a closed book.' Walpole smiled wryly. 'We must make the best of what we have.'

'Should we show our hand, then?'

'Not yet. I want our discredited emissary safely lodged in a Dutch gaol before we make the threat to the King public. Horace is ready to leave for The Hague tomorrow. How many troops do you think he can persuade Hoornbeeck to promise us?'

'Not as many as Heinsius would have done.' (The previous Grand Pensionary of Holland had indeed been an unswerving ally. His successor was a notably cooler one.)

'Hoornbeeck may feel more accommodating when Horace tells him that the Englishman who murdered one of Amsterdam's most eminent citizens last year and then escaped from custody can now at last, thanks to us, be made to answer for his crime. We've neatly, if inadvertently, attended to the destruction of the blackguard responsible for his escape as well. All in all, I reckon the burghers of Amsterdam are greatly indebted to us.'

'So, it's the noose for your redundant mapmaker?'

'Indeed. Which is nothing less than he deserves.'

Walpole took a thoughtful puff at his pipe. 'Irksome as the fellow is, though, I've done my best for him. Horace will ask for an assurance that he won't be tortured into confessing.'

'Nor into disclosing anything not strictly relevant to the case, presumably.'

'True enough, Charles. But mercy was naturally my prime consideration.' Walpole blew a noose-shaped smoke-ring towards the ceiling. 'As ever.'

CHAPTER FORTY-TWO

Dutch Reckoning

Spandrel spent a week of comfortable if scarcely contented solitude in the Tower of London. By coincidence, his quarters were next to those previously occupied by Sir Theodore Janssen. But though the view they commanded of the river and the wharves of Bermondsey was the same, there was an important difference ever to the fore of Spandrel's thoughts. Sir Theodore had been waiting for his case to be heard by Parliament, fearful about how much of his lovingly accumulated wealth – of land and houses, jewels and china, paintings and tapestries, horses and carriages, cochineal and pepper – he would be allowed to keep. But his life had never been threatened. He sat now at his house in Hanover Square, less wealthy but at several fortunes' remove from poverty, contemplating an old age of ease and security. For Spandrel, old age had joined a long list of experiences he knew he would never have.

Being led in chains through Traitors' Gate, loaded aboard a launch and conveyed downriver to a waiting Dutch frigate was, by contrast, an experience he had never expected to have and would have preferred to be spared. But his preferences counted for even less than they ever had. The *Kampioen* took delivery of its prisoner in Limehouse Reach on a dull May morning of spitting rain. And turning for a last glimpse before he was led below, Spandrel took his leave of the city – and the country – of his birth.

The day after Spandrel's unheralded departure, Viscount Townshend wrote to the Lord Mayor of London, instructing him to expel all papists and non-jurors from the city by reason of the Government's recent discovery of a Jacobite plot to overthrow – indeed, assassinate – the King.

Even as the papists and non-jurors left in their paltry hundreds, the troops arrived in their armed thousands to set up camp in Hyde Park. The King, it was announced, would not now be going to Hanover. A threat to his life, as well as his crown, was said to have been revealed in an anonymous letter to the Duchess of Kendal. Arrests, trials and executions were promised. And the London mob settled to await an exciting summer.

For Spandrel summer was less of a prospect than a memory. Not that the seasons made themselves apparent in the cells beneath the Stadhuis in Amsterdam. There the shadows were always deep and long and the days very much the same. Spandrel's cell was not the one he had been incarcerated in fifteen months before, but might as well have been for all the differences there were. Big Janus was still the friendliest of the turnkeys, bearing no grudge, it seemed, over the affray at Ugels' shop. He seemed, indeed, positively sorry to see Spandrel back, though not as sorry as Spandrel was to be there.

How and when the authorities would deal with him Spandrel did not know. Soon and summarily was his expectation. This time, he felt certain, the British vice-consul – if one had been appointed in succession to Cloisterman – would not come calling.

In that he was correct, though only because the dandily

attired visitor shown into his cell a few days after his arrival was not the vice-consul. Evelyn Dalrymple, as the plum-voiced fellow introduced himself, was at pains to emphasize that he held a senior post at the British Embassy in The Hague. He would not normally endure a *trekschuit* journey halfway across Holland for the dubious privilege of visiting the Stadhuis cells. That he had done so was a measure of the British Government's concern for the due and proper process of the law.

'I'm not sure you appreciate how much we've done for you, Spandrel.'

'Oh, I do appreciate it, Mr Dalrymple, believe me.'

'We've specially requested that you be spared torture.'

'That was good of someone.'

'Indeed it was. But it *was* only a request, you understand. Throw wild accusations around at your examination – muddy the water, so to speak – and the Sheriff may seek what he conceives to be the truth by rack and screw. The Dutch are a tenacious people, especially if you try to put them right. Are you familiar with the concept of Dutch reckoning, Spandrel?'

'I don't believe I am.'

'Query a bill at an inn in this country and the landlord's apt to send it back to you with further additions. In the same way, if you protest your innocence overmuch, you may find yourself punished more harshly. Hanging can be mercifully swift, if competently done. And the Dutch are a competent people. I should look more to their competence than their tenacity, if I were you.'

'Thank you for the warning.'

'Don't mention it.' Dalrymple glanced around at the four dank walls and up at the ceiling – though he scarcely needed to, given how close it was to the crown of his hat. 'It's not too bad here, is it?'

'No, no. A regular home from home. I can't think why I wanted to leave it.'

Dalrymple looked at him sharply. 'I shouldn't recommend sarcasm at your examination, Spandrel.'

'I'll remember that.'

'I have to ask you . . . if you'll require the services of a priest.'

'Won't that question arise only after I've been condemned?'

'I suppose so.' Dalrymple shrugged. 'But there's no harm in looking ahead.'

'In that case . . . no.' Spandrel forced out a smile. 'A priest might muddy the water.'

In London, muddied water was available by the bathload. Hardly a day passed at the Cockpit without the questioning of one or more specimens of unpatriotic riff-raff. But where were the serious plotters, where the genuine conspirators? Ten days after the papists and non-jurors had been sent packing from London, an answer seemed to be supplied by the arrest at his lodgings in Little Ryder Street of George Kelly, secretary to the Bishop of Rochester.

It soon became common knowledge, however, that Kelly had been able to hold the arresting officers at bay for some time, thanks to his distinctly unsecretarial skills as a swordsman, while most of his presumably incriminating correspondence burned merrily on his sitting-room fire. Walpole, it was said, would make someone suffer for such bungling, not least because he was bound to suffer for it himself.

'We'll have to release him,' was Walpole's conclusion when he and Townshend met two days later to consider the Deciphering Department's report on those papers of

Kelly's not consumed by the flames. And it was a conclusion that clearly pained him. 'There's nothing here.'

'But if we can't touch Kelly . . .'

'We can't touch his master. I'm well aware of that, Charles. Damnably well aware.'

'What's this about . . . Harlequin?'

'Atterbury's dog, damn his paws. Half Europe seems to have been writing to Kelly enquiring after the cur's health, obviously as a cipher for the vitality of the plot. But we can't prove that's what it means.'

'How are we to proceed?'

'Stubbornly, Charles. That's how. Stubbornly and tirelessly. We can't dig this fox out of his hole. But he'll have to come out of his own accord eventually. And when he does . . . we'll be waiting.'

At the waiting game Walpole knew no peer. For Spandrel, however, waiting was a game he could only lose, though one he was nevertheless forced to play. While in London the First Lord of the Treasury and the Northern Secretary pored glumly over the Deciphering Department's report, in Amsterdam Spandrel was taken before Sheriff Lanckaert for examination.

Lanckaert himself said very little, and that in Dutch. His English-speaking deputy, Aertsen, conducted the brief but pointed interrogation. He and Spandrel had last met on the occasion of Spandrel's escape from custody, an event to which neither of them referred directly. In short order, however, the long dormant evidence of Spandrel's association with Zuyler that had emerged just prior to McIlwraith's dramatic intervention at Ugels' shop was cited as confirmation that Spandrel and Zuyler had conspired to rob Ysbrand de Vries and had ended by murdering him. The even hoarier accusation that

Spandrel was a secret agent of the government of the Austrian Netherlands was not revived, due, Spandrel assumed, to some subtle change in the balance of political expediency. Instead, Aertsen invited him to admit that he had killed de Vries when discovered by him in the act of breaking open the chest in his study in search of the money and valuables Zuyler had told him he would find there.

'No,' Spandrel hopelessly declared. 'That's not so. Zuyler tricked me into sneaking into the house so that I'd take the blame for his murder of de Vries. I told you the truth last year and it hasn't changed.' No more it had. But he knew more of the truth now. He knew it all. Yet there was nothing to be gained by telling it. 'You should be looking for Zuyler and Mrs de Vries.'

'We have looked for them. But we have found only you.' They had in truth not even done that. Spandrel had been served to them on a plate, lacking only a sprig of parsley by way of garnish. Zuyler was dead, but they did not seem to know it. And Estelle de Vries had transformed herself into Mrs Davenant, mistress of Phoenix House *and* Robert Walpole, for which information they would probably not be grateful. 'We have a sworn statement from an elderly servant of Mijnheer de Vries that you killed his master, Spandrel. Against that all your denials and allegations count for nothing.'

'I didn't do it.'

'Then why did you flee when you had the chance to prove your innocence?'

'Because I had no such chance. As this examination demonstrates.'

'That is enough.' Aertsen glared at him. 'That is quite enough.'

There was a lengthy conferral in Dutch, then a

rambling pronouncement of some kind by the Sheriff, of which Aertsen supplied a brisk translation.

'Your guilt is established, Spandrel. Formal judgement and sentence will be passed tomorrow. Do not expect leniency.'

Aertsen's parting warning had hardly been necessary. Leniency did not feature in Spandrel's expectations. He tried, as far as he could, to harbour no expectations at all. A future governed by the forces pressing in upon him was unlikely to be either long or relishable. The authorities had to bend over backwards to avoid confronting the inconsistencies and contradictions in the case they had made against him. But it was clear that bend they would. And equally clear that Spandrel would be the one to break.

Back in his cell, he thought, as he often had of late, of McIlwraith, and wondered what that indomitable champion of lost causes would do in such a situation as this. Try to escape, perhaps. But the solid walls and thick bars of the Stadhuis would probably prevent him. Proclaim the truth as he knew it in open court, then – the whole truth, Green Book and great men's greed and all. But that would only win him hours of useless agony in the torture chamber. He would be as helpless as Spandrel to avoid the fate that lay in wait.

Between the bars of his tiny window, Spandrel noticed a spider spinning a web. He half-remembered some legend of McIlwraith's homeland, in which Robert the Bruce had been inspired by the indefatigable spinnings of a spider. But, more clearly, he remembered a superstitious saying of his mother. 'A spider in the morning brings no sorrow; a spider in the afternoon brings trouble on the morrow.'

413

Was it still morning, or had the afternoon already come? For a few moments, Spandrel struggled to decide. Then, irritated with himself for making the effort, he stopped. What difference did it make? Morning *or* afternoon, he knew what the morrow would bring.

CHAPTER FORTY-THREE

The Wheels of Justice

In the Stadhuis of Amsterdam, two flights of stairs were all that separated the cells from the civil chambers. The short journey between them, which Spandrel had never previously undertaken, was a bewildering transition from gloom and squalor to opulence and grandeur. The Magistrates' Court was a vast and glittering chamber, the magistrates themselves a sombrely clad half-score of solemn-faced burghers arrayed beneath pious paintings and allegorical friezes. Sheriff Lanckaert directed proceedings, with occasional interventions from one of the magistrates who seemed to outrank the others. Aertsen perched mutely at a desk to one side. Spandrel, guarded by Big Janus, was required to do nothing but stand and listen, understanding none of the words spoken but having a shrewd idea what they would amount to.

It was not long before the chief magistrate was intoning a formal verdict, a translation of which was helpfully muttered into Spandrel's ear by Big Janus. 'Guilty, *mijn vriend*.' It was no surprise. But somehow, until that moment, Spandrel had half-believed it would not happen. It had been the purest self-deception, of course. It had been bound to happen. Telling himself otherwise was merely an indulgence in one of the few comforts not denied him. But even those few were being stripped from him now, one by one. And soon there would be none left – none at all.

Spandrel was marched back down into the bowels of the building, which he thought strange, since no sentence seemed to have been passed. An explanation of sorts was supplied by Aertsen, who led the way and glanced back over his shoulder once to say, 'The Chamber of Justice is on the other side.' Spandrel took him to mean the other side of the Stadhuis, an indirect route to which was presumably used to spare any wandering city fathers a distressing encounter with an unwashed prisoner. Any figurative significance to Aertsen's words Spandrel dismissed as improbable.

Re-emerging in a hall yet vaster than the court and glimpsing a gigantic statue of Atlas supporting a star-spangled globe at the far end, Spandrel was taken into a marble-lined chamber where the Sheriff and the magistrates, accompanied this time by a pastor, were waiting for him. He was tempted for a moment to object to the pastor's presence, having told Dalrymple he had no use for one, but he supposed Dutch law insisted a pastor be there and to the insistences of Dutch law he was clearly a slave. With little ado, the chief magistrate pronounced sentence on 'Willem Spandrel'. And there really was no need for Big Janus to tell him what it was.

As it happened, Aertsen took it upon himself to remove any doubt there might be about the import of the words used. 'It is death, Spandrel. You understand?'

'I understand.'

'The sentence must now be publicly pronounced. This way.'

They descended some stairs to another marbled chamber, this one boasting open windows at ground level on one side, through which passing Amsterdammers could observe the scene. Spandrel noticed half a dozen or·so of them watching, their figures outlined against the bright sunlight filling the square, before he was turned to face the magistrates once more, seated now on the marble steps that ran along the opposite wall. Above them were statues of weeping maidens and above the maidens a frieze filled with gaping skulls and writhing serpents. The Old Bailey it was not. And for that Spandrel was grateful. He had seen men condemned to die at the Bailey amidst cat-calls and laughter. Here a dread dignity prevailed.

The chief magistrate said his piece again, less perfunctorily than in the Chamber of Justice. A clerk scribbled something in a book. And it was done. Big Janus sighed soulfully, then led Spandrel away, as gently as a shepherd leading a lamb.

Aertsen accompanied the pair as far as the door of Spandrel's cell. There he looked Spandrel in the eye for several seconds before saying, 'You have been sentenced to die by hanging from the public gallows at Volewijk. Do you have any questions?'

'When will it be?'

'The next hanging day is eleven days from now.'

'What is today?'

'Do you not know?'

Spandrel shrugged. 'I lose count.'

'It is the second of June.'

'The second?'

'Yes. Does it matter?'

'It's my birthday on the seventh.'

'Not here, Spandrel. Here, that would be the eighteenth. And you will not see the eighteenth. Lucky for you, I think.'

'How is that lucky?'

'You do not have to grow any older.' There was a faint curl at one edge of Aertsen's mouth.

'Is that what they call Dutch reckoning?'

The curl vanished. Aertsen turned to Big Janus and snapped, '*Sluit hem op.*' Then he stalked away.

Viscount Townshend climbed the stairs of the Treasury in Whitehall with a lightness of tread only the carriage of good news can impart. The gloom that had hung over Walpole since the farcical mishandling of Kelly's arrest was about to lift, or at least to thin, thanks to the intelligence Townshend was bearing. And his brother-in-law's gratitude was always a wonderful tonic.

As he approached the door of Walpole's outer office, it opened and a familiar figure emerged – that of Walpole's brother and loyal man-of-all-work, Horatio. As a Treasury Secretary, whose financial duties were confined to buying elections and selling favours at the First Lord's direction, Horatio was commonly to be seen about the place. Townshend was nevertheless surprised to see him on this occasion. There had been a letter detailing his discussions with the Dutch Government concerning troop loans, but Townshend would have expected a personal report from Horatio upon his return. His tread grew fractionally heavier.

'I didn't know you were back, Horace.'

'What? Oh, Charles, it's you.' The younger Walpole looked distinctly flustered. 'Yes. I arrived last night.'

'When shall you call on me?'

'I can't. Confoundedly sorry, old fellow. There it is.'

'There *what* is?'

'Robin's sending me on my travels again.'

'Where to?'

'Can't say. Sorry. Sworn to secrecy. He'll tell you, I'm sure, but I can't. He leads me a dog's life, you know.

418

And, like a dog, I must run.' With which Horatio did precisely that.

Townshend was wise enough not to ask Walpole what manner of mission he had sent his brother on. Walpole would tell him or not, as he pleased. Of late, he had told him less and less, which grieved Townshend as much as it irked him. They had once trusted each other completely. Now . . . But perhaps, he reflected, his news would bring some of that trust bubbling to the surface.

'We have him, Robin.'

'Who do we have?' came the frowning response.

'Plunket.'

'We were bound to, sooner or later.'

'But Plunket's the weak link in the chain. He'll give us all the rest in time.'

'You think so?'

'Yes. Don't you?'

'I'm not sure. Perhaps.'

'Are you quite well, Robin?'

'Yes. Just a little . . . distracted.' Walpole rubbed his forehead and gave a crumpled smile. 'It's nothing you need to worry about.' Which really meant, Townshend well knew, that it was nothing he was going to be *allowed* to worry about. 'As for Plunket . . .' Walpole's shoulders sank. He pushed out his lower lip. 'We'll see.'

'Wake up, Spandrel. It's McIlwraith. I'm back. And I'm heezing you out of here before you have your neck stretched longer than an Edinburgh Sunday. Put your boots on, man. We're leaving.'

'Captain? That can't be you. You're—' Spandrel woke and McIlwraith vanished into the dream that had summoned him. There was no-one there. Spandrel was alone in his cell, save for the spider that still kept him company, morning *and* afternoon.

He looked round at the patch of wall on which he had been keeping a tally of the passing days since his sentencing. The broken toothpick he had found wedged in a crevice, doubtless left by some previous prisoner, served well for the purpose. There were five scratches. He would make a sixth today. It was the halfway point of his journey from court to gallows and nausea swept over him at the very thought. He held his breath until it had abated, then stretched up for the toothpick.

'It'll be good to see you again, Captain,' he murmured to himself as he swung round and scratched at the grimy surface of the wall. 'And it won't be long now.'

'Mrs Spandrel?'

'Yes.' Margaret Spandrel looked doubtfully at her visitor. 'What can I do for you, sir?'

'Don't you remember me?'

'I don't . . .' She peered closer. 'My Lord, it's Dick Surtees. After all these years. Come to finish your apprenticeship, have you?'

'Not exactly.' Surtees smiled awkwardly.

'Not remotely, dressed like a dog's dinner as you are.'

'I was, er, sorry to hear about . . . Mr Spandrel.'

'Were you now?'

'Billy told me . . . just recently.'

'You've seen William?' Some mixture of hope and anxiety lit her features. 'When?'

'Oh, a month or so ago.'

'Oh.' Mrs Spandrel's shoulders sagged. Her expression shrank back into disappointment. 'I thought . . . Well, he didn't mention it to me.'

'Is he here?'

'Who?'

420

'Billy, of course.'

'No.' Mrs Spandrel sighed heavily. 'Gone abroad to better himself, apparently.'

'Abroad? Where?'

'He didn't say. The truth is . . .' She wiped away a tear with the back of her hand. 'I haven't the faintest notion where he is or what he's doing.'

'Oh.' Surtees too looked disappointed. 'I see.'

'What do you want with him?'

'Nothing, really. It doesn't matter.'

'It must do, to make you come here.'

'No. It *really* doesn't matter. It can't—' He stood looking at her for a moment, rocking back and forth on his heels. Then he blurted out, 'I have to go,' and turned for the door.

Such money as Spandrel had had about him when taken into custody was still his, at any rate notionally. For a genuinely modest commission, Big Janus had agreed to put it to good use: supplying Spandrel with a daily flagon of *jenever* that drowned the sour taste of fear and reduced his expiring allotment of life to a painless haze. There were eight scratches on the wall now and the coiner in the next cell, destined to hang the same day as Spandrel but denied the soothing effects of *jenever*, could often be heard wailing in sheer terror at the prospect before them.

There was no good or noble way to approach death, Spandrel decided in one of his long stretches of inebriated lucidity. It was the same for everyone. The variously pattering and shuffling footsteps he could hear in the street outside were leading their owners to death as certainly as Spandrel's sojourn in his cell was leading him. The only difference was that he knew when his journey would end. And that end was close now, so

421

close he could almost smell it. He reached for the flagon of *jenever* and raised it to his lips. And death shrank back into the shadows. But only a little way. Only a very little.

Alone in his study at Orford House, Robert Walpole threw another log onto the fire and watched it blaze up the chimney. It was not a cold evening, but he had need of flame and heat. He walked across to his desk, picked up the green-covered ledger lying there and leafed randomly through its pages. So many names. So much money. So many glorious secrets. It went against the grain to part with them. It offended his every political instinct. But this latest turn of events had shown him how dangerous the Green Book was, to him as much as anyone. Even if Horatio could manage the present crisis, there was no saying another would not flare up. The entire Spandrel affair had been partly Walpole's own fault, after all. The Green Book was simply too tempting. Ultimately, there was only one way to solve the problem it posed. With a regretful sigh, Walpole walked back to the fire and sat down in the low chair beside it. Then he began tearing the pages out of the book and feeding them, one by one, into the flames.

There were nine scratches on the wall now. The light was failing in the world beyond the window of Spandrel's cell. Tomorrow would be the last complete day he spent in it, the last complete day, indeed, that he spent anywhere, unless there really was a place beyond the end of life.

His reverie was interrupted by the unlocking of the door, which came as a surprise to him, so regular and predictable had the guards' ways become. He looked round to see Big Janus framed shaggily in the doorway.

'*Opstaan, mijn vriend. Opstaan.*'
'What's wrong?'
'Mijnheer Aertsen. He wants you.'
'What for?'
Big Janus shrugged. '*Ik weet het niet.* You come. Now.'

CHAPTER FORTY-FOUR

The Quiddities of Fate

Aertsen was waiting for Spandrel in the examination chamber. But he was not waiting alone. Seated next to him at the long table beneath the chandelier was Dalrymple, whose purse-lipped expression suggested that a second journey from The Hague had pleased him no more than the first. On Aertsen's other side sat a narrow-shouldered, black-wigged fellow with a face the colour and texture of an old saddle. At the far end of the table, lounging back in his chair with one hand thrust inside his waistcoat, the better it appeared to attend to an itch somewhere near his armpit, was a fourth man, less smartly dressed than the others but somehow giving the impression of being in charge of them. Sheriff Lanckaert was nowhere to be seen.

Aertsen fired some instructions in Dutch at Big Janus, who led Spandrel to a chair in front of the table and sat him down, then left, without troubling to shackle his leg to the block. Spandrel thought that almost as strange as the absence of pen and paper from the table. There was something strange about this gathering altogether. That much was clear before a word was addressed to him.

'Mr Dalrymple you know,' said Aertsen, after eying Spandrel for a moment with his strange squinting indirectness. 'This gentleman is Mijnheer Gerrit de Vries.'

He nodded to the grim-faced figure on his right. 'Son of the late Ysbrand de Vries.'

'And I'm Horatio Walpole,' said the fourth man. 'Brother of Robert.' There was indeed, Spandrel realized as he looked at him, a distinct resemblance. Horatio was fat, though not quite as fat as Robert, with a round and ruddy face, though neither quite so round nor quite so ruddy as his brother's. And there was a softness to his gaze Spandrel did not recognize. Horatio was the poor man's Walpole, but no doubt impressive enough to those who had not encountered the real thing.

'What can I . . . do for you, sirs?' Spandrel ventured.

'It's more a case of what *we* can do for *you*,' said Walpole.

'I'm a condemned man, sir. There's nothing anyone can do for me.'

'What if you were no longer condemned?'

'I . . . don't understand.'

'Tell him, Dalrymple. This isn't a Commons debate. We gain nothing by dragging it out.'

'Very well.' Dalrymple cleared his throat and glanced at Aertsen. 'By your leave, mijnheer?'

'*My* leave?' Aertsen tossed his head irritably. '*Mijn God*. Tell him, yes. Why not?'

'Your . . . situation, Spandrel,' Dalrymple began, 'has altered.'

'Altered?'

'Yes.' Dalrymple seemed to wince. 'Shortly after sentence was passed on you . . . someone else confessed to the crime for which you were convicted. Since you have all along maintained your inn—'

'Someone else?' Spandrel stared at Dalrymple, half-stupefied. 'Someone else has confessed?'

'Yes.'

'Who?' But there was, of course, only one person it could be. 'Not . . . Estelle?'

'Mrs de Vries,' said Dalrymple flatly. 'That is correct.'

'She can't have done.'

'But she has.'

'She . . . admits it?'

'Fully and completely. Thus exonerating you . . . fully and completely.'

'I don't believe it.'

'It is hard to believe, certainly. But it is true. The confession was made in person to Sheriff Lanckaert. Mijnheer Aertsen was also present.'

'It is true,' said Aertsen through gritted teeth.

'Why? Why would she do such a thing?'

'To save an innocent man from hanging was the reason she herself gave. Was it not, Aertsen?'

'*Ja.*'

'I'm not going to hang?'

Dalrymple shook his head. 'You are not.'

'But Estelle?'

'Worried about her, Spandrel?' asked Walpole.

Yes. He was. Almost in spite of himself, he was suddenly very worried indeed. '*She* will hang? Instead of me?'

'As in our country,' Dalrymple replied, 'a wife who murders her husband is not hanged, but, er, burned at the stake.'

'Oh my God.'

'Fortunately,' said Walpole, 'it needn't come to that.'

Spandrel turned to look at him. 'What do you mean, sir?'

'We have a proposition for you, Spandrel. Get on with it, Dalrymple, for pity's sake.'

'The circumstances are complicated as well as delicate,' said Dalrymple, choosing his words with palpable care. 'Mrs de Vries's confession establishes the primary

426

guilt of her husband's secretary, Zuyler, who, according to Mrs de Vries, has since—'

'He's dead,' said Spandrel.

'Quite so.' Dalrymple smiled tolerantly at him. 'To proceed. Mrs de Vries could not be tried without your conviction first being quashed. Such a public admission of judicial error would be . . .'

'Damned embarrassing,' said Walpole.

'The embarrassment is not all ours,' snapped Aertsen.

'He's referring to Mrs de Vries's confessed reason for the murder.' Walpole looked at Spandrel and shrugged. 'A certain green-covered book.'

'The contents of which we would prefer, especially at this sensitive juncture of national affairs, not be bruited abroad,' said Dalrymple. 'You follow?'

'I . . .' Spandrel glanced at each of the four men in turn and was no clearer about their intentions. 'I'm not sure I do.'

'Our proposition,' Dalrymple continued, 'is simply this. If your conviction were allowed to stand, but you somehow . . . escaped from custody . . . again . . ' He paused, marshalling his thoughts, it seemed, setting aside his scruples. 'Mr Walpole and I have persuaded the Dutch authorities to release you, Spandrel. Formally, you will have escaped. Informally, you will be allowed to return to England on the clear understanding that no attempt will ever be made to re-arrest you, provided that you never visit Holland again.'

'You'll let me go?'

'You have it, Spandrel,' said Walpole. 'It must almost be worth the fright of being condemned to hang for the relief of learning you don't have to after all.'

Spandrel was tempted for a moment to tell Walpole how very far from being worth it the experience had been.

But there was a puzzle here he did not understand. He was naturally eager to snatch this unexpected chance of life from the jaws of death. Yet he had the strange impression that the two Englishmen and the two Dutchmen were almost equally eager that he should snatch it. And one of them was de Vries's own son. 'What about . . . Mrs de Vries?'

'The V.O.C. will look after her,' said Dalrymple.

'How will they "look after her"?'

'*Mijn stiefmoeder,*' said Gerrit de Vries suddenly, '*doet wat ik zeg.*'

'Mijnheer de Vries has succeeded to his father's position within the V.O.C,' said Dalrymple, smiling awkwardly. 'He has interceded with them on his stepmother's behalf.'

'I don't understand,' Spandrel protested. 'What has the V.O.C.—'

'Your understanding is not required,' Aertsen cut in, so loudly that his voice echoed in the shadowy recesses of the chamber. 'Do you accept the proposition?'

'I . . .'

'She'll come to no harm,' said Walpole, with a reassuring grin. 'My brother wouldn't hear of it.'

'Do you accept?' Aertsen repeated.

'Yes. I do.' A sudden fear that his salvation was about to be rescinded gripped Spandrel. 'I'm sorry. I didn't mean— I'm grateful, sirs, more grateful than I can say. I accept . . . unreservedly.'

'Of course you do,' said Walpole, a grin still fixed to his face. 'Who wouldn't?'

'*Mijn stiefmoeder,*' growled Gerrit de Vries, '*is mijn zaak.*'

'What—'

'Enough,' declared Aertsen, frowning at de Vries. 'We have said enough.' He rose abruptly from his chair, took

428

a key from his pocket and tossed it onto the table. 'Can we leave you to end this as agreed, Dalrymple?'

'Most certainly, Aertsen.'

'Thank you. Mijnheer?' Reluctantly, it seemed, and with a scowl at Spandrel, de Vries also stood up. '*Laten we gaan.*' Aertsen glanced round the table. 'Good evening, gentlemen.'

The two men strode off into the shadows that shrouded the door, which was heard to open, then slam shut behind them. Silence settled over the unlikely gathering. Walpole scratched under his wig. Dalrymple adjusted his cravat.

'What is to happen, sirs?' asked Spandrel.

'What is to happen is that you are to pick up that key,' said Dalrymple. 'It opens the back door of this chamber, beyond which steps will lead you to a store-room, where someone has negligently left a window unfastened. You will climb out of the window, cross Dam Square and make your way up the near side of Damrak to the harbour. A boatman will be waiting for you near the toll-house. You will identify yourself as William Powell.'

'Powell?'

'That is correct. The boatman will row you out to a pinnace sailing tonight for the Texel roadstead, where she is to deliver mail to an East Indiaman, the *Tovenaer*, shortly to embark for Java. The master of the *Tovenaer* has instructions to deliver you by launch to any convenient port along the south coast of England and to furnish you with money for your onward journey. At that point, you will become a free man, in fact if not in name.'

'And Mrs de Vries?'

'Is already aboard the *Tovenaer*. But she will not be leaving the ship . . . until it reaches Java.'

'Is that what you meant by the V.O.C. looking after her?'

'Reading between de Vries's pouts and grimaces,' said Walpole, 'I reckon his stepmother knows more about the V.O.C.'s inner dealings than's good for their peace of mind. Hence her banishment to Java. Which is good for *our* peace of mind as well, in view of all she knows about the South Sea Company. You're a nonentity, Spandrel. But the fair Estelle? *Her* trial? *Her* execution? Too much attention. Far too much. For everyone. So, we've compromised. You go free. She goes . . . a long way away. And we breathe more easily. You're a lucky man.'

'Thanks to Estelle.'

'Yes. That's the damnably unaccountable part of it. You and I both know what she's given up. *How much* she's given up. And it might have cost her her life. Her life, for yours. Not a bargain that my brother gives me to believe a woman of her character would dream of entertaining. But she has. Why? She doesn't love you, does she?'

'No. She doesn't love me.'

'And there's nothing you can do for her.'

'Not a single thing.'

'So, why did she do it?'

'I don't know.'

'I should ask her, if I were you.'

'Yes.' Spandrel reached unsteadily for the key. 'I will.'

CHAPTER FORTY-FIVE

Homeward Bound

The *Tovenaer* made way slowly as she headed out into the North Sea. The weather was clear and settled, sunlight dancing and sparkling on the gentle swell. The following wind was scarcely more than a breeze. It was a fine early summer's afternoon, the last afternoon, as it had threatened to be, of Spandrel's life, but instead the first of the rest of a life restored.

Spandrel and Estelle de Vries stood on the quarter-deck, watching the Dutch coast drift away behind them. It was the first time they had been allowed to leave their cabins since Spandrel's dawn arrival from Amsterdam, the master of the vessel, Captain Malssen, following the instructions in this regard of a senior V.O.C. merchant, identified by Estelle as Gustaaf Dekker, who was also aboard. Dekker apparently no longer feared the two might jump ship or play some other trick on him and was content to leave them to their own devices. This was thus also Spandrel's first opportunity to thank Estelle for what he still found it hard to believe she had done.

'You saved my life,' was the lame but simple truth he finally put into words. 'I shall always be in your debt.'

'And you will always be in my heart,' said Estelle, smiling at him. 'Even though you don't believe I have one.'

'I believe it now.'

'But it's a surprise, isn't it?'

'I admit it is.'

'For me too. After all I've done. If you'd asked me, I'd have said there wasn't any burden my conscience couldn't bear in exchange for a life of ease and pleasure. That's what Walpole gave me. And that's what I could have gone on enjoying.' She breathed deeply as the mizzen-sails filled and flapped above them. 'All I had to do was forget my promise to Captain McIlwraith. Oh, and I had to forget you as well, William, which I couldn't seem to do. I begged Walpole not to send you to Amsterdam. I pleaded with him as I'd never pleaded before and never would have again. But he refused me. He told me it was a matter of . . . political expediency. But there he lied. The truth was that he was jealous of the place you hold in my affections. And angry, of course, because he believed you'd endangered his son. He sent you to Amsterdam out of spite. And he thought there was nothing I could do to save you. Well, he was wrong, wasn't he?'

'Did you know what you were risking? Worse than the noose – the stake.'

'Risk agrees with me. Besides, I felt sure it wouldn't come to that. Don't over-estimate the sacrifice I've made. I left Walpole a note, telling him I still had a copy I'd made of the contents of the Green Book, which, while not as damaging as the original, would still cause him a great deal of embarrassment if it fell into the wrong hands.'

'*Do* you have a copy?'

'Leave me with some of my secrets, William, please. The possibility that I had a copy was enough for Walpole to send his brother racing after me. Poor Horace has but recently negotiated a troop loan with the Dutch Government. He wouldn't have wanted them to think better of it, as they well might have if they'd felt the British Government had placed them in an intolerable position. The Dutch are no friends of King George. As Elector of Hanover, he has trading ambitions in the Baltic which they keenly resent. A copy of the Green Book could be a potent addition to their armoury. Trade is, after all, their lifeblood. I was married to one of them. I know how their minds work. When you were first arrested last year, you were accused of working for the Marquis de Prié, weren't you?'

'Yes. But—'

'Ysbrand was in secret communication with de Prié on behalf of the V.O.C.'

'What?'

'How much do you know about the Barrier Treaty of 1709?'

'Nothing. I've never even heard of it.'

'Be grateful I have. It granted the Dutch control of a series of fortresses along the border between France and the Spanish Netherlands – now the Austrian Netherlands – as a barrier against future invasion. The Dutch are supposed to be paid an annual subsidy towards the maintenance of the fortresses by the Flemish provinces they're sited in. Those subsidies are in arrears, amounting to many millions of guilders. The V.O.C. was worried – still is – lest de Prié persuade the Emperor to establish a Flemish East India Company to compete with them. Ysbrand was Flemish by birth and thus the obvious choice for a secret mission to negotiate a compromise with de Prié. The V.O.C. would use its considerable influence in the States General to have the arrears written off if de Prié would use *his* influence to have the idea of a Flemish East India Company quietly forgotten.'

'How do you know all this?'

'I've been the wife of an eminent Dutch merchant.

And the mistress of a *pre*-eminent British politician. I know more than either of them thought I had the chance of learning. Secrets aren't for telling. They're for storing against the day you may need to *threaten* that you'll tell them. That's why I told Sheriff Lanckaert last year that you'd admitted to travelling to Amsterdam by way of Brussels. Partly to incriminate you, of course. But partly also to let the V.O.C. know that I could, if I chose, reveal their secret dealings with de Prié, causing a rupture within the States General.'

'What a deep game you play.'

'Oh yes. Deep and dark. A man may have me as his mistress, if he is rich and powerful enough. But I am ever my own gamestress. I judged how it would be. Neither Walpole nor the V.O.C. could afford to let me answer for the crime to which I confessed, for fear of what I might make *them* answer for. So, I do not burn and you do not hang. I am sent away and you are allowed to escape.'

'But you've given up so much, Estelle. Ease and pleasure. You said so yourself.'

'All for you, William. I wasn't certain I could when I left England, you know. But when I stood outside the Stadhuis and watched you being condemned to—'

'You were there?'

Estelle nodded. 'I was. And when I saw the weary, hopeless despair on your face as the death sentence was passed, I knew I had to do my best for you. You didn't abandon me in Rome, did you, small thanks though you had for it? Well, *I* couldn't abandon *you*. It was a bewildering discovery to make about myself. That there really was someone in the world I cared about, even though he's neither rich nor powerful, nor ever likely to be.'

'Didn't you care about Zuyler?'

'If you're asking me whether I'd have done the same

for him, the answer's no. You're a different kind of man, William, I'm glad to say. You should be glad too. But don't let the difference go to your head. I think I was looking for an excuse to leave Walpole anyway. It was a beholden life. And I prefer to be beholden to no-one. Besides, ease and pleasure cloy after a while, don't you find?'

Spandrel laughed at the absurdity of the notion that he would have any way of knowing and shook his head at her sheer incorrigibility. 'What in Heaven's name will you do in Java?'

'I can't imagine. Fortunately, I don't have to. I'm not going to Java '

'You're not?'

'Certainly I'm not. You've met my stepson. If he's an example of the effects of the East Indian climate, not to mention East Indian society - and I'm assured he is - I'd be mad to go. Gerrit has me marked down as good marrying material for the wife-hungry merchants of Batavia. He - and they - are to be disappointed, however.'

'But Dekker and Captain Malssen have orders to take you there.'

'Indeed.' Estelle lowered her voice to a whisper. 'I intend to come to a private arrangement with one or both of those gentlemen. I have it from the boatswain that we're to call at Madeira on the way. I shall disembark there.'

'They won't allow you to.'

'Do you doubt my powers of persuasion?'

'No. But—'

'Then leave me to employ them. On which subject . . .'

'Yes?'

'Don't look round. Dekker has just commenced observing us from the shelter of the companion-way. It

435

would be helpful to my managing of him on this voyage if you and I appeared to be at odds. You'll forgive the pretence, I know, disagreeable as it will be for both of us. All will be well for you from now on, William. You have nothing to fear from Walpole. He knows certain bargains must be honoured, especially those struck by his brother in his name. He will leave you completely alone. And you will prosper. Of that I feel strangely certain. Finish your map. Maps *are* the coming thing, you know. People have need of them. At any rate, they think they do, which is even better.'

'Not you, though?'

'No. I prefer an unmapped future. Now, I hope we will be able to contrive a more fitting leavetaking closer to the time, but for the moment—' Suddenly, she tossed her head and raised her voice. 'It is all very well for you, Mr Spandrel. What do I have to show for it?'

'Enough, I think, madam,' he snapped back, rising to the occasion so well that there was the sparkle of a smile in her eyes that she did not allow to reach her lips. 'Go to the Devil.'

'I very likely shall.' She turned on her heel and strode towards the companion-way, where Spandrel glimpsed Dekker's black-clad form shrinking back out of sight. There was no way to tell Estelle's simulated anger and frustration from the real thing. That was the wonder of her. And for Spandrel it always would be.

Early the following evening, the *Tovenaer* hove to off Hastings and set down a launch, with Spandrel aboard. He could see Estelle watching from the quarter-deck, her pink dress turned blood-red by the wash of golden sunlight. She did not raise a hand and nor did he. The rules of the game she was playing had still to be observed.

Each knew what the other's gaze conveyed and that was enough.

Spandrel wondered if he would ever see her again. If not, this last, fading sight of her was the end. He did not want to believe that, likely though it was. She was still alive and so was he. There was no telling what the future might hold. Except that, throughout as much of it as lay before him, he would think better and more fondly of her than he would once have supposed to be possible.

'Fare you well, Estelle,' he murmured under his breath as the launch drew further and further from the ship. 'Fare you ever well.'

CHAPTER FORTY-SIX

Looking to the Future

After a night at the Smack and Mackerel Inn in Hastings – named, he decided, because a stomach-turning tang of stale fish pervaded everything, including the bedding – Spandrel was eager to be on his way. But it was Sunday and no coaches were running. The skipper of a coaster sailing for London that afternoon was willing to take on passengers, however, so Spandrel left Hastings as he had arrived, by sea.

The coaster had many calls to make on its way, the number and duration of which far exceeded Spandrel's expectations. Tuesday morning found the vessel no further on than Deal. There Spandrel lost patience. After a salty exchange with the skipper, who declined to refund any portion of his fare, he went ashore and continued his journey by road.

He spent that night at Faversham, whence the mail-coach bore him on to London the following day. He could have reached Leicester Fields by early evening, but a whimsical notion had occurred to his mind. He put up for the night at the Talbot Inn in Borough High Street.

After a meal and several reviving mugs of ale in the tap-room, he walked up to London Bridge and stood by the railings in a gap between the houses, watching the light fade over the city he had never thought he would see again. It was good to be back. And better still to know that, this time, he could stay.

The following morning, Margaret Spandrel breakfasted in low spirits. Her attempts to shake off the sadness William had caused her by his second abrupt and un-explained departure had been undermined by the realization that today was his twenty-seventh birthday. Sighing heavily and deciding to set off for Covent Garden in the hope that haggling over vegetables might improve her state of mind, she rose from the table and walked across to the window to judge the weather.

But what the weather was like she suddenly did not care. For there, standing at the edge of the lawn in the square below, was a familiar figure. And he was waving at her.

She flung up the sash and leaned out. 'William?' she called. 'Is that really you?'

'Yes, Ma,' he called back, smiling broadly. 'It really is.'

Later that day, another traveller returned to London from the Low Countries. Horatio Walpole, devoutly hoping he would not be sent straight back again this time, reported promptly to his brother at the Treasury.

Resilience was one of Robert Walpole's abiding traits. He had long since rid himself of the despondency that had gripped him on the occasion of their last meeting. It seemed to Horatio, indeed, that he had already forgotten the charms of Estelle de Vries, alias Davenant, thanks either to the alternative charms of some newly discovered mistress or to a happy turn in his pursuit of Atterbury. As it transpired, both emollients to Robert's mood had been applied.

'You've done well, Horace,' the great man and grateful brother announced over a bumper of champagne. 'The

East Indies is as far from harm's way as anyone could ask for. As for Spandrel, I suppose the fellow's never really *meant* any harm. And now he can do none. We have Atterbury by the tail.'

'Has he been arrested?'

'Not yet. But Plunket is beginning to see the attractions of turning King's Evidence. When he does . . . we'll have them all.'

'I can rest my weary limbs at home for a while, then?'

'Indeed you can. Take a well-deserved rest.'

'And what will you do with Phoenix House?'

'Oh, I have someone in mind for that.' Robert winked at his brother. 'When a mare throws you, mount a sweeter-tempered one, I say.' At which they both laughed immoderately and recharged their glasses.

Two days later, at the Goat Tavern in Bloomsbury, Sam Burrows' customary Saturday evening soak was enlivened by the not entirely unexpected arrival of William Spandrel.

'You've heard, then, Mr Spandrel?'

'Heard what?'

'Come on. It's why you're here.'

'I've been away, Sam. Apparently, Dick Surtees came looking for me. But, when I called at his lodgings, his landlady told me he'd moved – without leaving a forwarding address.'

'Shouldn't wonder at that.'

'What's it all about?'

'Bigamy, Mr Spandrel. Well, it would've been bigamy, if the marriage had gone off. Seems old Mr Chesney reckoned your friend was too good to be true, so made some inquiries. And what pops up but a wife, in Paris, legally churched and well and truly living. Didn't see Mr Surtees for dust, did we? Handsome of him to try and let you know the coast was clear, though.'

'How's Maria taken it?'

'Oh, much as you'd expect. Whey-faced and weeping at first. A little better lately. But she still keeps to her room a lot. In need of consoling, I'd say.'

'Would you?'

'I would, now I've met the man to do it. Not got a wife tucked away somewhere, have you, Mr Spandrel?'

'Definitely not.'

'Nor any skeletons in the closet likely to rattle their bones?'

'Not a one.'

'There you are, then. You're just the man she needs. And an altogether finer one than Mr Surtees, if you don't mind me venturing the opinion.'

'No, Sam. I don't mind at all.'

Spandrel took his place early for matins at the Church of St George the Martyr in Queen's Square the following morning, then settled back to watch as the pews filled around him with the pious pick of local society. About ten minutes before the service was due to begin, Mr and Mrs Chesney, accompanied by their daughter, Maria, entered the church and moved to their private pew near the front. They did not notice Spandrel. But Spandrel noticed them, Maria in particular. She was looking pale, as Sam had led him to expect, and thinner than he remembered.

A tender feeling of pity for Maria stole over Spandrel, a feeling he knew, in favourable circumstances – beginning with a brief but telling encounter at the conclusion of the service – might lead to a revival of the affection they had once proclaimed for each other. It would be a delicate business, at least at first. But he was confident

441

that he could manage it. He could not in fact recall feeling so confident about anything before in his life.

Many of the congregation were kneeling in prayer. So as not to appear out of place, Spandrel dropped to his knees, folded his hands and closed his eyes. As he did so, a strange and exhilarating thought came to him. Queen's Square stood at the very limit of London. Beyond the gardens at its northern end lay open fields to north and east and west. This was the edge of the map. It would not always be so. The city would grow, around and beyond it. The map Spandrel had not yet even finished – the map he had helped his father draw – would be redundant. What then? Why then, of course, as the future unfolded, he would draw another. And quite possibly another after that, helped, perhaps, by *his* son. In its way, the thought was a kind of prayer. And Spandrel uttered it solemnly.

POSTLUDE

July 1722–March 2000

CHAPTER FORTY-SEVEN

Tragedy, Comedy and History

History is the geology of human experience, a study, as it were, of tragedy and comedy laid down in the strata of past lives. In death there are no winners or losers, merely people who once lived but can never live again. What they thought, what they believed, what they hoped, is largely lost. That which remains is history.

The *Verenigde Oostindische Compagnie* vessel *Tovenaer* called at Madeira early in July 1722. It is not known if any passenger disembarked. Certain it is, however, that none of its passengers can have reached Java. The *Tovenaer* was lost with all aboard in a storm off the coast of New Holland (later to be renamed Australia) in the middle of October 1722. She has lately become the object of the eager attentions of aqualunged treasure-seekers, by virtue of her cargo of gold and silver bullion, intended to be traded for tea, textiles and porcelain, but which has served instead as a waterlogged memorial to Dutch commercial enterprise.

This disaster is unlikely to have been reported at the time in England. It almost certainly therefore did not intrude upon the early married life of William and Maria Spandrel, whose wedding had been solemnized at St George the Martyr's Church, Queen's Square, Bloomsbury, on Michaelmas Day of that year.

By the time of the Spandrels' wedding, the evidence given by John Plunket had led to the arrest on charges of treasonable conspiracy of Christopher Layer, George Kelly, Lord Grey and North, the Earl of Orrery and, of course, Bishop Francis Atterbury. As soon as Parliament met in October, the Duke of Norfolk joined them in the Tower. Walpole then pushed through the suspension of Habeas Corpus for a year and the imposition of a special tax of five shillings in the pound on Roman Catholics and non-jurors to meet the alleged cost of putting down the conspiracy.

Layer was tried and convicted of high treason and sentenced to be hanged, drawn and quartered. In the hope of extracting information from him to use against the others, his execution was many times delayed, but in vain. Eventually, Walpole had to acknowledge a lack of clinching evidence. He therefore proceeded against Atterbury and Kelly by a Bill of Pains and Penalties, calling only for presumptive evidence. The delinquent peers were released on indefinite bail. Kelly was sentenced to life imprisonment (as was the wretched Plunket), Atterbury to permanent exile. Layer was at last put out of his misery in May 1723. A month afterwards, Atterbury was loaded aboard a man-of-war and despatched to France, whence he was never to return. Of the multitude of Jacobites Walpole feared and/or hoped might come to see the Bishop off, only the Duke of Wharton put in an appearance.

Layer's head was duly displayed at Temple Bar, only to be blown down in a gale some years later, almost literally into the hands of Dr Richard Rawlinson, the Oxford theologian and non-juring bishop, who was so taken with this relic of Jacobite fervour that he asked to be buried with it in his right hand. It is not clear whether the request was carried out. Kelly languished in the Tower for fourteen years, then staged a dramatic escape and re-entered the Pretender's service. He was one of the 'Seven Men of Moidart' who sailed with Prince Charles Edward, the Young Pretender, from Nantes for Eriskay in June 1745. He later served as the Prince's private secretary. He died in Rome in 1762. Plunket, meanwhile, had died in the Tower two years after Kelly's escape.

Power breeds jealousy, especially in him who wields it. Robert Walpole, *Sir* Robert as he soon became, can hardly have expected to remain at the head of the nation's affairs for the next twenty years, but remain he did, growing more lonely and more ruthless in the process. He had his private griefs to bear, no question. His invalid daughter Kate died in the midst of his campaign against the Jacobites. His other daughter, Mary, was also to die young. His sister Dolly, Viscountess Townshend, and his brother Galfridus died within a few months of each other in 1726. And with Dolly died also his forty-year friendship with Charles Townshend.

Walpole had already engineered the disgrace and dismissal of Lord Carteret, whom he saw as a potential rival. Now, without Dolly to unite them, he began to weigh Townshend's loyalty in the balance and find it wanting. King George I expired unexpectedly of a stroke en route to his beloved Hanover in June 1727 and many thought the new King would give Walpole short shrift. But Walpole had been assiduously cultivating the Princess of Wales with just this contingency in mind and Queen Caroline's favour enabled him to manage George II much as he had managed George I. Townshend's ministerial days were thereafter numbered. Offended by

Walpole's ever more frequent interferences in foreign policy, he resigned and retired to Norfolk to pursue his theories on crop rotation, which were to win him a form of immortality as 'Turnip Townshend' of the Agricultural Revolution. He died in 1738.

By then Walpole was a stubborn and bloated old man, twice a widower, tortured by the stone, baited by the press and plagued by a rising generation of ambitious young office-seekers. He was forced into a war against Spain he had no wish to fight, thanks partly – irony of ironies – to a long-running dispute between the Spanish Government and the South Sea Company. The war went badly, the general election of 1741 hardly better, and at length, early in February 1742, he resigned, retiring to the Lords as Earl of Orford.

The newly ennobled Lord Orford was an immensely wealthy man. No satisfactory explanation of his extraordinary accumulation of riches has ever been advanced. He put much of it to use in assembling, at vast and heedless cost, a collection of the very finest paintings and sculptures. Raphaels, Rubenses, Rembrandts, Titians, Vandykes, Poussins, Murillos and Domenichinos found their way to Houghton Hall, his Norfolk residence, by the priceless crate-load. A less likely connoisseur is hard to imagine. But posterity has proclaimed his taste, if not his morals, impeccable.

Walpole died at his London home, of a remedy for the stone that turned out to be worse than the disease, in March 1745, aged sixty-eight. The doctor who attended him in his final illness, James Jurin, is now believed to have been a crypto-Jacobite. The earldom – and with it the bulk of Walpole's fortune – passed to his eldest son, Robert junior, while his surviving brother, Horatio, lingered on in the Commons until belatedly granted a peerage a few months before his death in 1757. By then

Robert junior had been succeeded as Earl of Orford b_
his son, George, who devoted the prime years of his
manhood to the seemingly impossible task of squan-
dering his inheritance. In this he was so successful that
in 1779 he was forced to sell the entire Houghton collection to Empress Catherine of Russia for a meagre
£36,000. Most of the pictures now adorn the Hermitage
Museum in St Petersburg.

Walpole's youngest son, Horace, the famous dilettante
and epistolizer, lamented the sale. 'It is the most signal
mortification to my idolatry for my father's memory that
I could receive,' he wailed. 'It is stripping the temple of
his glory and of his affection. A madman excited by
rascals has burnt his Ephesus.' What Horace's elder
brother, Edward, thought about this is not known. His
many years as the inactive and almost completely silent
Member for Great Yarmouth had been succeeded by an
increasingly reclusive existence, from which even his
nephew's gross sacrilege failed to rouse him. He died in
1784. His brother Horace inherited the earldom from the
profligate George in 1791. With Horace's passing, in
1797, the title became extinct.

The end of the Robinocracy brought an end also to the
long exile of Robert Knight. Upon payment of £10,000
for a royal pardon and another £10,000 to appease the
South Sea Company, he was permitted by the new
Administration to return to his homeland. It appears that
financial consultancy had not been unprofitable. He was
able at once to buy back his estate in Essex that had been
sold in his absence. And there he died in 1744. His son
later sat in Parliament as the Member for Castle Rising,
a Norfolk pocket borough in the gift of the Walpole
family, made over to him for reasons that can only be
guessed at.

Whether Knight senior ever visited Sir Theodore Janssen at his house in Hanover Square following his overdue homecoming is unknown. Certainly the wily old Flemish financier was still to be found there by those who sought him out, though not for a great deal longer. This founding director of both the Bank of England and the South Sea Company died in September 1748, aged ninety-four.

The South Sea Company itself lost its only tangible commercial asset – the *Asiento* for the supply of slaves to Spain's American colonies – in an opaque and tardy sub-treaty of the none too transparent Treaty of Aix-la-Chapelle in 1750, for a flat payment of £100,000. The company lingered on pitifully for another hundred years until Gladstone arrived at the Exchequer in 1852, noticed that it was still in being and promptly administered it out of existence.

By contrast, the last gasp of the Jacobite cause was in many ways its most glorious. What would have happened had the Young Pretender's army marched on south from Derby in December 1745 will never be known. The fact that a yacht loaded with King George II's valuables was kept ready at Tower Quay while news from the Midlands was anxiously awaited suggests that the conclusion was far from foregone. In the event, the rebel army marched back to Scotland – and destruction at Culloden four months later. Among the unanswered questions they left behind is whether Walpole would ever have allowed them to get so far in the first place. But Dr Jurin's ministrations had ensured that Walpole's counsel was not available to the Government of the day.

James Edward, the Old Pretender, died in Rome in

1766. By the time of his son's death, in 1788, eve
pretending had ceased to seem worthwhile.

While the King was packing his valuables, politicians
were pondering their allegiance and depositors were
clamouring for their money at the Bank of England
during those tense December days of 1745, calmer heads
were mapping the present for the benefit of the future.
*An Exact and Definitive Map of the City and Environs of
London in the Reign of His Britannic Majesty King George
the Second*, the work of William and James Spandrel,
father and son, was published in sixteen separate sheets
at monthly intervals between November 1748 and
February 1750. It can be assumed to have taken anything
up to ten years to produce.

The surviving subscription list shows the commercial
bias one might expect. But commercial considerations
are unlikely to account for the presence on the list of Sir
Nicholas Cloisterman, retired Ambassador. There are,
of course, many reasons for wanting to buy a map. Some
of those reasons have less to do with planning journeys
than remembering them.

Every map has its history, largely lost though it may
be. That which remains may become, if it survives long
enough, the stuff of saleroom speculation. Two hundred
and fifty years after its last sheet was published, an
original bound copy of the Spandrels' map was sold at
auction in New York for $148,000 – not far short of
£100,000. Back in 1721, such a sum would have made
a man rich beyond the dreams of avarice. It would
have been, quite literally, a King's ransom.

Appendices

APPENDIX A

Directory

A complete list of named characters featured in the course of the story in alphabetical order of title or surname (or forename where only this is known), with a note of their circumstances in 1721/22. Those listed in italics will not be found in any history book.

AERTSEN, Henrik. Deputy to Sheriff Lanckaert of Amsterdam.

AISLABIE, John. Chancellor of the Exchequer until forced to resign over South Sea scandal.

ALBEMARLE, Arnold van Keppel, Earl of. Allied Commander at Battle of Denain, 1712.

ANNE, Queen. Last reigning British monarch of the Stuart line. Died 1714. Succeeded by George I.

ARRAN, Charles Butler, Earl of. Jacobite landowner in Windsor Forest.

ATTERBURY, Francis. Bishop of Rochester, Dean of Westminster. Jacobite plotter.

BARLAEUS. Supposed name of Zuyler's landlord in Amsterdam (see Ugels).

BLAIN, Percy. British Consul in Florence.

BLAIN, Elizabeth, 'Lizzie'. Wife of Percy Blain.

BLAND, Dr Henry. Provost of Eton College.

BLUNT, Sir John. Director of South Sea Company.

RTOLAZZI, *Cardinal*. Pro-Governor of the City of Rome.

OUVIN, Host of card-playing and musical evenings in Geneva.

BRODRICK, Thomas. Chairman of House of Commons Secret Committee of Inquiry into South Sea Company.

BUCKTHORN, *Giles*. One of two supposed Grand Tourists whom Spandrel meets with Estelle de Vries in Switzerland (see Silverwood).

BURROWS, *Sam*. Footman to the Chesney household in London.

CADOGAN, William, Earl. Army general, sometime British Ambassador to The Hague and Windsor Forest landowner.

CALDERINI. Banker used by Spandrel and Estelle de Vries in Rome.

CAROLINE, Princess of Wales.

CARTERET, John, Lord. Secretary of State for Southern Department from March 1721.

CASWALL, George. Banker to and former director of South Sea Company. Also Member of Parliament.

CHANDOS, James Brydges, Duke of. Former Paymaster-General.

CHARLES EDWARD, Prince. The Young Pretender. Son of James Edward, the Old Pretender and heir to the Stuart line. Born December 1720.

CHESNEY, *George*. Businessman. Director of New River Company.

CHESNEY, *Louisa*. Wife of George Chesney and mother of Maria.

CHESNEY, *Maria*. Daughter of George and Louisa Chesney.

CLEMENT XI. Pope until March 1721.

CLEMENTINA, Princess. Wife of James Edward, the (Old) Pretender.

CLOISTERMAN, Nicholas. British vice-consul in Amsterdam.

CRABBE. Engraver of the Spandrels' map.

CRAGGS, James the elder. Postmaster-General until March 1721.

CRAGGS, James the younger. Son of James the elder. Secretary of State for Southern Department until February 1721.

DALRYMPLE, Evelyn. Chargé d'affaires at British Embassy in The Hague.

DAVENANT, Mrs. Name used by Estelle de Vries in London.

DEKKER, Gustaaf. V.O.C. merchant aboard the *Tovenaer.*

van DILLEN, Jacob. Deceased mutual friend of Sir Theodore Janssen and Ysbrand de Vries.

DIRK. Pickpocket with whom Spandrel shares a cell in Amsterdam Stadhuis.

DRUMMOND, Lachlan, Colonel. British Government spy at Pretender's court in Rome.

DUBOIS, Cardinal. Foreign Minister of France.

EDGAR, James. Secretary to James Edward, the (Old) Pretender.

GEERTRUID. Maid at de Vries house in Amsterdam.

GEORGE I, King of England and Elector of Hanover. Governor of South Sea Company.

GEORGE, Prince of Wales. Son and heir of George I. Governor of South Sea Company.

GODOLPHIN, Francis, Earl of. Brother-in-law of Earl of Sunderland, both having married daughters of the Duke of Marlborough.

GORDON, Sir William. Commissioner of Army Accounts. Also Member of Parliament.

REY AND NORTH, William, Lord. Jacobite plotter.

HARLEQUIN. Francis Atterbury's pet dog.

HARRIS. Clerk at British Embassy in The Hague.

HATTON, John, Captain. Soldier. Fiancé of Dorothea Wagemaker. Died of wounds during War of Spanish Succession, 1712.

HEINSIUS, Anthonie. Former Grand Pensionary of Holland. Died 1720. Succeeded by Isaac van Hoornbeeck.

HENRIK. One of three ruffians who try to kill Spandrel in Amsterdam (see Jan and Roelant).

HONDSLAGER, Cornelis. Name given by Zuyler to Spandrel as that of leader of the ruffians who try to kill him in Amsterdam (see Jan).

van HOORNBEECK, Isaac. Grand Pensionary of Holland.

INNOCENT XIII. Bishop of Osimo, elected as Pope in succession to Clement XI, May 1721.

JACQUINOT, Madame. Proprietress of Auberge du Lac, Vevey.

JAMES EDWARD, Prince. The (Old) Pretender. Son of King James II of England and claimant to the British throne.

JAN. Leader of the ruffians who try to kill Spandrel in Amsterdam.

JANE. Maid-of-all-work taken on by Mrs Spandrel after her move to Leicester Fields.

JANSSEN, Sir Theodore. Director of South Sea Company and Member of Parliament.

JANUS, 'Big'. Turnkey at Amsterdam Stadhuis.

JOHNSON, James. Alias of George Kelly.

JOYE, Charles. Director and Deputy Governor of South Sea Company.

JUPE, Nicodemus. Valet to Sir Theodore Janssen.

JURIN, James, Dr. Physician. Secretary of Royal Society.

KELLY, George. Secretary to Francis Atterbury. Jacobite plotter.

KEMP, Mr and Mrs. Travelling aliases of Estelle de Vries and Pieter Zuyler.

KEMPIS. Alias used by Pieter Zuyler in The Hague.

KENDAL, Ehrengard Melusina von der Schulenburg, Duchess of. Mistress to King George I.

KINGSTON, Evelyn Pierrepoint, Duke of. Lord Privy Seal.

KNIGHT, Robert. Chief cashier of South Sea Company.

LANCKAERT. Sheriff of Amsterdam – the city's chief law and order officer.

LAYER, Christopher. Lawyer. Jacobite plotter.

LAYTON. Alias of Christopher Layer.

LONGRIGG, Esmund. Chief woodward of Windsor Forest. Local landowner.

LORENZINI Chancellor to Grand Duke of Tuscany.

McILWRAITH, James, Captain. Soldier of fortune. Secret agent for Brodrick's Committee of Inquiry.

MALSSEN. Captain of V.O.C. vessel *Tovenaer.*

MAR, John Erskine, Earl of. Commander of Jacobite army in Scotland during the Fifteen.

MARABOUT, Gideon. Shopkeeper who sells Spandrel a map of Windsor Forest.

MARLBOROUGH, John Churchill, Duke of. Captain-General of the Army during War of Spanish Succession.

MARLBOROUGH, Sarah Churchill, Duchess of. Wife of Duke of Marlborough and mother-in-law of Earl of Sunderland.

MASTER, Harcourt. Director of South Sea Company.

MAYBRICK. A tile merchant Spandrel meets on his way to Amsterdam.

de MEDICI, Cosimo, Grand Duke of Tuscany.

MEHMET. Turkish Groom of the Chamber to King George I.

MONTEITH, Father. Secretary to Cardinal Bortolazzi.

NEGUS, Francis, Colonel. Deputy Lieutenant of Windsor Castle.

NEWCASTLE, Thomas Pelham-Holles, Duke of. Lord Great Chamberlain.

NORFOLK, Thomas Howard, Duke of. Jacobite plotter.

ORRERY, Charles Boyle, Earl of. Jacobite plotter.

PELS. Sir Theodore Janssen's banker in Amsterdam.

PHELPS. British Consul in Milan.

PLATEN, Clara Elizabeth von Meyerburg Züschen, Countess of. Secondary mistress to King George I.

PLENDERLEATH, Josiah. Deceased father of Estelle de Vries (according to her).

PLUNKET, John. Jacobite plotter.

POWELL, William. Alias used by Spandrel when leaving Amsterdam for the last time.

de **PRIÉ**, Ercole di Turinetti, Marquis de. Minister Plenipotentiary to Governor-General of Austrian Netherlands.

RAWLINSON, Richard, Dr. Theologian at Oxford University.

ROELANT. One of three ruffians who try to kill Spandrel in Amsterdam (see Henrik and Jan).

ROGERS, Captain. Adjutant to Colonel Negus.

ROSS, Charles, General. Member of Brodrick's Committee of Inquiry; former commanding officer of Captain McIlwraith.

SCHAUB, Sir Luke. British Ambassador to Paris.

SIEGWART, Frau. Proprietress of Pension Siegwart, Berne.

SILVERWOOD, Naseby. One of two supposed Grand Tourists whom Spandrel meets with Estelle de

460

Vries in Switzerland (see Buckthorn).

SLOPER, William. Member of Brodrick's Committee Inquiry.

SPANDREL, Margaret. Mother of William Spandrel.

SPANDREL, William. Mapmaker. Son of William and Margaret Spandrel.

SPANDREL, William senior. Bankrupt mapmaker. Died 1720.

SPENCER, Hon. William. Infant son of Earl of Sunderland.

STANHOPE, Charles. Treasury Secretary until forced to resign over South Sea scandal. Cousin of Earl Stanhope.

STANHOPE, James, Earl. Secretary of State for Northern Department until February 1721.

STOSCH, Philip von, Baron. German bibliophile recruited by Carteret to spy on the Pretender in Rome.

SUNDERLAND, Charles Spencer, Earl of. First Lord of the Treasury until forced to resign over South Sea scandal.

SUNDERLAND, Judith Spencer, Countess of. Wife of Earl of Sunderland.

SURTEES, Richard, 'Dick'. Former apprentice of William Spandrel senior.

TAILLARD, Jean-Luc. Surveyor for whom Spandrel works in Rennes.

TOWNSHEND, Charles, Viscount. Secretary of State for Northern Department from February 1721; old friend and brother-in-law of Robert Walpole.

TOWNSHEND, Dorothy, 'Dolly', Viscountess. Wife of Viscount Townshend and sister of Robert Walpole.

TURRETTINI. Banker used by Estelle de Vries in Geneva.

UGELS, Balthasar. Amsterdam shopkeeper who rents his basement to Zuyler.

S, Rebekka. Daughter of Balthasar Ugels.

RIES, Estelle. English-born wife of Ysbrand de Vries.

VRIES, Gerrit. Son of Ysbrand de Vries by first marriage.

de VRIES, Ysbrand. V.O.C. merchant and old friend of Sir Theodore Janssen.

WAGEMAKER, Augustus, Colonel. Secret agent of Robert Walpole.

WAGEMAKER, Dorothea. Sister of Augustus and Tiberius Wagemaker. Fiancée of Captain Hatton. Died in a fall, 1713.

WAGEMAKER, Henry. Father of Augustus, Tiberius and Dorothea Wagemaker. Died 1712.

WAGEMAKER, Tiberius. Brother of Augustus and Dorothea Wagemaker.

WALPOLE, Catherine. Wife of Robert Walpole.

WALPOLE, Catherine, 'Kate'. Eldest daughter of Robert Walpole. An invalid.

WALPOLE, Edward. Second son of Robert Walpole. Oppidan at Eton.

WALPOLE, Galfridus. Youngest brother of Robert Walpole. Postmaster-General from March 1721.

WALPOLE, Horatio, 'Old Horace'. Younger brother of Robert Walpole. Treasury Secretary from April 1721.

WALPOLE, Horatio, 'Young Horace'. Youngest son of Robert Walpole.

WALPOLE, Mary. Younger daughter of Robert Walpole.

WALPOLE, Robert junior. Eldest son of Robert Walpole.

WALPOLE, Robert, 'Robin'. Paymaster-General until April 1721. Thereafter First Lord of the Treasury and Chancellor of the Exchequer.

WELSH, Ann, 'Annie'. A neighbour of the Spandrel Cat and Dog Yard.

WHARTON, Philip, Duke of. Eccentric hell-raising Jacobite.

ZUYLER, Pieter. Secretary to Ysbrand de Vries.

APPENDIX B

Glossary

Recommended reading only for those with a taste for historical detail: an explanation of some eighteenth-century terms which may not be familiar to the contemporary reader, with notes on their significance in 1721/22.

THE AUSTRIAN EMPIRE AND THE AUSTRIAN NETHERLANDS

The Holy Roman Empire, a medieval attempt to unite central Europe under a single Christian Emperor, had long since become moribund. The Habsburg Emperors ruled effectively only in their Austro-Hungarian heartland, most of which actually lay outside the notional boundaries of the Empire thanks to recent conquests from the Turks – hence the growing trend to refer to this hotchpotch of territories as Austria. For finishing on the winning side in the War of the Spanish Succession (q.v.) Austria was rewarded with most of Spain's subject territory in Italy plus the Spanish Netherlands – the southern half of the formerly Spanish-ruled Low Countries, more or less equivalent to today's Belgium and Luxembourg. The Austrian Netherlands (as they were thereafter known) offered the Emperor a definite but far from straightforward opportunity to compete with the British, French and Dutch in maritime trade.

COFFEE-HOUSES

These establishments, which had begun to spring up the middle of the previous century, provided rather more than coffee. They were male-only eating, drinking, debating, gambling and newspaper-reading dens, distinguishable from taverns by virtue of (slightly) higher standards of décor and behaviour.

DEBTORS' PRISONS

Imprisonment for debt was a Sword of Damocles hanging over the head of anyone who accepted any form of credit. It was also a Catch-22, since, once imprisoned, how could a debtor pay his creditors? Even in debt, however, there was class distinction. In London, the King's Bench Prison was reserved for gentleman debtors, the Marshalsea and the Fleet for the lower reaches of society. There were also gradations of imprisonment, since not all debtors were penniless. Some could pay to live outside the prison itself but within its rules, in designated lodging-houses, from which base they might hope to earn some money and claw their way back to solvency. Alternatively, a debtor could flee to a different county (which in London meant crossing the river), where there was no writ for their arrest, or take refuge in one of the recognized debtors' sanctuaries, such as Whitefriars in London and Abbey Strand in Edinburgh (the sites of ancient and legally protected monastic foundations). Debt also enjoyed a sabbath. No debtor could be arrested on a Sunday.

THE FIFTEEN AND THE FORTY-FIVE

The two famous Jacobite (q.v.) risings of the eighteenth century, the first a recent memory, the second yet to happen. The Fifteen was intended to exploit popular resentment of the shipping over of a German prince to

...ed Queen Anne in the summer of 1714. The leader ...he rebel army, the Earl of Mar, proved a disastrous ...ilitary strategist and the rising was already a lost cause when James Edward, the Pretender, landed at Peterhead in December 1715. He retreated to France, along with Mar, in February 1716, leaving the remnants of their army to be hunted down by Lord Cadogan's forces. Thirty years later, the Forty-Five was to prove an altogether more serious rising under the personal leadership of Charles Edward, the Pretender's son.

HANOVER
The Electorate of Brunswick-Lüneburg, commonly known as Hanover, qualified as an electorate because its ruler was one of the German princes traditionally entitled to vote on the choice of Holy Roman Emperor. It became attached to the British crown at the death of Queen Anne in August 1714. The Act of Settlement of 1701 had settled the presumptive succession on Princess Sophia of Hanover, granddaughter of King James I and Anne's closest Protestant relative. Sophia died in May 1714 and it was thus her son George, who had ruled Hanover since 1698, who succeeded to the British throne. Hanover, however, remained officially a foreign country, with a completely separate (benignly despotic) form of government, coincidentally reigned over by the same man.

JACOBITES
Any person who maintained (as many did) that King James II remained the rightful King after and despite the Glorious Revolution of 1689 was, by definition, a Jacobite (the name being derived from the Latin version of James, *Jacobus*), but slowly the expression became limited in application to those who wanted to do something about it and engaged in treasonable conspiracy to

that end. Following James II's death in exile in
Jacobites recognized his son as King James III
succession of George I in 1714 outraged them
more, since Anne had at least been a daughter of the ro[
blood, but it also raised their hopes of a restoration of th
true line – hopes destined ever to be dashed.

THE MISSISSIPPI COMPANY

When King Louis XIV of France died in September
1715, he was succeeded by his five-year-old great-
grandson, Louis XV. Power was vested in a Regent,
Louis XIV's nephew, Philippe, Duke of Orléans, an
insecure and impressionable individual who was rapidly
seduced by the economic theories of the Scottish
financier, John Law, a far-seeing advocate of paper
money, who founded the Banque Générale in April 1716
and soon turned it into a quasi-national bank. In August
1717, Law took over the ramshackle Mississippi
Company, which held the monopoly on trade with
France's North American colonies, renamed it the
Company of the West (though the old name somehow
refused to go away) and transformed it into a vigorous
commercial enterprise with, it soon came to be believed,
such limitless wealth-making possibilities that only a fool
would refuse to invest in it. The company's stock soared
in value and soared again as it gradually acquired every
other overseas trading monopoly at the Regent's
disposal. It was accordingly renamed the Company of the
Indies (although everybody still called it the Mississippi).
In August 1719, Law played his trump card: the conversion of the entire National Debt of France (standing at
more than £100 million) into Mississippi shares. The
calculation on which the scheme was based – that the
shares would continue to rise in value – proved a self-
fulfilling prophecy, fuelled by generous instalment

nents for payment and a flood of paper money
Law's bank (by then the official Banque Royale).
at Law had failed to foresee, however, was the
sulting hyper-inflation, which soon began to dislocate
ociety. In his newly appointed role of Finance Minister,
Law resorted to ever more draconian measures to control
the beast he had let loose, culminating in May 1720
with an edict halving the face value of banknotes and
Mississippi shares. Three days of rioting in Paris
persuaded the Regent to overrule him. The shares sank
like a stone and the bank was besieged by mobs
demanding coin for their notes. Want and ruin had
suddenly taken the place of glut and prosperity. Not long
afterwards, plague arrived in Marseilles to add to
France's woes. By November 1720 paper money was
dead and the Banque Royale broken. Law fled the
country and a full-scale inquiry was launched into the
disaster, the laggardly conclusion of which, in October
1722, was that all documents relating to the affair should
be destroyed, by public burning in specially designed
cages. The Mississippi Company lived on, but its secrets
were not permitted to. The Duke of Orléans also lived
on, but only until the following year. He is commemor-
ated by the city of New Orleans, Louisana, named in his
honour. Law died in Venice in 1729 and is commemor-
ated by every colourful chapter in the subsequent history
of financial speculation.

NEW STYLE, OLD STYLE
The Julian Calendar (credited to Julius Caesar) counted
every fourth year as a Leap Year, an insufficiently precise
adjustment which led to a gradual separation of the
calendar and tropical years. The Gregorian Calendar
(promulgated by Pope Gregory XIII in 1582) solved this
problem by omitting the Leap Year at the turn of three

out of every four centuries. It was rapidly adop
most European countries, but not by Great Britain
1752. The result was that in 1721/22 the British calen
lagged eleven days behind most of the rest of Europ
This was further complicated by the British practice or
beginning the year for legal and civil purposes on 25th
March (Lady Day – the Feast of the Annunciation of the
Virgin Mary) rather than 1st January. Businessmen
dealing with the continent took this in their stride,
moving easily between the two systems and often
employing double dating. Hence Sir Theodore Janssen
would probably have dated the letter he sent to Ysbrand
de Vries after his meeting with Robert Knight at the
outset of this story 19th/30th January 1720/21. Dates in
the continental calendar were referred to as New Style,
those in the British as Old Style. (When Great Britain
finally adopted the Gregorian Calendar, it also moved
the beginning of the year to 1st January. Money-lenders
did not care to lose eleven days' interest, far less the
better part of three months', hence the financial year has
begun ever since on 6th April, being 25th March plus the
missing eleven days.)

NON-JURORS

To regularize the clearly irregular arrangement of 1689
whereby the deposed King James II was succeeded
jointly by his elder daughter Mary and her Dutch
husband, Prince William of Orange, all office holders
under the Crown were required to swear allegiance to the
new dual monarchs. The four hundred or so clergy
(including five bishops) who felt unable to do so because
they had already sworn allegiance for life to James were
expelled from their livings and described as Non-Jurors
(i.e. persons who had not taken an oath). Death and
recantation made steady inroads into this number. Those

ntinued to hold firm even after James's death in
were suspected (at least by the Government) of
nt if not actual Jacobitism. The most Jacobite prelate
. all, however – Francis Atterbury – had no difficulty in
swearing the oath, only in keeping it.

NORTHERN DEPARTMENT, SOUTHERN DEPARTMENT

The seemingly obvious and natural arrangement
whereby one Secretary of State deals with Foreign Affairs
and another with Home Affairs was not adopted by
the British Government until 1782. Back in 1721/22,
two Secretaries of State shared responsibility for
Home Affairs (according to which of them was on hand
at the time) but divided between them responsibility
for relations with the so-called Northern Powers
(Scandinavia, Poland, Russia, Germany and the
Netherlands) and the so-called Southern Powers
(France, Spain, Portugal, Italy and Turkey), hence the
names of the two departments. Seniority was vested in
whichever of the Secretaries had been in post the longer.
At the start of 1721, this was Earl Stanhope, by its end
Viscount Townshend.

THE OTTOMAN EMPIRE

The Turkish Empire was named after its ruling Ottoman
dynasty and was also known as the Sublime Porte, a
French translation of the formal title of the central office
of the Ottoman Government in Constantinople (now
Istanbul). It had recently lost control of Hungary to
the Austrian Empire, but still held sway throughout the
Balkans, as well as in the Holy Land and North Africa as
far west as Algeria. An ambassadorial posting to Turkey
was not without its complications. Edward Wortley
Montagu was despatched to Constantinople in August

1716. He and his wife (the celebrated poet and lett.
writer, Mary Wortley Montagu) arrived the following
spring after an arduous overland journey, only to be
recalled within months because of a ministerial upheaval back home (the resignations of Walpole and
Townshend). They ended up spending sixteen months
in Turkey (most of them waiting for the new ambassador
to arrive) and ten months on their way there or back.
Wortley Montagu's successor, Abraham Stanyan,
reached Constantinople in April 1718. He may well have
anticipated his own recall when he learned of another
ministerial upheaval back home three years later (the
return to office of Walpole and Townshend).

THE PAPAL STATES

A large area of central Italy (corresponding more or
less to the present-day regions of Latium, Umbria, the
Marches and Emilia-Romagna) was reserved for the
Pope in his capacity as a temporal sovereign. As such,
the Papacy was not revealed in a flattering light, the
region, beyond the city of Rome itself, being a byword
for poverty and maladministration.

POCKET BOROUGHS

Whilst the county constituencies of the British
Parliament represented local landowning opinion with a
fair degree of accuracy, many of the borough constituencies had such limited electoral rolls and arcane
electoral procedures that they were, to all intents and
purposes, in the pocket of a local magnate. The most
notorious example of this was Old Sarum, a deserted
Iron Age hill-fort near Salisbury, whose two Members
of Parliament were returned by an electorate of three,
tenants of Thomas Pitt, whom, not surprisingly,
they unfailingly elected. Many such boroughs were

nsparently for sale. Hence Robert Walpole's brothers, oratio and Galfridus, as well as his son, Edward, all sat at one time or another for the Cornish borough of Lostwithiel, controlled by a venal local landowner named Johns, who charged £20 per vote and a modest £300 for his travelling expenses on election day. (A very rare example of a pocket borough somehow slipping out of the pocket came in the 1722 general election, when Carr, Lord Hervey, son and heir of the Earl of Bristol – and father, persistent rumour had it, of Robert Walpole's youngest son, Horatio – failed to be re-elected for Bury St Edmunds, which his father had donated to him, apparently by reason of drink-sodden negligence. Hervey died the following year and it is not clear whether he was ever sober enough in the interim to appreciate his loss.)

THE SOUTH SEA COMPANY

The South Sea Company originated in the ambitions of a group of businessmen headed by John Blunt to turn the Sword Blade Company (which had originally manu-factured and sold sword blades but was, by the beginning of the eighteenth century, serving sharper purposes) into a bank rivalling the Bank of England, whose directors had been profiting handsomely from underwriting the currency since its foundation in 1694. Their hopes of doing so relied on the favour of Robert Harley, who became Chancellor of the Exchequer in the summer of 1710 and was immediately faced with the problem of how to manage unsecured war debts of £9 million. Blunt was ready with a solution, which Harley eagerly adopted: the unfunded loans were to be converted into shares in a new South Sea Company, which would hold the monopoly on trade with Spain's American colonies. The company came formally into existence in September 1711, with Harley (by then Lord High Treasurer and

Earl of Oxford) as Governor, the Sword Blade group prominent among the directors and one Robert Knight appointed to the post of chief cashier. Under the Treaty of Utrecht, which finally brought the War of the Spanish Succession (q.v.) to a close in March 1713, the company was granted a thirty-year contract for the supply of slaves to the Spanish colonies (the *Asiento*). They never actually managed to turn a profit on this business, but at political manoeuvring they knew no master. Oxford's fall from power and King George I's accession were smoothly accommodated, with the King and the Prince of Wales replacing Oxford as joint Governors. By 1719, Blunt and Knight had the entire National Debt of £31 million – and the consequent eclipse of the Bank of England – in their sights. This seemed to be rendered certain by the passage of the South Sea Bill in April 1720, the rapid conversion of most of the Debt into South Sea shares and the vertiginous rise in the value of those shares. But what went quickly up came even more quickly down. It came to be understood that even political corruption – the true basis of the entire scheme – had its limits. And there really was nothing quite as safe as the Bank of England.

THE WAR OF THE SPANISH SUCCESSION

As the seventeenth century drew towards its close, the dominant preoccupation of the European powers was how to carve up the Spanish Empire on the death of the ailing and heirless Spanish King, Carlos II. In October 1700, Carlos nominated his distant cousin Philippe of Anjou, grandson of King Louis XIV of France, as his successor. A month later, Carlos died. Great Britain, the United Provinces and the Austrian Empire were pledged never to allow the union of the French and Spanish crowns and formed a Grand Alliance in September 1701 to secure Spain's possessions in the Netherlands and Italy for Austria. War raged in Spain, Italy, Germany and the Low Countries for the next twelve years. When the war ended, in 1713, it did so very much on the Grand Alliance's original terms, with a guarantee that Philippe and his successors would never claim the French throne. An historically very significant feature of the peace treaty was that the British seizure of Gibraltar in 1704 was rendered permanent.

THE STONE

Why so many men and women of the eighteenth century – Robert Walpole among them – should have succumbed to stones and gravel in the kidneys and bladder is something of a mystery. Diet seems the likeliest answer. Most people were probably chronically dehydrated, the drinking of water being a hazardous undertaking at the best of times. Dehydration is now thought to be the primary cause of stone formation. The fashion for coffee consumption can have been no help in this regard. And the widespread use of chalk to whiten flour must also have played its part. The only effective treatment was lithotomy – surgical removal of the stone, without the benefit of anaesthetic. The odds against survival were long. As Walpole discovered, however, the odds against surviving such supposed cures as lithontriptic lixivium – the potion Dr Jurin poured down his throat in March 1745 – were even longer.

SWANIMOTE COURTS

Forest law was a thicket of ancient offences and penalties governing land use and peat, timber and game rights in the Royal Forests. It was exercised, inconsistently and irregularly, by local Swanimote Courts (the name Swanimote meaning literally a meeting of swains). Their judgments could only be enforced if confirmed at a trial before the Chief Justice in Eyre (*in Eyre* being a judicial term similar to *Errant*, indicating an itinerant circuit court function). No Chief Justice in Eyre had actually sat in Windsor Forest since 1632. This did not render the Swanimote impotent, however. It could detain offenders, confiscate their guns, dogs and traps, and bail them to appear before the next Justice Seat in Eyre (whenever that might be) on ruinous recognizances. Paying its fines tended to be a better course to follow. And fines there were aplenty in Windsor Forest during 1721/22, discontent at the acquisition of Forest land by Whig grandees being at its height. The Windsor Swanimote was allowed to lapse in 1728 when it began exercising its power of acquittal rather too freely for Walpole's liking.

THE UNITED PROVINCES

Those provinces of the Netherlands which successfully rebelled against Spanish rule in the sixteenth century (known today simply as the Netherlands) formed an independent federation, governed by representatives of the provinces meeting at The Hague as the States General. In practice, Holland, the largest and richest province, determined national policy, articulated by its Grand Pensionary, selected from the pensionaries of the States of Holland. They had deliberately left the office of Stadholder vacant at the death of William III in 1702, preferring a collective leadership. In the course of the seventeenth century, the United Provinces won a reputation as Europe's most orderly, prosperous and civilized nation. (In 1670, Amsterdam became the first city in the world to introduce a truly effective system of street lighting.) Crime was minimal, poverty hard to find. But nothing lasts for ever. By 1721/22, the country's power and wealth had begun to decline – even though most of its inhabitants probably did not know it.

THE V.O.C.

Spanish embargoes on trade with the Mediterranean drove the Dutch to develop the East Indies market far faster than either England or Portugal, their principal competitors in the region. To regulate this market, the States General established in 1602 a United East India Company – the *Verenigde Oostindische Compagnie*. The company was federally constructed, with directorships allocated to the provinces in proportion to their capital contributions, and was delegated the power to maintain troops, garrisons and warships, govern the inhabitants of the East Indian colonies (comprising most of what is now Indonesia) and treat with local potentates as it saw fit. The V.O.C. became, in a sense, a state within a state, albeit one exercising its power on the other side of the world. It reaped huge rewards as the years passed, supplying Europe with tea, coffee, spices, porcelain and textiles. But it also incurred serious losses, with one or two shipwrecks every year. Those wrecked vessels, lying still in the Atlantic and Indian Oceans, are ironically all that remains today of the V.O.C.'s once vast and mighty fleet. The company itself was dissolved in 1795 and not a single example of the many hundreds of its vessels that did not sink has survived.

APPENDIX C

Map

The map overleaf illustrates the political structure of western Europe in 1721/22, marking places and states featured in the story. (It should be noted that the mosaic of German states is a *simplified* version of the bewilderingly complex and virtually unmappable reality!)

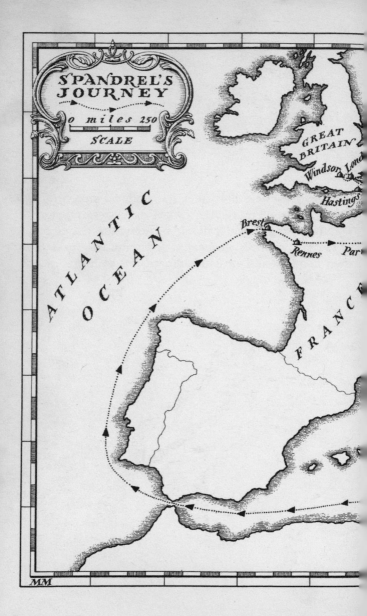

UNITED
PROVINCES

The Hague
Amsterdam
Antwerp
Brussels
Cologne

HANOVER

PALATINATE
Heidelburg

BREISGAU
Berne
Basle
Freiburg

SWITZERLAND
Geneva
SAVOY
Milan
Turin
Genoa

Leghorn
TUSCANY
Florence

PRESIDIO
Orbitello
Civita Vecchia

PAPAL
STATES
Rome

Naples

Vienna

AUSTRIA

OTTOMAN

EMPIRE

Gower

A LIST OF OTHER ROBERT GODDARD TITLES
AVAILABLE FROM CORGI BOOKS AND BANTAM PRESS

THE PRICES SHOWN BELOW WERE CORRECT AT THE TIME OF GOING TO
PRESS. HOWEVER TRANSWORLD PUBLISHERS RESERVE THE RIGHT TO
SHOW NEW RETAIL PRICES ON COVERS WHICH MAY DIFFER FROM THOSE
PREVIOUSLY ADVERTISED IN THE TEXT OR ELSEWHERE.

03587 9	BORROWED TIME (Hardback)	£15.99
14223 9	BORROWED TIME	£6.99
02492 3	CLOSED CIRCLE (Hardback)	£14.99
13840 1	CLOSED CIRCLE	£6.99
02489 3	HAND IN GLOVE (Hardback)	£14.99
13839 8	HAND IN GLOVE	£5.99
13281 0	IN PALE BATTALIONS	£6.99
13282 9	PAINTING THE DARKNESS	£5.99
13144 X	PAST CARING	£6.99
13562 3	TAKE NO FAREWELL	£6.99
54593 7	INTO THE BLUE	£6.99
03614 X	OUT OF THE SUN (Hardback)	£16.99
14224 7	OUT OF THE SUN	£6.99
03617 4	BEYOND RECALL (Hardback)	£16.99
14225 5	BEYOND RECALL	£6.99
04266 2	CAUGHT IN THE LIGHT (Hardback)	£16.99
14597 1	CAUGHT IN THE LIGHT	£6.99
04271 9	SET IN STONE (Hardback)	£16.99
14601 3	SET IN STONE	£5.99
04274 3	SEA CHANGE (Hardback)	£16.99
04758 3	DYING TO TELL (Hardback)	£16.99

IF YOU LIKE ROBERT GODDARD YOU MIGHT ALSO LIKE
GEMMA O'CONNOR

50586 6	FAREWELL TO THE FLESH	£5.99
50587 4	TIME TO REMEMBER	£5.99
81263 7	SINS OF OMISSION	£5.99
81262 9	FALLS THE SHADOW	£5.99
04719 2	WALKING ON WATER	£9.99

All Transworld titles are available by post from:

Bookpost, PO Box 29, Douglas, Isle of Man, IM99 1BQ

Credit cards accepted. Please telephone 01624 836000,
fax 01624 837033, Internet http://www.bookpost.co.uk
or e-mail: bookshop@enterprise.net for details

Free postage and packing in the UK. Overseas customers:
allow £1 per book (paperbacks) and £3 per book (hardbacks)

- 6 SEP 2014

3 0 SEP 2014

2 3 OCT 2014

- 6 DEC 2014

- 8 DEC 2018

2 9 JUN 2019

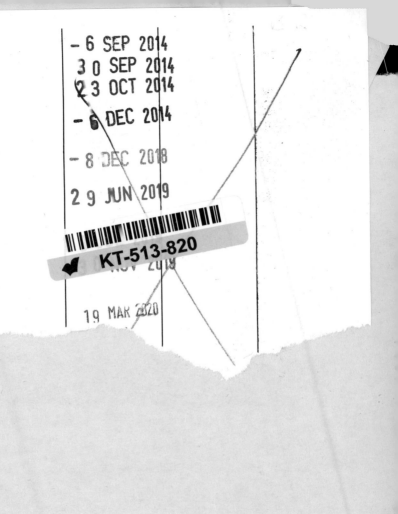

KT-513-820

NOV 2019

19 MAR 2020

C333563093

ALSO BY JENNIFER CLOSE

Girls in White Dresses

JENNIFER CLOSE

The Smart One

VINTAGE BOOKS
London

Published by Vintage 2014

2 4 6 8 10 9 7 5 3 1

Copyright © Jennifer Close 2013

Jennifer Close has asserted her right under the Copyright, Designs
and Patents Act 1988 to be identified as the author of this work

This book is sold subject to the condition that it shall not,
by way of trade or otherwise, be lent, resold, hired out,
or otherwise circulated without the publisher's
prior consent in any form of binding or cover other
than that in which it is published and without
a similar condition, including this condition,
being imposed on the subsequent purchaser

First published in the United States of America by Alfred A. Knopf,
Random House, Inc., in 2013

First published in Great Britain with the title *Things We Need* in 2013 by
Chatto & Windus

Vintage
Random House, 20 Vauxhall Bridge Road,
London SW1V 2SA

www.vintage-books.co.uk

Addresses for companies within The Random House Group Limited
can be found at: www.randomhouse.co.uk/offices.htm

The Random House Group Limited Reg. No. 954009

A CIP catalogue record for this book
is available from the British Library

ISBN 9780099563297

The Random House Group Limited supports the Forest
Stewardship Council® (FSC®), the leading international forest-
certification organisation. Our books carrying the FSC label are
printed on FSC®-certified paper. FSC is the only forest-certification
scheme supported by the leading environmental organisations,
including Greenpeace. Our paper procurement policy can be found
at: www.randomhouse.co.uk/environment

Printed and bound by CPI Group (UK) Ltd, Croydon, CR0 4YY

For Tim,
My favorite one

Part One

Chapter 1

From inside her apartment, Claire could hear the neighbor kids in the hall. They were running from one end to the other, the way they sometimes did, kicking a ball or playing tag, or just running for running's sake. They had their dog with them too, a big, sad golden retriever named Ditka, who always looked confused, like he couldn't understand why or how he'd ended up living in an apartment in New York.

Claire muted the TV and listened to see if the kids were going to stay out there for a while, or if they were just waiting for their parents to take them somewhere. She hoped it was the second option. It was Saturday morning, which meant they had hours ahead of them. Having them out there made her feel trapped in her own apartment.

Just because she was sitting on the couch in sweatpants and had no plans to leave didn't make the feeling go away. She could sense their presence on the other side of the wall, so close to her.

She could see the shadow of Ditka's nose as he sniffed at the bottom of the door. They were invading her space, what little of it she had. And it was interfering with her plan to be a hermit for the whole three-day weekend, something she was getting better and better at.

Last week, she was crossing Broadway and a man crossing the other way looked her in the eyes, pointed to her face, and said, 'I want to fuck you.' On the street, she'd blushed and walked away quickly. But when she got home she realized two things: The first was that the comment had pleased her. Claire was pretty, but it hadn't always been that way. She was the kind of girl who grew into her looks, who suffered through an awkward stage of braces, unfortunate haircuts, and overalls in her teen years. Now, when men called out to her, 'Hey, Princess. Looking good, beautiful,' she was grateful. She would duck her head and pretend to be embarrassed or insulted, but if they called out, 'Smile, pretty girl,' she always obliged.

The second thing she realized was that the man on the street was the first person to talk directly to her in almost three days. She didn't know whether to be impressed with herself or very disturbed. She chose a mix of the two.

*

The kids in the hallway were getting louder, and Claire turned up the volume on the TV, hoping that their parents would come out soon and tell them to come inside or at least quiet down. The kids' names were Maddie and Jack, and they were somewhere in the nine-to-eleven age range. Jack was older, and starting to get that shoulder hunch that preteen boys get, like the whole world was so embarrassing he couldn't even stand up straight. Maddie was the kind of kid who believed adults found her adorable, shouting out things like 'Purple is a mix of red and blue' in the elevator for Claire's benefit and then smiling and looking down at her shoes, as if she were shy. They both had dirty-blond hair and buckteeth, and Maddie would find out soon enough that she wasn't adorable or charming, so Claire always smiled at her.

She and Doug used to call them the Hamburger Helpers, because every night the smell of ground beef and onions came wafting out of their apartment. Sometimes Claire wanted to call the kids into her place to give them something to eat, anything that wasn't meat and onions in a pan. It used to be a running joke – whenever they'd smell the ground beef cooking, Doug would say, 'Is it tacos for dinner?' and Claire would answer, 'Nope, just some good old-fashioned Beefy Mac.'

Together, she and Doug talked endlessly about the family. They wondered what possessed the Hamburger Helpers to raise a family in an average New York City apartment. Every Sunday they watched as the dad took the subway with Maddie and Jack to Fairway, watched the three of them return carrying loads of groceries, struggle onto the elevator, and go up to their apartment. Wouldn't they have been better off in the suburbs? Wouldn't things have been easier?

Claire and Doug laughed when Jack failed his spelling test and they heard the fight through the wall, heard Jack say, 'Fuck spelling,' to his parents. They agreed that it was only going to get worse over at the Hamburger Helpers' as Maddie and Jack hit puberty and hormones crawled all over their tiny apartment. They pitied the family and what was in store for them.

Now Claire realized the family was probably pitying her – that is, if they'd even noticed that Doug had moved out. Either way, they seemed to be getting a lot more annoying.

When Doug and Claire called off their engagement, her friend Katherine had said, 'In some ways, it's worse than a divorce.' It was Claire's first night out since the whole thing happened, and she and Katherine were at a wine bar near her apartment. 'I guess it's because it ended before it even started, so it's like someone dying young.'

'Great,' Claire said.

Katherine wasn't listening. 'Or maybe it's because by the time people get divorced, they're usually like really sick of each other, and have done bad things and are ready to move on. With you guys, no one saw this coming.'

Claire figured this had to be the strangest response she would get. Katherine, a friend from high school, was so perpetually messed up that you got used to it after a while. Her first week in

New York, she'd watched a thirty-two-year-old woman leap off the subway platform at Twenty-third and Park, killing herself as she got hit by the number 6 train. Katherine had skipped work for two weeks, leaving her apartment only to purchase a small white Maltese for eight hundred dollars from the pet store on the corner with her parents' credit card. Things since then had been touch and go. Claire could forgive her strange reply. Surely everyone else would know how to be more appropriate.

But Claire was wrong. Apparently no one knew how to react to her news. Her two friends at work, Becca and Molly, decided that their mission would be to cheer Claire up by telling her all of the bizarre love stories they knew. Sometimes the point was clear ('My mom was engaged before she met my dad, you know!') and sometimes it wasn't, like the time Molly told her about her sister who worked as a nanny and ended up running off and marrying the father of her babysitting charges, leaving his first wife in their dust. 'Isn't that romantic?' Molly asked. *No*, Claire wanted to say, *that's not romantic, it's adultery*. But she stayed silent and smiled.

Becca and Molly had been nice coworkers to have. They were all around the same age, all enjoyed getting an occasional drink after work to complain about the office, and were happy to have lunch together. She had always liked them. Until now. One afternoon in her office, as Molly told her about all of the friends she had who were getting divorced, Claire said, 'Well, at least I won't have to be Claire Winklepleck. Now there's a silver lining.'

Molly stared at her for a moment, and then said quietly, like she didn't want to upset Claire, 'So many women don't take their husband's name anymore. You wouldn't have had to do that if it made you uncomfortable.'

'Right,' Claire answered. 'Right.'

She'd decided that day that Becca and Molly had to go. It was really for the best. She began to avoid them. Whenever she saw them coming toward her office around lunchtime, she'd pick up the phone and call her voice mail, so that when they popped their heads in, she could roll her eyes and point to the phone, then wave them along, as if to say, 'Don't wait for me, this could take forever, just go, go on!'

Maddie and Jack were now screeching and laughing in the hallway, the kind of laughing that often turned into hysterical crying, when one kid hit another and the game quickly went south. She waited for that to happen, but they quieted a little bit and resumed their game, some sort of crummy hallway soccer, she assumed. She hoped that they'd be out of there by the time she wanted to order dinner, because she didn't want to have to wave to them and say hello, have to pet the dog and smile as she accepted her food.

She probably shouldn't even be ordering out, considering her money situation, but what difference did twenty more dollars on her credit card really make at this point? The credit card balance was so high, so unbelievable, that she was able to ignore it most of the time, to pretend that there was no way she'd spent that much in the past six months. It just wasn't possible.

Her phone rang again, but she didn't bother to look at it. Her mom had been calling every day (a few times a day, actually) trying to persuade Claire to come to the shore with the family. 'It's important to me,' her mom said, over and over. If Claire had been anyone else, she could have told her mom the truth, that she didn't want to go and sit with her family for a week at the beach, that it would make her already pathetic life seem worse. But she wouldn't do that, because no matter how old she got, she still hated hurting Weezy's feelings, and the times that she did left her feeling so guilty she couldn't sleep. But for now, she let the phone ring. She had stuff to do, like looking at her bank accounts online hoping something had changed, and watching TV.

Claire sighed and switched the channel. She could always make something for dinner. There was a box of macaroni and cheese in the cupboard and that would be fine, she realized. Yes, if Maddie and Jack were still out there when she wanted to eat, she'd just make that. Calmed by the fact that she wouldn't have to talk to anyone today, she pulled a blanket over her and settled down on the couch to watch an old eighties movie. She figured watching people go to the prom would be soothing.

Claire first met Doug at a Super Bowl party of a friend of a friend on the Upper West Side. They'd sat next to each other on the couch and watched the game, eating guacamole and laughing at the commercials. Anytime Claire needed a beer, Doug stood up, took her empty bottle, and returned with a full one. At the end of the night, she was happy to give him her number when he asked.

'Doug Winklepleck?' her best friend, Lainie, had said. 'That's an unfortunate name.' Claire agreed, but continued to date him.

After they'd dated each other for a few weeks, Doug said, 'I would like to be exclusive with you, if that's what you want as well.' It sounded like a business proposal, but Claire was happy to agree. Doug was straightforward, and Claire appreciated that. He had a thin face, and a nose that was almost too big, but not quite. He was handsome in his own way. He was a systems developer for a fund of funds, a job title that meant nothing to Claire and that she never quite fully understood. He had his ties on a rotating schedule and contributed the maximum amount to his 401(k). He was, by all accounts, admirable.

On one of their early dates, Doug took Claire to see the elephants arrive in Manhattan for the circus. They were marched through the Queens Midtown Tunnel at midnight and Doug told her it was something she had to see. 'I can't believe you've lived here for five years and you've never seen them,' he said. 'That won't do.'

They went to a bar on Third Avenue that had a jukebox, long wooden tables, and smelled like yeast and bleach. They played darts and shared a plate of buffalo wings, which was a tricky thing to eat on an early date. And when it was time, they rushed out to the street to wait for the arrival.

Claire stood there, leaning against Doug, buzzed from the beers and the strangeness of the night. She shivered and watched the big, sad elephants march into Manhattan. They were wrinkled and dusty and magnificent. She wanted to cry for them, wanted to run up and touch their rough skin with her hand, to place her palms flat against their hides. It was all she could do to stay put in her place. She drew in a deep breath and said, 'Oh.'

'See?' Doug whispered into her hair. 'I told you. It's something to see.'

And right then, Claire felt like Doug was the right choice, the person she'd been waiting for, and anytime she started to think otherwise, she'd close her eyes and whisper, 'Remember the elephants,' until the feeling went away.

They moved in together nine months after they met, and then, about a year after that, Doug proposed. The ring was dull, silver, and thick, with a vine etched all around it. Along the vine were tiny dots of diamonds. Claire hated it. 'I knew you wouldn't want a big, showy ring,' Doug said. She'd just nodded and looked down at her hand. Of course she wanted a big ring. She'd always wanted a big diamond, even if she knew she was supposed to say it didn't matter.

And the thing that bugged her, the thing that really drove

her crazy, was that Doug had never asked her. If he had, he would have known. She suspected that he surprised her with this one so he wouldn't have to spend a lot of money, which was even more annoying, because he made a good amount of money – a lot of money by anyone's standards. It wasn't like she could look at the ring and think, *Well, this is all he could afford, but I know he loves me*. It wasn't. He could have bought her something spectacular, but he decided to be practical. And who wanted practical for an engagement ring?

They were engaged for four months. Claire tried to remember where the shift happened, when things started to fall apart, but she could never quite figure it out. There were no screaming fights, no cheating, no admission of an Internet porn addiction or a hidden drug problem. They just simply began to crack.

Almost every conversation they had led them to a disagreement. Had it always been this way? Claire didn't think so, but maybe it had and they'd just never noticed. Maybe now that they were facing the rest of their lives together, everything seemed bigger and more important.

'You only want two kids?' Claire said one day. Doug nodded. He'd said this before, but she'd always thought he was flexible.

'Two is a good number,' he said. 'Two is affordable.'

'What if one of them dies?' Claire asked. 'Then you only have one left.'

'Why would you say something like that?' He looked away. 'What's wrong with you?'

When Claire wanted to go out to dinner three nights in

a row, Doug said they shouldn't, to save money. When Doug talked about moving to Long Island, Claire told him he was out of his mind. When Claire watched reality TV, especially the singing competition show that Doug hated, he told her she was contributing to the downfall of American culture. When Doug wore his BlackBerry strapped to his hip in a holster, Claire told him he was a nerd. It went on like this, until most nights were spent in separate rooms of the apartment, watching different TV shows.

'You're always so mad at me,' Doug said, more than once. 'It's like whatever I do disappoints you.'

'That's not true,' Claire said. But she wasn't sure.

Then one night, after an argument about whether they should order Thai food or sushi that ended with Doug calling Claire overdramatic and Claire calling Doug controlling, he had sighed. 'What's going on with us?'

'It's just Thai food,' Claire said. But it was too late.

'Something's wrong. This isn't right.'

'You can get the crab wontons,' she said. Doug shook his head.

Claire stayed in the apartment and Doug moved out, saying that he would pay his part of the rent for two more months while she looked for a new place. It all happened quickly. There were two nights of talking and fighting, of Claire crying on the couch, and Doug crying a little bit too, and then it was settled and he was moving out and Claire still hadn't told anyone what had happened.

The Monday after Doug left, Claire got dressed, took the subway to work, and was standing in her boss's office talking about a grant proposal when she started crying. Crying! Like she was seven years old. It had been mortifying to stand there and try to hold back her tears, and even more so to have her boss jump up and close the door to her office, then guide Claire to a chair to ask her what was wrong.

Claire had told her everything – the engagement, Doug's moving out, the apartment, how she still needed to tell her family and cancel the plans that had been made for the wedding – and Amy had listened, nodding and handing her tissues, making sympathetic noises at certain places.

'It's such a mess,' Claire said. 'I'm sorry. It's a mess, I'm a mess.'

Amy had sent her home then, instructing her to take the week off. 'You have so much comp time. Take it. We're covered here. There's nothing that can't be done next week. Just get things sorted and settled.' Claire thought how strange this was, since the extent of her personal conversations with Amy up to this point had been about the salad place across the street that they both liked. When they ran into each other there, they'd laugh and say, 'Funny seeing you here,' and then they'd discuss whether it was better to get walnuts or pecans on your salad, or to leave them off altogether since nuts were so packed with calories.

'I don't need a whole week,' Claire said, but Amy held up her hand.

'Take it. This is your life and this is important. There's a lot for you to figure out. It wouldn't hurt to rest and be kind to yourself for a few days.'

Claire was forever grateful for this. She hoped that one day she could show the same kindness to someone who worked for her. But she was also deeply embarrassed and when she finally did return to work, she couldn't look Amy in the eye. It was like she'd taken all her clothes off in front of this woman and then expected it not to be awkward. It was awful, really.

Claire had spent the whole week in her apartment. She didn't leave once. She called her mom to let her know about the engagement and refused the suggestions to come home to Philly, and screamed, 'No!' at the idea of her mom coming to New York.

'I'm fine,' she said. 'Really. I just need to sort things out.'

'Oh, Claire,' her mom had said. And Claire had to get off the phone before she started crying, because those two words coming out of her mom's mouth were the worst. She'd heard them so many times before – when she got a D in calculus, when she crashed the car in the high school parking lot, when she got arrested at the shore for underage drinking.

Claire e-mailed her friends, but didn't take any phone calls. She made it seem like she wasn't in New York. *I'm sorting things out,* she typed. *I'm doing fine.*

That whole week, Claire took baths at night. She soaked in the tub, filling it with water as hot as she could stand. When the water started to cool, she would let some of it drain out and then turn on the faucet to let new, steaming water pour in.

She emerged from these baths pink-faced and dizzy. She would wrap a towel around her head and another around her body and stare at herself in the mirror. She looked like a newborn hamster before it got its fur – a doughy pink blob of see-through skin, unrecognizable and delicate.

Claire hoped for some revelation during these baths. She thought that soaking in the soapy water would clear her head. But it didn't. Mostly she just tried to figure out where she'd gone wrong. Sometimes she wondered what would happen if Doug were still there. Almost always she replayed the moment in her head when the actual breakup happened, when Doug said he was going to move out, and Claire said, 'What am I going to do now?' She hadn't meant to say it, didn't even realize it was coming out of her mouth until she heard it, and immediately she was ashamed. She didn't want to be that person, didn't want to hear her teary, pathetic voice in her head, admitting that she was lost, saying, 'What am I supposed to do now?' like she couldn't figure anything out for herself. And so she soaked in the water and hoped that somehow the words would steam out of her.

During the days, she watched talk shows. On Tuesday, the guest was a kidnapping specialist, who talked the audience through gory details of women being dismembered and raped. Claire forced herself to watch as a reminder that things could be much worse. More than once, the man looked at the audience with serious eyes as he repeated his most important advice: 'Never let them take you to a second location,' he said. He pointed at a different person with each word.

Apparently, the odds of being killed went up enormously when you let an abductor take you somewhere else. Claire let this thought run itself over in her head. She ordered takeout every night, and figured she was safest in her apartment.

Claire returned to work without one thing figured out. She had considered moving, but the thought of finding a new place that she could afford seemed impossible. And so she stayed put and dipped into her savings to pay rent after Doug stopped sending her checks. She told herself that it was actually less expensive this way, because to move she'd need money for a deposit and a broker fee and a moving company. It was the right thing to do, she thought, to stay where she was for the moment. *Never let them take you to a second location,* she'd remind herself.

Of course, six months later, all of Claire's savings were gone and she'd started charging anything she could on her credit cards – groceries, subway cards, taxi rides, the electric bill. It was easy to live in New York on credit.

At least ten times a day, she signed on to her bank accounts to look at the numbers, trying to make sense of them, trying to make them add up differently. She studied the numbers, like if she looked at them long enough, more money would appear in her bank account. But that never happened. After staring at it for about an hour, she'd begin to get a panicky feeling, and she'd have to sign out quickly, clicking the button at the top, like closing the screen was going to make the problem go away.

Sometimes at night, Claire dreamt about that crazy blond lady on TV, the one who tried to fix the financially irresponsible, adding up their bills, telling them, firmly, that they needed to change their habits. In her dreams, Claire saw this woman walking up to her in a no-nonsense suit, accentuating every word as she said, *You cannot live like this. You have got to take responsibility. You have got to live within your means or you are going to end up – Broke. Without. A. Penny. To. Your. Name. Or. A. Place. To. Live.*

In the dreams, Claire would try to run away from her. When she woke up, she'd always think, *Even my dreams have money problems.* Then she'd try to tell herself it wasn't that bad.

This past month, she'd realized that she was totally screwed, that she probably wouldn't even be able to pay her full rent next month. She wondered about this in a sort of abstract way, as if the apartment were so absolutely hers that the landlord wouldn't be able to kick her out. But she knew that wasn't the truth. She knew her borrowed time was almost up.

Every once in a while, Claire went to craigslist to look at apartment listings. She scrolled through them, clicking on the pictures of the tiny studios, usually in Brooklyn, or else so far up and so far east on the island, she wasn't even sure it could be considered Manhattan anymore. She looked at the pictures of the empty rooms, clicking through the bathroom photo that showed a bare toilet, naked and exposed in the empty white space. She'd click, click, click along, each one uglier than the one before, until she felt like she was going to throw up.

Even scarier were the apartment shares. She'd gone as far as e-mailing with one guy who was renting out a bedroom in a three-bedroom walk-up at York and Seventy-sixth. Claire set up a time to meet with him, got to the building, and then kept walking. She just couldn't face it. She knew what she'd find: a tiny place with thin walls, where she'd be able to hear everything her roommates did and said, would have to run into them in the kitchen while eating cereal, and wait her turn for the shower in the morning.

No. Sharing a place with randoms was out of the question. She was too old for that. Maybe a few years ago, it wouldn't have seemed so bad. But she was twenty-nine and she didn't want to have to negotiate refrigerator space with strangers.

What she wanted was to stay where she was. It wasn't fair that she had to leave. She hadn't done anything wrong. She'd always had a job, had worked hard, had been responsible. Why was she the only one being punished? None of her other friends had to deal with this. Even the dumb girls she'd known in high school seemed to be capable of living as adults. How had they all ended up fine and she'd ended up like this?

Claire loved the apartment that she and Doug had shared. It was a teeny bit run-down, but it was clean and in a beautiful old building. It wasn't big, but it was certainly the biggest place she'd ever lived in New York — a proper one-bedroom, with a kitchen that opened up into the living room with a counter and stools. What more could you want? Sure, she couldn't afford it, but maybe something would happen, maybe her circumstances would change.

Claire's phone had been ringing all weekend, which was really annoying. It was one thing to have to talk to people at work, but on Saturday and Sunday, she wanted peace. The first call was from her sister, Martha, reporting that a meth lab had been busted on the Upper West Side. Martha assumed that the meth lab was right next to Claire's apartment, possibly in the very same building. Martha left messages like this a few times a week. It was almost as if she searched for bad news to share, almost as if she liked it.

Her mom had called twice more, asking about the shore. Claire didn't even have to listen to the messages to know what they were about. Weezy wasn't going to stop until she got the answer that she wanted.

Her friend Lainie had also called three times, but hadn't left any messages. Lainie never left messages; she got too impatient waiting for the beep to come. Claire wasn't that concerned, because if it was a real emergency, Lainie would text her. But when her number came up a fourth time, Claire answered.

'You sound miserable,' Lainie said. She didn't even say hello. She was never one to sugarcoat things. Once in high school, when Claire was obsessing over a giant pimple on her forehead, searching for some sort of reassurance that it wasn't as bad as she thought, Lainie had said, 'Yeah, it's huge, but what are you going to do? Stay in your house until it's gone? Everyone knows you don't normally look like that.'

'Well, hello to you too,' Claire said now.

'Hi,' Lainie said. She spoke quickly. 'So what's going on? You sound awful.'

'I'm fine.'

'You're not fine. You sound like someone died. Katherine thinks you're depressed.'

'Katherine thinks everyone's depressed.'

'Fair enough.' Lainie knew this was true. Katherine loved therapy, thought everyone should be in it, and had encouraged Lainie to see someone after she gave birth to each of her children, just in case she developed postpartum depression.

'I'm fine,' Claire said again. She felt awkward on the phone with Lainie, like they were dancing on the offbeat of a song. They hadn't talked much since Doug moved out. Lainie had her third baby the month after, and was available only for quick calls, in which she often mentioned that her life was full of poop and that she sometimes forgot to brush her teeth. Claire was used to this, the way Lainie disappeared for a little while when each of her boys was born. She wasn't surprised by it anymore, or even hurt. It was just the way things happened, and Lainie always resurfaced after a few months. Just because this last baby had come at an inconvenient time for Claire, a time when she could have used her best friend, there wasn't anything she could do about it, except wait.

'Are you sure?' Lainie was saying.

'Yeah, I'm just . . . You know, trying to adjust, I guess.'

'It's been six months.' Lainie didn't say this unkindly, but it still made Claire's throat tighten up.

'I know. It's just weird, okay? It just sucks.' Claire heard a baby crying, and Lainie sighed. Claire could tell that Lainie was picking Matthew up and bouncing him around, trying to get him to quiet down.

'I know, I know,' Lainie said. But she didn't.

'I just have to figure a bunch of stuff out. I just never feel like doing anything. I have to move, I have to do tons of things, and I just feel like I can't.'

Lainie was silent for a moment. 'Maybe I'll come up to see you this weekend.'

'Really?'

'Yeah, really. That's what we'll do. I could come tomorrow and stay the night. It's a three-day weekend and Brian can watch the boys. We'll figure it all out. We'll find an apartment, get you signed up for online dating.'

'Funny,' Claire said. But then she did let out a little laugh.

'I'm serious. We'll get it all figured out.' Claire knew that Lainie was only half kidding. Lainie liked to solve problems and she probably thought she could come up for one weekend and easily sort out Claire's mess. Which was just a little obnoxious, but Claire didn't mind.

*

'It's amazing, really,' Lainie said, 'that this place hasn't driven you crazy yet.' She dropped her bag on the floor and looked around at the apartment. Claire had to admit it didn't look good. When Doug had packed up all of his stuff, it became clear that almost everything in the apartment was his. They'd both known this, of course, but somehow it was still a surprise to see him take it all with him.

He'd taken all of the framed pictures from the walls, the big TV, the dresser, the desk, the big couch, and most of the stuff in the kitchen. He'd left her the bed to be nice, and so Claire had insisted he take the duvet and pillows, which he had (except for one pillow), and now the bed looked like it belonged in an insane asylum, stripped down except for white sheets and an old knitted afghan that Claire had stolen from home years ago.

The only things left in the main room of the apartment were an old love-seat, a side table, a small TV, and a lawn chair that she'd found in the closet after Doug left. There were a few things in the kitchen, enough to get by, anyway – a couple of plates, a bowl, some silverware, a pot, and a skillet. She knew Doug had felt bad for leaving her with so few things, and he kept offering to leave more, but she insisted he take his stuff. 'It's yours,' she kept saying. 'You should take it, it's all yours.'

Doug probably assumed that Claire had waited a few days and then gone out to replace what was missing, that she'd moved things around, hung new pictures, or at least covered the holes that were left. But she hadn't done a thing. And now the whole place was practically empty, like she was in the middle of moving in or out, like the whole situation was just temporary.

That night, she and Lainie decided to just stay in and order food and when the deliveryman came, Claire realized that she wouldn't be able to charge it to her card. She hadn't paid the bill and there wasn't enough credit left.

'Oh shit,' she said. 'I forgot, there was some security thing with my bank and they canceled all my cards. I was supposed to get new ones, but they haven't come yet.'

'That's okay,' Lainie said. 'I got it.'

'Thanks,' Claire said. Her heart was pounding with the lie, but Lainie didn't seem to notice anything.

After they ate and drank wine and went to bed, Claire lay on her back for a long time and stared at the ceiling. Her room never got all that dark, since the light of the city came in through the blinds and she'd never taken the time to get curtains or a shade to block it out. This never bothered Claire, because when she woke up, she could always see everything in the room and never had to turn on a light to go to the bathroom, never tripped over a pair of shoes or walked into a wall.

'I have no money left,' she said. She wasn't sure if Lainie was awake or asleep, and she figured that was her gamble, that she could just say it out loud and if Lainie heard, then she'd have to deal with it.

But then she saw the pillow move, and then Lainie was squinting at her. 'What?'

Claire considered lying for a minute, or telling her that she was just exaggerating. But then it seemed too hard, and Lainie always knew when she was lying anyway. 'I have no money left,' Claire said again. 'I'm broke. And I don't mean, I'm broke, like I normally mean it. I mean that I've spent all of my savings and have been living on my credit cards for months and now there's no more room left on them, and I don't think I can pay rent this month. Not after I pay the minimum on the cards, and I seriously don't know what I'm going to do.'

'Oh shit.' Lainie was sitting up now.

'Yeah.'

'Can you borrow some money from your parents?'

'Yeah, I guess. I mean, I'm going to have to. But I don't know what good that'll do. Even if I get through this month, I'm going to have the same problem again next month.'

'Well, you need to move.' Lainie sounded firm, like moving would solve everything.

'I know, I know. I know I need to. I just put it off for so long because I didn't want to live somewhere shitty, and it costs so much to move – to pay the movers and put down the deposit and all of that. At this point, I'd have to borrow ten thousand dollars from my parents to move and that probably wouldn't even be enough. And I'd end up in some dungeon in Brooklyn.'

Claire felt her nose start to run and knew she'd be crying soon. Lainie patted her knee, got up, turned on the bedroom light, and went into the kitchen. She came back with Kleenex and two beers. She handed one to Claire and sat cross-legged in front of her.

'I'm so screwed,' Claire said.

Lainie nodded. 'We'll figure it out,' she said. 'It seems impossible, I know, but it's not. We'll figure it out.'

There were times in college when the size of a paper she had to write would overwhelm Claire. She'd sit there in front of the computer and try to get herself to start typing, but all she could think about was how much she had to do, the enormousness of the project. It would paralyze her. People sometimes said that fear was a motivator, but she never found that. Instead, she'd sit, all night, staring at the screen and not typing a word.

And it was happening again. The amount of her debt was too big, the size of her fuckup was too large. To act on it would be to acknowledge it, to start trying to fix it, and it just didn't seem like there was any way to do that. And so she sat, paralyzed, and waited.

The next day, Lainie left and Claire sat on her couch. She was exhausted. She and Lainie had stayed up almost the whole night talking, and right around five in the morning, Lainie had said, 'Look, don't freak out, okay? But maybe you should think about moving home.'

'Lainie. I'm not moving home. That's ridiculous.'

'Okay, that's what I thought you'd say. But listen, people do it all the time to pay off debt. You don't even like your job, and it would be an excuse to leave it. You could live rent free, get a random job, pay off all your credit cards, and then move back when you're more settled. You could take your time looking for a job and find one that you really want.'

Claire was annoyed at how rational Lainie sounded. She wanted to offer up another plan, another idea for how she could get herself out of her situation, but she didn't have one. From her calculations, after next month, she was done.

'You could even temp,' Lainie continued. 'So it wouldn't even be like you were staying there. Temping is just that. Temping. Temporary. Beth used an agency that loved her, that's always e-mailing her for referrals. They'd die to get you. I think most of the people that go there are sort of weird or something, but whatever. It would be easy. It would be like a break, and you deserve a break after this year, you really do.'

When she'd left today, Lainie had said, 'Think about what we talked about. I think it's the best plan.'

Claire had hugged her and closed the door, thinking there was no way in hell that was going to happen. But now here she was, alone in her apartment, and she felt trapped again, but this time it wasn't because the Hamburger Helpers were outside – it was because she had no money. None. This was it. Lainie was right. She couldn't stay, and her only option was to move home.

Last night Lainie had said, 'Look at it this way – at least you have this option. At least going home is a possibility.' Claire knew she should feel grateful for that, even if she didn't right now. She'd tell her parents at the shore, she decided. How bad could it be? It couldn't be worse than telling them her engagement was called off, could it?

And so, knowing that she couldn't get out of it, knowing that she had no better alternative anyway, Claire pulled her bag out of the closet and began putting together her clothes for a week at the shore with her family.

The woman that Katherine saw jump in front of the subway was named Joanne Jansen. It was a cute name – catchy and poetic, sort of like Claire Coffey. There were a few people on the subway platform that day that insisted Joanne Jansen had just fallen, that the whole thing was a horrible accident. But Katherine told Claire that wasn't true. 'She jumped with her arms in front of her,' Katherine said. 'She jumped like a superhero, like she wanted to make sure she got to where she was going.' Claire thought of that now as she packed, how Joanne Jansen had put her arms straight in front of her, determined and sure of her decision. She wished she didn't know that detail. It made it worse somehow.

Chapter 2

To be a manager at J.Crew, you had to be organized. That was what Martha always told people. She had, after all, risen to the position of manager faster than any other person at this particular branch. (Well, she was pretty sure of that. Someone had told her that once, and it seemed true.)

'You have to be willing to fold clothes all day if that's what needs to be done,' she always said. 'People don't want to scrounge around through a messy pile of pants to find the right size.'

Martha was being a little modest when she told people this. You did have to be organized, that was true. But you also had to have the right work ethic, and Martha knew she had it. Some of these people treated this job like it was nothing, like the store was lucky to have them. Well, Martha was a registered nurse who had graduated at the top of her class, and she still worked harder than everyone else. She wasn't too good to take the extra time to help a pear-shaped girl find the right kind of pants. If her job was to steer that pear of a girl away from skinny cords and point her in the direction of some wide-leg chinos, then that was what she was going to do.

The store was just a ten-minute drive from her parents' house, which was why Martha decided to apply there in the first place. She'd never worked in retail before, but she figured it couldn't be that hard, and so she dropped off applications at Banana Republic, Ann Taylor, and Anthropologie. She was turned down almost everywhere.

'But I went to college,' Martha would say, when the managers asked her about previous retail jobs.

Then they would shake their heads no and apologize. 'I'm sorry,' they'd say. 'We really need someone that has prior experience.'

It was a godsend, really, that the manager at J.Crew was someone that Martha had gone to high school with. They weren't exactly friends, but Margaret Crawford had sat next to Martha for years in school, and they'd had a sort of friendly alliance, since alphabetically they were always stuck together.

Margaret, it turned out, was pregnant. She told Martha that she was going to be cutting back on her hours and between that and all the college kids leaving to go back to school, they really needed help.

'You're pregnant?' Martha asked. She tried not to sound shocked, but she was. Margaret looked just a little tubby all around, but not pregnant. Martha noticed a tiny diamond ring on her left hand.

'Yep,' Margaret said. She smiled and rubbed her bloated tummy. 'Thirteen weeks. Can't you tell?'

'Oh, yeah,' Martha said. 'Now that you mention it, I can.'

'So why do you want to work here anyway?' Margaret said as she read Martha's résumé. 'I thought you were nursing. Career change?'

'No, not really. I was just in a job that wasn't a good fit and I thought I'd take a break from it for a while. From nursing, I mean. You know.' Martha prayed that Margaret wouldn't ask her what she'd been doing in the past year since she stopped nursing.

Margaret wasn't a very pretty girl. She was average height and a little hefty, with unremarkable brown hair and a splotchy complexion. She was the sort of person who was just average at everything. She'd been in all mid-level classes in high school, had played volleyball for one year on the B team, and had some friends, but not many.

But she was nice, Martha thought. A little dim, but not completely unaware. Martha wondered for a second why they never became better friends. They could have banded together in high school, enjoyed each other's company. It could have been a little less lonely.

Martha was mulling this over, thinking that maybe now

was the time when she and Margaret would connect and they would become great friends, the kind of friend that Martha had never really had before. Maybe Martha would be this baby's godmother, and they would laugh about it in years to come, about how they sat next to each other for so many years in school, but never really became friends until that one day when Martha just randomly walked into J.Crew.

'So where are you living these days?' Margaret asked.

'At home, for now.'

'You're living with your parents?' Margaret asked. 'Oh, no. That's awful.'

And just like that, Martha remembered Margaret. She remembered the first day of sophomore year, when Margaret told her that bangs were not in style anymore and that Martha should think about growing hers out. Not meanly, really. Just with a sort of honesty that comes with being clueless.

Martha looked at Margaret's chubby tummy and shrugged. She would not be the godmother of this baby. And she would get over it just fine.

That was almost six years ago, and Margaret had long since stopped working at the store. Sometimes she came in with her daughter, Addie, who always had a runny nose and the same blotchy complexion as her mother.

'Isn't she beautiful?' Margaret always asked Martha. Martha would just smile in response. She didn't believe in lying to make people feel good. The child wasn't the least bit attractive, and she didn't think it was right to say so. Besides which, what kind of person stated that their child was beautiful and then asked for confirmation?

Margaret's husband looked like Eddie Munster, with bushy eyebrows and pointy teeth. It was no wonder that their child turned out like she did. Martha could tell that Margaret believed her husband to be very handsome. Sometimes he'd accompany her when she came to visit the store, and Margaret would hold his hand with a tight smile on her face, like she thought Martha was jealous of them. Martha would look at this unattractive family, and Margaret's stupid smile, and feel nothing but sorry for the whole group of them, most of all for that eyesore, Addie.

Martha had seen people come and go from J.Crew. She trained the college kids in the summers and welcomed the good ones back over holiday vacations. She was a tough manager, that was for sure, but she was fair. And what more could you ask for?

Folding clothes in the store gave Martha a certain sense of accomplishment that was hard to explain to other people. She wasn't OCD or anything, but she loved the way it felt to stack the clothes on top of each other, all of them the same, crisp and ready for the customers. It was her favorite part of the job.

She especially liked folding the clothes in the morning or at the end of the day when the store was closed, as she did now. It was nice to be surrounded by quiet, to know that at least for a little while, the neat stack of shirts that you made would stay just that way, and no customer would go grabbing in the middle of the pile, looking for his size and knocking the whole thing to the side.

Martha folded a stack of navy pants, pulling the crotch of each pair tightly, so that it was taut, and then folding the legs just right to get a perfect crease. She put the sizes in order, big ones on the bottom and the small ones on the top, like the big guys were holding up the little ones. *2, 4, 6, 8, 10, 12,* she said silently to herself, making sure that each size was represented.

Martha took a size 12 out of the pile of pants and put them back behind the register. She'd try them on later. She was a little surprised at how tight her size 10 pants were lately. She'd ignored it for a few weeks, but that morning she wasn't able to button her favorite pair of khakis, and so she decided it was time for new ones.

It was a little hard to admit that she might have gone up a size. Again. She'd been a size 10 for so long now. Before she went on the medicine, she was a very respectable size 8, and once, a long time ago in high school, she was a size 6. She'd never been as thin as Claire, but she'd never been big. Even in college, when her diet of pasta and pretzels had bulked her up, she still wasn't fat. And then she'd learned to deal with being a 10, a little fleshier than she was meant to be, but nothing horrendous. But now there was this. She was a size 12 and it felt like she was sliding toward obesity.

Lately when Martha got undressed at night, she noticed that the waistband of her pants left a circle of angry pink teeth marks around her stomach. She was starting to feel like a sausage stuffed into a too-small skin.

Martha closed down the registers and began gathering the

receipts to bundle them. She couldn't wait for this day to be over. One of their best employees, Candace, had quit unexpectedly. 'I hate it here,' she'd said to Martha. 'You're like a Nazi.'

It was completely inappropriate to invoke the Nazis to describe anyone, and Martha told Candace just that. She asked Candace if she even knew the horror that the Nazis had caused. 'Because if you did,' she said, 'you might think twice about calling me a Nazi and disrespecting all of the people that were murdered by them.'

Candace made a strange sort of strangled sound, and threw up her hands. 'You're a freak!' she said. And she gathered her things and walked out. Martha tried not to let it show that Candace had embarrassed her, but she knew that her face was red. The other employee working that day, skinny little Trevor, gave Martha a small smile and she knew that he was pitying her.

'Good riddance,' Martha had said to him. Then she went back to the employee bathroom and put a wet paper towel on her cheeks until they cooled down.

Martha was stacking the register drawers to take them to the back when a teenage girl came to the door and, finding it locked, banged on the glass with her palm. Martha smiled and shrugged, then pointed to her watch to indicate that the store was closed. The girl outside gave her the finger and walked away.

Martha didn't deserve that. People felt like they could treat her however they wanted, just because she worked in the store. Customers were sometimes rude beyond belief, acting like she was their servant as they sent her to fetch them striped shirts and printed skirts. Martha muttered to herself as she finished up her closing duties. Maybe she would just leave J.Crew altogether. She was, after all, a registered nurse. Well, she wasn't exactly registered anymore, since she hadn't worked in so long, but she could be if she wanted to.

Martha had known that she wanted to be a nurse from the time she broke her wrist when she was twelve. It was the nurses who comforted her, with their matter-of-fact answers and soothing voices. She loved the uniforms they wore, how they all had matching scrubs, like they were part of some club. They looked so important, filling out charts and taking temperatures, and she knew that was what she wanted to be. Plus, she'd always had a mind for medicine, had always done the best in her science classes.

Nursing was not a major to be taken lightly. It wasn't like the other majors at her liberal arts college – English or sociology or philosophy. Nursing was different. There were high expectations for the nursing students. You had to keep your GPA up, or you were out of the program. You did clinical work in addition to your classes. People's lives depended on you, so you had to know your stuff. That was how Martha thought about it anyway.

The other girls in the program were different from Martha. They were sillier, flightier, than she was. But they all spent so much time together, studying for tests and carpooling to their clinicals, that Martha developed a fondness for them and even began to enjoy their company.

They used to drag her out with them sometimes, to bars or to a party to stand in a random kitchen in some off-campus apartment and drink out of red plastic cups. 'Come on, Martha!' they used to say. 'Blow off some steam.' They used to call her Serious Martha, like that was her full name. They used to think it was their duty to try to get her to have some fun.

Martha would let them pick out her clothes for going out, even sip some rum and Cokes with them while they were getting ready. They'd do her makeup and ignore her pleas not to put on too much. 'Mar-tha,' they'd say, and roll their eyes. It was the same way Claire used to say her name when they were younger, when she would get so exasperated by Martha's very being, saying her name like it hurt to get it out, dragging out each syllable — 'Mar-tha.'

She'd go to these parties and stand there for a while. She had a feeling that she was supposed to be enjoying them. At the beginning of the night, the girls would stand next to her and include her in the conversations. But as the night went on, each of them would wander away, distracted by some boy. They were all desperate for boys. The one male nurse in their year had seven piercings on his face, including a big plug in his ear. He was nice, but no one they would be interested in. They used to call him Leo the Male Nurse, right to his face.

Even if Martha found her way into a conversation at these parties, she never really had fun. There were some pleasant moments, but those were short-lived, and all that was left was a group of horny college kids waiting to get drunk enough that they could start making out with each other. It was like one big mono pool. She would wait until all the other girls were occupied, then she'd find one of them and tell her that she was leaving. She tried to find someone who was really immersed in a conversation with a boy, so that there would be no protests, so that no one would try to convince her to stay.

On the street, Martha would breathe with relief. She always walked home, even if it was the middle of winter. She didn't mind. She liked the way the air rushed into her nose and froze her nostrils. It made her look forward to getting back to her single room and making hot chocolate in the microwave. She liked the feeling of thawing out in her cozy room, finding an old eighties movie to watch while snuggled under her covers, knowing that tomorrow she'd wake up fresh and ready to do her work, while the rest of the girls would be groggy and hungover.

Those were great mornings, when her nursing friends groaned with their heads in their hands. 'Why did we do this?' they'd say. Martha would *tsk* at them, not meanly, just in a good-natured way. She'd smile sympathetically and indulge their requests for Gatorade and water. Martha was happy during those study sessions, pleased that she was learning more than the other girls, because her body wasn't wrecked from the night before. She always felt like she was a few steps ahead, so she was gracious enough to be nice to these girls, to agree to take a break so they could eat greasy food, shoveling french fries into their mouths as they said, 'Why didn't we leave when you did, Martha? Why did you let us stay?'

They didn't really mean it, Martha knew. Maybe at that moment they regretted their decision, but the thing that Martha always knew was that these girls wanted to go to parties and meet boys just as much as they wanted to be nurses. And that was the difference. Martha was in school *only* to be a nurse. For these girls, it was just part of the whole package. For Martha, it was everything.

It was only after she'd left college that Martha realized how much she'd loved it there – she loved the structure of it, the study schedule, and the forced socializing. She loved her single room, where she could be alone but keep the door cracked open so she could hear people chattering in the halls, the excited way people greeted one another, their shrieks of laughter. Of course, at the time, if anyone had asked her, she would have said that she couldn't wait for graduation, that her dorm was noisy and filled with immature girls who made it nearly impossible to get any work done.

But when it was all gone, she mourned it. She would never be back there again. Ever. Her life was a big silent white space. There were no tests to study for, no groups to meet. When she wasn't working, she could do anything she wanted to, but she found that she didn't like the openness of her time. It was startling, all that free space, and she ended up watching a lot of TV.

Martha got a job at a large hospital in South Philadelphia. She was hired as a floater, which meant that she rotated among departments, filling in wherever she was needed. One night she'd be in the pediatric ward and the next she'd be in the emergency room. She was always on the night shift, because she was new, and they told her she'd have to earn her way to the more desirable hours.

The hospital was large and understaffed. Martha would arrive at seven p.m. and be thrown into a pit of need. That was what it felt like. There was always so much to do, and so many people who needed things from her. The older nurses weren't particularly nice or friendly. She'd imagined that they would take her under their wing and show her the ropes. But that's not how it was. They were frustrated with her, impatient and bossy. And since she moved around all the time, she never really got to know any of them well.

Martha couldn't adjust to her new schedule. Getting to work in the evening gave her a bad feeling in the pit of her stomach, the kind that she used to get on Sunday nights in high school. She worked until seven thirty a.m. and then she'd take the train home, rumpled and exhausted, while everyone else was just starting their day. It made her feel anxious, to see them freshly showered and dressed, holding coffee and reading the paper, while she was on her way home to sleep. *I'm living life backward*, she used to think. And the thought of being a backward person made her heart pound loudly, strangely, so that sometimes it even felt like it was beating the wrong way, like it was going backward along with her

When she got home in the mornings, she couldn't sleep. She could never quite get used to climbing into bed as the sun was shining. She would lie awake for hours, wondering if she'd done everything she was supposed to. Had she given all of her patients their medications? Had she measured right? Had she filled out the charts? She was sure she was killing her patients, and that kept her awake, always. She was so tired that her whole body ached, but her mind was always moving, always thinking, and no matter how hard she tried, she just couldn't fall asleep.

With each day, it felt worse. Martha was antsy, but never wanted to leave her apartment when she didn't have to. She didn't want to wash her dishes or do her laundry. She ate in her bedroom and let plates pile up on her desk, let glasses full of iced tea sit on her nightstand until they started to mold and little black ants crawled in them. Her laundry lay in piles, and when you first opened the door to her bedroom, it smelled like the home of a dirty person — sour and stale. This wasn't the way Martha kept things. She'd always been clean, always been disgusted by people who sat around in their own filth. But it didn't seem to matter anymore, and leaving things to rot where they were was easier than trying to clean it all up.

Her roommate, a girl she knew from nursing school, told her that she couldn't live like this and that she was moving out when their lease was up. Martha started skipping work, napping during the days and watching TV at night. Her parents came over to see her, and her father stood in the doorway to her bedroom, looking all around, while her mother said, 'Oh, Martha,' and began to pick things up, gathering dirty laundry in her arms, as if the mess were the problem.

Martha quit her job and moved home. Her parents packed up the apartment for her, boxing up all of her books and clothes. 'It's just my job,' she told them. 'It was too much. I'm burned out. I just need to rest.'

But she was still so tired all the time. She slept almost all day, glad to be in a bed with clean sheets, back at home. Her parents would come upstairs to see her, insist that she get out of bed for meals. Her mom would take her on errands. 'You can sit in the car if you want,' she'd say. 'But you have to get out of the house.' And so Martha would put on clothes, and sit in the passenger seat of the car while her mother went to the dry cleaners and the bank.

Sometimes her dad would come upstairs and sit next to her bed, to talk or just read. 'It will get better,' he'd say to her. And for some reason, this made her cry, tears running down her face to her pillow.

Finally, her parents made her go see someone. 'You need someone to talk to,' they told her. 'It will make you feel better.' She could hear them whispering about her when she walked out of a room. But she didn't care. She knew they were worried about her. If she'd had more energy, she would have been worried about herself.

She'd gone to see a therapist and a psychiatrist. The psychiatrist she didn't much care for. He didn't seem interested in her, and she'd sat there and answered his questions, and at the end of the session he'd written her prescriptions. Just like that. When she started to take the medicine, she felt loopy and in her own world, and she wanted to tell everyone that this wasn't going to work.

Dr. Baer was her therapist, and at first Martha thought she wasn't going to be of any help either. But she kept going, and little by little, Dr. Baer began to grow on her. It was strange, like she didn't even notice anything was changing, but slowly she seemed to feel the tiniest bit better, then a bit more. The medicine seemed to balance out, or at least she didn't feel so out of it anymore. Things weren't perfect, but she slept less and got dressed more often. And one day she realized that her father had been right. Things had gotten better somehow.

A few months after that, she'd felt good enough to apply to J.Crew, and she'd gotten the job and worked hard and done well. It had really all been going well – until today. Today, Martha couldn't stand all the people yelling at her about sizes and sales. She couldn't stand the Candaces of the world thinking they could act however they wanted to, like they were special somehow. Today, for the first time in years, Martha almost wished she was a nurse again.

Martha left Dr. Baer's office, but stood right outside the door and leaned against the brick wall. She needed a minute. Even though it was August, she was chilled and she pulled a cardigan out of her bag and put it on. The air-conditioning in Dr. Baer's office was insane. Dr. Baer was always warm (hot flashes, Martha assumed), and now, because Martha had been forced to sit in the freezing room, she probably had a cold.

Early on, when Martha first started seeing Dr. Baer, she used to go home after each session and write down what her therapist had said, so that she could remember everything. Martha wanted to remember all the advice that Dr. Baer gave. She was always so calm, so practical. Martha used to carry that notebook around with her, so she could read Dr. Baer's words whenever she wanted. It made her feel in control.

Now, after so many years of therapy, she was able to hear Dr. Baer's voice in her head wherever she went. When she was at the store, about to buy ice cream, she heard her say, 'Sometimes we comfort ourselves in physical ways instead of emotional ways.' When Martha turned down an invitation to anything, she heard Dr. Baer say, 'It's scary to put yourself out there. But sometimes you need to be uncomfortable to live in the world.'

But this visit was different. Martha got the feeling that Dr. Baer was less interested in her problems. She seemed to sigh a lot, to tap her pen before she addressed Martha. And at the end she said, 'You know, Martha, it feels to me that you've had time to recover and now you may just be hiding. Maybe it's time to push yourself. Find a job that challenges you more. Maybe go back to nursing. Move out, take a trip, do something that will get you going.'

This seemed to be inappropriate shrink talk. All Martha had been saying this session was that she was having some problems with her family. She was complaining about how it seemed to be her curse that whenever she tried to help people (like her sister) they acted like she was butting in. Dr. Baer had sighed and said something about small problems seeming large under a microscope. What was that supposed to mean?

At first, Martha hadn't wanted to see a shrink, but her parents hadn't really given her a choice. For the first few visits, all Martha did was cry. Dr. Baer just sat with her, handing her tissues and waiting. Dr. Baer was a petite woman with short brown hair and thick-framed glasses. She was compact, and looked like she worked out for many hours a day. She handed Martha tissues with purpose, pulling them straight up and out of the box, in one quick motion.

Martha took them, always taking notice of how muscular Dr. Baer's arms were. She didn't even know why she was crying, exactly. She just knew that she didn't want to be there.

As the sessions went on, Martha began to appreciate Dr. Baer's firm voice. She looked forward to the weekly appointment, picking out her outfit to go to the office downtown, walking down Walnut Street, looking in the windows of the clothing shops. Martha always felt important when she walked down the street to the office, like she had somewhere special to be. Dr. Baer's office was on the second floor of a building that was squished in between a Rite Aid and a Lacoste store. Sometimes when she entered the door from the street, she felt like she was entering a secret passageway. There were no markings on the door, just a small mailbox card that said md baer. If you didn't know what you were looking for, you'd walk right by.

Martha wasn't embarrassed about seeing a shrink (although Dr. Baer hated that word. 'I'm a therapist, Martha,' she would say whenever Martha called her that). She was very honest about her appointments with everyone at J.Crew. 'I can't work Tuesday afternoons,' she would say. 'That's my shrink appointment.'

When Dr. Baer took her vacation in July, Martha felt a hole in her life. The hour appointment was easily the best part of her week. Martha began to think of Dr. Baer more as a friend than as a doctor; a confidante she could talk to. That is, until today.

Outside the office, Martha watched as Duncan walked inside to see Dr. Baer. Duncan had had the appointment right after Martha's for almost two years now, and they often ran into each other in the waiting room or right outside on the street. They always gave each other knowing nods as they passed. Today, Martha wanted to grab Duncan's arm and warn him. *Watch out,* she would say. *Dr. Baer is in a mood.* They would look knowingly at each other, Duncan understanding just what Martha meant. But Duncan walked quickly past her before she could say anything.

Martha pulled a dusty Kleenex out of her pocket and blew her nose. Then she decided to walk to the coffee shop a couple of blocks away to get something to drink. She needed to sit and make sense of her last hour.

She hadn't even gotten a chance to tell Dr. Baer about the dream that she'd had last night, where she'd seen a giant orange ant and grabbed a shoe to kill it. When she smacked it with her shoe, the ant turned to look at her with big eyes. Then the back half of the ant kept moving and Martha had to chase it around and hit it again. She'd been excited to talk about the dream, since she never had dreams that vivid. It must have meant something – she was sure of it. She'd told her mom about it that morning, but her mom had just sort of stared at her in a fuzzy way over her coffee. Dr. Baer would have had to listen as she described the body of the ant, how strange it made her feel. But she hadn't gotten to talk about it. And now she would never know what the ant was supposed to be.

The coffee shop was more crowded than Martha expected. There were several people banging away on laptops with a sense of purpose, a couple of people reading the paper, and one pair of girls with their heads bent close together, whispering seriously. Martha found a small table in the middle back of the shop, and edged her way through the other customers to get there. A few of them looked up as she passed and she wondered if she looked distressed to them. She tried to catch the eye of one scraggly-looking guy who had his hands resting on his laptop and was staring off into space, but he looked back at the screen as soon as he saw her looking at him.

Martha sighed and flopped her bag onto the table. It made a satisfying thump, and a couple of people jumped. Then she sighed again and sat down, pushing her chair back so that it screeched on the floor. No one looked up. She wanted just one of these people to acknowledge her and give her a sad smile. *I just had a fight with my shrink,* she would say. Although that wasn't really true. Maybe she'd say, *My shrink just told me I'm worthless.* That would get their attention. But that wasn't true either. Martha sighed again and leaned back in her chair.

A waitress with hair that hung down her back all the way to her waist came to take Martha's order. She looked like someone who wanted to be a singer or a songwriter. She probably had a guitar at home. Maybe she even played at small clubs around the city, or at this very coffee shop.

'Do you know what you want?' the waitress asked. She had a harsh voice, kind of rough, really, and Martha hoped she hadn't pinned too much on the idea of becoming a singer.

'I'll have a mocha,' she said. 'But with skim milk.' She was trying to cut back on her calories this week.

The waitress nodded without writing anything down, then turned to head back to the counter. 'Wait,' Martha called. 'Can I also have a muffin? Or coffee cake? Whatever's back there.' She shrugged like she didn't really care what she got, like she was just realizing that she hadn't eaten breakfast and should order something. Of course, she *had* eaten breakfast. She'd had a bagel and then a big bowl of cereal, but that was hours ago. No sense in starving herself to lose weight. That's not how it was done.

'Is cranberry okay?' the waitress asked. Martha nodded. She'd really wanted chocolate chip, or cinnamon, but cranberry would do. Yes, cranberry would do just fine.

Martha rooted around in her bag, hoping that for some

reason she had the Dr. Baer notebook in there, even though she knew it was in her nightstand. She hadn't used it in so long. She did manage to find an old to-do list and a pen. She uncapped the pen and smoothed out the paper, which had been folded up into a tiny square. Now she was ready. Ready to write down all of the horrible things that Dr. Baer had said to her and to deconstruct them.

But when she wrote down, *You need to push yourself,* it didn't have the same effect. The problem was that when you wrote something down, you couldn't hear the tone of voice. And really, it was Dr. Baer's tone of voice that was the biggest problem.

At the top of the page, she wrote, *Tone of voice was disapproving and harsh.* There. That explained it better. Then she continued. *Go back to nursing,* she wrote. *Challenge yourself. Stop hiding.*

The waitress came to deliver the coffee and muffin, and Martha made a show of moving her paper over and giving the waitress a look like, *Do you believe this? Look what I'm dealing with.* But the waitress just set the oversized coffee cup and the plate down, and placed the bill on the table next to her.

'Anything else?' she asked, but she was already walking away before Martha could answer.

Martha read over her list. She really couldn't believe the nerve of Dr. Baer, suggesting that she go back to nursing. After that nightmare of a job pushed her over the edge? All of those patients that didn't have enough care? It was too much. Way too much. She had a job now, and it was a good job, even if Dr. Baer didn't see it that way. Sure, it had gotten a little boring, but

49

that was to be expected. And yes, Dr. Baer was right when she said that Martha was in a more stable place now. And maybe she was even right when she said it might be a time for Martha to challenge herself. Maybe.

'I hate my job,' Martha had said, as soon as she walked into Dr. Baer's office that day. 'Retail is killing me.' She threw her bag on the floor and waited for Dr. Baer to say something comforting, something about how hard it was to wait on people, but that it taught you patience and taught you how to treat others. But Dr. Baer had just sighed, leaned back, and said, 'Tell me why you hate it.'

And so Martha had. She'd talked about how rude the new workers were, how she couldn't stand the way the customers talked to her. 'I'm a college graduate,' she said. 'I could be a nurse if I wanted to.'

'So, why don't you?' Dr. Baer asked her.

'I'm . . . well, you know why.'

'I know why you stopped nursing six years ago. I don't know why you don't do it now.'

'I have a job,' Martha said. 'It's not easy. And some days I complain about it.'

'You don't just complain about it some days. It seems you complain about it most days. Almost every day, in fact, in recent months.'

'Because I hate it,' Martha told her. 'But I need a job. I don't have a choice.'

'It sounds to me like you do have a choice. You're making the choice to be there. So, if you're complaining about something, then make another choice.'

'It's not that easy.'

Dr. Baer kept pushing. She kept asking her questions about the job, asking her why she hated it, telling her that it sounded like she was avoiding things. It was really rude, when you got right down to it. That was the only way to describe it.

At the end of the session, Martha had cried a little bit. She was tired of defending her job and then trying at the same time to explain why it was so awful. Because she did hate it, she did. But she couldn't hate it completely, and she knew that too. J.Crew had saved her, and maybe that was pathetic but it was true. When it had felt like she was never going to be able to be productive again, when the world seemed really awful, she was able to go there and fold clothes.

It hadn't always been easy, but she'd been able to get up and go, at first just for a few hours at a time, and when she got home, she'd go right back to bed. But at least she felt like she'd done something. And as time went on, it got easier, and then she didn't have to convince herself to get up and go to the store. She just did it, and now it was almost effortless. But always, in the back of her mind, was the thought that she might slip back to that place, to that time when getting out of bed seemed almost impossible.

Was she fixed now? Was that what Dr. Baer was trying to tell her? It couldn't be. No one in her life would ever consider her 'cured.' At least once a day someone told her to lighten up.

Every time she talked to her sister, Claire said, 'Calm down. Stop worrying.'

But she couldn't. That was the thing. Martha would have loved to stop worrying, but she didn't know how. Maybe Claire thought it was crazy, the way Martha always thought there was a murderer around every corner, or that she had stomach cancer, or that she was going to die in a car crash. But the thing was, those things happened. They happened every day to lots of people. And so she couldn't understand how other people just walked through life, unconcerned, not even considering the possibility that tragedy could strike at any moment.

How did these people just assume that they were going to live a full and safe life, when all evidence pointed the other way? When there were so many ways for people to die, so many different ways that people could get hurt – just walking down the street, or even sitting at their desks at work – wasn't it a miracle that anyone made it through the day at all?

As the session was ending, Martha had stood up and looked straight at Dr. Baer, to make one more attempt to try to get her to understand. And now, the last thing she'd said was playing over and over again in her head: 'I can't fold another pair of pants with whales on them,' she'd said. 'I'll die if I do.'

Chapter 3

In the Coffey house, there was always a list taped to the refrigerator. At the top, it was titled: THINGS WE NEED. When the list got too full, or most of the items had been crossed off, someone would tear it down and start a new list with the same heading. The title was always capped and underlined, as if to stress that yes, this is important, these aren't just things we want, these are things we need.

Weezy couldn't even remember when the list had started. She supposed it was when she and Will first moved into the house, over thirty years ago. They were so young then, barely out of college, and at that time they needed everything. But times were different, and they didn't ask their parents for help or just charge everything, like kids would today. Neither of them even had a credit card yet, and they had a whole house to fill. So they made a list to prioritize what they were going to buy first. Weezy remembered their deciding to buy a bed and a couch, but waiting almost two years to buy a dining-room table. Most of the house sat empty for those first few years, but the list always made them feel like it was only temporary.

It was on that list that Weezy told Will she was first pregnant. She'd gotten home from the doctor, so excited, and she'd added *A Crib* to the list. *So clever,* she thought. She stood back and looked at it and laughed and even jumped up and down a little bit. She was giddy the whole day, waiting for Will to come home and find out that they were going to start their family. It was almost perfect, the way she asked him to check the list to see if she'd added milk, and how he scanned it quickly, taking a moment to let it sink in, to believe what he'd read. He turned around to face her with a look of disbelief on his face. Neither of them could believe it, really, that they were capable of something so amazing, so fantastic. They were so proud of themselves, as if no one before them had ever accomplished such a thing.

Of course, when Martha was two months old, and Weezy found out that she was pregnant again, there was no such moment. Instead, she'd sat on the kitchen floor and cried up a storm. She never told Claire this story. They were delighted when the baby came, of course, but on that day, newly pregnant with a fussy infant, she had cried. Holy moly, had she cried.

Once the list had been up there for so long, it just seemed necessary. Each family member wrote down whatever it was they needed, and it was all in one place. Today, the list contained the following items: *Grape-Nuts, lightbulbs, car inspection (Volvo), AA batteries.*

When Max was home, the list was filled with food: *Cheetos, Oreos, turkey, Honey Nut Cheerios.* Max still ate like a teenager, ravenous, shoveling food in his mouth like he hadn't eaten in days. He was twenty-one now, going to be a senior in college, but he seemed younger to Weezy. His limbs still looked too long for his body, his smile a little sheepish, like he knew that he had grown up to be handsome, but he had no idea how or when it had happened.

Once, when Claire was in high school and in a particularly foul adolescent mood, she added *A Life* to the list. It was after they'd forbidden her to go on a weekend trip with a group of friends to someone's unsupervised shore house. Claire had screamed in the way that only a fifteen-year-old girl can. She'd narrowed her eyes and accused them of abuse, and denying her the right to any fun at all. 'Just because you have no lives,' she'd said, 'and just because you are socially void, doesn't mean that I have to be.'

Will had found the list in the morning while making coffee, and he'd brought it upstairs to Weezy, who was still in bed, and the two of them had laughed and laughed. 'What a little shit,' Weezy had said, and Will snorted. They saved the list, thinking that someday they'd show it to Claire, maybe when she had a teenager of her own. 'To show her what a horror she was,' Will said.

Martha had once added *Peace* to the list, during the first Iraq War, and Weezy was touched that she had such a sensitive daughter. (She was also a little concerned about Martha's obsession with war, natural disasters, and just horrible news in general, but she tried to focus on the sensitive part.) Claire had ripped down that list, saying that she didn't want any of her friends to see it, because it was 'beyond embarrassing.'

'Why do we even have this list?' Claire had asked that day. 'Things we *need*? It makes us seem so desperate. God, we aren't poor.'

Weezy loved lists. They made her feel powerful. Today she sat down with her coffee to make a list for the day. *Shore*, she put at the top. Then underneath that she wrote, *grocery store*. She put her pen down and took a sip of coffee. She'd been trying to get commitments from all of her children to go to the shore house for a week in August. She and Will would stay on for another week after, but she wanted all of her children there together. Was that too much to ask?

They'd all been responding in a casual way, 'Sure, Mom, probably.' And now here it was, August 1, and she still didn't have a real answer from any of them. Not even Martha, who was living with them. It was like none of them knew that things took planning, like they all expected her to just wait for them to make up their minds, and then rush around to get ready for it.

Weezy called Claire for the third time that week. As soon as she said, 'Hello,' she could hear Claire sigh. 'Mom, I told you I'd try. I'm not sure if I can take the time from work.'

'It's less than a month away,' Weezy pointed out. She tried to stay calm. 'Have you even talked to them about it? Have you asked? I'm trying to finalize everything.'

'I'll ask today, Mom. I promise. But they might say no.'

'Well, see what you can do. Your sister would love to spend some time with you. And Max, too. He's bringing Cleo. And your Aunt Maureen will be there for sure, although it's looking like Ruth and Cathy can't make it. Neither can Drew, which is too bad.'

'Max is bringing Cleo?' Claire asked.

'Yes. He asked if he could, and I said it was okay, of course.'

Claire stayed quiet for a few moments and Weezy wondered what she was thinking. They'd all met Cleo last year, when Max had brought her for a visit. Right after they'd all been introduced, Weezy and Claire went to the kitchen to get drinks for everyone, and Weezy whispered, 'She's a bombshell.' It was the only word she could think of to describe Cleo.

'Mom.' Claire laughed. She'd started to say something, but then stopped and nodded. 'She really is, isn't she?' And the two of them had bent their heads together and giggled like girlfriends at the pretty little bombshell that Max had brought home.

Weezy had warned her sister before she came over for Thanksgiving. 'Just so you know, Max's girlfriend is quite a show-stopper.' Maureen had laughed and said something about Weezy's being a protective mother. 'No, it's not that,' Weezy said. 'She's just . . . she seems older. She seems, well, very sexual.'

Maureen had laughed again, but when she got to the house and met Cleo, she was visibly taken aback. She recovered, walked over to Cleo to introduce herself, and tripped just as she got near her. Maureen put her hands straight out, ended up pushing Cleo down on the couch to break her fall, and the two of them landed tangled together. They pulled themselves up and off of each other, and then sat side by side on the edge of the couch.

'I'm Max's clumsy aunt,' Maureen had said. Claire, Martha, Cathy, and Ruth had watched the whole thing with their mouths hanging open. Cleo brushed off her arms and insisted she was okay, that there was no problem. She'd even laughed.

Later in the kitchen, as Weezy poured Maureen a glass of wine, she said, 'I told you.'

'You weren't kidding,' Maureen said. 'Good lord.'

It wasn't that she didn't expect Max to bring home a lovely, pretty girl. She did. But Cleo was something else altogether. She seemed out of place in their house, like a runway model that had been dropped out of the sky and into their Thanksgiving. She was nearly as tall as Max, and she wore strange, funky outfits that looked amazing on her, like the fake fur vest that kept shedding, so that little tufts flew behind her when she walked, making Will sneeze.

Weezy was immediately worried that she was too much for Max. She wanted Max to date someone just a little less stunning, someone who didn't seem like she would break his heart so easily. And so, although Cleo seemed perfectly polite and nice, Weezy prayed every day that they would break up.

Claire had defended Cleo. 'Just because she's so pretty doesn't mean she's not a good person,' she'd said. Claire was always protective of Max, and she'd gone out of her way to be nice to Cleo.

But Weezy could hear something in Claire's voice now, like she didn't want Cleo to go to the shore for some reason. Maybe Claire finally sensed that Cleo wasn't the right match for Max? Weezy started to ask Claire about it, but Claire interrupted her.

'Okay, Mom. I'll ask at work and let you know, okay? I'll call you later.'

Weezy hung up and started to cross the item off her list, but then realized she couldn't because it wasn't taken care of yet. She did add *Empty dishwasher* to the list, and then crossed it off, because she'd already done that and it made her feel like she had accomplished something.

She sipped her coffee, which was starting to get cold, and tried to plan out her day. There was so much to do, and already she was exhausted. How was it that even as her children got older, it seemed harder to get things done? It was supposed to be the other way around, she was pretty sure of that. But it seemed like the more she tried to get things in order, the more she tried to corral them, the more they squeezed out of her grasp like a group of little greased pigs, determined to do the opposite of whatever she wanted.

*

Weezy Coffey had once been Louise Keller. No one called her Weezy until she met Will, when they were freshmen at Lehigh University and were seated next to each other in World Civ class. She'd introduced herself as Louise, but the next day Will called out to her from across the quad, 'Hey, Weezy!' It made her laugh, made her heart beat faster to hear him call her that. (Of course, if she'd known it was going to stick, she would have put a stop to it right away.)

They were in college, and everyone was new to everyone else, and this crazy nickname took the place of her real name. Half of her friends from college never even knew her as Louise. With time, even her parents and sisters adopted the name, and eventually she just stopped fighting it. She almost forgot that she'd ever been Louise in the first place.

Even her own children sometimes referred to her as Weezy when talking to each other or to their friends. And a couple of times in high school, when Claire was annoyed, she'd say, 'Chill, Weeze,' which made her sound like a frozen treat.

Weezy had graduated from Lehigh with a degree in education, even though she had never really wanted to be a teacher. Her mother had pushed her toward it, telling her that it was a doable profession for women. Weezy took a job in a sixth-grade classroom for one year, and then she'd gotten pregnant with Martha and then Claire, and she never went back.

She hadn't missed it. After her first week of teaching, she knew she wasn't going to like it, but she had committed to it, so she gave it a try. The kids she taught were right on the brink of adolescence, that time when they don't quite fit in their bodies, when they can turn nasty in a second and gang up on each other, on teachers, on anyone, really.

It didn't make sense for Weezy to work those first few years, not with two babies at home. When both of the girls were in school, she'd started looking into other jobs. 'But not teaching,' she told Will. She wasn't even sure that she wanted to go back to work, but she felt like she should. Not for money reasons – they'd actually been quite fortunate, inheriting enough from Will's father to buy the house, and it wasn't like they lived an extravagant life. No, it was more that Weezy had always talked about how women had the right to work, how they were equal, and now she felt that she should act on it.

She'd worked on and off for years – at the front desk of a medical office, as the office manager of a small law firm, and most recently at an accounting firm running the day-to-day operations of the office. She'd been there for almost six years, and she couldn't say she was sorry when they started suggesting they were going to eliminate the position.

The secret she never told anyone – not Will, not Maureen, and certainly not her mother – was that she much preferred the times when she was at home, when she wasn't working. During those years she was able to make her life more orderly, was able to spend more time with the kids and Will. And even though it had felt chaotic a lot of the time with three kids and a dog, she still loved it.

Her favorite times were Sunday nights, when the house

was clean and picked up, the laundry was done, the lunches for school were made and sitting in brown bags in the refrigerator, homework was done, and everyone was asleep. It was those nights when Weezy felt she'd accomplished the most, when the quiet of the house buzzed through her, made her feel like she'd won a prize.

Maybe it would have been different if she'd majored in something besides education, something that she was interested in. But then again, maybe not. Her parents had always told her she was the smart one, right in front of Maureen, like Maureen wasn't even there. In their eyes, Maureen was the pretty one. 'Maureen will marry well,' her mom said once, but that wasn't true. Maureen had married an awful man, and they'd stayed together long enough to have two kids and then he'd left, moved clear across the country and barely saw his children.

No, it had been Weezy that had married well, married a kind man who was a caring father and a good provider. It had been Maureen who had found a career she loved and raised Cathy and Drew practically on her own. Sometimes Weezy wondered if they'd almost done it on purpose, fulfilled the part of their lives that their parents doubted they would, just to show them they could.

Weezy found herself overcompensating when she talked about women in the workplace, as if her children were going to pick up on her desire to stay at home and get some sort of subliminal message that told them women couldn't make it. No, she didn't want that. She couldn't raise two daughters and let them think there was anything they couldn't do.

Her rants became almost background noise to her children. They were so used to hearing her go off on the way the world viewed women, in a commercial, or a TV show, or a billboard. She wanted to make sure that they knew it wasn't right, but sometimes she wasn't even sure if they were listening.

She remembered once overhearing a friend of Claire's say that she 'wasn't a feminist or anything,' and Weezy had scolded her. 'Do you know what a feminist is?' she'd asked. 'Do you even know what you're saying by denying that? Do you think you're worth less simply because you're a woman?'

The girls had all giggled at being called women. They were twelve and uncomfortable at the thought. Claire had sat there, her face red and hot, trying to get Weezy to stop talking, rolling her eyes to the top of their sockets, saying, 'God, Mom, come on, stop!' But Weezy didn't care. So her child was humiliated by her — so what? Wasn't that the job of a parent? And when Claire was embarrassed enough to answer back, embarrassed enough to react, well, then at least Weezy knew that she'd been heard.

Weezy could hear Will walking around in his office upstairs on the third floor. Sometimes it sounded like he paced back and forth across the room all day long. Will was the head of the sociology department at Arcadia University, a small liberal arts school near their house. He'd started working there in the eighties, when it was still called Beaver College. It had existed as Beaver College for over a hundred years, but as the Internet grew, parents who went searching for 'Beaver College' didn't find the school's homepage – instead they found themselves on some pretty disturbing pornography sites. And so the school decided to reinvent itself.

Will was a popular professor at the school, teaching classes in sociology and in cultural anthropology. His most popular class was Society and the Cyberworld, which looked at the way culture changed because of technology. He used the name change of the college as his first example, pretending to be a prospective student as he searched the Internet, then faking his surprise at what he found. He always made the kids laugh, as he covered his eyes and shook his head at the results. His students loved him, found him entertaining and engaging. They begged to get into his classes, even after they were already full. He was almost a campus celebrity.

Will had written a book in the late eighties called *Video Kids,* which had become something of a phenomenon. It was a look at the effect that television and video games had on children. He hit something in the culture at that moment, and his book had become a best seller. He'd appeared on talk shows, and was still invited to sit on panels and give speeches.

It had been somewhat of an amazing time when the book came out. They'd been plugging along just fine, and then all of a sudden Will was a celebrity. He'd gotten a two-book deal with the publisher, and the movie rights to the book were snatched up. The good news just kept coming, and Will's job as a professor turned into something much more profitable.

Of course, the next two books that he'd written, *Video Adults* and *The Anger We Teach,* hadn't done nearly as well. The movie rights were still being optioned by the production company, but at this point there was almost no hope of those books ever being made into anything. Will was at work on his fourth book, which he was reluctant to talk about at all. Weezy understood that. She knew he'd been shaken after the mild reception of his two follow-up books. She reminded him that since he started out so high, anything would seem like a letdown. And *Video Kids* was still used as a textbook for college classes all over the country, which made for some nice royalties. But Will had seen his requests for speaking engagements and panels diminish in the past few years, and Weezy knew that he was anxious for another success.

Will had even cut back on his classes this year, and now was home three full days during the week, which took some getting used to. He was teaching three different sections of Society and the Cyberworld, but he could do the class in his sleep and he had teaching assistants, so it wasn't a big time commitment.

It was amazing to Weezy that Will could spend days locked away, studying how other people lived their lives and what it meant for them, and how the culture influenced choices, and vice versa, but she could barely get him to talk about his children for more than five minutes. His attitude was that they were grown, that he and Weezy had done their job and now it was up to the children to choose their own paths. It drove Weezy up the wall.

'What do you want me to say?' Will would ask sometimes, when she went on about Claire's calling off the engagement.

'I want you to have an opinion,' Weezy said. 'I want to know what you think.'

'I think Claire's a smart girl. I think if she thinks it was the right decision, then it was.' And that was all he offered. *Claire's a smart girl.* Like she was just a distant relative he didn't know that well, instead of their own daughter. They'd always assumed Claire would be fine. She was the most independent one, the one who was ready to live on her own by age five. But then, last year, Claire's plans had all fallen apart, and Weezy felt like they'd failed her, like they hadn't been paying enough attention. Will still believed she'd work it out.

Weezy wanted to shake him until he got some sense. 'These are our children,' she wanted to say. 'Our flesh and blood, the people we made, and you really don't care what they do with their lives?'

Why did everyone act like it was so wrong of her to want her children to be happy and healthy and successful and settled? Wasn't that what everyone wanted for their children? Was she really supposed to stop caring, stop getting involved, now that they could vote and drive?

Will always pointed out that he and Weezy hadn't had the

same support that they gave their kids. 'Once I was eighteen, I was on my own,' Will said. And Weezy knew that he was right, but why did they have to raise their children the same way they'd been raised? That didn't seem right. Wasn't there some sort of cultural evolution that took place? Will of all people should be interested in that.

Her children were her greatest accomplishment. Wasn't that what every mother said? Well, it was true. And Weezy didn't know how she was supposed to stop being a mother now. She'd grown them, raised them, and now she was still raising them and she probably would be until she died. What was wrong with that?

Weezy had loved being pregnant. It had agreed with her — everyone said so. She didn't have any of the vomiting or swollen ankles that Maureen and her friends had. Her cheeks got rosy when she was pregnant, and she loved the feeling of her babies swimming inside, loved watching her stomach move with the fists and the feet of the baby. Toward the end of each pregnancy, she mourned just a little She was excited for the baby to come, but she knew the things that went with it: bottles, diapers, spit-up. She loved how neat and tidy being pregnant was, carrying everything with you, giving the baby everything it needed without having to think about it.

It was harder once they came out, harder with each year that went by. Weezy wanted her children to have everything they needed and more. But it was hard to figure out just what that was. Sometimes she got fixated on things that she wanted the kids to have. She was determined to get bunk beds for Claire and Martha, something she'd always wanted so badly when she was younger. She used to picture herself and Maureen building forts, and talking to each other in their bunks, late into the night. What little kids wouldn't want that?

Her girls hadn't seemed as interested, but Weezy pushed for it. 'You'll love them,' she kept saying. It turned out that they were both too frightened to sleep on the top bunk. Martha cried the whole first week she was up there, so Claire agreed to switch, but ended up falling out of it a few days later and spraining her wrist. Weezy tried to remain hopeful that they'd end up falling in love with the bunk beds, but after waking up to find them both squished into the bottom bunk for almost a month straight, she gave in and had Will take the bunk beds down.

So maybe Weezy hadn't always been right about what would make the children happy. But that didn't mean she was going to stop trying or step back and let them search all by themselves. They didn't know what they wanted. She was their mother, and she couldn't help it. She was involved.

That was why she was hell-bent on getting them all to the shore. They didn't know how important this time would be to them later. Maureen seemed to have given up on her kids' coming to the shore. 'They're busy,' she said. Maureen's daughter, Cathy, was living in Ohio with her partner, Ruth, and her son, Drew, was all the way in California, and somehow this didn't seem to bother her. It seemed absurd to Weezy – they'd all gone to the shore together when the kids were little; it had been a tradition. Maureen should have encouraged her kids to keep coming. Didn't she want them to be able to look back on the family vacations and appreciate all the time they'd had together?

'They're adults now,' Will said, when she complained about getting the kids to clear their schedules for the shore. But they didn't really seem like adults to Weezy – Claire didn't even do her own laundry. She had it sent out to the cleaners around the block. Martha was still living at home. And Max was practically a child, still in college, likely to eat cereal for dinner if no one was there to cook for him. They weren't adult enough to know what was good for them, that was for sure. So she was going to get them to the shore, come hell or high water.

Weezy and her family had been going to Ventnor City since she was a little girl. Her father's family had acquired the house, and every summer her father and his brothers used to pack up their families for the summer and head out there. The husbands went back to the city during the week and returned each weekend to the shore, where the children greeted them like long-lost explorers, running out to meet them at the car, jumping on them like monkeys, wrapping their sunburned arms around their necks and saying, 'Daddy, we're so glad you're back.'

There were four bedrooms in the house where the adults stayed. Weezy and Maureen and their cousins were crowded on cots on the sleeping porch, lined up like little soldiers, waiting for a breeze to cool them down. From there, they would listen to the sounds of their parents outside on the front porch, getting drunk with the other neighbors, laughing and singing, smoking cigars, and saying, 'This is the life.'

Those were the best summers of Weezy's life. She firmly believed that. She was shocked when her own mother, Bets, had told Weezy that she'd always hated going to the shore. 'It was so crowded, and no one had any privacy. Your aunts weren't the best company, and anyway we had to cook and clean and what kind of a vacation is that?' After Weezy's father died, Bets never went back to the shore house.

But Weezy didn't care what Bets thought. She wanted her kids to have the same summers that she did, full of hot dogs, taffy, and sea salt. Of course, it was different now. The house was split between Weezy, Maureen, and nine other cousins, and no one (including Weezy) wanted to double or triple up on families and be squished the way they once were. She and Maureen always went together with their families, which was plenty. And for the past few years, Maureen's kids hadn't come, so it was just one extra person.

Weezy had claimed the last two weeks in August early on, and thankfully no one had challenged her on it. She and Maureen had brought their families there every summer for the past thirty years. Weezy was afraid to miss even one year, worried that if she did, one of the other cousins would take her time slot. Even the year that Will's mother died in August, they packed up the week after the funeral and went. It was good therapy to be by the ocean, Weezy thought, and what good would it do to sit at home?

The end of August was Weezy's favorite time, right before the end of summer, when fall and responsibility and schedules were so close that you could smell them in the changing air, and everyone rushed around to get as much sun and ocean as they could before they had to return home. That was all she wanted for her children, who were no longer children – to smell like sunscreen and play mini-golf and shuffleboard, and jump in the waves. If she could give them this one thing to carry with them, then maybe it would make everything else okay. And so she forced this gift on them, summer after summer, whether they wanted it or not.

Weezy was in the TV room sorting through the beach towels and her summer clothes. She had them all spread out on the couch, trying to decide which things to give away and which things she could keep. She needed to make a list of things to get for the shore and start shopping, because really she was already behind.

She held a black one-piece bathing suit in her hand, debating whether or not to just pitch it. She hadn't bought a new bathing suit in years, and she knew it was time, but the thought of standing in a dressing room to find a new suit that would (to be honest) just stay hidden underneath her cover-up seemed like a waste of time. Not to mention an unpleasant errand, to say the least.

She was still holding the suit when the door slammed, making her jump. Then she heard Martha clomp to the kitchen and open the refrigerator.

'Martha? Is that you?'

Martha came around the corner with a glass of Diet Coke in her hand. 'Mom,' she said, 'that bathing suit is like a million years old.'

'I know, I'm tossing it.' Weezy put it down on the couch. 'How was your afternoon?'

'Fine,' Martha said. She sounded down and Weezy felt her heart drop. She was used to Martha's moods, but she'd hoped for a good one today. Now dinner would be strained and silent. Maybe they would eat in front of the TV.

'Is everything okay?' Weezy asked. She tried to make it sound like a light question, so Martha wouldn't think she was prying.

Martha sipped the fizz off the top of the glass and sighed. 'It's fine. Just a bad day at work.'

'I'm sorry to hear that.'

'Yeah.' Martha sighed again. 'I'm just kind of over it. J.Crew, I mean. I'm thinking about looking for some other jobs. Maybe even think about going back to nursing.'

Weezy stayed silent, not wanting to say anything that would make Martha change her mind. She had wanted Martha to do something else for so long, but she hadn't wanted to push it. It had driven her crazy to watch Martha rot away at that store. It was a waste of talent. But she hadn't been able to say so. She'd remained quiet and patient, at least in front of Martha. At night to Will, she would whisper, 'What is she going to do? Work there for the rest of her life?'

'Really?' Weezy finally said. 'That's interesting.'

'Whatever. It's just something that I'm thinking about. I don't even know if I'll go through with it.' Martha took her Diet Coke upstairs, leaving Weezy to worry in the TV room.

Will teased her that she spent twenty-three hours a day worrying about the kids. But what did he expect? Of course she worried about them. That was what mothers did, wasn't it? Will had the luxury of knowing that she was taking care of the worrying and so he didn't have to. He could rest his head on the pillow at night and sleep well.

When the kids were little, she'd worried about their getting hit by a car. She was a firm believer in hand-holding. Max and Martha had been like obedient little suction cups when they reached the street, holding their hands up to her, clinging to her with trust. Claire was the first one to pull away, to hold her arm stiffly by her side, glaring up at Weezy, wanting her independence.

When they were in high school, Weezy worried that they'd get in a car with someone who'd been drinking. When they were in college, she worried that the girls would be raped, that Max would be mugged, that they'd fall down the stairs at a wild party and break their necks, that they'd try drugs, drink too much, or vanish. The list went on and on. She kept most of her worries to herself, knowing that if she shared them with Will, he'd just think she was overreacting.

And then she worried that all of her worrying had made Martha the way she was. Maybe as a child Martha sensed Weezy's fear of the world, absorbed it as a little person, and let it overtake her. Or maybe it had been passed down in her genes, a worrying gene that mutated and grew in Martha.

She wondered if having the girls so close together hadn't given her enough time with either of them. They were less than a year apart and so different in every way. Had she made them the way they were? She would never know.

And so she continued to go through her clothes and worry. She worried that Claire was unhappy, that Max would get hurt by Cleo, that Martha wasn't going to be able to get back to nursing. There was always something. That's what Will never got. You could worry from morning until night, and even then, there'd be something more, something else that you needed to add to the list.

Chapter 4

Right from the start, Cleo knew she wanted to go to a college with a campus. She wanted green lawns and trees. She wanted a quad with brick buildings and college kids reading books on the grass. Basically, she wanted to go to college in a picture.

'Why?' her mom kept asking. 'Why narrow it down before you even start looking?'

'Because,' Cleo said. She left it at that. Cleo had grown up in New York, lived on the Upper West Side her entire life surrounded by buildings and people, and she was ready for something different. There was no explaining to Elizabeth why she wanted — no, *needed* — a campus. She couldn't say that she was craving greenery, that she imagined herself walking across grass, wearing a backpack, while leaves fell in front of her. She couldn't say that she wanted to go to a school that had a campus because that was how she'd dreamt it would be. Elizabeth was not a dreaming woman, and would never understand.

Cleo also couldn't say that she wanted to go somewhere different, somewhere no one else from her high school had even considered going. She'd listened as the guidance counselor had listed all the usual colleges, and she'd pressed the woman for more options until she'd come up with some.

When she stepped onto Bucknell's campus, she knew it was the place for her. Their tour guide was a cute girl named Marnie, with a brown ponytail and a raspy voice. She was the kind of girl that looked like she always had a party to go to. Marnie laughed as she pointed to all the brick buildings, told them that she was a philosophy major (which made Elizabeth snort), that she was from Quakertown, Pennsylvania, and that her boyfriend was on the baseball team. 'He's the pitcher,' she said proudly, like they should all be jealous. Cleo found that she was.

After the tour, she and Elizabeth went to have lunch in Lewisburg, at a little place called Maya's Café. Cleo tried to contain herself as they walked down Market Street, even though she wanted to point at the old-fashioned movie theater and squeal. Elizabeth didn't like squealing and wouldn't be amused.

They each ordered a BLT and as they waited, Elizabeth pointed to the glossy brochure and then ran her finger down it, like she was trying to read it a different way. 'I've never even heard of this school,' she finally said. 'You should keep exploring other options.'

'Okay,' Cleo said. She took a sip of her Diet Coke and slid the brochure back across the table toward her. She didn't want Elizabeth touching it.

'I mean, my God, it's small. What did they say? Nine hundred people in the freshman class.' Elizabeth shuddered, like this was unthinkable.

There was no point in arguing. Cleo knew she'd end up at Bucknell, but she also knew it wouldn't happen by pitching a fit. She was only a junior. She would go on other college visits, she'd pretend to consider them. And when it came time, she'd make her choice and Elizabeth would let her go.

Cleo's dad was 'never in the picture,' which was a phrase she heard her mom use once, so she stole it and used it whenever anyone asked questions. She found that it shut them up right away. There was something final and not quite nice about it. He was 'never in the picture,' as if to say, don't ask anything more.

Even if people had asked questions, Cleo wouldn't have been able to answer them. Her mother told her that her father had been someone she worked with in Chicago at the Board of Trade, when she was 'right out of college and dumb.' Once, when Cleo pressed for more information, her mom said, 'He had a wife and a family and he wasn't interested in a new one.' Cleo never shared that information. Even if her own mother wasn't ashamed that she'd had an affair, Cleo found the whole thing humiliating. She was constantly afraid that her classmates would find out, that she would let it slip one day that her mom was a homewrecker.

After Elizabeth got pregnant, she moved to New York and got a job at a consulting firm, where she worked long hours and loved every minute of it. When Cleo was younger, she'd hated to listen to Elizabeth on work calls – she was always pushing people to do what she wanted, always sounded so angry and annoyed. Cleo knew why everyone caved around her, why Elizabeth just kept rising at the company. A coworker of Elizabeth's once told Cleo, 'Your mother is a force to be reckoned with,' as if Cleo didn't know that already, as if that wasn't the most obvious thing in the whole world.

Elizabeth was different from other mothers – Cleo knew that from the time she was about four. Some of the other mothers who worked hugged their children tightly when they dropped them off at school, declared how much they'd miss them, and surprised them by showing up early and taking them out of school for the day.

When Elizabeth dropped Cleo off, she'd walk her to the door, give her a light pat (usually on the head or back, sometimes on the arm), and walk away quickly. The few times that Cleo whined or clung to her, Elizabeth had been annoyed. 'I have to go,' she would say. 'That's how it works. You stay here, and I have to go.'

It wasn't that Elizabeth was a bad mom – she was just different. Cleo never felt bad for herself or imagined that she was missing out on anything. Mostly, she just wondered how they were even related.

'If I'm adopted,' Cleo said once when she was twelve, 'just tell me now. I can handle it.'

Her mom had looked up from the computer, serious, and for a moment Cleo thought this would be the big reveal, when her mom admitted everything. Then Elizabeth had thrown her head back and laughed. Cleo had been insulted. 'It's not funny,' she said over and over, until Elizabeth was able to talk.

'I promise you, you're mine. You're not adopted. I grew you, I gave birth to you. Sorry, kid. This is it.'

Elizabeth wasn't a liar, and she certainly wasn't one to lie to protect feelings, and so Cleo didn't argue. (Though she was deeply disturbed by the idea that she'd been 'grown' by Elizabeth, like a plant or a sea monkey.) As she got older, Cleo could see that she looked just like Elizabeth, almost identical, really, and so she tried to ignore the thought that her real mother was living somewhere else.

How else could she explain the differences? Elizabeth was entirely unsentimental. She barely kept photographs, let alone souvenirs or letters or any sort of memorabilia. Cleo kept it all. She kept every birthday card she'd ever gotten, even the ones from people she didn't like. When she tried to throw them out, she found that she couldn't – they looked so sad in the trash, the balloons and smiling animals staring up at her, and so she ended up pulling them back out and putting them safely in a box.

Cleo saved tests and old notebooks, papers that she was

especially proud of, notes from her classmates. She saved the cap from the first beer she ever drank (a Miller Lite). She hated to give away clothes, even if she never wore them or they didn't fit anymore. It seemed so mean to just discard them, like they had feelings and would be hurt when boxed and sent to Goodwill.

It was problematic to be a 'low-level hoarder' (as Elizabeth called her) while living in New York. Their apartment at Seventy-ninth and Riverside was nice – spacious even, by most standards – but it was still an apartment in New York. Sometimes Elizabeth would reach her breaking point, and lay down the law, sounding more like a mother than she usually did. 'You need to get rid of this stuff,' she'd say, looking in Cleo's closet. 'What is all this junk?' She'd hold up a stuffed elephant by its ear, and toss it on the floor, like it was going to be the first thing they threw out.

'No,' Cleo would say. She'd rescue the elephant. 'I'll clean it out, just don't touch anything, please don't touch a thing.'

It was the same thing she'd made her mom promise when she went off to college. 'My room is off limits,' she said. 'You aren't allowed to throw out one thing – not one thing – while I'm gone.' She made Elizabeth swear up and down a million times before she was satisfied. And still she sometimes worried that Elizabeth would get the urge to clean and would throw out all of her memories – her stuffed animals and dolls, her favorite books, her journals – would bag them up in big black garbage bags, until there was nothing left of her.

*

Elizabeth was impatient when Cleo moved into the dorm. Most of the other mothers were making the beds, dusting, or folding clothes. Elizabeth sat on the desk chair and watched Cleo do all of these things, looking at her BlackBerry or her watch every few minutes. Elizabeth hadn't offered to help, but even if she had, Cleo would have declined. Cleo wanted to put everything together herself. She knew that if her mom helped, she'd rush through it, and she didn't want her underwear thrown in a messy pile in a drawer. She and Elizabeth didn't have the kind of relationship where she trusted Elizabeth to fold her underwear.

Every so often, parents or other kids moving into their rooms on the hall popped their heads in to say hi. Elizabeth, who was wearing jeans that looked crisp and pressed, flats, and a button-down, barely smiled at these people. 'Hello,' she'd say quickly, nodding her head at their response as if agreeing with them, *Yes, it is a pleasure to meet me, isn't it?*

Cleo was used to the way her mom didn't quite fit into social situations. It wasn't that she didn't know what to do or say to come across as normal and friendly – she just didn't care. 'Be your own person,' she always said to Cleo. As if there were a choice to be someone else.

Once in sixth grade, when Cleo was crying because Susan Cantor cut her out of the lunch table, told her she couldn't sit there anymore, Elizabeth had said, 'Why do you care about those girls? If they don't want to be your friend, why do you want to be theirs?'

Whenever Cleo went out of her way to be nice to people,

writing letters to her grandmother, being polite to her friends' parents or to her teachers, Elizabeth would sometimes comment later, 'Good God, Cleo, you can't get everyone in the world to like you. Why try?' Elizabeth was used to being disliked – Cleo suspected she even enjoyed it – and she couldn't imagine why her daughter wasn't the same. 'You're such a people pleaser,' she'd said on more than one occasion, in the same way people said, 'You're such a liar,' or 'You're such a cokehead.'

Cleo's roommate, a small Asian girl named Grace, had already moved her things in and gone off to try to meet up with the dance troupe she wanted to join. 'I'm passionate about dancing,' she'd said when they met. Cleo had nodded and tried to think of a fact she could share. 'I was on the school paper,' she'd finally said. Grace had nodded like this was satisfactory.

'I'm almost done, Mom,' Cleo told Elizabeth. She was done with her bed and was on to unpacking her clothes into the drawers. Just then she turned and saw a man at the door to the room, 'Knock, knock,' he said. Cleo screamed, and he smiled apologetically.

'Sorry,' he said. 'I didn't mean to sneak up on you! I just came to offer my services.' He held up a hammer and a box of tools. 'My wife and daughter suggested I see if anyone on the hall needed help hanging things up. I suspect they just wanted me out of the room.' He winked at Elizabeth, and she gave him a small smile. Cleo laughed loudly to make up for her mom.

'That would be amazing,' she said. 'I wanted to put this shelf up, but I'm actually not sure how to do it.'

'That should be no sweat. I'm Jack Collaruso, by the way. My daughter, Monica, is moving in down the hall.' He stopped to shake Elizabeth's hand and then Cleo's, and then he turned to the wall and began making marks with a pencil. 'Monica's our oldest, so my wife's not handling this so well.'

Elizabeth made a sound then, a sort of agreement grunt that made it clear she wasn't very interested in Monica or her mother's emotional turmoil. For twenty minutes, the conversation continued like this. Jack would say something, trying to include Elizabeth in the Club of Parents Dropping Their Children Off at College, and Elizabeth would give a borderline rude reaction, while Cleo went out of her way trying to be charming and polite to make up for it. By the time the shelf was hung, Cleo was sweating.

As Jack was finishing putting up the shelf, a dark-haired mother and daughter poked their heads in. 'There you are,' the woman said. 'We thought we'd lost you.'

'You told me to go be helpful,' Jack said. The two smiled at each other and Cleo got the feeling of watching a play or a sitcom about a couple taking their daughter to college.

'This is my wife, Mary Ann, and my daughter, Monica,' Jack said. He put his arm around Monica's shoulders and smiled. Monica looked at the floor, and Cleo wanted to tell her that she had no reason to be embarrassed for her parents when Elizabeth, who was clearly the most embarrassing parent, was sitting right there.

'I was going to run down and get a cup of coffee somewhere.

All this unpacking and crying has made me tired,' Mary Ann said.

'Mom.' Monica rolled her eyes, but smiled.

'Why don't you come with us?' Mary Ann was smiling and looking at Elizabeth, who looked at Cleo and then stood up.

'Coffee sounds good,' Elizabeth said. Cleo let out a breath and Elizabeth gave her a look that said, *You need to relax.*

'That's great. It will give these two a chance to get to know each other.' Mary Ann squeezed Monica's arm and smiled.

After their parents left, Cleo and Monica looked at each other for a few seconds. Cleo wondered if they were just going to stay like that forever, just silently staring until their parents got back, and then Monica said, 'So, where are you from?'

'New York. What about you?'

'Boston. Well, just outside. Lynnfield.'

Cleo nodded. 'I've heard of it,' she said, although she hadn't.

'Hey,' Monica said. She was staring at Cleo's bed, where the gray ears of a formerly pink bunny were sticking out from behind a pillow. It was Cleo's baby blanket – a bunny head attached to a blanket, which used to be pink but was now faded. Monica walked over to the bed, and Cleo tried to think of something to say. Should she deny it was hers? Say that Elizabeth brought it? Or would that make it worse? Cleo had had the blanket for as long as she could remember. It was a thing that you gave babies – they were called snugglies or something like that. Cleo always called hers Bunny Nubby, and when she was younger, she had liked to hold it in her right hand and press it against her face while she sucked her thumb. She'd thought about leaving Bunny Nubby behind, but when she imagined sleeping in a strange room, she knew she wanted him there. When Elizabeth had seen her pull it out earlier that day, she'd made a face and said, 'Oh Cleo, really?' And so Cleo had hidden it behind the pillow so no one else could see it and so Elizabeth wouldn't make any more comments.

And now Monica was walking right over to it, leaning over and plucking Bunny Nubby out from behind the pillow, dropping it on the bed and then running out of the room. Cleo stood there. She felt dizzy. What was Monica going to do? Announce to the hall that she had a baby blanket with her? Wasn't this sort of behavior supposed to be done with? Wasn't this the kind of thing that girls in junior high did to each other? Bunny Nubby was lying crumpled on the bed, and Cleo was just about to go and rescue him, put him in her drawer or somewhere safe, when Monica came running back in the room, breathing hard and holding her own matching bunny blanket.

'Look,' she said. She sounded delighted and held her blanket next to Bunny Nubby. 'Twins!'

From that point on, Cleo and Monica were always together. Most people they met assumed the two had known each other before they'd gotten to Bucknell, that they'd gone to high school together or had been friends for a long time. Their names were almost always said together, Monica and Cleo, like they were

85

some sort of celebrity couple. Cleo loved this. She'd had friends before, but never a best friend. She was always the girl that was the addition to the group, the peripheral friend that was nice to have there but wasn't missed if she wasn't; and while she was fond of her high school friends, she didn't miss them all that much.

Monica's roommate, a girl named Sumi Minderschmidt, had never shown up. A week into the semester, Monica found out that Sumi had decided to go to Villanova instead. 'Poor Sumes,' Monica said. 'Confused until the very end.'

They loved Sumi's name, and would often say things to each other like, 'You know who loves Lucky Charms? Sumi Minderschmidt,' or 'Who do you think you are? A Minderschmidt?'

Cleo was in heaven. She and Monica had inside jokes that could make them double over with laughter, make everyone else look at them with jealousy. They were a pair, a team. And so, a few days after they found out that Sumi wouldn't be joining them, Monica blurted out, 'You should just move in here.' She said it quickly, like she was professing her love for Cleo and was afraid she was going to be rebuffed.

'Okay!' Cleo said. She was delighted. She'd been thinking the same thing, but hadn't wanted to be the one to bring it up. It was Monica's room, and she thought maybe she would want it all to herself, but Cleo was so sick of Grace and her spandex dance outfits, and the way she slept with an eye mask and a noise machine set to 'Babbling Brook' that made Cleo have to pee. If Cleo ever left the room while Grace was sleeping, she'd hear about it the next day. 'You woke me up,' Grace would say. 'We can't have that happen. I just really need my rest for dancing.'

And so the girls got permission from the RA, a senior named Colleen, who was never there much anyway, and moved all of Cleo's things into Monica's room. They were perfect together as roommates. They ate pretzels dipped in peanut butter and talked seriously about which famous person they would choose to be their boyfriend. 'It can't just be about looks,' Monica would always say. 'It has to be about their personality, too.'

Monica's Boston accent was surprising and harsh, and at first Cleo found herself reaching out her hand and placing it on Monica's arm, as if that could somehow soften the edge of her words. But soon she got used to it, the way that she could hear Monica talking loudly down the hall, the way her voice was sort of like a chicken squawk. Cleo found that she started to like the way it sounded, and she sometimes used the word *wicked* herself, when the situation called for it.

They made up dance routines in their room, after drinking vodka mixed with orange guava juice that they carried back from the dining hall in huge cups. They accompanied each other to parties of upperclassmen, where they were always welcome. Cleo found that their prettiness was somehow multiplied when they were together, that people seemed to notice them more and gave them more attention. She thought maybe it was because when they stood next to each other, Monica's hair looked darker and hers looked blonder and the difference was striking. But that was just a theory.

They shared each other's clothes and Cleo always put eye makeup on Monica, after suggesting nicely that sometimes she was just a tad too heavy on the shadow. It was everything Cleo could have hoped for college, and so midway through freshman year, when Monica suggested they move off campus, Cleo was all for it.

'My cousin is a senior and living in one of the best off-campus houses. If we don't take it now, some junior will get it and keep it for two years. We have to do it. It would be a crime not to.'

'But are we even allowed?' Cleo asked. She hadn't heard any other freshman talking about moving off campus.

'Well, legally it's allowed,' Monica said. She bit her bottom lip. 'I mean, they don't really like sophomores to move off, but they make special exceptions sometimes, and my dad thinks he can help.'

Monica never said specifically, but Cleo got the feeling that her dad, who was a Bucknell alum, donated a lot of money to the school – money that had helped Monica get accepted, and also get into the best freshman dorm, and into any classes that were filled.

They decided to ask two girls from their hall, Laura and Mary, to move in with them. The four of them sometimes went to eat dinner together, or pre-gamed in one of their rooms, and it seemed like the logical choice. All four girls got permission from their parents and then from the housing board to move off campus. For the rest of freshman year, the four of them talked endlessly about how amazing their house was going to be and the parties they could have. Sometimes, in the dining hall, Cleo would say to Monica, 'I can't wait to have our own kitchen next year,' just to remind whomever was around them that they were special, that they were moving off campus.

In New York that summer, Cleo felt like she was just counting the days until she could get back to Lewisburg. It seemed now that Bucknell was her real life, and New York and Elizabeth were just a holding place to wait until she could get back there. Cleo went to visit Monica in June, and stayed in her big sprawling house in Lynnfield, slept in the spare twin bed in her room, and went with her to a party at a high school friend's parentless house.

While they sat outside that night, drinking Keystone Lights by the pool, the two girls talked about their sophomore year, told all the other kids there about their new house and the parties they were going to have. She and Monica sat at the edge of the pool, their feet in the water, and they laughed at everything.

'I've missed you so much,' Monica said. 'You're just so much more important to me than my high school friends.'

Cleo loved everything about Monica. She loved where she grew up, how she was meticulous about putting her clothes away as soon as she changed, the way she drew little animals on the corners of her notebooks. She had a best friend and everything just fit. Cleo was filled with happy; everything was right in the world.

*

Sophomore year started perfectly. The girls moved in at the end of August, tripping over each other as they unpacked and ran from room to room. They hung up posters and bulletin boards, bought throw pillows and pots from Target, stocked up on macaroni and cheese and big plastic bins of pretzels. They were as happy as four little clams.

For the first few months, things went amazingly well — swimmingly, as her mom would say. Then two things happened, although Cleo couldn't say which had happened first, or if one thing caused the other, or if they just happened at the exact same time. The first thing was that Monica became severely anorexic. She started running for hours each morning, first at the gym on campus and then, when spring came, outside. After her run, she'd do sit-ups in the common room. As they all stumbled out of their bedrooms to make it to class in the morning, they'd find Monica flying up and down as she worked her abs, her arms crossed in front of her chest in an X, counting her progress in an angry, loud voice. 'One, two, three, four,' she would huff. When she got to 'twenty-five,' she'd stop for a few seconds, lying on the floor and staring at the ceiling, and then she'd start all over again.

'She's like a soldier,' Laura whispered one morning. It was an accurate description and it made Cleo nervous.

This seemed to come out of nowhere. Monica was anything but fat, and while both of the girls drank Diet Coke and frequently looked in the mirror and said, 'I'm a cow,' or 'Look at my giant ass,' it didn't mean anything. It was just what girls did. Cleo hadn't seen any behavior that would have led her to believe that Monica was going to be one of them: an Eating Disorder Girl. At Cleo's high school, there was one in every group of friends – a thin, chilled girl with bags under her eyes who was eventually taken out of school to go to a rehab clinic and returned eating measured foods and seeing the school counselor once a week. She couldn't understand how she'd missed this in her best friend.

Monica kept a notebook to write down every piece of food that she ate. Once, Cleo looked over her shoulder as she wrote down, 'Baby carrots, lettuce (NO dressing!), gum, water.'

'It doesn't seem like you're eating enough,' Cleo offered.

Monica slammed the notebook shut. 'I'm being healthy,' she said. 'Not like the rest of you, eating candy and french fries all day.'

She stomped off to her room, where she spent most of her time with the door closed listening to music. She was always tired and cold, sometimes coming out to nap on the couch in the common room, because the sun came through the windows, and she could curl up there like a cat trying to warm itself.

When the rest of them ate, Monica watched them closely. 'Is that a waffle?' she'd ask, sniffing the air. She'd sit and stare as Cleo put syrup on her Eggo, suggesting that she add butter, or maybe more syrup. Then she'd fill a glass of water and drink it while she watched Cleo eat with an almost erotic look on her face. It was really freaky.

Cleo noticed one day that Monica's arms were covered with

peach fuzz, and she knew she had to call her parents. They came right away and took Monica out of school for the last month of sophomore year, keeping her home all summer and the first semester of junior year. They left everything in her room, paid her rent, and told the girls she could return when she was better. Sometimes Cleo would open the door and look in Monica's room, which was just as she'd left it – the bed was made, there were books stacked on the desk, a box of Kleenex on her nightstand – except there was a fine layer of dust over everything, so that it made Cleo feel like time had stopped. She would stand there and stare at it, until it made her feel too lonely, and then she'd shut the door and go to her own room.

Once Monica was gone, Cleo wished she wasn't staying in Lewisburg for the summer. The house felt empty, and even though Monica had been in her own calorie-counting world for most of the year, Cleo missed her greatly. But the arrangements were made, and it was too late to back out of the summer job working in the Visitors Center. And so she stayed.

The second thing that happened that year was that Laura and Mary turned into complete and total bitches. The house had always been a little divided, like they were on two teams – Monica and Cleo on one and Laura and Mary on the other – but they still all got along pretty well. And then once Monica got sick and left, the other girls seemed to blame Cleo in some way. They were annoyed at her all the time, made passive-aggressive comments about her jacket being left on the couch, or the amount of noise that she made. Post-it notes were left on milk cartons and said things like, *This is Mary's Milk. Unless you're Mary, then hands OFF.*

Cleo had used Mary's milk on her cereal exactly once, and then she found the note there the next day. She honestly couldn't figure out how Mary could have known, until she looked at the side of the plastic carton and saw little black lines to mark the level of the milk. She placed the carton back in the refrigerator carefully, and closed the door softly, as if someone was going to jump out and catch her.

It became clear that it had been a mistake to move in with these girls so soon. Everyone else in their class had waited an extra year to make their permanent living choices, giving them time to weed out the crazies, to form real friendships, and now they all had their own living pods that were full and had no room for Cleo.

In June, right after sophomore year ended, Cleo went to a party with a girl she knew from her Foundations of Accounting class. It was at that party, standing by the keg in a dirty kitchen with a sticky floor, that she met Max. They were both holding red plastic cups, and waiting in line to get them filled. This was a story that pleased Cleo. It seemed like such a perfect way to meet a boy in college, the way he'd started talking to her in line, then pumped the keg and taken her cup to fill it first, tilting it perfectly to make sure there was no foam on top.

She liked him immediately, mostly because he was taller

than she was. Cleo was five nine, and it was surprising how many boys she towered over, especially when she wore heels. But Max was well over six feet tall, and her head just cleared his shoulder. The two of them hung out the whole night at the party, and once when she went to the bathroom and they were separated for more than ten minutes, he came up behind her and put his arm around her shoulders. 'There you are,' he said. 'I was afraid I lost you.'

At the end of the night, Max said, 'I really liked talking to you.' He said this like it was something that boys in college said all the time, when Cleo knew from experience that it certainly was not.

Max was so easy – and not in a bad way. He was so sure of himself, so honest, so happy. After that first night, he was always around and Cleo was thrilled to have someone to hang out with, someone to distract her from her haunted house of eating disorders and milk Post-its. He always wanted to actually do things. Unlike most of the boys at Bucknell, who sat around in sweatpants and played video games, Max suggested real activities, like playing tennis or going to see a movie.

By August, they were a serious couple, by the college definition. When Max's parents came up to visit one weekend, he asked Cleo to come to dinner with them, and so she put on a sundress and waited for them outside of her house, feeling more nervous than she ever had before.

They ate dinner at a steakhouse, and Max's mom encouraged Max to get the biggest steak, made sure that all the leftovers were wrapped up for him, and asked about ten times what he was making himself for dinner these days.

Max's mom fascinated Cleo. Weezy was doting. Cleo had never used that word much before, but it was the only word to explain Weezy's relationship with Max. When she walked into his apartment, she almost immediately began to clean it, stocking the kitchen with groceries she'd bought, dusting shelves and changing sheets.

During her first visit to the Coffey house, she and Max were sitting on the couch when Max mentioned in an offhand way that he was hungry. 'Do you want a snack?' Weezy asked. She got up and went to the kitchen, began returning with options, holding up bags of chips and cold cuts, like she was one of those ladies on a game show, presenting the contestants with their prizes.

It was no wonder Max was such a happy person. Sitting there, watching Weezy fall all over him, she got it. His whole life, people had been doing things for him, telling him how cute and funny he was – and he was all of those things, but still. Cleo couldn't remember the last time her mom had made her a snack. She might have been around five years old, and the only reason her mom got involved was because the granola bars were on a shelf that was too high for her to reach. After that, the granola bars were put on a lower shelf so that Cleo could help herself to one whenever she wanted.

The first time that Cleo met the whole Coffey family, she was overwhelmed, to say the least. They were loud and could be crass. They hugged often, sometimes for no reason at all. With no warning, they'd just reach over and pull the person standing next to them into an embrace. They touched each other's hair and squeezed shoulders when they passed by. More than once, Cleo jumped when a hand surprised her.

'You have a family of touchers,' she told Max. Then she tried to take it back and explain what she meant, because it sounded like she was accusing them of something. But Max just laughed. It was nearly impossible to upset him.

When Monica returned, halfway through junior year, Cleo was ecstatic. She couldn't wait to introduce her to Max, to talk to her every night, to have a friend in the house again. But Monica wasn't interested in any of it. She spent most of her time shut away in her room. She seemed mad at everyone, like they'd all betrayed her. Cleo apologized for calling her parents, but it didn't make a difference. Monica just shrugged like she couldn't care less. When Cleo talked to her – about school or Max or parties – she'd just look back at her, visibly bored. It was as if they'd never known each other before.

Cleo didn't know how to make it better. For a few days, she'd give Monica space, and then she'd decide that it would be better to spend more time together, so she'd force her way into Monica's room, sit with her and do homework. But nothing seemed to work. Monica was different and no matter what Cleo did, it wasn't getting better. It was lonelier than when she'd been gone.

Max lived on the top floor of a house in Lewisburg that was converted to a two-bedroom apartment. At the end of junior year, his roommate, Charlie, was asked by the college not to return the following year (a polite way to kick someone out), and Max asked Cleo to move in with him.

'Come on,' he said. 'It's perfect. I don't want to get some random to move in, and you're here all the time anyway.'

That was true, but Cleo wasn't sure. 'I'm not sure my mom would like that.'

'My mom wouldn't like it either,' Max said. 'We just won't tell them.'

Cleo was, first of all, just a little offended at the thought that Max's mother wouldn't like their living together, even though she'd just said the same thing about her own mom. Still. It was different.

'Just think about it,' Max said.

And so she did. She thought about what it would be like to give up her house and move in with Max. How she could use his milk whenever she wanted, how he would never yell at her if it was her turn to buy the toilet paper. It was tempting. Very tempting.

But it was a crazy idea. Couples in college didn't live together. They'd barely been dating a year, and what were they going to do? Live together for the rest of their lives?

'You're overthinking it,' Max told her.

But Cleo didn't think she was. She tried to picture herself living there, tried to imagine what it would feel like to wake up with Max every morning, to have all of her clothes there in a real dresser instead of the Tupperware box that she kept them in now. But then she thought about what would happen if they broke up, how she'd probably end up sleeping in the other bedroom since it would be impossible to move midyear.

That was enough to make Cleo decide to stay in her own house. Also, she felt disloyal leaving Monica, even if she barely spoke to her anymore. It was just one more year, and really she could do anything for a year. Maybe things would change and senior year at the house would end up being fun. Maybe Monica would go back to her old self. Anything could happen.

A few days later, Laura came out of her bedroom holding a cardboard wheel and looking full of purpose. Laura, a sturdy girl from Iowa, had gained all the weight that Monica had lost over the years, and was now bordering on being truly fat. People always used to say that Laura 'had a really pretty face,' but Cleo didn't think they even said that anymore.

'What is that?' Cleo asked. She was sitting cross-legged on the couch, eating a bowl of Life cereal and flipping through a gossip magazine.

'It's a chore wheel,' Laura said. 'Well, more than a chore wheel, really. See, there's a part here that also reminds us whose turn it is to buy toilet paper and toothpaste and dishwasher soap. So it's fair.'

Fairness was something that Laura talked about often. When Cleo first started dating Max, Laura mentioned that she thought they should have a rule for how many times a boyfriend could sleep over in one week. 'It's not fair to the rest of us if there's a stranger here all the time.'

'He's not a stranger,' Cleo said. 'He's my boyfriend.'

'Still,' Laura said. 'We have to be fair.'

And that was why Cleo ended up spending all of her time at Max's, keeping clean underwear and pajamas in the Tupperware box that he had in his closet.

Now Laura stood in front of Cleo, clutching her cardboard wheel, and called Mary and Monica out of their rooms to show them her creation.

'See?' She pointed to the wheel. 'For one week, it will be someone's responsibility to clean the bathroom, and someone else will be responsible for the kitchen and so on. Then we'll switch.'

'Fine,' Monica said. 'Fine with me.' She sat on one of the futons in the room, hugging her knees to her chest and looking bored. She was pretty agreeable these days. 'The bathroom's disgusting anyway.'

Cleo tried to catch her eye, to look at her so that she could see that Monica really thought this was stupid too. She wanted them to roll their eyes at each other and then go into one of their rooms and laugh about how crazy and annoying Laura was being. But Monica kept her eyes down, picking imaginary fuzz and stray hairs off of her leggings.

'Wait,' Mary said. 'What if, like, let's just say it's my week to clean the kitchen and then Cleo leaves her cereal bowl in the sink. Do I have to clean that?'

'I don't leave my bowl in the sink,' Cleo said.

'Okay, sure,' Mary said. She snorted and shook her head.

'I don't. I don't leave my dishes in the sink.'

'Okay, guys,' Laura said. 'I mean, the fair thing is for the kitchen person to just be there for the big stuff, like emptying the dishwasher and just making sure it's clean. We're all still responsible for our own mess.'

'Are we?' Mary asked. She looked at Cleo.

Cleo was still staring at Monica, willing her to look up and defend Cleo, or at least acknowledge that the girls were ganging up on her. But Monica only looked up to say, 'So are we done?'

Cleo stood up and put her cereal bowl on the coffee table. Her hands were shaking and she knew she was about to cry. 'Actually, I think a chore wheel sounds like a great idea,' she said. 'Fantastic, actually.'

'Really?' Mary said.

'Yes, really. I'd also like to say that I won't be living here next year. I'm moving out.'

'What?' Laura asked. 'You're just telling us now? What if we can't find a new person? This is so unfair.'

'Everything's unfair,' Cleo said. She knew she wasn't making sense and she didn't care.

When she told Max, he screamed, 'Yes!' He hugged her around the waist and her feet came up off the ground. 'This is going to be great,' he said. 'You'll see.'

*

They moved all of Cleo's stuff into the apartment right away, and spent the summer working and going to barbecues. Cleo had gotten a marketing internship, working for the Little League World Series in Williamsport. Elizabeth had advised her to take an internship in New York, but Cleo remained firm.

'You don't even want to go into marketing,' Elizabeth said. 'And you don't even like sports.'

'I like sports,' Cleo said. 'And maybe I will want to go into marketing.'

'This is a mistake, Cleo. When you're up against another candidate that did an internship at a well-known firm in New York, and then they look at you and see you wasted away your time as a ball girl in some stupid town, do you really think you'll win?'

Cleo was determined to show Elizabeth that she was wrong. Also, she didn't want to be away from Max, so an internship in New York was out of the question. She didn't give Elizabeth too much information about her job. She wasn't a ball girl, but she was mostly just typing out schedules and directions to send to the parents of the players, and getting coffee for people in the office. She was pretty sure there was no marketing involved whatsoever.

At the apartment, Cleo pretended they were married. They played house, making dinner (usually just pasta and jarred sauce) and drinking wine, like they were adults. She knew that her old roommates were wrong when they told her she was making a mistake. 'This will end in disaster,' Mary had said as she packed up.

Cleo had become friends with some of Max's friends, but

it felt like they were on loan, like they never really made the switch to being hers. She had really started to like his friend Ally, had started to think that maybe she would be the one that Cleo clicked with, until she heard her say at a party, 'Cleo's totally nice. She's supersweet. She's just, you know, sort of a loner.'

A loner? Cleo had been waiting for the bathroom when she heard this, and Ally was around the corner, out of sight, talking to someone else. She wanted to ask Ally what she meant by that, but she didn't. Instead, she stood there praying that she could get into the bathroom before Ally saw her.

Later that night, she'd told Max what she'd heard. 'Do you think I'm a loner?'

'No.' Max laughed.

'It's not funny. Why would Ally say that? I thought she liked me.'

'She does like you,' Max said. 'Don't let it bother you.'

'I can't help it.'

'Look, Ally can't be alone for five minutes without going crazy. You know that. She can't eat alone, she can't walk to class alone, and she certainly can't study alone. She's probably just jealous of you.'

'It didn't sound like she was jealous.'

'Well, then she's intrigued. You do your own thing, that's all. You don't need a clan of girls around you at all times.'

'I guess,' Cleo said. But it wasn't that she didn't need it, she'd just never had it. She'd learned to live without.

Cleo felt like she'd failed in some very real way, to be almost a senior in college and not have one single girlfriend to show for it. It was her mom's fault, probably. Elizabeth didn't have any friends, not really. She had work people that she went out to dinner with sometimes, or to the Hamptons with, but not real friends that she relaxed and spent time with. And now Cleo was all fucked up because of it. She'd never seen an example of how to have friends and now maybe she never would. She could go on a talk show about it.

One night she and Max were watching TV and she said, 'You're my best friend, you know.'

Max smiled. 'Why do you sound so sad about it?'

'Don't you think it's weird? That you're my best friend? My only friend, really? That I don't have any girlfriends?'

Max thought for a minute. 'No. I think you got in with a bad crowd early on.'

'A bad crowd?'

'Yes, a bad crowd. Any house with a milk tracer and a chore wheel is a bad crowd. In my book, at least.'

'I guess so.'

Max came closer to her and pulled her head down to his chest. 'You're my best friend, too,' he said.

'You're such a liar.'

'I'm not. I'm not lying at all.'

'What about Mickey?'

Max wrinkled his nose. 'He's fun, but you smell way better.' He lifted up her shirt and started kissing her stomach. 'Way better.'

*

In the middle of August, they packed their bags and headed to the shore for a week-long vacation with the Coffeys. They'd agreed to keep their living arrangement a secret from their families, and Cleo was terrified that she was going to blurt it out during the trip. Max told her she was being paranoid, but she knew better.

Around the Coffeys, she became a strange version of who she was. She tried to be chatty, but her voice came out higher than it usually was. She tried to be casual, but she felt uncomfortable everywhere. It was exhausting.

Cleo was almost certain that Aunt Maureen was bordering on a drinking problem, although when she suggested this once, Max laughed. 'She just likes to have a good time,' he said.

On the drive to the house, Cleo asked how Claire was doing. She was nervous about seeing her after the whole engagement disaster.

'She's good,' Max said.

'Well, she can't be good. She just called off her wedding.'

Max had shrugged. 'I mean, it sucks, but I think she's handling it fine.'

'It's just so sad. I feel so bad for her,' Cleo said.

'Well, don't ask her about it.'

'You don't think I should say anything?'

'No,' Max said. 'You know Claire. She doesn't like to dwell on things.'

'Yeah, but I'll feel weird not mentioning it.'

'Trust me, she doesn't want to talk about it.'

So now there were two things that Cleo wasn't supposed to talk about. She took a deep breath and looked out the window.

'Are you okay?' Max asked.

'I'm just nervous, I guess,' she said.

Max reached over and took her hand. 'It'll be fun,' he said. 'I promise.'

Cleo felt very grown-up just then, driving with her boyfriend to join his family on vacation, discussing the things that they weren't to discuss with the rest of the family. And the two of them drove almost the whole way like that, holding hands, sometimes linking their fingers, sometimes just resting against each other. It thrilled Cleo a little bit to be doing this, traveling in a car, with her live-in boyfriend, driving through the night with their secrets between them.

Chapter 5

The house at the shore looked like it belonged in a fairy tale. When Claire was little, she used to call it the Gingerbread House, because it was tan and pink with sculpted posts, and rising turrets that looked like the perfect place for hiding a princess. She'd been there every year since she was a baby. Even the year she was in college, when she had her own shore house with friends in Ocean City, she still stayed at the Gingerbread House for the last two weeks of August.

She'd pretended to be annoyed that summer, pretended that her parents were making her stay with them, but really she was grateful. She'd been sharing a room with Lainie, which meant that she was also sharing a room with Brian. The room smelled like mildewy towels and had two twin beds with thin mattresses that dipped in the middle. Every night, Claire had to get upstairs before Lainie and Brian, put on her Discman, face the wall, and pray for sleep so that she could ignore whatever happened when they came in. The alternative was to sleep on the couch downstairs, which always felt wet and smelled worse than the bedroom – a mix of feet and old cheese.

There was sand all over the house, dirty dishes everywhere, and every morning Claire woke up sunburned and hungover. She was filled with relief when it was time to go to the Gingerbread House. She packed up her clothes quickly, saying, 'This sucks, I can't believe I'm missing the end of the summer here. Yeah, my parents are so annoying.'

Claire loved the Gingerbread House, loved waking up to the sound of waves and the smell of sand. It was part of the reason she'd finally agreed to go this year. Well, that and also because she didn't have enough money in her account to pay September's rent.

She'd taken the train to Philly on Saturday, and her parents and Martha had picked her up at the station and they'd all headed right for the shore. Everyone was in a great mood. Her dad was whistling, her mom was almost bouncing up and down in her seat, and Martha wasn't discussing any recent tragedies. Claire started to feel calm for the first time in months. This was exactly what she needed. She had three new books to read, and the thought of lying on the beach and resting in the sun sounded like the most wonderful thing in the world. And then when the time was right, she'd tell her parents that she was broke. And moving home.

But that would all come later. She could wait until the end of the week to fill them in. Actually, it was preferable, since she could just leave right after. In the meantime, she'd enjoy her vacation, go for a walk on the beach or the boardwalk. Eat saltwater taffy. Just relax.

When they were younger, all of the cousins stayed in the same room. Cathy, Martha, Claire, Drew, and Max were all tucked away in bunk beds and sleeping bags. One summer, Martha forgot to put sunscreen on her feet and they burned, badly. She'd insisted that the fan in the room had to stay pointing right at her feet to cool them down, instead of circulating the room like it normally did. They'd all disagreed, of course. But as soon as Martha thought they were all asleep, she'd pull the lever on the fan to make it stop, and one of the other kids would realize it and yell, 'Martha!' But they were all laughing, not really annoyed, just thrilled with their own little game they'd created.

Had they ever slept during those summers? They must have at some point, but Claire didn't remember it. She remembered sandy beds and Cathy telling them stories about girls that were kidnapped. 'I knew a girl,' she said, 'that was taken right out of her room, pulled right through the window.'

'You did not,' Claire said. But she wasn't sure. Cathy always sounded sure.

Usually, as they were drifting off to sleep, Drew or Max would fart loudly and all the girls would scream, and there'd be a big to-do over airing out the room and running into the hall. Weezy and Maureen tried their best to get them back to their beds, yelling threats and using their full names, 'Claire Margaret, Martha Maureen, Catherine Mary.' It rarely worked.

During the days, they'd run as a pack, going to the beach and then to the boardwalk to play skeet ball and walk around. The girls would get wrapped braids in their hair, feeling very special and exotic when school started and they still had a tiny seashell attached to their hair.

They always went to the same little candy store. It was made to look like one of those old-fashioned places, with bins of colored candy balls, swizzle sticks, and fudge. They always chose Atomic FireBalls and Super Lemons – candy that was more pain than pleasure, that tested the will of all the sunburned kids that ate it. They'd stand in a circle outside the store, count to three, and pop the little sugar balls into their mouths. They'd groan and scream, wriggle back and forth and bend over laughing in a mix of agony and total pleasure, drooling colored sugar and waiting to see who could keep the candy in their mouth the longest. Martha always won. Usually the others would have to spit the candy out in their hands, take a break, and try again.

It was funny – her cousins hadn't come to the shore in years, but whenever she thought about it, she imagined them there. The house had been redone and the sets of bunk beds in the big room replaced with a huge king bed. But still, when Claire pictured the house, she saw all of them bunked down in the big room, scaring the bejeezus out of each other and laughing until they thought they were going to die.

They arrived at the house a little after five o'clock, and when they opened the front door, they heard music playing and saw smoke coming from the back patio. They heard laughing, and even though they all knew it was Max because his car was right out front, and because he'd told them he'd arrived the night before, Weezy stepped in nervously and called, 'Hello? Max?' as if an intruder had broken into the house and started grilling out back.

Max appeared at the screen door with a big smile on his face. 'Hello, family,' he said. He raised a spatula in the air. 'Cleo and I decided to cook you a welcome meal!'

He was pretty drunk, Claire could tell, and she wondered what time he'd started drinking. Weezy just clapped her hands together. 'Oh, Max,' she said. 'How sweet is that?'

It would, no doubt, be something she talked about for months, the way Max cooked for them out of the blue; went to the grocery store all by himself, with no one asking (as if he were an incompetent), and then made dinner, like he was performing a miracle of some sort. Once, when Max was in high school, he'd folded towels that were in the dryer and Weezy had gone on about it for weeks, until Martha said, 'Claire and I fold laundry all the time,' to try to shut her up. It was one of the few times that they'd been on the same side, Claire and Martha, but they were just so sick of listening to Weezy talk about Max and his amazing laundry abilities.

Max turned to Claire and gave her a hug that lifted her off the ground. 'Clairey!' he said. 'Clairey's here.' He set her down gently and Claire laughed. This was, of course, why he was Weezy's favorite, after all. He was adorable and charming, even when a little bit tipsy – maybe especially when he was a little bit tipsy. He turned to Martha and bowed. 'Welcome, miss,' he said.

Cleo walked in from the patio then, carrying an empty platter and wearing nothing but a bikini. 'Oh, you're here already,' she said. 'We thought we'd be done cooking by the time you got here.'

'Well, this is such a treat,' Weezy said. 'Personal chefs on our first night here.' Cleo smiled and looked down at the ground. Then Weezy hugged Cleo, which must have been awkward since the girl was practically naked. Claire noticed that her father stayed on the far side of the kitchen and just waved. She didn't blame him.

'We made chicken and salad,' Cleo said. 'We thought you'd be hungry when you got here.'

'That we are,' Will said. He looked around the kitchen, still averting his eyes from Cleo. 'You didn't happen to pick up any brewskies, did you, son?'

Claire closed her eyes for a second and took a deep breath. Her father had never used the word *brewskies* in his whole life. He'd never called Max 'son' either. She was embarrassed for him, but figured it wasn't fair to judge. After all, when you had a twenty-one-year-old near supermodel standing in all of her naked glory in the kitchen of your summerhouse, you were bound to be a little rattled.

She would change eventually, Claire figured, but it never happened. Cleo ate dinner in her bikini, she cleared the table in her bikini, and then she sat and had a glass of wine with the whole family in her bikini.

When Maureen arrived later that night, she walked in, looked right at Cleo, and let out an 'Oh!' Then she tried to recover and said, 'I guess you're ready for the beach.' Cleo just smiled.

And that was just the first night. It seemed that Cleo intended to wear nothing but her bikini for the entire vacation. In the mornings, she was in the kitchen, sipping coffee, bikini-clad.

'I mean, she's great, but don't you think it's a little weird that she never puts anything else on?' Claire asked Martha. Martha just shrugged, which bugged Claire. Normally, this was the kind of thing that Martha would jump right in on, getting upset and whispering behind Cleo's back. But she barely seemed to notice.

'I can't believe we have to share a room,' Claire went on. This surely would make Martha angry. 'Just because Mom doesn't want Max and Cleo in the same room, we have to share. They each get their own space.' Martha just shrugged again, and Claire grabbed a towel and left the room.

On Sunday night, the whole family sat outside making s'mores after dinner and Claire drank glass after glass of white wine.

Weezy kept talking about what activities everyone wanted to do, like they were at some sort of summer camp; Will read the paper and called Max 'son'; Maureen kept getting up to sneak around the house and have a cigarette, like they all couldn't smell the smoke on her when she got back; Martha was lost in her own thoughts and stared at the stars; and Max and Cleo used any excuse to touch each other, which would have been inappropriate for a family vacation anyway, but since Cleo was half-naked, it was downright pornographic.

'Aren't you cold?' Claire asked.

Cleo laughed. 'No, I never get cold at the beach. It's like the sun warms me all day and stays with me into the night. I could live at the beach.'

Claire snorted into her glass. Then she let herself admit that if she looked like Cleo did in a bikini, she would consider wearing one as much as possible too.

The night ended with everyone playing Scrabble, which Claire thought would make her feel better since she would surely win. She ignored it when Weezy said to Cleo, 'Watch out for Martha! She's a killer at this game.' Claire wanted to point out that Martha almost never won Scrabble. It was Claire's game.

It turned out that in addition to having a body that was meant to live in a bikini, Cleo also had an incredible vocabulary. After she got a triple word score by turning *dish* into *dishabille*, Claire made a comment about memorizing the dictionary and Cleo actually blushed.

'My first nanny was French, and she always had trouble

with English. She was always asking me, "What's the word for this?" and I wanted to make sure that I could tell her, so I kept a dictionary with me. Then it just became a habit. I read dictionaries all the time. And thesauruses. I just love words, I guess,' Cleo said. She shrugged and smiled a little bit and Claire made herself smile back. Of course Cleo read the dictionary for fun. If life was going to be unfair, it was going to go all the way.

The end of the Scrabble game was a bit blurry to Claire, but she did remember dropping her glass of wine on the floor, the glass smashing and spraying everywhere. She tried to clean it up, until Maureen came in to help and sent her out of the kitchen because she was barefoot.

Claire woke up on Monday, groaned, and rolled over to bury her face in her pillow. She could feel a burn on the edge of her scalp where her sunscreen had, of course, worn off the day before. She could hear everyone downstairs in the kitchen, dishes clinking, her dad telling some story about peaches, or something that sounded like that. Claire pulled the covers over her head. If she waited long enough, maybe they would all go to the beach without her.

At first, Claire thought she'd tell Weezy about her situation. Then she changed her mind and thought she'd tell Will, because he'd be calmer and would keep Weezy calm too. But then she thought no, that wouldn't work. Will would just sit there and listen, not sure how he was supposed to respond. Will was never the one they would go to when they asked permission for anything. And if it ever happened that they did come across him first, and asked to go to a friend's house or anything of the sort, Will always looked surprised to see them, like he couldn't quite place who they were, and then he'd say, 'Ask your mom.'

So it would have to be Weezy that she told. It would be fine. She'd just wait until the end of vacation, go up to her mom, and say, 'I'm out of money. I'm moving home.' Simple. She was going back to New York on Sunday, which meant that she had seven more days to do it.

Claire took a shower and then threw her wet towel on Martha's bed. If Martha came up and saw it, she would lose it. She was such a neat freak. Growing up, whenever they got new sneakers, Martha made a point to keep hers as white as possible for as long as she could. She'd step over puddles, avoid any dirt, and stare at her unblemished shoes with pride. Claire's Keds were usually dirty by the end of the week, and it used to drive Claire crazy, to watch Martha step around messes, so pleased with herself and her white shoes.

'That's probably the only reason why you wanted to be a nurse,' Claire told her one time. 'Because you knew you'd get to wear really white shoes.'

Once, when they were playing kickball outside with the neighborhood kids, Martha refused to take her turn for fear that her shoes would get filthy. Claire walked right up to her and stepped all over Martha's feet with her own dirty sneakers. Martha looked down at her shoes and let out a howl, then pushed Claire on the ground.

'Why did you do that?' her mother asked Claire. 'Whatever possessed you to do such a thing?'

Claire had no reason to give and was sent to bed right after dinner that night – no TV, no Jell-O Pudding Pop. She couldn't explain to her mom why she wanted to get Martha's shoes dirty. She wasn't even sure she knew herself. All she knew was that she couldn't watch Martha protect their whiteness anymore, couldn't stand to hear the other kids laugh at her while she stood to the side and refused to participate. And so she'd put a stop to it.

Martha was still being unusually quiet. On Tuesday, she and Claire sat on lounge chairs at the beach, and Martha wrote in her journal, sighing and turning her face to the sun with her eyes closed. Cleo and Max were frolicking in the ocean – that was the only word for it, *frolicking* – splashing each other and embracing as the waves crashed over them.

'What's going on with you?' Claire asked. It really wasn't normal for Martha not to be talking all the time.

'If you must know,' she said, 'I'm considering a career change.'

'Going to the Gap?' Claire asked. Martha shut her journal loudly and started gathering her things. 'I'm kidding, I'm kidding.' She put her hand on Martha's arm. 'I'm sorry, come on, I was just kidding. Tell me.'

Martha sniffed, acting like she wasn't going to say any more, but Claire could tell she wanted to talk about it. Finally she said, 'I'm thinking about going back to nursing.'

'Really?' Claire asked. 'Wow.'

'What's that supposed to mean?' Martha asked.

'Nothing, just – wow. I haven't heard you talk about nursing in a long time.'

'Well, I've just been thinking about it lately. I think it's time. But not in a hospital. Maybe at a doctor's office or something.'

'I think that's great,' Claire said. 'Really, I do. You always wanted to be a nurse and you were good at it.'

Martha looked over at Claire. 'Thank you,' she said, and then she started writing again.

Claire considered telling Martha everything. Confessing about the apartment and the credit cards and all of it. But she knew that if she did, Martha would let her mouth fall wide open, stare at her, and then go tell Weezy. She wouldn't be able to stop herself. Martha told Weezy everything, which was weird. It should have been the other way around, her loyalty to Claire, but it never had been and it wasn't going to start now. So Claire kept her mouth shut.

She wished that she could tell Doug about everything. It didn't make sense, of course, because if she and Doug were still together and he was there to talk to, she wouldn't be in this situation. It had helped a little to tell Lainie, but it wasn't the same. She missed having one person to give her undivided attention and advice, to be almost as responsible for her actions as she was.

Probably it was just loneliness that made her wish for Doug. That was normal, right? It was a shitty situation and she just wanted help, that's all. She sighed and rolled over on her stomach so she wouldn't have to watch Max and Cleo anymore. It was dumb, but it made her feel worse to watch them being happy. And she found she couldn't stop watching them, even though it made her feel horrible. It was like when you had a cut on your lip that you kept biting at – it hurt, but you couldn't leave it alone.

Now Doug and her money problems were all in a mix in her head. She shouldn't have started thinking about it. Lately, she tried to remember only the really annoying things about him. The way he read only nonfiction books on truly boring subjects. How when he slept he let his limbs fly everywhere, and how she was never really comfortable when she was in bed with him; how she remained still and rigid, right on the edge of sleep, tucked in the corner of the bed.

But then she remembered other things, like how he always unpacked her laundry when it was delivered, and stacked her mail on the desk. Or she remembered the time they were at a bar, drinking beer in the afternoon, watching a baseball game. The bar was pretty empty, just a few people watching the game, and one single guy on a stool at the end of the bar, wearing a knit hat and frowning at his beer and then at the TV. And Doug had leaned over and said, 'Hipsters are so joyless,' and Claire had been so surprised that she'd spit her beer on the bar.

The thing was that it didn't really matter what she thought about when she remembered Doug. Because the truth was that she would have married him if he hadn't ended it. And that was the scariest thing of all. Because it meant either that she was stupid enough to commit to someone who wasn't really right for her or that she did love him and he left her and broke her heart. And honestly, sometimes she wasn't sure which one it was.

On Thursday, Cleo asked Claire if she wanted to go shopping on the boardwalk with her. The shops down there were full of animals made out of seashells and T-shirts that said things like aa is where i go to meet drunk sluts, and rehab is for quitters. But Cleo looked eager and so Claire agreed. Who knew? Maybe Cleo would find a beach cover-up that she liked.

They walked in and out of the little shops, quietly browsing through the ashtrays and postcards. Every once in a while, Cleo would hold up a T-shirt for Claire to read, and they'd both laugh.

Claire turned to examine a shelf of glass pipes, as though she were really looking to buy one. She picked up a red and brown swirled pipe, looked at it closely, and then put it back down. Cleo was watching her, probably wondering if she was a secret pothead, and Claire was just about to make a joke about it, when she heard someone calling her name.

She turned to see a girl in a jeans skirt and bikini top running toward her. 'Claire!' the girl called out. 'Claire, hi!' It took her a second to realize that it was Heather Foley, a girl she used to babysit for, and before she had a chance to say hello, Heather had thrown her arms around Claire's neck and was squeezing tightly.

'I'm so happy to see you,' she said. 'I didn't even know you were here.'

The Foley family owned the house next to the Coffeys' and had been going to the shore for as long as Claire could remember, before they even had any kids. For a couple of summers, Claire had been a mother's helper for the family. It was a job she liked, holding the children's hands as she walked them toward the ocean, making peanut-butter-and-jelly sandwiches for lunch, putting them down for naps in their stuffy summer rooms, promising that they could go back down to the beach as soon as they woke up.

Once when she was trying to get Bobby Foley ready for bed, begging him to put his pajamas on, he'd declared, 'No pajamas. I want to sleep naked like my dad does.' As soon as Bobby finished saying this, Claire looked up to see Mr. Foley standing in the doorway. He'd walked away as though he hadn't heard anything, and Claire almost died of embarrassment. To this day, when she saw him at the shore, she always thought, *I know that you sleep naked.* It seemed too much information for her to handle, too personal for her to process.

Heather finally released her grip and Claire stepped back to look at her. 'Oh my God, Heather. Look at you!' She sounded like an old person, but she couldn't help it. Heather looked so grown-up. She'd just finished her freshman year at GW, she told Claire. She'd gained a little bit of weight in her hips and breasts and had that happy, pudgy look that freshman girls get. She was deeply tan, almost unnaturally so, like she'd been working on it all summer long.

'This is Cleo,' Claire said. 'Max's girlfriend.'

'Hi,' Heather said. Claire could tell she was trying not to stare.

'So what are you up to this summer?' Claire asked.

'I'm waitressing at the fishery. It's so fun. There's tons of kids working there that I know from high school and stuff.'

'That's great,' Claire said. She was about to ask how her first year of college was, just to make sure that she sounded completely like an old lady. But she noticed that Heather was looking at something, her face getting red. Claire turned around to see a college-age guy in a bathing suit, taking huge bites out of a cheeseburger, as though it were just a little snack.

'Oh my God,' Heather said.

'Who's that?' Claire asked.

'Bradley.' Heather was barely whispering and Claire had to lean in to hear her. 'He works at the restaurant with me. We're sort of – I don't know.'

'Ohhh,' Claire said. She smiled. She remembered summers at the shore, running around with her friends and chasing boys. Every day exciting, not knowing who you were going to see or what was going to happen. Claire hadn't felt like that in a long time. She hadn't even wanted to feel like that, which was maybe more disturbing. The thought of dating again, of getting back into that whole mess, was so tiring. But watching Heather skitter around, trying to pretend like she wasn't watching Bradley, almost reminded Claire of why it was so fun. Almost.

When Heather was about three, she always wanted to brush Claire's hair, which really always ended up getting it in knots. But one time, she'd sat there patiently, letting Heather run the brush back and forth so that her hair covered her face. All of a sudden, Heather had started laughing, really laughing, like she'd seen something so funny she couldn't believe it.

'What?' Claire had asked her. She peeked out from behind her hair and saw Heather lying on her side, still laughing.

'You look like a donkey,' Heather said, and she rolled back and forth on the floor.

That was how Claire always remembered her. And now, here she was all giddy and excited about a guy, a Bradley. How had that happened?

On Friday night, they had a Mexican feast. That's what Weezy kept calling it, when it was really just fajitas and refried beans. She moved around the kitchen with a great sense of purpose, repeating the phrase 'Mexican feast,' while Maureen sat at the counter and chopped jalapeños and Martha used the blender to make margaritas from a thick syrup, ice, and tequila.

Max and Claire set the table, and each time that Weezy said, 'Mexican feast,' Max held up another finger to count. They were up to eight.

'Martha, did you tell Maureen about your job?' Weezy asked. Martha shook her head.

'What's going on?' Maureen asked.

'It's nothing, really. I've just been thinking about maybe leaving J.Crew. Maybe going back to nursing.'

'That's great.'

'Well, it's just an idea. I actually have to look into getting recertified and all of that. I'm not exactly sure what I need to do.' Martha looked overwhelmed just getting the words out.

'You'll do it. We'll figure it out. We can look it up online after dinner. I'm sure it will be no trouble.' Weezy's peppy comments came out all in a row, and Max and Claire smiled at each other.

'You know . . .,' Maureen started. She held the knife in her hand and looked off in the distance, like she was trying to remember something. 'I have a friend that runs a high-end caretaker business. Well, more of a friend of a friend, really. She places really smart, bright people in the homes of the elderly – the really rich elderly.'

'Really?' Martha asked.

'Yeah, and I was just thinking. That might be a nice way to ease your way back into it, you know? You could look into getting recertified, sort of reacquaint yourself with some parts of the job. And it pays pretty well.'

'That sounds interesting,' Weezy said. She looked so hopeful that Claire wanted to smack her. Weezy couldn't hide how badly she wanted things to go well for Martha, all the time. 'Don't you think that sounds interesting?'

'Maybe,' Martha said. 'Of course, the work I did as a nurse is totally different than a caretaker.'

'Oh, of course. We know that. But just like Maureen said, it would be a good way to ease your way back in.' Weezy was holding her hands together and staring at Martha.

'Okay, well, I'll think about it.'

'I'll get you in touch with the woman when we get back,' Maureen said. Martha nodded.

Weezy practically danced the fajitas to the table. She made a big deal of sipping her margarita and proclaiming it delicious. They all sat down and began assembling their fajitas. Max took three right away and piled on every topping there was, while Weezy repeated the conversation about Martha's possible new job to Will, who had been upstairs while it happened.

'It's very exciting,' Weezy said. 'It just sounds great.'

They'd be talking about this all week. Whenever Martha did anything – got a raise, had a fight with a coworker, folded a shirt at her job – they all talked about it like it was the most interesting thing in the world, like she had done something so fantastic they couldn't believe it.

'Max, when do classes start?' Claire asked. She wanted to change the subject.

Max looked up from the huge fajita he was about to put in his mouth. 'Um, next week. I have only four classes, though, so I don't have anything until Wednesday.'

'How can you have only four classes?' Martha asked.

'Got 'em all done,' Max said. He smiled and shoved the fajita in his mouth.

'I had full semesters all through college,' Martha said. She was looking at Cleo, who was the only one polite enough to listen. 'Nursing is tough, I'll tell you that much.'

Max put his hand on Cleo's thigh, which was bare, since she was of course still in her bikini. Claire wondered if her dad still felt uncomfortable eating with a half-naked stranger, or if he was getting used to it.

'What's your major Cleo?' Martha asked.

'Economics and French,' she said.

'That's an interesting combination,' Weezy said. 'I wouldn't have thought those two go together.'

'They don't, really.' Cleo laughed a little. 'I wanted to study French, but my mother told me it was a waste of time and that I had to pick something in the business school. But I figured out I could do both if I took some summer classes and a couple extra here and there. I just love my French classes.'

'That's great,' Weezy said.

'See?' Max said. 'Cleo balances me out with her classes.'

'That's just how Martha was with her nursing classes,' Weezy said. 'She always had a mind for medicine, always got A's in her science classes.'

'So did I,' Claire said. 'I always got A's in science too.'

Weezy turned to look at her and gave her a small nod and a little smile. Claire knew she shouldn't let it bother her, the way her parents talked about Martha's success in school, but it did. It was like they thought if they focused enough on how smart Martha was, no one — maybe not even Martha herself — would notice that she didn't have any social skills; like if they talked about it enough, they could make up for everything else. It was just that in the process, they made it sound like Claire and Max were dumber than dirt.

'Martha, do you like the fajitas?' Weezy asked. Max and Claire laughed. 'What?' she asked.

'Of course she likes the fajitas,' Claire said. 'It's her favorite meal. Isn't that why we had them in the first place?'

'Everyone likes fajitas,' Weezy said. 'You all like them.' She sounded defensive.

'I wish Cathy and Ruth and Drew were here,' Martha said. She looked at Maureen and smiled.

'Me too,' Maureen said.

'We all do,' Weezy said. 'Hopefully they'll be able to make it next year.'

Claire wasn't all that upset about Cathy's not being there. They got along fine now that they were adults, but when they were kids, Cathy used to love teasing Claire, finding any reason to leave her out of a game or trick her into eating sand.

One summer Cathy had repeatedly called Claire a virgin, and Claire — assuming it had something to do with being Jesus's mother and sure that it didn't apply to her — had yelled back,

'I am not! I am not a virgin!' They were all on the crowded beach, and Claire had yelled this over and over, until finally Weezy came over and told her to stop, then leaned down to explain in a quiet voice what that word meant. Claire only partly understood what Weezy was saying to her, but she knew enough to be mortified. She thought she was going to die right there on the beach.

That's still how she remembered Cathy, even now, all grown up. Claire thought of her as that girl who loved to make her cry, who took so much pleasure in bossing other people around.

'We should go to Atlantic City tonight,' Max said. He looked at Claire. 'Come on, let's do it. I'm finally legal to gamble.' Cleo perked up and looked at Claire for her answer. She was probably dying to get out of the house. If family time was hard when it was your own family, it had to be twice as hard when you were the girlfriend.

Claire was tired from the sun, the talk of Martha, and the whole week. She'd been planning to go sit on the porch after dinner and read. She was trying to think of a way to let them down gently, when Martha said, 'I'm in, let's go!'

Max let out a whoop and Weezy laughed. 'Blackjack,' he said. 'We can play blackjack. I've gotten really good.'

'You're gonna go?' Claire asked Martha.

'Yeah, I'll even drive. I barely touched my margarita.'

Claire was trapped. She couldn't say no now that even Martha was going. 'Let's do it,' she said. She figured it couldn't hurt. Who knew? Maybe she'd win big, hit the jackpot, and be able to pay her rent next month and put off telling her parents and moving home for another month or so.

Cleo was laughing and clapped her hands like she was a child. 'Just give me a minute to change,' she said, and ran out of the room. Well, at least she wouldn't be wearing her bikini to the casino. That was a plus.

Weezy was telling them all to go. 'Have fun,' she said over and over. She was so happy to have all of her kids heading out together, especially happy to have Martha be a part of it, and so she took the plates out of Claire's hands as she tried to clear the table, and said, 'Leave this for me. Just go have fun.'

The casino was full of crazy people. Crazy, dirty people. Claire noticed that an abnormally high percentage of people were missing a limb. They'd gone to the Taj Mahal casino partly because it was one they'd heard of and partly because in the car Cleo had said she'd heard it was beautiful there.

'Beautiful?' Claire had asked. 'I'm not sure any casino can be called beautiful, but sure, we can go to that one.'

'I've never really gambled before,' Cleo said to Claire and Martha. 'Have you guys?'

'Not a lot,' Claire said. 'We came last year, and Max gambled, even though he wasn't legal.' Claire laughed and kicked the back of the seat.

'Hey, that wasn't my idea,' Max said.

'You made Max break the law?' Cleo said. She was smiling as she looked at Claire.

'No,' Claire said. 'It was my – it was Doug. He was here last year, and he wanted Max to do it.'

'He's like the worst gambler ever, too,' Max said quickly. 'He talked about statistics the whole time and made it so boring.'

'Gambling makes me nervous,' Cleo said. 'The possibility that you can gain or lose so much in a second is scary.' No one answered her, and they drove the rest of the way in silence.

Once they walked into the casino, Martha headed straight to the slots and began feeding twenty-dollar bills into a machine called Wild Cherry. 'I'm not going to waste my money gambling on blackjack,' she said.

'Right,' Max said. 'Because slots are really the smart way to go.'

Martha pursed her lips at him and kept playing. They left her at the slot machines and went to the bar to get a drink because Cleo had wrinkled her nose at the free drinks they were passing out. Then they walked around looking at the different minimums for the tables and trying to find one they liked. When they passed Martha again, about forty-five minutes later, her eyes were glazed, and her lips were parted, with a little string of spit between them, as she pushed the button to make the slots go, and listened for the *bing, ring,* and *ding* of the cherries and sevens and big-money signs.

'I think we've created a monster,' Claire said.

'Martha,' Max said. She didn't look up right away. 'Martha,' they all called together, and she looked up, spacey and surprised.

'Have you won?' Cleo asked.

Martha shook her head. 'Not yet, but I have a good feeling about this machine.'

'Are you sure you don't want to come with us?' Claire asked. Martha shook her head.

'No, no. I'm good here,' she said, turning back to the machine.

'Okay, well, if you need us, we'll be over there, okay?' Claire pointed in the direction of the tables. Martha nodded distractedly.

'Good God,' Max said. 'We're gonna have to call Mom and Dad to drag her out of here.'

'The scary thing is, she kind of fits in,' Claire whispered to Max. It was true. Martha was wearing a large tented flowered dress, and her hair was pulled back in a messy ponytail. She looked older than thirty, and she clutched her purse on her lap while she touched the machine like she was communicating with it. On either side of her were older women, just as sloppily dressed, petting their own machines. Claire got the chills watching her.

'Well, at least if she started coming here, it would be something social she could do,' Max offered.

'Max, that's mean,' Cleo said. She looked shocked and Max muttered an apology.

'Come on,' he said, putting his arm around her. 'Let's go gamble.'

At the blackjack table, there were only two seats open, so Claire and Max sat down in the middle and Cleo stood behind them. 'I just want to watch first,' Cleo said.

The man to Max's left looked a little off and anytime someone else at the table got a good card, he pounded both hands in front of him and said, 'Sonofabitch,' all as one word. Max leaned over and squeezed Claire's shoulder and the two of them bent their heads down, trying not to laugh.

Claire watched Cleo place her hand on Max's back, just lightly, like she wasn't even thinking about it. It was almost like they were the same person, and Claire felt a sharp pain. She was jealous of her younger brother and his girlfriend. Max had a life, a love life, and she didn't. Even Heather Foley had a love life. It was like somewhere along the way, Claire had stopped being a real person.

When Cleo finally sat down, she got blackjack on her first hand. She squealed and clapped her hands again. She was very careful to place her winnings to one side, and when she was up about forty dollars, she decided to stop. 'I should quit while I'm ahead, right?' she said.

'That's very mature of you,' Claire said. She had lost eighty dollars and was trying to stop herself from going back.

'You can't win if you don't keep playing, though.' Max said. Cleo just smiled and shook her head.

They went to retrieve Martha from the slot machines, and

she printed out her slot ticket and went to get the rest of her money. 'I lost forty dollars,' she said on the way home. 'But I know if I could've kept playing, I would have won big.'

That night, as Claire tried to fall asleep, she heard the sounds of the casino in her head – cards being flipped, people cheering or groaning, and the *bing* of the slots as they rolled around and around.

Saturday at the shore was cloudy and cool, but Claire and Martha went down to the beach anyway, bundled up in sweatshirts and pants. They were leaving the next day, so they figured they would try to get as much out of the end of their trip as they could. They sat on beach chairs and watched the wind chop up the water. A storm was coming in, and the dark clouds were getting closer.

Both of the girls held books in their laps, but neither of them made a move to open them. Martha took in a deep breath and let out an audible sigh, which Claire knew was a sign that she wanted to say something.

'What?' Claire asked her.

Martha shook her head and sighed again. 'It's just watching the ocean like this, right before a storm, it makes me think of the tsunami in Thailand, and how all of those people were just minding their own business, living their lives, and the ocean just swallowed them.'

'That's what you're thinking about right now?' Claire asked.

She shouldn't have been surprised, but she still was. Claire had been thinking about how she still had to tell Weezy everything, and how maybe it was a good idea to go back to New York first and do it over the phone, because then she could just hang up right after and be done with it. Yes, that made more sense. And so she was wondering what she was thinking before, planning to tell Weezy in person, and Martha was thinking about a natural disaster that had happened six years earlier. She wasn't sure whether she should be annoyed at Martha or ashamed of herself for thinking only about her problems.

'I think our brains work differently,' Claire finally said.

'Yeah,' Martha said. 'I think they do.'

The two of them sat there for another hour, books on their laps, watching the storm crawl closer and closer, witnessing the waves getting bigger and angrier, until they felt drops hit their faces and heads, and were forced to pick up their chairs and walk back to the house in the rain.

When Claire opened the door to her apartment, she was hit with a wall of hot air. This was always how it was when she got back from a trip; the air seemed unbreathable, like no one would ever be able to survive living here. She saw the rent envelope slipped under her door and her stomach twisted. She moved it aside with her foot, dragged her suitcase inside, and went to sit on the couch.

All the years that she'd lived in New York, Claire always felt giddy when she returned after a trip. It was nice to get away, to get out of the crowded city, but she always had the sense that when she got back, she was where she belonged. But now, looking around at the dusty old apartment that she couldn't afford, she didn't feel that. She just felt dread. She didn't belong here anymore, in this apartment. And it didn't even matter if she did, because she was going to be kicked out soon anyway.

And so, she took out her cell phone and called Weezy, who was still at the shore. There was no time like the present, especially if you were totally out of options.

Part Two

Chapter 6

When you live in a house your whole life, you know all of its noises. You know that two short buzzes is the end of the dryer cycle, that one short buzz is the back doorbell. You know that when the furnace kicks up, it starts with a clank, waits about thirty seconds, and then you hear the air coming out of the vents. You know every corner and twist in the house, that it takes sixteen steps to get up the stairs, three large leaps to get down the hall. You could find your way around the whole place blindfolded if you had to.

Claire loved this about going home – loved that she knew every corner, that everything was familiar, that the house would creak and groan her to sleep. But this time, the noises were not comforting. Each squeak of the floor made her want to cover her ears. She could hear her father breathing heavily as he walked down the hallway (was he that out of shape?), could hear her mom humming as she made coffee, could hear Martha in her room, thumping her feet against the headboard as she always did when she read, so that it bumped against the wall, over and over, until Claire was sure she was going to scream.

This reaction shouldn't have surprised her, but somehow it still did. Moving home wasn't exactly what she wanted; it was just the only possible way out of her mess. When she'd finally gotten the courage to call Weezy, she didn't waste any time. As soon as Weezy answered, she said, 'I'm having money issues.'

She had sounded like a polite older woman who didn't want to give the specifics of her financials, who thought that talking about money was rude. But at least it was out there. It had taken almost an hour for Claire to fully explain the situation, to really make it clear that she was in trouble. And still, when she'd said, 'I think I have to move home for a while,' Weezy was surprised.

Once things got moving, they happened quickly. Claire gave her landlord notice and said she'd be using her security deposit as her last month's rent. It was unclear if this was legal or not — everyone had a different opinion — but it didn't matter. If they were going to come after her, let them. She just needed to get out of this city. She figured she wasn't even staying the whole month of September, so maybe they'd look the other way.

At work, they weren't all that surprised. Amy had nodded like she'd seen it coming. 'Sometimes you just need a change of scenery,' she'd said. Claire had agreed and quickly left the office.

Becca and Molly were surprised, but not sorry. They wished her luck and said they'd miss her, but didn't sound very convincing.

On her last day, they all stood around and ate cupcakes, as was the tradition, and they all said things like, 'Enjoy those cheese steaks' and 'Bet you won't miss the crowded subways in the morning!' At the end of the day, Claire wasn't the least bit sorry to leave the office and never go back.

Her apartment was packed up easily, partly because it was still almost empty from when Doug left, and partly because she sold what little was left of the furniture on craigslist. She didn't want to pay for storage and didn't want a bed – or anything else – that she and Doug had shared. She was happy to open her door to strangers, let them come in and give her cash, and watch them leave carrying her possessions.

Martha had warned her to have someone else in the apartment with her and to leave the door open while the buyers entered. 'You should also alert your doorman to the situation. Make sure he knows why they're coming to see you.'

'Why?' Claire asked.

'Claire. Come on. People looking to murder innocent people use craigslist all the time.'

'Right,' Claire said. 'I'll be careful.'

There was no good-bye party, no send-off with her friends like they'd done for everyone else. 'I'm not really leaving,' she kept telling everyone. 'I'm just figuring stuff out.' Her friends nodded like they didn't quite believe her and hugged her like she was never coming back.

It shocked her, really, how quickly it had all been done, how fast she'd ended up back home and sleeping in her bed. For the first few days, she felt relief. Her debt was still with her, but at least she could stop worrying that she was about to get evicted. The worst was over, and she started to make a plan, set up an interview with a temp agency, and unpacked her bags. Then on the fourth day, she'd woken up and listened to all the noise around her. And that was when the panic had started to set in.

Her bedroom still had faded stuffed animals on the shelves, collages of old high school friends that she hadn't seen in years, plastic glow-in-the-dark stars on the ceiling (why had she thought that was so cool?), and a poster of Dave Matthews on the back of the door. It was like moving right back to high school. Nothing had changed.

There was a point each morning (and this had been happening since the breakup) when Claire first woke up and didn't remember what had happened. It was about a thirty-second window, give or take, when her mind was free of everything, when she didn't think about the wedding being called off, about Doug moving out, about her mounting credit card debt, about moving home. It wasn't that she forgot exactly – it was just that her mind didn't remember right away, and for those seconds she felt normal. And then it all came rushing back in, her head filled up with the events of the past year, and she was embarrassed and horrified all over again, like it had all just occurred. She'd lie there as it happened, roll over so that her face was in her pillow, and start thinking about how she was going to undo everything, how she was going to go about fixing the mess that was her life.

At night, she would look at the stupid plastic stars and think, *What the hell was I thinking?* She let the thought run through her head over and over. She let herself repeat it, stressing different words each time — *What the hell was I thinking? What the hell was I thinking? What the hell was I thinking?*

Even the dog seemed confused by the situation. Ruby walked around at night, poking her head into each room to make sure all of the family members were there. She'd go to look in Max's room, staring at the bed as if she just wanted to make sure that he *wasn't* there. When she came to Claire's door, she'd perk up, her ears springing alive, and she'd wag her tail and come to greet her. But Ruby seemed overwhelmed by this change, and she'd sometimes tilt her head at Claire before leaving the room, sighing as she walked away to continue her inspection.

Claire's first night home, Weezy made a special dinner and they all toasted, 'Welcome back,' like Claire's return was something to be celebrated, like it wasn't a total failing of her attempt to live as a successful adult.

At the temp office, Claire took a typing test and a computer proficiency test. The woman kept looking up at Claire and then back down at the résumé like it was going to answer the question of why Claire was here in the first place.

'Now, why did you leave your last job again?' she asked.

'I'm looking for a change and I thought it would be easier to figure out what I wanted to do if I took some time off and moved back home for a little while.' Claire had said this exact sentence to her about four times now. She was pretty sure the woman thought she was lying.

'Well, we shouldn't have any trouble placing you. There's a spot I'm thinking about that's just a three-month placement.'

'That would be great. I'm not looking for a permanent job.'

'Right.' The woman nodded. She looked again like she didn't believe Claire. 'Well, I think it would be a great fit. It starts in a week or two, and I can get you in there to meet them tomorrow if that works?'

Claire nodded. They set up the appointment and shook hands. Then Claire went back home, took off her skirt and jacket, put on pajama pants, and got back into bed.

Weezy was trying to be helpful, but it was getting on Claire's nerves. Which of course made her feel awful, since Weezy had been so nice about everything, had accepted Claire back home like it was no big deal. But still, every time Weezy asked about her plans or asked her how she was feeling, Claire thought she was going to lose it.

The morning that Claire was scheduled to meet with the office, she and Weezy sat at the kitchen table drinking coffee together in their pajamas.

'Are you nervous?' Weezy asked.

'No.'

'Not even a little?'

'No. It's not a real job. It's just a temp job.'

'Still,' Weezy said. 'It can be scary to interview.'

'I guess.'

'You know,' Weezy said, 'there are so many kids your age that have moved back home. Remember Mark Crowley? You went to first grade with him, but then he transferred to the public schools because he had all those learning problems? Well, anyway, I saw his mother in the grocery store last week and she told me that he'd lost his job in New York and moved home. Just like you.'

'I didn't lose my job,' Claire said.

'Well, you don't have one. You know what I mean,' Weezy said. Claire was sitting in her pajamas at ten thirty on a Tuesday morning, drinking coffee with her mom. Yes, it was pretty clear that she didn't have a job.

'I'm just saying,' Weezy continued, 'that it's an epidemic, a trend. It's the economy, of course, but still it's interesting, isn't it? All these adult children returning home again? Moving back in with their parents? It says something about this generation, I think. And our generation for welcoming you back.' Weezy looked off into the distance, thoughtful with this new revelation.

'You sound like Dad,' Claire said.

Weezy leaned forward in her chair and looked out the window at the house across the street. 'For a while, I thought the younger Connors girl was living at home, but now I think she just stays there sometimes. I think she brings things to her parents, their groceries and all of that.'

'Hilary?' Claire asked. 'Hilary still lives around here?'

Hilary and Sarah Connors had grown up across the street. They'd never been friends, but they knew each other and played with each other sometimes out of convenience. When Sarah went to college, she started dating this boy and eventually dropped out. There were rumors that he was a drug dealer, but no one really knew what was happening. Then Sarah and her boyfriend went on a crime spree through a neighboring suburb, shooting a gas station clerk and robbing seven different people, before the two of them holed up in an old hardware store that had closed down. The police surrounded them, until they heard a gunshot and then they stormed in to find that Sarah had shot her boyfriend in the head. It made national news, and reporters and police cars were outside of the Connors' house for months.

'I can't believe they still live there,' Claire said. She looked out at the house, a normal two-story brick house with yellow awnings. It looked dark and quiet.

'It's their home,' Weezy said. 'They shouldn't feel like they have to run away.'

'I would. I would leave the town, leave the whole state, probably go all the way across the country. I'd go somewhere where people didn't recognize my name and my face. Wouldn't you?'

'Maybe.'

'It has to be so miserable there. To stay in that house with all of those memories.'

'Maybe they remember the good things that happened there.'

'Would that really be what you remember?'

'Some people don't have the tools to start over when something like that happens,' Weezy said. 'Some people could, but other people – they just stop, and stay where they are and that's that.'

'Sarah was always weird,' Claire said. It was the first thing that she and Martha had agreed on after the strange and tragic day happened. 'She was always a little off,' Martha had said. Sarah had been a year ahead of Martha in school, and Hilary was a year younger than Claire. There was one picture of the four girls playing in the backyard one summer, all in bathing suits, laughing and running through the sprinkler. Claire couldn't remember it.

'It was the drugs,' Weezy said. 'She got mixed up with the wrong people.' They'd had this exact conversation dozens of times since the whole thing had happened, but somehow it never got old.

'I guess,' Claire said. 'Poor Hilary.' She imagined the girl grocery shopping, lugging bags over to the house that her parents didn't leave. How creepy.

Sarah had once stolen a toy of Claire's, a little plastic Care Bear that had been a Valentine's Day present. Claire had asked Weezy if she could take it to school to show her friends, and Weezy said no, so Claire snuck it in her backpack in the morning. That night, when she realized that she'd forgotten it in her desk, she started to cry.

The next morning, Weezy walked into the classroom with her, assuring her that it would still be there, but it wasn't. That day, on the playground, Sarah Connors had a little blue bear in her hand.

'That's mine,' Claire yelled. She told the teachers, but no one could prove that Sarah had walked through the classroom and stolen the bear. She told Weezy that night, but there was nothing to be done.

'I told you not to take it to school,' Weezy said, as Claire cried. She was firm on this point, although when Claire woke up that Saturday, there was a new little blue bear on her nightstand.

But it wasn't the same. Claire wanted the original bear, the one that had been taken. She hated the thought of it's being at the Connors house, which was dirty and smelled like mothballs. 'Your sister stole my bear,' she said to Hilary once. Hilary just shrugged and looked embarrassed. You couldn't blame her, Claire knew. She couldn't pick who her sister was.

Claire put on the same outfit that she'd worn to the temp interview and drove to the office of Proof Perfect, where she was set to meet the woman she'd be filling in for and a few others.

Amanda Liebman met her at the elevator, looking like she was about to give birth right there in the front lobby. She had both of her hands on her back, and was red in the face. 'Claire?' she asked. Claire nodded and Amanda puffed a little as she turned and motioned for Claire to follow.

Amanda sat at a desk at the front of the office. Behind her, on the wall, hung letters that spelled out proof perfect. There was a hallway to the right and left, but all the offices that Claire saw had their doors closed. Once they were seated at her desk, Amanda seemed a little calmer. 'I'm carrying around so much extra weight at this point that even standing feels impossible.'

Claire nodded again. 'When are you due?'

'In two weeks, but I want to keep working up until the very end so that I can take all of my time with the baby. I've already saved up all my vacation and personal and sick days, which wasn't easy, so I don't want to waste it now just lying around and waiting.'

'Right.'

'So, my title is Office Manager and Senior Executive Assistant. Basically, that means that I answer the phones, and then do whatever the account managers want me to do, or don't want to do for themselves. It's a lot of Xeroxing and other random stuff. All the higher-up people have their own assistants, so you don't have to worry about them.'

'Okay.'

'Some of the managers are a pain in the ass, but it's not rocket science, so you'll be fine.'

Amanda went on to show her the phones.

'So, will they let me know if I get the job?'

'Oh, you got it.'

'Really?'

'Yeah. Everyone else that comes in here wants a permanent

job. They're hoping to get placed here after this job is done. You're the only one that wants it for what it is. So, congratulations, it's yours.'

'Great,' Claire said. She wasn't sure that it was.

Amanda started to get up to walk her to the elevator, but Claire told her she could get there on her own. She was just walking out into the lobby when Amanda called her name.

'One more thing,' she said. She stuck out her foot from behind the desk. 'The dress code says no sandals, but my feet are too fat to wear any of my shoes right now, so fuck it. But if you come in wearing sandals, they'll go ape shit.'

'Got it. Thanks.'

Claire went over to Lainie's that night to drink wine. It was still pretty warm out, even at the end of September, and the two of them sat on chairs on the porch, a bottle of wine between them. Brian was inside on the couch, asleep with his mouth open and the TV on.

She couldn't get over the fact that Lainie lived with her husband and three children in a house that was down the street from where Claire grew up. How had this happened? Lainie became more adult every day, and Claire was back sleeping in her childhood bedroom.

'So you got a job already,' Lainie said. 'That's good news.' She held up her glass and Claire clinked it, then the two of them drank.

'I guess so. The thing is I don't start until this lady has her baby. It could be tomorrow or it could be in three weeks, which sort of sucks.'

'Then just relax. You've been not working for like a week. You should sleep in and enjoy yourself.'

'I can't. At least not in that house. I just feel like I should be doing something, not sitting around all day with my parents and Martha. It's driving me crazy.'

'Really? It sounds amazing. You can do whatever you want.' Lainie had grown up in the middle of five sisters, who shared everything from underwear to makeup. She'd never had her own room, and Claire was pretty sure she'd never want to.

'It's not. It's just really boring. All I want is to not stay there all day.'

Lainie looked sideways at her. 'Do you want to babysit?'

'For you?'

'Yeah, for me. Our nanny's mom is sick and she's going home for a couple of weeks. I was going to ask Kristen to do it, and then get my mom and Brian's mom to fill in, but if you're really looking for something to do, that would be awesome. It's just for the mornings, mostly, and some early afternoons.'

'Sure,' Claire said. 'Why not?' She hadn't babysat in years.

'Great,' Lainie said. She smiled and sat back like she'd figured everything out. 'Plus I'll give you free classes at the studio.'

'You already do that.'

'Yeah, but now you'll really earn it.'

*

Claire had forgotten how boring babysitting actually was. She'd blocked out the way that when a four-year-old is building a tower out of blocks, sometimes all you can do is keep looking at the clock, sure it's standing still or maybe even going backward. Babysitting could be so quiet, so devoid of conversation, and just when she thought she'd go crazy, it became loud, a fever pitch of whines and screams and toys hitting the floor.

Claire remembered babysitting for Bobby Foley once, the summer he was obsessed with Pokemon, and they'd been sitting on the floor in his bedroom playing. He started showing her all the Pokemon cards that he had, explaining to her the difference between the characters, how some could fly and some could run fast, and she'd been nodding and then just lay down on the floor while he went on, seriously, ranking his favorites, telling her what who would win in a fight.

She'd murmured, 'Mmm-hmm' every once in a while, closed her eyes for just a second, and then woke up twenty minutes later when the door downstairs slammed shut. Bobby was still next to her, babbling on, and she didn't even think he noticed that she'd been sleeping. Claire had shot straight up and wiped the drool off her face, her heart pounding as she tried to look awake before Mrs. Foley came in the room.

She'd been horrified after that, felt like the world's most irresponsible babysitter. And now she was babysitting again, spending her days with three little boys, who seemed just as bored with her as she was with them, glancing at her every once in a while to see if she was still there. Tucker screamed every time Lainie left, and then spent the rest of the time wandering his pudgy baby body around the house, picking up anything that wasn't nailed down — shoes, the remote control, cell phones, coasters — and rearranging all of it. Every once in a while he'd stop to stare at Claire, trying to figure out if she was responsible for the absence of his mother.

Jack didn't seem to be taking to the situation any better. He was a judgmental child and always had been. When he was a baby, he'd look around the room at everyone, his mouth turned down, his dark eyes taking everything in. Lainie had taken Jack everywhere with her, to bars or friends' houses, where they would put him to sleep in a bed, with jackets stuffed on either side of him so he wouldn't roll off. He'd stare at them while they drank wine, his little baby lips pursing and un-pursing as he listened to them talk. Now, when Claire arrived, he gave her the same look, as though he couldn't quite figure out what she was doing at his house. She wanted to tell him that she didn't know what she was doing there either.

Each morning when Claire arrived, the boys were half-naked — sometimes in just a diaper, sometimes wearing a shirt, or one sock, or a pair of pants. Lainie was always rushing around no matter what time it was, pausing to put an item of clothing on one of the boys, or stopping to smell their butts to see if they needed a new diaper. Claire would stand in the corner and watch as Lainie raced around and finally ran out the door. It made her tired just to watch.

The third morning she was there, Claire poured Jack some

cereal and leaned against the counter to watch him eat. Jack took a bite and then looked up at her. 'This milk tastes spicy,' he said.

'It tastes spicy?' Claire asked and Jack nodded. Claire picked up the carton and sniffed it, and a thick, sour smell hit her nose right away. She gagged twice and ran over to the sink, sure she was going to throw up.

'What's wrong?' Jack asked.

'Nothing,' Claire said. 'Don't eat that, okay? The milk is bad.' She took the bowl from him and poured it down the sink, holding her breath as she washed the little O-shaped pieces of cereal down the disposal. She went to the refrigerator and looked at the options. 'Do you want some toast?'

'Are you having a baby?' Jack asked.

'What? No.'

Jack shrugged. 'That's what my mom does when she's having a baby,' he said.

'Right,' Claire said. 'It was just that the milk made me feel sick.'

'Milk is good for you,' Jack said.

'You're right, it is.'

'Do you have any babies?'

'Nope. No babies.'

'Who is your mom?'

'My mom is Weezy. You know her, she lives down the street. And you know my dad, Will, and my sister, Martha. And you've even met my brother, Max.'

'Weezy is your mom?' Jack asked. He looked like he didn't believe her for a second.

'Yep.'

'Do you live with her?'

'I do now. I was living somewhere else, but I moved back.'

'I'm never leaving my mom,' Jack said.

'Okay,' Claire said.

'I don't think Weezy is your mom,' Jack said. 'Because we see her when we go to the playground sometimes.'

'Okay,' Claire said. 'Whatever you say.'

'What?'

'Nothing.'

Claire was exhausted by these conversations. Exhausted from sitting around and watching Jack and Tucker play. The one thing she did like about babysitting was holding Matthew. He was at a great age – small enough that he was nothing but a bundle of baby, but big enough that she wasn't afraid she was going to break him.

She liked holding him while the other two boys napped, feeling his solid little weight in her arms. He was totally relaxed, his mouth slightly open, and every once in a while his chin would quiver, and he'd sigh. Claire was jealous of him while he slept, and hoped that if she held that warm little body, some of his calmness would rub off on her.

Sometimes after Lainie would get home, Claire would just end up staying at the house for a little while. It was so much easier to be there than to be at her own house. She'd watch as Lainie and Brian came back from work and still never stopped moving, making the boys dinner and getting them ready for bed. Claire at least liked the feeling of being able to sit and watch, knowing she wasn't responsible for any of it.

It also amazed her how easily Lainie had become a mother. When she was first pregnant with Jack, Claire couldn't believe it. But then Lainie had the baby, and she walked around with Jack popped out on her hip, like he'd always been there. Then she had the next two, and she was a mother of three. There was no adjustment period, she just did it. How had it been so easy for her? Claire had barely gotten to the first step of creating that life and it had all fallen apart.

'We're going to have a party,' Lainie said one night. She was walking around the room, gathering all of the toys and shoes and socks that had been thrown around during the day. She picked it all up in her arms and then dumped it in the bin in the corner of the room.

Lainie loved having parties and used any excuse to do so. Claire suspected that she loved having everyone come to her, but no one minded because Lainie always threw a good party.

'Yeah, doesn't that seem like a good idea?' Brian asked Claire. 'Lainie just put a banana peel into the toy box and she wants to have a hundred people over here this weekend.'

'I didn't put a — oh, wait. Yes, I did,' Lainie said as she pulled a banana peel out from the toys. 'Why didn't you tell me? Anyway, it's not going to be a hundred people.' She turned to roll her eyes and shake her head at Brian. 'Just a party for fall, one last time to barbecue before it's too cold. Plus, Claire's back, so we should celebrate that. We have to have a party.'

'Sounds like fun,' Claire said. It was her last day babysitting for the boys. The nanny had returned earlier in the week and was coming back to work. ('Thank God,' Brian had said. 'I had this feeling she was never coming back to the country.') Claire would be starting work soon anyway. Amanda had called to tell her that if she didn't go into labor this week, they'd be inducing her on Monday.

'Do you want to come take a class tomorrow?' Lainie asked. She was always trying to get Claire to the studio, trying to convert her to the world of Pilates. But Claire was hesitant – the machines frightened her. Still, she agreed since she had nothing else to do.

At the Pilates studio, Lainie was treated like a celebrity. She introduced all the women to Claire as though they were her close friends. 'This is Barbara and this is Joanie. I'm so glad you are getting a chance to meet!' She acted like these middle-aged women with fallen stomachs and wiggly arms were the same age she was, just a bunch of gal pals getting ready to work out together.

Lainie had started taking Pilates right after Jack was born, and the teacher was so impressed with her that she suggested she do the teacher training. 'But you've been going to the classes for like two months,' Claire remembered saying to her.

'I know, it's crazy,' was Lainie's response.

And it was crazy, how Lainie stumbled onto this career. She'd never done well in school, which Claire thought was mostly because she never wanted to sit down long enough to study or do homework. She rushed through everything, scribbling down answers to tests, knowing that they were probably wrong. It was like she was just trying to get on to the next thing. She was never bothered by her grades; she'd just look at her B's and C's and nod, like *Yep, that's about what I expected*.

But at the studio, Lainie excelled. She quickly became one of the most popular teachers there. Her classes were always full, and they kept adding more to her schedule. One day, a student of hers approached her and asked if she'd ever thought about starting her own studio. 'I'd back you,' the woman said. 'I'll be an investor. I know you'd be wildly successful.'

And she had been. Lainie always called that woman her Fairy Godmother, which seemed perfect to Claire, because at least then Lainie was acknowledging that she was living in a fairy tale. Two years later, a large portion of the studio's mortgage had been paid off, Lainie had hired three other teachers, and the place was thriving.

Claire was always amazed when she went to the studio. Amazed at the way these women flocked there, not for Pilates, but for Lainie. They seemed to think that if they remained devoted, they would one day turn into her. There were loads of women in their thirties who had just had children and believed that Lainie could save them, could get them back to the body they used to have. They'd look at her and think, *Well, she's had three children, and look at her. All I need to do is some Pilates!* They were Lainie's disciples, her faithful following. They believed.

Claire wanted to pull these women aside and whisper to them, leaning in close to say, 'Look, I know you think you can have a stomach like that if you take these classes that if you do enough Pilates, your arms will look just like hers. But they won't be. She always looked like that, even before she ever started this, when she never exercised and ate fast food all the time. It's not real.'

It was like when you were younger and believed that it was just a matter of time before you would become a gymnastics gold medalist, or a Broadway star. But then you got to a certain age, and you realized that the gymnasts at the Olympics were all younger than you, and that you couldn't sing either; and just like that your visions of being a balance beam superstar or playing Annie onstage were gone.

Claire's friend Allison, who was extremely flat-chested, once confessed that she'd believed for years that her breasts would grow. 'In high school, I just thought I was a late bloomer,' she said. 'In college, I just figured it would happen later for me. And now, I'm twenty-nine and I think it's time to admit that this is it. I'm never going to have boobs.'

People couldn't help but hope for what they wanted to become – even if it meant deluding themselves. And so Claire felt bad as she watched the parade of women that marched into Lainie's Wednesday afternoon mat class, their bodies wrapped in expensive, cute spandex outfits, their hair pulled back in ponytails. Claire set herself up in the back corner, and as the class went on, as they all struggled through the exercises, she felt nothing but pity for these sweating women, who lay on their backs and sent their arms flying around, believing that they would be different soon.

That Saturday, Claire walked over to Lainie's to help her get ready for the party. Jack was on the sidewalk, drawing what looked like a monster with chalk, and when he saw her he stood up and said, 'My mom's not going to work today.'

'I know,' Claire said. 'I'm here for the party.'

'The party didn't start yet.'

'I know. I'm here to help. Plus, remember Silvia's back. I'm not even babysitting you anymore.'

Jack looked at her, like he was trying to figure out if she was lying, if she was really there to babysit him again and just trying to trick him. Finally he nodded at her and went back to his drawing, and Claire walked into the house.

Lainie had invited a random group of people to the barbecue. There were some old friends from high school, her older sisters and their husbands and kids, her younger sisters and their boyfriends, some people that Brian worked with, some women that worked at the studio. Claire was enjoying this randomness, and was talking to a woman named Susan about New York, when the front door opened and Fran Angelo walked in wearing a Phillies T-shirt with a hole in the collar, and an old, faded Eagles hat, like he was an ad for Philly sports fans.

Fran was a friend of Brian's in high school, but she hadn't seen him in years. Probably not since she moved to New York. Was it possible that it was that long? She was trying to figure it out, thinking that he actually didn't look all that different – a little older, sure, and maybe worn down, but no, not that different – when he took his hat off, pushed his hair back and then replaced it, and Claire realized that she was staring and looked away.

He had been a handsome teenager – the kind of boy everyone was in love with. His full name was Frances John Callaghan, and it said a lot that he was never, not once, teased for having a girl's name. All through high school, Fran had dip in his mouth and a bored look on his face. He was tall, well over six feet, and had dark brown hair that was just long enough to tuck behind his ears.

Susan was still talking, but Claire had lost track of their conversation, and nodded energetically to make up for it. She was no longer staring right at Fran, but was tracking his movements from the corner of her eye, and watched him walk through the front hall and out the door to the backyard. Claire excused herself from Susan, and went upstairs to use the bathroom. She closed the door behind her and let out a breath that she'd been holding. She shook her head, telling herself that she was being really pathetic acting like this, getting all nervous just seeing a boy she used to like about a million years ago.

Claire and Fran had made out just once, during a party at their friend Brad's house. She never really knew why Fran decided to pursue her that night. Maybe he knew that she had a crush on him, maybe she was the only girl there that hadn't fooled around with him yet, or maybe he just didn't feel like trying very hard. Whatever the reason, as soon as she got to the party that night, he'd called her name and waved her over to the couch where he was sitting, then pulled her down onto his lap. He put his arm around her waist, and used his other hand to hold the can he was spitting his dip into. Claire tried to suck in her stomach, tried to make herself lighter so that she wasn't putting all of her weight on him, which just resulted in her body's being completely stiff.

'Relax, babe,' he'd said.

They sat like that for a while, and Claire drank a beer, wishing to be drunk so she wouldn't have to track every movement that she made, be aware of every single breath. They didn't talk much, although she kept bringing up different topics, like where Brad's parents were, and how he'd moved all the breakable things upstairs. Fran seemed bored, she remembered, just watching everyone at the party like he was waiting for something good to happen. That was the main difference between them, really. Claire was always excited to be at a party, and if it turned out to be fun, that was just a bonus. There was always the promise of a great night, always the chance that something good could happen, and so she was often visibly enthusiastic. Fran, on the other hand, looked like he'd done this a million times before, like high school was so boring to him he couldn't even stand it, and like he had very little hope that anything truly exciting would happen.

Finally that night, Fran had squeezed her leg and said, 'Come on.' They stood up and he led her out of the room and up the stairs, like he knew just where to go. Claire let herself follow behind him, holding his hand, and thinking, *This is really happening right now.*

His mouth tasted like cinnamon gum and tobacco, and she kept rubbing her hands on his face and through his hair. They basically just kissed — well, and she took her shirt off, which she confessed only to Lainie — and when the whole thing was over, Claire wondered if it had really happened.

The events of that night just made her crush grow, and for the rest of high school she liked him so much that she found it nearly impossible to talk to him or be around him without losing her breath or having her heart beat so loudly that she thought people could see it through her shirt. He also made her sweat, which was the most unfortunate part, although it didn't really matter, because he never seemed interested in her again.

Claire waited all through high school for something more to happen, or at least for someone to mention it to her. She thought maybe Brian would tease her about it, but he didn't, which seemed like a bad sign since she figured that maybe Fran had said something bad about her and Brian didn't want to get involved. Claire would have almost thought she'd made the whole thing up, until the end of senior year, when Brad told her that Fran had made a list of every girl he hooked up with in high school and had given them all grades. 'You got a B-minus,' he told her. And Claire felt relieved, of all things, so happy that she was above average, that she hadn't failed or done anything ridiculous that would have earned her a bad grade.

Claire washed her hands in the bathroom and talked to herself in her head. It was ridiculous, all of it. First of all, where did he get off grading girls? And second, how disgusting was it that she was happy about the grade? She dried her hands on the towel and walked back downstairs and into the kitchen, where Lainie was peeking in the oven.

'Fran Angelo is here,' Claire said. She said it quietly and looked around to make sure no one could hear her.

'Oh, good,' Lainie said. She leaned down and pulled out a tray of mini hot dogs wrapped in dough. 'Brian thought it was dumb to make pigs in a blanket, since we have hot dogs for the grill too, but I told him he was crazy.'

'You never told me he was coming,' Claire said. She watched Lainie poke at the little hot dogs and start taking them off the cookie sheet with a spatula.

'So? What's the big deal?'

'Nothing. I just haven't seen him in forever.'

'Oh, yeah. Well, Brian's been seeing a lot of him lately.'

'Really?'

'Yeah. And anyway, I thought you'd be happy to see him. You were the one that was obsessed with him.'

'Lainie, shhh. I wasn't obsessed with him. I just, you know.'

'Yes, I do know. You were obsessed with him.' Lainie smiled and popped a hot dog in her mouth.

'Shut up. Anyway, he was such a jerk.'

'No, he wasn't.'

'Yes, he was. Remember he graded me? He graded everyone?'

'Oh my God, Claire. That was like a million years ago.'

'Still.'

Claire found it fascinating how Lainie could distance herself so much from high school when she was married to her high school boyfriend. Did she really not care about any of that stuff? Because Claire felt each memory freshly, like it had happened just the week before, like it was still happening twelve years later.

'You know . . .' Lainie said. Now she was the one to look around and lower her voice. 'He was engaged to this girl, Liz. She broke it off a couple of months ago and now he's living back at his parents' house.'

Lainie finished arranging the hot dogs on a tray and filled some little dishes with ketchup and mustard. 'Are you coming?' she asked.

'I'll be right out,' Claire said. She poured herself a glass of water and drank it down all at once. So she was in the same position as Fran Angelo. She'd gone to a good college, and he'd gone to some random small state school. She'd moved to New

York and gotten a good job, and then what did you know? None of it mattered. She and Fran Angelo were basically living parallel lives, tied in the exact same place in their lives. Well, wasn't that just a pickle?

Claire wasn't at all surprised to learn that Fran Angelo still made her sweat. She walked outside and waved to him from across the lawn, and he smiled and waved back, so she walked over to him. They stood for a while, each of them holding a bottle of beer, and then they moved over to some lawn chairs that were a little bit out of the center of the party, and conveniently located next to the cooler. Claire watched as the table next to them filled up with their empty beer bottles, two at a time.

Maybe it was because she knew Fran's situation, or maybe it was because she was getting drunk in the afternoon, but Claire felt free to share. It didn't take long before she was telling Fran about Doug and the apartment and moving home. He'd nodded and then told his story. And before long, the two of them were deep in conversation, cutting each other off to tell the details of their own broken engagement.

'She kept the ring,' Fran told her. When he said this, it almost felt like he was sharing too much, but Claire didn't care. She was fascinated.

'Did you ask for it back?' Claire asked.

'No,' Fran said. 'That would've been a dick move. But she should have given it back anyway, you know?'

'I wonder why she wanted it.'

'Because she's a bitch.' Fran was drunk now, and honest and angry, and Claire didn't judge him one bit for it. They sat together and drank more beer, watching the party from the sidelines as it got dark outside, their own little angry team.

After everyone left, Claire sat on the porch with Lainie and Brian, having a glass of wine and discussing Fran and the whole situation. Brian called Fran's fiancée a bitch, and Lainie interrupted.

'You can't just call her that because she broke up with him, like that's the end of it. There's a whole other huge part to the story.' Lainie's teeth and lips were a little purple and she was speaking loudly.

'What am I leaving out?' Brian asked. He leaned back in his chair and lit a cigarette.

'Well, first of all, you know I love Fran and I'm on his side, but it's not like he was the best boyfriend. He went out all the time.'

'Going out isn't a reason to break up with someone.'

'Brian, come on. She told me once that he sometimes didn't come home, and yeah, maybe he just got drunk somewhere and passed out, but maybe not. Who knows where he was? I'm not so sure he didn't cheat on her.'

'What makes you think that?' Brian asked.

'Are you serious? Remember last Fourth of July? We were

at the parade and then we went out with them after, and he was with that random girl at the bar?'

'So? Sometimes guys talk to girls in a bar. It doesn't mean they're cheating.'

'He was sitting there with his hand on her thigh. I'm just saying, you don't sit there and put your hand on some other girl's thigh, do you?'

'No, Lainie. I don't. And I wouldn't. But he did, and we don't know what else happened. Maybe nothing.'

'Claire, wouldn't that piss you off?' Lainie asked. 'Wouldn't that be totally out of line if someone you were engaged to did that?'

'Yeah,' Claire said. 'I mean, I guess so.'

Lainie nodded and sat back in her chair and took a sip of wine. She looked satisfied that she had finally convinced them of something.

That night, Claire had trouble sleeping. She was a little drunk, and had been out in the sun and eaten too many little hot dogs and received too much disturbing information. The hot dogs and stories were swimming around in her head and threatening to make her sick.

The year she was in third grade, she had developed insomnia for no apparent reason. She would just lie awake at night, wondering and worrying why she couldn't sleep. She'd read sometimes, and made her way through the Baby-Sitters Club books, one right after the other. 'Don't worry about sleeping,' Weezy always used to tell her. 'Just lay there. Resting is just as good as sleeping.' The problem went away one day, just as quickly as it had appeared, but whenever Claire couldn't sleep she always thought of Weezy's advice: 'Resting is just as good as sleeping.' (Which was total bullshit, by the way.)

Figuring she was less likely to get sick if she was sitting up, Claire finally got up from her bed and started looking through her dresser drawers. They were all still stuffed full of random things – a couple of the old Baby-Sitters Club books, collages made from magazines, notes from Lainie, a couple of games of MASH, and tons of those fortune-teller things, made by folding paper and filling them with predictions from the future.

It was around sixth grade when she and Lainie became obsessed with telling the future. They played games to find out what their professions would be, used a Magic 8 Ball, a Ouija board, whatever they could find. They never pulled a top off of a Coke can or the stem off an apple without believing that it would tell them the initial of their future husbands. Even now, sometimes, Claire would find herself twisting an apple stem around, silently saying the alphabet, waiting for the letter when it would fall off. It was funny to think of it now, the way they thought these things would just happen to them. You'll be a Lawyer and Live in a Mansion and marry Michael Kelly! When did they start realizing that there was more to it than that?

Farther down in the drawer, Claire found a couple of mix tapes with titles like *Claire's Driving Songs* and *Spring Fling Mix.*

She wondered briefly what high school kids did these days instead of making mix tapes for each other. Did they trade playlists on their iPods? That seemed so boring and sad. They'd have nothing to show for their years in high school.

Claire sorted through all this stuff, and she thought about Fran and his ex-fiancée's ring. She'd given her own ring back to Doug when things were final, handed it over to him and said, 'Here,' like she was giving him a pen that he'd asked for. He didn't insist that she keep it, and at the time she wasn't sorry to see it go.

But now, she kind of wished that she'd kept it, just so she could hold the ugly thing between her fingers and know that she hadn't made the whole thing up, that it had actually happened. She had all this shit in her room, all these pieces of paper with sixth-grade fortunes written on them, all these tapes in their plastic cases that were proof that her life had happened. But for Doug? For Doug she didn't really have anything. Not even a stupid, dull ring.

Chapter 7

Martha resigned from J.Crew the week she
got back from the shore. 'I am giving my
notice,' she announced to the staff that day. 'I want
you all to know that this is a personal decision and
has nothing to do with my relationships with each
of you. I have loved our time together, but it's time
to make a change.'

One girl, who had just started the week before,
kept looking around at everyone as though they
could explain just what was going on. Martha
thought somebody should tell her that it was rude
to keep swiveling your head around during a
speech.

'I'll miss you all,' Martha continued. 'But not
as much as I'm going to miss my discount.' She
had practiced that line in front of the mirror the
night before, and was expecting a big laugh, but

there were just a few chuckles. Her speech was wasted on these people. She wrapped it up and sent them back to work.

'I really am going to miss some things,' Martha said to the other manager, Wally. They were going over the schedule, moving things around so that in two weeks, when Martha was gone, they wouldn't be shorthanded. 'I wasn't just saying that. I'll miss when the new shipments come in, the excitement of opening the boxes and seeing the new things. It's like Christmas, sort of.'

'Sweetheart, I say go and don't look back. Live a life without these plaid skirts and ruffled tops. You'll be free!'

Once, Martha had gone out for margaritas with Wally and his boyfriend, Anthony. Anthony had called J.Crew a 'preppy hell,' and Martha had been beyond insulted. She'd thought that Wally would be too, but he just laughed and so she tried not to show how hurt she was, since she liked Anthony and he was generally very pleasant.

'You're right,' Martha said. She deleted her name from the schedule and felt a little thrill. One second it was there and the next it was blank. 'You are so right.'

Aunt Maureen's friend Linda, who ran the caretaker business, had been thrilled to hear from Martha. 'You're perfect,' she kept saying during the interview. 'You're just the kind of person we look for.'

Martha was flattered. Linda explained how their client

base was 'wealthy and sometimes high profile.' She whispered this sentence, as though someone were spying on them. These people wanted a higher-level caretaker than was usually offered, and it took the right kind of person to fill that job.

At dinner that night, Martha told her family all about the company. 'It sounds pretty amazing,' she said. 'Which is good, because it's going to be a long trek back to nursing.' She sighed and put her fork down.

'One step at a time,' Weezy said. 'You'll get there.'

Martha was sent on an interview on the Main Line in Villanova, which was almost forty minutes away. Linda explained that this was a new client, a family that needed someone to stay with their father on the weekdays. 'It can be tricky to navigate a new client,' she said. 'Often the patient doesn't feel that he needs the extra care, and the family is uncomfortable about the whole thing. Tread lightly.'

Martha kept repeating that to herself as she drove to the house. 'Tread lightly,' she said. She wasn't sure exactly what it meant, but it sounded important and sort of tricky. She could handle it.

Martha set out early to get to the house, afraid that she was going to get lost even though she'd printed out the directions and had a GPS in her car. She figured she could just sit in the car and drink her coffee if she was early, but when she pulled up to 24 Rock Lane, she didn't think that was such a good idea. It was the biggest house she'd ever seen, and since there were only about three giant houses on the block and each one of those houses had an enormous driveway, hers was the only car on the street. If she parked there, they'd probably report it to the police.

She drove down the windy road once, then around the block and came back to the house. She was only about twenty minutes early, which wasn't too bad. It would just show them that she was punctual, so she pulled into the semicircle driveway and parked her car.

When Martha rang the doorbell, she heard a deep and echoing chime ring through the whole house. She waited at the door for about five minutes, and just when she was about to ring it again, the door swung open. Standing there was a woman in her mid-forties, wearing dark slim jeans and a light pink button-down shirt. She had long blond hair that hung straight down her back, much longer than women her age normally wore it, but somehow it looked just right. She was very slim – almost bony – but in an attractive way, Martha thought.

'Come in, come in,' she said. 'I'm Ruby.'

'That's my dog's name,' Martha said.

'Really?' Ruby didn't smile. 'My real name is Ruth, but no one ever calls me that.'

'That's my cousin's girlfriend's name.' Martha couldn't stop herself from saying these things. They just kept coming out. Ruby just nodded, like this was a fact she already knew.

'Would you mind taking off your shoes?' Ruby made an apologetic grimace, and Martha saw that she had a gap between her two front teeth, like that actress whose name she couldn't remember. It seemed a strange thing, to have such a glaring orthodontic disaster on that face. Surely they had money for braces in this family. How had that been overlooked? Martha slipped off her shoes and prayed that her feet wouldn't smell. She wished she'd painted her toenails, but she didn't know that she'd be baring her feet in this interview.

'It's just that the nurses have said that any dirt in the house could cause a problem, and we have the cleaning lady only a few times a week now. But the house is so big and it gets so dusty in here.' Ruby made another face, like she was put out by how huge the house was.

'Not a problem,' Martha said. She noticed that Ruby was also barefoot, and that her toes were painted a perfect deep red. Her feet looked tan, and even her toes looked thin and elegant. Martha covered her left foot with her right foot and hoped Ruby wouldn't look at her toes.

Ruby motioned for Martha to follow her, and she led her to a sitting room off the front hall. Martha sat down in a light-pink flowered chair, and crossed her feet again. Ruby perched herself on a strange little piece of furniture in the corner, a green stool, that was shaped like a mushroom. Was it a muffet? Martha had never seen one, but she was pretty sure that's what it was.

'So, I brought a copy of my résumé, although I know you've already seen it.' Martha handed the piece of paper over to her, and Ruby took it but didn't look down.

'I don't know how much the agency told you, but I can fill

you in. My father's almost eighty and he's been having some trouble lately. He's generally been in really good health, but a couple of months ago they found some tumors on his spine. They were benign, but they had to operate, and the surgery was hard for him to recover from. We got night nurses to come in, just to make sure that he didn't need anything, and that seemed like it was enough. But then last week, he was walking to the bathroom and he fell. He was alone, because Jaz had run out, and so he was on the floor for almost an hour.'

'Oh no,' Martha said. She wasn't sure if Ruby wanted a response, but she felt like she should give one. Ruby nodded and looked pleased.

'He didn't break anything, thank God. But there was some bruising and he's still a little sore.'

'Who – who is Jaz?'

'Oh, Jaz is sort of the keeper of the house. She was our nanny when we were little and then she just stayed on, because we couldn't have made it without her. She does the grocery shopping and just sort of makes sure things run. You know, some light cleaning, the daily dishes, garbage, that sort of stuff.'

'Great,' Martha said.

'We thought it would be enough, to have Jaz here during the days when my father was here, you know, to stay with him until the night nurses came. But Jaz has said that she can't do that, that she needs to be able to run errands. She's kept a pretty loose schedule for the past few years, so I guess that's hard to change.' Ruby shrugged, like she didn't really believe this, but there wasn't much to do about it. She closed her eyes, arched her back, and stretched her arms up in the air.

'So, you need someone during the days,' Martha said.

Ruby righted herself and opened her eyes. 'Right. Sorry, I'm just exhausted. I've been filling in most days until we got this solved. Anyway, it's not such a hard job. He really doesn't need much attention, just someone here to make sure that he has what he needs, that he can get his meals, all of that.'

'Great,' Martha said again.

'He's not much for television, though, which can limit his entertainment. I should tell you that.'

'Mmm-hmm.'

The doorbell rang, and the chimes went through the house again. 'Would you excuse me?' Ruby asked. 'That's probably the cleaning lady. I've told her to use the key, but . . .' She turned her palms up, like, *What can you do with these people?* Ruby pronounced *cleaning lady* very clearly, like she wanted to say *maid* but knew she shouldn't.

Martha heard the door open in the other room and heard Ruby say to the lady, 'I'm not going to tell you again, use your key!' She said it in a funny tone, like she was trying to make a joke, but it came out sounding kind of mean. The woman scooted through the hall and into the other room without looking at Martha.

Ruby came back into the room and shook her hair back, gathered it in her hands like she was going to pull it back in a ponytail, and then let it go again.

'So, do you have any more questions? I'm trying to think if I forgot to tell you anything. Let's see. My brother and I come by pretty often. We take turns, and try to check in at least every other day, although sometimes we can't make it. And what else? Well, we'd need you to start right away.' Ruby looked at Martha as though she was waiting for an answer.

'I think that sounds perfect,' Martha said. This was the easiest job interview she'd ever been on.

'Really?' Ruby asked. She clapped her hands together and smiled. 'That is just great, just so great. You have no idea what a stress this has been.'

'I can imagine.'

'Would you like to meet him? My father?'

'Yes, that would be great.'

Ruby led her down a long hallway and they turned left past the kitchen. The walls were dark wood and the floors had dark oriental runners. Martha had trouble seeing, her eyes not adjusting to the lack of light right away.

'My father's bedroom used to be upstairs, of course, but a few years back we converted his study into a sort of bedroom area. It's just easier for everyone.'

Martha nodded, even though Ruby wasn't looking at her. 'That sounds efficient,' she said.

Ruby stopped outside of two double doors. She knocked lightly on one and then slid it open. 'Hello, hello!' she sang out. Behind her, Martha saw a man in a leather chair with a blanket over his legs. His hair was neatly combed and he was wearing a deep blue sweater. He looked sort of tiny. He had the paper on his lap, and looked up slowly when they came in. On the other side of the room, a large black woman sat reading a book with a vampire on the front cover. She put it down when they walked in and stood up.

'Well, look who it is,' she said. 'It's Ruby.' Ruby smiled and looked down.

'Hello,' Mr. Cranston said. He looked back down at his paper.

'We were just having some reading time,' the woman said. She looked at Martha, and then back at Ruby.

'Jaz, this is Martha,' Ruby said, but her eyes stayed fixed on her father.

'Martha Coffey,' Martha said, extending her arm out. Jaz laughed and shook her hand.

'Nice to meet you, Martha Coffey. Are you the person the agency sent over?'

'That's me.'

'Well, come meet Mr. Cranston.' Jaz led her over to the man, and Martha shook his hand, and he said hello again, but it was clear he just wanted to get back to the paper.

'Let's give Mr. Cranston some peace,' Jaz said. They all walked out into the hallway and Jaz shut the door behind her.

'Well,' Ruby said, 'do you want to just hang out here with Jaz for a while and she can fill you in on the details of the job?' Ruby looked at Jaz hopefully.

'Oh, chicken, that's fine,' Jaz said. 'You can get out of here.'

She sort of swatted Ruby's butt, which surprised Martha, and Ruby jumped and laughed.

'Thanks, Jaz,' she said, and she walked away quickly.

Martha and Jaz looked at each other in the hallway for a moment.

'So, that's it?' Martha asked. 'I got the job?'

'Oh lord, yes. That girl would've given the devil himself the job if it meant she could have her days free again.'

'Oh,' Martha said. She looked down at her naked feet.

'Oh, now, I don't mean that you're not qualified. We're lucky to have you. Come on to the kitchen and we'll have some tea and talk.'

The kitchen, unlike the rest of the house, was bright and inviting. The wallpaper was covered in colorful fruit, and the tabletop was a shiny marble. Martha took a seat on one of the wooden stools and waited as Jaz filled the red teakettle and arranged the teacups.

'I was Ruby and Billy's nanny when they were little,' she said. Martha nodded and she went on. 'And then when they were older, I just stayed on, to drive them places and make sure that things were in order. It's funny, you know. Not what I had planned for my life, but that's how it works sometimes.'

Jaz set down the mugs and a wooden box full of all different kinds of tea. Martha picked out a mint tea bag and put it in her mug, while Jaz filled it with boiling water. She blew on her tea and waited for Jaz to start talking again. She already liked her a great deal.

'It's hard here, for Mr. Cranston alone in the house. His wife died about five years ago now, but he doesn't want to go anywhere – refuses, actually, to leave the house.' Ruby lowered her voice for this part, like Mr. Cranston was eavesdropping outside.

'I can imagine it's hard,' Martha said.

'It would be easier if he went somewhere with more care, but he wants to stay in his house, so what can you do? The children can't talk him out of it, and Lord knows, he has the means, so here we are.'

Martha and Jaz talked for almost two hours. Jaz told her about Ruby's teenage years, how she ran away, stole some of her mother's jewelry, crashed a car. 'That child caused her parents so much heartache,' she said. She told Martha about Billy and Ruby, how they weren't on speaking terms anymore, how she was the only way that they got messages to each other. 'Despicable,' she said. 'Their father is in the last part of his life, and they can't even get over themselves to come together for him.'

Martha told Jaz about nursing, how she wanted to get back to it, how she had failed at it before. She told her about J.Crew and how she excelled there but wasn't happy. Jaz listened, nodding her head and saying, 'Mmm-hmm' every once in a while. When Martha was done, Jaz set her cup of tea down and put her hand over Martha's.

'Child, listen. You're on a journey. You didn't like the way life was going, so you're rewriting your own story. That's what you have to do. You don't see it now, but this is the most important part of your life. If you don't like the story that's being told about your own life, you've got to change it. You've got to tell a different story.'

When Martha got home that day, she took out her notebook and wrote down Jaz's words. *You've got to tell a different story.* She looked at it before she went to bed that night and smiled. Who needed Dr. Baer? She had Jaz, who seemed much smarter, was nicer, and gave her tea to boot.

Chapter 8

It was Weezy's secret. No one needed to know.
She wasn't hurting anyone, not even a little bit.
It was just something to fill her time, something
to lift her spirits. But if Will found out, he'd
think she was crazy. And her kids – well, they
would probably call the nuthouse and make her a
reservation right then and there. That's why she
kept it to herself. No one needed to know.

It wasn't like she meant to do it. No, it had all
been innocent enough. Weezy had been smack
in the middle of planning Claire's wedding when
it was called off. Just like that, it was over. She'd
been talking to caterers and venues, had meetings
set up, had been enjoying all the research, and
then one day Claire called and it was all done.

She'd never thought she'd be the type of person
to get so involved in wedding planning, but she

was wrong. It was a whole different ball game since she and Will had gotten married in the Starlight Room, with a lovely, simple lunch reception. For her own wedding, she'd made her dress, worn her hair straight and down. They'd all eaten and danced and that was that.

But when she started researching for Claire's wedding – oh, the excess! There were photo booths to be rented, personalized matchbooks and napkins to be had. Caterers sent her sample menus, with wonderful descriptions of bacon-wrapped dates and Boursin-wrapped snow peas. They sent pictures of the food, names of signature cocktails, options for monogrammed cupcakes and chocolate fountains. And that was just the food! There were also blogs of local brides, detailing every step of their weddings. There were forums of angry brides, trashing photographers and caterers and florists. It was a whole new world, and Weezy was fascinated.

Claire called off her wedding on a Monday. Weezy had already arranged to meet with one of the caterers the very next day, and she was too shocked to call and cancel. How do you explain a thing like that over the phone? That morning, she found herself driving toward the offices. She didn't tell Will where she was going. No, he wouldn't have understood. He would have picked up the phone and canceled the appointment himself, just said she couldn't make it, with no explanation. But he didn't understand. She'd been dealing with Sally Lemons, the owner of Lemons and Limes, for weeks now. They had a relationship, a correspondence e-mailing menus back and forth. She couldn't just cancel over the phone. That would be extremely rude. And so she got in her Volvo and drove to the office.

She had fully intended to tell Sally in person that the wedding was off. It was the right thing to do, to end this face to face. But when she walked into the room, the table was already set with the ivory and taupe liners that they had discussed, and a man handed her a glass of cucumber lemonade. 'This is what your guests will be greeted with,' he told her. She took a sip and decided to stay. She could tell Sally later.

And so they ate. They ate pan-roasted halibut with fingerling potatoes, and beef tenderloin with goat cheese medallions. They tried bruschetta and marinated mozzarella. They sampled wedding cakes and pecan diamonds. Weezy left Lemons and Limes, stuffed full and a little guilty. She'd drunk several glasses of wine without meaning to; every time she came close to finishing one, it was refilled right to the top. At the end, Sally had given her a warm handshake, saying how sorry she was that Claire couldn't make it, that they could do another tasting when the menu was decided, that she'd be in touch to work out the details.

Weezy had sat in her car in the parking lot for almost an hour after the tasting. When she'd stood up to go, she was dizzy and, she realized, a touch drunk. She felt almost giddy, like she'd stolen something, only she hadn't. It had all been free. Sally had talked to her like she was in charge of something big. She'd treated Weezy with respect and that was nice. The wine was just a bonus.

And that was how, months later, Weezy still hadn't told any of the vendors that the wedding was off. She'd told them it was postponed, of course. She had to. The date she had originally given them was looming, and there was no way around that. 'You know kids these days,' she'd said. 'Their lives are so busy they can't seem to find the time to get married!' But she still sent a note to Sally every couple of weeks, just to ask about new items on the menu, or to discuss what to do for a guest with a gluten allergy.

And so what? So what if Weezy was planning an imaginary wedding? People did far worse things, and anyway, maybe she'd use this information somehow at some point. Still, if anyone had caught her, she would have been completely mortified. And so, when Will walked into the kitchen and she was on her laptop, pricing out letterpress invitations as opposed to engraved, she slammed her computer shut and sat up straight.

'Hi,' she said. She tried to act casual.

'Hello,' he said, and stretched his arms out to the side, which made his shirt pull tight against his round belly. 'Just taking a break to get a drink. Don't let me interrupt.'

Weezy was just the littlest bit annoyed (as she was at least once a day) that Will had a room to work in all to himself, while she was relegated to a built-in desk in the kitchen. When had she agreed to this arrangement? Her desk was often littered with things that people just dropped there, receipts or empty envelopes and sometimes even food wrappers. And there was no privacy with people parading through the kitchen. Will came down several times throughout the day. Of course he was going to interrupt. Why even say that? *Don't let me interrupt.* It was ridiculous.

'How's the writing coming?' she asked. This question was a reflex. She asked it so often, with so little real interest. It was like saying, 'How are you?' to an acquaintance in the grocery store.

'Good,' Will answered.

'Are you ready for your class today?' This was another pointless question. Will had been teaching the same two classes for the past five years now and he could do them in his sleep.

'Yep. I'm all set.'

'Mmm. What time are you headed over?'

'I have office hours at four.'

They were silent for a few minutes and Weezy looked out the kitchen window. 'The Connors are having some work done on their house,' she said. 'I wonder if they're getting it ready to sell. There's been people coming and going all day.'

'Huh,' Will said. He half looked out the window, as though he was curious about this, which Weezy knew he wasn't. Will didn't really care or keep up on any of the neighborhood news.

It was the mothers that remembered everything anyway. That's what Weezy had learned after three decades in this house. The mothers knew what was happening in the neighborhood.

They knew the history, the scandals, the stories, the transgressions. They were the ones that kept the details straight, that passed information to the new people on the block. They gave the prompts to the fathers— 'You know who I'm talking about, the one that got pregnant, no, not the Brennan girl, the other one, the Sullivans' daughter.'

They knew who had gotten divorced, who was getting divorced, and who would probably get divorced soon. They knew who had cheated and who got the best settlements. And the fathers would always just nod as they listened to all of this, the stories sounding vaguely familiar, or at least more familiar than unfamiliar, like it had been overheard at a picnic somewhere, discussed at a barbecue, or whispered in the kitchen while dinner was being prepared and the kids were in the next room doing their homework.

As the kids had grown up, the neighborhood gossip had slowed down. Everything had slowed down, really. For some years in the midst of it, when the children were growing up, Weezy had spent a fair amount of time talking with the other mothers on the block about everyone's business. It wasn't mean-spirited, or at least Weezy liked to think it wasn't. It was just something to get them through the day, at a time when their days were always so busy – school projects, money worries, shuttling Max to hockey, and grounding Claire. It was all so fast that sometimes it felt like you needed a reminder to breathe.

Weezy and Will used to talk about what they would do after the kids moved out, when they had their own lives and no children to take care of. 'We'll be those crazy old people that buy an RV and drive cross-country,' Will said once. Weezy had laughed. She would be happy with an apartment in the city and a cottage by the shore. They had looked forward to that time, when they could relax and just enjoy themselves. It was still coming, Weezy believed. It was just put on hold for a while.

Ten years ago, if Weezy could have predicted where her children would be at this point, she would have guessed that Claire would be married and maybe even have a baby or two. Martha was harder to guess, but Weezy thought she'd be living on her own, nursing, and enjoying every minute of it. Max was still in school, so for the moment, he was still on track. But who knew? These things could get derailed at any moment. She knew that much.

Sometimes Will got a surprised look on his face when Martha or Claire walked into the room, like he'd forgotten that they lived there now. It wasn't that he disliked having them there. Sometimes Claire would say something that would make him laugh loudly, a huge, surprising guffaw. And he and Martha enjoyed spending quiet time together, reading the paper in the mornings and drinking coffee. Sometimes he seemed confused by their presence, and sometimes he treated them just as he always had, as if they were still children.

Just the other day, Martha had walked into the kitchen to get some aspirin, and Will said, 'You still have a headache? Poor baby.' And something unsettled itself in Weezy, hearing him say that. Martha wasn't a baby. It didn't seem right to call her that, to say *poor baby* and pat her on the head.

It didn't help matters that when the kids were home they seemed to start acting like teenagers again. They left shoes and bags and jackets scattered all around. Glasses were missing from the kitchen, only to be found in bedrooms or the basement. Dishes rarely made it to the dishwasher. The best you could hope for was that they'd get rinsed off and left in the sink. Usually they were just abandoned in the kitchen, on the counter, presumably waiting for a fairy to come and clean them up.

This was not how Weezy had raised her kids. Not at all. She taught them to clean up after themselves, called them back to the kitchen to clean up the apple and peanut butter snack that was now smeared on a plate. But that was when she was younger and had more energy, when she was able to take the time to yell and insist and ignore the rolled eyes and sighs of injustice. Now, most of the time she couldn't quite face it, and so she ended up picking up after them, throwing armfuls of possessions back into their rooms, rinsing off dishes, wiping crumbs from the table.

After Weezy had stopped working last year, Will had suggested that they get rid of the cleaning lady. 'Should we let Sandra go?' he'd asked, like it was the natural thing to do. He had just left his crumby toast plate, an egg pan, and a coffee cup right in the sink.

'Let Sandra go? Why would we do that? So I can fulfill my life goal of cleaning up after you? Believe me, I do enough of that. Who is it that you think is going to come along and clean up from your breakfast? The elves that live under the sink?'

Will had thrown up his arms and sighed like a martyr. 'It was just a suggestion,' he said. He went back to the sink and started cleaning up his dishes.

Sandra came in only once every two weeks now anyway. Did he really think that Weezy would be happy to spend her days scrubbing toilets? Sometimes she didn't know where he got these ideas. She had remained angry for weeks, and whenever she started to get over it, she'd hear Will saying, *Should we let Sandra go?* and get annoyed all over again.

'Don't you think you're overreacting just a little bit?' Maureen had asked her.

'No,' Weezy said. 'I don't think I'm overreacting at all. My husband would like me to spend my days dusting and mopping. Maybe that's what he always really wanted.'

'I think you're reading too much into this. Will says stuff all the time that doesn't mean anything. He just said it without thinking, that's all.'

Somewhere, deep down, Weezy knew that Maureen was probably right. Will said stupid things all the time. She tried to let it go. But every time Sandra was due to come, and Weezy had to go around the house picking up stuff to make sure that the poor woman could actually get to the vacuum cleaner and dust without tripping over a pair of shoes, Weezy would say out loud, 'It's a good thing Sandra's coming tomorrow. Look at this place. No one's picked up a thing in weeks.' She couldn't help herself.

She wanted Will to know that she had better things to do than to be his personal maid.

Once a month, Sandra was allowed to go into Will's office to clean it. It was disgusting in there. There were Kleenexes on the floor (near the garbage but not in it), dust all around the computer and desk, papers stacked everywhere. And as much as Weezy begged Will to bring dishes down as soon as he was done with them, there was always a glass or two that was left behind. The last time that Sandra was up there, she'd come down holding a coffee mug that had mold growing up the sides.

Weezy was embarrassed and also horrified for Sandra. Even if it was your job to clean someone else's house, it didn't mean that you expected to find a cup of mold while doing so. Will hadn't really understood. 'That's her job,' he'd said. 'Sorry, I didn't know it was up there.' But he wasn't sorry, and now Weezy was never going to be able to let Sandra back into the office without checking it out herself.

Will was still clunking around the kitchen, and Weezy wanted him to finish up so that she could go back to the blog post she was reading, the one that was all about the personal touches you could add to your wedding – old family wedding pictures, naming the tables after favorite books, designing your own guest book!

'So, what's on the agenda for today?' Will asked. He took out some lunch meat and sniffed it, as if he thought it had been left there to go bad.

'That's brand new,' Weezy told him. 'I just bought it yesterday.'

Will nodded and grabbed some cheese, bread, lettuce, and mayonnaise and started assembling a giant sandwich.

'Go easy on the mayo,' Weezy said. Will nodded and then moved so that he blocked the sandwich from her view. 'I'm going to meet Sharon, from work, in a little bit.'

'Oh really?'

'Yeah, she said there's some things she wanted to talk to me about.'

'I hope she's not trying to lure you back to work.' Will took a large bite out of his sandwich and chewed while standing. This was a habit of his that got more annoying with time. 'Sit down,' she was always telling him. 'Sit down and chew.' But he insisted on eating standing up, like a teenager or a farmer.

'I'm not sure what she wants to talk about. I told her I'd meet her for a cup of coffee.'

'Sounds good.' Will's answer came so easily that Weezy almost felt guilty for lying. Almost.

The florist was located clear on the other side of the city and it took almost an hour to get there. Sally Lemons had been the one to recommend him to Weezy. 'I love working with Samuel,' she'd said. 'He's so creative. A true artist.'

And so Weezy had called him to make an appointment. This was actually the first appointment she'd made since the wedding was called off. All of the others were ones that were already set up, and this felt in some ways like she was crossing a line. It was one thing to peruse websites, and to e-mail for information, but now she was actually meeting with someone. But she was so curious to see what he had to show her, and she loved flowers, and really, what was the big deal?

Samuel worked out of his own florist shop, which was small and damp. There was some temperature-controlled room to the left that housed plants, and a large refrigerated portion up front that held cut flowers. The smell of flowers was thick, but not overwhelming. Then again, Weezy loved the smell of flowers. She loved everything about them, watching them bloom and flourish in her backyard. It was so satisfying to plant something and know what would spring up from the ground – that is, as long as the squirrels and chipmunks minded their own business. You always knew what you were getting when you planted a flower, and Weezy liked that.

When she opened the door, the shop was empty. She walked to the desk and waited a moment, then rang the little bell that was there. A large, balding, sort of roundish man peeked out from the back. 'Mrs. Coffey?' he asked, and Weezy nodded.

'I hope you don't mind,' she said, pointing to the bell. 'I didn't mean to be rude, I just wasn't sure . . .'

'Of course not! Come on, let's take a seat over at the table.'

Samuel was not what she expected. He had the build of an old high school football player, his voice was deep and booming, and he was wearing a blue-checked button-down polo shirt, which was identical to one that Will owned.

'It's so nice to meet you,' Weezy said. 'Sally said the nicest things about you.'

'She's great, isn't she?'

The two of them sat at a long table and Samuel spread several glossy books filled with pictures of floral arrangements in front of them. Weezy couldn't help but sneak looks at Samuel. She was surprised at how, well, manly he was. Then she was ashamed of herself for being surprised. What did she expect? That just because he owned a flower shop he was going to be a tiny, delicate, feminine man? Well, yes, that's exactly what she had expected.

'So, how long have you been doing this?' Weezy asked.

'Oh, forever,' Samuel said with a laugh. 'This was my parents' shop, and I worked here growing up, helping out as a little guy, then part-time during high school and college, and full-time after that. I really took to it, and I was lucky because when my parents got ready to retire, none of my eight siblings was even the least bit interested.'

'Eight!'

'Yes, eight.' Samuel laughed again. 'You'd think there'd be a few more green thumbs in the bunch, but there was just me.'

'I love to garden,' Weezy said. 'I think of myself as a green thumb too.'

'Great,' Samuel said. 'Then this will be fun.' He placed his hands, palm down, on top of the books. 'So what I usually do is flip through these books, and just have you point out anything that grabs your attention – good or bad. Then we can look through some of my photos from weddings I've done. We can talk a little bit about what you imagine for the day, what flowers are favorites of yours, and so on. Then once we've worked through it all, I can draw up a proposal and we can go from there.'

'That sounds perfect,' Weezy said. 'And of course, it's so unfortunate that my daughter couldn't come with me today.'

Samuel nodded. 'Not a problem. As long as the two of you have talked and are on the same page, it should be fine. And we can show her what we come up with and alter it if we need to. Nothing is set in stone – this is a work in progress.'

Sally Lemons was right – Samuel was amazing. Weezy loved him right away, and the way he knew flowers, oh! He was a wonder. All she had to say was 'those little round green ones,' and he said, 'Kermit flowers.' They talked about bachelor's buttons and hydrangeas, lisianthus, and pincushion proteas. He knew the name of every flower, could describe the textures and colors so vividly. A couple of times, he went into the refrigerator and came out holding samples. He had flowers in every shape and size; he had green, and orange, and ivory. He talked about pairing textures and tones to complement each other. He agreed with her on the flowers she felt were a little tired (roses) and the ones that were timeless and elegant (lilies).

'Now, there's one more thing I'd like to show you,' he said. 'When the guests walk in, I like to give them a Wow!' He gave her some jazz hands when he said this. 'One of my favorite things to do is a tall vase with monochromatic gerbera daisies, maybe in a dark orange, surrounded by a spray of tall grass. Now, it's a little pricey, so don't feel pressured. I just wanted to throw it out there.'

Samuel opened a photo album and pointed to a picture of the arrangement he just described. 'It's fantastic,' Weezy whispered.

On the ride home, Weezy's flower high wore off. She got more deflated as she drove. What was she doing? How could she not have anything better to do with her free time than to have a fake meeting with a florist to plan a fake wedding? What was the matter with her?

Weezy thought of her mother, Bets, and how committed she was to attending daily mass. Weezy was almost jealous of her. Not because she herself wanted to actually go to daily mass (she didn't, and anyway, if she did she could just go) but because it was an anchor in Bets's day. Every morning she woke up and met her friend at the church at seven thirty, sometimes getting there a little early to say the rosary together. Afterward, they walked down the block to a little bakery and got donuts and coffee. It was simple, but it seemed nice to have an activity like that every day.

There was nothing worse than feeling bored and restless at the same time. Maureen could always find something to fill her time, but Weezy always felt like there was something else she should be doing, even if everything was marked off her list. Maureen and Bets both loved those cheap Harlequin romance novels, and every so often they'd exchange grocery bags full of them, passing the overflowing bags to one another. Weezy tried to read them, but she just didn't get it. They were all the same. Why waste your time reading something that was just going to be thrown into a bag when it was done, and confused with the rest of the bunch? There was nothing special about any of them; you knew what the ending was before you even started.

She drove home slowly and pulled into the driveway feeling very low. When she opened the door, she smelled garlic and onions cooking. Claire's head popped out of the kitchen. 'Hi, Mom. I'm making dinner. Hope you didn't have anything planned. I tried to call you, but your phone was off.'

Weezy walked toward the kitchen. 'That sounds great,' she said. 'I'm pooped.'

'I'm making sausage and peppers and some pasta thing to go along with it.'

'Mmm,' Weezy said. She smiled and sat down in a kitchen chair. 'Do you need help?'

'No, I'm good. Where were you? Your phone kept going right to your voice mail.'

'I had some meetings. How was work?'

'Fine,' Claire said. 'The same. Pretty boring.'

Claire had announced that she wanted something to do, a job, but she didn't care what it was. This disturbed Weezy. She suggested that Claire look at grad school programs or research some non-profits here, but Claire wouldn't hear of it.

'I just want a job,' she'd insisted. 'Just a job. I don't care if it's boring or what it is.'

Weezy wanted to tell her that this wasn't the attitude to take. She'd spent years working at places that were 'just a job' and it didn't make it easier that you didn't care about it. If anything, it made it harder.

She'd always known that Claire would be able to thrive in a work situation. It was Martha that she had to constantly build up. 'You're so smart and capable,' she'd said to her last week. Martha needed reminding, needed to be shown how to showcase herself. Sometimes her skills didn't translate in the real world.

Claire didn't go into much detail on her temp job, which was nothing new. She was always private with her information, never offered up anything unless Weezy was there to pry it out of her. Even after she and Doug called off the wedding, Weezy had to push to get any sort of answer. 'It's over, Mom,' was all she said. 'What else do you want me to say? It's done.'

'Was he unfaithful?' Weezy had asked.

'No, God, Mom. No.'

'I'm just trying to understand. Were you unfaithful?'

'Mom, stop. No.' Claire had breathed loudly on the phone, as if she was trying to calm herself down. 'No one cheated, Mom. Nothing happened. We just don't want to get married.'

Weezy had started to say something else, but thought better of it and stayed silent. She didn't quite believe Claire, but there was no point in pushing further, she knew. Claire was the most stubborn of her children, and the more Weezy tried to put pressure on her, the more she dug in her heels and refused to move.

When the girls were little, Weezy sometimes resorted to trying to scare them into behaving. Once, in the grocery store, when they both refused to walk next to the cart, choosing instead to run in circles in the cereal aisle, she'd turned her back and left them. 'Okay, then. I'll see you later. I'm going home.'

Weezy walked down the aisle, turning once to look back at them for dramatic effect. Martha had screamed, 'Wait! No! I'm coming,' and raced after her, snotty and red-faced, already crying in a panic. Claire had remained where she was. She sat herself down on the floor of the grocery store and didn't budge. She just looked up at Weezy, daring her to go, her jaw clenched and her arms crossed, refusing to move.

And so Weezy went to the checkout, paid for her groceries, and then started walking to the car, sure that Claire would follow behind at any moment. Martha was still snuffling with fear because she'd almost been left behind. Weezy stood at the car, trying to remember what her child-rearing books had said. Should she give in? Should she hold her ground? At what point did this become dangerous? Kids could be kidnapped anywhere at any time. Even if she was watching the front door, to make sure that Claire didn't come out, you never knew.

She probably stood there for only a total of two minutes at the most, although it felt like an hour, and finally, convinced that Claire was in some sort of danger, she'd grabbed Martha and run back inside, and found Claire sitting right where she'd left her, staring straight ahead, refusing to move.

Dinner that night was wonderful, mostly because Weezy hadn't had to cook and Martha offered to clean up the kitchen. 'Maybe having you two home isn't so awful,' Will said, and the girls rolled their eyes at him.

Reading in bed that night, Weezy thought about the large flower arrangement of orange daisies, and how if she was really going to do this, she'd splurge for it. Even if it meant scrimping somewhere else in the budget, she'd do it. They were so beautiful and breathtaking. She could just imagine everyone's faces as they walked in and saw them.

Will leaned over to give her a kiss good night, and his lips stayed on her for just a moment longer than usual. 'You smell nice,' he said, smiling at her. 'Like flowers.' He kissed her one more time, and then rolled over and fell asleep.

Chapter 9

The people at Proof Perfect (or 'PP,' as they affectionately called themselves) took themselves very seriously. They wrote each other e-mails that said things like, 'As we discussed,' and 'FYI,' and 'Per our earlier conversation,' and 'Loop me in.' It was as if they'd all just read a book on office jargon and were in a competition to see who could use the most terms in one day.

People walked quickly, as if they couldn't waste a second (not one second!) by walking at a regular speed, and so they raced from their offices to the restroom, and back again, presumably to continue their proofreading. As they passed each other in the halls, they often called out to each other, 'Shoot me an e-mail,' because wasting time to stop and talk was clearly not an option.

Sometimes it was funny and sometimes it made

Claire a little sad to watch them. They all seemed to have just discovered Microsoft Outlook meeting invitations and they sent them to each other for everything – weekly meetings, morning coffee breaks, birthday celebrations in the break room. It was the cause of many a scuffle when someone chose not to respond to an invite.

One of the women that Claire assisted, Leslie, called her anywhere from seven to ten times a day. She mostly called her Amanda, even though Claire was certain that she knew her name and remembered that Amanda was on maternity leave. Claire answered to it, figuring it was Leslie's way of trying to tell her that she was very important and couldn't be bothered to remember everyone's name.

The job was easier than Claire had imagined. It was also a lot more boring. She mostly just sat around and waited for someone to ask her to Xerox something or for the phone to ring. If Claire had had any desire to write a book or a screenplay, this would have been the perfect opportunity. She could have sat all day and typed, mostly uninterrupted. But she had no such desire, and so instead she played solitaire, and perused cooking sites for recipes. Sometimes, she added up how much she was earning each day, and how much closer she was to paying down her credit cards. That was usually the most exciting part of her day.

At home, Martha kept saying, 'It's good timing that you moved home now, since I'll probably be buying a place soon.' Martha had been talking about buying a place for years now, so Claire didn't pay much attention to her.

Each morning, Claire got up and was in the shower by seven, in order to beat Martha, who took forever in the bathroom. The two of them still often ended up in there at the same time, brushing their teeth or putting on their makeup, which made it feel like they were in high school again. Claire left the house around eight thirty and then was home by six, where she immediately changed into pajamas, or headed over to Lainie's to drink wine. It was one or the other.

The first time that she came back late from Lainie's, Weezy started to say something about coming home at a regular hour, and wanting to know where Claire was. While she talked, Claire just stood and stared at her and finally said, 'Mom, I'm almost thirty. This isn't going to work.'

Weezy let out a little laugh then, and looked just a touch embarrassed, as if she'd actually forgotten how old Claire was. 'I guess it's hard to get used to you living here as an adult,' she said. But then she made Claire promise that she would still just leave a message so that they knew where she was. Claire was too tired to protest, so she agreed. 'Just Twitter me,' Weezy said, by which she meant send a text.

They ate dinner together every night, and Martha talked about her new job, Will talked about his students, Weezy asked Martha about nursing, and Claire tried to figure out how she'd ended up there. After a week of the same routine, Claire felt like she was right back in high school. Or jail.

The other thing about living at home (which Claire had forgotten) was that all of a sudden, she was expected to be so many places, to attend so many random things — Lainie's niece's baptism, lunch with Weezy's cousins, dinner with Will's professor friends. When she tried to back out of anything, they would all just shake their heads. 'You're here,' they'd say, as if that explained it. As if her presence back in the state of Pennsylvania required her to participate in everything.

She even got roped into going to a wake for the father of an old high school friend. 'I haven't seen Kelly in, like, six years,' she said, but Lainie wouldn't hear of it.

'You have to go,' she said. 'It's Kelly's dad.'

And just like that, Claire was in the car with Lainie and Martha (who'd taken a math class with Kelly in high school) and they all stood in line at the wake, which was incredibly crowded, and then talked to Kelly's mom, who looked really drugged up, hugged Kelly, and then stood and looked at the dead body at the front of the room.

'Doesn't he look great?' Kelly's mom said.

No, he didn't look great. He looked dead. Kelly's mom grabbed Claire's hand, although Claire was pretty sure that she didn't know who she was. Lainie, meanwhile, was nodding and telling stories and saying gracious things, like she was an expert at wakes now.

Claire hated wakes. It was a bizarre tradition to stand around and look at a corpse. And so, as soon as she could, Claire excused herself and walked outside and around the corner of the building, where she almost ran right into Fran Angelo, leaning against the wall, his head tilted back and his eyes closed as he smoked a cigarette.

For a second, Claire wondered what he was doing there. Was everyone in town required to go to this thing? Then she remembered that he was related to Kelly somehow, a cousin or a second cousin or something like that.

'Hey,' Claire said. He opened his eyes, but didn't look all that surprised to see her, like he'd been waiting for someone to come find him. He smiled at her and she looked at the ground.

'Hey,' he said. 'What's going on?'

'Not much. Just, you know.' Claire motioned toward the wall of the funeral home, like that explained everything. She shifted from one leg to the other, hating that he made her feel like she was fifteen again.

'I haven't gone in yet,' Fran said. 'I hate wakes.'

'Me too. I was just thinking the exact same thing.'

'Do you want a cigarette?' He shook the pack and held it out to her.

'I don't really smoke anymore,' she said. 'But sure.' She didn't bother to explain that she'd never really smoked in the first place, except when she was drunk and sometimes in college if she was bored. But now seemed like an appropriate time to smoke, and so she took one out of the pack and leaned forward to let Fran light it. She remembered parties in high school, clumps of teenagers standing around a backyard, smoking and looking bored. She inhaled and felt dizzy almost immediately. Fran smoked Reds, which seemed like a serious, old-man cigarette. He would probably smoke for the rest of his life.

'I was going to call you to hang out,' Fran said, 'but then I realized I never got your number the other day.'

'Oh really?' Claire said. She sounded like an idiot. A teenage idiot.

'Yeah, we should get together.' He reached into his pocket, pulled his phone out and handed it to Claire.

'So, should I put my number in?' she asked. He nodded and she typed herself into Fran Angelo's phone.

'I should probably go in, I guess.' He closed his eyes and leaned his head back, aiming his face at the sky. Claire remembered him in high school, how he was always tilting his face up like that to drop Visine into his eyes, like he was stoned or wanted people to think he was.

'Okay,' Claire said. 'I'll see you.'

Fran opened his eyes and looked at her. 'I'll call you,' he said. He walked back toward the front door of the funeral home, and left Claire standing there, holding her still-burning cigarette.

Lainie came out of the funeral home as Fran was going in. Claire walked around the corner of the building and called out to Lainie.

'Hey,' Lainie said. 'I wasn't sure where you went. Are you smoking?'

'Not really,' Claire said. She dropped the cigarette on the ground. 'Are you ready?'

'Yeah. We just have to wait for Martha.'

'What's she doing in there? Making plans to go to the burial with the family?'

'She's just saying good-bye to a couple people. What were you doing out here anyway?'

'Nothing. I just didn't want to be in there anymore. I hate wakes.'

'I don't think anyone really likes them,' Lainie said.

'Martha,' Claire said. 'I think Martha likes them.'

Fran called Claire two days later and invited her over. She'd lost her breath for a second when she heard his voice on the phone, and it was hard to recover and answer him when he said simply, 'Want to hang out?'

'Sure,' Claire said. And then, 'Sorry, I'm out of breath. I just got back from a run.'

'Cool,' Fran said.

Fran was living in the basement of his parents' house. It looked just as she'd imagined it would. There were two old red-plaid couches that were scratchy when you sat on them, a banged-up coffee table, wall-to-wall brown carpeting, and a queen-sized bed in the corner. There was a small bathroom down there with a stand-up shower, a tiny refrigerator (the kind that kids keep in their dorm room), and a flimsy-looking desk with the oldest computer Claire had ever seen on it. In an adjoining room were the washer and dryer, and every so often, a whiff of dryer-sheet-smelling air would come drifting out, which was always surprising and pleasant.

'Here it is,' Fran said when she walked down there. 'My new place.'

'It's nice,' Claire said. She knew that since she was living in her parents' house at the moment, she didn't have a lot of room to judge, but it seemed worse that Fran was in the basement. Like it was more permanent or something.

Claire's friend Natalie had a brother who had lived in the basement for as long as she could remember. He was eight years older than they were, and by the time they were in high school, he was a permanent fixture in the basement of the Martin house. He smoked pot down there, and he and his parents seemed to have an agreement — as long as he sprayed air freshener and pretended that he wasn't smoking, his parents would pretend that they didn't notice the smell of weed drifting up to the kitchen.

When they were freshmen in high school, they were all in love with Dan Martin. They'd giggle when he came upstairs and talked to them, kept their makeup on when they slept over, just in case he was around. As they got older, they sometimes went down to the basement with him to hang out, and by the end of high school, they sometimes drank beers down there or even smoked a joint.

But by the time they graduated from college, Dan no longer seemed cute or even a little bit appealing. He was thirty then, and even though he was thin everywhere else, he had a gut that hung over his pants. They never went down to the basement to see him anymore, and when he came upstairs they didn't giggle. He transformed into Natalie's creepy older brother, who was sort of a perv, and everyone seemed to forget that they used to worship him. Even Natalie started rolling her eyes at him, calling him a loser, blaming her parents for letting him live there. 'What a waste of life,' she used to say. 'What a complete waste of a person.'

Claire sincerely hoped that Fran would not live in the basement forever, but as she looked around she heard Weezy saying, 'It's a trend, an epidemic.'

Fran told Claire that he'd let Liz keep their apartment, which was a loft on the edge of a trendy new neighborhood. 'I didn't want to stay there anyway,' he said. 'She picked out all the furniture and decorated it. I didn't want that place. It was full of fake posters and dreamcatchers.'

He got them both beers and they sat on the couch with the TV on, but they didn't watch anything. Instead, he told her about Liz, who was a waitress and an artist who made jewelry that she sold at street fairs and some small boutiques.

'She thinks she's going to make it,' Fran said. 'She stays up half the night baking beads in a kiln that's in the middle of the fucking apartment, thinking that she's really going to make it.' He took a sip of beer and sniffed. 'I mean, her stuff's good, don't get me wrong. But how many people actually make it big designing jewelry, you know?'

'Probably not a lot,' Claire said.

'Yeah, exactly. I used to tell her I wanted the kiln out of

there, and she'd freak, like me saying that I didn't want a huge fire pit in the middle of our apartment was single-handedly killing her career. Like, because I didn't want to live in a fire death trap, I wasn't supporting her.'

Claire laughed, and he smiled at her. He got them each another beer, and they set the empty ones right on the coffee table in front of them.

'Doug used to sleep with his BlackBerry. And I don't mean he had it by the side of the bed. He had it *in* the bed, right next to him, sometimes on the pillow like it was a little pet. No matter what time it went off, he'd read it and respond. Like he was so important that he couldn't even wait a second, like someone would die if he didn't answer them right away.'

Fran nodded like he understood. He was just as confident as he'd been in high school, which surprised her. She thought maybe time or the breakup would have taken something off of him, but it hadn't. After their second beer, he got them each another, and when he sat back down, he put his hand on her upper thigh, just letting it rest there right next to the crotch of her jeans.

He didn't move his hand, just started moving his fingers, drumming them. Then he started moving his thumb in circles on the top part of her thigh, and rubbed his fingers on her inner thigh, his pinky just sometimes brushing against her, lightly, until she couldn't sit still.

He kept talking while he did this – about his job, his old apartment, what he missed about the neighborhood – just kept circling his fingers, as though he had no idea what he was doing, until she couldn't listen to him anymore, and when he leaned over to kiss her, she turned to face him, straddling one of his thighs, moving back and forth, grinding against him, both of them making appreciative noises as they moved.

Later, as they lay in bed and sniffed the dryer-sheet air, Fran laughed. 'What?' Claire asked.

'I'm just surprised, that's all,' he said.

'Surprised at what?' She rolled away from him and sat up, holding the sheets in front of her and feeling very, very naked.

'At this. You were always so quiet in high school.'

'I wasn't quiet,' Claire said.

'Well, you didn't talk to me.' He stretched his arms above him.

'I talked to you. We hooked up, remember?' She felt like digging her nails into his arm until it hurt.

'I remember,' he said. 'Don't get so worked up.'

'I'm not worked up.'

'Okay,' he said. He put his face next to her and started to kiss her, then pulled her on top of him. He still tasted like tobacco and cinnamon gum, but his face felt different now. He had stubble that seemed harder, more grown-up. As they kissed, she was aware of all of this, and still had time to think, *This is a dumb move.*

Lainie and Brian had sex freshman year of high school, and when Lainie told her about it, Claire tried to listen, but she was so far away from it, so far from that actually happening to her, that it didn't make much sense. It was like somebody telling you about a safari that they went on; you understood why they were excited, but you couldn't actually imagine a giraffe coming up and licking your hand, and so you just nodded and smiled.

After that happened, Lainie joined the Group of Girls Who Have Sex With Their Boyfriends. It was like a club. Claire never totally understood how they all identified one another, but somehow girls from all different groups of friends would smile knowingly at each other during the health portion of gym class, nod at each other in the hallways. Sometimes, Claire would walk into the bathroom at school and find Lainie whispering with Margie Schuller and Tracy King, two girls they weren't even friends with, and she knew without asking what the three of them were talking about.

When Claire finally had sex, her junior year in college, she didn't tell Lainie right away. She didn't want Lainie to welcome her into the club, like she was the president, like she owned sex because she'd done it first.

And even now, as she told Lainie about Fran, it was strangely uncomfortable. Claire just blurted it out, knowing that Lainie would be hurt if she didn't tell her.

'You're sleeping with Fran?' Lainie asked her.

'Not sleeping,' Claire explained. 'Slept. Once.'

'Why didn't you tell me?'

'I'm telling you right now. What did you want me to do? Call you from his bed?'

'I can't believe this.'

'I sort of can't either.'

'I do not see you guys together,' Lainie said.

'Yeah, I know, right?' Claire was offended, but tried not to show it.

'So, do you think you'll see him again?'

'Who knows? Probably not,' Claire said.

But Fran called her the next day, as she thought he would, and they saw each other that night. And then the next night and the one after that.

'It's fun,' she said to Lainie, as if that explained it all.

The truth was that most of the time when they were together, they talked about Doug and Liz, telling stories and trading information with a sense of urgency, like the faster they could get it all out of their heads, the sooner they'd be back to normal. They talked about them when they were still in bed together, often when they were still naked. Claire wondered what Doug and Liz were doing at that moment, and she thought that it would have been nice if they could have been together, doing the same thing.

They were a good balance; Fran was angrier than she was, and Claire suspected he was a little more heartbroken too. Claire was mostly confused and embarrassed, and Fran was neither of these things, so it seemed to work out well. Claire never minded when Fran talked about Liz, even when she didn't have clothes on. She understood what was happening here, that they were trying to get rid of their memories, trying to figure out new bodies to forget the old ones.

Claire waited to come to her senses, waited for her grown-up self to show up and tell her to cut it out, to tell her that Fran Angelo was not who she should be spending time with. But every time he called, she happily went over there, ran down the steps to the basement as quickly as she could, to get to Fran Angelo and his dryer-sheet-scented room.

Claire had been dreading this weekend for a long time. All of her high school friends were getting together, 'for a reunion,' they kept saying, like they didn't all see each other a few times a year at least.

Their friend Jackie was the one that demanded this reunion happen. 'I miss you girls,' she kept saying. 'Come to my house and I'll send the kids to my mom's and we'll have a GNI.'

'A GNI?' Claire asked.

'Girls' Night In,' Lainie said.

'It sounds like an STD,' Claire said.

They suspected Jackie just wanted to show off her new house, but for some reason they all still agreed to go to Red Bank, New Jersey, for the weekend. Claire, Lainie, and their friend Paula drove from Philly, and their friends Katherine, Clancy, and Erin came from New York.

Paula was recently engaged, and on the drive down there, every time she talked about the wedding, she turned to Claire and said, 'Sorry.'

'I'm fine,' Claire said. 'Really, you can talk about your

wedding.' She was already planning to drink as much wine as she could.

'I can't believe we're going to Jackie's,' Claire said. 'We could have at least gone somewhere fun. Why did we agree to go there again?'

Lainie just shrugged. They'd all been friends with Jackie in junior high, mostly because they were scared of her. Jackie was the queen of three-way calling, orchestrating one girl to stay silent, while she encouraged another unsuspecting girl to rip the listener to shreds, and then she'd announce the secret guest like she was a talk show host. She was like an evil preteen Oprah.

In seventh grade, Jackie left fake notes in Claire's locker, signed from Luke, the boy in the class that they all loved. It still made Claire's face burn to remember the excitement she felt when she found those notes, how she hoped they were real, as if any seventh-grade boy would ever declare his love for a girl on a piece of notebook paper and stuff it in her locker.

Jackie confronted Claire at a sleepover, announcing to everyone that the notes were fake. 'You believed it, though,' she said to Claire. 'I saw your face and I know you believed it.'

'I did not,' Claire said. It still remained one of the worst nights of her life, as she found out that every one of her friends had known that Jackie was leaving the notes, including Lainie, who cried later and apologized.

'I wanted to tell you,' she said. 'But she told me that she'd get me if I did.'

To distract Jackie from Luke and the fake notes, Claire

suggested that they TP Molly Morrisey's house. 'You know,' she told Jackie, 'she said you were the fifteenth-prettiest girl in our class. The only one lower than you was Lacey. And she said it was because she thought you were fat.'

Claire was still ashamed that she'd thrown Molly under the bus like that. But looking back, she realized it was normal to crack under a regime of terror. She was just trying to survive.

In high school, Jackie had gone through a klepto phase. She had piles of bras and underwear in her room with the tags still on them that she'd stolen from Victoria's Secret. 'It's so easy,' she told them. 'You just bring a bunch of stuff to try on in the dressing room, and then you wear it out underneath your clothes.'

Sometimes if she grabbed the wrong size or was simply feeling generous, she'd dole the stuff out to the girls. Claire never wanted to take any of it, since it felt like stealing once removed, but Lainie didn't seem to have a problem with it. 'What?' she'd always say. 'It's not like *we* stole it.'

The fact that they'd lived with Jackie as their evil ruler for all of junior high was hard to believe. Harder to believe was that they stayed friends with her throughout high school, where her power was diminished a little bit when it became clear (as Molly Morrisey so accurately pointed out) that she wasn't very pretty; but whatever power she lost, she made up for by always being the one to take beer to parties in her backpack, to be unafraid to talk to boys. She was not to be trusted.

Jackie had married a boy from high school, Mike Albert,

who was a roundish guy with glasses and a fuzzy stare. He'd been friends with all the cool kids, even if he was a little on the periphery of the group, and Claire figured that this was very important to Jackie, that she had probably bullied him into dating and then marrying her.

As they pulled into the driveway at Jackie's house, Claire said, 'I can't believe we agreed to this.'

'Of course you can,' Lainie said. She turned off the car and the three of them sat there for a moment. 'Come on, we'll get drunk and it won't be so bad.'

'I can't believe that I have two under two,' Jackie said. It was probably the twentieth time she'd said it, but who was keeping track? She sounded so pleased with herself that she almost couldn't stay seated.

'I'm so glad we're doing this,' Jackie said. 'And I'm so glad you guys get to see my house. Don't you love it?'

The girls just nodded and looked around. Clancy was eight months pregnant and was sitting so far back on the couch that it looked like she'd never be able to sit up again. Claire didn't envy her, having to stay sober this weekend. Clancy and her husband had just moved to Long Island. 'It's really boring,' she answered, when they asked her how it was. 'I mean, I know we had to do it. We were running out of space and we would have had to put the baby in a drawer or something, but still. You can't order any takeout past like eight thirty, and it's just really boring.'

Erin and her boyfriend, James, had just bought a new place in Brooklyn. She showed them all pictures of the huge new loft, and when she left the room, Jackie leaned forward. 'What does James do?' she asked. 'I mean, I know it's just an apartment, but still it's really nice.' Jackie was easily threatened. 'I mean, I'd sooner die than live in Brooklyn. There's a lot of immigrants there, you know. And gangs. It's really dangerous.' Claire was almost positive that Jackie had never been to Brooklyn.

Jackie poured them all some more of the deep yellow Chardonnay from the huge bottle, unaware that they were all looking at each other. They'd begun to notice in the past few years that Jackie was definitely racist. At first, they'd thought she was just a little clueless, maybe had some bad timing or judgment with her jokes. But her comments kept getting harsher and way more embarrassing. 'Don't be a Jew,' she'd say, when someone tried to itemize a restaurant bill.

'Even my grandmother wouldn't say that,' Claire whispered.

'Bets would totally say that,' Lainie whispered back.

'Okay, fine, but she's like a hundred years old.'

They all took large gulps of the wine, which was tangy and bordered on unpleasant but thankfully seemed to go down easier the more you drank. When Jackie went into the kitchen to get another bottle, Katherine picked up the empty one and said, 'I think my great-aunt Janice drinks this. And she's, like, the world's cheapest person.'

The weekend went slowly. The next day, as they walked around the neighborhood and down a bike path, Jackie made an announcement. 'We've decided to teach Emma to sign,' she said, like they'd all been waiting for this news about her daughter. 'We've all read the reports about its possibly delaying language. But Mike and I just really believe that it's positive, you know. We really think it will help her.'

No one said anything, but Jackie didn't seem to notice. She was so sure that everyone was dying to know the details of her life that it probably never occurred to her that she could possibly be boring them.

Later that night, they ordered pizza and drank more wine. Erin suggested going out for dinner, but that idea was quickly shot down by Jackie. 'It's so cozy in the house,' she'd said. 'Let's just stay here.'

They drank more wine that night than they had the night before. Katherine told them all how she had broken up with her latest boyfriend, Jed, a computer programmer of some sort that looked like he really wanted to be a hipster, but was just a little off.

'What happened?' Claire asked.

Katherine shrugged. 'I read his e-mails and found out that he'd been posting online ads for meeting men,' she said. Lainie choked on her wine and started coughing. Erin leaned over and patted her on the back. 'It happens sometimes, you know?'

Jackie nodded knowingly. 'That's why you should always read your boyfriend's e-mails,' she said.

'Seriously?' Clancy asked. 'That's seriously what you just took from that story?'

Katherine sighed and drank her wine. She'd cut her hair short and dyed it blond. She looked tired, like she'd given up fighting. Even when she'd climbed out of Clancy's car the day before, it had seemed like she didn't want to be there but didn't have the energy to resist.

'So,' Jackie said, turning to Claire. 'I heard you and Fran Angelo have a little thing going on.'

Claire turned to Lainie, who shook her head just a little, meaning that she hadn't said anything. 'Who told you that?' Claire asked.

'I have my sources,' Jackie said.

'It's nothing,' Claire said. 'Really.'

Jackie let it drop, and Claire was relieved. But on the ride home, she was angry. 'What are we doing still hanging out with her?' she'd yelled at Lainie and Paula in the car. 'She's disgusting. I'm done. I'm serious, I'm ashamed of myself that I even spent this much time with her. What does that say about us? What is wrong with us?'

Paula and Lainie had muttered in agreement, which made Claire even angrier. She was silent the rest of the way home, arms crossed, hating herself for not cutting off all contact with Jackie when they were twelve. What was wrong with her? Why was she still putting herself in situations where she was around this person? Jackie was nothing but bad energy. She was pure evil. And how on earth had she ended up married and living in a house with two kids? How had she tricked people into not seeing that she was horrible?

It seemed to Claire that Jackie was a symbol for everything that had ever gone wrong in her life since junior high. She couldn't stand up for herself then and it had probably just spiraled from there.

Fran was sitting on the couch in the basement playing video games when Claire walked in. 'How was your weekend?' he asked. He didn't look away from the TV, or pause the game.

'It was fine,' she said. 'Sort of boring. We just stayed at Jackie's house mostly.'

'Oh yeah? Did you see Mike?'

'No. Jackie made him leave for the weekend.'

'Jackie was always sort of a beast,' he said. 'I don't know what he was thinking.' Claire felt better.

At least sitting in the basement with Fran, she didn't feel like the messed-up one. Even around Katherine and her boyfriend that dabbled in men, Claire felt like she was the one that was a disaster. It was only here, on the red-plaid couch, that she felt like things weren't totally falling apart. She sat and watched Fran play his game.

'Remember what video games looked like when we were little?' Claire asked. 'The people were basically just little geometric shapes. You could barely see them. These look like real people.'

'I know,' Fran said. 'It's awesome.' He stood up and put his arms straight up in the air when the game was over, and Claire assumed that meant he'd won. 'Want to watch a movie?' he asked her.

'Sure.' Claire sat with her arm resting against the back of the couch, her feet right at Fran's thigh. She let him pick the movie. It was some story about gangsters or a fighter or something. It was mindless. She watched it without talking, just nodding whenever Fran said something.

'You okay?' he asked.

'Yeah, I'm fine.'

Fran picked up her foot in his hand and held it on his lap. He started running his fingers over her toes, pausing to hold each one for a second, before moving on to the next one.

'What are you doing?' Claire asked.

'I'm looking for the one that ate roast beef,' he said. He held on to her middle toe and squeezed it. 'He's my favorite.'

Claire leaned her head back and laughed, a big loud laugh that surprised her. She held her stomach and laughed until it hurt. Her whole body shook, and she laughed harder than she had in as long as she could remember.

'There we go,' Fran said. He patted her leg. 'There we go.'

Chapter 10

Cleo never even went to the bathroom when Max was in the apartment. That was her first thought when the nurse told her. Of course, if she just had to pee that was one thing. But to really 'do her business,' as her mother would say, she waited until he left and then she'd run in there. A couple of times, when she really couldn't hold it, she'd pretend to take a shower, letting the hot water run (which she knew was wasteful), and just pray that he couldn't hear or smell anything on the other side of the door.

She wanted to say this to the nurse, but she couldn't quite get the words together. Instead, she said, 'I'm sorry, that can't be right.'

The nurse nodded and said, 'I'm afraid it is.'

'I don't understand,' Cleo kept saying. 'I don't understand.'

The nurse was sympathetic, but firm and removed, which was annoying as all hell. Cleo wanted her to be just as shocked as she was. She wanted her to say, 'I can't believe it either!' But she just stood there calmly. She probably thought Cleo didn't understand how the body worked, that it was possible she was one of those girls who would give birth in a bathroom, leave her baby in a garbage can, and then head back to the prom. This could not be happening.

'This is a mistake,' Cleo said.

'There is no mistake, the nurse said. 'You're pregnant.'

'But I'm on the pill.' It sounded like she was making excuses, even to herself, but it was the truth. She was on the pill. This wasn't right.

'It can happen.' The nurse shrugged her shoulders, like, *What can you do about it? Isn't life a bitch sometimes?* Cleo wanted to punch her in the jaw, give her a side hook, like a boxer.

'Yes, it can happen. But it doesn't happen often, does it? There is a very minimal margin of error in these things.' Cleo thought to herself that she sounded just like Elizabeth. And then she thought, *Elizabeth. Oh fuck.*

The nurse was giving her pamphlets, asking her when the date of her last period was, looking unsurprised when Cleo said, 'Ummm, let's see.'

'It looks like you're about five weeks,' the nurse finally said.

'Five weeks?'

She wanted to ask the nurse how many pregnant students she'd seen in her time here. Cleo would feel better if there were lots of them. She always felt better when she was part of a group.

Cleo could have stayed there all day, going round and round with the nurse about how this really wasn't possible, but the nurse told her she had another patient and told Cleo she should make an appointment with an ob-gyn to get more information. Then she'd herded Cleo out the door, nudging and guiding her like she was some sort of sheepdog.

When she went to health services, she really hadn't thought she was pregnant. Maybe it crossed her mind, the same way that cancer does — it's a possibility, sure, but really, not very likely. Cleo had been feeling nauseous and tired, but she thought it was the flu or maybe a parasite or something.

It had never occurred to her to take a pregnancy test at home. She'd never ever taken one. Cleo had slept with her high school boyfriend senior year, mostly because she thought she should before she went to college. He was a lacrosse player with nice hair. She'd never really had any sort of pregnancy scare — she was careful! — but there were a few times she was a day late, and she'd panic.

Her friend Violet took pregnancy tests like they were going out of style, sometimes just to reassure herself, sometimes because she was bored, sometimes because she thought it seemed adult. Cleo thought maybe she bought them in bulk.

If Cleo ever breathed a word that maybe she was worried, Violet would offer her a test and encourage her to take it. 'Don't you just want to know?' she'd always ask. Cleo always refused.

To take a test would be too final – you might get the answer you were dreading. If you didn't take it, there was always the hope that things were still okay. And so Cleo preferred to lie in her bed at night and pray and imagine that she would get her period the next day. It had always worked.

After she left health services, Cleo walked for a while. She left the campus, because she couldn't look at all of the students, just walking around with their stupid backpacks, thinking that they had real problems because they had a paper due or a test to take, when really none of it mattered at all.

She walked into town, and then around the neighborhoods, winding in and around streets, hoping to get lost. Just then, she missed Monica so much that it was a little bit like a stabbing pain in her stomach. She wanted so badly to find her, to be able to tell her what had happened, to cry hysterically on her bed, while Monica rubbed her back and said, 'What are we going to do?'

And the strangest thing about it was that she missed Monica so much in that moment that it seemed to override everything else. Cleo didn't want to tell Max. It was embarrassing or shameful or something. What if he got mad or broke up with her or thought she'd done it on purpose? Even if he wasn't that kind of person, you had no idea how someone was going to act when he was in a situation like this.

Cleo ached to be able to tell Monica, but she knew she couldn't. The day she packed up her stuff, she knocked on

Monica's bedroom door. 'I'm sorry about this,' she said. 'I don't want things to be weird between us.' This of course didn't mean much, since things had been weird between them for a while now.

Monica had shrugged. 'It's pretty shitty, but I guess I understand.'

She'd felt awful then, leaving her best friend who wasn't well. What kind of a person was she? To give up on a friend when she hit a rough patch. Well, she was paying for it now. She had no one. No friend to talk to, no safe place to go. And so she walked up and down the streets, hoping that maybe she'd wake up and it would be one of those dreams that you talked about for days, saying, 'It was so real, you wouldn't believe it.'

Cleo went back to the apartment, and took a cigarette out of the pack that Max had left on the table. Max was a drunk-smoker, as he put it, buying packs when he was out at night, and then letting them sit untouched until the next time he was out drinking. Cleo had never really liked smoking all that much. Usually, if she got drunk enough to smoke a couple of cigarettes, she threw up the next morning.

She opened the window and leaned over the back of the couch. The lighter was running out of fluid and she had to click it a few times before she finally got it to light the cigarette. She inhaled and coughed, then inhaled again.

Of course, she wasn't supposed to smoke. But she wasn't

supposed to drink either and she reasoned that drinking was worse. Maybe the cigarette would jostle the pregnancy, cause a miscarriage. She could smoke this baby out. But that was stupid. If that was the case, anyone would just smoke a cigarette when they were pregnant and no one would ever have to get an abortion.

Was that what she was going to do? She couldn't imagine it. But imagining a baby, a creature that was going to grow inside of her and then come out of her, was even harder. She was so screwed.

When Cleo got nervous, she balled up her hands into fists and played piano exercises from memory. It probably made her look strange, if anyone noticed the way her fingers pulsed, how her mouth sometimes counted. She explained it to Max once, and he'd said it was something you'd think an autistic kid would do.

She wanted him to come home and didn't want him to come home at the same time. Once it was over with, it would be done. She could tell him and she wouldn't have to worry about that part anymore. It would just be all the shit that came after it.

When he finally came in the door, she'd stopped crying but her face was still red, and she knew she looked strange sitting there, her legs underneath her, a blanket wrapped around her.

'What?' Max said. 'What happened?'

It occurred to her later that he probably thought someone had died. And then after she told him, just blurted it right out, he probably wished that it had been that — because if someone had died, it would be sad, sure, but not unthinkable. They would know what to do and how to deal with it. There would be things they had to do, actions they had to take. But with this, they were left on their own.

Sometimes when Cleo was in a moment that she knew was an important one, she could step back from it like she was watching it, like she wasn't part of it, like she was just an observer. And she knew she was going to remember for the rest of her life how Max responded when she said, 'I'm pregnant,' simply and without any lead-in. Because he'd remained standing and put both hands on either side of his head so that he looked the way people on TV look when they're witnessing a tragedy or an accident, like someone jumping from a building. And then he looked straight at her, waiting for her to take it back or say she was kidding, but she remained silent.

'Oh fuck,' he said. And then again. 'Oh fuck.'

They didn't sleep that night. They tried; when they were exhausted with talking and Cleo was drained from crying, they lay on the bed facing each other with their eyes closed. But neither of them slept, and soon they'd just start talking again.

'What are we going to do?' Max said. It was just what she'd wanted to hear Monica say. But it didn't sound comforting coming out of his mouth.

'I don't know,' Cleo said. 'I really don't know.'

'Do you think you want to keep it? Or do you think you don't?'

He couldn't even say the word, which was driving her crazy. All night, he'd talked around it. It wasn't his fault, she tried to tell herself. It was a hard word to say, but if they were going to talk about it, they were going to have to say it.

'I don't know if I can have an abortion,' she said.

'Okay.'

'But I don't know if I can have the baby.'

'Okay.'

Cleo started crying again, quietly. Tears just rolled out of her eyes and she had no idea how she still had any left inside of her. She was surely dehydrating herself. She hadn't cried this much in her whole life. Never.

'I'll do whatever you want,' Max said. He put his hand on the side of her head. 'Whatever we do will be okay.'

Cleo moved away from him and sat up to blow her nose. He sat up too, put his hand on her back. She knew that he was trying to make her feel better, trying to touch her so that she would know he was there, but it was suffocating. She blew her nose and added the Kleenex to the pile that was on the nightstand.

'I can't imagine doing either,' she said. 'But if I had to pick one that I really couldn't do, it would be having an abortion. I can't. I know I just can't.'

'I know,' Max said.

'And I don't want to even think about giving the baby away.

I don't want to do that. I mean, we're young but we're not, like, thirteen. People our age have babies all the time.'

'So that's the decision, then,' Max said. He reached over and put his arms around her shoulders, pulling her down until she was lying in his lap. She was so uncomfortable, she wanted to scream. It felt like Max was trying to act like a straitjacket. But she knew if she moved then, he'd be hurt, and so she willed herself to stay still.

'We shouldn't tell anyone,' Cleo said. 'Not now. Not for a while. Anything could happen. I could have a miscarriage. It happens all the time.' She tried not to hope for this, but she couldn't help it. It was one thing to decide to have the baby, but if nature intervened, well, then, who was she to stop it?

'How long should we wait?' Max said.

'I don't know,' Cleo said. *Forever,* she thought.

They decided they would wait until Thanksgiving to tell their families. It was three weeks away. If she was still pregnant by then, they'd suck it up and tell them.

'They're going to kill us,' Max said. He sounded so young then, like a seven-year-old in trouble, and even though it was the exact same thing Cleo had been thinking, she found she was annoyed.

They went through their days, going to class and watching TV. Cleo studied for midterms harder than ever, trying anything she could to keep from thinking about being pregnant. She stayed in the library for hours, eating only bananas and drinking water.

There was one cubicle she liked, on the fourth floor near the back. It was right by a window, and she could watch people below as they scurried around the campus, sometimes laughing with a friend, sometimes staring down at the ground with a serious look.

Cleo got more done at this cubicle than anywhere else. She began to think of it as only hers, and a couple of times when she arrived at the library to find it taken, she sat nearby, keeping her eye on it until the person there decided to leave. Once, when someone left an empty Coke can there, like it was his own personal garbage can, she'd followed him out.

'You forgot this,' she said, and handed it to the boy.

'Oh, I'm done with that,' he said.

'You're not supposed to have food or drink in here,' she told him. He'd just shrugged. She felt like someone had come into her home and littered.

Two weeks later, Cleo felt like she was losing her mind. She was still pregnant, there was no doubt about it. And even though almost every night she or Max would say, 'Let's not talk about it tonight,' they couldn't help it. They always came back to it. Even if they were just watching TV or a movie, there was always a baby somewhere on the screen, and one of them would look at the other, or Max would lean over and rub her leg, and just like that they were in the middle of it again. There was no escaping it.

Cleo managed to avoid talking to Elizabeth much on the phone. She was afraid if they talked too long, Elizabeth would hear it in her voice. It was a lot like after she had sex for the first time and was afraid to look Elizabeth in the eye, like she'd be able to tell right away. Cleo kept her phone calls short, told her that she was really busy with schoolwork, that she was spending every minute studying.

'I'm glad you're focused,' Elizabeth said. 'Senior year is important.'

Max stayed in the apartment with her every night. She wondered what his friends must think. Maybe that they were fighting, that they'd break up soon. Or maybe that she was making him stay home, controlling every part of him. If she thought about it too long, her head hurt.

One afternoon, Max was at class and Cleo was walking around the apartment. She felt jittery, like she'd been drinking Red Bull. And before she could think about it, she pulled out her phone and called Monica.

Monica answered on the first ring. She probably thought something was wrong, since even when she and Cleo were a pair, they mostly just texted. They preferred talking in person.

'Hey,' Cleo said. She suddenly felt nervous. 'I was just thinking about you and thought I'd call.'

'Oh, hi,' Monica said.

'I was – do you want to get lunch? I haven't seen you in forever.'

'Sure,' Monica said.

They met in the cafeteria. Monica looked thin, but she got a salad and she seemed a little less angry. The frown line between her eyes was gone.

A new girl that had transferred, Trish, had moved into Cleo's old room and Monica said she was nice. 'She's clean – like almost OCD – so, you know, Mary and Laura like her.'

'That's great,' Cleo said. She felt weirdly jealous, like she was being cheated on.

'So, how's Max?'

'He's good. He's really good.'

Monica poked at her salad. 'I can't believe you guys are living together. It's so grown-up.'

'Yeah, I guess so.' Cleo knew she'd never tell Monica now.

Monica told her that she was almost definitely going back to Boston at the end of the year. 'My parents want me close by.'

'That seems like a good idea.'

'Yeah, I guess. They want me to live at home for at least a year, which seems unnecessary, but whatever.'

Then Monica went on to tell her about a party they'd had at the house. 'We got all these boxes of wine, and had people dress up like it was fancy, and Laura made Jell-O shots, which I've never had.'

'Really?' Cleo asked.

'Yeah, it was so funny.' Monica stopped poking at her lettuce and put her fork down. 'Oh shit, we should have told you about it. I don't know why we spaced on it.'

'That's okay,' Cleo said. She wouldn't have gone anyway. She couldn't have stood to be sober at a party where Laura and Mary were fun and took Jell-O shots.

'I feel so bad,' Monica said.

'Really, it's fine. Laura and Mary probably wouldn't have let me in anyway, unless I spun the chore wheel and cleaned the bathroom or something.'

'Oh, them.' Monica waved her fork. 'I think they're over it.'

'Really?'

'Yeah, you know how they are. They get all bent out of shape, but then they get over it. You should have seen them with this party. They really went all out.'

Cleo picked up her drink and took a long sip of her Diet Coke through the straw, even though it was hard to swallow. Monica and her old roommates were getting along just fine without her. Better, really. They were having parties and Jell-O shots. How did she get here? How did she end up pregnant and friendless, about to graduate from college with nothing to show for it?

Monica was watching her, like she knew she was upset but didn't know what to say. Cleo pulled the straw out of her mouth and set her drink down.

'That's crazy,' she finally said. 'I can't imagine it.'

It started to make sense to her now, how people that undergo terrible loss or tragedy manage to keep living. She'd never really understood it before, but the thing was that the body will shock you, so that maybe you don't believe it all at once. And then, if you keep moving, a day goes by, and then another. And since the worst thing you ever imagined actually came true, that becomes your reality, something else takes the place in your mind, and you continue on.

Once. One day she had forgotten to take her pill. And she'd taken it the very next day, just like she was supposed to. Just like they said to. In what world did that make a baby? In what world? Cleo never really did much wrong. She'd always been a rule follower. She always went to class, always did her assignments, did her reading, handed in her papers on time. The worst thing she'd ever done was get drunk in high school. And who didn't do that? She'd forgotten to do the right thing for one day and that was it. Life was shit sometimes, it really was.

Thanksgiving was getting closer. Every time Cleo saw a paper turkey anywhere, she felt like she might throw up. She thought often about the presidential pardon of the turkey. It was a weird tradition and when she was younger it upset her. It still did, if she was being honest. Why on earth would everyone gather to watch one bird be spared when there were millions of others being eaten for dinner? Were you supposed to feel really happy for that one turkey that made it when the rest of his family was getting their heads chopped off? It didn't make any sense. It was cruel, really, and it made her stomach turn. It was enough to make anyone a vegetarian, and she found that she couldn't stomach the thought of it. During those weeks before Thanksgiving, she stopped eating meat altogether.

Walking around campus, Cleo just watched everyone and thought, *I fucked up more than you, and more than you, and more than you.* It was like nothing she'd done up to this point mattered anymore. Everyone else was free and she had a human growing inside of her.

Every day, Cleo thought about what it would be like after they told everyone. Max's family would hate her for sure. And Elizabeth was going to be so mad, she couldn't even imagine. She'd always talked about birth control, always made sure that Cleo knew what she needed to know. It was like she was telling her, *You were a mistake and believe me, you want to make sure you don't do what I did.*

Maybe they were some sort of hyper-fertile family. It was possible. She could tell Elizabeth that it wasn't her fault, it was biology. That would go over well.

Cleo hated when people were mad at her. She couldn't stand to disappoint anyone. The thought of Elizabeth and Max's family being so thoroughly disappointed in her made it hard to breathe.

Elizabeth used to always tell her she needed a thicker skin. 'Not everyone is going to like what you do all the time,' she'd say. 'Sometimes you have to say, screw you, and do it anyway.'

Senior year in high school, Cleo had decided not to play soccer. It had gotten to be too much, and she liked her other activities better, so it only made sense. She was sleepless for weeks, knowing that she'd have to tell the team, knowing that the girls and the coach were going to be disappointed in her. She hated disappointing people.

'Oh, for Christ's sake, Cleo,' Elizabeth had said. 'This is your life. You're the one that has to live with the decision you make, not anyone else. Just remember that. What you do in life is yours and it doesn't matter what other people want from you.'

It was sort of funny, actually, that for the first time in her life, Cleo was going to take Elizabeth's advice, that for once she was going to do something that was going to make everyone around her angry as all hell. She repeated Elizabeth's words to herself every night. *What you do in life is yours.*

Cleo thought that maybe when she told Elizabeth, she could point out how ironic it all was, how she was finally doing just what Elizabeth suggested. 'That's the thing about giving advice,' she could say. 'It might come back to haunt you.'

Chapter 11

Martha's new job smelled like death. Or actually, it smelled like dying, which was worse. Death was at least clinical and final. Dying lingered. It was urine-stained couch cushions and shirts with drool on them. It was labored breathing and fake cheery voices that tried to distract the patient from the fact that this was it — his life was coming to a close.

Her first day, Martha showed up to find Jaz scrubbing the wood floor in the den with Pine-Sol. 'Just a little accident,' she said. Her voice was pleasant and no-nonsense, the kind of voice you would use when dealing with a child, to let them know that accidents happen, but they're nobody's fault, and it's nothing to be embarrassed about.

Mr. Cranston sat in his chair and stared straight ahead, not acknowledging Martha or Jaz's comment. Martha, unsure of what to do, stood in the corner and folded her arms across her stomach. 'Accidents happen every day,' she'd said. Then she wanted to die, because Mr. Cranston gave her an accusing look that meant he thought that either she was a moron or she was against him.

'Mr. Cranston loves to read his papers first thing,' Jaz said. She wrung out her rag into the bucket. 'Why don't you go grab those for him – they're by the front door – and go ahead and put them in the sitting room? When we're done here, I'll show you how to get breakfast ready.'

Martha nodded and almost ran from the room to the front of the house, where she picked up the *Wall Street Journal,* the *New York Times,* and the *Philadelphia Inquirer.* She was so grateful to get out of that room, that she almost hit her head when she opened the door.

When they met in the kitchen, Jaz told her not to get overwhelmed. 'I'm going to be here with you for a couple of weeks until you get it down. Any questions you have, you just ask. I'm not going anywhere, so there's no reason to get nervous, okay?'

Martha nodded and swallowed. Ever since her stupid comment about accidents happening every day, she felt like she might start crying. But Jaz was kind. And for that, she was very grateful.

'Okay, now. First thing you'll do when you get here in the morning is make breakfast. It's the only meal you'll have to make, but he's pretty particular about it. He has the same thing every day – two soft-boiled eggs and a piece of wholewheat toast. He used to have bacon too, but that ended about five years ago, when his cholesterol went through the roof. Every once in a while he can still have it, but don't let him fool you into thinking that he gets it every day, okay?'

Martha nodded again. She was trying to remember everything that Jaz told her, and then, without a word, Jaz handed her a black leather-bound notebook and pen. The breakfast was just the beginning of the instructions. Lunch and dinner were prepared by a cook who came in a few times a week, and stored the meals.

Jaz opened the big shiny refrigerator to reveal shelves full of delicious-looking meals, stored in clean, labeled Tupperware containers. It was the kind of refrigerator that Martha would love to have, full of meals that made her hungry just to read the labels – cold salmon and homemade mayonnaise, mini beef tenderloin sliders with horseradish sauce, fresh arugula with shaves of Parmesan, and little lamb chops, tiny and perfect.

'Don't worry about getting the food ready,' Jaz said. 'The cook writes everything down on this pad over here, and you just follow her instructions. It's easy. Also, there's always plenty, so help yourself to whatever you want.'

Martha wanted to stand and stare at the shelves all day. They were so neat and orderly. Imagine having this be your refrigerator! You'd never find an old peach or a soft sweet potato in there, never find a block of moldy cheese and have to wonder when you bought it. Martha was still staring as Jaz shut the door.

The instructions continued. Mr. Cranston could go to the bathroom by himself, but he sometimes needed help walking there, or getting up from his chair. He did not want or need help once he got there. 'For now,' Jaz said.

He read all three papers every morning. He did not like to watch TV, except for the seven o'clock news, and sometimes *Jeopardy* if he was in the mood. If he was extremely tired, you could sometimes persuade him to watch a show; just suggest it like it was something you'd heard about and thought he would like. Nothing popular. No sitcoms. He did not like to watch shows where groups of adults lived together in the city and whined and acted like children. Stick to things like BBC miniseries, as long as there wasn't too much melodrama.

He was an avid reader and would (at least twice a month) make a list of new books that he wanted. The local bookstore could be called — they had his account information — and they would drop off the books the next day. He had a computer, although he didn't use it all that often. He did not e-mail. He did sometimes ask to dictate a letter, to an old friend or work acquaintance, which he would want typed up so that he could sign it. 'He had a secretary for years,' Jaz explained. 'It's just something he's used to.'

Mr. Cranston enjoyed crosswords sometimes, and did not like to be interrupted while he worked on them. He did not like to go outside, but Jaz insisted that he get out at least once a day, to go for a walk in his wheelchair. It made him feel like a baby, to be pushed around the block, but Jaz was firm. He needed fresh air and he knew it. If you were firm with him, he would be okay. Just a quick walk, maybe fifteen or twenty minutes, down the street and maybe over by the park, but not *in* the park, because there were almost always children there, and they were so noisy, and he didn't like to see the way that children were raised these days, like wild animals let loose. Why did they always have snacks with them, their grubby hands full of yogurts and drinks and crackers, like they were going to starve before they got home? 'Just trust me,' Jaz said. 'Stay out of the park.'

Ruby came over a couple of times a week, whenever she felt like it, really. She usually brought some sort of gift, a book, or a pint of frozen soup that she picked up. 'She tries to help, bless her,' Jaz said. But Ruby was often in the way. She insisted that he go on an outing with her, to the store, or maybe to a restaurant for an early dinner.

'Even when he was healthy as a horse, Mr. Cranston never shopped. Never. And he never liked eating out,' Jaz said. 'That man would rather eat a peanut butter sandwich than sit in a restaurant.'

His son, Billy, usually came only on the weekends, so Martha would probably never see him, but when he did come he just liked to sit with his father and wasn't a bother.

Martha wrote everything down. It was a lot of information, but she felt like she could get a handle on it if she could just write it down. The nurses came at night, and as soon as she let them in at six o'clock, she was free to go.

'Don't take it personal if he gets crabby,' Jaz told her. 'He's an old man and he's used to having things his way. And now his body's failing him and that's hard for him to handle.'

'Okay,' Martha said. 'That's so sad.'

'It's sad, sure. But it's just life. We're here, we live, and we die. Not much you can do about it, so we might as well enjoy it while we can. No use worrying about that.'

Martha couldn't believe that Jaz really thought this. Who in their right mind wasn't afraid of dying? She was probably just putting on a brave face so that Martha would feel better about the whole thing. She must be.

Jaz moved around the house with so much purpose. Martha watched as she informed Mr. Cranston that it was time for lunch, suggested that he'd like to take a rest, announced that it was time for a walk. Martha walked behind her, afraid of what Mr. Cranston was going to say, her feet following Jaz's, stepping right where she had stepped, hoping that this would give her some sort of strength.

When she got home at night, she was so tired she could barely move. The first week, she was in bed by nine each night. She resolved every night as she went to bed that the next day she would act just like Jaz. She would be firm and purposeful. But each morning she woke up and she was still herself – nervous and unsure, following behind Jaz, afraid of upsetting Mr. Cranston.

*

'It's sad,' Martha told her family at dinner. 'It's like everyone is just waiting for him to die, including him! Like they're just killing time. Literally.'

'Well, what did you expect?' Claire asked. 'You knew you were going to be a caretaker for an elderly person. It's not like there's a lot of different endings to that story.'

'I know, I was just saying that it's hard. That's all.'

If Martha was being honest, she missed J.Crew. She missed bossing people around the ribboned shirts and sparkly scarves. She missed her work smelling like new clothes. It had been so clean at the store. There'd been an order to the polos, a calmness to the khakis.

Every night, Weezy asked her how her day had gone as soon as she walked in the door. She asked it nervously, like she was waiting for bad news.

'I think people are waiting for me to fail,' Martha told Dr. Baer.

'Are you waiting for yourself to fail?' Dr. Baer asked. 'Do you think you want to fail?'

'No, I don't want to fail,' Martha said. 'Of course I don't want to fail.' Sometimes Dr. Baer was an idiot.

Martha found herself losing patience during her sessions. *I'm a patient losing patience,* she often thought when this happened. Dr. Baer didn't seem all that impressed that she had a new job, that she was practically back to nursing.

'Well, I don't think that people are waiting for you to fail,' Dr. Baer said. 'I think you have a good support system around you, and when people ask you how things are going, they're really asking just that and nothing more.'

'I guess so.'

'So, how do you feel at the end of the day with Mr. Cranston?'

'Good, I guess.' The truth was that sometimes it was very, very boring. Martha sat still and watched the clock during the days, just waiting for the next activity.

'That's great,' Dr. Baer said. 'It sounds like this job was the right move for you then, something to challenge you a little more.'

'Retail is very challenging,' Martha said. She tried not to sound too offended. 'People don't understand that, but it's not easy. You don't just show up and sell things. Plus, I was a manager, which entailed a lot of responsibility. So actually, I don't think that this job is more challenging in that sense. Not at all.'

'That's a good point,' Dr. Baer said. 'I guess what I meant was that it's different and new. And new things are always challenging, especially when you've gotten comfortable somewhere.'

'Right, I guess that's true. New jobs are hard,' Martha said. 'Actually my sister just got a new job too.'

'Really?'

'Yeah, she's temping for an agency, and they already placed her somewhere for a few months.'

'You sound impressed.'

'With Claire? No. I mean, not that I'm not impressed, but I'm not surprised, I guess.'

'No?'

'No. She wanted a job and so she got one.'

'That's all there was to it?'

'Pretty much. Things come pretty easily for her.'

'Really?'

'Yeah, I've told you that before.'

'You have,' Dr. Baer said. 'I just find it interesting that you're still so sure of that. She's had a tough year, hasn't she?'

'Yeah, but still. It's not like things have happened to her . . . She's made the decisions. She ended her engagement, she quit her job, she moved back home. I mean, it's a lot of changes, but it's all stuff she wanted to do.'

'But haven't you made your decisions too?'

'Well, yeah, but it's different.'

'Different how?'

'Claire has more choices?'

'How so?'

'She just does, she always has.'

'Okay.'

'It's true.'

'I didn't say it wasn't true. I just think you can't be so quick to be so sure of other people's situations. Examine your own situation. You also have a lot of choices. It's not always easier for other people. It doesn't work like that.'

'Sure it does. A lot of times it does work like that.'

'Well, sometimes, I'll admit it might seem that way. But things aren't always what they seem.'

After that session, Martha thought about her choices. She thought that maybe she should have been a therapist, so that she could say things like, 'Your life isn't so hard,' and 'I see,' over and over again. Now that seemed like an easy life.

Now that Claire was temping and she was at the Cranstons', they were getting up and getting ready at the same time each morning, which they hadn't done since high school. Sometimes Martha knocked on the bathroom door, pretending to be in a hurry, so that Claire would let her in and they could brush their teeth together, put on makeup side by side.

Martha loved when Ruby came to the Cranston house. She was the prettiest person Martha had ever seen in real life – she always looked a little bit tan, her hair was always shiny. Once, when Martha commented on how glamorous Ruby was, Jaz said, 'She should be. She works at it like it's a job.'

Sometimes, Ruby would sit in the kitchen with Martha and have some tea. Martha always made it, but she didn't mind. Ruby sort of seemed like a little kid that needed things done for her. The first day that she came, she kept staring at the teapot and saying, 'I'd love some tea,' like it was a puzzle she couldn't figure out. Finally, Martha got up to make the tea, and Ruby smiled at her like she was relieved.

Now Martha offered as soon as Ruby walked into the kitchen,

setting out cookies and starting the water boiling. Then, Martha would sit and wait for Ruby to start talking – Ruby loved to talk – hoping that she was going to spill some family secrets.

'We're not speaking,' Ruby said one day. 'My brother and me, I mean. We're on upsetting terms.' Ruby had a strange way of talking, of putting words together, almost like English wasn't her first language, or like she wanted people to think that. She dotted her sentences with random phrases, arranged verbs and nouns in odd places, throwing them wherever she pleased.

'Oh really?' Martha asked. She didn't want to sound too eager, but she was dying to know about Billy.

Ruby sighed. 'He's impossible, if you must know, my brother. He thinks of himself as the most important person in the world. Or rather, he thinks he's more important than he is, in truth.' Ruby paused to think this over. 'I don't know which one it is, or if there's even a difference. I'm just telling this to you, so that you understand why we won't be in the house at the same time. This is why the schedule exists.'

'Of course,' Martha said. 'I mean, I understand. Has this been going on for a long time?'

'Forever, it seems like. But in actual time, only a few years. Since my mom died, really. Billy thinks he's in charge of everything.'

'Families are tricky,' Martha said.

'Isn't that the truest thing,' Ruby said, and Martha felt like the cleverest person in the world.

*

Martha loved sending her cousin Cathy long e-mails about her job and the Cranstons. She told her about Jaz and Ruby, and talked about how degrading it must be for Mr. Cranston to basically need a babysitter at this point in his life. Cathy loved hearing about her work, always responded by telling her how funny and insightful she was, sometimes suggesting that Martha should be a writer, which always thrilled Martha.

Martha and Cathy had always gotten along well, mostly because they found each other entertaining. Martha always said how lucky she was that her best friend was her cousin too. And the fact that she was a lesbian was just an added bonus. Martha thought it made her sound very cool and accepting when she said things like, 'I'm going to visit my cousin Cathy and her partner, Ruth. She's great, Ruth is. They've been together for a while now, my cousin and her partner.'

She used to talk about Cathy all the time at J.Crew, partly because she wanted Wally to know that she was not only accepting of his lifestyle, but that she too had gay friends and family. She made references to Cathy a lot, until one day Wally said, 'You don't have to call her *Cathy my cousin who's a lesbian* every time you talk about her. We get it, sweetie. You're related to a dyke.'

Martha wanted to tell him that she didn't like that term, that she found it offensive, but she wasn't sure she was allowed to, since Wally was gay himself. She just cut back on her talk about Cathy at work.

Cathy had come out via e-mail to the family during her

freshman year in college. Martha had read the note, and then called home immediately, knowing that Weezy wouldn't have checked her e-mail yet. She was excited to be the one to break the news, basically yelled it out as soon as Weezy answered the phone.

'Oh,' Weezy had said. 'Well, honey, you aren't surprised, are you?'

Martha actually was surprised, but not because she couldn't imagine that Cathy was a lesbian – she actually could, now that she thought about it. But she just hadn't thought about it one way or the other before. Cathy was just her cousin, who was sometimes bossy and always knew the most scandalous information growing up, like what French kissing really entailed, and what the definition of third base was.

'No,' Martha had said. 'I guess I'm not surprised.' She was, however, sad that she wasn't able to shock Weezy with this information. Martha loved a good piece of gossip and this one was a doozy.

Cathy was very excited about Martha's new job, and even more excited at the idea that Martha might get a place of her own. Martha had mentioned this idea briefly one time, and now Cathy wouldn't let it drop.

'Things are cheaper in Ohio,' she reminded Cathy one night on the phone. 'I can't afford a place just yet.'

'Martha, you're thirty. You can't afford not to afford your own place.'

*

After two weeks, Jaz started leaving Martha alone with Mr. Cranston. First, she just ran little errands, but with each day she left for longer stretches of time. 'I need to run to the store,' she'd say. Martha knew that she was being tested during this time, to see if she could handle it and also to see if Mr. Cranston was okay with her being there.

'I get the feeling that if he doesn't like me, they'll just fire me,' Martha told her family one night.

'Of course he'll like you,' Weezy said. And Will had nodded in agreement, and that was that.

Most of her time with Mr. Cranston was quiet, sometimes just sitting together and reading. Martha learned to bring a book with her, so that if Mr. Cranston wanted to read all afternoon, she could do the same. At first, she would walk around the house, trying to find something to do, refolding blankets and hanging them over the edge of the couch, or getting Mr. Cranston a fresh glass of water.

Eventually, Jaz told her to settle down. 'There are people that come to this house to do all of these jobs. All your job is, all you have to worry about is keeping him company and making sure he gets what he needs. Most of the time it's not too hard, right? So just settle down and enjoy the quiet time.'

Martha had nodded, although her feelings had been a little hurt. She was a doer. She couldn't help it. That's why she'd been so great at J.Crew. She loved moving around and keeping busy, making things look pretty.

But after a few days, Martha realized that Jaz had been

trying to help her. She could see that it annoyed Mr. Cranston when she moved around too much, that it disturbed his reading when she walked in and out of the room. He didn't like to call for help, would never shout to the next room that he needed something. He liked someone to be right there, so that he could just turn his head and Martha could say, 'Did you need to go to the restroom?' or 'Are you thirsty?'

Jaz was agitated lately, on the phone with her family often, and she confided in Martha that she didn't like the 'no-good' man that her daughter was dating.

'If she marries him, so help me God, I will kidnap her and leave the country.'

'Is he abusive?' Martha asked. She was imagining Jaz and her daughter running for their lives.

'Is he what? No, child. He's just a lazy shit.'

'Oh.'

'Mark my words, if they end up getting married, my Marly will work herself to the bone, while he lays around the house smoking dope in his skivvies and watching talk shows.'

'Did you tell her that you don't like him?'

'Did I tell her? I tell her every day that he's worthless. I tell him, too, when I see him. It doesn't seem to help. He don't scare easy, I'll give him that.'

Martha tried to imagine what it would be like to have Jaz as a mother, or to be in a family where people just said exactly what they were thinking, shouting their opinion no matter what it was. She didn't see how much good could come from that.

One afternoon, Martha was in Mr. Cranston's office, looking for a new credit card to give to the bookstore. 'The old one expired,' Jaz told Martha on her way out the door. 'The new one is on his desk, I think. Just call them with the new number. He's getting cranky and needs his books.'

The desk was covered with folders and file cards that had notes and lists written on them. Martha felt like she was snooping, even though Jaz had told her to go through the papers. She carefully lifted one set of folders and placed them to the side, then picked up a couple of loose pieces of paper and that was when she saw the manila folder, labeled FUNERAL.

She couldn't believe it. She glanced at the door and then opened the folder before she could even stop herself. It was full of old funeral mass booklets, some of which were marked with Mr. Cranston's handwriting. There were readings that were circled, and some that were crossed over with a big X, sometimes a NO written next to it for good measure.

Martha heard a noise in the hall and she shut the folder quickly. She spotted the new credit card, grabbed it, and ran out into the hall holding it in the air, like it was a badge proving that she wasn't snooping. But no one was there.

All afternoon, Martha kept thinking about what it must be like for Mr. Cranston to plan his own funeral. How scary it must be to know that death was coming. Of course, she knew that death was coming for everyone, but it must be strange to know without a doubt that it was coming soon. He was so organized, so efficient. It looked like just another business file on his desk, just one more thing to cross off his list.

Sometimes, imagining her own funeral, Martha could make herself cry. She didn't sob, but if she pictured her parents and siblings sitting in a pew, pictured Cathy bent over with grief, she could get a tear or two out. After all, it would be such a tragedy, such a shame if she were to die now.

There were times when Martha imagined that she'd died of a long and drawn-out disease, which would give her time to prepare, as Mr. Cranston was doing. She would write letters to all the people that were important to her, and leave instructions for them to be opened on the day of her funeral. And of course, she'd write an open letter to be read at the actual service. She'd probably have Claire read it – her parents would be too distraught, and Max wasn't great at public speaking. She could have Cathy do it, but she was a little rough sometimes, and Martha would want the letter to be read with quiet emotion. Claire would be devastated too, of course, but Martha would explain that it was her last sisterly duty, and Claire would come through.

Martha wondered if she was the only one who thought about these kinds of things. She could daydream about her funeral for hours, imagining the people from her past that would show up, the ones that would be shocked to hear the news. She worried sometimes that this wasn't normal, but then she told herself that people talked about death all the time. At least once a month, usually after she'd had to go retrieve something from the attic or the basement, Weezy would say, 'I pity you children, if your father and I die unexpectedly. It will take you a decade to clean out this house.'

Once, her grandma Bets had announced at a family dinner that she'd like to be cremated and have her ashes split between her two daughters. Later that night, Martha overheard Weezy and Maureen talking about it.

'That gives me the heebie-jeebies,' Weezy said. 'What do you think possessed her to say that?'

'I think she wants to make sure that she'll always be with us,' Maureen answered. 'Judging and disapproving our every move from her urn.'

The two of them had laughed, but Martha was disturbed. Maybe she'd like to be cremated too. Then she could be with her family, instead of underground, and they could take her with them wherever they went. But then what would happen after all of them were gone too? Her ashes would be passed around, and then, eventually, generations later, someone would say, 'What is this thing?' and they'd get sick of taking care of the urn, probably find it creepy, and put it in the garbage. So maybe cremation wasn't the best choice.

When she was younger, she'd seen a mausoleum in a graveyard and asked Weezy what it was. 'Can we get one of those?' she asked. To her, it seemed like the perfect solution, to be with your family, above ground, so that no critters could get to you. It was just like a little house. But Weezy had told her no.

'You'll grow up and have your own family,' she'd said.

'And you'll want to be buried near them too.' But that seemed impossible to Martha at the time, to grow up and have a family of her own. She'd always secretly thought that she could buy a mausoleum after her parents died, but then for their fiftieth birthdays, Bets had given each of her parents a plot in Saint Ambrose's graveyard.

Ruby kept bringing presents for her father – a blanket, a CD, a new movie for him to watch. Mr. Cranston never seemed to like any of the things that she gave to him, but she seemed determined to keep trying. Once she brought him an iPad, and insisted that he try to play Angry Birds.

'Here, Dad, put your finger here and then shoot the bird like this.'

'What? Why am I doing this?' he asked.

'To try to kill the pigs,' Ruby explained. 'I know it seems strange, but I think you'll really like it. It's totally addicting.' Ruby had a tendency to sound like a teenager when she talked to her dad.

Mr. Cranston humored her, putting his finger to the screen, and then looking surprised when there was the sound of a bird screaming and pigs snorting. 'What the hell is this thing?' he asked.

Ruby had just laughed. 'We can put it away for now,' she said. 'But you should try it later. I really think you'll like it.' Martha was pretty sure that Mr. Cranston never touched the iPad again, and sometimes it made her sad, how badly Ruby wanted to find something that would make her father happy.

Martha had started to dream about the Cranstons. She figured it was just from spending so much time there. After all, she'd had more J.Crew stress dreams than she could even count. The number of times she'd woken up in a panic, sweating, because no matter how hard she tried she couldn't get the sweaters to stay folded and in a pile. Oh, those were the worst! As soon as she managed to wrangle one sweater, another one fell out, and another. Around the holidays, when the store was at its craziest, Martha barely slept.

But the dreams about the Cranstons were a little different. In them, Martha was part of the family. They weren't stressful at all, except for one where Ruby's hair fell out and she screamed at Martha. But usually, the dreams were just Martha sitting around with the family, watching TV or eating dinner. They sort of reminded her of the dreams she used to have when she was younger, where she was a part of the Huxtables or the *Full House* family.

Dr. Baer told her she might be getting a little too involved. 'I understand it's hard when you spend so much time with a family, and you get wrapped up in their business. But just remember to keep a little distance. You're there as the caretaker.'

People were always telling Martha not to get too involved. She didn't understand it. How could anyone be too involved?

Didn't that just show people that you cared? What did people want? Did they want everyone to just walk around, pretending that they didn't see anyone else, didn't notice a thing? That was ridiculous.

In college, Martha was always the first one to step up and tell one of the girls if she needed to break up with her boyfriend. 'He's not treating you right,' she'd say. She'd demand that the girl end it. How could she not step in when she saw something bad happening?

The girls that she was trying to help almost always got annoyed with her. 'Mind your own business, Martha,' they'd say. But she wouldn't let it drop. After all, they were the ones who offered up the information in the first place, who told her about the things their boyfriends said, the suspicions they had about cheating. What else was she supposed to do?

'People don't want to hear that they're with the wrong person,' Claire told her once. 'And unless they're being abused in some way, the most you can really say is that you think they can do better. Or that they should be treated better. But that's it.'

Martha disagreed. She'd just ended a friendship with a girl in her nursing program, Ann, who had refused to break up with her boyfriend.

'Look,' Claire said. 'I get what you're saying. But at the end of the day, it's not really your business. People don't always want the truth, and you don't always know what the real truth is. It's not worth losing a friend over.'

But Martha had lost a friend. Ann never forgave her for the things that she'd said, and she ended up marrying the guy. Martha didn't get it. Weren't friends there to tell you the truth? Weren't you supposed to get involved?

When Mr. Cranston had a doctor's appointment, either Jaz or Ruby took him. He preferred Jaz, because Ruby usually got herself all worked up, thinking the doctor was going to find something fatal during these visits.

'Don't worry about it,' Mr. Cranston told her once. 'I'm already dying. What else could they tell me?'

'Oh, Dad,' Ruby said. She went to the upstairs bathroom and shut herself in for almost fifteen minutes.

'Well, now we'll never get out of here,' he said. He crossed his arms and waited for her to come downstairs.

'Why does he have so many appointments?' Martha asked Jaz. 'Is there something wrong with him?'

'He's old, child. Things have started failing. He's having trouble breathing, his heart's giving out, you name it, it's happening to him.' She didn't know how Jaz could be so matter-of-fact about it.

It seemed to Martha that Mr. Cranston got a little smaller each day, just a tiny bit weaker than he was the day before. Could she be imagining it? When they sat together and read, sometimes he fell asleep in the middle of a page, the book open on his lap, his mouth open with a little bit of drool at the corner.

His skin looked so thin while he slept, the veins so close to the surface. Martha knew he should rest if he was tired, but what she really wanted to do was make noise until he woke up and moved around, until he looked alive again.

Martha couldn't help but talk about the Cranstons when she was at home. She was always dying to share new information about them, or tell her family what she thought was behind the rift between Ruby and Billy.

'You sound a little obsessed with them,' Claire said one night. Claire had started cooking dinner for the family, claiming that she was so bored at her temp job, all she could do was look up recipes on the computer. She'd made some truly amazing things, like tonight's dinner of tarragon chicken in cream sauce, scalloped cherry tomatoes, and twice-baked potatoes.

'You're going to send us all to the fat farm,' Weezy said when she sat down that night.

'I'm not obsessed with them,' Martha told Claire. 'I'm just interested. They're interesting.'

'It's a fine line between interested and obsessed,' Claire said, but Martha wasn't offended. Claire had never met them, so she didn't understand. The Cranstons were the kind of people who had an interesting story, who had many interesting stories. They were the kind of people that once you met them, you just wanted to learn everything you could about their lives.

Chapter 12

Thanksgiving started weeks before it actually happened. It was the way it always had been. There was shopping to get done, the house needed to be cleaned, silver needed to be polished. There were logistics that had to be figured out – who was coming, who was staying where, who was a vegetarian this year, who was lactose intolerant. There were phone calls to be had with Maureen, to complain about their mother and her absolute refusal to cooperate with anyone on anything. 'She doesn't want to come?' Maureen said every year. 'Great, let's leave her in Michigan. I'm good with that, are you?'

Years ago, when they were both first married and had little babies in the house, they used to switch off hosting Thanksgiving. This didn't last long. Weezy ended up doing all of the cooking anyway, and most of the cleaning, and honestly it was just easier to have it at her own house in her own kitchen.

The past few years had gotten more complicated, since they started to think that Bets shouldn't travel by herself. Cathy and Ruth had taken on the responsibility of driving almost three hours from Ohio to Auburn Hills to pick up Bets and fly with her from Detroit. It wasn't convenient, but none of them could think of a better alternative. Bets, of course, still thought she was fine to travel alone, so Cathy and Ruth had to think of excuses for why they were going to be up that way anyway. 'We're visiting friends,' they always told Bets. She acted like she was doing them a favor, letting them stay at her house for a night before they all flew to Philadelphia.

'Cathy's coming again this year,' she told Weezy. 'I guess some of her lesbian friends live up this way.'

'Great, well, that works out for everyone.' Weezy didn't know how many more years they could realistically keep asking Cathy and Ruth to escort a crabby old lady on a plane.

Weezy and Maureen still alternated who Bets would stay with, and unfortunately this was Weezy's year. 'Tough break,' Maureen said. She didn't mean it. Bets was a horrendous houseguest. If Will emptied the dishwasher, she commented on Weezy's lack of housekeeping skills. Once, Weezy put out cocktail napkins and Bets had called her hoity-toity. There was no winning.

They used to invite their cousins the Nugents from Pittsburgh, but thankfully that had stopped after Bets's sister, Linda, died and all of the children's children had reproduced so many times that it was impossible to fit everyone in the same house. They were an odd bunch. Linda had once brought a basket of stuffed reindeer to the house, and Weezy assumed (as one might) that she'd brought them for the kids. 'How nice of you,' she said. 'I'm sure Martha and Claire will be thrilled.' She tried to take the basket away from Linda, who held on tight.

'These are my pets,' she'd said. 'Our last dog died and we're too old to get another one, so now these are my pets.' She'd walked into the house with her basket and proceeded to tell anyone who would listen about each of the reindeer. 'This is Misty, she's shy. Bernie is bossy.' Martha and Claire were six and seven that year, and they'd petted the stuffed animals with wide eyes, as if even at that age, they knew that their great-aunt Linda had really gone bat shit crazy.

Linda was the only person who Bets refused to say a bad word about. She once admitted that she thought her sister had 'married down,' but that was all. Bets still went to stay with her sister's children between Thanksgiving and Christmas, taking the train from Philadelphia to Pittsburgh and spending a week or so with each of them. She bought their children gifts and raved about the cooking. 'Your cousin Patty really knows how to fry a chicken,' she'd say, while watching Weezy prepare chicken cutlets.

Weezy didn't really keep in touch with any of her cousins anymore, except for a Christmas card each year, and a call to talk about Bets's stay. But she was eternally grateful to them for taking Bets for the stretch between the two holidays. Getting her back and forth from Michigan twice a year would have been a nightmare, and while Weezy suspected that Bets was much kinder and more charming to her nieces and nephews than she was to her daughters, she still couldn't have been an easy guest.

Maureen was coming over today to talk about menus. Ruth was a vegan, which was a choice that Weezy respected, but it made cooking for her almost impossible. The girl was so nice about it, always brought over a side dish of her own, and assured Weezy that she was getting enough to eat, but Weezy didn't see how that was possible, considering that pretty much all she could eat was plain vegetables and nothing else. Last year, they'd made a special pecan pie for her, and out of curiosity, Weezy took a bite. She'd made herself swallow, but it wasn't easy. *Poor, thin Ruth,* she'd thought. *No butter or meat, what a sad life.*

She was happy that none of her children had entered into the world of vegetarianism. Unless you counted the two years in high school when Claire refused to eat red meat, but even then she'd eat chicken occasionally. She was just doing it to be difficult, really. Even Cleo ate meat, thank God. Not that she considered Cleo one of her children – it was way too early for that. So at least she had that much to be thankful for, that her children were getting enough protein. Ruth should probably be taking iron pills, and Weezy made a note to ask her about that.

Maureen was late, which was not unusual. In fact, it was almost expected. It surprised Weezy how Maureen could be so

264

organized and efficient in her work, and have none of that spill over to her personal life. Maureen was an executive assistant for John McLaughlin, one of the VPs at Price Waterhouse. She had been there for over twenty-five years and as he got promoted, she went with him. He called Maureen his 'right-hand man' and he meant it. She kept his schedule, was loyal to him, and always had her ear out for talk among the assistants of any rumblings in the company. She kept his office running tightly and smoothly, and you would never know that she often ran out of dishwasher detergent at home and forgot to replace it for weeks.

Maureen had gone back to college after her husband left, and it had taken her almost three years, during which Cathy and Drew spent a lot of nights eating dinner with the Coffeys, and sometimes spent whole weekends there so that Maureen could make it to class and study. But she'd done it, and landed the job with John right after she graduated.

'You went back to college to be a secretary?' Bets asked when she got the news. 'I was a secretary for years, and I didn't need to go to college.'

'An executive assistant,' Maureen corrected her. Bets had rolled her eyes, but her job was one thing that Maureen never doubted. She loved working for John. She was friendly with his wife, attended his children's first communions and graduations, and accepted his investment advice. Maureen loved everything about her job, feeling in control and having lunch with her friends in the office. Hearing her talk about it always made Weezy a little jealous.

Now, John was over sixty and his role in the company was getting smaller. He wanted to retire. He and his wife wanted to move to Maine full-time. For the time being, he still had an office at the company, but he'd been moved to a small office, and while Maureen went in every day, she was done by one o'clock at the latest. There just wasn't much to do. She set up his golf games and answered e-mails and phone calls about when he would be in the office. Sometimes he came in and they organized files or went over things. But by next year, he would be gone, and Maureen would be retired as well. She wouldn't need to work, thanks to the investments she'd so wisely listened to him about, but she wasn't looking forward to it.

'All those days, stretching on, spending them all by myself,' she'd said. 'It seems so definite.'

'You're not by yourself,' Weezy told her. But she knew what Maureen meant.

Maureen kept suggesting that they start a business venture together, but she was just talking, just trying to grasp at something so that she wouldn't feel lost. She'd mentioned a dog-walking business and a paint-your-own pottery store in the same sentence, and Weezy knew that she was just going a little bonkers over the change.

The feeling of loss was understandable. It was like Max and his hockey. He'd played since he was four years old. He took to skates right away, a natural, which surprised Will and Weezy, since neither of the girls liked it at all. The few times the girls had gone skating when they were little, Weezy and Will had to drag them around on the ice, their little mittened hands gripping their parents' tightly.

But Max stood up on his own right away. It was really something to see. For a while there, Weezy was convinced that he was going to be an Olympian or a professional athlete. It was amazing, to watch this little boy glide on the ice, forward and backward, like it was nothing. And then, when the Pee Wee coach handed him a stick, he just smiled. It was like he'd always been holding it.

They threw him into the sport wholeheartedly. Will loved hockey, and Max's being the star of the team was just a bonus. What Will and Weezy learned about the sport very quickly was that they were required to be just as involved. There were club teams and tournaments. There were day camps and sleepaway camps. Soon, their weekends were filled with driving Max to different locations (often different states) to play hockey.

Weezy loved watching Max play. Her sweet, even-tempered baby turned into something else on the ice. He was fluid and graceful and also could be ruthless and sneaky, coming up beside someone, checking them with his shoulder, and then skating on, like nothing had happened.

Hockey took up almost all of their time, and they often grumbled to each other about it, but it was too late to back out. It was exhausting and it seemed that they were always trying to schedule around a hockey game of some sort. Holidays were cut short, and long weekends were spent in Canada and Michigan.

And then, just like that, it was over. Max went to college and decided that he didn't want to try out for the team. He didn't think he'd start, he told them, and it seemed like a lot of time and work to sit on the bench. He decided to play on the club team, which was really just a bunch of boys getting together at eleven o'clock at night to play around on the ice and drink.

After that, Weezy felt like part of her life was missing. Did she really miss the hours in the car? The nights spent in questionable hotels in random Canadian towns? No, she told herself, she couldn't miss that. But there was a loss when it was gone. And so Weezy understood it when Maureen talked about missing work. Even if the whole point of a job was to be done with it someday, to be able to relax, it could become a part of you, it could become how you saw yourself. And when it was gone, it left a hole.

Maureen let herself in the back door, apologizing before she was even inside. 'I know, I know,' she said. 'I'm sorry, I got stuck talking to someone at work.'

'That's okay,' Weezy said. And it was. They didn't have all that much to go over, actually. She'd spread the cookbooks out on the table, and had the lists of what they'd made for the past five Thanksgivings.

'So, Cathy and Ruth are all set with Bets?' Weezy asked.

'Yep. They're leaving Ohio on Tuesday, and they'll stay over with Bets that night, and they all fly out bright and early on Wednesday.'

'God bless them.'

'No kidding. But you know, I'm paying for their tickets, so it's not like they're getting nothing out of the deal.'

'Still.'

The two of them talked about the pies that they wanted to make. Pumpkin, of course. Pecan was Max's favorite. Bets always wanted something with chocolate in it, and then there was an apple-cranberry crisp that looked good.

'Four desserts?' Weezy said. 'That seems like a lot, doesn't it?'

'Yeah,' Maureen agreed. 'I guess we'll lose the crisp?'

Weezy nodded. The crisp was actually her favorite, but there was nothing else that could be cut from the list without a lot of whining and complaining from the group. And none of them needed four desserts. Especially not Weezy or Maureen, who were starting to both look just a little barrel-shaped in the past five years, no matter how much they exercised.

'So this is the trade-off?' Maureen had asked, when she'd started to go through menopause, just a year and a half after Weezy. 'No more cramps, but now I'll just be hot as hell and fat?'

Weezy couldn't even find it in herself to tell her it would get better. Her hot flashes had persisted, well past the time when she thought they should have stopped. 'How long will this go on? How many years is normal?'

'I don't like the term *normal*,' her doctor had said. Weezy told him that was too bad, because she did like the term *normal*, loved it even, and so she would be getting a new doctor.

Will and the kids had learned not to say anything when in the middle of winter she'd open the back door and stand there, while the rest of them shivered and moved to the front of the house. She was glad when Maureen started, just so she could have someone to complain with. Weezy's new doctor had told her that there was a slight chance that she'd have hot flashes for the rest of her life. Maureen never had hot flashes like Weezy. She did, however, have raging mood swings that once caused her to tell Bets to go fuck herself on Christmas Eve.

Weezy filled in her calendar. She entered in when Max and Cleo would arrive, when Bets would get in, who needed to be picked up at the airport when. She woke up every morning and went for a walk, then came back and a few times a week went to that weightlifting place with Maureen, the one that was made just for menopausal women and had popped up in every suburb across the country.

She was trying to keep herself busy, to keep away from the computer and the wedding blogs and websites. Thanksgiving was a good excuse, she figured. During the day, she did pretty well. But it was at night, when she couldn't sleep, that she crumbled.

Her favorite wedding blog was called WeddingBellesand Whistles.com and featured a different DIY project every day. It was also filled with tips, and once a week a guest bride wrote an article about an aspect of her wedding. That night, Weezy read about a bride who'd been left behind at the venue, after all of the buses that they hired to take the guests back to the hotel (forty-five minutes away!) had driven off. 'Oh no,' Weezy whispered out loud. 'What a nightmare.'

Weezy told herself that staying away from weddings during the day was a good start. It was like the patch for smoking, and she felt virtuous when, at the end of the day, she hadn't checked in even once.

She went to the store and stocked up on all of Max's favorite foods. She got his room ready for Cleo, washing sheets, vacuuming and dusting, airing everything out. She set Max up in the basement, which was a shame really, that he wouldn't be able to stay in his own room when he came home, but they couldn't very well put Cleo down there. She got everything that was on Bets's list: creamer for her coffee, bran cereal, pistachios, and hard caramel candies. Bets had called several times to go over the list, and Weezy assured her that it was all taken care of.

Maureen had offered to have everyone over for dinner on Wednesday night, which was a nice thought, but just made extra work for Weezy since she'd have to make everything at her house, then pack it all up to take over. Maureen didn't cook, and she'd suggested ordering pizzas— 'Why make it complicated?' she'd asked – but Weezy had shot her down and told her she'd whip up some meatballs.

By the time Max and Cleo arrived on Wednesday morning, everything was ready. Claire was at work for just a half day, and Martha was working all day, so Weezy was the only one there to greet them. She was so happy to see her son, her Max, who walked right in and gave her a huge hug.

Cleo, if it was possible, looked even more gorgeous than she had before. 'Hi, Mrs. Coffey,' she said. They gave each other a tentative hug.

'I brought these for you,' Cleo said, and held out a box of chocolates, which was a nice gesture, but Weezy's first thought was that more food in the house was the last thing that they needed, and when was she going to put these out for people when there were already so many desserts?

But of course she just smiled and said, 'Thank you.'

The two of them stood there and smiled at each other, as though they both thought it would convey how thrilled they were to share Thanksgiving. Max was on the ground with Ruby, letting the dog lick his face, bending his head down so she could smell his hair and press her head against his. Ruby wagged her tail more for Max than for anyone, and she was always a little depressed when he left.

'Do you two want something to eat?' Weezy asked. 'Max, I got some cold cuts for you. I could make you a sandwich or maybe you want something else? We're having spaghetti and meatballs at Maureen's tonight, so you probably don't want pasta.'

'We're okay for now,' Max said. 'Actually, we're going to throw our stuff down and head over to John's to see him and meet up with some people. I think we'll stop at Gino's for a cheese steak.'

'Not Pat's?'

'We went there last time. Cleo has to try both so she knows which one she likes better.' Max gave the back of her neck a squeeze, and she scrunched up her shoulders and laughed.

And then they were gone. They dropped their bags in the rooms and were out the door a few minutes later. 'Be sure to be back by four, because Bets will be here and then we'll head over to Maureen's.' Max gave her a kiss and they left. She noticed that Cleo looked relieved to be leaving, even though she'd just gotten there.

Maureen burned the bread. She basically had just one thing to do for the dinner, which was to cook the garlic bread, and it was black when they got there. Smoke filled the kitchen. 'I didn't want to forget it, so I just popped it in,' Maureen said, as if that explained it.

Will was sent out to get more. 'Just get some frozen stuff,' Weezy instructed. There was no telling what he'd come back with, but it was a risk they'd have to take. Bets was already sniffing and coughing in the kitchen over the smoke, and Maureen was in the corner sipping a glass of wine.

Weezy turned the fan on and cracked the window in the kitchen, then set to work warming up the meatballs, and instructed Maureen to empty the bags of prewashed salad that she'd gotten that day and to toss them with Italian dressing. She sat Bets down and got her a glass of wine. All of the kids were already in the next room, laughing about something.

'Maureen was never much of a cook,' Bets said.

'Thanks so much, Mom,' Maureen said.

Parents would probably be arrested these days if they talked the way their parents had. Sometimes she still heard her dad's voice: 'Louise is the brains,' he'd say to strangers, 'and Maureen's the looker.'

Will came back with the bread and asked Bets how things were going in the retirement village. 'I call it Death Valley,' she told him, 'because every other day, there's a body taken out of there on a stretcher.'

'Bets, you're a funny one,' he said. He laughed and put his hand on his stomach, and Weezy was amazed, as she always was, that her husband was good-natured enough not just to put up with Bets but to actually seem to enjoy her company.

They finished getting the dinner ready – after sending Will out one more time to get meatless sauce for Ruth, which they'd forgotten – and everyone sat down to eat. The kids were chattering, all happy to see each other, and that made Weezy so happy. When she had Claire, everyone had told her, 'Those girls are sure to be best friends,' but they weren't. And then, when she'd had Max, she was worried that he'd be raised as an only child, not close to his sisters at all, but right from the get-go, he and Claire had been thick as thieves and still were.

She was always happy that Martha and Cathy were so close. It wasn't the same as a sibling, but at least it was a family member that was a friend. It was Cathy's poor brother, Drew, really, that was always the odd man out when he was around. Although most of the time, he didn't even seem to mind.

Will poured them all more red wine and made a toast, and the whole family ate, spilling sauce all over the tablecloth, which would have driven Weezy nuts if it had been her house, but Maureen didn't seem to notice or care, and so she relaxed and let herself enjoy the dinner.

It occurred to Weezy, after Max was born, that she now had the exact same family that she'd grown up in – two girls, a year apart, and then a boy. Of course, their baby brother, Jimmy, died when he was just a few weeks old and – this was awful, but true – sometimes she forgot that he'd been there at all.

After he'd died, her father delivered the news, very matter-of-factly. 'He went to heaven,' he said one morning. He'd already been to the hospital with Bets and Jimmy in the middle of the night. The girls had never even been woken up. A neighbor was called to come and sit in the house with them.

They'd had a funeral for him, a small and quick ceremony. ('Thank God he was already baptized,' their grandmother kept saying. 'That's why you do it right away. Right away. You don't waste a second.') There was a baby picture of him placed alongside pictures of Weezy and Maureen on the side table in the front hall. But he was rarely mentioned.

If that had happened these days, if a baby died, people would talk to the kids. They'd probably be in therapy before the funeral was even planned. But Weezy and Maureen never really talked about Jimmy. They knew it was sad – unthinkable – to lose a baby, and after they'd both had kids they maybe understood that a little bit more. But they didn't feel the sadness, really. Not the way Bets did. She never talked about it, but something changed in her after that. The pictures before were of her smiling widely with lots of lipstick, and after she looked sharper, and always smiled with her mouth closed.

Bets had always hated Philadelphia, still referred to Michigan as home even after she'd been gone for years. She had met James when he was working in Detroit, and she'd been impressed with his 'East Coast ways,' as she always put it. They dated for a few months, and when his company transferred him back to Philadelphia, he'd proposed and she'd accepted.

But she'd never liked the people in Philadelphia; she missed her friends and family back home. She seemed to blame James in some way for taking her there, although Weezy always thought, she'd agreed to go, so she couldn't really complain. After Jimmy died, it was just one more thing that Bets hated about the place.

When James had a heart attack and died Weezy's freshman year in college, Bets wasted no time. She packed up the house, sold it, and right after Maureen graduated from high school, she moved back to Michigan. Both Weezy and Maureen thought this was a mistake, and they were devastated at losing their childhood home so soon after losing their father. 'She's not going to be happy there,' they told each other. 'She has a memory of it, but it won't be the same when she gets there.'

But they were wrong. Bets thrived back in Michigan. She reconnected with all of 'the gals' she'd known growing up, and it was like she'd never been gone for those twenty years. She had no problem leaving Philadelphia, even if that meant moving away from her children. 'That was never my home,' she always said about it, as if all of her time there, raising her children, was just one little pause in her real life.

They all got home, stuffed and tired, and Weezy figured everyone would just go to bed, but Claire announced that she was going over to Lainie's with Max and Cleo.

'You're going over now?' Weezy asked. 'It's so late already.'

'Mom, it's fine. It's not even that late.'

'What about Martha?'

'What about Martha?' Claire repeated.

'Did you invite her?'

'Yep. I told her we were all going but she wasn't interested.'

'Well, why don't you invite her again?'

'Why? She already said no.'

'You know sometimes she needs to be convinced to go somewhere,' Weezy said.

'You want me to go beg Martha to come with me, to a party that she doesn't want to go to?'

'Claire.' Weezy gave her a look, and Claire let out a sigh, but she went upstairs, and returned with Martha in tow. The four of them headed out the door and Weezy called, 'Have a good time!'

Weezy settled herself on the couch and turned on the TV. There was so much to be done for tomorrow, but she could rest for just a minute. *It's a Wonderful Life* was on, which made it seem like Thanksgiving was already over, like time had just raced by and it was already Christmas.

She watched a little bit of the movie, but her heart wasn't in it, so she snuck over to the computer and pulled up Wedding Belles and Whistles. She read an article by a bride who was to be married that weekend, and how she'd already arranged to have a plate of Thanksgiving food set aside for her, since she wouldn't be able to indulge that day. She was making place card holders in the shape of turkeys, which sounded a little silly to Weezy, but they were actually sort of whimsical looking. *Just a few minutes,* she told herself as she settled into her chair and read all about Thanksgiving Bride's big day.

Chapter 13

Claire knew before she opened her eyes that it wasn't good. Her head was throbbing, and it felt like she was on a boat, or something that was moving very slowly, back and forth. She opened her eyes to find that it was just a couch – Lainie's couch – and not a boat. Her right hip ached, probably because she'd been lying on it for hours without moving. She looked in front of her and saw a full glass of wine on the coffee table, and Jack standing and staring at her. He was still in his pajamas, which were dark blue with light green monsters printed on them, and he was holding some sort of Transformer-looking toy, although Claire realized with a horrible throb of her head that it couldn't be a Transformer because kids didn't even play with those anymore – or did they? Were they back?

She couldn't remember, and thinking about it was making her want to vomit.

'Hi,' Jack said. He rubbed his nose with the heel of his hand. 'Hey, you're still dressed for the party.'

Claire closed her eyes. She was still wearing the same clothes she'd worn over last night. Sleeping on Lainie's couch wasn't a first – she'd done that plenty – but being so drunk that she couldn't bother to borrow a T-shirt and sweatpants was a new low. In the kitchen, someone was banging drawers open and closed, like they were in a hurry. Lainie walked out into the room holding a cup of coffee.

'Hey, bud,' she said, touching Jack's head. Then turning to Claire, she said, 'I feel awful.'

Claire sat up slowly, and held on to the arm of the couch in an attempt to stop the spinning in her head. 'Really? I feel great.'

Lainie laughed. 'You kept me up way too late last night. And made me drink way too much wine. I'm so screwed. I have to bring a pie to Brian's mom's house.'

'Really, well, I have to actually stand up at some point today. And right now I'm not sure that's possible.'

'Do you want some coffee?' Lainie asked. She was now moving quickly around the room, picking up the last of the party remnants, taking the empty glasses into the kitchen, and throwing out the napkins. Ever since Lainie had had kids, she didn't really get hungover. She claimed she did, but she never sat still and moaned about it. 'I can't,' she said once. 'I don't have a choice, so it's like my body figured out how to get through the hangover while letting me move around.' It made Claire feel worse to watch her up and cleaning.

'No coffee for me, thanks,' Claire said. 'I just need to lay here for a minute.'

'Sure. Your phone has been ringing, by the way.'

'Oh God.' Claire knew it was Weezy. 'I should go home soon.'

Jack was folding and unfolding his little toy into a truck and then a robot. He was making those noises that little boys make to mimic an explosion, or a rocket, or a bomb.

'Hey, bud, you want to help me make a pie?' Lainie asked. Jack looked up and nodded. 'All right, then, go get dressed.'

Jack ran out of the room, and Claire sat up. She told Lainie what Jack had said to her about still being dressed for the party, and the two of them snorted with laughter.

'Okay,' Claire said, finally standing up. 'I think I might make it.'

'Oh, Claire,' Weezy said when she walked in.

'What?'

Weezy sighed. 'Look at you. You're going to be exhausted. I need your help today.'

'I'm right here, ready to help,' Claire said. She smelled like liquor and cigarettes, and she stood on the other side of the kitchen so that Weezy wouldn't notice.

Weezy went back to stirring the stuffing, sighing as though Claire had just caused a huge inconvenience. The stuffing was in three different pots, each one overflowing, little stale bread pieces jumping onto the counter at random. 'I just wish you hadn't stayed out all night. We've got a big day.'

'I'm fine,' Claire said. She was reminded of the recurring fight that she and Weezy had had after every grade school sleepover. Claire would get angry, Weezy would accuse her of being tired, and then Claire would scream that she wasn't tired, and then Weezy would threaten that she'd never go to another sleepover again.

All Claire wanted was to go to her room and lie down just for a minute, but Bets was in her room, probably going through her drawers, and snooping through her things. There had been some issues with the sleeping arrangements. Normally, Max stayed in the basement and Bets stayed in his room, but with Cleo here, they needed an extra place for her, so Claire was sent packing to Martha's room, which had twin beds, Cleo took Max's room, and Bets got Claire's room. No one was happy.

Claire grabbed a bagel from the counter, spread it with cream cheese, and ate it in huge, quick bites. She hoped that it would make her feel better. She headed upstairs to take a shower, but Martha was in the bathroom, so she lay down on one of the twin beds and waited.

Martha came out of the bathroom in a cloud of steam. She closed the door and then listened to make sure that no one was outside the room. 'It smells like an ashtray in there,' she whispered. 'Last night, I woke up and there was smoke coming out from underneath the door.'

Claire laughed. Bets was a secret smoker, but it was a secret that wasn't very well kept at all. When they were little, they used to ask Weezy, 'Why does Bets smoke in the bathroom?' and Weezy would shush them.

'It's her secret,' she told them. 'She doesn't want anyone to know, so we can't say anything. She'd be embarrassed.'

And so, for years now, Bets would disappear into a bathroom and emerge with smoke billowing behind her. Sometimes she'd cough. 'I'm getting a cold,' she'd say. And none of them would say a word.

Once, Claire and Doug had been sitting on the back deck, and Doug touched Claire's arm and silently pointed up to the bathroom window, where a hand holding a cigarette was going in and out of the window. Claire had shrugged. 'It's her thing,' she said. 'She doesn't want anyone to know. We just let her be and pretend we don't see anything.'

'Your family,' Doug had said, 'is just so Catholic, it kills me.' Claire never exactly knew what he meant, since secret smoking didn't really seem like a Catholic trait to her.

Claire had also warned Doug that Bets was just a little bit racist. She wanted to give him fair warning. 'You know,' she told him, 'not like *really* racist but like old-people racist.' Doug had tilted his head like he didn't quite understand, and she said, 'You'll see.'

'The president looks blacker on my TV,' Bets told Doug that

night. Doug coughed on his water. 'I don't know what it is, but it's true. He looks so much darker on my TV at home. He looks practically white here.'

'Mom,' Weezy said, 'that's enough.'

'What? I'm just making an observation. Come over and watch him on my TV and you'll see what I mean. He looks blacker there.'

'Mom, drop it.'

Bets turned to Doug and shook her head. 'No one can say anything these days. You can't say a single thing without someone being offended, without the polite police coming to tie you up.'

That was Bets, always full of inappropriate comments. They spent every holiday whispering about her while she was in the next room. At least she made things interesting, and gave them something to talk about.

In her room, Martha was now drying her hair with the towel, then stopped and sprayed a can of air freshener in the direction of the bathroom and Bets. 'One day,' she said to Claire, 'she's going to burn down the house.'

'I know,' Claire said. 'And then we're all going to have to lie to the firemen about what started it.'

Claire stood in the shower for a long time. She let the hot stream run over her, and then she had to sit down because she started to feel a little nauseous. Even from inside the shower, Claire could hear Weezy yelling up the stairs at people, giving orders.

'I can do this,' she said to herself as she shampooed her hair. It was fine. She could make it for an hour, then have a drink and some appetizers and she'd be fine. Thank God their cousin Drew wasn't coming this year. Not that Claire didn't love him, but when he came to family gatherings, they all abstained from drinking out of support. It was miserable. Well, all of them abstained except for Bets, who once told him that she thought alcoholics were people that couldn't handle their liquor. 'Maybe you'll get the hang of it as you get older,' she'd said to him. Maureen was out smoking on the deck, but Weezy had stepped in to defend him.

'Mom, Drew has a disease and he's been very brave in dealing with it,' she said, in a speech that would have made any Lifetime Movie writer proud. It was embarrassing to watch Weezy standing there, knowing that she thought she was doing something very important.

Weezy put her hand on Drew's shoulder and the three of them stood in an awkward triangle, until Bets said, 'Cancer is a disease. Not being able to drink is just a goddamn shame.'

Claire was all for abstaining when Drew was there, although sometimes she wondered if he really was an alcoholic or if maybe that was just where his problems showed themselves. He was only twenty-two when he went into rehab – a baby, practically. Which one of them wasn't an irresponsible drinker at that age? But Claire kept this thought to herself, since Drew seemed to be doing well in the program and had gotten his life back on track.

The last time he'd come, two Thanksgivings ago, the dinner

seemed to drag on forever as they'd sipped at Diet Cokes and some stupid raspberry spritzer that Weezy had made in an attempt to have a fun non-alcoholic cocktail. Bets had gotten drunk by herself, not needing any of them to join her. She was happy as a clam to down glass after glass, and all of them realized that she was much harder to deal with when they were all sober. As Drew had pulled out of the driveway that night, Weezy was already opening a bottle of red.

'Good God,' Claire said to Max. 'It looks like Mom's going to rip the cork out with her teeth.'

So, yes, it was better that Drew wasn't coming. After all, Cathy was enough to deal with. The first year after she came out, she'd made a point to mention her sexuality at every turn. When she first brought Ruth to meet the family, she'd made a point to introduce her to Bets in a way that left no room for misinterpretation.

'Bets, this is my girlfriend, Ruth,' she said. 'And by *girlfriend,* I mean *sexual partner.*'

'Oh, sweet Jesus,' Max had said under his breath, and he and Claire had laughed. Martha shot them a look, like they were being rude, but really. She didn't know why Cathy had to talk about her sex life all the time. No one else did. Claire was all for it, thought it was great and that Cathy should be who she was and they could all live life together. Cathy was the one that talked about it all the time, and that got tiring. It wasn't like she'd invented being a lesbian.

*

'It's interesting,' Cathy said once at a family dinner. 'Some people would think that my father being a misogynist had something to do with me being a lesbian. I don't believe that sexuality is something we choose, but others disagree. Some think it's something we learn.' Then she'd turned to Claire. 'What do you think?'

Claire had just shrugged. How was one supposed to even answer that question? She didn't remember Uncle Harold all that well. He'd been around when they were younger, and then he and Maureen had separated and he'd moved to Oregon. Claire hadn't seen him since.

She remembered the time (the only time, she was pretty sure) that Cathy and Drew went to visit him there, how Cathy had called Maureen from some strange person's house to tell her that she and Drew had been left there, that their dad had gone out and told them to 'stay put.' Maureen had come over to the Coffeys' that night, screaming and crying, was on the phone with the police in Portland, trying to get them over to her children. She'd flown out there the next morning and had come back with Cathy and Drew.

Maybe Harold visited once or twice after that, maybe he'd come to a birthday party that Cathy had, but Claire was fuzzy on that. And soon, as the years went by, they stopped talking about him at all. It was like he'd never even existed. Claire had no idea if he was a misogynist or not. Mostly she just thought he was a really shitty dad.

*

Downstairs, Weezy had a new apron on that was already covered in stuffing and potatoes. The kitchen table had casserole dishes spread all over it, with different Post-it notes stuck to each one that said things like, *Bake at 350 for 20 minutes, uncover for last 10,* and *Vegan Stuffing!* And *Put in the same time as sweet potatoes.* And then there was one note that said, inexplicably, *Will and Green Beans.*

Weezy kept reaching up to push her hair out of her face. She looked hot and annoyed. Cathy, Ruth, and Maureen had arrived and all crowded themselves into the kitchen. They were chatting away, believing themselves to be kind in keeping Weezy company, but Claire knew that all Weezy wanted was for them to get the hell out of her kitchen so that she could spill and curse and cook in peace.

Will and Bets were in the living room, watching the TV in silence. They both seemed happy. Will just wanted to watch the football game, and Bets was probably just gauging the blackness of the NFL players on this screen as opposed to her own.

Max and Cleo were in the basement. They'd been kind of quiet all weekend, and she thought they might have had a fight of some kind. Poor Max. It wasn't easy to deal with a significant other in this household.

Martha was at the stove, stirring apples and cranberries and looking worried. She'd made this dish every year for the past ten years, and still every time she fretted about it and tasted it, apologizing to everyone that it wasn't quite right, until people praised it so much that she smiled down at her plate and said, 'It's not that hard.'

When Claire walked into the kitchen, Weezy was arranging appetizers on a platter and Cathy was eating crackers and talking about her job, which had something to do with computer programming. Ruth saw Claire and gave her a hug. 'Hi!' she said, like they hadn't just seen each other the night before. Claire always liked Ruth, and sometimes wanted to pull her aside and say, 'You know you can do better than Cathy, right? You're way nicer.'

'Okay then,' Weezy said. She clapped her hands and then held them together like she was praying, which maybe she was, for strength to make it through the day. 'Ruth? Would you take these out to the family room and then why doesn't everyone head out that way to spend some time with Bets.'

Ruth nodded and picked up the tray of cheese and crackers. Cathy followed behind her, still talking about her job – something about a man named Brett, and why he was responsible for spreading a virus throughout the company.

'What can I do to help?' Maureen asked.

'Nothing. Really, we're all set. You can go relax.'

'I think I forgot to add cinnamon,' Martha said. 'Oh shoot!' The mixture boiled and spit a little bit, and Martha jumped back to avoid it.

'I can stay in here,' Maureen said. But Weezy just shook her head, and Maureen got up and headed out, looking like she was being punished. During Thanksgiving, Maureen ended up sulking and smoking in corners of the backyard, looking like a teenage version of herself.

'I'll go see if people need drinks,' Claire said. She took orders in the family room – white wine spritzer for Bets, beer for Cathy, white wine for Ruth, and for Maureen 'anything with vodka.'

'Do you want some help?' Will asked, but his eyes were still on the game.

'I'm good.'

Claire went to the bar and first made herself a large Bloody Mary with olives. After a few sips of that, she took the drinks to the family room and delivered them to each person with a napkin. She took her drink and walked down to the basement, knocking on the doorframe.

'You guys? Are you in there?'

'Hey,' Max said. He sounded tired. Claire peered around the side of the door and saw both of them sitting on the bed. Cleo's eyes looked a little red. They were definitely fighting.

'You should come up soon,' Claire said. 'Cathy's talking about her job, which is fascinating, and Bets is getting ready to tell us all why we're a disappointment. You don't want to miss it.'

'We'll be up in a minute,' Max said. He didn't smile.

Claire felt bad for them. Once, during a trip with Doug's family, she and Doug had gotten into a fight about the cable bill. It was so stupid, but at the time she was so mad she thought she was going to scream at him, right in front of his parents.

She'd found the bill and saw that he'd added this crazy football package that basically doubled the price.

'We split this bill,' she'd hissed at him in their room. 'And you didn't even have the courtesy to tell me about it? To ask me?'

'It's not a big deal,' Doug said. 'I'll pay for it.' Then he tried to shush her, which she hated.

'Don't you shush me,' she'd said. 'Don't you dare shush me.'

The Winkleplecks were a quiet family. They never yelled. At dinner, if someone accidentally interrupted another person, they'd say, 'Oh, I'm sorry. Go on.' There was no talking over anyone else. When someone started telling a story, the whole family turned and gave that one person their total attention. It made Claire feel very nervous to ever talk around them.

She knew Doug was scared that his parents were going to hear them fighting. 'Shhh,' he kept saying. 'It's fine. I'll pay for it, okay?'

'That's not the point,' Claire had said. But she couldn't quite say what the point was, exactly. Just that she was so mad at him that she wanted to scream, and she wanted him to scream back. But they couldn't, and that made it worse. And Mr. and Mrs. Winklepleck were always there, quietly reading or watching TV at a very low volume. There was nowhere to go, and Claire stayed mad at him the whole trip.

And now it looked like poor Max was in the same situation. 'Okay, guys,' Claire said. 'See you up there. You want me to bring some drinks down here for you?'

'No, thanks,' Max said. 'We'll be up soon.' Claire left them down there, wondering what it was that they could be fighting about.

Claire freshened her Bloody Mary, and sat down next to Cathy on the couch. She reached forward and grabbed some slices of cheese. *The worst part is almost over,* she told herself.

Cathy turned to her and lowered her voice. 'I didn't get a chance to tell you, but I'm really sorry. About Doug and everything.'

'Thanks,' Claire said.

'I really mean it,' she went on. 'I know how sometimes news can be worse when everyone else gets ahold of it. You forget how you even feel about it. But just remember that however you feel about it is fine.'

'Thanks,' Claire said again. But this time her eyes watered a little bit and Cathy squeezed her arm. Maybe being with Ruth had made Cathy a nicer person. And maybe Claire should ease up on the Bloody Marys a little bit.

Last night, Fran had told her that she was 'D-runk.' That's how he'd said it, pronouncing the *D* and the *runk,* as if they were two different words. She'd protested, telling him she was just tipsy. And then, as they walked into the kitchen to look for snacks, she'd tripped on her heel and ended up face down on the kitchen floor.

'I've fallen,' she said, 'and I can't get up.'

'Come on,' Fran said. He lifted her up and brushed the front of her, like she was a little kid that had fallen in dirt. 'Time to go home.'

'No, I was just kidding,' she said. 'Don't you remember that commercial? I was just pretending.'

Fran had walked her across the street and down the block to her front door. 'I should get home anyway,' he said. 'People are coming over early tomorrow. Why do people eat so early on Thanksgiving anyway? Who wants to eat mashed potatoes at noon?'

'We don't eat until late,' Claire said. 'Like six o'clock, usually.' She sat on the front cement steps and rested her head on her knees.

'Okay, then,' Fran said. He knelt down. 'Do you want to go inside?'

'I think I'm just going to sit here for a while.'

'What?'

Claire lifted her head. 'I said, I'm just going to sit here for a while.'

'Do you want me to wait with you?'

Claire shook her head. 'No, you can go home.' She put her head back on her knees and waved her arm. 'Go, I'm serious.'

'I'd feel better if you were inside,' he said.

Claire stood up and walked down the steps. 'Okay, I'll go in the back door, then.'

She waved good-bye to him as he walked down the driveway

and the sidewalk, and then when he turned the corner, she walked across the street and back to Lainie's.

Almost everyone had gone home, but Lainie's two younger sisters were still there, and they cheered when she walked in. 'You're back,' Lainie said. 'Yay!'

They sat on the back patio and smoked cigarettes, until Claire started feeling like it was going to make her puke. Lainie smoked only when she was drunk, but she didn't like to smoke in the front of the house, in case any of her clients walked by. 'Pilates people do not smoke,' she always said.

They talked about Fran, and Claire re-created her 'I've fallen and I can't get up' scene for Lainie, who loved it.

'What do you want with Fran?' Lainie asked. Claire shrugged. She really didn't know.

'I don't think I want anything,' she said. 'Or maybe just a little something. I don't know.'

She barely remembered their moving back inside the house, and vaguely remembered sitting on the couch and then just laying her body down sideways to sleep. Then the next thing she remembered was waking up to Jack calling her out on sleeping in her clothes.

'Ruth, aren't you going to have any turkey?' Bets asked.

'Bets, Ruth is a vegan,' Cathy said.

Bets sniffed. 'Right, I forgot.' She asked the same question every year, and Claire was pretty sure that she put 'Vegan' right along with 'Alcoholic' on her list of things she didn't believe in.

'Martha, how's the job going?' Maureen asked.

'Fine. I mean, good. It's going well.'

'You must be the only white caretaker out there,' Bets said. 'All of ours are foreign, probably illegals. You'll be in high demand.' She smiled at Martha.

'Mom,' Weezy said. Bets just shrugged and held up her hands, like, *What do you want me to do?*

'Should we say grace?' Will asked. They all bowed their heads, and afterward Will raised his glass and said, 'Let's eat!'

Claire noticed that Cleo was just poking her food around on her plate. 'Are you okay?' she asked her quietly, but everyone heard her anyway.

'What's the matter, Cleo? Are you not feeling well?' Weezy asked.

'There was a bug going around the retirement community last week,' Bets offered. 'Four people died.'

Claire and Ruth caught each other's eye and smiled, then looked down at their plates. It wasn't funny, of course, that four people had died. It was just that the first time Ruth met Bets, she'd been going on and on about all of her friends that had died. Ruth had very nicely asked Claire later, 'Does your grandmother talk about death a lot?' and Claire had laughed so hard she'd peed a little bit. Ever since then, the two of them were in serious danger of getting the giggles when Bets announced that another bridge partner had dropped dead.

'The sweet potatoes are wonderful,' Will said. 'And so are the apples and cranberries. Martha, you've outdone yourself.'

Martha smiled as everyone chimed in, 'Yes, they're amazing, they really are. So tasty.'

Claire had moved on to white wine and she finished her glass and refilled it from the bottle at the table. Thankfully, it was making her headache go away. There would be another one tomorrow, she knew, but for the moment it was worth it to get through this dinner.

'We'll call Drew after dinner,' Weezy said.

'Where is Drew?' Bets asked. They'd told her maybe ten times already.

'Drew stayed in California. He's having Thanksgiving with some coworkers,' Maureen said.

'Well, that sounds downright depressing,' Bets said.

'I think it sounds nice,' Max offered. 'To be someplace where it's warm, I mean.' He got up and returned with another beer. On his way back to his seat, he patted Cleo's shoulder. The table got quiet and all Claire could hear was chewing and forks hitting the plates.

'Do you like train travel?' Bets directed this question at Ruth, who looked as surprised as the rest of them.

'Um, yes, I do. I haven't done much of it, but I do like it.'

Claire saw Weezy and Maureen give each other a meaningful look across the table. They were always on the lookout for signs that Bets was losing it, and bringing up train travel out of the blue was a bit strange.

'Should we go around and say what we're thankful for?' Weezy suggested. It was something they'd done when they were little, and every so often, when conversation was lacking, they did it again. One year, Drew said he was thankful for the dirt bike that he'd gotten for his birthday, and Bets tried to make him choose something else. He'd refused, telling her that really was what he was most thankful for. Bets got mad and told Maureen that she'd raised materialistic children. Weezy had come to her defense, and all the kids went upstairs to play and listen to their mothers fight with their grandmother. Will had gone into the kitchen to clean, which was more desirable than staying at the table and fighting over a dirt bike.

Now, when they went around the table to say what they were thankful for, everyone gave up and just said 'Family' and 'Health' as their answers. Weezy was about to start, when Cathy interrupted her.

'Well, actually, I have an announcement to make,' she said. She looked around the table and smiled, looking a little nervous. 'Last night I asked Ruth to marry me, and she said yes!'

Claire thought she felt time stop. Bets had her fork in her hand and she held it right above her plate, a strange little smile on her face. Everyone else stared at Cathy, as though it would take a minute to understand what she had said. Finally, Martha squealed and jumped up to run around the table and hug Cathy and Ruth. Once she moved, everyone seemed to get unfrozen.

'This is so exciting,' Martha said over and over.

'Will you be my maid of honor?' Cathy asked. Martha started to cry and Claire rolled her eyes before she could stop herself.

'Of course,' Martha said.

'Well,' Maureen said. 'What a surprise. Well. What a happy Thanksgiving.'

'To the engaged couple,' Will said, holding up his glass. Claire knew he would repeat the story later, to friends and coworkers, saying, 'You can't pick who you love, you know. As long as they're happy, we're happy.'

They all raised their glasses and clinked them to the right, to the left, and the center. Now Claire knew why Cathy had mentioned Doug. She really did feel bad that she was going to announce her engagement so soon after Claire's ended. That's why it was sincere.

Cathy turned to Claire. 'Will you be my bridesmaid?' she asked.

'Of course,' Claire said. 'I'd be honored.' She took a sip of wine.

Later, after the table was cleared and the dishes were stacked, and the dishwasher was started, they all rested in the family room. It would probably be two days before the kitchen was really clean again. It never seemed worth it to Claire, to make all that mess for one meal. But then again, Thanksgiving was not her favorite holiday.

Someone suggested playing a game, but no one really wanted

to, so they just sat around for a while. Will fell asleep in his chair and started snoring loudly. Claire leaned her head back on the couch and closed her eyes, and when she opened them, Maureen, Cathy, and Ruth were getting ready to leave.

Everyone hugged, and Bets went up to bed. Will stood up and stretched, pretended that he hadn't been sleeping and said that he was heading to bed as well. The house smelled like turkey grease, which made Claire feel a little sick.

Claire and Martha unloaded the dishwasher and got another group of dishes in, and then they started washing the china and crystal by hand. 'Oh, thanks, girls,' Weezy said. She was on the couch with her feet up. 'You don't have to do all that. I'll be there in just a minute.' But her eyes were closed, and she looked like she couldn't have moved if she wanted to.

Martha kept talking about Cathy's wedding. 'I'll have to give a speech,' she said. She almost dropped the wineglass she was drying. 'What will I say? Oh, I'm already nervous. What do you think she'll want us to wear?'

'Burlap sacks,' Claire said.

'Very funny. Ruth has a great sense of style.'

'Yes, but we're Cathy's bridesmaids. I think she'll be the one picking out the dresses.'

'Oh, well, we can suggest some things. Don't worry.'

'I'm not.'

They finished the second round of cleaning, and Claire went upstairs to get ready for bed. Martha came up a little while later, when she was already under the covers.

'I tried to get Mom to go to bed, but she's still on the couch. She kept saying, "I'll get up in a minute."'

'Mmm-hmm,' Claire said. She was half-asleep.

'Happy Thanksgiving,' Martha whispered.

Claire woke up with a start, in the middle of a nightmare where she was falling off of a balcony. She sat up to steady herself, and saw Martha squatting by the door, which was cracked open.

'What are you doing?' she asked.

'Shhhh,' Martha said. She motioned for Claire to come next to her.

'What?' Claire said. But she got up and went to the door. She could hear her mom's voice, but couldn't quite hear what she was saying. Then she heard Max, who sounded like he was crying.

'What's going on?' she asked Martha.

Martha turned, her eyes wide. 'I think Cleo's pregnant,' she said.

'No – did you really hear that?'

'I think so. It's kind of hard to hear.'

'No way. Max is probably just failing a class or something.' But even as she said it, Claire knew that she was wrong. She couldn't hear what Max was saying, but she knew he was upset. And not much upset Max. In fact, almost nothing upset him. Claire tried to ignore the excited look in Martha's eyes.

Claire never understood the way that Martha got almost

giddy when there was tragedy or drama. She fed off of it. She could find a problem in any situation, even the most pleasant. But when there was a real problem, like this, that's where she really thrived. She got involved, she talked about it constantly. It was like being a part of the drama made her feel included and important.

They sat crouched together, listening to the rise and fall of Weezy's and Max's voices. They heard Cleo's name and something about her mom. They heard Weezy say, 'Decisions to make,' and 'young' and 'difficult.' And once, they heard an 'Oh, Max,' from Weezy, and then they heard Max really start to cry.

They looked at each other, and Claire knew that it was true. Cleo must be pregnant, because what else could it be? Unless Max had killed someone, but even then, Weezy would be on the phone with a lawyer or the police. And she wasn't. She was just talking to Max, her voice filled with disappointment. And that was never a good sign.

Poor Max, she thought. *Poor, poor Max.*

Chapter 14

Weezy didn't handle it as well as Max had thought she would. He'd said, 'It won't be that bad' so many times that Cleo almost believed him. She agreed that he should tell Weezy by himself, and not just because she didn't want any part of that conversation. Weezy wouldn't be able to react truthfully if Cleo was there, and that didn't seem fair.

Max went upstairs late, after everyone had gone to bed. Weezy was asleep on the couch, but he'd woken her up. Cleo had stayed in the basement, sitting on the top step and listening.

Weezy had started crying almost immediately. At first Cleo felt bad, but after a while as she listened to Weezy heave and gasp, with what seemed like unnecessary drama, she started to get annoyed. She thought about storming up the stairs, looking her in the face, and saying, 'What are you crying about? You don't have to have this baby.' She didn't, of course. She stayed put and listened to Weezy repeat that she was so disappointed. Not *in* them, but *for* them. Whatever that meant.

Somehow, during the conversation where Max told Weezy that Cleo was pregnant, it had come out that they were living together. 'You're what?' Weezy had said, like that was the real problem, like living together was the reason she got pregnant in the first place.

Max stayed calm until the very end when he started to cry. She couldn't blame him. She was about to cry herself, just listening to Weezy repeat herself, letting him know that she really was just so disappointed.

Cleo heard the word 'options' and she sat up straight. She didn't want Weezy up there talking about her like she wasn't there. She was right here. They weren't Weezy's options, they were hers, and she had decided.

When Max finally came back down, she had moved one step down and had her head resting on her arms on the landing. She was exhausted. Max was walking quickly, and he still had tears running down his face, which embarrassed her so much she had to look away. She was embarrassed because she knew he wouldn't want her to see him cry. She never had before, and if this hadn't happened, she wondered how long, if ever, it would have been before she'd seen it.

'I think we should go,' Max said. He was already grabbing his bag and putting stuff in it.

'Now?' It was five in the morning.

'Yeah, let's get out of here. I want to leave before anyone wakes up.'

'Can you even drive? You had kind of a lot to drink.'

'Yeah, I'm fine. It's morning now.'

'What did she say?' Cleo already knew, but she wanted to hear it from him.

'I'll tell you about it later. Let's just go.'

'But my stuff is upstairs,' Cleo said. The last thing she wanted to do was to walk up there by herself, and run into Weezy in the hall, or see crazy Bets on her way to the bathroom. Her heart started to beat quickly just thinking about it.

'I'll run and grab it,' Max said. 'Can you finish packing my stuff?'

Cleo nodded and he ran up the stairs, taking them two at a time. They looked like a couple that was late for the airport.

It was still dark out when they got in the car, and they drove in silence for almost an hour. Cleo was afraid to say anything to him. Every once in a while she reached over and put her hand on his leg, or rubbed the back of his neck, but he didn't react much. Cleo forced herself to keep her eyes open, even though all she wanted to do was sleep. It used to be that she couldn't sleep if she was worried, but now she felt like she could sleep anywhere and anytime Finally they passed a sign for a rest stop that was coming up, and Max turned to look at her. 'Are you hungry?' She nodded, and he turned on his blinker and got off the expressway.

Max said he'd run in and get the food, and Cleo asked for an egg sandwich and a cup of coffee. Max shook his head. 'I don't think you're supposed to have coffee.'

'Oh,' Cleo said. 'Not even a cup?'

'I'm not sure.'

'Forget it. Just get me a bottle of water.'

Max nodded and got out of the car to go get their food. She was so sad just then, for both of them, as she watched him open the door and go in. It was so sad, just fucking depressing, really. Neither of them had any idea what they were doing. They didn't even know if she could have coffee or not.

Cleo started to cry a little bit, her nose running, and she dug around until she found an old napkin in the car to blow her nose. She was trying to stop the tears before Max came back, but when she saw him walk out with a drink tray and a bag of fast-food breakfast, she started crying all over again.

'I got you orange juice, too,' he said. He put his hand on the back of her head and ran it down to her neck.

'What're we doing?' she asked.

'We'll be okay,' Max said. This sounded like such a complete lie that Cleo let out a little laugh. 'Here, you should eat.' He handed the sandwich to Cleo and she unwrapped it in her lap.

'We're really in a lot of shit, aren't we?' she said. Max was pulling out of the parking lot and onto the ramp to get back on the highway, and he didn't answer her.

When Cleo told her mom, there was a pause and for a second she thought her mom hadn't heard her and she was going to have to repeat herself. And then she heard her mom say, 'Oh god*damn* it, Cleo.'

Cleo had breathed in quickly, like someone had surprised her, and then she'd started to cry. On the other end of the phone, her mom sighed. She hated when Cleo cried, she always had.

'Well, have you thought about it?' Elizabeth asked.

'Mom, of course I've thought about it.'

'And?'

'And what? I'm keeping it. I wouldn't be telling you about it otherwise, would I?'

'Cleo, you really need to think about this.'

'What do you mean, I really need to think about it? You think I haven't thought about it?'

'I'm just saying, it's a big decision.'

'Yeah, no kidding. And I've thought about it. I have. You're talking to me like I don't think things through, like I'm some idiot who got knocked up and just decided to go with it.'

'Well, right about now, that sounds pretty accurate, don't you think?'

Cleo hung up the phone and threw it at the couch. Then she

started to really let herself cry, with big, indulgent, dramatic sobs. She waited for her mom to call her back, but all she got was an e-mail an hour later.

Cleo,

I'm upset at the way things were handled today. I understand that you are upset as well, so when you're ready to talk in a calm manner, I'll be available.

Mom

'Do you believe this?' she screamed. She ran into the bedroom to show it to Max, holding her phone right in front of his face until he took it from her and read it. Her first instinct had been to hide it, to hide the fact that she had a mom who was such a monster. But then her rage had taken over and she didn't care about that.

It sounded like a fucking business e-mail: *The way things were handled. I'll be available.* Good God, her mom was a crazy person. She didn't even know how to talk to people normally, didn't even know how to act when her daughter told her she was pregnant.

'I'm never talking to her again,' Cleo said. 'She can die alone.'

'Okay,' Max said. 'You're upset.'

'Of course I'm upset. My mom is a horrible person. And can I just point out that she also got pregnant by accident? With me. You'd think she'd be a little more understanding.'

'She's just surprised.'

'I'm surprised too,' Cleo said. 'Didn't she think about that?'

Cleo was still throwing up almost every day. They kept waiting for it to stop, but it never did. Max read the pregnancy books they bought and reported back to her. 'It says it's normal for some women to be sick through the whole pregnancy. Mostly it's just the first trimester, but some people have it the whole time.' He looked up at her with wide eyes.

'What a relief,' she said.

In class, her lips were red and raw from all the retching. She could feel her professors looking at her, probably thinking that she was on a bender, that she was perpetually hungover, that her life was spiraling out of control. The last part was true, of course, just not for the reasons they thought.

As soon as she got home in the afternoons, she'd lie on the couch and watch TV. Sometimes she'd try to eat saltines, but the only thing that ever had any chance of staying down was Fig Newtons, which she'd never liked before.

'Our baby is going to grow up to be a fig,' Cleo said. She was kidding, but Max looked worried.

'Maybe I'll call my mom to see if she has any ideas,' he said.

Weezy had called them before they'd even gotten back to school. She apologized for the way she acted, Max relayed to Cleo. She was sorry that they'd already left. And she wanted them to know that the whole family would be there to help them through all of this.

Max was relieved, and Cleo was too. She was. For the most part, anyway. She still wished that her own mom would have come around, and if not, it would have almost been nicer if she and Max could have commiserated on how awful their parents were being. Instead, he talked to his mom every single day, filling her in on doctor's appointments and asking her advice on every little thing.

Cleo was tired. More tired than she'd ever been in her whole life. Sometimes when she'd be walking to class, she'd think that she was going to fall asleep standing up, because she couldn't keep her eyes open, and they would close and her head would bob. One night, after dinner, Max came in the room to tell her that Weezy had said that her nausea would be worse if she lay down after meals. 'She said to stay upright, just walk around or sit up until you've digested.'

Cleo was lying on the couch when he told her this, and she opened one eye to look at him standing there, so eager. 'I'd rather throw up all over myself, than sit up right now,' she said. She closed her eyes again and heard Max walk out of the room.

Sometimes Max would be talking to Weezy and he'd just hand the phone to Cleo, without giving her a chance to say no, or even just prepare. She wanted to tell Max that it hurt her feelings, that it made her feel sad when she heard Weezy's voice over the phone, telling Cleo what it was like when she was pregnant, asking her how tired she was, promising that it would get better. But she couldn't tell him that, because even she knew it sounded ridiculous, that talking to his mom hurt her feelings, and so she kept it to herself.

There was one night, though, when Max was on the phone with his mom, again, and Cleo was lying on the couch, trying to watch TV, which was hard since Max was talking kind of loud. She turned up the volume, but all she could concentrate on was Max's voice.

'Yeah, she's been having trouble with that for a while now,' he said. 'It's making her feel sicker, I think.' Then Max turned to her, lowered the phone from his mouth, and said, 'My mom says to drink hot water with lemon. She said it really helps constipation.'

Cleo opened her mouth to say something, but nothing came out. Then, when Max got off the phone, she finally found her words. 'Could you please not talk to your mom about my constipation?'

Cleo made Max promise that he wouldn't tell any of his friends. 'Please. Please don't say anything. I don't want to be the pregnant girl at college.'

'Okay,' Max said. 'But people are going to find out eventually.'

'I know, but let's just wait, okay? No one needs to know right now.'

'People are going to think something's wrong when we just hole up in the apartment.'

'Well, you can go out. Just because I can't drink doesn't mean you have to stay home.'

'Really?' Max asked.

'Definitely. You can just tell everyone I'm studying or sick or out with other people.'

And she had meant it. Or at least she had meant it until Max came home drunk one night with a bag of McDonald's and crept into their bedroom to say hello.

'Hey, baby,' he said, and put his face next to hers. He smelled like rubbing alcohol.

'Hey,' she said. She'd been asleep. She rolled away from him and heard him rustling in the bag of food. She looked back to see him unwrapping a Filet-O-Fish.

'Have you ever had one of these?' he asked her. 'They're pretty good. I don't always feel like them, but tonight I wanted an appetizer to my Big Mac.' Cleo now smelled tartar sauce in addition to the rubbing alcohol.

'Ugh, Max,' Cleo said. She sat up and put her hand over her nose.

'What's the matter?' he asked. He was slurring just a little bit. 'Do you want a bite?' He held the sandwich out to her.

'No! Just get out,' she said.

Max looked hurt. 'Do you want some french fries?'

'No, Max. Really, please just leave me alone.'

'Fine,' Max said. 'I was just trying to be nice.' He stood up and walked to the door, leaving a few french fries in his trail. He slammed the bedroom door shut behind him and turned on the TV in the other room.

Cleo found him there the next morning, fast asleep, mouth open, with the McDonald's bag resting next to him. They didn't talk for almost the whole day, just huffed around each other. Then, just when it was starting to get dark, Max apologized.

'I'm sorry,' he said. 'I didn't mean to make you mad.'

'I know.'

'But I did.'

'Yeah.'

'You're the one that yelled at me to get out.'

'Yeah, but that was because you woke me up with a Filet-O-Fish on my pillow. Can you blame me?'

'I just wanted to say hi.' Max smiled the tiniest bit.

'Max.'

'I know, I'm really sorry. I am.'

'I'm sorry too, for yelling,' Cleo said. She went over and sat next to him on the couch.

'What a fucking mess,' Max said. Cleo wasn't sure if he was talking about the apartment or their life.

'I know,' she said.

Max kept assuring her that she wasn't showing, but she didn't believe him. 'Look at this,' she'd say, pulling her shirt tight across her stomach. 'This is not what I normally look like.'

'Well, I know that,' Max said. 'I just mean that no one else can tell.'

'But I can tell,' she said.

Max insisted she didn't look any different, like he thought that was the nice thing to say, but it wasn't. And so, she finally said, 'If I'm normally this fat, then kill me.'

At the first doctor's appointment, she'd been poked and prodded and had blood drawn and everything else. She kept waiting for him to say, 'It's a mistake, you aren't pregnant,' but he didn't.

'Your due date is July fifteenth,' he told them.

It was already cold outside, the start of winter, so July seemed far away, which comforted Cleo. They bought a calendar on the way home, the kind that you hang on the wall, because it seemed like they should have one, and they hung it up on a nail in the kitchen, and circled July 15 with a red marker. In the circle, Cleo wrote, due date.

'Well, there it is,' Max said. They stood and stared at it.

'Yep. There it is.'

When she was four months along, Max started telling people. 'We can't just wait until your stomach starts to get huge,' he said. He told his friend Mickey first, and then his friend Ben, and then more and more people. And those people told other people and Cleo figured that a few days after Max first told Mickey, the whole school knew. She didn't tell anyone. Who would she tell? Her old roommates that seemed to be thriving without her? Could she really call up Monica and tell her that she was pregnant, that she'd fucked up? She could just imagine Laura and Mary when they found out, sitting on the futon and saying to each other, 'I knew it was a mistake for her to move in with him. I knew it. She's getting what she deserves. It's only fair.'

Cleo felt like people stared at her wherever she went on campus. She felt like as soon as she passed, people whispered to each other, or pointed her out to the friend they were walking with. *There she is, that's the pregnant girl, can't you tell, her butt looks huge.*

'You sound paranoid,' Max said.

'Well, I'm not,' she told him.

Cleo and her mother were on e-mail terms. That's how she put it to Max. They had tried to talk on the phone once more, and Cleo had ended up screaming while her mom said, 'This is not the kind of conversation I want to have,' over and over. E-mail was better for both of them, they agreed. Maybe they'd just stay on these terms forever. Maybe Cleo could just e-mail pictures of the baby to her when it was born and then when the baby was old enough, it could start e-mailing with Elizabeth, have its own online relationship with its grandmother. It would be like they were all virtual people, like they were bodyless and floating in cyberspace.

Max went with her for the first ultrasound, even though she kept telling him that he didn't have to. It was so weird, that before she was pregnant, the thought of having Max in the room while she went to the gynecologist would have been disgusting, silly really, and so strange that no one would ever allow it. But now that she was pregnant, it wasn't just common but it was expected? Max was supposed to be there while she put her feet in the stirrups.

'Well, we can see the baby here,' the doctor said. 'And it is just one baby.' The thought of its being more than one baby had never even occurred to Cleo.

'That's it right there?' Max asked. He pointed to the screen.

'It looks like a little doll,' Cleo said. 'Or a peanut.'

The ultrasound technician froze the screen and told them that she'd print out some pictures for them.

'Can we get an extra copy?' Max asked the technician. 'I want to send one to my mom.'

'Really?' Cleo asked.

'Yeah, I think she'd like to see it. She'll probably hang it on the refrigerator or something.' The thought of a picture of the inside of her uterus hanging in the Coffeys' kitchen made Cleo feel strange. But Max seemed excited, so she let it go.

They hung the ultrasound on their own refrigerator, and

whenever Cleo went into the kitchen, her eyes went first to the picture, and then to the calendar that hung on the wall. And each time she glanced back and forth, between the calendar and the grainy ultrasound picture, she thought about how they were that much closer to that little baby's actually being a baby and coming into the world. As if she needed reminding.

Chapter 15

Weezy had a high horse. And she could get on it whenever she wanted. Maureen used to always tease her, when she'd go off on other people's behavior. 'Uh-oh,' she'd say. 'Giddyup! Here comes the horse.'

Even when she was younger, her parents used to act like Weezy thought she was too good for people. 'Don't get too big for your britches,' her father would say.

It was silly, really. It's not like Weezy believed herself to be so morally superior to everyone. It was just that sometimes she simply couldn't believe the way that people acted. (Like Cleo's mother, for instance.)

Because what kind of mother would abandon her child at this moment? No matter how disappointed or upset a person was, to sever contact while your only daughter was pregnant? Well, it was disgusting. That's what it was. There was no other word for it, really. Except maybe *despicable*. And *selfish*.

'You know,' she told Maureen, 'I'm not thrilled with this either. I'm not jumping up and down that my son that's still in college is going to be a father. But I'm helping. I'm still talking to him.'

'I know,' Maureen said. 'But you never know the details of other people's lives.'

'I know enough. I know enough to know it's wrong. I have half a mind to call her up myself and talk to her.' She'd said as much to Max, but he'd begged her not to.

'Don't, Mom. Please don't. They're figuring it out, and Cleo would kill me if you did that.'

'Fine,' she'd said with a sniff. 'I'll give it a few more months. But then she's going to have to be involved.'

Right after Max told her the news, she'd been floored. This wasn't what she expected. Not that anyone expects this news, but still. She had to admit that this hadn't even crossed her mind. She'd thought about what would happen if one of the girls got pregnant, but not this.

'It's easier, probably, that it's your son and not your daughter,' Maureen said.

'What's that supposed to mean?' Weezy asked.

'It just is. I don't know.'

Weezy did know what Maureen meant, but she wasn't going to give her the satisfaction of admitting it. At least not without faking some sort of innocence. She had always made a point of being more open-minded than Maureen. When Cathy came out, Maureen admitted (when she was about three bottles of Chardonnay deep) that she was sad about the whole thing.

'I don't love her differently, I don't. I just wish . . . I just wish it wasn't the case,' she'd said.

'Well, there's no use thinking that now,' Weezy had said. She'd secretly been thrilled that Maureen had admitted such a thing to her.

'I know that,' Maureen had said. She sounded annoyed. 'I just mean, I had a picture in my head of how it was going to be. And now it's not. It could have been so much simpler.'

They'd never spoken about it again, or at least not really. Weezy had found an article about how parents need to mourn for their straight children when they find out that they're gay. She'd been excited to give it to her, since it made so much sense. It said that you needed to mourn and fully understand that your child was going to lead a different life than you had imagined. And once you did that, you could fully accept who they were.

'Thanks,' Maureen had said. She took it and folded the paper, and put it right in her purse.

Weezy knew why she didn't want to talk about it anymore. There was nothing worse than wishing that your children were something other than what they were. She'd had those moments, where she wondered what it would be like if Martha could function on her own, what it would be like if she were able to have normal relationships with people.

And of course, she wished that things had gone differently for Claire. It's not that she thought marriage and children were the answer to everything. Certainly not. She just wished that things had worked out between them, that Claire was settled now instead of lost.

When Max first told her about Cleo, she'd thought his life was ruined. So there it was, all three of her children in a mess, and yes, she wished things were different. She was ashamed at these thoughts, and she would never admit it to anyone. Maureen probably regretted even speaking the words out loud, and so Weezy swore she would never do the same.

Weezy had been paralyzed for the weeks between Thanksgiving and Christmas. She'd managed to call Max, to tell him that they would be there for him, of course. But then she'd felt like she couldn't move. Christmas was a struggle. She'd do one thing, like get a box of decorations out of the attic, and then she'd have to lie down. Little by little, everything got done, but not before Weezy was convinced that she was anemic or possibly had some kind of cancer, because it just wasn't normal to have so little energy.

Max called her at least three times a day. He called to report on doctor's appointments and to ask her questions and to tell her what was happening. She knew that he was looking for reassurance. He'd been the same way as a little boy, needing to talk about things, needing to hear someone say that things were going to work out.

She talked to him whenever he called. She was happy to. At least this wouldn't tear their family apart, right? She felt righteous and good when they talked. She suggested that he and Cleo start taking walks for exercise, because it was never too early to start thinking about keeping in shape for the baby. Yes, she was happy to talk to him. But she did wonder if possibly that was what was taking all of her energy.

When she woke up in the mornings, her limbs felt heavy. She tried to explain this to Will, who suggested that it was just a reaction to Max's news. (That's what he was calling the whole thing. He hadn't said the words *pregnant* and *baby* at all.)

'I think I should see a doctor,' she told him. She was still lying in bed when she said this.

Will turned to look at her. 'Maybe,' he said. 'Or you could just give yourself some time to get used to this.'

'Maybe there's a gas leak in the house,' she said. There had to be something, some reason why her body felt like this.

'If there was a leak, wouldn't we all feel sick?' Will asked. Weezy had sighed and rolled over on her side. It was the kind of comment that could make you really hate Will.

Maureen brought soup over after Weezy told her on the phone that she was coming down with something. 'I don't know what it is, but it's bad. A virus of some kind.'

When Maureen arrived, she found Weezy sitting on the couch in her pajamas and robe. She arranged the soup without saying a word, and then the two of them sat and watched some talk shows.

One morning a couple of weeks after Thanksgiving, Weezy walked down the stairs and surveyed the house. She decided that she'd do one thing every day to get ready for Christmas. How hard could it be to do one thing? She stood at the bottom of the stairs and looked all around. Dozens of little turkeys smiled at her from all around the house, sending her right back upstairs to bed. They all had such creepy gobbles, and she couldn't face that today. She could start tomorrow.

One day, she managed to arrange all the Santas that she'd collected over the years on the mantel, and then she'd gone over to the couch and lay there, staring at them. She'd cried a little bit, because her heart was breaking for her Max and she really didn't know what would happen.

Will brought the tree up from the basement and put on the lights, and the girls hung the ornaments. (They'd gone to a fake tree a few years ago, when getting a real tree seemed like too much of a hassle. Claire and Max had both protested, saying that it was pointless to put up a piece of plastic. Weezy tried to tell them that the pine-scented candles would make it seem like the real thing without all the needles on the floor that couldn't be vacuumed up no matter what. Even in April, she'd still be finding them hidden behind furniture and under rugs. This year she was even more grateful that the tree was in their basement, or they might not have had one at all.)

She didn't know how she was going to manage to buy presents and she put it off, until it was the week before Christmas and she had no more time to waste. She got in the car and drove to the mall. It was cold, but there was no snow on the ground, so she could be grateful for that.

For the first time in her life that she could remember, Weezy had no Christmas list with her when she shopped. She walked into department stores and bought generic gifts, scarves and mittens. She shopped in groups. When she found something she liked for one of the girls, she bought three of them. Will and Max got the same sweater in different colors, the same gloves, the same socks.

She was surprised at how quickly it went, buying piles of books at the bookstore, not caring who got what, just knowing that there'd be something to wrap. She had to buy for Cleo this year, who was coming for Christmas, but that just meant buying more duplicates. All of the shopping was done in one day, with Weezy making a few trips to the car in between.

When she pulled into the driveway after her shopping trip, she left all the bags in the car, poured herself a glass of wine, and got into her bed in her pajamas. It was five thirty. When Will found her, she was watching TV and had the comforter pulled up to her chin.

'I'm not feeling well,' she said. Will looked at the glass of wine and nodded, then let her rest for the night.

Weezy spent her time in bed on the laptop, looking up information on weddings where the bride was pregnant. There were many tips. Ruching seemed to be a popular way to hide the stomach, although it didn't really look like it worked that well. There were some brides that decided to wait until after the baby was born, some that waited years and then had the child as a ring bearer or flower girl. (Which just seemed downright trashy.) She wondered what it would take to convince Max and Cleo that they should get married. She scoured the sites for tips and tricks, and thought at least they weren't the first couple to get themselves into this mess.

She had no idea how she was going to manage to have everyone home for three days. That was all it was going to be, but it seemed impossible. She could fake sick, she thought, if things got really bad. It would be like the year that she had gotten the stomach flu and could barely make it downstairs for twenty minutes to watch the kids open their presents. They'd all eaten breakfast without her, gone to mass without her, and she'd stayed upstairs in bed, watching old movies.

Weezy felt safer that she had a backup plan. No one could argue with a sick person, and it wouldn't even be like she was lying. She was sick. She just didn't know what she had.

Somehow she managed to make it through. Will and the girls had helped with the cooking and while she had imagined that this year, the days would go on forever, it was like any other year and Christmas seemed to be over in a flash.

Now she could rest. She imagined sleeping all day, not having to shop or decorate. This is what her life would be like from now on. It was like she'd aged twenty years in the past month.

But then, after Christmas, things changed. She woke up one

morning with her heart pounding, thinking of all the things that had to be done. And instead of feeling tired, she felt full of energy. She drank a pot of coffee each morning, and darted around the house, cleaning and organizing.

Claire told her that she had to slow down. Actually what she said was, 'Mom, you're going to give yourself a heart attack.' But Weezy couldn't stop. She sent out an e-mail to all of her friends, telling them that Max's girlfriend was pregnant and that she hoped they could all be happy for the family, even if things were happening a little out of order.

Weezy knew that they were all giving each other looks behind her back, but she didn't have time to deal with them. There was too much to do, too much to figure out.

'I'm glad you're feeling better,' Maureen said. She raised her eyebrows and waited for Weezy to say something.

'Thanks. Me too,' she said.

Will continued on through his days like nothing had happened. 'What do you want me to do?' he asked Weezy. 'It's happened and we're dealing with it.'

But *they* weren't dealing with anything – *Weezy* was dealing with all of it. She made the plans and ran them by Max, who ran them by Cleo, and then she told Will what was going to happen.

'They'll be moving back here at the end of the school year,' she told Will. It had taken weeks to convince Max that this was the right thing to do, but she'd done it.

'That's a good idea,' Will said. And that was all.

Will spent almost all of his time in his office, typing away.

He took all his meals straight up there, probably to avoid Weezy and talking about Max. Whenever she brought it up, when she talked about how worried she was about Max, Will just nodded.

'Don't you care?' Weezy asked.

'Of course I care,' Will said. 'I just don't think we need to pretend like Max isn't responsible, like this is something that happened to him and not something that he did.'

But Will's inaction just made Weezy move faster. She began to redo the basement, since she figured that Max and Cleo would be staying down there when they returned. It would be more comfortable for them, and easier on the whole family, if they had their own space.

The challenge of course was to make a basement look like a place where you wanted to spend time. There was something damp and chilly about the room down there, and Weezy had never liked it. But now, she would get it done. She felt like she was on one of those home-decorating challenge shows, where they find an unused space and make it into something amazing.

She got the floors redone, and bought new throw rugs to cover the tile. (They couldn't put wall-to-wall carpeting down there, because there was always a chance it would flood. But she made it look cozy.) She bought new furniture, a new dresser and two bedside tables with matching blue ceramic lamps. She had the walls repainted a soft yellow, which seemed welcoming and calming, and she bought new bedding that looked inviting and soft.

The bathroom in the basement was old and rusty and the floor was always freezing, no matter what time of year it was.

She had some people come in to look at it and two days later it was all ripped up. 'We've been meaning to do this for years,' Weezy said when Will acted surprised. 'Now this just gives us a reason to get it done.'

She bought a bassinet for the baby and put it right next to the bed. That would do for the time being. They'd have to figure out a crib at some point, but for now this would be enough. Although she did go out and buy a couple of extra soft baby blankets, and just a few little stuffed animals to put in the bassinet so it didn't look so empty.

When she showed Claire and Martha the finished room, she was extremely proud of herself. They were shocked, she could tell. 'Well?' she asked them. 'What do you think?'

'Whoa,' Martha said. She kept turning in circles looking at the walls.

'It looks great,' Claire said. 'It doesn't even look like the same place.'

'Oh, it was just a few things here and there,' Weezy said.

'I don't know how you did this all so quickly,' Claire said. 'Now you're all set.'

But she wasn't all set. The room was just the beginning. There was so much more to do. Maureen told her to slow down. 'You're running yourself ragged,' she said. But no one understood. No one understood that Weezy had to keep moving, had to keep doing things, or everyone around her would fall apart.

The rest of her family seemed to go on just as usual. Claire was spending a lot of time with that boy Fran, which worried

Weezy, although in the grand scheme of things she couldn't worry too much about it now. Unless Claire got pregnant as well, there just wasn't time. And of course once she had that thought, it was stuck in her brain. Imagine if that happened – if Claire and Cleo were both pregnant and living under her roof. *See?* Weezy thought. *Things could be worse.*

Weezy got the feeling that her family was talking about her behind her back. Whenever she came into a room, it seemed that Will and Martha and Claire had just been whispering about her, just been sharing some information. 'Just humor her,' Will probably told them. 'Just be helpful.'

It reminded her of when the kids were young, when every once in a while she'd lose her temper and stomp off to her room, and when she'd come back down, she'd find Will playing with them or making them lunch and they'd all look up at her and say hello, cheerfully, as though nothing had happened. Will would be spinning the wheel for Candyland or making bologna sandwiches, and she just knew that they'd talked about her while she was upstairs. 'Mom's upset,' Will would have said, 'so we need to be on our best behavior.'

It should have made her feel better during those moments, that Will would step in and run interference, that her kids were so willing to put on a smile to appease her. But whenever she came downstairs, it just made her feel left out, like she was the moody member of the team, that needed special treatment, and they had all kept going without her. Will always looked so satisfied, like he thought that he could take over with the kids. He was so pleased that he could handle them for all of thirty minutes, and it didn't make her feel better – it made her angry, made her feel like she wasn't even a part of this family that she was running.

One Wednesday, Will had called from his office to suggest they go to dinner. 'Somewhere nice,' he said. 'Just the adults.'

It occurred to Weezy that their children were now adults too, that there were really four adults living full-time in this house, soon to be six. But she didn't say that.

'I don't know,' she said. 'There's so much to do.' Really, the thought of washing her hair and finding something to wear out seemed overwhelming. But Will had insisted.

They'd gone to Pesce, a seafood restaurant that was a favorite of theirs. Usually it was saved for anniversaries or birthdays.

'Well, this is fancy,' Weezy said, when they pulled into the parking lot.

'I thought you deserved a nice night out,' Will said.

They walked in and were seated at a corner table. The restaurant was dark and the table had a small votive in the center, as if that would be enough to help people see. Will ordered a Scotch and Weezy ordered red wine. It came in an oversized glass, the kind that almost looks like a bucket, which pleased her. She took a few sips and felt the warmth in her chest and stomach.

'I've been worried about you,' Will said. 'Because you've been so worried about everything. You're going to collapse if you keep this up.'

Weezy sighed. 'I have to worry. Just for a little while. Just until things settle down.'

Will nodded and tilted his glass to the left and right, causing the ice cubes to clink against one another. 'You're a fantastic mother,' he said. He raised his glass. 'To you.'

He and Weezy clinked glasses and then took a sip. Weezy wanted to tell him how strange it was that she felt so energized lately. How for the past few years, she'd felt like there was nothing surprising to look forward to – that is, until Claire had gotten engaged, but then that had all gone to hell. Her children were mostly grown, they'd gone off to college, and she had just been waiting, stalled really, for the next stage of her life to start. And she thought that it was far away, many years down the line.

But then this had happened. And, of course, she was not pleased at first. Disappointed, really. Embarrassed, for sure. But once that went away, once she dealt with that, she was excited. She couldn't admit that to herself for a long time, but it was the truth. She was needed again. Max needed her and Cleo needed her. She was useful. And there was going to be a baby.

She thought of how to explain this to Will, who was looking at her with a mix of concern and pity. He felt bad for her! He still thought she was the martyr who was putting everything aside to help their child. So she didn't say anything except, 'It's what any mother would do.'

Will reached out and patted her hand, leaving his to rest on top for a few moments. 'That's not true,' he said. 'It's what you do. And so you deserve a night out.'

With that, he took his hand back and opened the menu. 'Good God, can you see any of this?' He squinted and brought the menu close to his face, then picked up the votive and held it next to it. 'I can't see a thing!'

Weezy pulled the magnifying card that Will had given her a few years earlier out of her purse. It had lights on the side to help as well. He'd put it in her stocking as a surprise one Christmas, as a joke about their old age. But lately she'd really had to use it. It had become their custom for Weezy to look through her menu with it, reading aloud the things that she knew he'd like.

'Seared scallops with asparagus risotto,' she read. 'Pecan-crusted tilapia, maple-glazed salmon.'

Will got the scallops, which she'd known he would. Weezy got the tilapia, which Will had guessed. They both ordered white wine with their dinners, and ate slowly. Will cut one of his scallops in half and deposited it on her plate with a scoop of the risotto. She did the same with her fish.

They even split a dessert, at Will's insistence. 'My diet is already shot,' he said. 'So we might as well go all the way.' Will's 'diet' consisted of his complaining about his weight and spending a few days each month doing sit-ups in his office and trying to give up butter.

'This was a perfect night,' Weezy said as they left. Will had ordered a glass of port for each of them and they were both a little wobbly as they left the restaurant. Will had started slurring just the tiniest bit, and Weezy knew it probably wasn't smart for them to drive home, but it was only a couple of miles.

She woke up in the middle of the night with a headache and stomach cramps and spent the next hour in the bathroom. Will came in at one point to get the antacids. The rich food and all that alcohol. Oh, what was she thinking? There was a time when that wouldn't have bothered her one bit, when she would have slept peacefully through the night. But now? Well, now she was old. Practically a grandmother.

She thought of Will then, the way he'd said 'just the adults' as if Claire and Martha were still little children they needed to escape from. She thought of the way that she'd passed Claire's room the other night, seen Claire asleep on the bed, her mouth wide open, her arms around an ancient stuffed moose. How Will had said 'Poor baby' to Martha. Her head pounded and her stomach threatened to revolt again. What was going on? She took two aspirin and drank a glass of water and tried to go back to bed.

The next week, Weezy told Max that she needed Cleo's mother's number. Enough was enough. She understood that families work things out in their own way, but Max and Cleo were not in any position to deal with things on their own. 'Just have her tell her mother that I want to talk to her,' Weezy said.

She found she was nervous when dialing the number, and

even more so when she heard someone else answer the phone. 'Elizabeth Wolfe's office.' Weezy identified herself and was put on hold. She wondered what Elizabeth would say, if she would even take the call. And just when she was beginning to think that she'd never get through, the line clicked.

'Am I ever glad to talk to you,' Elizabeth said.

'Oh! Well, I'm glad to hear that.'

On the other end of the phone, Elizabeth let out a breath, blowing straight into the receiver. 'Can you believe this?' she asked. 'Cleo is driving me absolutely insane.'

'I've said the same thing about Max every day since I found out.'

The two women laughed a little, and Weezy felt relieved. Elizabeth was just a mom after all. Weezy felt guilty for all the things she'd been saying about her, and even though there was no way Elizabeth could have known about them, she almost apologized. 'I didn't want to intrude,' she said. 'I just thought we should talk.'

They made plans to meet that weekend for lunch. 'I can take the train there,' Weezy said. 'It'll give me an excuse to do some shopping.'

The two women met at a restaurant on the Upper West Side, not far from Elizabeth's apartment. 'I can't imagine raising a child here,' Weezy said. 'I admire you for it. If I hadn't been able to run mine like dogs outside, I think I might have gone crazy.'

Elizabeth just nodded and Weezy was afraid she'd insulted her. 'It really is admirable,' she said again. 'Cleo's a lovely girl.'

'A lovely pregnant girl,' Elizabeth said. Weezy looked up, embarrassed that the waiter was standing right there and had heard, but Elizabeth didn't seem to care. She ordered a glass of wine and raised her eyebrows at Weezy, who nodded in agreement.

'I'm just so furious,' Elizabeth said.

'I know, I know.' Weezy found that Elizabeth's anger made her want to be even more understanding.

The two women talked about what was to come, agreed that their children had no idea what to expect, but promised to help in any way they could.

'I've told Max they can move in with us after graduation.'

'That's a very generous offer,' Elizabeth said.

'Of course, if you'd rather have Cleo here, I understand.'

'It's really up to her. I doubt she'll want to come back here.'

Weezy felt very sad for Cleo just then. If Martha or Claire were pregnant and abandoned, she'd drag them back home whether they wanted it or not. She'd make sure they knew they had their mother for support; she'd be in their faces every day.

'You're handling this all quite well,' Elizabeth said.

'I'm just handling it,' Weezy said. She tried to sound humble, but it actually came out sounding like she was bragging.

After lunch, Weezy wandered up Amsterdam, popping into some of the little boutiques. She was a little light-headed from the wine, but found it refreshing not to care who saw her. She ended up buying a ridiculously expensive pair of booties with giraffes on them. They were so tiny and perfect. She tucked them into her purse and went out to get a taxi back to the train station.

Chapter 16

This was what a psychotic break looked like. Claire was pretty sure of that. Sometimes, she wanted to stand up in the middle of the office, at dinner with her family, or while she was in Fran's basement watching ESPN with him, and scream, 'I am having a psychotic break, people. I am having a breakdown and no one is noticing.'

But that only happened if she let herself think about it which she tried not to do most of the time. She found it was easier to ignore everything that was going on and just get through the day. She stayed busy.

If she wasn't at Fran's watching a movie or drinking a beer, she was running around the neighborhood with her iPod on, sprinting down the dark streets in the cold until her chest was too tight to breathe and her legs hurt. Anything to make sure that when she got into bed that night, she'd fall asleep quickly.

At home, the air was filled with Max and Cleo. Weezy was acting like someone with a brain injury, sometimes slow and spacey, sometimes sharp and wild. The day after Thanksgiving, she'd told them the news in the kitchen, and although they'd already guessed, it was still a shock to hear.

'Don't tell anyone,' Weezy said. She looked nervous, like they might have already spread the news around town.

'Of course not,' Martha said. 'Oh my God, we won't tell anyone.'

'People are going to find out eventually,' Claire said.

'I know that,' Weezy said. 'But let's just hold off. It's no one else's business.'

'People are so gossipy in this town,' Martha said. Her eyes filled with tears.

'Why are you crying?' Claire asked.

'They're so young. How can they handle this?' Martha's nose was running.

'Martha,' Claire said, 'stop acting like you're the one that's knocked up.'

'Claire, that's enough,' Weezy said. 'This isn't easy on your sister. This isn't easy on any of us.'

'Why isn't this easy for her?' Claire said. 'What's so hard

about it? Just because you're embarrassed doesn't mean you can act like this is all about you.'

'This has nothing to do with being embarrassed,' Weezy said.

Martha looked up at the ceiling then, just as the tears poured down her cheeks. She let out a strange squeak and left the room quickly. Weezy turned to Claire with a look that said, *Are you happy now?*

'Jesus,' Claire said.

'It wouldn't kill you to be a little nicer to your sister.'

'It actually might.'

None of them spoke to one another for the rest of the day. Will looked like he wanted to get out of the house. He'd been angry in the morning, but by the afternoon, he looked exhausted. He and Weezy had been holed up in their bedroom having whispered conversations. Around dinnertime, Will tried to act normal, asking if anyone else was interested in warming up some leftovers, then going ahead and taking out the Tupperware containers and warming up the turkey, stuffing, and gravy until the whole house smelled like Thanksgiving again. He was the only one who ate.

They didn't apologize to one another. That isn't how they worked. The three of them were just short and chilly to one another for a few days, and then eventually it went away. Even Martha and Weezy spoke to each other with pursed lips and stilted conversation, although Claire was pretty sure they hadn't been fighting with each other. It was like no one could keep track of who was mad at whom.

Even Ruby the dog was upset by the situation. She knew that

everyone was out of sorts, and she spent her time walking up to each member of the family and licking them on the hand, as if to say, *Don't worry, it will all be fine.* At the end of each day, she looked exhausted, lying on her green bed in the corner of the TV room, her head on her paws. Ruby had taken to eating her food quickly, like she was afraid someone was going to take it away from her if she paused or looked up.

'She's not even chewing,' Claire pointed out. And it was true. The dog was just scarfing down her food, swallowing the pieces whole.

'Maybe she's an emotional eater,' Martha said.

'A what?' Claire asked.

'An emotional eater,' Martha repeated. 'You know, like she's eating her feelings because she's upset about Max.'

Both Weezy and Claire stood and stared at Martha without saying a word.

After Thanksgiving, Max had taken to calling Claire's cell phone every day. 'Just checking in,' he'd say.

'Things will get better,' Claire told him. She could think of nothing else to say.

'I can't even imagine that right now,' Max said.

'Trust me. I know it seems bad, but in a few months it will be fine.'

'Months?'

'Just give it time.'

Claire convinced Max to come home for Christmas, telling him it would be worse if he didn't. So he'd arrived with Cleo in tow, who still wasn't talking to her mother and was so quiet that she didn't even seem like the same person. All of Christmas was quiet, actually. They sat around reading books most of the time, which seemed to be the perfect activity since they could ignore each other and still pretend to be spending time together. Everyone took a lot of naps. And even Bets, who didn't know that Cleo was pregnant yet, seemed to sense that something was off and was on unusually good behavior.

'Won't your mother miss you?' she asked Cleo.

'Oh, no. She'll be fine.'

One night, Claire got up and had a cigarette in the bathroom. She never would have dared if Bets hadn't been there, but who was going to know the difference? She sat on the tile floor, her back against the wall, and smoked slowly, letting the cigarette burn down to her fingers. She sort of understood what it was that Bets liked about this. It was secret and solo. It was just one little thing that she had for herself. When she was done, she flushed the butt down the toilet and went back into Martha's room and climbed into the twin bed.

'Did you just smoke in there?' Martha asked.

'No,' Claire said. 'I didn't.'

They all went to midnight mass on Christmas Eve, and came back home to have eggnog by the fire. Bets excused herself, telling everyone that it was well past her bedtime.

'I'm an old woman,' she said. 'Practically on death's door.

I'm not cut out for this anymore.' She'd worn her best red suit, which seemed too big for her. Bets had always been tiny. 'I barely eat,' she sometimes said. But now she was practically miniature. She seemed to be proof that old people really did shrink. It was a frightening thought.

The rest of them settled in the living room and Will started a fire. Claire was certain that they all wished they could go to bed like Bets had, but this was their tradition and they didn't really have a choice.

Weezy poured everyone eggnog with a shot of whiskey, except for Cleo, of course. 'This one's a virgin,' she said, handing the glass to Cleo. Cleo blushed and took it. 'Well, that's an awful term, isn't it?' Weezy asked. It was like everyone was trying to be as awkward as possible.

Claire even wished that Cathy was there with them. It would have been lovely to have someone to talk loudly and hog the conversation. But Maureen, Cathy, and Ruth had decided to visit Drew in California for Christmas. 'We're just in need of some sunshine,' Maureen had said. But that was a lie. Maureen just didn't want to be anywhere near the Coffey house that Christmas. And really, who could blame her? She'd offered to come back and fly home with Bets on the twenty-seventh, which was her way of apologizing, and Weezy had seemed to accept it gladly.

Christmas morning, they opened their presents politely, thanking each other like they'd met not long ago; like they were acquaintances or office mates who were fond of each other. They balled up wrapping paper and threw it into a big black garbage bag that Will held open. Anytime someone made it in, Will would shout, 'Two points for you!'

By the time they all sat down to eat ham at the table, their patience was thin and their small talk was bordering on nasty.

'Don't take so many potatoes,' Martha told Max.

'Calm down, there's plenty left for you, porky,' he said.

'I can't believe any of you are hungry,' Bets said. 'You all ate like pigs going to slaughter this morning. I can barely even imagine eating a meal right now.'

'I could use some help in the kitchen,' Weezy said.

'I'm right here, trying to help,' Will said.

'This ham looks really fatty,' Claire said.

Only Cleo remained almost completely silent. She was probably trying to will herself to be anywhere but there, thinking that no matter how much she was fighting with her own mom, this was worse. You could almost see her thoughts: *There's no place like home. There's no place like home.*

Fran spent the holiday in Florida with his parents, and when he returned, he brought her a little tchotchke, a tiny stage with a group of stones with googly eyes and little guitars. Underneath the label said rock band. Claire took it and laughed.

'It made me think of you,' Fran said. She wasn't sure what to make of that.

He also gave her a beautiful light tan leather journal. She realized that he probably found both presents in some little gift shop that was nearby, but she didn't hold that against him.

She gave him a plaid scarf that she'd bought at the last minute,

341

during a moment of doubt when she couldn't justify sleeping with someone for three months and not giving him a Christmas present. He seemed to like it.

It was a relief to go back to work after Christmas, which was the first time Claire had ever thought such a thing. Even though the heat in the office was on full blast and the place was always too warm, and everyone always seemed to have wet shoes that smelled like dogs, Claire was glad to be back. It meant that time was moving forward, that winter was continuing on. The people of PP loved talking about the weather, and even when it was barely snowing outside, they'd come in sniffling and saying things like, 'We're due for another whopper,' or 'It took me twenty minutes to clear off my car this morning!'

Right before Christmas, Leslie had called Claire into her office to tell her that Amanda had decided to take another three months off unpaid. 'It's company policy that allows you to do that,' Leslie said. 'So legally we have to let her. I won't get into the details, but let's just say I'm not surprised we're in this situation.'

'Uh-huh,' Claire said. She couldn't blame Amanda for not wanting to come back to PP right away.

'We're hoping that you'll be able to stay on for the next three months.'

'Sure,' Claire said.

'That's great. That really gets us out of a bind.'

It didn't seem like a bind at all to Claire, but she didn't say anything. If she couldn't do it, wouldn't they have just called the temp agency and gotten someone else? But she could tell that Leslie was the kind of person who enjoyed being annoyed at work, who liked to sigh deeply and tell her friends, 'You just have no idea what I'm dealing with at the office. No idea.'

'So you'll stay until the end of March?' Lainie asked when she told her. 'That's good.'

'I guess.'

'Well, it's a job. And that's what you need.'

'I know. It's just sometimes I feel like I'm going to be there forever. Like I'm just going to keep working at PP and keep living at home for the rest of my life.'

'Claire, it's three more months. Don't be so dramatic.'

'It's just when I look at the past year, I feel like I messed up so much that there's no telling what I could do.'

'That's ridiculous. You're not going to live at home forever. You'll move out, and probably soon. You're just taking time to figure out what you want to do. It's just a time-out.'

'Yeah, I guess.'

Claire thought about Lainie's words when she was at Proof Perfect, making copies or opening the mail. 'TV Time-out,' she'd whisper sometimes at her desk. It was something they used to scream when they were little, when they were in the middle of a game and someone needed a break. They'd be running around, playing tag or kickball, and someone would yell, 'TV Time-out!' and just like that, they'd all stop right where they were, put their hands on their knees, and catch their breath.

*

Every week, Max forwarded an e-mail from a baby website to Claire that had been forwarded to him by Cleo. Claire was familiar with the website. Lainie had been obsessed with the same one when she was pregnant with Jack. 'Do you believe this stuff?' Max would sometimes write at the top. The e-mail gave weekly information about skin and organs and fingernails. It gave comparisons to objects, so that you could imagine how big the baby was: The baby was a peanut, a grape, a kumquat, a cucumber. Okay, maybe they didn't use that last one, but Claire couldn't bring herself to read the e-mails. She knew that Max was overwhelmed, knew that he needed her to talk to, so that she could tell him that it was all going to be fine. So she did try.

Your baby is an orange, your baby is a peach, your baby is a plum, a watermelon, a fig. This is what Claire thought each night before she went to sleep. She listed them out of order, then went backward, making the baby smaller and smaller. Sometimes she'd keep going, creating her own list of objects: Your baby is a basketball, a watermelon, a dachshund, a couch. The list of items ran in her head fast, until it felt like she wasn't in control of them anymore. How could you tell the difference, she wondered, between hearing voices in your head and your own thoughts?

And then one day, when the IT guy was working on her computer, she saw his eyes get wide and he turned to her with a smile. 'Well, I guess congratulations are in order.'

'What?' Claire said.

'Your baby is a lemon,' he said. 'You can barely tell.'

'Oh no, that's not me. That's my brother's baby.'

'Oh, sorry about that.'

After he left, Claire tried to figure out what he meant when he said, *You can barely tell.* Barely tell? 'I can barely tell that you're a huge loser,' she muttered. And then she felt mean. And she deleted the e-mail.

Fran's parents were still in Florida and Claire started sleeping there a few nights a week. Whenever she left the house with a bag and said she wasn't coming home that night, Weezy raised her eyebrows.

'What?' Claire would ask. Weezy would just shake her head.

It wasn't much different with Fran's parents gone all the time, since they'd seemed oblivious to Claire's presence anyway. She'd met them a few times and they'd seemed uninterested and bored. His mom was a thin woman with short gray hair who wore sweat suits and looked tired. His dad was the same.

Claire knew without having to ask that these were not the kind of parents who asked after her, or asked Fran much about his life, for that matter. They were the parents who were truly surprised when Fran was caught smoking pot in his car at the high school, who were annoyed about it mostly because it meant they'd have to go in and meet with the dean.

One Saturday, Claire went over to help Fran watch his niece. Fran's sister lived a few towns over, in an apartment building.

She was divorced. Claire vaguely remembered her from high school. Bonnie was a couple of years older, and used to stand with the group of kids that huddled at the edge of the parking lot to smoke cigarettes in the morning and the afternoon.

Fran's niece was about three years old, and was not an attractive child. It seemed horrible to think that, but it was the truth. She had stringy blond hair and her nose was way too big for her face. She always had food on her clothes and cried often and loudly. Also, she was a hitter.

When Claire got to the house, Fran was smoking a cigarette in the basement and Jude was sitting on the floor playing with a doll. Two lines of snot were running out of her nose.

Claire tried, but she couldn't take an interest in the little girl. She pretended to, kneeling down to talk to her, but Jude just snatched up her doll to her chest and reached out to smack Claire. After that, she just watched. Fran seemed fond of his niece, or at least not opposed to her. He made her macaroni and cheese and got her milk in a sippy cup, which she immediately poured down her shirt. For the rest of the day, the little girl was slightly damp and smelled sour. When Claire got up to leave, she leaned down and touched the top of Jude's head.

' 'Bye, Jude,' she said.

' 'Bye, stupid,' Jude replied.

She and Fran never went out, which suited her just fine. Sometimes they picked up food or got takeout, but mostly they just sat in the basement. 'Don't you two ever want to go out to dinner?' Lainie asked. Claire knew she thought it was weird, but to her it would have been weirder if they ever left the basement.

'Not really. We're fine just hanging out,' she said.

It wasn't just that she never wanted to spend money (which she didn't), but it was like they both knew that their relationship, or whatever it was, worked best in the basement. If they took it out into the light of day, it would be different.

All through high school, Claire had imagined what it would be like to date Fran. Fran now seemed like a different person than the one she used to spend hours thinking about. In high school, Fran had worn a gas station shirt to school almost every day. It was navy and had the name bud stitched above the left breast pocket. She would wonder what it would be like to lie next to him, rest her head right on top of the bud.

She remembered the way Fran would sometimes take huge sandwiches to parties, how he would sit, stoned, in the middle of a room and shove a sub in his mouth, letting lettuce and onions drop all around him, like he was the only person in the room, or really, like he could give two shits about what these people thought of him anyway. In her whole life, Claire was pretty sure she had never felt that comfortable.

Sometimes when she was with him now, she would have a moment where she'd think, *I am lying in bed with Fran Angelo.* It was a strange, out-of-body experience, like when she used to get stoned in college, stare in the bathroom mirror and think, *That is me. That is me looking back at me,* until she got dizzy and had to leave the room.

*

Winter seemed lonelier, although Claire couldn't say exactly why. She was barely home, but when she was, the idea of going somewhere else seemed so hard. It was like the idea of putting on boots and a coat exhausted her.

She didn't spend as much time at Lainie's, mostly because with the three boys stuck in the house, it seemed smaller and much more crowded. The last time she'd been over there, Jack spent most of the time leaping from the couch to the table to the chair. 'I can't touch the ground,' he screamed. 'It's lava and if I touch it, I'll die.' Then he'd leapt back over to the couch and hit his arm on Claire's nose. 'Ow!' he yelled. He cradled his arm against his chest with his other hand and glared at Claire like she'd hit him. 'That hurt,' he told her.

Martha had gotten in the habit of coming into Claire's room every night. She'd sit on the edge of Claire's bed and rattle off a list of things she'd done that day. She talked about her job and Max and Cleo. It didn't matter if Claire answered her or even really listened. It was like Martha just needed to hear herself talk.

Claire tried to be patient with her, but it wasn't easy. Most of the time she just wanted to be left alone. She found herself shutting her bedroom door early, turning off the lights and getting into bed so Martha would leave her alone.

One night, Claire woke up outside the house in her pajamas. She stood there, heart pounding, and realized that she must have sleepwalked out of her room, down the stairs, through the garage, and outside.

There she was, barefoot, staring right into the living room

and trying to figure out what had happened. It felt a little like waking up in a hotel room on vacation and not knowing where you were for a few minutes – only so much worse. Claire hadn't sleepwalked in years. As a child, she'd occasionally wander out of her room and down to the kitchen or into her parents' room. Once, she'd walked out the front door, but Will had been following her and managed to guide her back to her room.

At camp, she'd once woken up a few feet from the cabin, and her counselor, a snarly teenage girl with horrible acne, was behind her, looking like she'd just seen a ghost. 'What the hell?' the counselor had said. 'You're, like, possessed or something.' From then on, Claire had a note in her camp file that said: prone to sleepwalking. please monitor.

But she'd thought she'd outgrown this little habit. All those years that she lived in apartments in New York, she never even worried that she'd do such a thing. And here she was, standing outside in winter in the middle of the night.

A few nights later, it happened again and Claire woke up standing on the front porch. Ruby was right behind her, her head tilted as if she was getting ready to bark. Claire hurried back into the house, locked the door, scooped Ruby up, and headed to her room, where she scrunched underneath the covers and tried to get warm again.

Telling her family was out of the question. Weezy would freak out, Martha would insist that she needed to go see a therapist, and Will would start trying to figure out how to lock the doors so that she couldn't get outside. The whole family would talk about it at dinner for weeks. Martha would pretend that she knew the medical reasons for sleepwalking, as if being a nurse qualified her to diagnose Claire. No, it was out of the question.

The next night, Claire put a stack of books in front of her door, so that she couldn't open it without knocking them down, which she hoped would be enough to wake her up. She was pleased with the plan, pretty sure that this would keep her safely inside. Although she did go to bed every night a little afraid that she was going to wake up somewhere strange.

At the end of February, the whole family came down with the flu. It was a flu that sent each of them running to the bathroom again and again. Just when one would flop down on the couch, dehydrated and exhausted, the next one would hear a rumble in their stomach and get up, clutching their middle and running out of the room.

Martha and Claire lay on the couch, trying to watch a movie, but they couldn't get through much before one of them had to leave. They were starting to get delirious. The flu had been going on for almost three days now and there was no sign of its slowing down. They had all said out loud that they might be dying.

'We look like a diarrhea commercial,' Claire said. Martha started to laugh. 'What?' Claire asked.

'A diarrhea commercial? I know what you mean, but it sounds like you're talking about an ad that's selling diarrhea.'

'Oh yeah,' Claire said. She started to laugh too. 'I meant like Pepto-Bismol or whatever.'

The family shuffled around in their pajamas, getting ginger ale and toast from the kitchen and then heading back to the couch or their beds. For the first time, when Max called, Claire told him truthfully that they hadn't talked about him and Cleo in days. 'We're too busy talking about each other's shit,' Claire told him. 'You're off the hook.'

'I think I might be coming down with something too,' Lainie said to Claire on the phone.

'Well,' Claire said, 'you would know if you had this.'

'Yeah, I just feel so pukey all the time. Great. I'm sure the worst is coming.'

But then a couple of weeks later, Lainie called and asked Claire if she could go out for a little bit. 'Brian's watching the boys,' she said. They met in Lainie's driveway, and Lainie drove to the Post Office Bar, a place that they used to frequent during the summers when they were home from college.

'This okay with you?' she asked.

'Sure,' Claire said. 'I haven't been here in forever.'

They ordered two drafts of some sort of amber beer, and a basket of Parmesan-garlic fries, which looked like frozen french fries that had been warmed and covered with grated cheese, but were actually not bad. The bar was empty, except for one older man at the end of the bar, who was doing a crossword puzzle and drinking. Claire wondered where he went in the summer, when this place was overrun with underage kids and a DJ came in on

Friday nights. She wondered if he was mad when that happened, if he felt like his house had been taken over, or if he had a different place that he found, another quiet place for the summer.

'I'm pregnant,' Lainie said. She was addressing a thin, limp fry that she was holding. It seemed to bend further with the news.

'What?' Claire said. 'When?'

'I just found out last week. It wasn't the flu.'

'Oh my God. Well, congratulations.'

Lainie's eyes had started to fill with tears. 'I can't be pregnant,' she said. 'What am I, that reality TV woman that has like a hundred kids? I'm barely recovered from Matthew. I can't be starting this all over again.' She took a sip of beer and the tears fell on her cheeks.

'Should you be having that?' Claire asked.

'It's just one beer,' Lainie said. 'It won't do anything.'

'Okay,' Claire said. She was unsure how to continue.

'It's just so fucked up. I can't believe I let this happen. We have, like, just barely enough money now, but not even really. And that's with me teaching, which I can't do much longer.' Lainie's nose had started to run, and Claire handed her a napkin.

'You'll be okay,' Claire said. 'I know you will. It seems crazy now, I'm sure, but you'll be okay.'

Lainie lifted the glass of beer to her lips and then put it down again without drinking. 'I don't even want it,' she said, pushing it away. 'Not really. I just ordered it because I'm annoyed I can't have it.'

'What did Brian say?'

'Same as me. He just doesn't know how we're going to afford it, or even fit in our house anymore, not that that matters, because we're not going anywhere. We can't.'

They sat together for a while, Claire reassuring Lainie that it would be fine, and Lainie listing all the things that would be different. They picked at the fries, and Claire drank both of the beers, even though by the time she got to Lainie's, it was a little warm.

'Well, maybe it will be a girl,' Claire finally offered, as they paid their tab. 'You did always want a girl, too.'

Lainie laughed and put the last group of french fries in her mouth, dragging them through the cold grease that was dotted with garlic before eating them. It was a bitter sort of laugh that sounded like she was a wise old person who'd seen it all. 'It will be a boy,' she said. 'I know it. We're just going to have all boys.'

When Claire got back home, she didn't even bother going inside before she called Fran. He was sleeping, but he answered the phone. 'Come over,' he said. And so she ran there, all six blocks to his house, like she was in a race. She stopped when she got to his driveway, and rested for a minute, putting her hands on her knees.

She walked down the stairs on the side of the house, and turned the doorknob carefully. Fran never locked the door, which usually bugged her, but tonight she was grateful. The room was dark, and she stood in the doorway for a minute, letting her eyes adjust, so that she could see enough not to crash into anything.

She walked to the side of the bed and looked down at Fran, who had fallen back asleep. He was so handsome, but when she looked at him, she thought what her high school self would have thought: *He's so hot*. She touched his head and he opened his eyes and gave her a sleepy smile.

'Hey,' he said. 'You're a nice surprise.'

She bent down over him, putting her face in his neck and smelling him, all cinnamon and smoke, and for one scary second, she thought she was going to start crying. Fran pulled sleepily at her shirt and then her pants.

'Off,' he said. 'Take these off.'

And so she unbuttoned her jeans, fumbling with the zipper, like she couldn't make her fingers move fast enough. She slid out of them quickly, tripping a little as she pulled them off her feet. Then she took off her shirt with one movement and finished the rest before getting into bed, sliding in between the sheets and moving over next to him so that her skin was touching his. 'Come here,' he said, and so she did. She would have done anything he told her to at that moment, would have listened to anything he said.

Chapter 17

Her mom had said not to tell anyone, but
Martha knew that she'd meant not to tell
people who knew them, like family friends and
neighbors and that kind of thing. It didn't hurt
anyone that Martha told Jaz. She had to. This was
the kind of thing you had to talk about, so that you
were able to process it.

'Can you believe it?' she'd asked. 'Can you
believe that in this day and age, someone could be
so careless?'

'It happens,' Jaz said. 'I believe it.'

'I mean, at colleges these days, people
are practically forcing condoms on kids. Well,
not at my school they didn't, but that's
different. It was a Catholic school. Still, you
can get them anywhere.' Martha had heard
Will say this exact thing the night before.

wondering aloud how on earth his son hadn't been able to find a simple condom.

'It happens every day,' Jaz said. Martha thought Jaz was probably trying to calm her down, but what she was really doing was making it seem like this wasn't a big deal. When it was. Her brother had gotten someone pregnant. There was going to be a baby. She was going to be an aunt. This was a very big deal.

Martha had been spending more and more time with Jaz in the kitchen. Mr. Cranston was sleeping a lot more and they'd all decided it was a good idea to have the nurses look in on him more often. Now they came in the afternoon as well as at night. Martha was sure that meant her job was gone, but Jaz assured her it wasn't.

'There's still no one here in the mornings. Plus, we need you for all the things that nurses don't do,' she said. She was trying to reassure Martha, but it just made her feel worse. She was a nurse. She should be doing more than buying books and retrieving the TV clicker.

When she asked what was wrong with Mr. Cranston, she always got the same answer: everything. It was the winter, the recovery from the surgery, just general exhaustion. Martha had imagined that she'd come in as the caretaker and nurse Mr. Cranston back to health, then leave when he was better. She never told anyone this, of course. They'd all told her from the beginning it wasn't going to go like that. It was just harder to see in person.

Jaz asked Martha what Cleo was going to do. She said it

very carefully, like she wanted to remove all judgment from her words.

'She's going to keep it,' Martha said. She tried not to sound like that was a stupid question, but really. If Cleo was going to have an abortion, would Martha even be talking about this? 'We're really happy about it,' she added. Just in case Jaz misunderstood.

Martha had a lot on her plate. In addition to her new job and the Max-and-Cleo family crisis, she was officially house hunting again. She'd called up the Realtor she'd been working with last year and told her she was ready to resume the search. When she'd told Cathy this, she hadn't gotten the response she was looking for.

'Martha, what are you waiting for? Just do it already,' Cathy said.

Martha was too surprised to talk at first. She was used to Cathy's blunt way of speaking; it was one of the things that she admired about her actually. But this sounded mean, impatient almost.

'I am,' she said. 'I'm going out with the Realtor tomorrow. I'm just waiting for the right place for me. Last year just wasn't the time to buy.'

Martha hadn't actually told anyone what had happened last year. The truth was that she'd been sort of fired by her Realtor. And even though she knew that's not how it worked, it still felt that way. She'd been working with Sarah for almost a year, meeting on Saturdays and driving around to different apartments. Sarah was a few years younger than Martha, and was funny in a predictable and not terribly clever way. She wore her hair in a high ponytail, and always talked in an upbeat manner when describing the places they were going to see, using Realtor short-speak that Martha liked – *washer and dryer in unit, en suite bathroom, outdoor area.*

She was peppy, which you had to be in realty. There were lots of awful places out there, and you had to be persistent to find the right one. Martha figured that Sarah identified with her, wanted to find her the perfect place in the right neighborhood. It had been fun to meet with her every weekend, sometimes stopping for lunch in the middle of their day, eating pizza and taking a break to go over what they'd seen so far. And then one day, when Sarah dropped her off, she turned off the engine and said, 'Martha, can I ask you something?'

'Sure,' Martha said. She thought maybe Sarah wanted her to rank the places they'd seen that day. But that was not what she wanted.

'Do you really think you're looking to buy an apartment?' Sarah asked.

'Of course I am,' Martha said. She sniffed.

'Okay, well, I'm happy to help you find a place. And I want you to find a place that you love. But at this point I'm getting worried that you're not going to be happy with anything we see.'

'I don't want to compromise,' Martha said. 'You're the one that said I could find my perfect home.'

'I did,' Sarah said. She put her hands on the steering wheel and breathed in and out like she was trying to figure out what to say. 'But at some point, there's going to be something you're not thrilled with. I'm not saying you have to settle for a place, but there's trade-offs. A place with a balcony might not have a washer and dryer and you just need to decide which one you want more. Does that make sense?'

'I need a washer and dryer.'

'Right, I know. That's why we put it on the top of your list.' Sarah tapped the pad of paper and bit her lip. 'Martha, I just need you to really think about this. We've spent seven of the last ten Saturdays together. And again, I'm happy to take the time if it's going to end in a sale. But I'm starting to think that this isn't going to. That you aren't going to find anything that you feel comfortable buying.'

Martha didn't know why people said that they were happy to do something and then followed it up by saying they weren't happy about it. It didn't make any sense.

'Look,' Sarah was saying, 'maybe we just need to take a break for a month or so. Take all the flyers for the places we've seen and look them over and think about what you want. Maybe you're just oversaturated with looking.'

Oversaturated? Martha was pretty sure that didn't make any sense at all. Sarah was kind of stupid sometimes. She used words wrong all the time, but Martha let it go because she felt bad for her. She just wasn't book smart, not at all. She'd told Martha where she went to college, but it was nowhere that Martha had ever heard of before. It was probably some online university, the kind that accepted anyone.

'Fine,' Martha said. She started gathering up her papers.

'Martha, please don't be angry.' Sarah put her hand on Martha's arm. 'I'm not trying to upset you. I just have to be practical here. I hope that you'll call me in a few weeks and want to look at more places and that we'll find one. I'll keep e-mailing you with anything I think you'll like, okay?'

'Okay,' Martha said.

When Martha got out of the car, she was embarrassed, although she couldn't say why exactly. She'd told Weezy that night that she was taking a break from looking. 'I just think I need to take a step back,' she'd said. Weezy tried to ask more about it, but Martha shut it down. 'I'm just not finding what I want.'

When she told Dr. Baer, she said that it was hard to commit to buying something. 'It's a big step. There's a lot to consider.'

'Maybe you should start smaller then,' Dr. Baer said. 'You could rent.'

Rent? Martha had to take a deep breath before she said something rude. Why would she throw her money away, month after month? Money she worked hard for and spent so long saving. It was a buyer's market. But maybe Dr. Baer didn't know a lot about real estate. It seemed a little ridiculous to have her try to give Martha financial advice, especially when it was so bad.

'I'll think about it,' she'd said.

But she hadn't. She hadn't thought about it at all. Once she stopped looking, it was easy to forget. And even if she did want to try again, the thought of calling Sarah was too humiliating. But now it had been a year, and she was ready to look again. She thought about finding a new Realtor, but that seemed silly. Sarah knew what she was looking for.

Sarah answered her phone, perky as ever, and for a second Martha considered hanging up. But then she thought better of it.

'Hi, it's Martha Coffey.'

'Martha! How are you? I'm so glad to hear from you.'

Martha smiled before she could help it. She told Sarah that she was ready to start looking again.

'I'm so glad to hear that,' she said.

'Things are really busy now,' Martha said. 'I have a new job, and I'm the maid of honor in my cousin's wedding. And there's just a lot of stuff going on with my family at the moment.'

Sarah didn't ask about specifics, and Martha figured she didn't want to pry. They made a date for the next weekend.

'I'm really looking forward to it,' Sarah said.

'Me too.'

Martha was beyond excited for Cathy's wedding. Every day, she called or e-mailed Cathy with an idea for the bridesmaid dresses or the ceremony. Cathy told her that she was thinking simple — an outdoor ceremony somewhere.

'Just because it's simple doesn't mean it can't be lovely,' Martha said. She didn't want her cousin to get married in a campground somewhere with Porta-Potties and hot dogs.

Martha talked about the wedding often at home. She figured the more that she talked about it, the better. She didn't want Claire to feel awkward about it, to feel strange discussing someone else's wedding when hers was canceled. Martha thought the more they discussed it, the easier it would be.

Cathy wanted to do it soon. 'We're thinking April,' she said.

'April? That's not enough time,' Martha said. She was already panicked.

'I think you're imagining the wedding a little differently than we are,' Cathy said. She said it gently, as though she knew she'd be letting Martha down if she admitted this.

'Different how?'

'We just want it a little more casual than your typical wedding. You know, just a fun party but nothing crazy.'

'Well, okay. Have you thought about what you want the bridesmaids to wear?'

'You can wear whatever you want.'

'You mean, like all wear a black dress or something?' Martha hated this new trend where brides let the bridesmaids pick their own black dresses. If it was your one day to tell people what to wear, wouldn't you take advantage of that?

'No, it doesn't even have to be black. Just wear a dress that makes you happy.'

'Makes me happy?' Ever since the engagement, Cathy had talked a lot about letting yourself be happy. Martha figured it was a good sign, but it was still a little annoying.

'Yeah. Just wear something you feel good in. It's just going to be you, Claire, and my friend Carol anyway. You'll all look great.'

'Um, okay. Hey, how about this? Why don't I look into getting the dresses from J.Crew? They have cute bridesmaid dresses, I promise. And I can probably still get my discount, because I'm really good friends with the manager there now. I'll just get Carol's measurements and we'll be all set.'

'I guess that would be okay,' Cathy said. 'Whatever you guys want.'

Martha was relieved. She could at least do this for her cousin, who was apparently under the impression that weddings were the same as potluck picnics.

'I'll pick out something really pretty,' she promised.

'Whatever you want,' Cathy said.

On Wednesday, Martha got home from the Cransons' and found a package waiting for her. 'Bets sent something for you,' Weezy said. 'I'm not sure what it is.'

Martha tore into the package. It wasn't even her birthday. What could Bets have sent? Maybe some sort of congratulations present for the new job? Inside was a little statue of a saint and a note. Martha read Bets's letter a few times, trying to understand.

'What is it?' Weezy asked.

'It's a statue of Saint Jude. She says to bury him in my closet and that it will help a husband find me. She said that a few of her friends have seen it work for their grandchildren.'

'Oh lord.' Weezy closed her eyes. 'Your grandmother is a real piece of work.'

'I thought Saint Jude was the cancer saint. No?' Claire asked.

'There's no such thing as a cancer saint,' Martha said. 'The note said he was the saint of lost causes.'

'Is she kidding?' Claire said. 'How rude is that?'

'She's probably just trying to be helpful,' Martha said. Bets was old, and Martha figured she no longer knew what was insulting and what wasn't.

'Honestly, girls. Your grandmother doesn't know what she's doing or saying half the time.'

'She probably thought it was a nice thing to send,' Claire said. She laughed a little bit.

'I think I'll put him in my closet anyway,' Martha said. 'It can't hurt, right?'

'Look at it this way,' Claire said. 'At least she thinks you're worth sending it to. She probably thinks I'm past the point of a lost cause.'

Martha took the statue upstairs and wrapped it in an old shirt that she never wore anymore, then stuffed the bundle in the back of her closet. It seemed a little sacrilegious, and she knew this wasn't how things were supposed to work, but why not? She was surprised that Bets thought such a thing was possible. How did such a religious woman end up thinking that her beliefs basically boiled down to voodoo?

*

Martha dragged Claire to J.crew to get fitted for the bridesmaid dress. 'I know what my size is,' she kept saying, but Martha insisted.

'It's better to get measured. I've seen it happen a million times that girls think they know their size and then the dress doesn't fit them properly. Plus, I want your opinion on what style we should get. We can all do the same or do it a little different. Cathy said it was up to me.'

'Okay, fine. Whatever.'

It was strange to walk back into J.Crew. It felt sort of like going back to visit your grade school after you'd been gone for a couple of years. Things looked the same, but also Martha was overwhelmed with the brightness of everything the sheer amount of stuff that was in the store. She felt dizzy at first.

'Did things move around?' she asked Wally.

'Nope. Same as it's always been, Squirrel.'

Wally took Claire back to put her in some of the dresses and to measure her. The two of them were fast friends, which irritated Martha just a little bit. She could hear them giggling behind the curtain.

'Everything okay in there?' she called. It was not only a waste of time, but also pretty unprofessional of Wally to be giggling away instead of helping customers.

'We're fine,' Claire said. She came out in a strapless light gray dress.

'Oh, I love it,' Martha said. 'That's the one I was thinking. Driftwood, right?'

'Yep,' Wally said. 'She looks amazing in it.'

Again, Martha felt just a little irritated because first of all, he didn't say that Martha would also look amazing in it, and that was just rude. He should know that if you were dealing with bridesmaids, you shouldn't single one of them out. That was Retail 101. And granted, she wasn't a regular customer, but still . . .

'Do you like it?' she asked Claire.

'Yeah, it's cute actually. It's fine.' She shrugged as if she couldn't care less.

'Just fine? Do you want to look at some of the others?'

'No, this one's good.'

'Claire, a little help here would be nice. A little more enthusiasm and effort, please.'

'It's fine. I'm going to wear this dress once, to a wedding at a yoga retreat that's probably going to be filled with lesbians, so it's fine.'

Martha was horrified and turned to Wally to apologize, but he was laughing. 'Probably not going to meet a man at this wedding, are you?' he asked, and the two of them laughed and laughed.

On the way home, Martha told Claire, 'You know, maybe you're having trouble with this wedding because of your situation, but I don't think it's fair to not put any effort forth as a bridesmaid for Cathy.'

'Excuse me?'

'I'm just saying, this is Cathy's day. We need to be there for her, no matter what our feelings are.'

'Are you serious right now?' Claire asked.

Martha hated that people (especially Claire) always asked her that. Did it seem like she was joking? 'Yes, I'm serious.'

'Martha, didn't I just go with you to pick out the bridesmaid dresses? And that wasn't even something that Cathy wanted — that was something that you wanted. Plus, the only reason I'm a bridesmaid is because you are and Cathy was just being polite.'

'That's not true,' Martha said. 'Don't think that.'

'Um, I don't care, so you don't have to use your voice like you feel bad for me, but of course that's true. And it's fine. Cathy and I have never been close. She used to basically torture me when I was little, remember?'

'She had a lot of issues,' Martha said.

'Yes, she did.'

'I'm just saying, maybe you should be a little more enthusiastic about the wedding.'

'And I'm just saying, if you don't shut up now, I'm going to jump out of the car.'

By that time they were just about home anyway, and they drove up the street in silence. Claire slammed her door shut and was inside the house before Martha even got out of the car. She sat for a moment, then pulled herself together and went up to Claire's room, where she knocked, but then opened the door right away.

'You know, Dr. Baer said that she once knew two adult sisters that moved back home and had so much trouble, that they went to couples counseling.'

'Jesus.'

'It's just something to consider.'

'We are not going to couples counseling.'

'You shouldn't judge therapy so much. You know, you might benefit from it.'

'Martha, seriously. If you don't get out of here, I'm going to push you out. I mean it.' Claire stood up from her bed, like she was going to come after Martha, like they were going to have a physical fight, which they hadn't done in about twenty years. Even then, it rarely happened, where they actually pulled each other's hair or pinched one another. But Claire was moving toward the door, and Martha turned and ran, hearing the door slam behind her.

Mr. Cranston slept more and more. At first Martha thought maybe he was just coming down with something, but he never really seemed to bounce back. Everything exhausted him. He never even read the papers anymore. He would start to, and then get tired or frustrated, and they remained folded up on the table until the next morning, when Martha would throw them in the recycling bin and replace them with the new ones.

Jaz seemed to be around more, like she was nervous to leave. Martha didn't mind, since it gave them a chance to talk. She told Jaz about the Saint Jude statue, which made her laugh, but then she said, 'It can't hurt, can it?'

'No,' Martha agreed. 'It can't.'

Most mornings, Jaz was there to fix breakfast for Mr. Cranston. Martha noticed that she started giving him bacon every once in a while. 'He needs a pick-me-up today,' she said, whenever she fried the bacon slices up in the pan.

All of a sudden, it felt like everyone was waiting. There was no more talk of new doctors, and even Ruby and Billy decided to get over their fight and began spending time at the house together.

'I decided to start looking for a place to buy,' Martha told Jaz one day.

'That's good,' Jaz said. 'You should keep moving forward for as long as you can, until you can't move forward anymore.'

Martha started to write that one down, but found it was too depressing. She ended up tearing the page out of her notebook and throwing it away.

She was happy to be spending her weekends with Sarah again. She'd been a little nervous, but they fell back into a routine pretty quickly. Sarah would come and pick her up, they'd stop at Starbucks and go over the listings for the day, and then they'd head out.

On the second time they were out, they looked at an old converted loft. It had two bedrooms, two bathrooms, an open kitchen, and a balcony.

'I know you said you didn't want a loft space,' Sarah said.

'But I think you should look at this one. It's all brand-new, which I think you'll like. Brand new appliances, a washer and dryer, the works. It's really beautiful.'

Martha was sure she wouldn't like it, especially when she saw there was still sawdust in the lobby. 'They're still working on most of the units,' Sarah explained.

It wasn't at all what Martha had pictured as her new home. It had high ceilings and exposed brick and pipes. But there was something about it.

'Do you think it will be loud?' Martha asked.

'There might be some echo,' Sarah said. 'That can happen in spaces like these. But I don't think it will be too bad.'

'Okay,' Martha said. She walked into the smaller bedroom.

'So what do you think?' Sarah asked. 'Should we say it's a maybe?'

'Yeah,' Martha said. 'Let's put it at the top of the list.'

In May, they threw Cleo a baby shower. Weezy kept saying, 'It's the right thing to do. This baby is coming, so let's get on board.' She pretty much just kept repeating this to herself as the days went on, but Martha figured whatever helped her was okay.

Martha and Claire put together the invitations, rolled-up pieces of paper in actual baby bottles that they mailed out. Martha had seen this on a crafts show once and she'd been dying to try it. Claire had sort of grumbled about the idea, but finally agreed, and the two of them went to Target to buy all the supplies, stocking the cart with baby bottles ribbon, and confetti shaped like little rattles.

'We should get some streamers,' Martha said.

'Really? Streamers?'

'You don't think so?'

'That seems more junior high dance than baby shower.'

'Yeah, I guess you're right.' They continued walking up and down the aisles. 'I still can't believe this is happening. I feel so bad for Mom and Dad.'

'Don't you feel bad for Max?'

'No. I mean, look what this is doing to Mom and Dad. He's the one that put himself in this position.'

'Martha, it was an accident. You think he meant to do this?'

'I'm just saying it was irresponsible. And he's always been that way. I'm just worried about Mom being able to handle this.'

'She's fine.'

'She's not fine. Haven't you noticed? And it's really affecting the whole family.'

'Have I noticed that she's being dramatic because that's how she is? Yeah, I've noticed.'

'You're being really insensitive.'

'I'm being insensitive? You're the one that doesn't even feel bad for our twenty-one-year-old brother who's about to be a dad and is scared out of his mind. Stop making this about anyone else. It's Max that has to deal with this, and he's the one you should be worried about.'

The two of them pushed the cart down the aisles, sighing and shaking their heads. 'Have you thought any more about coming to therapy with me?' Martha finally asked.

'Oh my God, Martha, I'm not going to couples therapy with you. Seriously, what is your problem?'

'It's not my problem. We're having trouble communicating.'

'No, we're not. You're just looking for something to be wrong. You're looking for a problem to have. It's like you like it when you have issues to deal with.'

'That's not true.'

'Well, it seems like it is. It seems like Max is taking a lot of the attention lately, and you want some disaster of your own to focus on, and so you want to go to couples therapy with your sister, which isn't just ridiculous – it's totally weird.'

'People have done it,' Martha said. She sniffed.

'I'm sure they have. But we're not going to. Look at us – we're communicating right now. So let's finish shopping for this baby shower and go home.'

'Fine,' Martha said. Later that afternoon, she sat on her bed and evaluated her behavior. This was something that Dr. Baer had suggested she do. She wasn't being insensitive to Max, like Claire suggested. That was absurd She just didn't think that everyone needed to be falling all over themselves feeling bad for Max and Cleo, when really, they were the ones who got themselves into this mess in the first place.

*

Mr. Cranston came down with a cold, that turned into bronchitis, that turned into pneumonia. When he coughed, his whole body shook, and sometimes it sounded like his chest was going to rip right out of him.

Ruby and Billy agreed that it was probably smart to have nurses there round the clock, at least for a little while. 'He's having so much trouble breathing,' Jaz told Martha. 'They just want to make sure that there's someone here to help.'

Martha wished that she could be the nurse that was there, but she couldn't. She hadn't done one thing – not one thing! – to start getting recertified. What had she been doing this whole time? She was ashamed of herself for wasting these months. Sure, there had been family drama that had taken her attention away, but still. That was no excuse. She promised herself that she would start looking into it.

The baby shower was a success, despite the arguments that had taken place. She and Claire strung a clothesline across the living room, and hung little onesies on it. Claire had wanted to make strawberry cupcakes, but Martha thought that made it look like the baby was going to be a girl.

'I think it's fine,' Claire said. 'It's a girlie cupcake, the kind you would have at a shower.' But Martha was really against it, and eventually Claire gave up and made chocolate chip cupcakes instead, which were delicious.

Martha was dying to meet Cleo's mom at the shower. Cleo

had described her once as 'driven,' and Martha wanted to know what that meant exactly. Elizabeth arrived a few minutes after the shower started, as though she were just another guest and not the mother of the mother-to-be. She wore a suit, and stood out among all the other women. Martha wasn't surprised to see that Elizabeth was a very attractive woman, although she noticed that her beauty was a little different from Cleo's, more focused and angular. Elizabeth had a firm handshake and she was direct and in command, which Martha admired. When Cleo opened the presents, Elizabeth stood in the very back of the room, like a Secret Service agent watching the crowd.

Cleo got so much gear that Martha couldn't even imagine where she was going to put it all. People had so much stuff for babies these days. There was a bouncy chair, a vibrating chair, and a swing. There were mats and mobiles and play sets. It was craziness.

But at the end of the day, when Cleo was done unwrapping her presents, sitting among the piles of her loot, she thanked Weezy, Martha, and Claire for the shower, and even started to cry a little bit. Martha felt satisfied, like she'd done a good deed. She wanted to point out to Claire that an insensitive person wouldn't have felt that way, but she kept it to herself.

Chapter 18

Winter finally started to melt, and after a quick and wet spring, it became hot. The weather people kept calling it 'a burst of summer,' like it was something fun, when really it was just miserable. No one was ready for the weather. People still walked outside with jackets, confused. They hit eighty degrees at the end of March and it just kept going up from there. And Cleo, who was already hot all the time anyway, became more annoyed with each day.

'Tell me there isn't global warming,' she said to Max one morning. He was eating cereal at the little table they had in the kitchen, and he just raised his eyebrows.

'I mean, are people kidding when they try to pretend it's not happening? Eighty-seven degrees in April? What the hell is going on here? It's like those people that try to say the Holocaust didn't happen.'

'I know,' Max said. He ignored her comment about Holocaust deniers. 'The air conditioner isn't doing much, is it?'

'It sounds like it's dying,' Cleo said. They had only one air conditioner in the apartment and they kept it in the bedroom. It was an old one that Max had taken from the Coffeys' attic, and it growled and whined as it tried to spit out cold air. If you stood directly in front of it, you could sort of feel a breeze.

'Even I'm going to the library today,' Max said. 'It's too hot to stay here.'

'Actually, I think I'm going to stay here today.'

'Really?'

'Yeah, I just need to work without distraction.'

'Okay,' Max said. 'But I'll save you a seat just in case you change your mind.'

The weather was a problem for lots of reasons, the main one being that all the kids on campus stripped down like it was spring break, and Cleo, who was not ready to show her stomach to all, still wore sweaters, as if the extra layering could hide what was happening underneath. She ended up sitting in her classes, sweating and uncomfortable, trying to cool down by pulling the fabric away from her skin and fanning papers at her face. When she was alone in the apartment, she usually wore nothing more than a tank top and boxers, and she'd sit on the couch with her feet on the coffee table in front of her, hands stretched across her stomach. She sat like that for hours, not moving, just holding her stomach like that was going to stop it from getting bigger.

They opened the windows wide, in an attempt to cool the apartment down. All it did was invite every fly to come in through the screenless openings. Once they were inside, they buzzed around, too dumb to figure out how to get back out. Cleo watched them frantically fly around, hitting the blinds and the walls. Sometimes she tried to sweep them out with papers, but it didn't help much. Always, right before they died they got especially crazy and aggressive, looping around and dive-bombing Cleo and buzzing out of control as if that last burst of energy could save them. A few hours after that happened, Cleo usually found a little black corpse on the ground, and she'd scoop it up and throw it out the window. One morning, she woke up to find a bunch of dead flies on the table. 'A massacre,' she whispered, and then cleaned them up.

After Monica heard that she was pregnant, she came by the apartment. 'You could have told me,' she said.

'I couldn't,' Cleo said. 'I couldn't even say it out loud.'

She finally had what she wanted: Monica was here with her to talk to her about being pregnant. She could have cried or screamed or told her that she was so scared all the time, that she felt like they were making every single decision wrong. They weren't living in a movie. Things weren't going to work themselves out offscreen and result in a cute baby. There was going to be blood and fighting and a lot of crying. She knew that much. But she couldn't say any of that to Monica. What she'd really wanted was her old friend before they'd fallen apart. Now she had someone who looked familiar but felt sort of strange. It was almost better when she was gone altogether.

'It's pretty messed up,' is all she said.

Monica started to come by the apartment more often. Sometimes she brought an orange or a bag of licorice or a gossip magazine, like little offerings. Most days they ended up sitting side by side on the couch, watching bad reality TV.

'You know,' Monica said one day, looking at Cleo's stomach, 'you'll get used to people staring. Or not used to it, but it won't bother you as much after a while. Like when you get a haircut and it feels so different, you feel the missing ends, and then one day you wake up and it's just your hair again. It's like that.'

'It doesn't feel like that,' she said. She knew that Monica was trying to help, but what she wanted to say was that being pregnant was way worse than being anorexic. She wouldn't say that, of course, because it sounded horrendous. But still, she thought it.

And it was true. There were things that college professors were used to. They were used to kids getting drunk, or getting overwhelmed, or failing a test and then crying. They were used to girls like Monica getting pulled out of school and returning a semester later. But they weren't used to seeing pregnant seniors wander around the campus. They could barely look at Cleo. When it finally became clear to her economics professor that she was pregnant, he started avoiding her eyes when he taught. The staring was bad, but it was worse when people pointedly didn't look at her, when they just avoided her altogether, fixing their eyes on the air around her.

Cleo was ready for the school year to end, ready to be away from everyone her age that was celebrating and talking about where they were going to move. They talked about Manhattan and Boston and Chicago and San Francisco. Sometimes they changed their minds just because they felt like it. They were going to live on the East Coast and then decided to try the West Coast. Why not? They had choices. They could do whatever they felt like. She was moving into the basement of her boyfriend's parents' house in a suburb of Philadelphia. Was a sadder sentence ever said?

She and Max had both agreed to move to the Coffeys'. She didn't want to, but what other option was there? Where else were they supposed to go? Even if Elizabeth had wanted them, her apartment was way too small, and it was still too hard for her to really talk about the baby without causing a fight of some kind. The last time they'd spoken on the phone, she'd said, 'You have to understand, I just feel like I failed as a mother, Cleo. To have you pregnant in college is a nightmare and I can't help but think it was my lack of parenting.' Cleo wasn't sure if this was supposed to make her feel better, but it certainly didn't. Then Elizabeth said, 'I should have never let you go to that school,' like that was the cause of all this.

She and Max also decided to get married, although that still seemed not quite real. Max had brought up marriage the day after he'd woken her up with McDonald's on her pillow. The fight was over, but they were still talking carefully to each other, stepping out of the way when the other walked by, saying *sorry* and *please* more often than normal.

They were both in bed, but not sleeping. Max was on his computer and Cleo had her eyes closed, a book resting on her stomach. Max cleared his throat once and then again and again, until Cleo opened her eyes.

'I was thinking,' he said, 'that we should probably get married.'

'Married?'

'Yeah. I mean, we're going to be together anyway, and with the baby, I just feel like it's right.'

'I just . . . I don't know. It's a lot.'

'But don't you want to marry me? I want to marry you,' Max said. He shut his laptop and turned to face her. 'Will you marry me?'

She said yes, although she felt unsure. It seemed mean to say no. It was a horrible story, really. That was her engagement, Max saying, 'We're going to be together anyway,' and her saying yes, because that seemed the polite thing to do.

Later in the week, Max came home and threw his bag on the floor. 'I got something for you,' he said. He pulled a small box out of his backpack and opened it for her. In it was a ring with a large round diamond on it. Cleo looked up at him and tilted her head.

'It's fake,' he said. 'Sorry, I should have said that right away.' He took it out of the box and held it out to her. 'I just thought you should have something now, until I can get you something real.'

'Oh,' Cleo said. 'Thanks.'

'Should I kneel?' Max didn't wait for her to answer, before getting down on one knee. It felt like they were playacting and Cleo wanted it to be over soon. She took the ring and put it on her finger.

Cleo felt funny wearing the ring, like she was pretending to be some-thing she wasn't. She turned the ring around often, so that the fake diamond faced the other way. She was embarrassed whenever one of her professors noticed it.

When Cleo told her mom that they were getting married, Elizabeth was silent.

'What?' Cleo asked.

'Oh, Cleo,' her mother said. 'What do you think is going to happen? That you'll get married and live together, all happy playing house? Come on, Cleo. You're smarter than this.'

Cleo wanted to tell her mom that clearly she wasn't smarter than this. If she *was* smarter, wouldn't she be in a different situation? It reminded her of the time she got a B in calculus senior year, and Elizabeth had been angry, had shaken her head. 'No B's,' she'd said. 'You're smart enough to get an A.'

That never made sense to Cleo. If she was smart enough to get an A, wouldn't she have gotten one in the first place? She often wondered if she was even smart at all, or if Elizabeth just expected her to be, so she had to live up to it. Of course, the next semester she had brought home an A in calculus. Elizabeth had just nodded. 'I told you,' she said.

She wore the ring for Max, since it seemed to make him happy. After a while, her fingers got bloated and she had to take it off. She was scared it was going to get stuck on there, that her fat little sausage finger would lose circulation and have to be amputated.

A little while later, Max came home with an identical ring – except this one was bigger. She wore it until that, too, got too tight, and she placed it on her dresser. She was ringless until Max replaced it again. Sometimes she took all three rings and lined them up next to each other. She never asked Max where he got them. They were probably from Walmart but she didn't want to know.

When senior week came, Cleo was relieved. At least when it was over, people would stop talking about it all the time. Max kept insisting that he should skip it. 'I don't even want to go to Hilton Head,' he said. 'I hate it there.' Because he was nice enough to lie, she told him he had to go. It didn't go unnoticed that he was acting in a way that very few college boys would. She saw the way his friends looked at her, like she'd ruined his life, like he didn't have as much to do with this situation as she did. And so, because of this, she kept saying, 'You have to go.'

Max finally agreed, but tried to get her to come with. Cleo

was firm on this. There was no way in hell she was going to Senior Week with a huge pregnant stomach to be the only sober person in a sea of Bucknell students. She'd rather be trapped in a cave with Mary and Laura for seven days straight than go through that.

'Then I'm not going the whole time,' Max said. 'Just for a few days.'

Cleo figured that was better than nothing.

With Max gone, the apartment was so quiet. Even when she walked outside, the town felt empty, since all the seniors were gone. Before he left, Max went to the grocery store and bought Cleo enough food that she would have survived a war. She stood in the doorway of the kitchen and watched him unload frozen pizzas, boxes of cereal, macaroni and cheese, and soup. It made her start to cry, watching him pile up all this junk food for her, and she had to turn and go into the bathroom so she wouldn't bawl in front of him. These hormones really were a bitch.

Secretly, Cleo had been sort of looking forward to her time alone in the apartment. She realized that it would be the last time ever that she'd really be all by herself. After graduation, they'd be at the Coffeys' and then there'd be a baby. And while that was hard to imagine, hard to think that it was really going to happen, she knew enough to be grateful for this time.

She watched marathons of old TV shows, and stayed up well into the night, then slept past noon and ate huge bowls of cereal. She read stupid books and ate ramen. And after two days, she felt like she was going out of her mind. She'd started to have nightmares about the baby, where she forgot it someplace and left it behind. In one, she was buying shoes and Weezy came up to her and screamed at her for leaving her baby in her purse. Cleo was confused as to how the baby had gotten there in the first place, and tried to say so, but couldn't get the words right. She woke up sweating.

She had wanted time alone, but now she wanted Max. She felt desperate for him. She wanted someone else to be there when she woke up to tell her that the baby wasn't even there yet and to assure her that she didn't (and wouldn't) leave it in a purse. She couldn't help but imagine Max at the beach, drinking and talking to girls. Every night, she thought, *Please, God, don't let him make out with anyone. Please, God, don't let him decide to leave me.*

When Max came home, Cleo almost knocked him over. She sat with her legs on his lap while he told her about the week and who got really drunk, who hooked up, who threw up all over the floor. Cleo laughed at these stories, so happy to have him home. They talked into the night, and Cleo kept her leg linked around his in bed. She wanted to make sure that he was really there. What had she been thinking, taking him for granted? Was she out of her mind? This might not be what she had imagined, and this certainly wasn't perfect, and maybe she was wearing a ten-dollar ring from Walmart, but Max was still the best thing she had in her whole life at the moment, and she couldn't forget that.

*

Graduation was long and hot, but the upside was that in her robe, Cleo looked like she was just chunky and not necessarily pregnant. The downside was that both of their families were there, and they were all together for the first time ever.

Weezy and Elizabeth had been in touch and even met up for lunch a few months back. It was a strange thing to imagine, these two women getting together. Cleo waited for her mom to call and ridicule Weezy, to make fun of her coddling ways, how she talked about her children like they were all still toddlers. But she never did. She actually seemed to enjoy her. It was amazing how much an accidental pregnancy could bind you together against your children.

Weezy made the two of them pose in front of trees and buildings, with their caps on, then with their caps off, holding their diplomas, and just standing. She tried to make the two of them throw their caps in the air, which was when Max put his foot down. Then she made Cleo pose with Elizabeth, and then they took pictures of the whole Coffey family. 'I'll get you copies,' Weezy told Elizabeth. Elizabeth just nodded. Cleo was pretty sure she didn't even have a camera with her.

After the ceremony, Cleo and Elizabeth ran into Monica and her family. Cleo and Monica hugged, and then Monica's mom and dad each hugged her. Elizabeth looked at Monica with a fond but distant smile, like she was sure she'd seen her somewhere before, but couldn't say where. When they went to say good-bye, Monica's mom hugged Cleo again, and whispered in her ear, 'We're all thinking of you,' which made Cleo feel strange, and weirdly like Monica had told on her. She pulled away and said the only thing she could think of, which was, 'Thanks.'

They all went out to an Italian dinner at a restaurant where Weezy had made reservations months earlier. Every restaurant was booked, of course, and unless you remembered way ahead of time, you were out of luck. Cleo wondered what they would have done if they weren't with the Coffeys. Elizabeth probably would have just driven back to New York.

They all said good-bye outside the restaurant. Cleo and Max had to go pack up their apartment, and everyone else was driving back that night. It felt weird packing up the apartment with Max. 'I don't feel like we graduated,' she said. 'I don't feel like anything's over.'

Weezy made them unpack their bags on the driveway. 'Who knows what you're bringing back from that place?' she kept saying. Cleo wasn't sure if she thought they had bedbugs or that mice were hiding in their clothes, but she was offended. She managed to convince Weezy to let them bring the stuffed chair from their apartment down to the basement, after Weezy inspected it and sprayed it with some sort of foam that she then vacuumed off of it.

Cleo wondered what the neighbors must have thought, looking out to see Weezy in cropped workout pants and an old hockey T-shirt of Max's, sweating as she pulled the vacuum around, the orange extension cord trailing out of the house, while Cleo just stood there and watched, her hands resting on her stomach, which was as big as a beach ball.

After they moved everything in, Max sat on the edge of the bed and Cleo stood by the dresser. They were exhausted and sweaty. The room felt tiny, like it could barely hold the two of them.

'Well, here we are,' Max said.

'Here we are,' Cleo said.

Max started looking for a job the very next day, which was annoying. There was no point in her even applying anywhere, since no one was going to hire a girl that was almost eight months pregnant. Cleo looked at his résumé and wanted to tell him that she should be the one getting a job, that she'd be able to get a better one than he could. It was always understood between them that she was the smarter one, and now she wanted it acknowledged. She had to bite her lip to keep from saying something out loud. Instead, she sat and watched Max send out his résumé, feeling like a big blob of nothing.

Then Max got a job doing ad sales for a small business magazine, and Cleo spent her days sleeping late, wandering around the house, reading, sleeping, and waiting for Max to come home. Then when he did, she listened to him talk about his job. She wanted to hear everything about his coworkers. Who brought tuna for lunch every day and who napped in their cubicle? She herself had nothing to share, except for the day that she took Ruby for a walk and the poor thing got diarrhea. Max was so tired every night. 'I can't believe this is what a job feels like,' he said. Most nights, he fell asleep while they were still watching TV in bed.

The days got even more boring. Weezy tried to help, which some days Cleo appreciated and some days it made her want to scrape her teeth with her fingernails. 'Shall we go look at some strollers?' Weezy would say. Or, 'Why don't we go get you some new tops?' That last comment made Cleo cry a little, since she was sure that Weezy was telling her that her shirts were too tight.

One day, even Weezy seemed at a loss, and the two of them sat upstairs on the couch, reading. Weezy had given Cleo an old copy of *The Thorn Birds* that she'd found on a bookshelf in the basement. The book was wrinkled, like it had gotten wet and the pages had dried all wavy, but Weezy promised she'd enjoy it. 'It's so dramatic, full of love affairs with a priest, and – oh, I don't want to ruin it. You'll love it, I promise.'

And so, even if love affairs with a priest didn't really sound like a huge selling point for Cleo, she was reading the book, which actually seemed a little bit trashy to be on Weezy's bookshelf but did hold her attention, which wasn't easy these days.

'You know what we should do?' Weezy asked her. 'We should go get some yarn and start knitting blankets for the baby.'

'I don't know how to knit,' Cleo told her.

'You don't know how to knit?' Weezy sounded appalled, as though Cleo had just told her she didn't know how to tie her shoes. Really, what did Weezy think, that girls still took Home Ec classes? In what world was it that strange not to know how to knit? Cleo thought all of this, but just shook her head in response to Weezy's question.

'Well, then, I can teach you. It will be wonderful.'

Cleo was so bored that she agreed. She even hoped it really would be wonderful. Here she was, getting excited over yarn and books with philandering priests. She didn't even recognize herself.

She and Weezy went to the yarn store, to stock up on needles for Cleo and get some easy patterns and fun yarn. The place was called At Knit's End and was tucked in an old house off of a busy road. A few of the women greeted Weezy when she walked in.

'Hello,' Weezy said. 'Ladies, we have a first-timer! This is my daughter-in-law, Cleo.' The women didn't seem all that excited, and Cleo stood frozen, shocked to hear herself be called Weezy's daughter-in-law. She wasn't yet, but she didn't correct her. She guessed that's what she would be soon.

'Since we don't know what the baby will be,' Weezy was saying, 'we'll have to get some neutral colors. Yellows, greens, and I guess even light blue would work. We'll get you some yarn to practice on. And let's see . . .' She thumbed through a stack of books. 'Here. This looks like an easy pattern. Just knitting with increasing and a yarn over. Or you could do this one, it's a basket weave. Just knitting and purling. What do you think?'

Cleo hadn't understood one word that Weezy had just said, but she pointed to the simpler pattern, and Weezy nodded. She chose a light yellow yarn, which was super-soft and pretty. Weezy had found a complicated pattern, with sheep dancing across it, and she was picking up ball after ball of yarn and throwing it into the basket.

When the ladies rang them up, Cleo was surprised by the total. How did yarn cost this much? Cleo tried to offer to pay, but Weezy patted her hand away. 'This was my idea and it's my treat. It will be fun for me to get knitting again, and now I have a good excuse.'

The cashier, who was a large sour-looking woman, put their purchases into a bag and handed it to them without smiling.

' 'Bye, ladies,' Weezy called. Some of them grunted in response. When they got out to the parking lot, Weezy lowered her voice. 'Knitters are not friendly. I don't know what it is, you'd think they would be, but I've learned over the years that most of them act like they have a needle up their behind.' Cleo laughed and then Weezy laughed a little bit too.

It turned out that Cleo loved knitting. Well, that wasn't exactly true. She loved the feeling of concentrating, the magic of turning the yarn over the needles and coming out with a perfect little stitch. When Weezy taught her to do a yarn over for the first time, she gasped. 'Oh, look at that!' and Weezy looked pleased. It was magical, sort of.

She could knit for hours, sit with the TV on or music in the background and let her fingers go. She didn't enjoy the actual process; it sort of made her fingers ache, and sometimes it was so boring that she felt like her skin was going to split. But she liked the goal, and she loved checking off the boxes as she was done with each row, marking her stitches with the little stitch counters. She was determined.

At night, she'd sit up in bed and knit. Max thought she was becoming obsessed. 'Maybe I'm nesting,' she told him.

'Maybe that's it,' he said. He pulled her down for a kiss and then put his face on her stomach and kissed that. 'Good night, baby.'

She and Weezy took to knitting every night after dinner. They had different programs that they liked to watch, and Weezy could always help her if she knotted a stitch or did something wrong. She sometimes hoped that Claire or Martha would join them, but they seemed to have their own thing going on. Will always went up to his office to work, and Max was so tired with his new schedule that he went to bed early.

Weezy's blanket was really complicated. Sometimes she would explain it to Cleo, the stitches she was doing, and Cleo would watch, fascinated. It took Weezy more than an hour to do a row, and almost every row required something different. When she was done, she would knit the sheep over the blanket. 'It's not as hard as it seems,' she said. But Cleo could tell she was pleased at the attention.

Cleo finished her first blanket, and as Weezy taught her how to do the final stitch and tie it off, they both cheered. Cleo felt exhilarated. She couldn't believe that she'd made this thing. 'I love it,' she said over and over. She put it next to her and rubbed it on her face.

'We'll wash it in Dreft and it will be all clean and ready for the baby. It's really beautiful. You are a natural.'

They got Cleo more yarn and she started on the basket-weave blanket. This one she did in a light blue that was almost aqua. It was really more of a girl color, but you could use it for both. Plus, Cleo felt like she was having a girl, but she hadn't told anyone in case she was wrong. She didn't want to sound like an idiot.

'A baby can never have too many blankets,' Weezy said. 'And you can always give them as gifts. It's such a wonderful thing to receive.'

Sometimes Weezy had a glass of wine while she knitted, although one night, after she'd had a few, she ended up messing up the blanket so much that she had to take out two entire rows. 'This is why you don't drink and knit,' she told Cleo. They laughed, and Cleo wished that she could knit and drink, but it wasn't an option.

It was funny, those nights, how peaceful it was to sit together, the TV chattering in the background showing some silly sitcom or fashion reality show. She and Weezy could talk about the people on the TV, who their favorites were, or they could talk about their knitting. But most of the time they were silent, both pairs of hands working away, fingers moving in rhythm, and Cleo felt a certain sense of happiness, to be making something for the baby, to be sitting quietly with Weezy and creating something for this little person.

Ruby liked to sit on the couch next to Cleo while she knitted, sometimes resting her body on the completed part of the blanket, like she was testing it out. At first Cleo hadn't really liked Ruby all that much. The dog had goopy eyes and some strange-feeling lumps on her back. But after seeing how much Max adored her, and after being at the house long enough to get used to her, and the sort of foul smell that she carried with her, Cleo grew fond of her.

Ruby seemed to know that Cleo was pregnant, and she would come sit next to her and rest her head on Cleo's stomach, as if she were talking to the baby or protecting her somehow. 'Are you talking to the baby?' Cleo would sometimes whisper, and Ruby would press her snout into her stomach, as if to say yes.

Max was always worried about Ruby. 'She's walking weird,' he'd say. 'She's limping, on her right side.'

'She's just getting older,' Weezy would tell him. But she didn't sound so sure herself.

Ruby moved slowly around the house, and sometimes when they got ready to take her out, by the time she walked to the back door, she seemed to have forgotten where she was going.

Some days, if Cleo didn't think too much about anything, she was okay. But she was never much good at putting things out of her mind, and so most days she spent worrying. She thought about getting married to Max, and how silly it probably was. Then she thought about how, if they didn't get married, Weezy would probably sneak down to the basement one night with a judge and marry them in their sleep. She did not want her grandchild to be born to unmarried parents. She'd made that much clear.

Cleo loved statistics. But she knew that what they would tell her now was that she and Max wouldn't make it. Not for the long term anyway. Who knew what would happen ten years from now? She'd be only thirty-two. Not old at all. She tried not to dwell on these thoughts, but she couldn't help it. Look at what happened with Monica. She couldn't even keep a best friend. What hope did she have that she and Max would stay together?

There were nights that she lay in bed and stared at the back of Max's head, just thinking, *Well, this won't last long.* Or worse, sometimes when she woke up in the middle of the night, she'd stare at the lump of him in the bed and think, *Who is that?*

Sometimes if she couldn't stop thinking about their doomed fate, she'd remind herself that the odds of her getting pregnant while on the pill were small too. Almost impossible, really. If she was feeling good, she'd think that these slim statistics would revisit them again, that she and Max were some sort of magnet for the improbable, and that they'd have a long and happy life together. If she was feeling bad, she'd think that they'd used up all of their impossible odds, and that she and Max were bound to split up soon.

Chapter 19

Claire had broken even. Which was a miracle of sorts, really. She had barely any money in the bank, but her credit cards were paid off. And she felt rich. Now, when she signed on to her bank accounts, she felt like she could breathe, like her chest was open again. It hadn't even taken as long as she'd thought it would. Apparently having someone else give you a place to live and pay your bills was a great way to get rid of credit card debt. Moving home had been the right thing to do.

It was good to remind herself of that, to remember that living at home had saved her. Because at the moment, the house was so crowded it felt like hell.

How had they all lived there at the same time? Sure, there wasn't a pregnant Cleo living with them when they were growing up, but still. Claire didn't remember it being like this. It seemed like every time she went down the stairs, she ran into someone. She'd go to the kitchen to get a glass of water and find that there were no clean glasses. Bowls of cereal were left out, balled-up napkins were all over the counter, and there were always crumbs – on the floor, on the counter, in the sink. Everywhere. It made Lainie's house seem tidy and calm.

The bathrooms were a whole other story. The Coffey house was old, and some of the plumbing issues had never quite been resolved. If the dishwasher or washing machine was running while someone took a shower, there were bound to be shocks of cold water that spurted out. And if someone flushed a toilet while someone else was in the shower, the water turned scalding for about five to seven seconds. They'd all lived with this before, coming out of the bathroom looking to accuse whoever was rude enough to flush the toilet while they were in there, but they hadn't had to deal with it in a while, and now it just seemed absurd and impossible.

'I'm sorry,' Claire heard Weezy saying to Will one morning, 'but there is too much laundry to do, and if I wait until everyone is showered, it will never get done. Maybe if the people in this house learned how to use a washing machine instead of throwing their laundry down the chute for me to handle, we wouldn't have this problem.' Will grumbled something and walked away.

Trying to explain the water rules to Cleo proved harder than they thought. Over dinner one night – after Cleo had started the dishwasher while Weezy was in the shower and was faced with a screaming Weezy running down the stairs a few minutes later – Max tried to explain the situation.

'So if I flush the toilet, it will make the shower cold?' Cleo asked.

'No, it makes a spray of hot water come out,' Max said. 'So you can do it, but you have to warn the person.'

'So what you're saying is that you want me to knock on the bathroom door and tell whoever is in the shower that I have to use the bathroom somewhere else in the house?'

'Exactly,' Max said. He sat back and looked pleased.

'Maybe I just won't use anything if anyone's in the shower. Does that work?'

'You could do that too,' Claire said. She smiled at her and reached across the table to pat Cleo on the arm. She couldn't believe that her brother was asking his girlfriend to interrupt showers at his family's house. How stupid could boys be?

At the end of March, Amanda decided not to come back to Proof Perfect. Claire wasn't surprised one bit. As soon as Amanda had taken the extra three months, Claire could have guessed that she'd never be back. Who could blame her? The thought of returning from maternity leave to face crazy Leslie and all of the strange people here was pretty horrible. Leslie called Claire into her office to tell her the situation.

'What's unfortunate is that we've paid for her health care for the past three months. We believed her when she said she was coming back,' Leslie said.

'I'm sure a lot of people change their minds once they're home with the baby,' Claire said. But Leslie shook her head.

'The good news is that we've discussed it and we've decided to offer you the job full time.'

'Oh, Leslie, that's so nice, but I can't take it.'

Leslie wrinkled her eyebrows and tilted her head, like she couldn't possibly understand what Claire was saying.

'It's just . . . I don't plan to stay here long term.'

'Well, we all know that the best-laid plans always blow up in your face.'

Was that a saying? Claire really didn't think so.

'I think I'm pretty set on moving back to New York,' Claire said. 'But thank you for the offer and for the opportunity.'

'Why don't you sit with it for a while? We're not in any rush to find someone new. You can keep the job as a temporary situation and think about it for a month or two.'

Claire agreed, but her heart was pounding when she left her office. She felt like there was a chance she'd just end up trapped there. She tried to talk herself down, tell herself that it was a ridiculous thing to think. But she still felt a slight panic and she knew that sooner rather than later, she'd have to get out of there. June, she decided, was her limit.

Lainie and Cleo had taken to going for long walks together after dinner. 'You should come,' Lainie said, but Claire declined. She watched from her window as the two pregnant ladies walked down the sidewalk, their heads turned toward each other, Cleo laughing at something that Lainie said, while she gestured and shook her head. Lainie had invited Cleo over for lunch one day, and ever since then the two of them had been spending a lot of time together.

'She just needs someone to talk to,' Lainie said. 'She's scared out of her mind, and there's no one she can really ask about this stuff.'

'That's nice of you,' Claire said. She didn't really mean it.

The first time Cleo and Lainie had met, a couple of years ago now, they seemed to like each other immediately. They'd smiled at each other right away, and spent the night talking, bonding over (Claire could only assume) both being really, really pretty. And now, here they were, waddling off into the sunset together, talking about pregnancy and hormones and placentas. It reminded Claire of seeing Lainie talk to Margie Schuller in the bathroom that day, knowing that she was on the other side of something and that there was nothing she could do to join them. It felt a little lonely.

Her friend Katherine was calling her more often, asking her when she was coming back to New York. 'I don't think you should stay there any longer,' she said. 'You really need to come back.'

When Claire thought about going back to New York, she felt calm. Was it wrong that part of it was because she knew that there were so many other women there her age who had jobs and were unattached and weren't even close to having babies?

Was it such a bad thing to want to be surrounded by your own kind? People had been doing it for years, really. Look at the ethnic neighborhoods that popped up all over. There were Little Italys and Chinatowns in every city. And weren't there even midget colonies somewhere? She'd heard that once and it made so much sense to her, to want to be somewhere where everyone and everything was your size, where things were within your reach and you weren't struggling all the time to fit in a world that wasn't built for you.

That was all she wanted. To be back somewhere where no one looked at her strangely, where she fit in. And she knew that place was New York. Sometimes the thought of going back there overwhelmed her – she'd have to find a job, look for an apartment, and be shocked and disgusted at how much she was going to pay for a tiny place. But she could figure it out. She knew where she was supposed to be.

On the day that was supposed to be her wedding day, no one said anything to her. She wouldn't have forgotten anyway, but all of the places that she and Doug had registered sent her congratulatory e-mails. She had never bothered to take the registries down, or take her e-mail address off the list.

She wondered if Doug had gotten the same e-mails. It was so strange to think that Doug knew nothing about what was happening in her life, and she knew nothing about his. She'd e-mailed him when she left New York, because it had seemed like the right thing to do, to let your former fiancé know that you were going to be living in a different city. He'd written back and wished her luck, but they hadn't been in contact since.

She wondered what he'd think if he knew that she was living at home still, what he'd say about Max and Cleo having a baby, and about Martha's trying to get her to go to therapy. She couldn't imagine what he'd say if he knew that she was acting like a whole different person, smoking cigarettes pretty often, hanging out with Fran, sometimes smoking pot on weeknights just for fun. She would bet he wouldn't believe it.

When they'd split up their stuff in the apartment, they had both wanted the expensive ceramic Dutch oven that they'd gotten as an engagement gift. It was bright orange and cheerful, and Claire loved it. When they registered, Doug had wanted a blue one, but she fought for the orange. She pointed out that he would eventually be with someone else, and that girl wasn't going to want something that his ex-fiancée had chosen. He'd looked hurt when she said it, but nodded and let her have it. And she wondered now if he was with someone else, if he also was acting totally different than he had with her. Maybe he was engaged again. He could be married already with a baby on the way. (Okay, sure, it wasn't likely, but Max and Cleo were proof that things sometimes happened much faster than intended.) She thought about e-mailing him, just to see. But in the end she left it alone. He wasn't hers to know anymore.

*

At the end of May, they'd all trekked out to a yoga retreat in Ohio for Cathy and Ruth's wedding. The place was called Bear Den Cottages and they spent the weekend sleeping in cabins, doing Downward Facing Dog, and drinking green tea. She'd told Fran that it was family only, which wasn't true, but she didn't want to invite him and anyway, she didn't think he'd even want to go.

Claire had been dreading this weekend, but surprisingly it wasn't awful. Even pregnant Cleo seemed to enjoy her sun salutations. And while they all agreed that a lot of it was 'hippie nonsense,' as Maureen whispered to them, it was all in all a pretty pleasant trip. And when Claire stood up front with Martha and Cathy, wearing her Driftwood bridesmaid dress that Martha had freaked out over, all she thought was that Cathy and Ruth seemed really happy. And when she realized that this made her feel happy, she was relieved, because she figured that meant she wasn't a horrible, jealous person after all. And that made her even happier.

Her thirtieth birthday was at the beginning of June, and she really meant it when she said she wanted to ignore it. But that wasn't an option. Lainie insisted on throwing her a party. 'We'll have a barbecue,' she said. 'It will be fun.'

'I really don't feel like having a party,' Claire said.

'Don't tell me you're freaking out about turning thirty. Come on. It's not that big of a deal.'

'Fine,' Claire agreed. It seemed easier than trying to fight it. 'Fine.'

For three days out of the year, Claire and Martha were the same age. When she was younger, Claire loved this. She used to torture Martha with it, telling her that she was just as old as she was. Now it didn't seem that fun.

Martha was concerned that turning thirty would send Claire into a tailspin, and she talked to her often about it. 'It seems worse than it is,' she said. 'The idea of thirty can be scary but once it happens, you're totally fine.'

'I'm fine,' Claire repeated over and over again.

Martha thought Claire's birthday was even more reason to go to therapy with her. Sometimes Claire thought she should just agree to go to shut her up about it.

'You're probably stressed about things you don't even know that you're stressed about. That's the best part of therapy,' Martha said.

'Martha, I'm going to tell you for the last time. I am not going to therapy with you.' Claire couldn't help but yell it. That was another reason she had to get out of this house. Each day made her act more and more like a teenager.

'You are being really closed-minded,' Martha said. She yelled a little too.

'Good,' Claire said. She didn't care if she wasn't making sense. The two of them left the room and slammed their respective doors. Anytime Weezy looked at them, she just shook her head.

*

Lainie tied balloons to the chairs in the backyard and hung an old silver banner that read happy birthday. Claire hugged her when she arrived. 'This is a big birthday,' Lainie told her. 'You should enjoy it.'

Lainie's boys were all dressed alike, in khaki shorts and light blue polo shirts. When she got there, Jack ran right up to her. 'Remember when I was five and you babysat me?' he said. She nodded and he smiled. 'That was fun.' He had made her a birthday card and helped her blow out her candles. He seemed to have changed his mind about her. Apparently, they were now the best of friends.

Lainie invited a couple of her sisters, Claire's whole family, a couple of friends from high school, and Fran, of course. When she brought Claire's cake out, which was a yellow sheet cake with chocolate frosting she'd made from a box, she said, 'I just want to wish my best friend a happy thirtieth birthday. I don't know where I'd be without you.'

It was a funny speech, considering Claire had always thought that Lainie would be just fine without her. She was the one that needed Lainie more. But maybe that was how all friendships were – one person was the littlest bit needier than the other one. And maybe sometimes it switched. Not often, but sometimes.

Fran had shown up at the barbecue wearing a collared shirt and no hat. It looked like he'd made an effort to look nice, and seeing him stand there and talk to her family dressed like that hurt Claire's heart a little for reasons she couldn't totally identify.

After Claire blew out her candles, Lainie brought out a

cupcake with another candle in it and lit it for Martha. 'It's a few days early,' she said, 'but we can't forget the other birthday girl.'

Martha was pleased, Claire could tell. And Weezy was too. Even Claire felt good about it, and she realized that in every relationship, Martha was the needier one. And she knew that would never change.

Martha was closing on a condo, which took up a lot of the discussion at the dinner table. Cleo always looked happy to talk about it, since it took the attention away from her and the baby, and actually everyone else also seemed relieved to have another topic to discuss.

'It would make sense to rent out the other bedroom, but it would also be great to have it as a guest room. Cathy was saying that she and Ruth would love to come stay for a few days soon, and I'd love that too. I just have to decide what to do.' Martha sighed, like she'd just been faced with deciding whether or not she should euthanize a puppy.

'I'm starting to apply for jobs in New York,' Claire said. It seemed as good a time as any to let everyone know.

'Already?' Weezy asked

'I've been here for almost a year,' Claire said.

'What sorts of things are you looking for?' Will asked. He took a bite of peas.

'I think the same sort of thing I was doing before . . . nonprofit stuff.'

'But we'll miss you,' Cleo said. Claire smiled at her. She really did feel bad leaving her and Max, but at least they'd all be happier for the space.

'It might be a good idea to wait,' Weezy said. 'Until your money situation is more stable.'

'I'm fine,' Claire said.

'Well, it couldn't hurt to give yourself a cushion is all I'm saying. Just have a good amount socked away. You could stay for a few more months, get yourself in a better position,' Weezy said.

'I don't think so,' Claire said.

'Well now, don't dismiss the idea before you even think about it. You don't want to find yourself right back in the same situation.' Weezy shook her head just a little.

'Thanks for the vote of confidence. But I'm ready to go and I'm fine. You can't have all your children living with you for the rest of your life, you know.'

'Claire.' Will gave her a look.

'Who will be our babysitter?' Max asked. He tried to laugh.

Weezy sniffed. 'I'm just saying you should think about it, that's all.'

'It's not a bad idea,' Martha said. 'When you look at how much I've saved, how easy this buying process has been. It's worked out great.'

'So, we should have all lived at home for all of our twenties? Sounds like a great plan,' Claire said.

'Don't be nasty,' Weezy said.

'This is ridiculous.' Claire got up from the table. Cleo was looking down at her plate, like she wanted to disappear, like she'd been dropped in the middle of a loony bin and had no way to escape. Which, really, wasn't too far from the truth.

Claire grabbed her bag and walked outside, although she didn't really know where she was going. She hated the way she acted here. As soon as she stepped on the sidewalk, she felt guilty. What a brat she was. They'd let her come back and stay with them, and she couldn't even stand to listen to their suggestions. Why was she like this? The worst part was she couldn't help it. The anger seemed to come out of her before she even knew what was happening.

She wandered around for a while, pretending that she didn't know where she was going to go, before she finally called Fran. 'Come over,' he said. That's what he always said. She loved that.

He had a beer waiting for her on the coffee table. He was just in his boxers, even though the basement stayed pretty cool. 'Here,' he said, handing her the beer. 'You sounded like you could use one.'

Claire tried to tell him about the fight, about why she felt so bad. He listened, but she knew he didn't really understand. Fran wasn't one to feel guilty for being mean to his parents. It made sense, really, since they didn't seem to think about him so much.

'I just can't stand being there anymore,' Claire said. 'I feel like this horrible person, because I'm annoyed at them all the time. And they're just trying to help, I know that. But it's so smothering.' Fran made a noise like he agreed with what she was saying, but she knew he didn't. She put her feet in his lap and they fell silent, watching TV.

They were lying on the couch a few hours later, when she told him. She was wearing just her bra and underwear, and all she could think about was how scratchy the couch material was on her hip. Fran was lying on his back, and she was on her side, her head on his chest. He was holding a chunk of her hair in his hand, twisting it and then letting it unravel on his fingers. She knew he would fall asleep soon if she didn't say anything.

'I think I'm moving back to New York,' she said.

'You think?' He held his hand still, and she could imagine her gob of hair in his hand, raised above her head, like it was waiting for something.

'I mean, I know,' she said. She lifted her head to look at him. 'I'm moving. Soon, I think. I just need to figure it all out.'

Fran didn't say anything for a few seconds. He dropped her hair and put his hands behind his head. 'I'm not surprised,' he finally said.

'Really?'

'Yeah. I mean, last week you said you were going to kill someone if you had to live in your house much longer.'

'No, I didn't,' Claire said.

'Yes, you did,' Fran said. 'So, before it comes to murder, it's probably best if you get out of there.'

'I just think it's time,' Claire said. 'It just feels like everything is going on without me. Like I took a break, but no one else did and now if I stay here I'll just fall further behind. Does that make sense?'

'Not really,' Fran said.

'Oh.'

'But I mean, I get it. You're not happy here.'

'I'm not unhappy.'

'There's not that much room in between, you know.'

'I guess that's true.'

'It's probably a good idea.' Fran picked up her hair again and started twirling it.

'I just wanted to tell you. Because I don't know what we're doing, exactly, but I've liked it. I really have. You were one of the only good things here.'

'That's nice,' Fran said.

'I mean it.' Claire sat all the way up and moved her hair away from his hands. 'I might have been unhappy, that's true. But I wasn't unhappy when I was with you.' She got a feeling that she was going to start crying, so she looked at the far wall until it started to go away.

Fran pulled her back down and kissed the top of her head. 'Look,' he said. 'We had fun, right? It's okay, I swear. We're good, I promise.'

'Okay.'

'Claire, really. We're good. Both of us. We needed time to get over those fuckers, and we did. And you can't feel bad about that.'

'I don't.'

'You're such a liar. I mean it. Stop feeling bad. You feel guilty all the time, about everything. And you shouldn't.'

Claire didn't say anything. She was impressed that he had

been so observant. It didn't seem like he noticed. 'You should move out too,' she said.

Fran laughed. 'You mean to tell me a thirty-year-old living in his parents' basement isn't that attractive? Point taken.'

'I didn't mean that.'

'Nah, you're right. It's time. Soon.'

'I like this basement,' Claire said. She felt even worse now for saying that to him.

'It's all right,' he said. 'I bet you'll be happy to get back to New York. I have to say, I never really got it. I could never live there.'

'You could visit,' Claire said.

'Yeah, maybe I'll come see the elephants when they come to town,' Fran said. Claire didn't even remember telling him that story, but she must have. Had she left Doug out of the story when she told him or not? She couldn't remember.

'You should,' she said. 'It really is something to see.'

'Okay,' Fran said. 'Maybe we'll do that. Maybe I'll come and we'll see the elephants.'

They were both lying. They knew he'd never come to visit her in New York, that he would never see the elephants. But just then, she really wished he would, so he could see how weird, how unreal, the whole thing looked; how magical it was to watch these huge animals marching down the streets of Manhattan. Just thinking about it now made her homesick and a little sad. The way it felt like a dream, how even after you saw it with your own eyes, you never really believed it had happened.

Chapter 20

The wedding was ridiculous. All of it.

Max had insisted that it take place in the backyard, and at first Weezy tried to get him to change his mind. But now she was glad that they were at home, and not out in public for the world to see. The bride was walking down the 'aisle' eight months pregnant, in a flowy white dress that showed off the bump underneath it, like she was a movie star, some starlet that was flaunting the fact that she was getting married in this condition. *Look at me,* the dress seemed to say. *I'm pregnant and I don't care who knows it.*

Weezy tried to be open-minded. After all, her children were living in a different world than the one she'd grown up in. But honestly. A white dress? Really? Why even bother?

She'd suggested to Max early on that he and

Cleo should think about getting married. She waited for him to disagree, or to tell her that it was none of her business, but he surprised her.

'I think that's a good idea,' he said. 'I think it's something we both want.'

Even though Weezy had just suggested the same thing, she immediately wanted to tell him that marriage was a mistake. He barely knew this girl. They were children. How did they think they could make a marriage work? But she kept her mouth shut.

She imagined the children would want a quick justice of the peace ceremony, that maybe they'd all go out for a nice lunch afterward. And then after the baby was here, they could have a small church ceremony, really do it right. But Max told her they had other plans.

'We want our friends to be there,' he said. 'And our families. If we're going to do it, we want to do it in front of everyone.'

It sounded just like something Cleo would say, and Weezy knew that her son was repeating Cleo's words, and she resented that. It was enough to make her scream.

'You know, if you have it in the backyard, it won't be recognized in the church,' she finally said.

'It'll be recognized everywhere else, though,' Max said. 'Plus, Cleo's not even Catholic.'

And that was how Weezy found herself in early June, staging this spectacle, this crazy event for everyone to see. 'One day, we'll look back on this and laugh,' Will said to her that morning.

She didn't have the heart to tell him that she didn't believe that for a second.

The day of the wedding was warm, but not too warm, and Weezy felt that she deserved at least that much. 'Aren't you grateful for the weather?' Maureen asked her, and Weezy just shook her head a little bit. If your son got his college girlfriend pregnant, if her mother was still so angry she could barely speak to her, if they were going to live in your basement while they had the baby, then you deserved a beautiful day for the wedding. That was all there was to it.

Bets was over at Maureen's house, along with Cathy, Ruth, and Drew. And somehow Maureen knew enough not to breathe even a word of complaint. When Weezy finally picked up the phone to call Bets and tell her the news, Bets was surprisingly calm.

'Oh, Weezy,' she'd said. 'Don't worry about it so much. Once kids are out of your house, you can't control what they do. Not one bit. Believe me, I've learned that.'

And even though it sounded like Bets was placing some sort of judgment on her and Maureen (what on earth could they have done that would have disappointed her, really?), she didn't care. She kept waiting for Bets to start being, well, Bets. But it didn't happen. She'd been quiet during her visit, sitting and smiling at the family, and not even muttering anything about 'bastards' under her breath. It was a wedding miracle.

The girls had been fighting – were at each other's throats, actually – and it was driving her crazy. They were acting like they were back in high school, stomping up the stairs and knocking loudly on the bathroom door, screaming, 'I need to get in there!'

'Girls, *enough*,' she'd yelled that morning. They were in the kitchen, bickering about cereal, and she couldn't take it anymore. And the two of them, still in their pajamas with their hair messy, had turned to look at her like she was the crazy one. Cleo and Max had both just come up from the basement, and were standing at the kitchen door, staring at her as well. She felt like telling all of them to just shut up, to do exactly what she said. She had half a mind to just leave the house and let them all deal with the wedding on their own. But she knew she'd never do that. It wasn't her way.

'We all need to work together today,' she finally said. And all of them had nodded, like quiet, obedient children.

Outside, workers were setting up white wooden folding chairs in two groups, to create an aisle in the middle. At the front, there were two large potted plants, which sort of made it look like an altar. Sort of. All of the flowers were white, which is what Cleo wanted. And even though Weezy would have gone a different way, she had to admit that it looked pretty.

When they'd started planning the wedding, Weezy considered finding a new florist. After all, how could she explain this wedding to Samuel? But in the end, she knew he would be the best, and she called him to set up an appointment.

'This is a delicate situation,' she'd said. 'I'm actually not calling about Claire's wedding. It's – well, it's my son's.'

She'd gone on to tell Samuel the whole story – more than she'd told most of her friends, in fact. He'd listened kindly, told her gently that he'd done more of these sorts of weddings than she could even imagine. He told her that she was a lovely woman, a kind mother to be there for her son and his wife-to-be, promised her that once the baby was born, she wouldn't remember any of the mixed feelings she had about this.

When she'd gotten off the phone with him, she felt better than she had since the news had broken. (That was how she thought about it, like it was a news story that broke on television, of an awful event like a murder or the death of someone famous and beloved.) She met with Samuel alone, telling Cleo that the flowers needed to be picked immediately, promising that she would stick to her wishes for the white flowers. And she had. And now they were the loveliest part of the day – the hydrangea blooms that were tied to the chairs, the lovely textured bouquets, the potted plants.

Samuel had come to set up the backyard himself, which she knew he almost never did. He'd given her a hug and wished her luck, told Cleo that she looked beautiful (even though she was still in her robe). He arranged the pots up front, straightened the bows and blooms on the chairs, made sure that every detail was perfect.

She saw him talking to Claire outside, and for a moment Weezy hoped to God he wasn't talking about her wedding, but before she could head out there, the caterer had another question and she was drawn back into the kitchen.

Even though this wedding was almost nothing compared to what they had been planning for Claire, Weezy still found herself totally swept away with it. Maybe it was because they had so little time, or maybe that's how it always was with a wedding. They'd all been running around like chickens with no heads for weeks now, and the day of the wedding felt like a nightmare — the kind where you're trying to pack to go on a trip, and all your clothes keep falling out of the suitcase, no matter what you do.

They'd all gotten up early, but there still didn't seem to be enough time. Weezy had this fear that guests were going to start showing up and they were all going to be half-naked, running around the backyard barefoot. If anything was going to get done, Weezy was going to have to make it happen.

'Why don't you two go get dressed?' she said to Claire and Martha. They were both bridesmaids, although they had both just picked their own dresses (white, of course) and didn't really match. But when they came downstairs, they did both look very pretty. Even if Cleo did seem to be rubbing this white-themed wedding in everyone's face (*I'm pregnant, but I want everything to be virginal!*), it actually all came together beautifully.

She kept sending Will on errands, or out to check on the setup of the bars outside. He was driving her sort of crazy, just standing there all ready for the day, like he couldn't think of anything to do unless she told him. Weezy couldn't help but snap at him, more than once, for just standing there, or for not being in the same room when she needed something from him. Honestly, sometimes men were no help.

The caterers had taken over the kitchen, and set up strange little ovens on the countertops to cook the food. You could barely move in there without running into someone or something.

Cleo had been very opinionated during the meeting with the caterer. She wanted wine and appetizers served as soon as the guests arrived, before the ceremony, so that when the two of them said their vows, people would be eating and drinking, just snacking away, like they were watching a TV show. Weezy tried to talk her out of it. 'It's just not how things are done,' she said. But Cleo's mind was made up.

'I want it to feel like a party, like a celebration,' she said.

Weezy tried to give the caterer a look, to raise her eyebrows as if to say, *I know this is a ridiculous request, do you believe this?* But the caterer had just nodded.

'I love that idea,' she said. 'Very fun and relaxed.'

They'd gone on to decide on 'stations' of meat and sushi instead of a sit-down meal.

'I don't want any seating arrangements,' Cleo had said. 'I just want it so that people can eat whenever they feel like it, wherever they want.'

'I think that will confuse people,' Weezy said.

'That's very in right now,' the caterer said. 'People will catch on.' Weezy could only imagine what Sally Lemons would say about something like this. She was not one to throw seating arrangements away like they were nothing.

The kicker of the wedding planning was when Max announced that they wanted a friend of theirs to marry them. 'Absolutely not,' Weezy had said. 'It's not even legal.'

'Mom, it's legal,' Max said. 'Everyone does it now.'

'Why don't you have Deacon Callaghan? Or even a judge?' But it was like Weezy wasn't even talking, and somehow it was decided that Max's friend Ben (a boy who was once almost kicked out of school for ripping the doors off all of the bathroom stalls in their dorm freshman year) would be the one to marry them. They might as well have had a Muppet do the honors.

The ceremony was brief. Cleo and Max had put it all together on their own. After Ben was chosen as the officiant (Weezy still couldn't say that without a sneer), she decided to just let them do what they were going to do.

Claire and Martha walked down the aisle, and then Cleo followed them, alone. Her mother was sitting in the front row, and she looked just like Weezy felt: *Let this day be over with, please God, soon.*

One of their friends read a love poem by George Eliot, which Weezy had to admit was nice. Then Max and Cleo filled a glass jar by pouring two different-colored sands into it, Max with blue and Cleo with yellow, which seemed a bit silly. Another friend played the guitar and sang, a lovely but very sad song called 'Hallelujah.' Weezy had been excited when she'd heard the name of it, but then quickly realized it wasn't the least bit religious, and wasn't even joyful. There were parts about tying people to kitchen chairs, cutting hair, and bathing on the roof. She hoped that no one was really listening to the words.

Before they exchanged vows, Ben talked about the couple, and said how after Max had met Cleo, he'd told everyone that he'd met 'the hottest girl he'd ever seen.' People laughed at this, but Weezy was just plain embarrassed. Then the two of them were facing each other, promising to be friends forever, to love each other, and then Ben was pronouncing them husband and wife, which seemed impossible, Weezy thought, because it was just some words spoken in the backyard. It didn't seem real at all.

The whole crowd cheered as they walked down the aisle, and then someone handed each of them a glass of champagne and everyone was clinking glasses and hugging. Weezy went up to both of them and kissed and hugged them. She figured if she pretended like this was a real wedding, eventually it would start to feel like it.

One of Max's friends was a DJ, and he and Cleo had insisted that he should do the music for the wedding. So Weezy hired a twenty-one-year-old kid to be in charge, and just as she predicted, it was a mistake. As soon as the vows were done, he decided it was time for the music. He started off playing a loud song, and the only words that Weezy could make out throughout the whole thing were 'bad romance.' So, not only did all of the adults look shocked at the noise, but it didn't seem to be a very wedding-appropriate choice.

As the night went on, the older people made their exit

quickly. Weezy couldn't blame them. The music got louder with each song, and more vulgar. Her friends came up to say good-bye to her, hugging her and kissing her on the cheek, as though this was a normal wedding. Almost everyone had brought a card with money in it for Max and Cleo, and they'd deposited them into a birdcage that was set up for the purpose. (The birdcage was Samuel's idea, and it was a genius one. It gave the cards a safe place to go, but it wasn't so obvious that it looked like they were begging for money.) It seemed a little sad that all the new couple were getting was cash, but then again, what else would people give a young couple who were expecting their first child in the very near future? A place setting of china? A Cuisinart? No, cash was the only practical thing. Weezy would have done the same if she'd been a guest at the wedding.

Max and Cleo seemed to be having a good time, which was nice, although Weezy was a little shocked to see Cleo out there dancing, shaking her round stomach around the dance floor, rubbing it against Max and laughing.

She and Will danced just once, when the DJ found it in his heart to play a Frank Sinatra song, something for the old people, and Will found her right away and led her out to the dance floor. That was a nice part of the day, swaying and twirling with Will. Of course, right after that, the next song played repeated the words *sexy bitch* over and over, and everyone who had been dancing to Sinatra scattered like cockroaches.

Finally the day was over. It was funny, on all the sites that Weezy had looked at, the bride and the bride's family always commented that the reception went so fast, in the blink of an eye. But this one seemed to go on forever. At one point, Weezy thought they were going to have to kick the straggling college friends out of the backyard and tell them to go home. Thankfully, by the time it was getting to that point, they all seemed to get the hint and were on their way.

Maureen had hired a limo to take Max and Cleo to the Ritz-Carlton for two nights. 'My present to you,' she'd told them the week before. 'I know you won't be going on a honeymoon, so think of this as a mini trip.' She'd made them appointments in the hotel spa, and dinner reservations for the next night. 'Enjoy yourselves,' she said.

And so Max and Cleo had driven off in a limo, while the rest of the family finished saying good-bye to the last guests that were hanging on, and watched the caterers fold up the chairs and remove the leftover food. Weezy felt tired through her whole body, right down to the bones in her fingers, which ached just a little bit.

They'd all gathered on the back patio to have a glass of wine, although that was the last thing Maureen needed. She'd downed her glass quickly, then announced that she thought it would be a good idea if she went home, and Drew, who had been waiting quietly the whole day, piled Maureen, Bets, Ruth, and Cathy into the car and drove them off.

'And then there were four,' Weezy said. She felt sad, the way you do after holidays or vacations, just a little let down that the whole thing is over. Isn't that what she'd wanted the whole day, for the thing to be over? But now, she felt let down. Her own head felt a little swimmy from the wine, but she somehow didn't want to go to bed just yet.

'I think it all went well,' Will said.

'It did,' Martha said. 'Except when the caterers tried to set out the buffet before the ceremony even started. I went right in there and told them they'd have to cool it. I mean, can you imagine?'

Martha had repeated this story a few times already, and Weezy saw Claire close her eyes briefly.

'Well, thank goodness you were there,' Weezy said. 'It could have been a disaster.'

'I mean, really,' Martha went on. 'How hard is it to follow simple directions? What if the food had been out there for all that time, getting cold and congealing as they said their vows?' She sat back and shook her head.

'Well, it wasn't,' Claire said. 'So there's no need to keep talking about it.'

'I'm just saying it could have been a disaster,' Martha said.

'We know. You've said it only about a million times already. We understand – the caterers were incompetent and you saved the day. We heard you.'

'Girls, stop. Please stop.' Weezy felt the beginning of a headache.

'Give your mother a break, would you?' Will said.

'I'm not doing anything,' Martha said. 'I don't know what Claire's problem is. All I tried to do today is help.'

'You were a big help today,' Weezy told her.

'Oh my God,' Claire said. 'Can we please stop praising Martha for acting like a normal person for once?'

'Claire, stop it.' Weezy could tell that Martha was on the verge of tears.

'I'm serious. This is why she's like this, you know. This is why she thinks everything's about her. Because you make it about her. All she did was say thank you to people as they left today. And you're acting like she performed a miracle.'

Martha got up and walked inside, and Claire rolled her eyes.

'You should apologize to your sister,' Weezy said. Her whole body felt so tired. Had she ever been this tired in her whole life?

'I'm not apologizing to her. She needs to hear it. This isn't good for her, the way you treat her.'

'You should try to be a little more understanding,' Weezy said.

'Understanding is all I am. You make her worse, do you realize that? She thinks the world revolves around her because you make it seem like it does. You make it seem like every little thought she has is so important. It makes her crazy. She thinks the whole world is supposed to treat her like that. And God forbid we should hurt her feelings. How is she ever supposed to live like an adult if you never treat her like one?'

'When you're a parent, you'll understand this more.'

'When I'm a parent,' Claire said, 'I won't focus only on one kid.'

'You know what?' Weezy was mad now. 'Sometimes the

world isn't perfect, Claire. Sometimes you just need to be grateful for what you have. Sometimes you need to be a grown-up.' She hadn't yelled at Claire like this since high school.

'A grown-up?' Claire looked up to the sky and laughed. 'Right, a grown-up. Well, since you're such a great example, maybe you can explain to me why the florist somehow still thinks I'm getting married. Why he told me that the two of you have been planning things, and that my flowers would be beautiful.'

Will turned to Weezy, but didn't say anything. Weezy felt her face get hot. She hadn't felt like this since she was in high school, when Bets had found out that she'd snuck over to Steven Sullivan's house. She swallowed a few times and finally answered.

'I have no idea what you're talking about. He does tons of weddings a year. He probably just mixed you up with someone else.'

'Really?' Claire asked. 'He seemed pretty sure it was me. He knew Doug's name, he told me how even though we'd changed the date and postponed the wedding, he was still so excited to work with us. How he'd loved going over the flowers with you, how you had great instincts.'

'Claire, that's enough,' Will said. 'Your mother has had a long day – we all have – and we need to just step back.'

'I can't wait to get out of this house. I can't wait to get away from this crazy family. I hate it here.' Claire stormed out, and Weezy had a strange feeling of déjà vu, of the girls' being teenagers, when their storming out of the room in tears was just another Tuesday. It used to hurt less when Claire said she hated them. Now it stung, like someone had whipped her.

Weezy felt tears come to her eyes, and she tried to blink them back. Oh, she was so tired. Her children all thought she had failed them, probably even Max. Had she? Because even though Claire was being horrendous, she was right – they did treat Martha differently. They'd had to. All those years, ignoring her outbursts, doing anything to make sure that she was happy, or at least stable. Was it true that they'd made things worse for her? Had she ruined her even more? Weezy's head throbbed and she closed her eyes.

'Don't let this upset you,' Will said. 'It's been a long day for all of us. Hell, it's been a long year.'

'Yes, it has,' she said. She waited for Will to ask her about the florist, but he never did.

'We should get some sleep,' he said. 'Come on.'

'I'll be up in a minute,' Weezy told him. He nodded and walked over to kiss her good night.

Weezy sat there for several hours. She was so tired, she thought she might just fall asleep right there on the porch, like a crazy old woman. But she stayed awake. She wondered why Will didn't ask her about the florist. She let herself admit that she was secretly thrilled that Samuel had said that she was a pleasure to work with, that she had great instincts. She thought about her children – Martha, Claire, and Max – and how none of them was where she wanted them to be. None of them was where *they* wanted to be. She wondered if it was all her fault, wondered whether if she'd done things differently, they'd all have turned out okay.

She thought about Bets, and how she'd just left Pennsylvania after her husband died, just left her two daughters without a home base and gone back to Michigan to live her own life. She'd just assumed that they'd be okay, that they'd be able to manage. And they had. Was that what she should have done with her own children? She couldn't imagine it. Couldn't imagine how Bets had just separated her life from theirs.

When the sky started to get light out, and the birds started to sing, Weezy got up from the porch and went in the house to go to bed. It was no use torturing herself anymore, she thought. She couldn't fix anything by wondering what if.

She finally got into bed, and Will, who was snoring, turned over in his sleep and put his arm on her stomach as if to say, *There you are.* For a second, she felt a little bit calmer, a little bit less lonely. She pulled the covers up to her shoulders and closed her eyes. She thought she might just sleep all day.

Part Three

Chapter 21

Mr. Cranston's funeral wasn't as dramatic as Martha had imagined it would be. They didn't have a separate wake and funeral, just had an open casket for an hour or so before the mass started. Martha came early, and then sat in the back. When they finally closed the top of the casket, Ruby started crying, loudly. It echoed in the church, and actually was a little dramatic, which was probably what Ruby was going for. But her brother was the one to take her arm and lead her to the pew, so it looked like they were getting along now. Who could tell how long that would last?

There weren't too many people there, actually. Martha remembered Bets saying once that the older you got, the smaller the funerals were. Because everyone that you knew was dying and there weren't many people left, which was depressing when you got right down to it. Which was worse? To be one of the first to die and have a packed church or to outlive everyone and have almost no one at your funeral to show for it? Martha couldn't decide.

The funeral was at a Presbyterian church, and the service was just what Mr. Cranston had written down. Martha felt like she'd gotten a sneak peek, since she knew which hymns and readings she was going to hear. She was a little surprised to see Jaz get up to do a reading, but thought how nice it was that Mr. Cranston had chosen her. It was right.

Ruby and her brother both gave the eulogy, although Ruby didn't get too far. She talked about being a little girl and having her dad read the comics to her while she sat on his lap. Then she said something else that Martha couldn't understand, and her brother put his hand on her back and gently moved her out of the way. He spoke about Mr. Cranston like he was a businessman that he admired. But Martha tried not to judge, because maybe he had to keep his speech a little removed or he'd lose it like Ruby.

Martha went back to the house for the lunch, which was catered, but it was still Jaz that was in charge, taking over and giving orders. She seemed happy to have something to do, to be bustling around, arranging and rearranging cold cuts and tiny rolls. Switching out the serving spoons for the salads, inspecting the glasses. If anyone noticed that she was crying while doing all of this, they didn't say anything. Jaz just kept moving, and every once in a while reached up to wipe away a tear.

She didn't stay at the house too long. Since Jaz was so busy and Ruby and her brother were greeting guests and accepting condolences, Martha didn't really have anyone to talk to. She made herself a tiny ham sandwich and ate it standing in the corner of the living room, where she'd had her interview with Ruby. She wondered what they'd do with the house now, if they'd sell it, if they'd have to redecorate it before they put it on the market. To think of it cleared of all the personality (as stuffy as it was), to think of the pictures gone, the furniture taken away, made Martha sadder than she'd been all day.

After she ate, she put her plate in the kitchen and found Jaz to say good-bye. Jaz gave her a big hug, and cried a little in her hair, but Martha didn't mind.

'It was so great working with you,' Martha said. She meant it.

'You too, baby. Take care now. You take care of yourself.'

They squeezed arms and then Jaz kept moving, picking up plates and glasses that had been abandoned, picking up crumpled napkins. Martha looked around and saw Ruby, so she went up to say good-bye.

'It was really an honor to work for your father,' Martha said. It seemed like the right thing to say.

'That's sweet,' Ruby said. Oh, I almost forgot. Come with me.'

Ruby led her back to the office, and gave her an envelope with her name on it. 'To thank you for all your work,' she said, sounding strangely formal.

'Oh, no, I already got paid,' Martha said.

'This is just a little extra.'

'I couldn't.' Martha held the envelope out to Ruby.

'Take it,' Ruby said. She looked like she didn't really care if Martha was going to or not, but didn't want to deal with the back and forth.

'Well, thanks.'

'Sure. I know he wasn't always that easy to deal with.'

'Oh, no. He was great. Really. He loved your presents, I think.'

Ruby laughed. 'No, he didn't. I never knew what to get for him.'

'He did, I think. Even if he didn't use them all the time, I think he really loved getting them.'

'Thanks,' Ruby said. She looked around the office.

'Thank you again.' Martha felt like she'd done a good deed, like she'd made the day better for Ruby. She smiled as she let herself out the back door.

Martha had gotten a call from the caretaking company, just a few days after Mr. Cranston passed, which seemed a little insensitive, but it was their job, she supposed. They asked if she'd be interested in a new placement, and because she hadn't thought too far ahead, she said yes.

This was a different sort of job. She'd be with a woman in her early sixties who had fallen and broken her hip. The woman lived alone and would need help getting to the store and moving around. Martha was happy to take a job with someone who wasn't going to die anytime soon. Although sixty was fairly young to break a hip. This woman probably hadn't gotten enough calcium or done any of the light weightlifting that could help prevent bone deterioration. Well, no matter. Martha could talk to her about all of those things.

They met once, briefly. Sharon Cooper lived alone in a much smaller house than the Cranstons'. Her husband was dead, she told Martha, but she didn't elaborate on it. Martha wondered if he was older or if he'd had an untimely death. From what she could tell from the pictures in the house, she had a few children and a couple of grandchildren. Martha stopped in front of one picture of a blond girl, about three years old, hugging a teddy bear.

'She's so cute,' Martha said. Sharon just smiled. 'I'm just about to become an aunt. My brother's going to have a baby.'

'Congratulations,' Sharon said. And that was that. Well, never mind. They had plenty of time to get to know each other.

It would be strange to be in a new house all of a sudden, surrounded by a new family and a new story. It seemed not right to just leave the Cranstons when she'd been such a part of it. But she knew she could always go and visit Jaz over the next few months. Jaz would be happy to have a friendly face, she supposed, while dealing with the house and the loss of Mr. Cranston. Yes, that's what she'd do. She'd make a plan to go there next week and have tea with Jaz.

*

At home, Cleo seemed too pregnant to even breathe. Martha had never spent this much time up close with a pregnant person – other than when Weezy was pregnant with Max, and Martha didn't remember that much. It was fascinating. Sometimes Cleo leaned back on the couch, shifting around.

'The baby's feet are in my ribs,' she'd say.

'Really?' Martha asked. What a strange thought to have feet kicking you in the ribs.

Cleo nodded and puffed a little. She was pretty irritable, but it seemed to be that Max was the only one she took it out on. Martha couldn't really blame her. She looked like she was about to pop.

'You're so close,' Martha told her one day. The due date was just a week away. The two of them were lying on the couch watching TV, and Cleo's breathing was so loud it was almost distracting.

'I hope I make it until then,' Cleo said.

'You will.' Martha patted her big, swollen feet. It was the first time she'd seen any part of Cleo that wasn't pretty and perfect, and she couldn't help but feel just a tiny bit happy about it. 'You will.'

Dr. Baer told Martha that she was going to have to let Claire make her own decisions about therapy. 'Not everyone is ready or willing to give it a try. And if they're not ready, then it won't do them any good.'

434

'I know, but I just know it would help,' Martha said. Dr. Baer held up her hand, as if to say, *That's enough talking for now.* Martha sighed.

'It's not up to you. You made the offer, you told her why you wanted her to come with you, and she doesn't want to do it. Sometimes you just have to let it be.'

'Fine,' Martha said. She hated when people said to let things be. If everyone in the world just let things be, it would be a disaster.

Claire wasn't home much these days anyway. She took the train to New York for interviews and to look at apartments. Martha knew she'd be on her way soon. They had totally different schedules now, and even when Claire was home, they rarely ran into each other in the bathroom, which made Martha feel sort of sad. But then, the other morning, Claire had come in while she was brushing her teeth and gone over to put toothpaste on her own toothbrush.

They stood there and brushed their teeth, each at their own sink, looking in the mirror. Claire spit and then sang 'Brush, brush, brush, in a rush, rush, rush.' She looked at Martha from the corner of her eyes, and Martha started laughing. It was a song they had made up when they were little, and they'd insisted on singing it every night while they brushed their teeth together.

'Spit and rinse, spit and rinse, brush in a rush,' Martha sang. The song wasn't exactly genius, but they'd been little kids. The two of them smiled at each other in the mirror.

Claire cleared her throat and looked over at her. 'I'm sorry if I've been hard to live with the past few months. I really am. I didn't mean to take it out on you.'

'It's okay,' Martha said. And it really was. She knew that even when Claire was saying stuff about her, it was really more about Claire.

'Good,' Claire said. 'It's just not been the best year for me, you know? But I'm sorry if I was being an asshole.'

Martha opened her mouth and was about to say something about how maybe therapy would have helped her work through it, but thought better of it and just said, 'Thanks.'

'I'm glad you got your own place. Really. I think it's great.'

'Me too,' Martha said.

Martha was really diving into being a homeowner. She got paint samples and wallpaper books from the store, and spent hours studying each one. Some people thought wallpaper was old-fashioned, but Martha liked it. She thought maybe she'd do the guest bathroom in a small floral pattern. And who cared if other people didn't like it? It was her house after all.

She was starting to get a little nervous about moving out. It was strange to think she wouldn't see her parents every day. But with the baby coming, it was probably for the best. Even though once she and Claire were gone, Weezy wouldn't have nearly as much help around the house as she did now.

The great part about Martha's situation was that she didn't have to move at any specific time. She now officially owned the condo, but she was taking her time getting it set up. She went over and measured and thought about how she wanted everything to be. It was a pretty big job, actually, since she had to buy all new furniture

'Just take it piece by piece,' Weezy said to her one night. 'You don't have to have it all done in a day.'

That was true, Martha thought. And that calmed her down a bit.

Sharon Cooper turned out to be a tougher patient than Martha had thought she'd be. She was much tougher than Mr. Cranston, that was for sure. Martha was there every day from nine to five, and she helped her get into the shower and get dressed. She took her to the grocery store, which seemed like a big trip out, but Sharon insisted. She was using a walker and was not very steady, and it made Martha nervous to watch her shoot down the aisles of the store.

'Why don't you take it easy?' she said one day.

'I'm fine,' Sharon said. 'I'm not going to get better just sitting around.'

'No, but if you make yourself fall again, it's going to take you a much longer time to get better.'

Sharon didn't answer her but she did slow down a little bit. She had a fight to her, which was good. But it also made it seem like she was annoyed all the time, and that got tiresome. Mr. Cranston had been frustrated, sure, but that was different.

He was looking back at his life, mourning the fact that he was almost done. Sharon was fighting like hell to get back to the way she'd been. And you had to admire her for that. Still, it didn't make her an easy patient. Not at all.

Sharon's children took turns coming over at night, to bring her dinner and get her settled. They always looked frazzled and tired, and kind of put out to be there, which bothered Martha. If Weezy was in this situation, Martha would be happy to help out. Although maybe Sharon was a harder mother to take care of than Weezy would be. She could see that.

Her oldest daughter, Megan, was a nurse and often came by in her pink scrubs. 'You should change,' Sharon said to her one night. 'There's probably germs all over those things.'

Megan rolled her eyes, and Martha knew she was annoyed, but really, it was true. Her scrubs were probably festering with disease. The next day, she told Sharon that she used to be a nurse, that she was planning to go back to it.

'Really? What's stopping you?'

'I'm just figuring things out,' Martha said.

'I could never have been a nurse,' Sharon told her. 'I don't like seeing people sick and lying around in beds. Blood is not for me. Vomit even less. When the kids had the stomach flu, it was their dad that dealt with them.'

'It doesn't bother me so much.'

'That's like Megan. She never had to turn away from those things.'

'That's a sign of a good nurse.'

'Well, I can't say I understand your choice, but I have to say it seems better than this gig. You should figure it out soon, you know. Or you'll be stuck wiping the asses of old people like me for the rest of your life.'

Martha didn't say anything. She could see why Sharon's children weren't tripping over themselves to come here and help her. Yes, she could certainly see why.

That night, Martha had trouble falling asleep. She was annoyed at Sharon, at how harsh she'd sounded when she told her she should go back to being a nurse. What did she know? She had no idea what Martha had been through the past year. Good lord. Some people were so quick to judge.

Although, if she had to be honest, she was a little bothered with herself for not doing anything about it the whole time she worked at the Cranstons'. Not one thing. She had so much more free time there! She could have figured out what needed to be done, could have gotten started on it. It was always so quiet and peaceful at the house. Even when Ruby was making a scene or Mr. Cranston was crabby, it was nothing like being with Sharon. Martha hoped her hip healed soon.

She told herself that she deserved a break. Time had gotten away from her, but that happened. And she'd just bought a new condo, for goodness' sake. That was a big change, a life change, and anyone would need to take a breath after that, to take some time and regroup. She was okay. *One step at a time,* she thought.

That was also the motto for alcoholics, wasn't it? No, that was one day at a time. Well, that made sense too. She still had to adjust to her new place, decorate it, and get settled. She could only do so much at once or she'd drive herself crazy. *One thing at a time,* she told herself. There was always time for the rest of it later. Yes, there was always time.

Chapter 22

Cleo wanted a natural birth. And no one could talk her out of it.

'Take the drugs,' her mother had said. 'Oh, sweetie, believe me, you'll want the drugs.'

Weezy told her to keep an open mind. 'Sometimes you don't know what you want until you're there. Sometimes you don't have a choice. You might even need a C-section.'

Even Lainie told her that she should be flexible. 'It's good to have a plan,' she said. 'I didn't really know what I wanted, but then when it started with Jack, I was sure that I wanted an epidural.'

'What about the rest of them?' Cleo asked.

'Well, with Tucker, he came so fast that we didn't even have a chance. I started labor and then it's like he slipped right out as soon as we got to the hospital. And with Matthew, it took a while and I got the epidural right away. Just be ready to do whatever you want in the moment, okay?'

Cleo agreed, but she knew deep down that she was going to stick to her plan. She'd found a doula to be with her when she went into labor. The plan was to labor at home for as long as possible before going to the hospital.

'Think of the hospital as a drive-thru birthing center,' the doula said.

Cleo liked that idea. She didn't want to be in the hospital for any longer than she had to be. 'Hospitals make me nervous with all the germs and infections,' she explained. Max pointed out that the doctors were there too, and that was a plus, but he said it was up to Cleo.

It was nice of Lainie to offer advice, but Cleo wished she'd never said, *He slipped right out*. It made it sound like the baby came down a greased slide, made her want to cross her legs, as if that would keep the baby inside her. Sometimes when she lay down at night, she would hear the phrase *He slipped right out*, and she knew she was going to be awake for a while.

It didn't matter what anyone said anyway. She wanted a natural birth and she wanted a doula and that was that. Cleo explained this to Weezy and her mother while they were sitting around having tea after the shower, and talking about her like she wasn't even there.

'I don't know where she got these ideas,' Elizabeth said. 'Certainly not from me. She wasn't raised in a hippie house.'

And Elizabeth and Weezy laughed together, like they were friends now, like they were ganging up against her.

'It's better for the baby,' Cleo said.

'Next thing you know, she'll tell us about plans to bury the placenta or, worse, eat it!' The two women really got a kick out of that one, and Cleo pressed her lips together to keep from saying anything else. It was like when she told them that she wasn't going to find out the sex of the baby because she wanted to be surprised. Elizabeth had snorted and said, 'Because getting pregnant in college wasn't a big enough surprise for you?'

She relayed the whole scene to Max later that night. She was propped up against the headboard, with two pillows behind her back, and she was somehow still uncomfortable.

'They think they know so much more than me,' she said.

'Well, they did both have babies.' Max took her hand and tried to hold it with both of his, but she pulled it away and got out of the bed. She grabbed her pillow and held it in one arm.

'That's not the point,' she said. 'Didn't you hear what I said? They were mocking me, like I'm so stupid. Like I don't matter at all.' She stood there for a moment, thinking that she'd go sleep somewhere else, that she'd show Max. Then she realized there was nowhere to go. What was she going to do? Sleep on the couch in the TV room and be lying there with her giant stomach when the whole family came downstairs in the morning? She sat back down on the edge of the bed.

'I just want you to be on my side,' she said.

'I'm on your side,' Max said. He sat up and rubbed her

shoulders too hard, so that it almost hurt, but Cleo didn't say anything because she knew he was trying to help. 'I'm always on your side.'

Cleo never told anyone where she got the idea for the doula. She let them think it was in some article she'd read in a baby magazine, or in one of the how-to books, when really she'd read about it on some celebrity's blog and it had convinced her.

When she couldn't sleep, she searched the Internet for any article or website that would make her feel better about what was going to happen. One night Max woke up and rolled over to find her looking at birthing pictures.

'What the hell?' he said. 'That looks like murder.'

'I know,' she said. The computer glowed in the room and the two of them looked at the pictures in silence.

When her due date was one month away, Cleo honestly didn't know how she was supposed to make it any longer. 'I'm too big,' she said. 'I'm huge. I can barely walk and I think the baby is stuck in my ribs.'

'You're not huge,' Max said. But Cleo knew he was lying. He'd walked into the room the other day while she was changing, and when she turned, so that her bare stomach was facing him, he'd said, 'Whoa,' before he could stop himself.

'I just don't think there's anywhere else for this baby to go,' Cleo said. She sat back so that she was on an angle. 'It feels like it's in my chest. It's probably hitting my heart.'

'I don't think that can happen,' Max said. 'Plus, the doctor said all of what you were feeling was normal, remember?'

'Yeah. But maybe he doesn't know what he's talking about. Maybe the baby is ready to come now. Maybe it will be early.'

'Maybe,' Max said.

But she wasn't early. She kept waiting, each morning, to wake up and be in labor. She knew that the baby was ready to come out, could feel it inside of her, and sometimes could see its elbow or foot pushing at her stomach, like it was trying to get out.

'I know,' she'd whisper, when this happened. She'd touch the little bump that the baby's hand made, and rub it. 'I know you're ready.'

Two days before her due date, Cleo went into labor. She walked upstairs to find all of the Coffeys sitting around the table having breakfast together, which was weird, because they never did that. 'I'm in labor,' she said. All of them looked at her and Will took another bite of his toast. 'I said, I'm in labor.'

'Are you sure?' Max asked. He got up and walked over to her, touched her stomach like that was going to help him figure out if she was telling the truth.

'Yes, I'm sure. I feel cramping, like a contraction. I've had a few of them.'

'Why don't you sit down and have some breakfast?' Weezy said. 'It may be false labor or maybe you're just hungry. And if you are in labor, it will probably be a while.'

'I'm not hungry,' Cleo said. 'I'm in labor, I know it.' She turned to Max. 'I want to go to the hospital.'

'I thought you wanted to wait,' Max said. He was shifting his weight from one leg to the other, like a little kid, and Cleo reached out and held him still.

'I did, but I don't want to anymore. I just want to get there.' Cleo's heart was pounding and her breath was uneven.

Weezy stood up, took Cleo by the arm, and led her to the couch in the TV room. 'Okay, let's do this. You sit for a few minutes and we'll start timing the contractions, okay? Max, go get the stopwatch.' Max ran out of the room and up the stairs. He looked grateful to have an order.

'Okay,' Cleo said. 'But not too long. I want to be in the hospital. I don't want to have the baby here.' Her eyes filled with tears and Weezy patted her shoulder, which was the last thing she wanted. She didn't want to be here with these people, didn't want to be in this place.

'We're not going to let that happen,' Weezy said. 'I promise. We'll just sit for a few minutes, let you rest, and we'll get all your stuff together and get ready to go. Okay?'

Max came running back into the room, breathing hard. 'I got it,' he said. He held up the watch and Weezy stood and pointed to her seat.

'Great. You sit here and start timing. Remember what the book said and what they told you in class, okay?' Weezy was talking to them like they were schoolchildren, like she was instructing them how to tie their shoes. If she'd been able to catch her breath, Cleo might have said something.

'Can I get you anything?' Weezy asked. 'Water?'

'Maybe water,' Cleo said. 'Also, could you call my mom? Could you tell her to come here now? Or to go to the hospital?'

Weezy nodded. 'I'll do it right now.'

Cleo heard Weezy on the phone with Elizabeth. 'She thinks she's in labor,' she was saying. Cleo wanted to run over there, grab the phone, and yell. 'I *am* in labor,' just to set the record straight, but she stayed put.

Weezy called the doula too, informed her that Cleo wanted to head right to the hospital, and then she was quiet and then said, 'Mmm-hmm, yes,' over and over again. When she hung up the phone, Weezy told Cleo that the doula was coming to the house. 'She's very opinionated, isn't she?' Weezy asked.

No one at the hospital seemed to be alarmed that Cleo was in labor. After waiting at the house for a few hours, with everyone watching her and the doula trying to get her to lie in different positions, Cleo announced that she was really ready to go. She expected the hospital staff to at least react, but they seemed almost bored with her. A nurse told her that they'd have the doctor come in to see how far along she was. 'He might send you home,' she said. Cleo thought it sounded like a threat.

In the room, Cleo went into the bathroom. While she was on the toilet, her water broke. She couldn't wait to tell that nurse who wanted to send her home that it was too bad, because she was staying put. She sat there for a while, feeling too tired to get up. When she finally pulled up her leggings, she felt them get wet almost immediately.

Cleo waited on the examining table, feeling like she was leaking. When the nurse came back in, Cleo said, 'My water broke.'

'Are you sure?'

'Yes, I'm sure. Why is everyone asking me that? I'm sure that I'm in labor and I'm sure that my water just broke. I am inside this body. I am in my body and I know.' Max was typing something on his phone, and he looked up at her with his eyebrows raised.

'When did it happen?' the nurse asked.

'Right after I went to the bathroom.'

The nurse sighed. 'Are you sure you didn't just wet yourself?'

'Yes, I'm sure.'

'It's very common.'

'I know I didn't wet myself, okay? I know for sure because I just wet myself yesterday and I know what it feels like.' Max raised his eyebrows at her again, but stayed quiet.

'Well, then, get changed into the gown. You were supposed to do that already, and we can't check anything with you still dressed.' Cleo snatched the gown from her. She'd show that nurse.

The plan was for Max to stay by her head. 'There's no way he's going anywhere else,' she said. She told Lainie this one night while they were over at her house. Brian was in the other room and he laughed.

'Good luck to you,' he said. 'That was our plan too. But once it starts, it's like a war zone in there. You just go where you're needed, and you can't help but look.'

Lainie rolled her eyes at Cleo as if to say Brian was ridiculous, but now Cleo was more determined than ever to keep to the plan.

'By my head,' she kept saying. 'Stay right here. Up here.'

'Got it,' Max kept saying.

After being in labor for ten hours, Cleo was sure she was going to go crazy. 'I want an epidural,' she said. 'I want it now.'

The nurse nodded. 'We'll get the doctor and we'll talk about it.'

'I know my rights,' Cleo told her. 'You can't deny me what I want. I want the epidural.'

The doula quietly reminded Cleo of her birth plan, suggested that maybe she was just having a low moment and should try to get through it. 'We can do some breathing and meditation,' she said.

'Get out,' Cleo told her. 'Get out of this room.'

'I know you're uncomfortable,' the doula said. 'Let's try to switch positions.'

'I said get out of the room.'

The doula looked at Max and nodded. 'I'll give you two a few minutes, but I'll be right out in the hall.'

Max stood next to her and held her hand, and sometimes

smoothed her hair back from her face and put a wet washcloth on her forehead. She knew that he was trying to be helpful, but it felt like water torture to her for some reason. The washcloth dripped down the side of her face and neck, pooling at her shoulder. Finally, she picked it up and whipped it across the room.

'Okay, Dad,' the nurse said. 'I think we can take it easy on the cool compresses.'

Max gave Cleo a look like she'd hurt his feelings, and if she'd had any room left in her body to feel anything, she might have felt bad. He was so easily hurt.

Weezy had been surprised that Cleo didn't want her mother in the room. Cleo didn't know how to explain that they weren't that kind of family. She and her mom didn't talk about bodily functions the way that the Coffeys did, like Will's constipation or heartburn was just another normal breakfast topic. They never walked out of a bathroom and warned people not to go in there for a while, like she'd seen Weezy do, or announce that their cramps were just unbearable this month, as Martha had done last week.

No, she and her mother didn't talk about those things. When Cleo had gotten her period, she'd never even mentioned it, just put her underwear in the laundry and the next day there was a pack of pads and another of tampons. 'Any questions?' her mom had asked. And Cleo hadn't had one.

So she didn't want her mom in here while her water was breaking. She didn't want her here while the doctor explained that it was that color because the baby had just pooped inside of her. And she didn't want her mom to be here if she pooped on the table, or bled, or did all of the stuff that you do when you have a baby.

And she hoped to God that Weezy knew that she'd never consider having her in the room. That would be absurd. She wasn't even thrilled about having Max in the room, but she had to have someone and he was the dad so he was supposed to be there. He would probably never want to have sex with her again, she imagined. And who could blame him? This was why you were supposed to wait until you'd been together longer before you had a baby, because of all the gross and embarrassing stuff that happened along with it. They should advertise that when they tried to stop teen pregnancies.

The last thing that Lainie had said to her was this: 'You're going to be in the room, and you're going to think, "I can't do this, I take it back, what was I thinking, I changed my mind." And here's the best part: You can't change your mind. So there's no use thinking about it. You'll just have to do it. If there was any turning back, there'd be no babies in the world. So just remember, the decision is done and you'll just have to get through it.'

After she got the epidural, Cleo said to Max, 'I know why people are drug addicts.'

'Okay,' he said. He tried to smile, but he looked concerned.

Her labor went on and Cleo even managed to rest a little, to close her eyes, and even though she didn't think she really slept, it made her feel better.

Afterward, it was hard to remember the pain. It wasn't that she didn't remember that it was awful – she knew that much. But if she tried to talk about it, tried to imagine it again, she couldn't. It was like there were no words for it. Even saying that it was the most awful thing ever didn't do it justice.

Someone took pictures, but she didn't know who. When she looked at them later, she didn't remember the actual moments that were captured, didn't remember smiling and posing for anyone.

Elizabeth and Weezy were the first ones in the room, telling her she did a great job and marveling over the baby. They asked Cleo the name, but she let Max answer.

'Nina Grace,' he said.

'It's perfect,' Elizabeth said, and Weezy agreed.

Will came in later, looking uncomfortable at being so close to Cleo in her ragged state. But he did hold Nina in the corner, smiling at her as she slept. Claire and Martha came in together, hugged her, and then took turns passing the baby back and forth.

'She's perfect,' Claire said. 'She's so beautiful.'

'She really is,' Martha said. 'Are you two going to send her to the nursery for the night? You should, just so you can get some rest.'

After everyone had gone, she and Max stared at the little red face. Cleo had told him that he could go home, but he'd insisted on staying and sleeping on the window seat that turned into a bed. She was grateful that he was there – even though they did send the baby to the nursery like Martha suggested – so that when she woke up in the middle of the night, there was someone else with her.

'I can't believe they're letting us just leave with her,' Cleo said to Max. 'Don't you feel like someone's going to come and stop us?'

'Yeah, kind of.' Max had insisted to his family that they were going to take Nina home themselves.

'Why don't you just let us come to help?' Weezy asked. 'We can even take a different car, if you want.'

But Max wouldn't budge. And so, it was just the three of them in the car, Cleo riding in the backseat next to Nina, because she was just so small and they couldn't really see her, even with the mirror.

When they pulled in the driveway, there was a wooden stork in the ground and pink balloons tied to the front door. They walked in and found everyone waiting in the front hall, and they all gathered around the baby as if they'd never seen her before. Ruby came over to see them, and Max knelt down on the ground and held the little bundle out to her. She sniffed Nina's legs and then poked her snout on her arm.

Cleo almost told him not to let Ruby lick the baby, but she thought better of it and stayed silent. Ruby looked up at her, like she understood, like she was saying, 'I know this baby, I poked her with my nose when she was still in your stomach.'

'Here she is,' Max said to Ruby. 'Here's your new niece.' Then he looked up at Cleo. 'Right? Nina would be Ruby's niece, because Ruby's like my sister?'

'Yeah, that sounds right,' she said. Cleo was crying now, thinking that Ruby understood everything about Nina, which was absurd. She needed to sit down and she needed that weird donut thing that Weezy had gotten for her. She'd been mortified when she received it, but now she thought it might have been the nicest present anyone had ever given her.

The first night home with the baby, they were both too scared to sleep, not that Nina gave them much of a chance. She screamed and cried and nothing they tried seemed to work.

'She was so quiet in the hospital,' Cleo said. They were standing above the bassinet, looking down at Nina's red face.

'Maybe she was in shock from being born,' Max said. 'But she's adjusted now.' They were grateful when the morning came, like they had survived something. It had been only one night.

The days blended together, all of them sleepless and filled with feedings and diaper changes. Their time was marked by the cycle of Nina's sleeping and waking. Cleo gave up trying to breastfeed almost immediately. 'She doesn't like it,' she explained to Max. 'She seems to know what she wants and she doesn't want this.'

The doula was supposed to stop by to check on them, to help with breastfeeding if needed, but Cleo refused to call her back. She couldn't face the woman after she'd yelled at her and thrown her out of the room. She was fine with giving Nina formula. After all, that meant that Max could feed her too, which meant she could stay in bed sometimes.

Max stayed home with them for a week, and the first morning he went back to work, Cleo watched him get dressed and was filled with terror.

'I'll be back so soon,' he said. 'And my mom will be here all day. It will be okay.'

With Max gone, the days seemed longer and more tedious. Weezy was there almost all the time, making comments or offering to help. Whenever Weezy suggested anything, Cleo's first instinct was to do the opposite. She had to stop herself from yelling, 'You're not my mom' several times a day. It was just the hormones, she told herself.

Weezy often mentioned how Nina was such a good baby, and Cleo got the feeling that she was lying to her. If Nina was a good baby, what were the bad ones like? How much fussier and needier could something be?

Sometimes, she and Nina would wake up from a nap and outside the door would be a laundry basket, filled with clean, folded clothes for Cleo – onesies, pajamas, baby socks, and burp cloths. Things like this usually happened just as Cleo was thinking particularly horrible thoughts about what a beast Weezy was. She'd grab the laundry basket, more thankful than she could ever express, and hope that she'd be a better person soon.

When Nina cried for a long time, Ruby would lift her head and look at Cleo with sad eyes, like, *Really? This is really what our life is now?* Other times, she would come over and lick Cleo's hand softly, as if to say, *I know you didn't mean to bring this one home. It's okay. It was clearly an accident.*

One night, Cleo was up feeding Nina, and she noticed Ruby lying in the corner of the room. Cleo watched her for a while, and then became convinced that Ruby wasn't moving, wasn't breathing. She crept over to her, holding the baby in her arms, trying to figure out how she was going to tell the family that the dog had died. She wondered if Ruby had just given up, if she was so unhappy with her house being so noisy that she simply willed herself to stop living. Cleo didn't think she could handle being responsible for the death of the Coffeys' dog. But just as she bent down, she saw Ruby's pink tongue dart in and out of her mouth, licking her nose, and Cleo sighed with relief.

Cleo had never known tired like this before. It was constant and violent, like someone had beaten her up when she wasn't paying attention. She was still sore, everywhere, and sometimes the edges of her vision were blurry, like she was going blind. She was heavy-limbed and clumsy. She found herself walking into doorframes, tripping over her feet, and knocking glasses over. She had no sense of space. Once, she sat on the toilet and started going to the bathroom before realizing that she hadn't pulled her underwear down.

Cleo ached for her mom in a way she never had before. Elizabeth felt so far away when she was living in the Coffeys' basement, even though they talked every day, something they'd never done before. Elizabeth listened to her talk about Nina's spit-up and diapers. She drove to see them often, sometimes twice a week.

Of course, no matter how much Cleo ached for her, as soon as they got together, there was some sort of squabble. Often Cleo ended up snapping at her mom, then felt like crying when she left, like a guilt-filled toddler who had done something wrong.

Cleo prayed that this would be over soon, this feeling of wanting things and then not wanting them as soon as she got them. It was exhausting not to know your own heart.

Cleo and Max were afraid that Nina was going to die, always; or that they'd hurt her or break her in some way. Clipping her nails almost always resulted in drawing blood, and Cleo often wondered why anyone let them take this baby home. Surely they were not equipped.

Some days she and Max fought over nothing, over everything. They were so tired that it didn't take much to get them going.

Once she yelled at him for putting Nina in a day outfit in the middle of the night.

'It was the closest thing I could find, and who cares? They all look the same anyway? Her pajamas were all wet.'

'The yellow pajamas were there for her,' Cleo said. She held them up as proof.

'You and your yellow pajamas,' Max said. Neither of them was making any sense, but the anger was real.

Cleo often imagined packing herself and Nina up, heading to New York, never talking to Max again. There was power in this image, scary and absolute. Whenever she thought about it, she felt strong, then immediately sick and afraid.

They apologized all the time, and sometimes Cleo was grateful that they were in such a tiny space. There was nowhere else for them to go, so eventually one of them had to say something. After they fought, Cleo often felt a wave of panic rise up. But usually, she was too tired to let it overtake her, and she just let the fight go. She figured it was the only upside of exhaustion.

They probably weren't supposed to let Nina sleep in the bed with them, but almost every morning she got up to eat around four thirty, and they'd feed her and change her, and then take her back into the bed. They'd put her right in the middle, and the three of them would doze for a couple of hours before Max had to get up for work.

Right after she ate, Nina acted like she was drunk, eyelids fluttering, happily drooling. Max would always say, 'You hit that bottle hard, didn't you?' and lean down to rub his nose against her hair.

Those were Cleo's favorite moments, when they were all in bed together, before the day started. She and Max would both open their eyes every so often to check on Nina, and sometimes they opened them at the same time, looked at each other across Nina's full round tummy, and smiled.

When that happened, Cleo let herself feel happy, let herself believe that there really was a chance – no matter how small – that things just might turn out okay for all of them.

Lying in between them in bed, Nina would often wake up with a start, jerking her arms and legs, looking around like she was surprised to find Max and Cleo there. Then she'd settle down, ready to fall back asleep almost immediately. And with her little chin shaking, her eyes would close and she'd sigh like she was saying, *Okay then, everyone's here. Let's get some rest.*

Chapter 23

When the baby cried in the middle of the night, Weezy's first instinct was to get up and go downstairs to help. She'd wake up groggy and think, 'Oh no, the baby's up again,' and it would take a minute for her mind to catch up, to remind her that it wasn't her baby, that there were two parents down there to take care of it. So she'd stay right where she was in her own bed, listening as they paced the floor with Nina, sometimes singing or talking quietly, and sometimes pleading for her to stop crying.

Well, Weezy stayed in bed most of the time. Sometimes, if Nina was crying for an especially long time, she'd go down and offer her help. Even if it was only to hold the baby for a minute or two, while Cleo or Max went to the bathroom or drank a glass of water, or just got themselves together for a moment. She remembered how it was, the way it could drive you crazy sometimes, the endless crying for what seemed like no reason.

Once, when Martha was a baby, she'd been screaming all night and Weezy, who was already pregnant again at the time, was pacing back and forth and finally held the baby up, looked in her face, and said loudly, 'What? What do you want?' Martha had been so surprised, had started the way babies do at loud noises, and then after a few seconds of silence began screaming again. Weezy had felt like the worst mother in the world, had brought her into the bedroom and woken Will up, told him that he had to take her. Then she'd gotten back into bed and cried herself, feeling like the cruddiest person ever.

So yes, she remembered the exhaustion and she was there to help if they needed it.

It was a strange thing to have a baby in the house again. As much as Cleo and Max tried to pick up after Nina (which truthfully wasn't that much), there was stuff everywhere. Cloth diapers for burping, almost-empty bottles sitting on the coffee table, clean bottles drying in the kitchen, pacifiers on the floor, blankets and baby socks and onesies with spit-up strewn all over the couch and the floor.

Had it been like this with her own children? Weezy didn't remember it that way, but it must have been. Maybe you just got used to it, got used to the milk and dirty-diaper smells that seem to be on everything. But now, in her house that used to be orderly, every time she stepped on a pacifier, she got a little annoyed.

She worried about Cleo and Max. The two of them often sat on the couch in their pajamas, looking exhausted and sort of dirty, wordlessly passing the baby back and forth, staring straight ahead at the TV. Sometimes Weezy would take Nina, suggest a shower or a change of clothes, and they'd get up like zombies and go do what she said. Was this normal? Maybe. She couldn't remember. She tried not to judge. After all, she hadn't had an audience when her children were babies. And she did remember one day when Will came home from work and stepped on an open dirty diaper that was on the floor. So yes, she would try not to judge.

Cleo had tried to breastfeed, but the poor thing never really got the hang of it. Weezy tried to give her tips, told her to stick it out. Weezy had never had any trouble, of course, but she knew some women that had. But after a few weeks, Cleo gave up. Weezy was disappointed, but there wasn't too much more she could say. Max, in fact, got a little snippy with her one morning when she was just saying that she felt bad for them about it. So she kept her mouth shut after that.

And she did have to admit, that once Nina was only on bottles, things ran a little more smoothly. For one thing, Cleo wasn't crying most of the day because it wasn't working. Also, she got more sleep, was able to go for walks with the baby, seemed to get it together a little bit more. Nina started sleeping like a champ, since she was always full now. And the other good part was that once Cleo stopped nursing, her breasts went back to their normal size. Right after she came back from the hospital, Cleo had looked a little bit like a porn star with her huge chest, and it didn't help that she seemed not to notice, that she wore little tank tops without bras all around the house. So yes, she looked a little more decent now.

Of course, some nights Weezy would look down at Nina, snoozing away with her belly full, and hope that she wouldn't end up an obese child because of the formula. You never knew. You really never knew.

There were so many days when the only thing any of them ever talked about was Nina. Had she eaten? Was she fussy? How much had she spit up? Did she smile? It consumed their days and nights, and sometimes Weezy would be in bed before she realized that not only had she not called her other children, she had barely thought about them.

It was almost hard to notice that the girls were gone, since tiny little Nina took up so much of the space. But both of her girls were out on their own, and it was strange to remember that they had been there not too long ago.

She decided to make them both blankets, as housewarming presents. (She had shown the patterns to Cleo, who barely looked up at them. She hadn't had the time or energy to get back to her knitting.) Weezy's first instinct was to start with Martha's blanket, since Martha would surely see the one she was working on for Claire and wonder where hers was. But Weezy thought that maybe she would do it differently for once, and start Claire's

463

first so that she could take it with her when she went to New York. She would try not to worry about Martha's reaction, try to treat her like an adult, which she was. It didn't mean anything to make Claire's blanket first. And also, she thought, as she cast on the stitches, she could just hide it whenever Martha came over.

Martha was still getting settled in her new place, and she stayed with Weezy and Will at least one night a week, but usually more like two or three nights. Weezy tried not to worry about this. After all, it just took Martha longer to adjust to new things. And it was a big step. She came over with paint samples or catalogs so that she could show Weezy things she thought she might want to buy for the new place. She was even thinking about renting out the second bedroom, and was working on an ad. Weezy hoped that maybe she'd find a nice roommate that would become a friend, that she'd find a group of people that could be hers.

When Martha held Nina, Weezy felt her heart tear a little bit. She worried that it would never happen for Martha. She was already thirty-one, with no prospect of any sort of relationship in sight. And while she knew Maureen would make fun of her for wanting her babies to have babies, she couldn't help it. She wanted Martha to experience that, and at this point she had to admit to herself that it didn't seem probable. Martha had never had a boyfriend or, to be truthful, even a best friend. It was hard to imagine that she would just go through life like that, but with each year that passed it became more likely. Still, Weezy could hope. So she did. She hoped.

She remembered the way that no matter what, Maureen always cheered for the sports team that was supposed to lose. 'You have to go for the underdog,' she always said. And Weezy supposed that was true.

Claire was doing well. She and Will both agreed that she seemed happier than she had in a long time. And Weezy tried not to let it hurt her feelings that part of that had to be due to being away from them. She tried to remind herself that it was the natural thing to be on your own. But sometimes she thought back to the time when Claire was at home, and wished they could all do it over again, do it differently.

'What does it matter as long as she's happy?' Will asked one day as she was thinking out loud. And she said that he was probably right.

One night she tiptoed down the stairs to find Cleo leaning back on the couch, watching an old movie. It was a little after three in the morning, and Nina was snuffling in her arms, sort of sleeping, but she was fighting it. Any time she started to drift off, she'd wave her arms, like she was waking herself up.

'How's she doing?' Weezy asked.

'She's okay.' Cleo looked down at her face. 'She won't go to sleep. She's refusing. She is so stubborn.'

'Claire was the same way as a baby.'

'Really?'

'Oh yes. She seemed to know what I wanted her to do and then she did the opposite.'

Cleo laughed. 'What about Max?'

'Max? Oh, he was so easy. He was the kind of baby that makes you want a few more. He was so sweet, no matter what. I could put him in his seat for the whole day, and he just sat, content.'

'I can imagine that,' Cleo said.

'Do you want me to take her?' Weezy was tired, but she loved holding Nina while she was sleeping.

'I'm okay,' Cleo said. Weezy sat down anyway.

'I love this movie,' she said. It was the original *Parent Trap*. 'Martha and Claire loved it when they were little. They used to beg to watch it almost every day.'

'Really? I've never seen it.'

'What? Oh, it's a riot. Just a riot.'

The two of them stayed up to watch the whole movie, well after Nina was asleep. It was the moments like these with Cleo that made Weezy feel especially protective of her. When she was just in pajamas with no makeup on, holding Nina, and looking very young herself, Weezy wanted to take her in her arms and tell her it would be okay.

Cleo and her mother had been on better terms since Nina was born. Elizabeth came down a few times, and Cleo had been up there with the baby to spend a week or so, which made Weezy feel empty and almost panicked, like she was just going to take Nina away and never come back. Weezy imagined never seeing Nina again, pictured going to court to try to get visiting rights. But then they returned.

Cleo and Elizabeth were maybe on better terms, but they didn't have an easy relationship. There was one time when Elizabeth was visiting and made a remark about all the jobs that Cleo had missed out on this year. 'It will be a hard thing to explain this empty year on your résumé,' she said to Cleo, who left the room in tears. Weezy thought she sounded a little harsh, but then again, who was she to say? Mothers and daughters had their own language.

Cleo and Max fought fairly often, which was to be expected. They were in a small space in someone else's house, with a new baby and no sleep. But still. Whenever Weezy heard them arguing, she wanted to hold her breath. What if they split up? What if Cleo took Nina and never let them see her? Sometimes she would interrupt to take the baby, just to try to help so that the two of them could calm down and talk in peace; this was sometimes welcome, and sometimes Cleo and Max looked at her like she was out of her ever-loving mind.

It was a hard thing, to try to stay out of it. All she wanted to do was to get in the middle of their fights, sit them down, mediate, point out who was in the wrong. But she didn't. She stayed above it, and afterward always felt very saintly.

She kept suggesting that they start thinking about getting Nina baptized, that they should do it soon. But every time she talked about it, they just looked at her like she had suggested they take Nina to get a tattoo on her back. She complained about this to Maureen, who listened and then said, 'Well, in the end it's their decision, isn't it?' Weezy hadn't really seen it that way, and wasn't sure she really agreed. But she dropped the subject for the time being. She'd bring it up again later, when they were a little more settled.

Will was up in his office more than ever. He was in love with that little bundle of a baby, but he preferred to hold her while she was sleeping, or to feed her every once in a while. Anything else, and he was ready to hand her off. He complained more about the crying in the middle of the night. Even if they weren't the ones getting up with her, it woke them and it was hard to get back to sleep at their age. Many mornings, Will was grumpy, but what could you do? He knew what they had signed on for.

After the wedding, Weezy kept thinking she should tell Will about the wedding planning, but she couldn't quite find the words. She took all of her wedding stuff, her binders and folders, and went to throw it out. Then she thought better of it and put it all in a large Tupperware storage container in the back of her closet. It was a lot of information and it seemed a waste to throw it out. Who knew? She might need it one day.

One afternoon, Weezy decided she needed to come clean. They were both in the kitchen and Will was eating toast when she said, 'Do you remember how Claire accused me of lying to the florist?' Will nodded. 'Well, it was a little bit true. I just got so enamored with the wedding planning that after Claire called it off, I just kept doing research. It was silly, I know.'

It sounded much better when she called it research. Why hadn't she thought of that before? She looked at Will to see how he'd react, and her stomach fell. He was looking for something to say, but his face told her that he'd already known.

'Well,' he finally said 'I can see how that could happen.'

She'd nodded and begun loading the dishwasher. In the other room, Nina began to cry and Weezy had never been so happy for that little baby's ability to distract them from everything else.

Maureen was officially retired, which meant that she stopped by more often than ever. She loved seeing Nina, and spent many afternoons just holding her, walking around the house with her. Also, she used this time to pitch business ideas to Weezy. Maureen suggested starting a nanny company, buying a gym franchise, and once – in one of her strangest moments – starting a purse design company.

Weezy just listened to her talk, nodded when she'd say, 'Okay, I know you're going to think this one is crazy.' She was like a wind-up toy, and Weezy figured she just needed to wear herself out.

Then one day Maureen brought over a catalog with continuing education classes. 'I'm signing up for something,' she said. 'And you're doing it with me.'

A cooking class sounded a lot more pleasant than watching Maureen try to design purses, and so Weezy sat down and looked at the catalog with her. Paging through, she found a class on flower arrangement. 'What about this one?' she said. 'I bet it would be fun. I loved the florist we worked with for the wedding. He was amazing. If I could do what he could do . . .'

'We should open a flower shop,' Maureen said.

'I don't think we're really qualified,' Weezy said. 'But I will take the class with you.'

'Okay, great. Let's do it. And you never know. Maybe we'll be great at it. Maybe we'll start working for a florist, and then we'll decide that we should open our own shop.' Maureen was off again, and Weezy let her go.

'I doubt that working for a florist would pay very much,' Weezy pointed out. 'And they would probably never even hire someone our age. Plus, who knows what this course will be like? We don't even know if it will be worth it.'

'No one ever does,' Maureen said.

For the first time in a long time, Weezy began to wish for her house to be just hers and Will's again. No babies crying, no worrying about making dinner for more than just the two of them. And while it probably wouldn't happen for a while (they weren't going to throw Max and Cleo out on their ears!), it seemed like it was actually a possibility, that in a year or two they might be able to watch TV alone, just the two of them.

As much as she knew she'd miss the kids when they were gone, she also knew that she'd be happy to reclaim her house, to maybe just have a quiet dinner with Will one night on the back patio, with wine, no interruptions, no one handing the baby around to give everyone a chance to scarf down their food. Yes, she was looking forward to that.

Weezy was changing Nina's diaper one day, and the little buster was crying so hard her face was bright red. Nothing Weezy said or did seemed to do anything to begin to quiet her. 'Okay, sweetie pie,' she said. 'Let's just get through this. We're in it together. A dry diaper will make you feel better, I promise.'

Nina continued to scream and then Max came back to the house. 'Hey,' he called out. 'Who's that crying?'

Nina stopped and her eyes opened, looking around to find the voice that she recognized from all that time she was in the womb. Weezy stopped and stared at her, feeling tears start to form in her eyes. She blinked them back before Max came into the room, so he wouldn't accuse her of being just a sentimental old lady. She finished fastening the diaper and picked up Nina in time to hand her to Max, and he took her easily, put his face against hers.

'There you go,' he said. 'There you go.'

Anytime Weezy felt she was losing her patience with Cleo and Max, anytime she wanted to scream at them for being so irresponsible, for letting themselves get to this place, she would take a breath and observe them with Nina – the way they watched her, the way they rushed to her bassinet to make sure she was still alive. More than once, she watched Cleo place a hand on the baby's back while she slept, waiting to feel the little body rising and falling so she could make sure she was still breathing.

She wanted to tell them that it would never go away, that feeling, that worry that your child was going to be okay, but she was pretty sure that they were figuring that out already. They'd have to watch Nina start walking, watch her walk up the stairs, sure that she was going to tumble down. They'd have to take her to school, pray that she made friends, hope that no other little kids were mean to her. They'd watch her get in fights, get left out, get cut from a sports team, not get into the college that she wanted. They had so much heartbreak ahead of them.

And so, after she had watched them for a minute or two, she found that she wasn't angry anymore. Not much, anyway. At least, she didn't feel like yelling at them. What else could she have said anyway? What could she have said to make them feel worse, to make this bigger? They had Nina to take care of and worry about for the rest of their lives.

They were in it now.

Chapter 24

Claire slept on Katherine's couch for a few weeks, while she started her new job and looked for an apartment. It wasn't the most ideal situation, but Katherine offered and Claire didn't want to be rushed into finding a place she didn't love. Plus, Katherine had a new boyfriend and as long as she had someone at the apartment to stay with Mitzy the dog, she could stay over at his place as often as she liked.

Most mornings, Claire woke up with Mitzy breathing on her, asking to be taken outside. She wasn't the best-trained dog by a long shot, and she often just squatted in the apartment, relieved herself right where she was, looking right at Katherine or Claire, like she was daring them to punish her. The whole place smelled a little bit like urine, no matter how quickly Katherine cleaned up after her.

Also, Katherine had become very eco-conscious, and while Claire admired this, it could be a little hard to live with. She'd stopped one day to buy paper towels and cleaning supplies, and had spent the afternoon dusting and cleaning, but when Katherine came home to find her Windexing the front windows, she'd screamed like she was watching the execution of a near-extinct animal. 'What are you doing?' she'd said.

'I have rags for that. And this' – she held up the blue solution with two fingers—' is basically poison.'

Katherine also kept a compost bowl in the kitchen, which smelled and attracted flies. 'She's just a little *too* green,' Claire told Lainie over the phone. Claire was grateful for the place to stay, but she knew she couldn't stay too long.

Claire interviewed for almost a month before she contacted her old boss, Amy. She had just started to panic and think that she was never going to find another job, that she shouldn't have quit any job in this economy, and she felt desperate. Amy was happy to hear from her, probably because she was just happy to hear that Claire was still alive and functioning and hadn't had a complete breakdown. 'I'll put the word out,' Amy said. And true to her promise, Claire had three calls in a week, one from a nonprofit called Gallery 87 that was looking for a project manager to replace someone immediately. 'We're in a bit of a bind,' they kept telling Claire during the interview. She figured this worked in her favor.

The office that they gave Claire was a mess. All the drawers were still full, and there was a long sweater hanging on the back of the door, like the woman that had been there before had just not bothered to come back one day. The office assistant, Abigail, apologized when she showed Claire the office. 'She moved to California with her new boyfriend,' Abigail said. 'They hadn't even been dating that long, like two months, and one day she just came in and said she was leaving.' Abigail shook her head. 'We think she was dying to get out of New York and just looking for an excuse.'

Claire had no idea what she was doing at the job, but no one seemed to care. They were all just happy to have a body there again. The purpose of Gallery 87 was to pay high school kids to beautify the city – they painted murals on the sides of graffiti-covered buildings and in the subways, and spruced up parks, and playgrounds. Claire was thrown into the middle of projects that had been in the works for months, accompanied teenagers to parks and watched them paint benches with designs they'd created. They would descend on the park in the morning, and at the end of the day the benches were bright spots of color, some painted with checkerboards and swirls, one with tiny animals marching all over it. Claire was surprised at how much better the park looked when they left, how much it had changed. She wondered if she could get the kids to come paint her new apartment when she moved.

Every night when Claire left work she was so tired she was almost dizzy. Her head swam with information, and she felt like she'd never catch up. She slept better than she had in a year.

Whenever she had a few free moments, Claire would go

through the drawers and files in her office. She threw out old receipts and packs of gum, and kept paper clips and pencils. In a cardboard box, she put all of the woman's personal stuff – her sweater, an old pair of heels, a stuffed duck, and pictures that were on the bulletin board. She was going to throw it all out, but it seemed nicer to put it all in a box together first.

In one of the drawers, Claire found a shopping list that read: *Tulips, Carrots, Q-tips,* and *Celery.* She taped the list up on the wall behind her computer. It made her smile. She liked reading it out loud, reciting it under her breath like a prayer or a poem, a crazy little list of the things someone needed.

A broker showed her two apartments in Manhattan before Claire decided she was going to live in Brooklyn. Most of her friends were there now anyway, and she didn't want to go back to the Upper West Side. She'd walked by her old building one day, expecting to feel drawn to it, but instead she found herself speeding up to get past it quickly. She waved at the doorman when she passed, but didn't think he remembered her. He waved back like she could be anyone.

Katherine tried to convince Claire to live in Windsor Terrace near her, but Claire was set on Brooklyn Heights. She'd fallen in love with everything about the neighborhood. Even the street names were adorable – Poplar, Orange, Cranberry, Pineapple, and Vine. She didn't care how small her place was, she just wanted to be there. It was too perfect for words.

476

'I think you should try to widen your search,' Katherine told her. Sometimes she looked at Claire like she'd lost her mind, like she'd forgotten how hard it could be to find a decent apartment in New York and would end up living on Katherine's couch forever. But Claire remained hopeful.

The day that Claire moved out of the house, Max followed her around with Nina, making Nina's arm wave. 'Say good-bye to your aunt,' he said. 'Tell her how much you're going to miss her.' She remembered how, when she left for college, Max had cried in her dorm room. He was ten at the time, and tried to pretend it wasn't happening. He seemed sort of the same now, holding Nina up and talking behind her, saying, 'Aunt Claire, how can you leave me? You're going to miss me so much.'

And she did miss them, of course. As soon as she left, she missed them all, more than she had before she moved back. It was like she felt their absence more now. That was the worst part about leaving home – no matter what, it always felt a little sad. But not for one second did this mean that she doubted her decision. She was leaving and that was that.

When Claire told Lainie she was moving, she nodded like she'd been waiting for the news. 'I hoped maybe you'd stay. That you'd like it here so much you wouldn't want to go back.'

'Lainie,' Claire said, 'I can't stay here.'

'I know, I know. I knew you'd go. I just thought maybe you'd change your mind.'

477

'I'll come visit, I promise. Probably more than I ever did before.'

'Good,' Lainie said. 'Because once I have this baby, I'll probably never be able to leave the house again. I'll be under house arrest, so you'll have to come to me.'

'I will,' Claire said. 'I promise.'

And she had been home three times already since she moved out. She loved seeing Nina, holding that sweet little baby. And then Lainie had her fourth baby, a boy that they named Tommy. Lainie and Cleo got the babies together pretty often, would put them next to each other on blankets and let them play side by side. They referred to Nina as Tommy's girlfriend and talked often about their future wedding. Claire knew they were kidding, but she swore those little babies smiled at each other.

Every time Claire came home, Weezy made a big deal of it. They all had dinner, and Martha came home to be there too, like it was a special occasion, like they all hadn't eaten together every single night just a few months ago.

When the broker told Claire that there was a studio on Pineapple Street that was for rent, she almost screamed. She tried to stay calm, but she knew that barring a major disaster (a serious mice infestation, for example), she was going to take it. Pineapple Street had been her favorite one from the start, the place where she hoped to find an apartment. She started to think that she was getting very lucky.

The apartment was one of the smallest that Claire had ever seen. But it was clean and solid and the girl that was moving out told her that she loved it there. (And she seemed honest, even if she did have Care Bear sheets on her bed.) There was a little half wall that hid the bed from the rest of the apartment, and enough room to put a tiny couch and TV comfortably. Claire didn't have any furniture anyway, since she'd sold it all, and she promised herself that she was going to get only the basics – a bed, a couch, and maybe a little table.

Katherine had come to see it with her, had looked around and then at Claire. 'You could find a much bigger place by me,' she said. But Claire took it and Katherine just shrugged. 'It's your overpriced apartment,' she said.

The night Claire moved in, she had a few friends over and they sat on the floor and drank wine out of plastic cups. They ordered Thai food and ate it out of the containers, passing around spring rolls and noodles. After dinner, they left to go to a bar, since they were all feeling a little cramped by then. Claire was almost hyper that night, was excited at every suggestion someone made, could barely keep from skipping to the bar.

'You look like you just moved to New York for the first time,' Katherine told her. 'You're acting like a tourist or something.'

Claire knew it was true. She was so happy to be back in New York that sometimes she'd be walking down the street and she'd get a rise in her chest and a giddiness that bubbled out of her throat. It made her smile at strangers. She couldn't help it. These strange surges of happiness seemed to come out of nowhere. Even if she'd wanted to stop herself from bouncing up and down and smiling, she didn't think she'd have been able to.

It was strange. Claire was back in New York, working for a nonprofit, just like she had been a year ago. It was almost like she was right back where she'd started, but it didn't feel that way at all.

There were things that Claire didn't even know she'd missed until she moved back. At home, everything was done for her – grocery shopping, laundry, dusting, cleaning the bathroom. Now, she was responsible for all of it again. The first time she went to the grocery store after moving into the apartment, she had the best time. She bought a random assortment of things – sugar, cereal, Diet Coke, yogurt, cheese, crackers. There was nothing in all of it that could make a meal, but it didn't matter. She was only a little embarrassed at how free she felt, how grateful she was to throw whatever she wanted into her cart.

Weezy came to visit, carrying a potted plant and a new afghan that she'd made. 'Oh,' she said when she stepped into the apartment.

'I know, it's small,' Claire said. 'But I love it.'

'It's adorable,' Weezy said. She set the plant on the kitchen counter and arranged the afghan on the back of the new couch.

'It looks perfect,' Claire said.

Claire and Weezy walked around the neighborhood, and then on the Promenade. Weezy kept looking over her shoulder, like she thought someone was following them. She'd never been a fan of any of the places that Claire lived in New York, and this one was no different. Claire tried to ignore it.

They talked mostly about Nina and Max and Cleo, but also about Martha's new condo. They'd never really addressed the fighting that took place during Claire's year at home, the accusations that she'd made. Weezy had tried to bring it up before she'd moved out, saying, 'You have such a support system that we don't have to worry about you as much,' and she had looked like she was going to cry and so Claire just said, 'It's fine, Mom, it's fine.' Claire had apologized for her behavior, and then really wanted to drop it. There was no use in talking about it, in making everyone uncomfortable. It was just the way it was.

Now Weezy was talking about the shore again, telling Claire that they'd pay for her train ticket, that the whole family was going to be there, that Martha really missed her and would love it if she came.

'Of course I'll come,' Claire said. 'I wouldn't miss it.'

'Oh good,' Weezy said

It was so much easier to be gracious with distance.

The end of August was cooler than normal, and everyone seemed to shift with the weather. Usually when they were at the shore, it felt like they were waiting for summer to end, dreading the return to fall. This year it felt like summer was already over. There wasn't the same sense of longing in any of them.

They didn't spend much time at the beach. It was hard to

take Nina down there and everyone seemed just as happy sitting out on the deck in the morning and going for walks in the afternoon. Their days revolved around Nina, and they could spend hours watching her, talking about how much she ate or what she was wearing or how funny and cute she was. Nina was a topic they all agreed on, and Claire couldn't remember what they'd talked about before her.

One afternoon, they had Nina set up in the middle of the room, lying on her back on a blanket, a mobile set up above her. She was looking intently at a stuffed corn on the cob, frowning at it, like she didn't like the way it was smiling at her. She sized it up for a while, then wound up her arm and swatted it. She looked pleased when it went flying, and waited for it to settle down, then gave it another whack with her arm.

'I wonder what the corn said to piss her off,' Max said.

'She's so focused,' Claire said.

'Oh, she is so smart,' Weezy said. Everyone laughed a little, but Weezy just shook her head. 'She's one smart cookie, I'm telling you.'

Claire woke up one morning before anyone else and went down to the kitchen to find Cleo and Nina. She started a pot of coffee and then took Nina from Cleo. Nina had a habit of curling up when anyone tried to put her over their shoulder.

'She's like a roly-poly bug,' Claire said.

'That's what Max called her,' Cleo said. 'It took me a while to figure out what he was talking about. We used to call them pill bugs.'

'Max loved poking them with sticks and watching them curl. It used to make him laugh so hard when he was little.'

'That's what he told me. I can imagine it.'

'So, how's it been going?' Claire asked.

'Okay,' she said. 'I mean, it's good. Just overwhelming, you know? I keep thinking that this baby's parents will be by soon to pick her up and take care of her, and then I remember that it's me. I'm the parent. Is that crazy?'

'I'm sure it's normal.'

Cleo nodded. 'It's not that I want someone to take her, I just sometimes forget that I'm the one in charge of her. That she's really mine. Don't tell anyone, okay?'

'I promise. But don't worry, I think it's normal. Once, right after Lainie had Jack, we were out at the bar and she all of a sudden looked shocked and said, "I just forgot I had a baby. Just for a second."'

Cleo laughed. 'Thanks,' she said. 'That makes me feel better.'

It was strange watching Max with Nina. He picked her up with so much ease, changed her diaper and fed her with authority. He burped her with a great amount of confidence, patting her back hard, then smiling when he was successful, always laughing when she burped especially loud, saying, 'That's my girl.'

It was the first time ever that Max couldn't and wouldn't ask for Claire's advice. What did she know about babies that could help him? It was so bizarre and a little sad to watch Max going ahead of her, to picture herself having a baby someday and asking Max for tips. But most of the time, she was just impressed with him, how unafraid he was of Nina, how in control he seemed when he held her with one arm or buttoned her into a new outfit.

Martha kept saying, 'Thank God for this vacation,' and shaking her head. Her new patient was apparently difficult and Martha loved to talk about her. 'She's running me ragged,' she said. 'She's sort of a wretched old woman. Last week she told me that I should dress for my body type. Can you imagine?'

Claire found herself actually laughing at Martha's stories. Now that they weren't living under the same roof, and Martha was no longer pushing for sisters couple therapy, Claire found her kind of amusing. She even managed not to get annoyed when Martha talked to her about the benefits of owning her own place. 'You really should make that a goal,' she told Claire. 'What you're paying in rent, just throwing that money away month after month.' She shuddered, like the thought was repulsive.

'I'll think about that,' Claire said.

Maybe it was because of the weather, or maybe it was because she'd just had a baby, but Cleo didn't wear a bikini once. Whatever the reason, Claire was grateful.

The last night that everyone was at the house, they barbecued and ate outside. Claire and Weezy had marinated cubes of chicken and beef, and skewered them with red, green, and yellow peppers, mushrooms, and onions.

It was a nice night and everyone was laughing a lot. They were sharing Nina like a toy, passing her around nicely, even if

484

they were all a little reluctant to let her go. Claire noticed the way that everyone leaned down to smell Nina's head before they had to hand her off to the next person, how they breathed in deeply, like teenagers sniffing glue to get high.

Nina fell asleep while Claire was holding her, and she didn't make a move to pass her to anyone else. She wasn't trying to be a baby hog, but Nina was her goddaughter and they were all leaving tomorrow, so it seemed only fair. Nina snuffled in her sleep, like a tiny little pig. She was a beautiful baby, which wasn't a surprise to anyone.

Everyone talked late into the night, like they didn't want to go to bed and admit that it was the end of vacation. Claire was a little sad to leave, but also excited to get back to her new apartment, to spend time there. The apartment was new enough that it didn't quite feel like hers yet. She still had the sense when she opened the door that she was walking into an unfamiliar place. It didn't bother her, though. She knew that would change soon enough. She knew that one day, she'd walk in and it would be like she belonged there. All of the dust and dirt would be what she created, the smell would be her own. And she would be able to walk barefoot everywhere without thinking that someone else's foot germs were there. It would be like no one else had ever lived there before, like no one else would be there after; it would feel like home.

Maureen went into the house and came out carrying a new bottle of wine. 'Just one more splash for everyone,' she said. 'It's our last night here, we can't go to bed early.'

They all obeyed, holding out their glasses like children, while Maureen stood in the middle of the circle, turning and pouring. Claire wrapped the blanket a little bit more up around Nina's face, even though it wasn't cold out. Will was talking about his new teaching schedule, listing all of the things he had to do to get ready as soon as they got back.

It was quiet for a few moments, and Claire could tell that everyone was getting sleepy. But then Martha started talking about her job again, explaining how her patient sometimes tried to sneak away from her in the store. And they all turned to her to listen, gave her full attention, and watched her as she said, 'I have to chase her down, scream her name in the supermarket like a crazy person.' Martha looked pleased as everyone laughed, then looked down at her lap for a moment and twisted her hands around, like a middle-school girl, embarrassed by the attention. They were all silent for a few seconds, waiting. And then she recovered and went on.

ACKNOWLEDGMENTS

For my husband, Tim Hartz, who lets me take over the dining room table with piles of papers for weeks at a time and talk about my characters over dinner — when I come out of my writing haze, I'm so happy that you're the one there to greet me. Thanks for everything, friend. I think marrying you was a good decision.

My agent, Sam Hiyate, always, always believes in my writing and in me, which means more than I can ever say.

As far as editors go, Jenny Jackson is the very best. She is thoughtful and wise in her edits, so fun to gossip with, and always starts e-mails to me by saying, 'this is a no-pressure e-mail.' For all of these reasons (and because she makes my books better), I am delighted to know her.

I am a lucky writer to have such a great

family. My parents, Pat and Jack Close, are the best cheerleaders ever. They are willing to attend multiple readings, assure me things will work out if I get nervous (Mom), and try to sell my book to strangers (that's you, Dad). Thanks, you guys.

Kevin Close, Chris and Susan Close, and Carol and Scott Hartz are a constant support and eager readers. I couldn't ask for more.

My adorable and brilliant niece, Ava Close, responded to the cover art for this book by saying, 'Ooooh, Santa.' Ava, I am always happy to have your honest feedback.

Wrigley Close-Hartz keeps me company while I write and also makes sure that I get outside at least once a day, by demanding his walk.

I am also grateful to:

All of my students at George Washington University, who remind me of why I wanted to be a writer in the first place.

Tom Mallon, who was kind enough to give me a job teaching creative writing at GW.

My virtual coworkers – all of the people who make my days a little less lonely, by chatting over e-mail, answering writing questions, reading drafts, and always offering encouragement: Megan Angelo, Jessica Liebman, Martha Leonard, Lee Goldberg, Courtney Sullivan, and Molly Erman.

Moriah Cleveland is forever willing to talk to me about imaginary people as though they were real. There is no first reader/e-mail companion that I would rather have. You are invaluable.

My friends are constantly telling me funny things, and sometimes I have to steal bits of their dialogue and stories for my writing. Thank you, and I'm sorry, but if you guys weren't so funny I wouldn't have to do it — Becky Schillo, Margaret Hoerster, Mairead Garry, Erin Claydon, Erin Bradley, Mary Colleen Bragiel, and Hilary Murdock.

Being at Knopf has been a dream come true, and I am thankful every day for all the people there who support me, and my books. This team is superb at what they do and are also just genuinely nice people. I am indebted to: Sonny Mehta, Paul Bogaards, Ruth Liebman, Nicholas Latimer, Julie Kurland, Jennifer Kurdyla, Andrea Robinson, Elizabeth Lindsey, and Abby Weintraub.